WARPED

~BOOK 5~

BLENDED

WARPED

Copyright ©2017 Erica Chilson

Wicked Reads
PO Box 29
Nelson, PA 16940

www.ericachilson.com/wicked-reads

Printed in the United States of America
First Printing, 2017
ISBN-13: 978-0-9979899-5-3
ISBN-10: 0-9979899-5-5

Titles by Erica Chilson

Mistress and Master of Restraint

Restraint
Unleashed
Dexter
Dalton
Queen Omnibus*
Jaded*
Queened*
Checkmate*
King
Faithless
The Hunter
Integrated

-Coming Soon-
Hero

BLENDED

Good Girl
Wildly Wedded Wife
Widow
Wanton
Warped

RUSTY KNOB

Rusty Knob
Tarnished
Stainless
Polished

WILLOW PRYNNE

I need to buy a vehicle before a house.
I need to graduate college before I run a business.
I need to learn to be a girlfriend before I'm a wife.
I need to get married before I have a baby.
I need to learn how to be a daughter before I can be a mother.
I need to finish being a girl before I can become a woman.

ESSIE PRYNNE

I was that girl, ya know?
The girl.
The girl who developed early. The one every boy with testosterone firing in their veins wanted. The one every girl wanted to be– the one they hated out of pure jealousy.
I was *that* girl, but she wasn't me.

KIEREN MASON

I've seen things I can't unsee, things that ruined me. I've taken on the role of my father's wife, my siblings' mother, and my brother's enabler, because the guilt is suffocating. As those roles are stripped from me as my family moves on, I'm left behind without a purpose.

DEVON MASON

I'm just like my mother– bipolar and abusive, but I'm also a drug addict. Being manic is a high without a drug, to the point I have to take drugs to dampen my high. Imagine your mind is a heavy metal song, but all the instruments are giving conflicting sounds, and you're doing all you can do to make sure the bass doesn't overpower the guitar, and the drummer is pounding out a wicked solo, drawing the song in a new direction. I've yet to find anything to properly represent the depression aspect. Perhaps death is the only way to describe the low of depression. You just feel dead in a sea of hopelessness, without the ability to move as all life has to offer flies by in waves of fast-forward and rewind. Everything you once loved, no longer sparks any interest. Ever. The only thing the inflicted seeks is relief. Something to make you high again. Anything to make you feel alive for only a few seconds. A reprieve in an endless expanse of shadowy nothingness.

CHAPTER ONE

Essie Prynne

"How are you really doing?" Beth says out the corner of her mouth to me as we drive away from the scene of my humiliation. "And don't feed me any more of your '*I'm fine*' bullshit." She all but growls like a kitten finally growing her Hello Kitty fangs to match her wagging puppy dog tail.

Turning to her, I dramatically roll my eyes– a slight curve twisting my frown upside down.

Bethany taps one fingertip on the steering wheel, in time with Kings of Leon's *Sex on Fire*. My best friend's girl-next-door demeanor, her laidback jeans and girly pink t-shirt, and her stubby fingernails remind me of my other *best* friend, or as I've always dubbed Willow, my best *cousin*. Boy howdy, does that always rankle the girl. (Hehe!) The tunes rocking the stereo are Willow's, as is the seat beneath my ass, and the steering wheel suffering the out-of-tune tappage. My car is broken, and Willow's driving around Rob's Explorer, so I nabbed Willow's Beetle as our ride of the night.

Until recently, I never allowed the two halves of my world to collide: Bethany and Willow. Why, you ask? Because I'm not fucking stupid, that's why.

Jealousy.

Possession.

Fear.

I knew my best friends would connect more with each other than with me, leaving me all alone.

Bethany is sweet, beautiful, caring and giving. Beth is one of those people who makes the world a better place. She *will* make a difference, not only in one person's life, but in every person she comes into contact. She's brilliant, intuitive, and patient. I've always wanted to grow up to be Bethany Oman, but I'll happily settle with being someone she's content to hang out with.

Willow is snarly, aggressive, kick-ass and bad-ass. Willow is one of those people who makes the world a more interesting place. There is never a dull moment in Willow's presence. She thinks I drag her around because I don't like being alone. Not true. I drag Willow around because she makes me fearless. The girl has balls the size of a wrecking ball, not destroying everything in their path but altering it just for the hell of it. It's a rush like no other to see Willow work her magic.

If Beth is the angel on my shoulder, Willow is the devil.

What happens when they don't need me anymore?

To use Bethany's words: I'm filled with repressed anger. Misdirected, repressed anger. I'm angry at everyone and no one, filtering it until all that anger is bottled up and directed inward at myself.

Bethany, being the best frickin' person on the planet, asked about my welfare for the billionth time tonight. Why? Well, I'm angry, of course. Pick a reason, and you'd hit the nail on the head. Any reason.

There aren't many events on the face of the planet that make you want to drag a dull razor blade across your wrists. (Vertically if you want to do it right, boys and girls. Thank you, Advanced Biology, which means Bethany, of course). Earlier, I unsuccessfully tried with my *Venus* razor– it's like using a butter knife surrounded by moisturizing strips –where Bethany caught me and called me an attention whore. She showed me the correct way, taunting good luck on finding a sharp object in my house, and then proceeded to analyze the ever-lovin' fuck out of my ass. That was punishment enough alone.

Death and Taxes are the only things guaranteed in life, right?

Taxes, I've got that one down pat. A third of my pittance is torn from my hard-working hands every Friday afternoon to pay for bullshit I will never see. Do student loans count? If so, well, fuck me with a chimney brush. I can shove hope up my anal passageway as my future dissolves with my defaulted student loans. I work six days a week, and after taxes and miscellaneous bullshit, I can barely afford my car insurance. I'm three months behind on the loan for my in-the-shop Toyota, which is as old as my twin cousins. It will cost the bank more to repossess the piece of shit than for me to keep it.

Get ahead in life?

Fuck you very much!

Which leads to death, right? Well, apparently I'm not crafty enough for that activity. God has other plans for me, I guess.

I bought the lie. I bought the lie that if you educate yourself by getting a degree, you're guaranteed a better life. It's like the crossroads at the start of *The Game of Life*: play on or go to the university, where you will be *fined* so much before you can move on. In the end, the uneducated and the educated alike were dead even– just as in Fairport these days. Kieren deviously laughed his ass off every time he won when we played Life– his *un*educated ass, I might add. In the game and in real life, I had to pay a bazillion dollars (not really, but those suckass loan statements sure make it feel that way) just to be able to work at a job I could have done when I was thirteen. I'm a girly girl– proficient in all things girl. I didn't need to pay some instructor to show me how to do my thing, but I did...

When you're dirt-poor and debt-rich, your next line of defense is your parents, right?

Wrong.

Earlier tonight, my parents told me they are retiring, selling the house I grew up in, and are moving to sunny-fucking-Florida. I'm a mishmash hybrid like the majority of Fairport, Massachusetts' natives: Scottish, Irish, and English. Mom's a huge genealogy buff, tracking our migration to Ellis Island in New York City in 1909. Meaning, I burn in the sun like a vampire meeting its true death.

Floridian sun '*flame*' + Essie '*the wick*' Prynne = Whoosh.

I was given an ultimatum: leave my family, my best friends, the guy I've loved since kindergarten, my job, my home, my world– leave it all behind to cling to my umbilical cord... or I'm all on my own. Well, needless to say, I chose the box marked '*other*'.

What's other? Fuck if I know.

Taxes: check.

Death: uncheck.

Dead-end job with a degree: check.

Defaulted student loans: check.

Unmovable jalopy with an outstanding loan: check.

Broke-assed bitch: check. Check. CHECK.

Abandoning parents: check.

Supportive best friends: Check– Bethany. Uncheck– Willow on all fronts.

So, most people can't handle an empty wallet, abandoning parents, and the stress of a going-nowhere-in-life future. That's enough to grab a Venus razor and get to hacking, right? Wrong. If you have friends at your side, life is livable.

Willow.

My courage-creator. My blooded cousin, for my genealogy tells me so. My sister from another mother. My abandoner. My heartbreaker. The one who had me grabbing for that razor.

Willow: my betrayer.

I stifle a sob, hiding it beneath the rolling purr of Followill brother, Caleb, of KoL... or so I believe.

"Essie..." Bethany sighs, fingers stopping their rhythmic tapping to reach over to hold my hand.

"I love you," I say to avoid the inevitable conversation. "Seriously, Beth. You're my beating heart."

Laughing uncomfortably, "Jesus, Ess... dramatic much? Do I need to put Will and Ana on suicide watch again?"

"Probably should," I grumble beneath my breath, knowing she can't hear me over Followill's crooning.

I was that girl, ya know? *The* girl. The girl who developed early. The one every boy with testosterone firing in their veins wanted. The one every girl wanted to be– the one they hated out of pure jealousy.

I was *that* girl, but she wasn't me.

I went through puberty at nine, had a C-cup at thirteen, and a D-cup at sixteen. I was labeled a whore by my peers simply because I had big tits. Disgusting to my adult-mind, but debilitating to my child-mind.

I was *that* girl– the one who was a child in a woman's body. *The* girl who still played with Barbie, went trick-or-treating, all the while grown men looked at me like I was impersonating a ten-year-old child, labeling me the *babysitter*. I was playing with my friends, *needing* to play with my friends, because I was still a kid in my mind even though I wore a bra and was bleeding between my thighs.

I loved boys, sure. But I wasn't boy-crazy. I was the same height as the boys, even though I hadn't grown a single inch since I was nine. I still wanted those awkward, gangly idiots, even though the senior guys were staring at me like fresh meat on the first day of seventh grade at Fairport Area Junior/Senior High School. I wanted the boys in my class, not those guys who were as big and intimidating as my daddy. It was less than a week into seventh grade before I was assaulted (ass grabbed, tits tweaked, catcalled).

I was scared. I was all alone. No one understood but…

Bethany Oman: bless her heart.

Devon Mason: curse his blackened soul.

Beth and Dev were my support system. I survived the *'whore'* spewing (issued by the upperclassman girls), slut shaming (issued by the upperclassman guys when I turned them down), and the assaults to my private parts (both guys and girls), because I had my best friends at my side.

First love cuts the sharpest and the deepest, and it's a wound that fails to heal.

I spent every waking moment with my best friends, and then Devon and I changed. Puberty hit him *hard*– like a brick to the junk. We were fused at the lips and the hips (clothed). Every day I'd hang out at the Mason house since Chief Mason was at work, Mrs. Mason was lost in her mind, and Isis moved out. No supervision except for the tiny Masons. Ren was a trip– my board game terrorizer. Raven was a sulky beauty who loved it when I brushed her amazing hair. Weston was a ray of sunshine with a heart of gold.

It felt like home.

While Ren cooked dinner, Dev and I would detour into their bedroom– we'd make out, and more. (Isis caught the *more*) We almost had sex one afternoon. By almost, I mean, we pretty much did. I had just turned fourteen. As I said, puberty hit Devon Mason like a shot of testosterone to the nuts.

Highly clichéd: I didn't hear from any Mason for almost a week. Fairport gossip reported a break-in at their home. Next I saw Devon, he called me a whore… to my face.

"Your tits disgust me, Hester," Devon said coldly, tightly. "It's the mark of a whore. Masons aren't meant to marry whores."

Devon hasn't said a word to me since. Not. A. Single. Word. He speaks around me, never truly meeting my eye. If we are in a social situation, Devon directs his answers at whomever is nearby. Always. I've tested this hypothesis, as has Bethany, who was more pissed for me than for losing our mutual best friend when I lost my boyfriend. On principle, Beth hasn't said a single word to Devon since. Fun times.

At the time, the only person I'd ever kissed or touched, who had only ever kissed or touched *me*, said the same exact word that I had to swallow on a daily basis. If my best friend/boyfriend agreed with my bullies, must be it was true– so I made sure it was.

My greatest shame.

After Mrs. Mason died, I tried to talk to Devon at school– tried to comfort my ex-boyfriend/best friend. He sneered at me, wouldn't meet my eyes. Dev whispered seethingly, "*Whore*," and then he turned his back on me in the hallway at Fairport Area High.

I was so stunned, betrayed– ruined –my ass hit the floor. Leaning against my locker, heart fracturing, I ugly-cried with snot smearing my face. As I watched Devon's back disappear in the distance down the hallway, his hands tucked in his hip pockets, I remember my pretty pink skirt wrapped around my thighs (Devon's favorite skirt) showing my underwear. A senior girl, whose boyfriend accosted (assaulted) me that very morning, walked by, pointed and cackled, and then shouted, "WHORE! Essie Prynne's a granny-panty-wearing-whore!"

I learned many valuable lessons that day, none of which I heeded. #1: Girls are fucking irrational idiots. (Blame the girl with big tits, not the assmunch who is hand-raping her) #2: no matter how many times you tell yourself the *word* isn't you, you can only hear it so much before you start believing it– living it. Reveling it in. Hating it as much as you now hate yourself.

My greatest shame happened when I was sixteen… Kieren was shuffling down the street, trying his damnedest not to cry. So I pulled up and offered him a ride. Ren got in my car, holding my eyes like I was somebody he could *see*, and he still loved her just as his big brother used to. Ren looked at me like he always did– as I saw myself, not as a *whore*.

"Don't take me home," Ren begged. "I can't go back there."
Stunned, the "Why?" rolled quickly off my tongue.

"It's a secret," Ren whispered, rubbing at his eyes with the back of his hands. Even at almost fourteen, he looked like an adult. Already six foot and training for Varsity Football at the end of eighth grade. The guy was destined to break hearts: blond, blue-eyed, and built like… well, a heartstoppingly gorgeous football player. But Kieren was not my Devon– at least not for me.

Ren and I understood one another, already having that 'adult' conversation about being a kid trapped in a grown adult's body. Put it this way, Ren's hormones kicked in at the same time Devon's did. Not age-wise, literally at the same time. Devon was almost fourteen and attacking my ass, and his little brother was a confused eleven-year-old ogling Dev and me when we made out. I knew the feeling after having the misfortune of only being nine when those fucking hormones wreaked havoc on my body. Half your mind said Barbie/Board Games/Action Figures, and the other half wanted something it didn't understand and didn't know how to get.

"You can trust me," I whisper back, meaning it. I drove us down a rural path to a trailhead, parking half on/half off the dirt road until we were swallowed by the woods. I loved the kid, not like I loved his brother, but love nonetheless.

Respecting me while shutting my ass down, "Our secret isn't my secret to tell, ya know?" Blue eyes pierced mine, filled with trust, wizened knowledge, and stark fear.

"I feel ya," I breathed, voice tight with unshed tears. I read between the lines: Devon is the only person who will ever tell me that secret... as if!

Males are like wild animals, especially the Masons. Once pissed on by one brother, you are always his girl. In Ren's eyes, I will forever be Dev's, no matter if Devon threw my ass back for involuntarily growing mammoth tits or not.

Not blinking– Ren never blinks when you hold a conversation with him. You are his total focus, and it's intoxicating. Inside and out, Ren looked and sounded like a grown man, no matter how young he truly was. "I hate him sometimes, too."

Barking a sharp, humorless laugh at the ceiling of my parents' Buick, my head hitched backward as if struck in the gut. "Love him more, though, right?" I chuckled, suddenly feeling sick to my stomach, like I ate bitter soap.

"I wish I didn't," Ren breathed, sounding just as ill. "If I could, I'd empty it all out for you. I want to."

I reached over to take a crying Kieren's hand– tears skating down his sculpted cheeks. Squeezing tightly, "Doesn't matter where I am, who I'm with, or what I'm doing... I'll drop everything if you need me," I promised, and I've never broken a promise. "Got it?"

Turning to look away from me, overcome with grief, Ren took a deep, cleansing breath while staring out the passenger-side window. From one heartbeat to the next, his fierce gaze captured mine. "Prove it," he snarled. "Make me fuckin' forget 'em all."

My greatest shame– Ren's greatest shame.

My biggest regret– Ren's biggest regret.

I forget everything. Everyone. I forget my own freakin' name, as did Kieren Ewan Mason.

They say the path to Hell is paved with good intentions, but more so with regret and shame… and we paved that motherfucker proper.

With a promise kept, I earned the name **WHORE**! Not only did I earn it, I OWNED it! As did Kieren.

In no more than three minutes, I lost my virginity, my self-worth, my self-respect, as did Kieren.

I betrayed Devon, as did Kieren, even though Devon didn't deserve our loyalty. I betrayed Willow, as did Kieren, even though Willow had no claim. But more so, Kieren and I betrayed each other and ourselves.

They say when you get older, you come to regret your past mistakes. That heinous, awkward, painful, tear-filled three minutes… we didn't need time to tell us how fucking stupid we were. We knew it, lived it in less than a heartbeat.

With my skirt pulled up, my panty seat pushed to the side, Ren's pants unzipped with his bare dick only halfway shoved inside me– one thrust, no longer a virgin. Two thrusts, the weeping started– released from both our souls. By thrust three, our clothes were righted and I was holding Ren as he unknowingly wailed Devon's and his *secret*. Horrified for the both of us– all the Masons –all I could do was stroke Ren's silky hair with a shaky hand and keep his secret along with my promise. I was there for Kieren. Unconventional and shameful, yes. But I was there for him, goddamnit!

W. H. O. R. E. Every day I wake up and vow to prove those motherfuckers wrong, and every day I prove them right…

Tonight was no different.

Tonight wasn't even the worst.

I became *that* word after my three minutes with Kieren. I've blown no less than twenty dicks. Yes, dicks! Not just the appendage, but the guy– one of them being Devon. I've used my mouth to speak the word I couldn't utter. I became the word to the point that dicks who shoved their dicks in my mouth took advantage. I've had sex three times, a total of twenty minutes of my life, where I cried the entire time.

Kieren (never a dick): I just turned sixteen to his almost fourteen. I gave him three minutes because I loved him, and he needed me. We cried together, and it was as cathartic as it was catastrophic.

Dick #2: Devon glared at me while I bobbed some random's knob at a party in plain view of our entire class. I felt as gratified with his negative reaction (because I thought he cared) as I did disgusted with myself. When Dev proved he couldn't give two shits, I drank and smoked myself to near unconscious levels. I gave some dick almost ten minutes because I laid there frozen in a drunken, pot-induced stupor. Technically, I couldn't consent. But at the same time, I never tried to say no either. Pretty sure I deserved it. I cried silently the entire time.

Dick #3: Three years ago. My first week away from home with Bethany. My first frat party. Let's just say, if you give some dick head, the rest of his friends think you're fair game. With. Out. Fail. You are labeled as not having a voice– the word no meant jackshit, which I screamed behind a heavy, sweaty palm. I gave my rapist seven minutes of rough rutting with my face pressed into the front lawn of Delta-Kappa-Epsilon, with the entirety of their membership as witness. It was Rush Week, and I was the Pledge's *in*. I know I didn't deserve it, yet I can't get my mind to actually believe that bullshit lie, now can I? FYI: not only did I cry into the grass, I threw up on that dick's hand, not that he gave a flying fuck.

When I said Bethany was my world, I wasn't lying. I am the reason she abandoned our dream of all things girl for all things mental healing. When I said God had other plans for me, I wasn't lying. I overdosed on the pills in our medicine cabinet, and Beth had the hospital pump my stomach.

Angel.

I haven't sucked, touched, or looked at a dick's dick in three years– until tonight –and I puked on sight.

I could blame my tits. I could blame Devon. Hell, I should blame Willow. But I can't. The only one to blame is myself.

Why Willow? Because it was my fault I lost my voice, giving her the ability to betray me– burn my heart to ash.

You see, Willow thinks she's in love with Devon. She's lying to herself. The thing is, Devon *is* in love with Willow. Last night, they made love, and I learned about it tonight from Robin. Hence the reason why I dressed up in a strapless dress sans underwear, and I tried, *tried* to bob some dick's dick at a party to make myself feel worse than I already do.

As I said, it's all my fault. I zipped my lips, embarrassed and hurt with the way Devon had treated me, and shamed and guilty over what happened between Kieren and me. I wanted one person on this planet to look up to me, to think my shit was together, and that person was Willow. We all need someone who believes in us or else we are nothing.

Nothing.

Even now, when I'm more down on myself than ever, it's not as if I can forget Willow, even if I wasn't riding in her car. My best cousin is like my little sister. I can never call Willow my best *friend*, because I can never allow her to know the real me. I love her to the moon and back. I love Willow so much that I gave her the love of my life, because I love Devon that much too.

Devon made Willow laugh. Willow made Devon smile. I forced their kiss at the twins' fourteenth birthday party as a test, and it murdered something vital within me when I saw the spark. The connection. Devon and Willow had something Devon and I could never have– never *had*. I swallowed my pain, my jealousy, and strived to be a better person by being happy because they were happy.

It will be worth it if they can love each other as much as I love them, since neither of them can love me the way I need. Because I'm not worthy of either of their love. I hear this on repeat in my mind, as I try to forget how that afternoon kiss spawned evening sex.

"Essie," Bethany breathes, knowing the exact direction of my thoughts. As if a message from God above, rain splatters drops upon the windshield since I long ago lost the ability to shed tears.

"Is this what rock bottom feels like?" I muse more to myself than to Beth, while staring down at my knotted fingers.

"Um... Essie? What the fuck do I do?" Beth says in a panic, voice wavering. "Dude! Motherfuck! LOOK!" she shouts, laying on the brakes, careening my forehead into the dashboard.

Eyes slowing rising, I draw in a deep breath.

Déjà vu, motherfucker.

Pacing the sidewalk in front of Wreck & Ruin Repair, doing the Mason frustrated hair yank, isn't the brother I picked up on the side of the road as he cried in the rain. No, it's *my* Mason brother.

"Devon," I breathe, and as if he hears me, his head slowly rises in my direction. For the first time since I was thirteen, Devon looks at me– he looks at me like he sees *me*. *His* Essie.

Wrenching my door open, Devon yanks me from the car, only to pull me into his lap. He's sopping wet, and smells deliciously like Devon– like home.

"You ever do something for someone's own good, but it hurts like nothing has ever hurt before?" Devon says as he shuts us in the car– Willow's car –and I know he's speaking only to me. Speaking to me for the first time in more than seven years.

"Every single day," I whisper.

Pulling away from the curb, Beth whispers. "No, *this* is rock bottom."

CHAPTER TWO

Devon Mason

This would be hilarious if it were anything *but...* prowling around like a pair of caged tigers, Ren and I do our thing: scowling at the floor, pacing a hole into the carpeting, tugging at our hair until it sticks straight up. Basically, acting all a fool.

Brothers.

"What the fuck is up with you?" Dad barks when I almost smash his bare foot on my way by. He sits farther up in his recliner, jacking the lever until he's almost horizontal. I know he's stressed, but a thinly veiled insult is on the tip of my tongue anyway.

Kieren beats me to the punch, "I want Dev to tell Willow the truth."

The click of the lever on the recliner is louder than a gunshot, and we'd all know, seeing as how our house has been used for target practice twice in my lifetime. *POP* Dad sits up, staring at me with interest. "Ya gonna tell her, son?"

Dad and Ren stare at me with similar expressions of endless patience, and it just pisses me the fuck off. "Only if coerced," I snarl, teeth bared.

More patience from father and brother– *motherfuck*!

Guilt, we are old friends. The best of friends. "Willow needs to know." I agree just to shut them down. She does need to know, but does she need to know from *me*? That's the guilt talking, no doubt.

Guilt– a bastard more patient than my father and his youngest sons.

I hate every person on the planet tonight, but especially myself. With an about-face, knowing the matter is settled, I pace another circuit around the coffee table. Ren plunks down on the couch, size fourteens almost upending my ass. I glare on my way by– disaster averted. I see the judgment in their identical blue eyes.

Yes, I'm sober! Fuck you very much. Thanks for asking.

Another circuit, where I try my damnedest not to stare at the couch, at the coffee table, but I fail as usual. No surprise, since I'm the Mason equivalent of a failure. I'm the worst sort of human being. Instead of seeing my loving mother sitting on that sofa, the ghost of my girlfriend flashes before my eyes.

Essie.

Hester Prynne was the only bright spot in an otherwise shitty fucking existence. A veil of nostalgia descends on me, similar to a drug haze or a manic episode. I have the ability to do two things at once– in my mind –and I highly doubt that is normal. Like now, I hold a semi-coherent conversation with my dad and brother, all the while I draw inside myself. *Semi*-coherent, hence why they always think I'm trashed on something good– *bad!*

Bad, but oh-so fucking good...

My favorite time of day was late afternoon when I was a little shit. Essie and I would humor Ren by playing board games. That last time was the best time. Shoulder-to-shoulder, Essie and I sat in the center of the couch, with Ren sitting on the floor on the opposite side of the coffee table. Rae was begging to join our Monopoly game, as if she wasn't already helping Ren cheat. West was *washing* his Matchbox cars with a dusting rag and a can of Pledge, after driving them around outside and getting their tires dirty.

Dad was at work, saving the neighborhood while wearing his superhero badge. Mom was quietly zoning out on her latest pharmaceuticals– I come by my love of all things chemical dependency from Mommy Dearest. Aunt Isis escaped our shit to sink into her own, off sucking my uncle's dick and playing house with Robin above Rush. God, how I envied Isis, almost enough to take my turn at the Beast as payment out of Hell.

The best moments in life are the most mundane yet the most prolific. One glance, that's all it took. I looked over at Essie and saw the same look in her eyes that I saw when I gazed in the mirror. She was looking at Ren and Rae tickling the shit out of West, his high-pitched giggle infectious. Essie looked like she was home, like we were her family. Here was an outsider who wanted to be here when I wanted to escape. But with her here, it was worth staying.

Back then, I was the horniest motherfucker on the planet– I'm a Mason. One morning I woke up with wood, and it was a Divining Rod pointed at Essie. Essie was my best friend back then– a total sweetheart who would do anything I asked, and I asked and received.

Shameless, I leaned over to capture Essie's rosebud-shaped mouth, a tiny squeak fluttering against my lips. I pulled away quickly after showing Essie what I wanted, not wanting to corrupt the innocent in the room: Raven and Weston.

Kieren? That boy popped out Mom's cunt a full-grown Mason. Innocent? Never. He saw my first wood, figured out who caused it, and I swear to God, that asshole willed one of his own just to spite me. A week prior to my best day and worst night of life, I had to show the little prick how to tug one out to stop him from staring at Essie's tits like he was a thirsty baby craving milk. Ren would hole himself in our bathroom, jerking to visions of my girlfriend's tits.

Brothers are a special breed. We love each other like no other, and hate each other just as equally. We are our only competition. We are our only backup. It's a discombobulating feeling to simultaneously have the back of the one you're angling to stab for shits 'n' giggles. A little more than two years younger than me, I'd lay awake at night with visions of hacking off Ren's dick if it ever grew bigger than mine. Kieren's saving grace, we're exactly the same size. How do I know? I measured it– his and mine –every year on our birthdays.

I never said I was sane.

Why is this memory in my head while I hold a semi-coherent convo with Dad and Ren? Because those fucks want me to tell Willow our secret– a secret that happened *that* night. The worst night of my best day.

Taking my kiss as a hint, Ren whined, "But I wanted to finish our game first."

"It's Monopoly." I pointed at the board. *"It takes hours to finish a game."* Pointing at Ren's fangirl cheater, *"And you always win."* Raven worships Ren and loves West the best. She and I are too much alike to get along– we have too much of Aunt Isis and Mom in us, and not enough of Dad.

Shady eyes darting toward my girl's chest, "I'd rather lose," my brother mumbled, almost earning himself an ass kicking. *Pissed at me after asking the night before if it felt better to have someone else touch it, Ren punishes us all. "I'll make dinner, but we're having spaghetti again."*

Mock-groaning and rolling around on the carpet while clutching his stomach, Weston showed his budding proficiency for sarcasm– the only trait he gained from Aunt Isis, much to Dad's relief.

There are two shades of Mason: light and dark, and the dark seemed to only get darker with the addition of Camille Jamison's genes... and we aren't talking about hair color, either.

Light: Dad and Ren. The lightest of us all: West.

Dark: Isis and Rae. The darkest of us all, even darker than Mom: me.

"I love spaghetti," Raven chirped, hopping up to help her hero.

"Good," I said, tugging Essie to stand up next to me, causing her to giggle near my ear. "'Cuz we eat it six days a week." I pulled Essie through the living room toward Ren's and my bedroom for our afternoon snack. Ren bolted by us, slamming the bathroom door behind him. "Wash your goddamn hands before you cook dinner, you pervert!" I shouted through the wooden door, pounding it with the side of my fist. "I'm not eating traces of your spunk on my noodles."

Snickering evilly, Kieren was finished before I even closed Essie inside my bedroom. "Um..." Essie trailed off, looking a bit green. "I'm glad I'm an only child. Seriously gross."

Laughing, my only comic relief back then, "I wouldn't touch anything in this room if I were you. You'd get knocked up off the sheets." I laugh harder when Essie flashes across the room, avoiding all contact with its surfaces. "Be happy Ren's not in here with us– the boy is even tugging on it in his sleep. One of these days he's gonna wake up with it broken off in his hand."

The mouth I planned on sucking twisted up in revulsion, "Gross..." Essie wasn't a fan of jizz. Her tiny lips puckered up in remembrance over when I 'accidentally' didn't tell her I was about to blow.

"You're too cute." I laughed sinisterly, tossing Essie on my bed, hoping the sheets knocked her up. I stared down at her, marveling over how she was mine.

I wasn't very tall back then, with Ren towering over me and Weston quickly gaining ground, but Essie only ever reached five foot. Built like a tiny woman with huge tits, a fourteen-year-old Essie was my ultimate wet dream, one I've had since I could spurt– still do in my sleep after catching sight of her grown woman's body now.

The worst night of my life hadn't happened yet, so I was still a Mason. *Motor running at full tilt, the vision of my pinup girlfriend almost brought me to my knees. We'd been making out for months, and getting each other off for weeks with our hands and mouths. Ren's question from the night before put a singular thought into my mind– one that wouldn't leave. For the past week, no matter how many times I got off, my wood wouldn't go down.*

With a singular purpose, I stripped down bare-assed naked, shocking the hell out of Essie. If I live to be a thousand years old, I will never forget the look in my girlfriend's eyes. Fear and trust.

As a precursor, "Do you trust me?" I asked, even though I knew she did. No verbal reply necessary, Essie scrunched up, hitching her skirt above her hips, and then she tugged her pink panties down her thighs.

I should preface this– I'm a liar.

I lie.

About everything.

To everyone.

For no reason and for every reason.

But I'd never lied to Essie before, and it was the first of many. *"I'll only stick the tip in," I said slyly, knowing it was a bullshit lie as it rolled off my tongue. I knew once I was in there, I'd be 'in' there. I was a week away from my fourteenth birthday, too young but hormone-crazed. It was the least of my lies– a lie every guys tells at one point in their lives.*

The thing about Essie, she knew I was lying and was okay with it.

Breathless, feeling a bit high even though I'd never taken a hit of any drug– I just instinctively knew that was the sensation. I was too eager to make it good for Essie. I crawled over her, pressing my boy-sized junk up against her perfect pussy... and I got the tip in. Just the tip, and it was pure bliss– and then someone yanked my hair out by the roots and tossed my ass on the floor with a deep grunt. I hurt. My hair hurt. My balls ached as my tip leaked like a faucet.

With a shriek, Essie skittered across my bed to hide in the corner, her skirt tucked over her knees. Wrapping her arms around her legs with her knees pressed to her chest, Essie looked terrified.

I wasn't.

I'm a motherfucking Mason, and we have big balls– metaphorical ones, that is.

I rolled my eyes up to connect to my furious aunt's. Haloed from the light of the hallway, my aunt's hair was wafting around her head like her anger fueled static electricity. "Way to ruin the moment, Isis," I snarled. This was the first changing point in my life. It was the first time I felt rage boil in my blood.

"What. The. Fuck?" Isis bit out, talons curled to her palms, blood dripping to the carpet along with chunks of my hair. As I said, Aunt Isis and me, one in the same.

Evil.

"Pretty sure I was trying to fuck my girlfriend for the first time. Thanks for the save, Auntie," I spit sarcastically– bitterly. "Don't get all sanctimonious on me, bitch. You were my age when I walked in on you and Tweety."

Blue eyes turning as black as night, mirroring my own, "And your Dad shot Rob's dick," Isis reminds me, causing me to bark a laugh.

"What?" Essie gasped as she reached for her panties. She hid them in her palm, like it changed a damn thing.

"The gun wasn't loaded." Isis tosses it off, like Dad didn't hold Rob down on the couch with his forearm pressed into Rob's windpipe with the barrel of his service piece shoved up against Robin's crotch... and then Dad pulled the trigger. Robin pissed his pants and all over the couch cushions. Bad at learning lessons, Rob still didn't behave after that. Just as bad at learning lessons, neither did I.

"You do realize Malcolm won't be pointing his gun at Essie, right?" Isis said, smirking evilly.

"Right," I grunted as I rolled to my feet to yank on my jeans. "Right."

"Malcolm has two spares and he can always make more," Isis reminds me I'm the oldest of many. "He doesn't need grandchildren from you, especially at fourteen."

"I don't know what you're talking about," I muttered absentmindedly. I did know, though. If Dad had caught my ass, he would've castrated me on the spot. This was premeditated, and not driven by my hormones. When Essie looked at my siblings like they were hers, I wanted her to be part of the family forever. We're Masons, and we're only good at making more Masons. Instead of running away, I would be content staying here. But only if Essie was with me.

"I'm sorry, hun," Isis said softly, and she sounded sorry. Aunt Isis was always about girl power. "You're not in trouble, and I'm not mad at you," sounding understanding. "You better go home, sweetheart."

Skittishly, Essie got off the bed, like if she made herself smaller we wouldn't notice her. There was nothing in the world that could make me forget about the girl. Brushing by me, I said the hell with it and kissed her goodbye– really, really kissed her: hand fisting the hair at the nape of her neck, lips mashing, tongues fighting violently. Call it a premonition, I knew it was goodbye– the kiss to last a lifetime.

I never said I was sorry, because I wasn't.

I didn't realize I was crying until after my bedroom door was closed, shutting Isis inside with me. Palming my forehead, my aunt drew her knee up and gave me something to truly cry about. With a deep grunt of pain, I collapsed on the floor and vomited, shuddering in fiery agony.

"You make me sick," Isis spit at me, literally spit on me. "You shouldn't fuck before you're full-grown. I saw your stubby dick." Getting gradually louder with every word uttered, "But worse, you shouldn't try to trap a girl by not wearing a GODDAMNED CONDOM!"

That's not how my best afternoon turned into my worst night. Never learning, I'd planned on doing Essie the next afternoon, and *not* wearing a condom. I needed Essie to save me from this nightmare, to save me from this hell, to save me from myself. I needed Essie to give me a reason to breathe as the darkness descended.

Retribution for my abysmal plan came in the form of three convict rapists that very evening. The only saving grace is how Aunt Isis was so pissed at me, she took Raven and Weston with her when she left me lying on my bedroom floor. She tried to take Ren. But as I said, we're brothers. Ren had my back by cleaning up my puke and putting a bag of frozen peas on my swollen nutsack. Not knowing, if I'd had Ren's back, I would've made Ren go with my aunt and baby brother and sister... and he would've been saved from the nightmare.

Mom deserved what happened to her. The beginning of her end. The humane way to put herself out of her misery.

I deserved what happened to me– the loss of my Masonhood. Since that night, I've never felt the urge for sex again. Not even last night when I was with Willow three times. But then again, that wasn't fueled by passion or lust, and it makes me sick to even contemplate why I did it.

But I will never release the guilt of what happened to the one person on this planet I was born to protect.

Decision made, I finally turn to my brother and do the right thing. "Cowboy up. Let's go tell Willow our secret."

CHAPTER THREE

Devon Mason

There is an unspoken form of communication between Ren and me. Always has been, always will be. We have each other's backs because we're the only ones who can hurt the other– that's our twisted version of symmetry.

What happens when both brothers are doing their damnedest to balance the guilt and shame, to make things even?

A clusterfuck of epic proportions is what.

Retribution, bitch!

I hated myself, so I lost my girl. My brother hated himself and me, so he took my girl. I hate my brother, so I took his girl. My brother loves me, so he let me have her. If I loved Ren enough, I wouldn't have taken Willow from him. It's a test of our loyalty– our brotherhood –and an unending vicious circle.

I shoved Essie away because I loved her, because I was ruined inside and out. The sicker I got, the more I realized I couldn't be the person she needed me to be. I have Mom's illness growing inside my mind like a coil of black, angry smoke, eating my brain like the virus that turns you into a zombie. I've known this forever, but the nightmare unleashed it early.

The night Ren came home and told me he lost his virginity to Essie, taking what was rightfully mine, I snapped. It took both Dad and Auggie to tear us off each other. I ended up with a broken wrist and three cracked ribs to Ren's blackened eye and fractured collarbone. Dad said it was brothers forming a bond. Robin said it was attempted murder, and the cop should have recognized it. Dad smacked Rob upside the head and walked away laughing… that night, Ren woke up with me straddling his chest and my pillow smothering his face, proving Robin Prynne right.

Around the time Ren's legs stopped kicking and his arms stopping flailing, I changed my mind. I'm a Mason, and we're patient. I began a long-term game, playing more strategically than Ren does on the football field. The thing is, I had nothing to win or lose. I had nothing. I was nothing. I had no reason to breathe. But unlike Mom, I was too cowardly to end it all.

The cycle ends tonight, which means I have to turn into the biggest bastard on the planet for all of our sakes. How altruistic. Time to give Kieren his girl back, after I fucked her like he fucked mine. It's my turn to spill our secret to his girl, like he spilled it to mine… after he fucked her.

Symmetry.

Being the better person, Ren didn't try to kill me when I got home this morning after I gave him every single exaggerated, antagonizing detail of Willow's and my tryst. The lack of violence was unsatisfying, because I *needed* it to feel alive.

As usual, I decide I should probably get out of my head and determine what kind of situation I've been in for the past half hour. I find myself pacing a small space in front of Willow and Kieren as they sit on a futon mattress above Wreck & Ruin's service bay.

Of course, half my brain is running my mouth while the other half is plotting in misery. "NO! I'm the big brother! I'm the one who's supposed to protect you, Goddammit!" I scream bloody murder until my voice cracks and my mouth runs dry– I scream the truth. Tortured, I realize I shouldn't have done what I did last night. When will I ever learn?

A deep keen rumbles up my chest, a sound of pure agony. The sound echoes back, over and over from the service bay beneath us. Stunned by my outburst, I freeze, feeling haunted and ashamed.

Last night, while I was inside Willow, the only thing I could think of was my brother and Essie. What got my dick up was fury. It was laughable how Auggie and Willow thought it was my nightmare that stopped me. Not once did my mother and the rapists enter my mind. That's the beauty of my sickness; I choose what to think of, and I've never relived the nightmare.

I was able to penetrate Willow because I kept seeing Ren *inside* my woman. What kept me going to the end, I had to win. Ren never finished, but I did. Round two and three were a disaster. I was suffocating on guilt, realizing retribution meant jack-shit, and as much as I was hurting Willow, Ren, and Essie, I was hurting myself more… and if that didn't feel satisfying and horribly fascinating.

"It's been you and me, side-by-side, since I was twelve and you were fourteen, bro. None of that superhero bullshit outta your mouth again! This isn't just about you anymore, Dev. Willow needs the truth, because she has to make an informed decision on whether or not she wants her family connected to ours. We have to tell her the truth. *Now*," Kieren demands softly.

I whip my head around, tears splattering my cheeks when I didn't even realize I was crying. It's laughable, Ren thinking I'm reluctant to tell Willow the truth. But in reality, I'm fighting myself. Retribution and balance versus brotherhood and loyalty. If I tell Willow, the circle is complete. If Ren tells her, I'm selfless enough to give them one of the most intimate, bonding moments of their lives. The moment Ren took away from me with Essie.

"I can't do this sober," I groan, needing something to numb my mania.

"No! No, fucking way. Not around me, and not around Willow, you selfish asshole. It's bad enough you have me taking your piss tests," Kieren snarls.

Ren offered, and now he's bitching about it?

"What?" Willow breathes, tiny face twisting up in pain. "What...You're still using?" Willow begins to shake as betrayal floods her veins, just as I knew it would. Within seconds, she's silently crying. I feel a twinge of hurt for her, but that's about it. A slight twinge of regret.

Do I love Willow? Yes.

Am I *in* love with Willow? No.

I see Willow as Kieren's, which makes her family. I love her. She's a comfort to me– a friend. She's an incredible person, but not *my* incredible person. Spending time with Ren's girl was a blast, a distraction I enjoyed. Hugging her was like going home after a long vacation. Kissing her was to hurt myself as much as I was hurting Essie. Fucking her was torture– for all of us. A torture Willow deserved just as much as the rest of us. The girl should've said no. She should've loved Ren enough to push me away. Willow should have realized *Mr. Kline* is never right, and he belongs to Isis and Robin.

Do I want to hurt Willow? No, but it's necessary for her future happiness. Now, if Willow hurts Ren, the #2 person in my life, I'll smother her. If Willow hurts the #1 person in my life, I'll tear her fucking head off and shove it up Ren's ass without a second thought.

I never said I was sane. In fact, I said I wasn't.

Do I want to tempt Willow with my pot-smoking ways? No. It's not about Willow. Pot is the medication for my manic phase. I'm scared to get a real diagnosis of being Bipolar, because it will destroy my dad. So I use street drugs as medication. I smoke pot to calm myself on nights like tonight. When I'm in the depressive stage, I go for the hardcore uppers to drag my ass out of my suicidal thoughts.

I take drugs for Dad's sanity and happiness. HA!

"Willow," Kieren sighs her name while reaching over to hold her hand. Technically, Willow is my girlfriend, and the only thing I feel the moment their hands connect is relief. On the heels of that is the perfection of it all. "No matter what he's told you, or what excuses he will undoubtedly begin to make, Devon's never stopped. Not one day."

"You can join me," I offer just to be an ass. I'd rather throw both of them over the edge of the loft and onto the concrete floor below than let either one of them touch my medicine. I don't share. This shit is expensive... for the criminals I arrest and pocket any medicine they have on their person, which is why I became a cop in the first place. I pull my pipe out of my jacket pocket, testing Willow's resolve. I smirk when she flinches as if struck.

"You've got to be fucking kidding me," Willow mutters in utter disbelief. "I didn't work my ass off over the past 119 days to stay sober to have a drug addict pull me back in."

I unleash the bastard inside myself. With a snide voice, I crash Willow's world because I can. "So high and mighty–judgmental. Willow, who could keep up with the impossible goals you've set? In the end, you're still a lost, little girl, just one who's no fun anymore."

Trying to act nonchalant, I fish my lighter out of my pocket, but my shaking hands betray me. Willow narrows her eyes, gaze filled with disgust. No doubt the bitch thinks I'm tweaking, when in reality I'm battling my conscience. Redemption screams I need to leave. Retribution demands I stay to the end.

"Wow... Fuck. You. Devon. You self-righteous prick." Willow's voice quivers, breaks, and it satisfies the hate-filled person who dwells just beneath my surface.

Ren, half believing my act and half knowing I'm doing him a favor, turns on the dramatics. "Welcome to my world, Willow. The three stages of Devon Mason: the sober asshole, the tweaking bastard, and the high fucker posing as our local hero.

You've only known the poser." Kieren gestures toward me, and then back to Willow, "Meet the tweaker. This bastard says horrific shit as an excuse to light up. The damage is already done, right, Dev? So you might as well just light up and do your worst, right? That is your M.O. You're a victim of the past, and you use my resentment as an excuse to do drugs to punish yourself. I agree with Willow– Fuck. You. Devon."

"Fuck you, too," I say shamelessly, softly chuckling to myself. Victim of the past? I can't even remember that goddamned nightmare, let alone be its bitch. It's called Bipolar, brother. Welcome to Mom's legacy.

"You have no idea how selfish you are, or what I have to go through because of you. You're blind. You run around as Dad's pride and joy and Fairport's golden boy, while you leave me looking like a loser. I'm the one feeding two kids three square meals a day, making them do their homework, making sure they get to bed on time. I'm the one who gives the hugs. I'm the one that has to go to school and beat the hell outta guys who hit on Raven. Now I'm taking care of the twins' issues too! Last week West came home with a shiner for defending Seth, so I went to school and put the fear of God into three freshmen. Violet was getting harassed by some mean girls, so I sicced Rae on them– now *that* took a lot of convincing."

"Kieren, why didn't you tell me about that?" Willow squeaks out, amusing me to no end.

I'm doing them a favor. Really. They might not realize it tonight, but they will soon enough. Now they can have each other to lean on by getting the job done right as a team.

"The kids needed muscle not brains," Kieren mumbles to Willow, and then he turns rabid on me. "Every night I have to sit at the kitchen table and explain to two kids why their brother won't fucking eat so he can feel the high better. I'm the one whose bedroom stinks from when you pass the fuck out and piss yourself. I'm the one you manipulate into lying to everyone because the truth would kill them. I. Am. The. One. Who. Sacrificed. Their. Future. So. You. Could. Have. One… and you throw it in my fucking face. Hell, you throw it away!"

Now that was just mean– the piss the bed comment. I haven't done that since I took my first drink freshman year. I got pass out drunk after watching Essie blow some tool. The only reaction Essie got from me was when I handed the ass a condom and told him not to soil her pretty mouth because she hated the taste of spunk. I leaned back against the wall and forced her to blow him in front of me. We had an intense staring contest the entire time, and she hated every second of it. (The blowjob, not our eye-fucking) Essie should've never done it, but she did.

Mentally I wanted Essie. Thriving on our eye-fucking, I got the first hard-on since my nightmare. Sadly, since that night, only anger and drugs force blood to flow south. Since Essie acted like she wanted– *needed* –sex, and I couldn't give it to her, I watched out to make sure she was safe. No longer my girlfriend, Essie will always be my best friend. So, I embarrassed Essie and got the word out that her body was condoms-only. I stressed my point afterward when I busted the tool's taillights out with a beer bottle, dumped a bottle of Jack all over the interior of his car, and then sicced Colin McGregor on him for traffic violations and a DUI.

The only dude I know for a fact Essie screwed, besides my brother, was Mike– a kid a few years older than us who is kind of slow but girls found him *hot*. I knew Essie was shit-faced, so I stood in the shadows waiting for her to say no, ready to murder Mike. Not only did she not say no, she grumbled yes. Essie hated every second of it, but he was gentle and quick about it, and that's the only reason Mike still breathes. I think I owe that tool a visit.

As I said, I'm a Mason. Patient. Plotting. I get even in a way no one will ever see coming. It may take years, but it'll happen eventually.

Clicking back in with the conversation, I find myself annoyed. I turn defensive because Ren is rewriting history to suit his agenda. "I didn't ask you to turn the football scholarship down so I could go to the academy."

"No, but I had to because all the responsibility falls on my shoulders. With both of us gone, Dad couldn't do it alone. I didn't do it for you; I did it for our family. It's what a man should do. Here you are, Officer Devon Mason, living the life of a drug addict and a drunk while arresting people just like yourself. Hypocrite. It's a spit in the face how you use our past as an excuse. I was there with you throughout everything, yet you're the addict and I'm the one taking the responsibilities for the pair of us, big brother," he twists nastily.

Not wanting to argue how wrong Ren is on all accounts, I redirect the conversation. "You're just pissed about Willow," I snarl, needing him to say it out loud so I can rub it in, but mostly so Willow can hear it. "Admit it. Finally admit it, Ren," I demand.

"YES!" Kieren screams at me, eyes bulging from their sockets, with the vein above his left eyebrow twitching.

FINALLY! I grin like a dog lapping up a cat's spilt cream.

"Yes, you have *my* girlfriend because *our* family gave her to you, you entitled prick! And you're fucking it all up instead of appreciating what was given. You are an amazing actor, I'll give you that. You have them all wrapped around your drug addict fingertip, thinking you're getting better, so they give you anything you fucking want while I get denied. Denied. DENIED!" Kieren's scream of frustration and agony would have brought me to my knees if I hadn't heard worse from him before.

Veins visibly pulsing in his forehead, chest rapidly rising and falling from breathlessness, I worry if Kieren doesn't calm down, he may harm himself. Willow takes the comforting out of my hands, just as I'd hoped. My *girlfriend* reaches over to pat my brother's back, trying to soothe him.

Me? I point at myself. I'm the one to blame for that stupid-assed fiasco Auggie was pulling to get Auntie's attention, so Rob turned manipulative commando on all our asses. The fuck?

For fuck's sake, everyone always seems to forget how Willow could've said no to Auggie and me and just got it on with Ren like she wanted to do in the first place. My brother ought to be blaming Willow, not me.

"How do you think it makes me feel, Ren? How would you feel if Willow came to you only because Auggie manipulated her into it? How would you feel if you had to listen to Willow and Auggie talk about you while you pretended to sleep? How would you like to wonder whether or not Willow likes you for you, or because she's being brainwashed?"

"That isn't true, Devon," Willow interrupts Ren's reply. "If you listened last night, then you know that isn't the case. You're my friend. I thought you were my boyfriend. I was… intimate," her voice breaks, making me feel odd, "with you last night… and this morning you didn't seem to mind whatever you overheard… repeatedly, I might add."

"You don't know the real me, Willow," I caution. "But now isn't the right time to talk about this because I don't feel like myself." Running a hand through my dark hair, I begin to pace the small open space in front of the futon again. I have to think. I have to have some smoke.

"Humph," Kieren grunts out. "Let me answer your earlier question: how would I feel about '*insert your selfish, addict ramblings here*'? Gee, I don't know, Dev," Kieren twists sarcastically. "Probably about as good as it feels to watch Auggie warp Willow's mind against me, but I'm okay with that because it has helped Willow better herself. I'm guessing your wounds don't bleed as badly as mine– how would you have liked to lie in bed last night, knowing *I* was inside Willow. Hmm? It killed me." Kieren presses a fist to the center of his chest and releases a tortured sound.

Kieren sounds broken, so that part of Willow she tries to bury erupts. She tries to give Ren a hug, which pisses me the fuck off. As the eldest, it's my responsibility to comfort my brother– bitch. Bitch should've said no– should've been in Ren's bed, not letting Auggie brainwash her. Now she's hugging my brother...

Not that I want to comfort Mr. Perfect narcissist right now. I'm pretty sure I have a good idea how Ren felt last night, which is why I did it in the first place, since he started it all by fucking Essie. Asshole.

"You always make everything about you," I mumble, pointing at how my *girlfriend* is trying to comfort him.

"What?!" Kieren shouts, sounding incredulous. "Fuck. You. Devon. There, now you have an excuse to toke up. So toke the fuck up, buddy." Kieren spits the words out, filling his voice with humorless attitude. "C'mon, ya know you're gonna do it anyway. Punish yourself by punishing us– go on now," Kieren coaxes me to disappoint him.

I glare at them as they sit on the futon mattress, because they don't get it. Ren is my brother. Willow is supposedly my girlfriend right now– my friend. They are so blinded by the drugs that they don't seem to realize I'm doing it for something other than attention, and that maybe the issue isn't the drugs. It sickens me since Ren had a front row seat to the train wreck known as Mom. Don't they get that I can't get the words out? That they get stuck in my throat?

"I'm sick."

"I'm crazy."

"I need help– help me, please."

I've tried for the past few years to say the words to Ren and my dad, and they get stuck in my throat, suffocating me. I've never felt as alone as I do with two of the most important people in my life judging me, not *seeing* me for who I am. They're so blinded by what they think I did to them that they don't see what they are doing to me, what I'm doing *for* them.

Fuck 'em. I need my medicine. With the ease of years of practice, my lips automatically seek out my pipe while my finger flicks my lighter to life. With a deep draw of relaxing bliss, I thank Jimmy from my earlier traffic stop. Jimmy is a known pot dealer, so I tail him around, waiting for him to do something that warrants flicking on my lights. Jimmy rolled through a stop sign this afternoon, and I left him with a warning and a three day supply of medicine.

"How dare you?" Willow shouts, sounding aghast, which is now funny in my drug haze. I toke up again. "How dare you bring me here and close me in without escape and do the one thing I'm trying to avoid?"

I show Willow the real me for a second before I realize I'm supposed to be *bad* cop tonight– the bastard prick who's breaking her heart so she'll turn to my little bro. Voice dry from the smoke, "And you call me self-righteous? Your body will thank me for the contact buzz even if you won't."

Wordless, Willow makes a noise in the back of her throat that sounds like death. Her face turns red as she tries her damnedest not to breathe. For the first time ever, I see the family resemblance. I take another toke before I end up telling Willow she's almost as cute as Essie.

Knight in worn denim, "C'mere, Spanky." Kieren tugs Willow into his lap. He unzips his jacket and tucks her against his chest, and then zips his jacket, enclosing her face and shoulders. "There now," he whispers while rocking her back and forth. "The mean smoke can't get you in there. I'm so fucking sorry, Willow. I wouldn't have brought you here if I'd known Devon was gonna snap. I think last night was too much for him to handle, adding that to my pressure over telling you the truth. It's my fault."

I snort, roll my eyes, and then realize Willow can't hear or see me for the irony of it. "Mr. Responsible," I grumble at my brother, wondering what will ever make him toke up or drain more than a single beer in a sitting.

Ignoring me as my medicine seeps through my system, Ren proves who his #1 is. "So I bought a few tickets to the Comic

Expo in Boston next month," Kieren says to distract Willow. "I thought we could take the boys and see if we could find anything for you to hock on Revamped's website. That would be fun, huh? I'll have my buddy join us instead of Devon. I'm too pissed off at him to look at him at the moment."

Feeling like a mime, I flip my brother off, make a blowjob gesture with my pot pipe, and then a handjob motion. I finish it off with the roll of my fingertip, calling myself crazy, which earns me a big motherfucking grin from the blond giant.

I'm not really feeling that blissed out. My tolerance is hardcore now. I'm just mellow, no longer experiencing that intense feeling of anxiety. It's like creepy crawlies in my brain, taking over and making me do shit I'll regret. But I have to do it or explode.

Ren experiences Restless Leg Syndrome, and Weston is following in his footsteps from all the sports training. When they explained how it felt to me, a light bulb went on in my mind. My brothers said they had to get up and walk around, that nothing could keep their legs still– like their nerves just move on their own.

Being Bipolar is Restless Mental Syndrome, and you need something to soothe it. The manic phase is exactly how the nerves in their legs feel, how I feel when I clean at two in the morning because I can't sleep. How I will do one thing right after the next, never completing a task because there is always something else that needs to be done now. There is a signal in my brain that screams **MOVE! NOW!** So I do…

Being manic is a high without a drug, to the point that I have to take drugs to dampen my high. Imagine your mind is a heavy metal song, but all the instruments are giving conflicting sounds, and you're doing all you can do to make sure the bass doesn't overpower the guitar, and the drummer is pounding out a wicked solo, drawing the song in a new direction.

I've yet to find anything to properly represent the depression aspect. Perhaps death is the only way to describe the low of depression. You just feel dead in a sea of hopelessness, without the ability to move as all life has to offer flies by in waves of fast-forward and rewind. Everything you once loved, no longer sparks any interest. Ever. The only thing the inflicted seeks is relief. Something to make you high again. Anything to make you feel alive for only a few seconds. A reprieve in an endless expanse of shadowy nothingness.

My mother rode the sea of depression ninety percent of the time, with bursts of mania that were intoxicating to hitch a ride when I was a kid. I learned from an early age, the higher the high, the farther you fell. My mother succumbed to her depression, and I've never blamed her. Everyone who resents Camille Jamison Mason for taking her own life doesn't understand, and never will.

I understand.

I hate Mom for another reason– I hate her for passing this legacy onto me. The only saving grace is that our symptoms were in reverse. I'm almost always manic.

High. Riding a high with or without drugs.

"Ah, now that's better," Kieren murmurs to Willow while holding my gaze. No doubt he's searching to make sure the wildness has abated in the back of my eyes. "Dev's back to being Dev again."

"Sorry," I mutter, still mulling over my illness. I blush, embarrassed that I allowed Ren to see that much of my Jekyll and Hyde routine. "Jesus, I'm sorry. You know how I get. I haven't had anything in over thirty-six hours, not since just before the twins' birthday party."

"The only reason I don't go straight to Dad is because I'd rather have this Devon, the stable yet high Devon, versus the asshole who could verbally assault the kids."

"I apologized," I offer lamely, finally feeling semi-in-control of the firing of my synapses, my reactions, and my emotions.

"Yeah, 'cuz that right there is good enough," Kieren says sarcastically, shooting fury in my veins. It's a test of my well-honed patience not to strangle my brother when he doesn't get it. "You don't understand what you probably just lost, fuckface. Do you have any idea what you just ruined?"

Lost? More like handed you Willow on a silver platter, brother. You're welcome even though you never said thank you. "Willow will hate me as much as I hate myself by the time we're done with the truth," I say defensively.

As the oldest, I was supposed to protect my mother. My brother.

I failed on both accounts.

The look Kieren flashes me breaks my heart. It's that look of compassion that makes me choose redemption over retribution, even if it makes me look like a spineless asshole. Not only do I put Willow on a silver platter for Kieren, I drop her into his lap like a gift. I couldn't protect Ren from the three bad men and the nightmare, but I can be the bigger, better man for once. I decide to break the cycle before it's complete. I gift Ren the intimacy of sharing our secret, gaining us all closure. I give Ren the beginning of his happily ever after– the beginning I was never offered.

I mouth to Ren, "*I love you, bro*," and then I say for Willow's benefit, allowing my voice to waver, "I can't do it. I'm too much of a coward. You have my permission to tell Willow everything."

Awed, Kieren unzips his jacket, letting Willow loose, like seeing my *girlfriend* will make me fight instead of flee. With huge, watering brown eyes set in a tiny face, Willow stares at me like she's never seen me before. The real me. For a brief moment, I show her exactly who I truly am… and it's terrifying.

Breath caught in my lungs, heart hammering against my ribcage, I abruptly turn on my heel, and then nearly topple to the floor. "I'm sorry," is the last thing I say. I grab the ladder, hook it into place, and crawl down to the service bay. Running faster than I did during training at the academy, I sprint across Wreck & Ruin to the back door. With a forceful lunge, I exit into the night– rain splatters my face like God is washing away my sins.

I'm an Atheist.

A seventies sun parts the rain– a yellow Volkswagen screeches to a halt a few feet from me. Slowly I raise my face, and what I find is something to believe in, something to grab onto… someone who makes me feel alive.

Essie.

CHAPTER FOUR

Essie Prynne

With a casual voice, as if it hasn't been the better part of a decade since he acknowledged Beth's and my presence, "You ever do something for someone's own good, but it hurts like nothing has ever hurt before?" Devon shuts us in the car– Willow's car –and I know he's speaking only to me. Speaking to me for the first time in more than seven years.

"Every single day," I whisper in return.

Time stills.

The windows fog from the rain hitting the hot car, and I've never felt clearer-headed in all my life. Shock and awe are all I feel, as not only Devon speaks to me but he touches me. Not only does he touch me, he engulfs me in his very presence. Every single one of my senses ignite. But instead of burning out, they burn brighter than ever before. My nostrils inhale their fill of Devon– the leather from his jacket combined with his natural musky scent. My eyes stare down at the track pants pulling tightly over his strong thighs as I sit in his lap. My skin quivers with greed as his weight presses into me. His labored breath panting in my ear causes a ripple to run along my spine, beading my flesh with goose bumps.

Taste.

Grabbing my face with both of his palms, Devon tastes *me* with his mouth, lips, tongue, and teeth. He devours me, never giving me a chance to kiss him back. Faster than my mind can follow, Devon is attacking my mouth, tearing my strapless dress down to my belly button, exposing my tits and *owning 'em like he's grown 'em*, and then he's picking me up and turning me until I'm straddling his thighs, dress riding up past my ass, showing off the fact that I went without underclothing this evening.

"HEY!" Bethany shouts, laying on the brakes, jarring us all forward in a rush. But I don't move an inch where Devon doesn't want me. Both of us ignore my best friend as she tries to peel me off Devon, which is an impossible feat with her blunt fingernails dragging across my forearms. "Stop it!" Beth swats Dev's hand as he works his fingers between us, trying to free the hardest dick I've ever felt.

As if in slow motion, Devon turns to Bethany and says in a cold voice, "Leave or watch, I don't care. But we will not be interrupted again," he warns, sounding scary, freezing Bethany's words before they can release.

The cadence of Devon's voice and the tinge of pot tainting his tongue draws me into my right mind. Blue eyes as dark as night swing back in my direction, capturing me, and I find comfort in the sober look Devon levels me. "Are you clean?" he whispers, followed by a subtle hitch in his breathing as he waits for my answer.

I want to tease Dev, ask him if he's *clean* drug-wise when I know he's talking about sexually. "Still zero to sixty in the blink of an eye, I see," I breathlessly gasp out, motherfucking shocked out of my skull. Devon laughs, and it's the first real laugh I've heard him release since the last time we were in this position, when he said I was *too cute*. The memory makes me forget all the pain he's inflicted and loosens my tongue. "Yeah, only flesh-to-flesh was with–"

"A Mason," Devon finishes for me, sounding relieved yet proud.

"Don't do this, Essie!" Bethany pleads, trying to tug me out of Devon's vise grip of an embrace. "Think!" She swats me in the forehead, trying to beat some sense into me. But with all things Devon Mason, I'm senseless.

In a heartbeat, Dev smothers the angel on my shoulder's pleas. As always, if Devon Mason asks, I give. If Devon Mason takes, I give more. In one fluid motion, Devon wrenches his dick out of his pants and shoves me down on it. Hard. Unforgiving… punishing us both.

"OH! MY! GOD! Oh. My. God. OhMyGod… ohmygod… ohmygod…" Bethany's background hysterics reverberate off the metal of the VW to fill my ears. I cannot concentrate on Beth's screaming because Devon has me stretched to the limit. It motherfucking hurts. Losing my virginity was nothing compared to this. Being raped was more humiliating than painful.

Agony. Searing, stinging, burning pain as Devon rides me raw without preparation.

Owns me.

Devon Mason

Ignoring the harpy in the car, I continue to act on impulse, reveling in the manic, ecstatic high that overpowers me. When Bethany gets an inch too close, my palm meets her forehead with a vicious shove. We've known each other since Pre-K, she'll fucking deal. It's not like I haven't watched her ride my uncle half a dozen times, much to my disgust, including that time with Willow helping.

To silence Beth's pleas to a god I don't believe in, I'm thankful for my mental illness. I switch off the active part of my brain and just... chill. "Holy hell," I utter to combat Beth's prayer. "Satan, I'm so sorry I hurt you," I croon to the woman surrounding me.

An unexpected warmth fills my black heart. Essie's whimper of pain eclipses everything. "Shh..." I comfort, hands rubbing her back, hips, and ass in a massaging rhythm. My eyes nearly roll back in my head at the feel of her fleshy curves meeting my fingertips. "How long's it been?" I rasp out, voice thick with ecstasy. "You've been a good girl, Essie. I'm not surprised."

Essie is tighter than Willow– much tighter. There is only one way that is humanly possible. I don't want to compare them, but when the skin covering your dick gets sheared off on the first thrust, and your girl is wet, she's either a virgin or a born-again-virgin. Since I have first-hand knowledge of Essie's blooding, and watched Mike rut like a buffoon...

"Cutie," I purr the nickname I gave Essie in elementary school. "It's okay." I rock her back and forth, doing my damnedest not to move my cock. "We'll wait 'til you adjust."

Suddenly quiet with her mouth gaping open, Beth shuts her trap, teeth clacking loudly. Leaning closer, the head shrinker eavesdrops to hear what Essie whispers in my ear. "You're bigger," Essie says with a gulp and a swallow.

Fucked. Up. I laugh. "I hope so, Essie. I wasn't even fourteen yet, and I wouldn't want a four inch dick for life. I'm sure I feel like a baseball bat right now, but I'm only average. I've checked," I admit wryly. "How long?" I ask again.

Instead of scratching me, Bethany rests her palm on mine where I'm rubbing Essie's back. "Don't," Bethany warns, causing me to meet her horrified stare. Even if she didn't say what she says next, I instinctively know. "Please, don't go there. Please," she begs, forcing ice water through my fire-filled veins.

"You and I were friends once," I remind Bethany. "Expect a visit from me in the next few days, and all your secrets will flow like water from a broken spigot," I threaten as my voice goes colder than my veins. "One I broke to get it to flow. Ya feeling me, here?"

No one knows the lengths I went to in high school to protect Essie's reputation. Whore was the only name anyone ever called her. Yes, I said that word to her face *once*– the first words I said to Essie when I got into this car tonight were directed toward her for that exact infraction.

"You ever do something for someone's own good, but it hurts like nothing has ever hurt before?"

Just because I pushed Essie away from my tainted ass didn't mean anyone else was allowed to utter that word. Ever. Most kids spend their high school careers playing ball, acting in drama, smoking pot underneath the bleachers, or geeking it up over comic books.

Not me.

I tracked down every single asshole who ever hurt Essie, and I punished them. I was the invisible law of Fairport Area Junior/Senior High School, and I never got my hands dirty. I ruined lives to satisfy my thirst for vengeance. I didn't lie to Willow when I said I was born to be a police officer. I jumped at the chance to patrol FAHS as the Truancy Officer, just so I could continue on my duty of bully eradication.

Now I'm a bipolar drug addict with a badge… and Bethany is going to point me in the direction of my next prey. A shudder rolls through Beth, as if she finally realizes just how dark the vein of illness runs deep within me.

Soul-deep.

"Don't do this, Devon," Beth releases her plea again, only this time she's not crying over Essie and me having sex. It's too late for that; it's happening whether she likes it or not. Beth now knows some asshole is already a dead man walking. "What if someone drives by and sees? We're just sitting in the car… with your… um… dick in Essie. It's gross."

Problem solved. I shrug out of my jacket, not allowing Essie to leave my lap, then I settle it over her shoulders, effectively sheltering us from prying eyes. Needing more of her creamy skin in contact with mine, I lift my t-shirt so my chest cushions Essie's breasts. An intense shudder rolls throughout my body from the force of Essie's heart beating wildly against my stomach.

When I was a month shy of fourteen, Essie and I were almost the same size. Now, cradled against my chest, Essie feels fragile, precious. Breakable. As the smallest Mason in recorded history, I've always been bitter about getting the genetic '*fuck you*' from both my parents. But here, with Essie in my arms, I feel like a man. I close my eyes and nuzzle the side of her soft cheek, her wispy brown hair tickling my forehead. I could stay immobile like this forever, even if my cock is pulsing for action and Bethany is bleating morality like a dying animal.

I check into Bethany's ramblings when I think they are important, "What about Willow?"

Essie freezes in my arms. I mentally tear Bethany's head from her neck, envisioning her lifeblood filling Willow's VW. I want to say, "*Who's Willow?*" just to rankle Beth, but it would hurt Essie if I did.

As if reading my mind, "You know, your girlfriend," Beth reminds me, as if I could forget.

"A technicality," I admit as my arms seep beneath my jacket to tug Essie closer to me. My eyes drift shut at the pure pleasure of Essie's warmth radiating against my skin. "Let's be honest, Willow was just obeying her wayward Mr. Kline, which kind of hurts. Willow has to break up with me, or Robin is going to cut my dick off."

Head perking up, Essie meets my gaze. "Rob?"

"You too?" I ask, smiling for some wicked reason. Not only does Essie nod her head in assent, Beth does too. "Ah, I think Robin just earned my respect."

"Rob told me to come on to Auggie," Essie whispers, and when I turn to stone, she adds, "He laughed in my face, calling me little girl. Then Rob told me to do what I did at the twins' birthday party– taunt Willow about the *ruler* incident. I didn't want to, but it felt gratifying to hurt Willow as much as she's been hurting me."

"Sorry," I mumble, but I may have just thought it. I'm sorry for a lot of things. It's not Willow's fault Essie and I aren't together. It's my mother's fault. My fault. The nightmare's fault. I'm fate's bitch. Tonight is a relapse because I need to feel alive with the mania dissipating and the depression rolling in like a thick, black fog over my soul.

"I told Rob I was finished this morning when he came to me, gloating over how you and Willow…" Essie's voice breaks, killing me inside.

"What I did wasn't about Rob," I grumble, but don't say, "*It was about balance.*"

Without a lick of remorse, Robin Prynne has been maneuvering his family members like chess pieces to thwart my uncle's obsession with Willow. He's done everything in his power to sabotage it before it ever began. I learned how to do my best work without getting my hands dirty by watching Rob. Bethany shouldn't be studying Auggie– she needs to home in on Rob instead.

"Willow? Hello!" Beth starts in on the hysterics again, slapping and scratching at me. "You cannot do this in the poor girl's car!"

"Do I look like I give a shit?" I snarl. Ren owes me one, so I'm taking it out of his girl. "After how I just left things back at Wreck & Ruin, I'd say it's guaranteed that Willow is finished with me and moving on to Golden Boy Mason." I hate the edge of jealousy that creeps into my voice, and it's not directed toward Willow.

I hate how I'm not as pure as Kieren. Healthy. Our conception was a genetic lottery. While Dad's sperm was wiggling a hole into Mom's egg, I won the lottery where they draw names and stone you to death in the street. Ren won the lottery where they hand you a cocksucking check for a million dollars a week for life.

Starting the ignition again, Beth gets to driving, like she's trying to drive away from us even though we're in the car with her. I hold Essie while I order my thoughts. It's a relief to be in the presence of my girls again, and it makes me say things I shouldn't.

"I need this," I admit to Bethany. "Just for tonight, okay?"

"I know you're just using me," Essie breathes against the side of my neck, yet she tightens her arms around me. "And we both know I'm stupid enough to let you."

I could lie, and I usually do… "Yes," I admit, voice cracking. "This isn't a beginning, Ess. It's more like a–"

"Goodbye?" Essie provides for me, but she's wrong. I can't tell her what it truly is. I want to though. Tonight, being with Essie, it's my punishment. Because I'm going to fall into her and fly high, and later when I want another hit, I'm going to deny myself. My denial is because I love Essie enough to be selfless when I'm a selfish piece of shit. Essie deserves better than a bipolar drug addict who will pass those same fucked up genes to her adorable, innocent children.

Here goes nothing. "You're my medicine for the night," I breathe into Essie's ear so Bethany can't overhear. With a whimper, as if she understands, Essie hugs me so tightly tears spring to my eyes.

Still driving us toward my house, "Why? Why should I just swallow the fact that you're balls-deep in my best friend– just taking what you want from her without any regard for her feelings, just like those other creeps?"

I mull Bethany's words over while she drives. I'm being selfish. I know I am, and yet I can't muster up the conscience to give a shit. Beth pulls Willow's car into an abandoned lot that's about a block from her house, so I assume she's walking home from here.

I reach over and grab Beth's arm when she goes to exit the vehicle. I don't care what Bethany thinks of me, because it can never be worse than what I think of myself. But it does matter how she thinks about Essie.

I wait until Beth looks at me, and then the words roll unbidden off my tongue. "For one night only, I want to play pretend. I want to experience life as if nothing ever happened. What would it have been like for us to go through high school as friends, with Essie as my girlfriend, to be the one who was with Essie first, to go off to college together… Right now, Essie and I would be married and happy in a home of our own, with me as a cop and her at the salon. Maybe we'd be telling our parents that we're trying for a little Mason brat. We'd fight over whose house we were going to spend Thanksgiving or Christmas, and then we'd ask Aunt Bethany to tag along."

"Devon," Bethany cries, trying to get closer to me to comfort me. "It could still happen."

"No, it can't," I say in a stiff voice filled with tears. "It really can't. Because I'm not that Devon anymore. I could blame my mom for passing her illness on to me. I could blame Mom for beating me when no one was looking because it made her feel better– but I know how she felt in the moment, because I do bad things to people… and. I. Like. It," I bite out. "So I can never blame Mom. I could blame our rapists for setting off the ticking time bomb that was waiting to go off in my brain–"

Essie gasps and Bethany almost falls out the open car door when I say more than I planned. "I trust you to never speak of that." Turning feral, I snarl, baring my teeth. "As Essie's best friend, I need you to put her back together after tonight, because I'm incapable of ever giving her what she needs and deserves. Because tonight, I'm using her– using Essie as my medicine. Using Essie to give Ren and Willow the chance neither of us will ever get. With us out of their way, they can have that fucking picture postcard life."

"Devon, please don't," Bethany cries out. The wealth of compassion in her eyes stunned me. "You can have that too, but you need help."

With a forceful shove, Bethany is out of the car, almost falling on her ass. I grip the driver's side door, ready to close Bethany out of Essie and my fictitious world. A second before the door slams, rattling the car, I whisper in a cold, dead voice. "You don't get it, Beth. I'm warped."

CHAPTER FIVE

Essie Prynne

Heart beating erratically against my rib cage, I sit stiff with shock in Devon's lap. Frozen beneath me, not even breathing, the only sign of life he exhibits is his heart hammering against my left breast. Even though he's still resting inside me, he's completely limp– has been since he hurt me when he slammed into me.

I don't feel so completely alone anymore, like a stranger among a crowd of family. I find a purpose as I sit here with Devon, as if God is spotlighting him. "*Your path in life is to heal Devon Mason,*" the light announces. I willingly accept my purpose, even knowing Devon will tear my heart to shreds. But if I can just make a small difference in his life, it will all be worth it.

With a gulp, I ask in a tentative voice, "Were you? Is that why?" In this moment, I feel closer to Devon because I've never talked about what happened to me. With Devon, I won't need to since he knows exactly how I felt in that moment.

Powerless.

"I don't know," Devon croaks out. "I can't remember anything from that night." Releasing a sharp bark of bitter laughter, "Ren won't tell me– the bastard. Of all the shit I'm jealous of over him, that's the only thing he's jealous about over me."

"Is that why you…" I'm unable to ask why Devon broke me, because if the answer is yes, I'd forgive him anything.

"My nightmare taught me I was sick in the head," Devon snarls. "That's why I pushed you away. After a life at Mommy Dearest's hands, I couldn't do that to you or any kids I put in your belly."

In a small voice, I utter, "You could get help," knowing it might set him off.

"No, I can't," he says with finality. "I can't do that to my father. He didn't have to deal with Mom's bullshit like the rest of us, but he dealt with the doctor's appointments, medicine, and the psych wards at the hospital. I know my grandmother was functioning, how she lived a good life and was happy, that her medicine helped and she didn't have many episodes. But I'm *not* my grandmother's son– I'm my mother's son. I can't do that to Dad, not now. Maybe if he convinces Clover to marry him."

"Does Malcolm know?"

"No, no one knows. The only reason I said it in front of Bethany is that if she didn't figure it out, she'd be the world's worst psychologist. Seeing as she's the smartest person I know…" Devon takes a deep breath as if he's exhausted. "Anyway, I'm pissed because they haven't figured it out. Always thinking the worst of me. The drug addict. It's insulting, and it makes me hate them. Fuck 'em!"

"They will be angrier at you for not telling them, for not getting help." I tell Devon what he needs to hear, not what he wants me to say. "Subconsciously you must know what happened that night with your mom, or else you wouldn't have blurted it out like that."

Devon's fingertips unthaw and roar to life at the small of my back. If he were a musician, I'd say he was composing a tune. By the erratic beat, I assume he's using it to release excess energy.

I hate Devon so much right now, it renders me speechless. My only weakness is that I love him more than I hate him. I lean back a bit, so I can look Devon in the eye– eyes that aren't as dark and wild as usual. The endless chasm of sadness mirrored back at me causes my breath to catch in my throat.

Fingertips picking up speed, legs joining the jangling, dick starting to swell… "I get that– I do. It startled me when I said *our* rapists. It's always tickling the back of my brain like an infection I can't cure." Devon moves his hand to scratch at his scalp. "But I can't remember what happened. I just know it triggered my illness early. Hell, maybe I was always fucked in the head. All I know, it broke me. Nothing worked." Snorting, "My dick only gets hard when I'm furious or high now. How is that for disgusting?"

"Are you furious or high right now?" I ask wryly to cover my worry. If his cock could get any harder, I'd be in more pain. Devon's like Dr. Jekyll and Mr. Hyde. I've watched him go from calm and sedate to despondent. Now he's reverberating with energy.

Laughing, truly laughing, and looking frightened by it, Devon smiles up at me. "Neither. This is going to sound totally lame and clichéd, but my dick has always had a thing for you." Taking in a large gulp of air and expelling words with it. "Not to bring up bad shit, but if Willow will talk to you after what we're doing tonight, you should probably help her deal with last night."

Terrified, hurt, dying inside at the reminder of Devon screwing Willow last night, I shriek out, "What'd you do?"

"I confused her," Devon mumbles, looking confused himself. "I told her it was because of what happened to my mom. Probably some of it was. But anyway, it was good *and* bad."

"I understand," I whisper, remembering my first time.

"I know you do," Dev says just as quietly as I did. He reaches up to smooth my hair off my forehead in a tender gesture. "The roles should have been reversed on both accounts, that's all I'm gonna say about that because what's done is done."

"Is Willow really with Ren now?" I ask, hope thick in my voice.

I tried on Willow's birthday, tried my damnedest. Ren pestered me for weeks, setting up their *date*. He was so damned cute, like an eager puppy. He even made me fix his hair and pick out his shirt. Our three minutes of torture and Ren's inability to keep his eyes off my tits aside, he's like my kid brother. Nothing would make me happier than for Willow and Ren to be happy, especially together.

On Willow's eighteenth birthday, I left the decision up to her, asking her for confirmation on whether she wanted Ren or not. Young and dumb, she made a fatal error– just like we all did. I only told her the truth about losing my virginity so she wouldn't make such a dumb fucking mistake by choosing the wrong guy.

Willow chose the wrong guy anyway.

Sighing, "Willow's a stubborn bitch," Dev drawls, causing me to laugh. "Willow's physically with Ren right now, hearing his version of our mutual nightmare. Probably verbatim to the one he told you."

"The version devoid of any mention of you," I mutter, just now realizing that when Ren cried out their secret, he still managed to keep Devon's.

"Bastard," Devon snarls. "The only reason I've stopped my murder attempts, is because if Ren dies, my secret dies with him."

Shaking his head like he's surprised he just said that, I wonder if Dev was being serious or not.

"Umm... Dev–"

Ignoring me, Devon lifts his hips slightly, pressing farther into me. Both of our eyes pop in shock. "Tonight has a purpose." He sounds deadly serious, and I know he's about to break my heart. "Your arrival at my exit was a sign."

"From God?" I squeak out, finally seeing just how nuts Devon truly is.

"The Devil? Fuck if I care," Devon mumbles. "You're going to hate me. If Willow's a good person, she won't hate you." Dev arches an eyebrow in question over that, since Willow has a propensity for violence. "Blame me every time Willow attacks you– it will lessen any heartache you feel from me. Finally get your ass to hate me, it will."

I try again, "Dev?"

"Stubborn Spanky will not fall into Ren's coddling, suffocating, patient embrace if she's still attached to her Mr. Kline. Rob was going to have somebody text Auggie, saying Willow was smoking pot again. So Auggie is going to be dead to Willow from now on."

"What?!" I shriek.

"C'mon," Dev growls. "Auggie's influence is more toxic to Willow than pot, and you know it. Rob's fucking sick to death over it. Imagine how you felt about Willow and me last night, because I know it felt like death when Ren told me about you and him. Now multiply that when the love of your life is acting like a PedoBear hell-bent on your–"

"Niece," I fill in, letting Devon know I know Clover's secret. "Alright, but I'm not doing this for you. I'm doing it for Rob and Willow." Moving to get off Devon's lap, "But we can just say we did, and not actually do it."

Strong hands bruise my hips with their merciless grip. "For once, we're doing something for *us*." Devon growls in my ear, and then he attacks me.

"DEVON!" I shout, the sharp intensity ringing in my ears. Devon turns into an octopus– hands grabbing and groping my ass, thighs, tits, trying to pull me closer, push himself deeper inside me. I feel no pain except the inevitable doom of heartbreak. Unlike any time before, I want this. I want Devon. Ruthlessly, he sucks at my mouth– his groans of violent ecstasy spilling between my lips.

Pumping into me from beneath, Devon grabs my ass in both hands and pounds me raw. With a forceful shove, my head careens into the ceiling, time and time again. Sweating, my fingertips slip off the headrest, so I sink my fingernails into Devon's shoulders for leverage instead.

Our intimate moments when we were kids were sweet, awkward. Loving. This is dirty. Fucking dirty.

Grunting, growling, panting, with sweat dripping down his forehead, Devon reminds me of a wild animal. The VW's suspension is creaking under the stress of his onslaught. I should feel violated. Forced. But this is nothing like before. I didn't have to say yes because it was a given. I close my eyes and just glorify in the reality that Devon Mason is finally thrusting inside me– seven years too late.

Mauling my breasts with both hands, Devon is transfixed. I gaze down in shame, hating how his hands only cover my areolas and nipples, with a huge expanse of flesh still exposed. As fast as a lightning strike, Devon shoves his face between my tits and moans. His dick gets even harder inside me, pulsing as if he's about to explode.

I freeze, hating my breasts, hating the reaction I get out of people when they see them. I've always planned on getting a reduction when I had the money– *if* I ever had the money. But then Devon rolls his eyes up to connect to mine, and I change my mind. He doesn't touch me like he covets the slutty bags of fat. He touches me like he finds them beautiful because they are attached to *me*.

Slowing the jackhammer routine, "I'll make it good for you, love," Devon croons, reaching down between us. "I remember what you like," he teases as a finger flicks my clit. Spreading my lips farther apart, Devon shifts until the base of his cock is sliding, grinding against my clit.

"Uhng…" an unintelligible word spills from my lips, as if Devon flipped a switch in me, moving me from pleasured to *ohmyfuckinggodimgonnacum*.

Quivering, shuddering, I enter a drug-like state of bliss I've never entered before. I've orgasmed. A lot. Devon gave me my first orgasm, then he made me touch myself over and over again until I had another one. We did this for weeks on end. I'm not my nickname, but I'm no saint. Some of the guys I've blown returned the favor, with more than half of them getting me off. But I've never had an orgasm during sex. Ever.

Is it different because it's during sex, or because it's with Devon?

It was always a couple seconds of muscle clenching, followed by relief, and sometimes I felt relaxed. I always felt empty while my pussy spasmed for something it didn't have. A deep grunt in my ear changes everything– heightens everything. Devon's arms embrace me in a constrictive manner at the same time he thrusts up so hard it hurts me inside. With a suffocating squeeze, he moans again, cock pulsing inside me.

I don't fall into my orgasm– I'm ruined by it. Every single muscle clenches in my body, all gripping Devon closer to me. Moaning and shuddering, I find myself wrapped tightly around Devon, but not as tightly as he holds me while he cries my name and spills inside me.

Coiled tightly, I instantly relax as a wave of satiation rolls over me. I tuck my face against Devon's neck, and cling to him. I know I'm going to regret this moment for the rest of my life on some level, but I can't muster up the energy to give a shit at the moment.

Not angry, not high, Devon proves it's all me. Holding me in the most intimate of embraces, whispering promises he'll never keep, Devon never goes soft as he rocks slowly, spilling inside me over and over again.

CHAPTER SIX

Devon Mason

When I was five years old, I learned the word *Masochist*. My mother was in a rage, laughing the word demonically as I let her verbally punch me. She'd get that way; just fucking snap. Out of the blue, she'd go from comatose on the couch to a raging fucking lunatic with flailing hands and a venomous, forked tongue. I'd walk by, and it was like looking at me set her off. When I was little, I didn't understand why I was Mom's only target. Now I do. By some miracle, I was the only one of us who was afflicted with her poison, and she knew it from the time I was born.

It was just me and Mommy Dearest back then. Being a bitch, Isis made me watch the movie Mommy Dearest one night to scare the hell out of me. She got a kick out of the fact that I was the only five-year-old terrified by wire hangers. She didn't understand why none of our closets had any clothing hanging in them when I was finished. Isis kept buying more hangers, hanging our clothes back up, and I kept removing them while she was asleep. Finally Isis brought in plastic ones, and I left them where they hung.

Mom hurt me with her tongue more than her hands, but I was scared what would happen if she got a hold of a wire hanger like the demonic bitch in the movie.

Isis was never around when Mom was manic. Only two people ever witnessed Camille Jamison outside of her catatonic, depressive state: Dad and me. Kieren was too small, being toted around by Aunt Isis like an adorable puppy, and I was tasked with watching Mom. Raven wasn't born yet, but Dad had already put her in Mom's gut.

Mom wouldn't take her medication. Ever.

"Baby, I feel off when I take my pills. They're poison," Mom would tell Dad, and then they'd fight until he shoved them down her throat– literally. I had to hold her legs down while she tried to de-man Dad. Seething, Dad would rush out of the house to play

Super Cop. As soon as the door smashed against its jam, I'd be holding Mommy Dearest's hair out of her eyes while she threw the pills up in the toilet.

Back then, I thought I was helping Mom. Now, as I suffer from the same illness, I don't understand her. I feel more *off* when I'm not *on* something. Drug-free for me is probably how most feel when they are on drugs.

Aunt Ginny was a big help back then. She sat me down and told me how Grammy Maeve and Mom had the same illness, telling me how Grammy was always even-keeled because she took her medicine. I saw Grammy every day of my life before she died, and I knew Aunt Ginny was telling the truth.

The trick was drugging Mom's food, and since it was my job to feed Mom, life was easier for a while. But as anyone who has ever been truly depressed knows, you lose your appetite when you lose your will to live. You also lose your appetite when you have morning sickness, so that meant I had a manic, hormonally-charged lunatic mothering my ass every time Dad knocked her up.

Mom was perpetually in stasis. She'd sit on the couch, eyes tracking me around the room, while she watched television. The only time she moved was when she had to do something we couldn't do for her, like take a shit. Ren nicknamed Mom *Gimme*. Gimme this. Gimme that. Even when you gave Mom something she asked for, it was never right, never good enough for the bitch.

I was five years old when I learned I was a masochist… and a sadist. I am my mother, so everything she and everyone else had said about her was directed at me. I just didn't know what it meant at the time. It meant I was bipolar because half of me liked to hurt the other half. Bi: Two. Polar: opposite ends. High and Low with no in between. If not properly medicated, you become your own victim as you victimize yourself and all those around you. I do things that hurt because it relieves the pressure. I also hurt other people, and enjoy it because it hurts me.

When someone yells at you, it hurts, but no one can see your inner pain. When someone punches you, the bruise is proof of the injury. Mommy Dearest lashed out because she was harboring invisible, unexplainable agony, and I let her because I did, too.

Mom didn't mean it. But at the same time, she did.

I loved my mother– the more she hurt me, the more I loved her. As an adult, I finally understand her, and I wish I could turn back time and save her.

Every single human being is closer to one parent than the other. I'm not speaking of love; an emotional and biological connection that binds you tightly. It's hard when the parent you emulate is the one person everyone in your family despises. When they talk negatively of Mom, it's a sucker-punch to the gut.

Reason #1 of why I'm jealous of Kieren and Weston: they have Dad– Dad understands them. Not that he loves them any more than me, but they don't have to go through life feeling lost, like half of them is… dead. Not only do Ren and West emulate Dad, they are a better version than Dad himself.

No one in their right mind would want to be like Mom, and even when I'm in my right mind, I'm still exactly like her.

With a burst of energy she'd saved up over the past week, Mom lunged off the couch after me. "What the fuck is this?" Mommy Dearest shouted, shaking the bag of chips in her hand.

"You wanted potato chips," I stammered, pointing at the chips I just handed her.

"These are sour cream. I hate goddamned sour cream!"

Shaking, I squeeze my legs together, scared I might pee my underpants again. Last time Mom got really angry when I peed on the carpet. I walked back into the kitchen, crawled up onto the chair, and tried to reach the upper cabinet where I got the sour cream chips. Straining, I couldn't see into the cupboard because I was too short. Hand searching– empty. With dread, I shuffled back to Mom, empty-handed.

"We're all out. Gonna have to have Daddy get some more."

"You back talking me?" The words connected at the same time as her open fist across my cheek, flinging my head to the right. Stunned, Mom stared down at her hand for at least a minute.

Fingers curling into a fist, Mom looked up at me with wild eyes filled with tears. "You make me hurt you because you're just like me," she whined, explaining how it was my fault. "I don't want to hurt you, baby. But I feel so rotten on the inside that I have to show you by hurting you. Does that make sense?"

I nodded my head yes even though it didn't make sense. Satisfied, energy released, Mom plopped back onto the couch and tore open the potato chips. She pouted while looking into the bag. "They're crushed," she cried out, and then began to sob… and sob… and sob… rambling about feeling dead inside and how she had to hurt me to feel alive, how she couldn't help herself.

"I'm sorry," I whisper inside my mind to Essie while I hold her against my chest. Bipolar: opposite ends with no in between–a delicate balance to remain even. My mother loved me the most, and I know this because I was the only person she said goodbye to. I just didn't realize it at the time. I cannot hurt the one person I love the most like she did.

Balance.

I will *not* perpetuate the cycle.

It would be so easy to fall into a life with Essie, and then I would destroy her. I'm going to love her enough to walk away like my mother walked away from all of us. The only difference, I haven't fallen into the endless dark abyss yet. I can see light–hope. Just as in high school, I can protect Essie from afar, never leaving a trace of myself behind.

"What's it like?" Essie breathes against the side of my neck, and I realize letting her go tonight will be the hardest thing I'll ever have to do. If it's only a fraction of what my mother felt before she ended it all, she was the bravest person I've ever met. It's just too bad she didn't use that courage to overcome her illness instead of succumbing to it.

Connected by more than just our bodies, I understand Essie's vague question. "I have no normal– no baseline. I have no concept of normality," I admit for the first time in my life. "People go through life, always feeling the same way. So outside forces create a strong reaction. When someone hurts them, they hurt. When something awesome happens, they get excited. That isn't what it's like for me."

Hesitant, Essie stumbles over her words, "How do you feel now?" She plays with the tips of my hair along the nape of my neck.

I wait a moment, enjoying the gentle way Essie straightens my wavy hair with her fingertips. "Spiraling downward," I grumble, surprising myself. Eyes popping wide, scared shitless, "I've only hit the low a couple of times, and it wasn't too bad. Nothing uppers couldn't handle. It's been more than a year since the last time."

Essie moves away from my chest so she can look me in the eye. "I don't understand."

I draw from personal experience with Mom, Aunt Ginny, Isis, and especially Raven, because it's the only way I know how to explain it to someone who is… normal. "You know when you have PMS and everything annoys the fuck out of you? After you snap at them, you feel bad. Manic is like that. Snapping at random people because they offended you just because they breathe, even though rationally you know they didn't do anything to you. You know that rush you get when you win, how giddy you are? Or when you're bored but you have a dozen things that sound like fun but none of them satisfy you? Well, combine all that and you'll know my normal– my baseline."

Essie mutters, "Fuck," then releases a sharp whistle. "And pot calms it?"

"Yeah, like smoke to a disturbed beehive." I snort at my analogy. "On the opposite end of the spectrum is the depression. It's normal with the usual stuff: broken hearts, lost dreams, mourning the dead. But there is a beginning, a middle, and an end. Eventually you're going to heal, and the whole time you still have a spark of life."

"I know the feeling," Essie grumbles, and I laugh because I know she's thinking of me and how much she'd love to hack my dick off.

"Exactly," I say to prove my point. "But you're feeling anger with your sadness, which fuels that spark of life I was talking about. Imagine not having a purpose to the sadness, and without a purpose there is no other emotion but dread. It's like being lost in a never-ending, dark landscape with no hope of rescue, and you wish you were dead just to end it. Death is a sweet surrender to the unexplainable, invisible, unjustified, irrational, never-ending misery you're experiencing because you're already dead on the inside anyway."

"Oh, Devon," Essie cries, doing her damnedest to comfort me.

"Like this," I say, capturing her hand, and then I kiss her palm. "Right now, I know you're comforting me because you care about me. But at some point, if I follow down my mother's path, I won't know it, and nothing will make me see it. There will be nothing anyone can do to make me feel the love, the comfort, the happiness. There is no '*Snap out of it!*' or '*look at what you have!*' that will make a difference."

"None?" Essie whispers, finally realizing why I'm showing her I love her by letting her go.

"None. Nothing. There is no reason we feel this way. If someone breaks your heart, you mend it. If someone breaks your bones, you heal it. If your mind breaks itself… your only recourse is hope that drugs can chemically alter it. There is no way to accurately describe it to someone who's never experienced it. Which is pretty much the definition of insanity, isn't it?"

Essie's words spill in a torrent of fear. "What are you going to do? You have to tell someone. Get some help."

"Tonight you're in luck, because as I said, I'm sliding downward. Right now I'm the most lucid. When I'm manic, it's like the Energizer Bunny on crack. When I'm depressed, I see no hope, so why try. I can't see reason during my high or low. On the downward, I can at least hear you out. Right now, I'm going to live my life and try to see what good I can do for others. I'm not worth shit, and I deserve even less, but it makes me feel better to help those who are worthy. It's the only thing that keeps me putting one foot in front of the other. I'll take my medicine like a good boy. At some point, I'll grow the balls to tell Dad."

"Devon, you're worth so much." Essie sounds so compassionate that it makes me laugh.

"This is the closest I'll come to explaining this. You were a child– a virgin –and you believed yourself a whore because jealous assholes called you one. Even at your worst, giving blowjobs out as party favors, you were never a whore. So unless you start selling your snatch–"

"Shut the fuck up," Essie growls, causing me to laugh harder.

"I see you get my point. Nothing will change your mind on that front. I'm inherently evil. I do evil shit. I hurt people just because I can, and it doesn't matter if I feel badly about it afterward because it doesn't change shit. So there is nothing you can do or say to make me see myself as anything but evil. This was my point about there being no '*snap out of it!*' It's the mind of madness, and it's irrational. So don't even try to argue over whether or not I'm worth it, because I'm not."

In a rush to say it all before I can stop her, Essie breathlessly spits out, "So you say you're evil, yet even right now you're with me to help Willow, Ren, Rob, Isis, and Auggie."

Laughing harder. "Don't even ask about the bullshit I did to get us here tonight. I'm cheating on my *girlfriend* with her cousin, who just so happens to be my ex-girlfriend, in said girlfriend's car. I came four times, and I plan on it some more before I go. How altruistic of me and not at all evil."

Stunned, looking guilty, I leave Essie speechless.

"I've gotta move. I can't explain the sensation, but I have to do something because it feels like my skin is about to crawl off my body and run away if I sit still. C'mon." I reach over and hit the door latch, allowing the night air to chase away the intense scent of sex filling the VW. I miss our smell before it completely dissipates.

CHAPTER SEVEN

Essie Prynne

It stopped raining, but the air is cold and invigorating. Alive. The night promises new life– the ground soaks up the spring rain, ensuring the grass will grow, the flowers will bloom, and the leaves will unfurl.

I look at Devon, wondering if he's deadened to the intensity. I'm truly trying to understand, but I doubt I will ever get a grasp on what or how he feels. All I know, this is one of those moments where normal feels more. Everything is heightened– for the better or worse, only time will tell.

Standing outside of the cramped, hot car did wonders for Devon. The vibrating energy has dissipated some, but he's still not quite even. Only wearing a pair of sneakers and track pants, he stares at me like he's hungry.

Clothed in my dress and Devon's leather jacket, I feel uncomfortable, unsure, and embarrassed. I squeeze my thighs together to stop the cool slide of Devon's jizz from making its way to my knees.

"I can't believe I did this," I direct to the night sky. It's surreal. Anti-reality. "Willow is going to make my life a living nightmare."

Dev's snort turns to bitter laughter. "Ya think?" He pulls his cellphone from the pocket of his pants and hits a few buttons. "Hey!" he barks to someone. "She's still with Ren. How's Auggie?"

I make my way closer, hoping to overhear, but not wanting to look like a nosy bitch. Smirking while nodding his head, Dev pulls the phone away from his ear and pushes *speaker*.

"Auggie thinks he's home alone, and I wanted it that way. He was rummaging in Willow's room like an angry bear. Now he's standing sentry at the front door, looking like a demented, red-headed Sasquatch guarding the Spook House against tiny, teenage potheads. Meanwhile, I'm burning while standing on the

widow's watch overlooking his mammoth ass. In a former life, Auggie was a DEA agent who was canned for incompetency."

"Is Willow going to be okay? Don't do this, Rob," I beg, on the verge of tears. "Don't let Auggie fuck her up like this. Please."

"Ess? What. The. Fuck. Are you doing with Devon?" Rob's voice wavers from the other end of the cellphone.

"Final nail in Mr. Kline's Good Girl trap, my man," Devon says without a lick of remorse. "Willow's trust in Auggie will be broken in all ways."

"What'd you do, dumbass?"

Snarling, face twisted in fury, "Auggie shouldn't have made my brother look like a womanizing bastard. He shouldn't have started that smear campaign calling Ren Date-Rape. Now he's gonna regret spreading my virtues to Willow. Now his judgment will be suspect since he hooked her up with the dick who cheated on her with her own cousin."

"You didn't!" Rob shouts, furious. *"Jesus, Dev. This is too much for one person to handle in one night, don't ya think? Why Essie? Our family life is going to turn into World War Prynne. If you did it because it would hurt Willow the worst, you did a good fucking job, douchebag!"*

"I did it because I'm a selfish bastard and I wanted Essie, consequences be damned. I also did it because nothing will bond Mr. Perfect and little Miss Wrecked together tighter. With Auggie out of the way, Ren and Willow can make a go of it. With Willow away from Auggie, maybe my aunt will get her head out of her ass. Don't make me regret my sacrifice," Devon snarls.

"Sacrifice?" Rob's laughter is sharp and grating, and never-ending. *"You're such a prick, Dev. I've got to go. I'll follow Willow after Auggie's through with her. Just don't go dropping the Essie Nuke until I say so. Got it?"*

"Let me tell her," I beg, not wanting Willow to hear it from anyone but me.

Devon says, "Sure," sounding incredulous, as Rob laughs out, *"That will fare well,"* and I can tell he's rolling his eyes. *"Later, cheaters. Make sure you put on a raincoat."*

"How did Rob know we were outside?" I ask Dev as he pockets his cellphone. With my fingers splayed in the air, testing for raindrops, sounding confused, I add, "And it's not even raining anymore."

Devon bites his lip while prowling toward me. "You're too cute," he chuckles. "Cutie," he adds with a grin. He looks invigorated, flushed. High. The plotting made him feel alive. In a heartbeat, I recognize the part of Devon shining in his eyes that he calls evil. But he's not evil...

Devious.

Naughty.

Bad-assed.

Sexy.

For every step Devon takes toward me, I back up two. It's so cold our breath creates visible puffs in the air. Dev's nipples are jutting out like pencil erasers and his body is beaded with goose bumps. But it's the potent look in Devon's eye that has me shivering.

"Uh!" I grunt out when the VW's bumper hits me in the ass. I watch in fascination as Devon prowls forward, trapping me at the hood of the car.

Leaning into me, pressing his weight into me, "You have no idea how freeing it is to finally have someone who knows my secret, and is trying to understand the unexplainable. I can be myself around you to a certain extent."

"You're going to wreck me." I gulp, voice quivering with anticipation. Devon's fingertips grip my hips, pulling me into him so he can grind his pelvis into my belly. Hard. Harder than before, and he is neither high nor angry. All me.

"Yes." Devon flashes me a sly smirk. "I believe we already covered that in intro to Bipolar Disorder 101. With a semester in *Devon is going to fuck you, and then fuck you over, leaving you to pick up the pieces.* Remember? I believe you scored a 99% on your last exam."

Even Devon's playfulness is a sharp stab and an agonizing twist to the heart. I know it's a rare gift he's sharing with me. Even though he's teasing, he's being blatantly honest with me. When we drive away tonight, our lives will return to how they were an hour ago.

An hour from now, I won't be devastated. I won't be wrecked. Devon will be my rock bottom, and just like any other drug addict, I will welcome the spiral into hell with open arms as long as I get one last hit of euphoria. No matter the consequences, I'll never regret. But one thing's for sure, I'll be damned.

"How did I lose a percentage off my grade?" I play along, never wanting this evening to end– wishing I could capture it and bottle it forever.

Chuckling wryly, dark eyes dancing with deviousness, "You let me in the fucking car," he rasps out. "You should have locked your door and told Bethany to put the pedal to the metal." Curling a strand of my hair around his pinky fingertip, demonstrating the power he holds over me, "You did the wrong thing, Cutie."

"Not me." I play innocent by breathing, "Never."

"Me neither," Dev says with a smirk and a wink. Descending, he proves us both liars. "Never," flutters against my lips.

Shuddering, my hands seek Devon's cool, whisker-stubbled cheeks as our lips brush together. This kiss is different. A hesitant, tentative, feather-light caress, unlike our kiss in the car. Dev had something to prove before, and he found it. So now he's being careful.

I grab a chunk of Devon's wavy dark hair, and tug, drawing his sight up to mine. I stare him down, refusing to say all the words on the tip of my tongue.

I hate you.

But I love you more.

I want you.

But I need you more.

Get help!

"I promise," Devon whispers as if he can read my thoughts. I know he's lying, and not for the first time tonight. Hell, not for the fiftieth time tonight. I'm starting to believe Devon's greatest flaw is his ability to lie to himself and not recognize it.

"I'm already going to hell," I rasp, voice curling into a husky tone. I close my eyes against the open, honest, and confused look that flashes over Devon's features. "Might as well fuck me again. One for the road."

Shocked, he gasps, and then the wild, passionate Devon who kissed me earlier reappears. It was as if he was waiting for permission to release the insanity. "I'll make it memorable," he promises, and this time he's not lying to me or himself.

I moan the instant our lips connect. My fingers twist in the hair at the nape of his neck, drawing him down to me. Needing a stronger taste, I suck his tongue into my mouth, performing fellatio on it as if it's a miniature cock. Weak-kneed, I suck and slurp in an intoxicating rhythm.

Grunting, Devon's hips jackknife, pressing his bulge into me as if he can enter me through my belly. It's cold, yet I'm feverish, as if I'm standing beneath the high noon desert sun.

Hester Prynne– the moronic, romantic idiot.

Instead of running in the opposite direction and licking my wounds, I channel my nickname. Like a seasoned whore, I suck Dev's tongue as I hook my leg around his hip in invitation.

With a feral growl, Devon's hands skate down from my hips, shaping my thighs, where they cup the back of my legs and lift me onto the hood of the VW. With a squeal, my bare-naked ass meets the damp, cold metal of the hood.

Mouth never leaving Devon's, I make the decision. I recognize why I gave so many blowjobs. It was obvious to anyone who noticed I was trying to prove everyone right who ever called me a whore. But subconsciously, it was the only time I was in control over what was happening to my body. Every time I've had sex, I had no power. Earlier in the car, Devon took that away from me too. His hesitancy now is because he realized this before I even did.

Kissing me back, massaging me with his hands, Devon makes no sexual advances, and it makes me love him even more. If I had lower self-esteem, I'd feel rejected. But I'd have to be paralyzed below the waist not to feel the pulsing bulge pressing into the apex of my thighs.

Devon makes no sound, and his lips don't move, but I swear he says, "Please."

Pulling away, I gasp out of breath. Leaning back against the hood on my elbows, I present Devon more flesh to worship. A gentle kiss beneath my ear has a greater impact than a forceful tongue-fucking. Moaning, every muscle in my body clenches as Devon peppers butterfly kisses down the column of my throat and across the tops of my breasts, never venturing further south.

Toes curling, fingertips slipping on the condensation on the hood of the car, I can't take it anymore. Reaching between us, I shove my hand under the waistband of Devon's track pants. He issues a sharp grunt when I wrap my fingers around his cock. Tacky from our combined, drying juices, I can't stroke him without pulling at his skin. So I use Dev's dick like a leash, pulling him closer to me.

The happy rumble of a chuckle against the top of my breast turns into a deep moan when I finally pull him into position.

Patient, Devon waits for my cue. I lean further back on the hood, wrapping my legs around his waist, trying my damnedest to force him to enter me. But the infuriating man is toying with me.

With just the tip in like we're adolescents fooling around on his twin-sized bed after a round of Monopoly, I sigh out in exasperation, "Uncle."

Expecting laughter, Devon leans up from my breasts to stare down into my face. Shifting slightly, he cups the back of my head in his palm. "It wouldn't have been this good, Essie. Seven years ago, it wouldn't have been this good."

Devon rolls his hips into me, the movement flowing from his strong thighs, across his taut ass where my legs are locked, and up his back where my hands are digging into his muscles. All that coiled power to move seven inches of flesh.

"Ahhh…" my mouth parts on a gasp, and stays open for the long seconds it takes Devon to slowly enter me inch by inch. My wondrous expression is mirrored in Devon's face.

Before we're fully connected, I know I'm never letting him go. Devon is worth the fight.

Devon is going to fuck you, and then fuck you over, leaving you to pick up the pieces.

Devon lied.

Devon made love to me, slowly and passionately, making it last. When he walked off into the night, I made a promise to myself. Devon can try to fuck me over, to leave me to pick up the pieces. But like Rob, we Prynnes never back down from a fight.

I'm going to get Devon Mason help, even if it ruins me.

CHAPTER EIGHT

Kieren Mason

You okay, bro? Text seen at 10:49 p.m.

Sighing, I hang my head, tossing my cellphone behind me on the mattress. Slumped on Devon's bed, I face the door, worried to death about where he ran off to. I've sent three texts, all of which he looked at but never replied. I've tried calling a few times, but he ignores my calls, pushing me straight through to voicemail.

Goddamnit!

"You rang?" has my head popping up. Devon's voice sounds upbeat, but he looks like shit. His track pants are soaked through from the rain, like he walked home. Strung out, skin pasty, eyes bloodshot, he's either been crying or doping.

Doping.

"You could have answered," I grumble, getting fed up with Devon's shit. Last night while Devon was off screwing Willow's brains out, both literally and figuratively, Dad and I were researching rehab centers.

Tugging off his jacket, Devon reveals he's missing his t-shirt. I narrow my eyes at him, completely baffled over yet another layer of strange behavior on top of the pile of shit he's already exhibiting.

I'm never taking a drug or drinking another drop of alcohol, because sure as shit, I'd end up like my big brother.

Noticing my gaze on his chest, Devon's lips curve up into a cocky smirk. "You sent me three texts and called me four times in the amount of time it took me to walk four blocks. Your voicemail said you were home, which is where I was headed. Stalker, much?"

"I was worried about you," my voice wavers, sounding pathetic. "Where were you?"

Kicking my foot, "Get your big ass off my bed," Devon demands, mood changing from cocky to furious in the blink of an eye. Sighing again, I get up, cross the room in two strides, and fall face first onto my dinky bed. My bedframe creaks and the mattress squeaks, protesting my heavy weight.

It's not like I'm not used to the asshole sharing our bedroom. Dev's being a prick, but other than being venomous, he's completely harmless if you do as he asks. He tends to not bite unless provoked. Which in turn makes him lose his shit when I refuse to provoke him, no matter what he does to me.

"Nice," Devon drawls, the innocent word taking on the cadence of pure fury. "Where was I?" he mocks. "You were worried about *me*?" Striding across the room, Devon stands in front of me, hunching down to get closer to my face. "It. Took. You. Two. Hours. To. Call. Me. Worried about me? Pissed I didn't answer when you rang? Funny how I ceased to exist when you were chatting up my *girlfriend*," he twists nastily.

Quickly righting myself, I sit up on my bed until I'm face-to-face with my brother. "It wasn't like that, okay? You wanted me to be the one to tell her." Here I go, sounding pathetic again.

Here's the thing, Devon has this bullshit in his head about balance and how we're playing this game together– Devon and me. But I'm not playing it. What I did with Essie was wrong, but not for the reasons Devon believes. It was wrong because I was a kid, and I took advantage of Essie and made her feel like a slut. It didn't have a damned thing to do with Devon. I don't care who pops whose cherry. It's a long life to worry about who you screwed when you were fourteen, especially with the fifty-four other girls since.

If Devon wanted Essie, he should've kept her. Cherished her– protected her from guys like me. As far as telling Essie about the night Mom was raped, it was both our secret to tell, and it was my right to share it with anyone I wished. I never betrayed Devon, not where it mattered– not about what happened to us.

I so badly want to scream at Devon. "**FUCK OFF!**" "**GET YOUR HEAD OUT OF YOUR ASS AND GROW THE FUCK UP!**" But that is provoking, which will lead to broken bones and a crying Weston and Raven.

Devon may be a grown man with a badge, but he's more juvenile than Weston. The guilt over what I did to Essie changed me for the worse. She changed, started acting slutty, and so did I. I understand how empty it is when you use your body as punishment. It took me fifty-four one-night-stands to figure it out, but I grew up before I hit nineteen years old. Here is Devon, almost twenty-one, with a position of power that holds a lot of responsibility, and he's stuck in the goddamned past, reliving something he can't even fucking remember, and taking it all out on me.

Devon's just like Mom, and I know better than to say it out loud. Devon's practically salivating for me to scream, "**YOU'RE JUST LIKE MOM!**" But I instinctively know he'd kill me if I did.

A man with a badge equals a man with a gun, with the knowhow to use it and the ability to cover it up. Dad taught us that nifty trick.

"You think I can't read your mind, you little shit?" Devon says calmly, belying the fact that he reaches down to wrench my head backward by my hair. "If you'd say all that shit you're thinking out loud, we could move the fuck on." Pulling tighter, strands snapping off in his hand, Dev shoves me backward onto my mattress. Sneering, "But you're too cowardly to say it. Say it," he demands.

I hold my ground, realizing it's going to be one of *those* nights. The nights Dev's out for blood, and will bait me until I provoke him to do something about it. "No," I say with finality, refusing to play his demented games. "If you want a fight, go look for it somewhere else."

Standing firm, Devon glares down at me. His words strike with purpose. "As of tomorrow night, Willow and I are through, so you better take care of her afterward. She's going to need you."

"You bastard," I snarl, fingers clenching into fists around my blanket. "What did you do?"

"Not just me, bro. We all knew when I walked out tonight it was over. Hell, even by round three last night, Willow was done with me. Said just as much to Auggie while she thought I was asleep."

I knew Devon was provoking me into a fight this morning, and that's why he's worse tonight. But I didn't give him the satisfaction. It backfired on him when he was giving me the disgusting blow-by-blow of what happened between Willow and him. He told me verbatim what Willow said to Auggie, and as much as he's pretending it didn't bother him, it did.

"Devon." I reach out, needing to comfort him.

Ignoring my out-stretched hand, Devon yanks my hair again, but he's not mean about it. It's his insane version of affection. "It didn't bother me that Willow was using me– that our uncle was using me. It's no big deal that Willow was just doing what she was brainwashed to do." Which means it did bother Dev, or else he'd never voice it. "Last night, we used each other for different reasons."

"Yeah," I mutter, voice strained since Dev is cranking my head backward again, making my neck go all taut. "If Willow's was about Auggie, what was yours?"

Fingers tightening, twisting the strands in his fingertips, Dev tips my head back farther. He leans down to me while I sit on the bed, expression fogged over with an emotion I cannot name. I'm not worried– I trust my brother not to kill me.

"I wanted to hurt you," Devon murmurs, and then quickly kisses my forehead because he regrets it. He steps back, refusing to look me in the eye. He turns his back to me and whispers, "Did it hurt you to know I was inside your girl? I know it did." He answers from his own experience.

Dev's as malicious as ever. "I deserved that, I guess." Sighing heavily, I slump against my mattress now that my brother isn't giving me a back adjustment from hell via the roots of my hair.

Rutting around in his top dresser drawer, Devon starts pulling out the tools of his trade that scare me shitless. Methodically going about his business as if he didn't just try to fight me, didn't just tell me he was tossing his girlfriend of four months at me. I always worry over Devon going into work while high. Humming to himself, Devon checks the clip to his handgun, ejecting all the bullets, inspecting and counting them, and then reloading them back into the clip– thank God, he doesn't pop the sucker into his handgun or I'd piss my pants.

Muscles bunching from his movements, I notice something alarming etched across Devon's back and all the way to the crack of his ass where his track pants are barely hanging on his hips. I didn't think anything of it a few minutes ago when he took his jacket off, but now… Willow has blunt fingernails. I love to tease her how if she chews on them anymore, she's going to get Sharpie ink poisoning. Devon's back is torn to shreds from the violence of sex– sex with a very satisfied grown woman.

Removing everything from his belt, Devon gingerly places everything on his bed after checking its condition. The meticulous bastard is even buffing the lens to his Maglite. I'd find this odd, except he does this routine before heading to work every single time.

"Dev?" I call out hesitantly.

He looks over his shoulder at me, as if he wasn't just threatening me with bodily harm. Yet again, I use this as fuel to never take a drug or a drop to drink. "Yeah?" He sounds mildly curious.

"Where were you tonight?" I ask again.

"None of your business," he replies matter-of-factly as he goes about removing his uniform from our closet. Lint brush in hand, he goes after his trousers in an anal-retentive manner, which means he's barely keeping his shit together.

Devon finally found something horrifying enough to bait me into provoking him. My fingers curl into my palms, creating a punishing fist. My breathing accelerates. My heart hammers a violent tattoo against my ribcage. Nothing angers me more than disrespecting women– especially Willow.

Prepared for Devon's venomous, verbal bite, I provoke him in a cold, tightly controlled voice. "Maybe not my business, but I bet it's Willow's business to know you were fucking some whore tonight," I spit, barely keeping myself on my bed, in fear I'd choke the shit out of my brother and he'd end up dead on our bedroom floor.

In the blink of an eye– "Ugh!" I'm flung backward, unprepared for Devon's quick and deadly right-hook. Rubbing my jaw, I test to make sure my teeth are still attached. "What the fuck?"

Devon doesn't say a word to me. He just stands three feet in front of me, wearing only a pair of pants, while holding a sticky lint brush loosely in his left hand like the dumbest fucking weapon on the planet. My brother stares down at me with my death reflected in his eyes, and I'm terrified.

"I cannot believe you," I sputter. "Fine. You wanted me to talk, so I'll fucking say it. You are the most irresponsible piece of shit I've ever seen, you selfish son of a bitch! You cheated on Willow while you made me tell her the truth of the past. Are you going to blame that shit on drugs, Dev?" I challenge.

In a flash, my head whips to the left, and I'm left rubbing my jaw again. "F-u-c-k," I hiss. "Stop hitting me, you bastard!" I look up at my brother, and he doesn't even appear as if he moved. I know I've crossed an invisible boundary since he's speechless.

Devon's usual modus operandi is to verbally lash out, using physical violence as a last resort since I'm almost half a foot taller than him now.

Calm, relaxed, Devon says to me in his everyday voice, "I'll keep hitting you until you look at me and actually see me." The psycho has the balls to roll the lint brush against his thigh, removing imaginary lint. He makes a noise in the back of his throat, satisfied that his pants are in working order.

Staring me dead-on, "Look at me. Am I high or sober, Kieren? Which is it?"

Confused, my eyes make a sweep of my brother's body. Tired. Half-dressed. Smelling strongly of sex and covered in scratches, especially on his forearms. Devon's not a big guy–strong as an ox, yet too thin because he never eats enough to fuel his body. He doesn't take care of himself because the drugs have a greater impact on an empty stomach, and he never sleeps because he's always high.

"I don't know," I mutter, feeling lost and overwhelmingly sad. "I can't tell when you're high or sober anymore, Dev, and I can't trust your word on whether or not you are or aren't."

"Am I drug addict?" Dev bites out between clenched teeth.

"Yes," I breathe, admitting it to myself for the first time.

Movement draws my eye, and all I can do is sit on my mattress and watch my brother rage. Devon is across the room in a heartbeat, arm extended to sweep everything off his dresser in one fell swoop. Shit flies around the room: Deodorant just missing my head to land at my feet. A bottle of cologne explodes against the wall, causing me to duck and flinch. A cloud of white talcum powder plumes in the air, falling in a layer on every surface.

Patient, I just watch Devon rage. It's not the first time, not even the hundredth– he only ruins his own shit, always leaving mine where it lies. Devon shreds the boxers he was wearing this morning when he came home, cursing himself for ever touching Willow. A torrent of tears spills down his cheeks, leaving a pasty trail of damp talc.

Gasping breathlessly, Devon finally looks at me, shame and anger mingling in the depths of his eyes. "Thanks for seeing me clearly, brother," he says in confirmation of his drug addict status. Charging across the room, Dev yanks the door open, only to be faced with Weston.

I don't breathe as I watch them interact. Devon's fists clench, but not in violence. It's surreal how old habits die hard. Our sign of affection was to ruffle the kid's hair on our way by, but now Weston is pushing six-foot-four, a couple inches taller than me and almost a foot taller than Dev. It takes the sweetness out of the act if you have to reach up to muss your baby brother's hair.

In a silent standoff, Weston wanting in the bedroom and Devon wanting out of it, neither of them moves. Both look terrified, neither blinking their tear-pooled eyes... Suddenly, Weston yanks Devon into a hug, wrapping him tightly to his chest, and Dev allows it. Assuming the position of big brother, Weston ruffles Devon's fucked up hair, and then kisses it. Stepping to the side, he allows Dev's escape.

Devon just looks Weston in the eye as he moves by, patting the kid in the center of the chest, and then he's gone, and who knows for how long.

Holding my breath on a sob, holding my eyes wide to abate the tears, I hate what Devon's doing to our family.

Hate him.

"You're working on sainthood, aren't you?" I ask Weston as he slinks into my room.

Ignoring me, doing what he came to do, Weston drops to his knees to collect all of Devon's scattered shit, tittering on about how I should help him. "You shouldn't enable him, West," I warn. "You'll be cleaning up his shit for life. Make Dev do it himself so he learns," I caution, knowing I'm being disregarded.

Picking up Devon's cracked alarm clock, West clicks a few buttons to see if it's still functioning. He stands up, and then begins righting everything on Devon's dresser. "You shouldn't provoke him. He can't help it," Weston says boldly.

"Can't help being a drug addict?" I choke on incredulity. "You sound just like Dev used to when he was your age, only he was enabling Mom. Big difference between a medical condition and being a selfish asshole who uses drugs to get attention, while whining about how bad he's got it. Fucker," I snarl.

Weston just looks at me pointedly like I'm a fucking moron, but he doesn't say a word. Saint. The kid is the most compassionate person I've ever met. He's patient enough to outlast a snail on a transcontinental voyage. Disappearing from the room without so much as a backward glance, Weston leaves me to look at the disaster in my room, like I'm the one who threw a tantrum and destroyed the place.

"Shit!" I stare at the clay figure I made in art class two years ago and gave to Devon on his birthday. He never destroys it– ever. It was the only thing left standing on his dresser. Fingers twitching, it takes everything in me not to clean up the goddamned disaster.

I will not be Devon's enabler.

I'm saved by the kid toting a bucket filled with cleaning supplies. I knew he couldn't leave well enough alone. Weston's all about order. I growl when he plunks the bucket on my bare foot.

"I'm going out," West says flatly, brooking no room for argument.

Staring down at the bucket, "Where?" I ask.

"None of your business," Weston gives me attitude.

"The fuck it ain't!" I bellow. "You're only fourteen."

"Let it be a comfort to you that I don't act like you or Devon," West says wryly. "I believe you have some work to do." He nudges the bucket with his toe.

I just growl and glare in response, and then I flick my eyes to the hallway.

"Rae's coming with me," Weston says, reading my mind. "You tripped Devon off, so you get to clean up the result."

"You're worse than Dad," I grumble, feeling admiration for the kid. "Your future dude is in for a rude awakening."

My baby brother blushes like a kid, but he's built and sounds like a grown man. It blows the mind. Reaching down into the bucket, he pulls out a wad of papers. "Here," he crams them into my hand. "Read it, and when Dad gets home, make him admit Devon to this program."

Baffled, I stare down at a set of admission forms for rehab. "Why this place? How did you find it?"

"I didn't," Weston says in a deep voice. "Rae did. She researched them for the past few months, finding exactly what Devon needs. He doesn't need rehab, Ren. Devon needs help. It's time."

"Don't be a naïve, kid. Devon's a drug addict." I shake my head at him.

Flicking me in the forehead with his fingertips, Weston gets my attention. "The program says Devon has a chemical dependency they will fix, but it won't matter unless they solve the underlying problem. This place in Arizona specializes in PTSD, emotional trauma, and mental illness, and Rae and I think that's what Devon needs."

"God, Devon's such a victim. Maybe we all better go with him then, huh?" I mutter snidely. If I said that to Devon, he would've punched me. Weston, he just sighs as if I'm exhausting him, and then leaves my wrecked bedroom.

Materializing out of nowhere, Raven sticks her head in the doorway. "Devon's just like Mom."

"No shit," I growl. "He's the toxicity in this family. A fucking menace."

Leveling me with the same look Weston threw me when he left, Rae states, "You should be thankful you're not like Mom," and then she leaves my room. I hear the front door click shut, the kids going where it's none of my business.

"Enablers," I grumble, and then I drop to my knees and do my own enabling by cleaning up the mess Devon made.

CHAPTER NINE

Essie Prynne

Shivering, teeth chattering, I go to the only place I could think of– Bethany's. I couldn't enter my house, knowing Mom and Dad are cuddled up on the sofa, eating rainbow sherbet and binge-watching shows on the DVR. I can't witness their love and devotion, how after twenty-five years of marriage they still hold hands and laugh together.

My parents wouldn't understand why I did what I did tonight. They won't be mad or disappointed in me, knowing we all make mistakes and *on purposes*, but they won't be happy about it either. They want the best for me– they want me to have what they have. They want me to move to Florida because they think it would be good for me to get away and start a new life.

My mom doesn't believe in high school sweethearts. She told me every girl needs to fall in love, and then have her heart broken at least once to recognize when the right guy comes her way. When I asked her if a boy breaks your heart, then comes back later, if that counted, she looked faint. I took her reaction as a yes and no.

Analiese Prynne is an awesome mother. She held me when Devon broke my heart, and didn't even tell me *I told you so* or ground me for being naughty when I was too young. Mom's not a Prynne by birth, but she thinks like us. The only thing she told me to do, *"If you see that little prick, give him a swift thank you from Ana Prynne. Knee him in his minuscule nuts."*

Mom's the one who bought me a jumbo pack of condoms and showed me how to use them by rolling it on a banana. She also taught me that men aren't really assholes, but all teenage boys act like teenage boys. *"Suffer through it, Hester. They have to grow up eventually, and if they don't, they aren't the right one for you."*

I want to explain to my mother, *"What if you met Dad first? He's the love of your life, but you would have thrown it all away because he had to break your heart so you could move on."* Something tells me my mother would say I was talking about Devon and not my father, and that is the difference.

My mom doesn't think Devon is worth it, but I know she's wrong.

"Get in here, ya flippin' idiot," Bethany says lovingly as she yanks me into her apartment. "I got the shower going while you ambled up the steps at a snail's pace."

I give Bethany a droll look. "I don't need a shower."

"Fuck do!" she mock-shouts while tugging at my dress. "You fucking stink to high heaven."

Annoyed, I wrench myself out of her grip. "Jesus Christ, you're a strong little bitch," I say in appreciation. I cross Beth's apartment to get away from her, but that's a laughable five feet. It's wall-to-wall Hello Kitty and nothing else in here.

Flashing me her patented *'I'm a genius, and you should listen to me'* bitch-glare, "You need a thorough scrubbing. First, you stink like Devon's spunk." Pointing at me while grimacing, "Not something I wanted to know, chick. Second, you have Devon's spunk running down both legs, and I don't want it impregnating my carpet."

Embarrassed, I burn bright red when I glance down. Sure enough, I'm sticky down to my calves. "Sorry," I rumble, blushing to my hairline.

"We'll talk later," Beth says with finality. Crossing the room in one stride, she traps me against her desk. Grabbing something behind me, Bethany smirks.

"Hey!" I shriek, trying to get away, but Beth has several inches and a good fifty pounds on my ass. "Don't do that!" I flail my hands like a girl, pin-wheeling yet coming up empty. She attacks my dress with a pair of scissors she keeps in a cup on her desk with her pens and pencils. "Stop it!" The loud protest of fabric ripping races my heart.

Dress rent away, leaving me buck-assed naked, Bethany issues a whoop of victory. "So disgusting!" She grimaces, holding the fabric in her fingertips. Turning to the side, she steps on her trashcan lever, flipping the lid open, and drops the offending article on top of her shredded paper. With a flourish, the can snaps shut, hiding my dress away.

Pointing at my feet, "Shoes too." I narrow my eyes. "Seriously, you've got that nasty shit speckling your ballet flats."

"These are my favorite shoes," I whine, staring down at my black and hot pink ballet flats, decorated with a mouse nose, ears, and whiskers at the toes. "No."

"Essie," Beth draws out my name, getting perturbed. "I don't want to know what kind of creature that union would spawn. Do you really want a pair of sneakers showing up someday, black with blue dots, a bubbly yet suicidal attitude, and a propensity for drug abuse? You'd be jogging someday, and your sneakers would just up and run away, leaving you with unprotected feet."

Toeing the shoes off, I roll my eyes. "Yes, Mommy," I grumble as I pitch my favorite shoes into the bin.

"That's better," she praises like I'm a child. Braceleting my wrist with her strong fingers, Bethany drags me into the shower. Not only that, she tugs off her jammies and climbs in with me, a bottle of hand soap in her clutches.

"What the hell?" I shriek as Bethany dumps the whole bottle of Dial Antibacterial Hand Soap over my head. Then she starts scrubbing me with a floor brush. "Ouch, fucker!"

"You're a dirty girly." Beth giggles sadistically. "Gonna wash that bad man right outta yer hair," singing, and taking great delight in it. "Jesus Christ, somebody likes sucking on tits."

I close my eyes, already knowing what Bethany's bitching about. Devon went a bit nuts all over my breasts, leaving fingertip marks and love bites as a memento. "Please don't make fun of me," I breathe, near tears.

"I know, hun." Beth sighs, sounding as hurt as I feel. "I get it. Let's get you clean, and then we will work on getting your head on straight. Kay?"

All I can do is nod in assent. Then I press my tear-stained face into the spray of the shower, letting it wash my misery away. I envision it swirling around the drain, going down the plumbing with all traces of Devon and the sperm-killing soap.

"Here, Ess," Beth hands me a body pouf, and I don't have to guess what she wants me to scrub with it. The unmistakable scent of Summer's Eve Feminine Wash wafts up my nose. Beth slips out of the shower and begins drying off, giving me privacy to sob and scrub my cunny Devon-free.

I step out of the shower, and I'm met with a huge, fuzzy Hello Kitty towel. Bethany wraps it around me, but doesn't move away. Hugging me dry, I limply rest against my best friend and cry.

"How ya really feeling, girl?" Beth asks as she tugs a hoodie over my head. It fits everywhere but my short arms. Treating me like a baby, Beth rolls the cuffs up until my fingertips are poking out. "Step in," she instructs.

I bark a laugh as I step into a pair of purple boxers. When we were in junior high, it was all the rage to wear men's boxers as shorts. Bethany and I each had a pair in every color, and we'd coordinate them with tank tops and matching hoodies, and then we'd wear identical outfits to school. "We were flippin' idiots back in the day."

"Back in the day, girl? Pfft!" Beth scoffs. "Puhleeeeeze," she draws out while tugging me to her bed, where a fuzzy blanket is waiting to envelop me. Tucking me in her twin-sized bed, she crawls in next to me, squeezing me tightly. Yet another reminiscent reminder from a few years ago when things were simpler and sweeter.

"You're still a flippin' idiot." It's a tease– Beth's not trying to insult me. "Do I need to ask again?"

I think for a minute, trying to gauge my emotions. "Blank. Numb. Scared. Worried. Sad. Awed. Shocked. Satisfied. I wonder if that is what Devon meant, how he feels so much at once it's overwhelming."

"Yeah," Bethany says, pretty face skewing up in concentration. "Devon has to get diagnosed, Ess. I can't confirm it, no matter what he thinks. It's out of my realm of study, even when I'm licensed. He needs a Doctor of Psychiatry."

"You could totally kick ass as Dr. Oman. Don't shortchange yourself."

"And you shouldn't change the subject." Beth chastises me, and then makes a tsk-tsk sound in the back of her throat. "Let me graduate with a PhD before I move onto an MD, kay?"

"Kay," I sigh.

"I don't doubt Devon's claims, Ess. As pissed off at him as I am, I still love the little psycho with all my heart."

"I'm so gonna tell your future patients that you once used the turn of phrase *little psycho*. That will go over like a fart in church."

"Oh, my God!" Beth shouts, and then starts giggling. Shoving at me, "Stop changing the subject, bitch."

"Wait!" I laugh as she keeps shoving me back and forth. "You've got this one coming. For the rest of my days, every time you say *oh, my God*, I'm so gonna see the expression on your face when Devon impaled me."

"You should have looked in a mirror. Dang, girl." Laughing, Beth takes a breath to sober up. "Seriously, though. With all the shit Devon said tonight, not only does he need to be diagnosed, he needs to go through detox and get that shit out of his system. It's doing him more harm than good, and he really is addicted. Chemical dependency doesn't care why you're taking it."

"I know. I'm thinking," I mumble.

"Then there is his past– major counseling sessions for life. Camille, I remember how she was when we'd hang out at the Mason's. She abused and neglected Devon... then there was what happened. Not to mention her suicide a few feet from the kids. That's enough to wreck a sane person. Add that to a bipolar kid trying to medicate with street drugs, it's a miracle Devon's still with us."

Hiding my face in the blanket, I release a sob. "Don't say that."

Patting the top of my head, Beth says softly, "Don't worry, Ess. Whether Devon realizes it or not, tonight was his cry for help. He came to us, and he told us shit he's never said out loud before. There was a reason for that, and we're going to get him the help he needs. You and I have to go to Malcolm. It's not an easy diagnosis, nor is it easy to find the right drug regimen, but it's not without hope."

"Promise," I whisper, feeling like a kid asking God for a favor.

"Promise," Bethany vows. "Now, I need you to do something for me."

"What?" my voice wavers.

Beth reaches over to her desk, grabbing a bottle of water. Handing it to me, I take it, and she goes for something else. Without ceremony, a box is plunked into my palm. In a rush, I'm out of bed, dropping the box on the blanket as if it burned me.

"NO! No! Noooo. No.no.no.no.no.no.no..." I howl in pain, screaming at the offending box resting sadistically on Hello Kitty's grin. "No!"

"Yes," Bethany says patiently. Her fingertips find the box, and then start tearing into the cardboard. As if time stills, I watch in horror as Bethany pops a single tablet from a pill packet.

"No!" I shake my head in utter defiance. "I. Will. Not. Swallow. That. Vile. Pill."

Palms stretched out, one with a pill, one without. "This is a crossroads, Ess." Presenting the empty palm, "This is your *too stupid to live* decision. It will be your biggest regret." Fingers pinching the pill, and then extending it in my direction, "This is the intelligent, responsible, and grown up thing to do– for you, but more so for Devon."

Staring at the pill like I'm looking into the pits of Hell, I reach out and grab it quickly before I can think the better of it. Bottle of water still in hand, my mind works a mile a minute. Body overpowering my mind, I do the right thing... for me... for Devon.

Bethany sighs so loudly it eclipses the flush of the toilet. "Yer shittin' me, right? That wasn't cheap for a college student eating Mom and Pop's Ramen."

"I'll pay you for the Plan B," I grumble, feeling guilty. "I just couldn't do it. You heard Dev tonight– Christmases, Thanksgivings, and Aunt Bethany. I'm not going to murder any hope we may have."

"Christians." Beth sneers.

I lash out, kicking Bethany's shin. "Bitch, Puhleeeeze. You sit in the pew next to me every fucking Sunday morning. Christians?" I roll my eyes. "Would you have taken it if you were in my position?"

Leveling me with an evil grin, "Devon's spawn? Fucking right I would have swallowed that cocksucking pill in a heartbeat."

Exasperated, I shout, "Rory, dumbass!"

Snickering, Beth sobers. "Not on your life, bitch. Nothing would have forced me to swallow that pill." Sitting up on the bed, Beth tucks her legs underneath her ass and gets comfy for a down to business chat. "You're guaranteed knocked up, you get that, right?"

"Not necessarily," I mumble, calculating in my head.

"I'm the one you want to go to med school." Juggling a pair of Hello Kitty erasers she nabbed off her desk, Beth concentrates on the matter at hand. "If I was worried about your rat shoes, don't you think I'd be worried about you? Hell, at this point, I think Masons breed by osmosis. Just get near one who has their sights set on you, and nine months later, you pop out another generation."

"I don't believe that." Blushing from embarrassment, shaking from fear, quivering from excitement, I start pacing around her apartment (plumbed bedroom).

"That boy was always insane– insane for you. I remember the last time he got near your puss-puss, refusing to wear a rubber. Devon might not have realized it tonight, seeing how he wasn't thinking straight, but his cry for help was his egg-seeking baby juice."

"Eww…" I shudder, just remembering the nasty taste of his baby juice. "Yuck."

"A baby isn't going to fix shit, Ess. I can see it written across your face– you're hoping and praying. But it's only going to get worse." Beth offers sage advice. Advice I can't heed because I'm TSTL.

I stop and look at Bethany, showing her the depths of my pain. Tears streaking down my face, I speak from the heart. "I know Devon can't love me, that he won't share a life with me, how he's unable. I realize that even with help and medication, we might never get there. But I want one guarantee in life– I want a part of Devon forever, a part he's been doing his damnedest to share with me since we were fourteen."

"Oh, Ess," Beth breathes, looking tortured. "You're so fucked. Warped." I nod my head, agreeing with her. When I sniffle, she parts her arms. "C'mere, girl. Let Auntie Bethany make you feel better."

Walking toward my best friend on shaky legs, I grumble a warning, "Don't analyze me though. I'm not one of your subjects." Enclosing me in her warm, comforting embrace, Beth's laughter is even warmer, more comforting. Sinking into her, I know I'll be okay no matter what with Beth at my side.

CHAPTER TEN

Kieren Mason

None of your business isn't a place per se. Said by anyone else, it's a rude way to tell someone to fuck off. But when said by a Mason, it's a location.

It took me a while to realize this because I was pissed and frustrated. About halfway through Dust-Bustering up baby powder, I had a light bulb moment. But before that, I just really wanted to know what the fuck Devon uses talc for in the first place. His sweaty, cheating nutsack?

You have to have an instructional manual when dealing with Devon. He never says what he means, wanting you to reason him out like he's a motherfucking challenging calculus equation. If you get it right, Devon's tossing another equation at you– this one harder than the last. If you get it wrong, he blows up into a rage and makes you clean up his mess. The rest of the time, Devon just lies straight to your face. Then there's the brooding, deep cop bullshit he pulls, where he keeps his trap shut so no one realizes he's wandered off and not paying attention to a thing you're saying.

I still have no idea if Devon's high or not, since I'm used to seeing him high. So after thinking about it, digesting his visceral reaction to my accusation, I'll take a 50/50 guess on him being sober. Odds are, he was high.

I hate my brother because he makes it impossible to love him. It's hard work just holding a conversation with Devon, knowing he's probably having a separate conversation with you that you're not even privy to. It's discombobulating. So as I was cleaning up his tantrum, I started to sympathize with him, wondering what it's like to be him during this bullshit.

Scary.

Devon is smoke and mirrors all the time. He throws a fit so you can't see him clearly, because you're too pissed that he's purposely baiting your ass. So it's afterward when you realize he was actually asking for a fucking hug– some kind of reassurance. This morning, he wanted a fight, but what he wanted more was for me to tell him it was okay that he was with Willow, that I didn't hate his fucking guts because of it.

Devon wanted to hurt me, and when he did, he was sorry and expected me to be upset. So when I wasn't angry, and when I didn't say it was okay, I left him in limbo. Dev cheating on Willow was a direct result of what I failed to do.

It's not my fault– it's all Devon's, because he's so emotionally stunted you have to have a handbook just to understand him. A handbook you need to read to Devon, so you can tell him what he's feeling and why. Doesn't matter, though. He's my brother, and I'd rather play Rubik's Cube than not have him in my life.

It took me an hour to put our room to rights, now I'm wandering down the street toward *None of your Business*, carrying Devon's cocksucking leather jacket that reeks of sex, fearing the bastard is cold. I hate that I have a good idea of who he screwed just by her scent alone. I don't mean her pussy juice, even though I'll never forget that fragrance for the rest of my life, which is why Dev tries to murder me in my sleep when the whim strikes him.

Every year since we were kids, I've bought Essie her favorite perfume on her birthday. I'd recognize the scent of Givenchy anywhere, and it's wafting from Devon's jacket.

No wonder Dev made me promise to be there for Willow starting tomorrow, not that I wouldn't be anyway. This is going to kill her. But I'm happy for my dipshit brother nonetheless. I get that cocky smirk Dev flashed me when he entered our bedroom and those wicked scratches– Devon had one hell of a ride.

My biggest clue, after Devon got back from None of your Business, and then ran off again, Weston and Rae were going there next, which meant they were tracking our big bro like I'm tracking them all now. If I can decipher Devon's moods, I can definitely find None of your Business in the dark.

"You shittin' me?" I mumble.

Only a Mason would play football in a cemetery.

Like a lone, lit candle on an emo's birthday cake, Weston is tossing the ball to some little shit I don't recognize. Almost six and a half feet topped with blond hair glowing in the moonlight, I know my burnt-out flames are hiding amongst the headstones.

As I wander closer to the Jamison/Mason section of Fairport's Memorial Cemetery, I realize the little shit is actually a guy, and he's pretty good at intercepting Weston's throws. But I also notice Weston is going easy on him, meaning he's not a football bud.

Mid-step, I almost fall on my ass in shock. The boy is agile, running fluidly, and blushing and giggling. The only thing he's missing is a *gay* nametag on his jacket. He's a cute, pocket-sized cocksucker, no taller than my chest.

Raven's easier to locate than Devon. Her skin glows in the moonlight even if her hair blends into Grammy and Pop's and Dad's parents' headstones. She always gravitates here, where all our dead are interred.

Barry Timothy Jamison – Maeve Camille Price Jamison
Johnathon Harlon Mason – Penelope Jean Sutton Mason

"Who's Weston's girlfriend?" I whisper spookily, hoping to frighten my baby sister, but she's made of sterner stuff.

Rolling her dark eyes up to me, Rae whispers back, "Shh… he's not here."

Confused, my eyes seek the kid as he lopes across the graveyard like a tiny gazelle. "He's not?"

Shaking her head, Rae flashes me a somber expression. "He's not really here."

"Is he a ghost?" I play along. "Because he looks flesh and blood to me. He's putting pink in ol' Wessie's cheeks."

Still shaking her head, "He's not here. You don't see him."

"O-kay…" I drawl out, laughter bubbling up. "Can you see him?"

"No," Rae replies immediately, causing me to bust out laughing.

"Can Weston see him?"

Horrified, "Absolutely not!"

"Can Seth see him?" I try a new tactic.

"Yes." Her little eyebrows knit together, and then she looks around for Seth.

"What the fuck, Raven? Seth's not here. You're confusing me so much, you're confusing yourself."

"We go to school with Sage, that's why Seth can see him," Rae reasons. "But he's not here *right now*. Got it?"

"Um, not really. I don't see what the malfunction is. What's all this cloak and dagger bullshit? Is this Sage kid grounded?"

"Nope, he's Opal's son," is Rae's only explanation.

"Wait, what?" I bark. "That freakin' fairy popped out of Opal's snatch?" Before the words are fully out of my mouth, Sage and Weston are glaring at me, either for the derogatory remark or for commenting about Opal's baby chute. "Sorry!" I give a wave. "I'm making an ass out of myself left and right tonight."

"Opal is Dad's buddy," I whisper to Raven, leaving out the part about how Dad's fingers have been where Sage was born. Maybe that's the malfunction.

"Sage is a junior," is all Raven has to say, and I get it.

"I see nothing," I mutter as I weave my way over a few headstones. Weston looks happy. When I was his age, I'd fucked four girls by then. If he wants to be a stud by snagging a junior when he's in the eighth grade, more power to him. But Chief Mason can't find out, or the prancing Sage will be in the slammer for molestation. "I see nothing," I repeat.

Looking like someone kicked his puppy, Devon's slumped on Mom's headstone. His back is covering up the engraving, but I have it memorized anyway.

Camille Helena Jamison Mason. Loving sister, mother, and wife.

I'd snort at the irony of Mom's everlasting epitaph, but I had an epiphany while I scrubbed *Right Guard* off the bedroom wall. Devon wants me to say he's just like Mom, which means he thinks he is. Here we are, all of us saying nasty shit just because we're angry at the bitch. I get why he'd think we feel the same way about him, but we don't. Mom was Mom. Devon's Devon… and we're angry because we miss her.

I don't want to miss my brother, so I'm going to keep him with me.

I plunk down across from Devon, resting my back on some dude's granite. My brother doesn't move. Hell, he doesn't even look like he's breathing. The only sign of life is the misery glowing from his eyes. I'd ask if he was high, but this is the opposite of high.

We know Devon visits Mom's grave once a week, but I suspect he comes here every damn day. What he silently says to her, I have no idea. When I come here, which is to visit Grammy and Pop, I never venture to this slab of granite.

Devon looks terrified, face paling, sweat beading on his forehead, eyes held wide in horror. Mortality is my only guess. I don't visit Mom because her birth and death years scare me shitless. The woman was only thirty-one when she took her own life. I can't imagine losing Aunt Isis, Auggie, or even Rob, in less than two years from now. It's like having a timer ticking down in your head– a bomb set to go off –and I bet Devon's the only one who hears it.

I tap the toe of Dev's sneaker with my own. "I'm not gonna say it, 'cuz it's not true, bro. You're not like Mom." Dark eyes move in my direction, but otherwise he's immobile. A shiver runs up my spine, remembering. "A'rite. Don't pull that spooky bullshit, 'cuz that was Mom's signature move, dude."

Dev doesn't move.

Shit.

"I'm sorry," I breathe. Creepy eye action again. But I can speak Devon's silent language. *Why?* "I'm an asshole, that's why." Sighing, I yank at my hair. Pain radiates across my scalp, and I wince. *You got me good, bro.* "I'm sorry because it takes me too damned long to realize you and I don't think the same way."

Ah, that got Dev's attention. I'm rewarded with an eyebrow raise.

"See, I've fucked over fifty chicks. Most of them I don't even remember. So for me, it's just a biological function, like taking a shit."

Dropping the stone routine, "You've been doing it wrong," comes dark and deep from the recesses of Dev's throat.

As Dev's reward, I toss him his jacket– a plume of Essie fills our noses, earning me a twitch in Devon's lips. "Thought you might be cold, but I see Wessie gave you his hoodie."

"Thanks." Devon hugs the jacket, and I hate the sheen to his eyes.

"Nah, I don't think I've been doing it wrong," I muse. "For me, anyway. Listen, dude." I lean forward, grabbing a hold of Dev's shoelace, toying with it as an excuse not to meet his eyes. "About Essie and Willow..." Deep breath. "Yeah, I love 'em both, but I don't get you, dude. Maybe because I've never had a girlfriend, or some shit. But to me, it doesn't matter who you screw."

"In this, you've got too much Jamison in you." Dev's voice is eerie. Before I can voice my '*what the fuck*', he answers it. "Masons are like wolves– we mate for life. Aunt Ginny, she's had what? Two girlfriends, and fucked around with hundreds more. You were a little slut, too."

"So what?" I say with a shrug, not offended in the least. "I wasn't with anyone, so what's the issue? I want Willow and all, but she's not mine *yet*. So who I've screwed shouldn't matter– who she's screwed doesn't matter. It's whether or not we're loyal when we're together. As a newfound cheater, I think you'd understand."

"I didn't cheat on Willow tonight." Voice thick with shame, Devon sounds tortured, and I don't dare look at him. "I cheated on Essie the night before."

"Oh, Christ," I blurt out, wincing. "You're such a head-case. That's why you exploded in our room?" I take a deep breath and expel it in a gust. "I know you hate me for being with Essie, and you were trying to punish me, and it's eating you alive because it backfired on your ass."

"FUCK! YOU!" Devon bellows, eyes going bloodshot, with a vein bulging in his forehead from the force of his fury. "I can never pay your patient ass back for shit. Now, you're fucking fine with what I did, and I'm not. Okay? I'm choking to death on guilt. It doesn't matter that Willow was using me– it matters how I was using her. It doesn't matter if Essie cares whether or not I screwed her cousin– it matters to me. I was the asshole, and the only one who was hurt was me."

"Just let it go, man, and move on. Stop looking at me like you want to kill me all the time. It creeps my ass out."

"I can't help it," Devon whines. "My hatred of you pulses in my mind, and it doesn't help that you still look at Essie likes she's a tasty treat."

"UGH! UGH!" I grunt, hammering my head backward against some poor dead dude's headstone. I close my eyes, frustrated. "You're like a dog pissing on its territory. I won't touch your girl ever again. Hug her, maybe."

With glaring, narrowed eyes, "But you want to, and that's why I want to cut your dick off."

"Seriously, bro? Essie's hot, and you're a lucky bastard. I ain't the only one who likes looking at her. But I do love her, okay? I love her like a really hot cousin I wouldn't mind fooling around with if I wouldn't get caught." I start laughing when Devon growls. I'm fucking with him, but I'm not.

Devon is channeling Dad right now. Dad killed the guys who touched Mom. Mom was a virgin when she came to Dad, and when those bad men touched her, Dad couldn't handle it. He shot each one of them twice– once in the head and once in the junk. Dad shot them in the junk first.

I can't even comprehend how Dad was feeling in that moment. What terrifies me is how Devon would've reacted in that moment if he were in Dad's position.

Devon's right about one thing; I'm more Jamison than Mason when it comes to this. I know deep down Willow and I will work out someday. I don't care that she was with Auggie and Devon first. It just rankles me that Devon did it to punish me, and it hurts me to know it's torturing him instead.

As a guy who has fucked fifty-four girls– and only came for two, not that I will ever admit it –I can't judge anyone for anything. I'm not a hypocrite. I'm not the jealous sort. I'm also not a cheating douchebag. When I finally get a girlfriend, I'll treat her right. Respect her. Cherish her. I'll make her want to stay with me because I'm a good guy and she's a good girl, not because I'm territorial and possessive. If she's the right girl, we'll be faithful to each other, no questions asked.

I've had a crush on the tiny tyrant for a few years. Willow's a cute girl, but who she is on the inside is my draw. Her wicked personality keeps me on edge, and I want to maul her like a wild animal when we're in the same room.

I just happen to have a problem with finding Essie's outside package tantalizing, which is why my brother will kill me someday. Can't help it. I got my first wood for Essie, and I've been cranking out Mason swimmers at a rapid rate while fantasizing about her ever since.

I'm a dude– what can I say?

Would I do Essie again? The old me from six months ago would have, and I would've enjoyed it. But I grew up, got smarter. Even back then I had a will to survive– kept my trap shut. What no one but Essie and I know, the reason we stopped on thrust three wasn't because we were bawling. It was because I was coming like a three-pump-chump losing his v-card without a condom.

Crying, snotting on Essie's awesome tit, she stroked me off while I jizzed all over her thigh. Essie was so sweet, understanding– loving. I was jealous of my brother because Essie wanted him and he threw her away because he's a fucking idiot. I developed a bit of a crush on Essie that lasted until Willow stopped looking like a little girl. Essie and I will never fit, but that doesn't mean I don't care about her or want her, and that also doesn't mean I will ever act on the impulse either.

I'm not a cheater, and I learned my lesson last time. I was a kid, and I didn't realize I had hurt my brother as much as I did. The beating wasn't what killed me. It was Devon crying himself to sleep, feeling betrayed– by me.

A sense of betrayal I didn't feel last night when Dev was with Willow, and he can't handle it because it's unbalanced. Life isn't about balance– it's about living.

"I'm sorry," I say again, and the hitch in my voice is proof I mean it. "If I could, I'd go back and erase what I did with Essie. But since I can't, you've got to move on. Seriously, move the hell on, bro," I plead.

"You don't think I've tried?" Dev releases a laugh that stings the back of my eyes. Good God, he's in misery. He sniffles, and I know he wants me to ignore it, so I do. "I thought being with Willow would fix it. Balance it. It's the only thing that kept me going while I was plotting. But being with her made it worse, made me feel worse."

"Did being with Essie make you feel better?" I ask hesitantly, knowing Devon's not much on giving details unless they are to punish me.

"You've been having sex wrong, Ren," Dev says wryly, giving me a glimpse of the brother I'd tear my beating heart out of my chest to make happy. "It means something if done right. Hell, with Willow, it even meant something because I care about her."

"I know," I breathe, and then I tell Dev a secret. "I've come before during sex."

"What?" Dev squawks, shocked shitless.

I've told everyone I can't get off unless it's in my own hand. Out of fifty-four girls, only two meant anything to me, and well… it's best if I don't mention Essie. The first time and, "The last time I had sex I came, and it freaked me out. So I stopped doing it, and set my sights on courting Spanky."

Devon leans forward, the intensity in his eyes is startling. You can visibly see his mind reeling. "Because you felt fixed? Fixed?" he says like the answer is life-altering. "I know you were avoiding Willow, worried if you... had sex with her, you'd cry like a little bitch and lose your chub."

"Thanks for that. *Really*." I roll my eyes, and then spit it out before I can change my mind. "It was Tina, okay?"

Making a gagging sound in the back of his throat, Devon's pale skin is tinged green. "Tina? She's like our cousin." Eyes narrowing with fury, "But then again, you seem to like cousins if you don't get caught."

Kicking out hard, my foot lands an inch from Dev's junk. "Shut the fuck up, ya prick. Tina's not that bad. She just has a bad rep."

"I love Tina. She's cool." Dev's eyes gloss over, like he's remembering his drug addict sister-from-another-mother. "Beautiful and bullied, like how everyone is jealous of Essie. I can appreciate how Tina's hot. I can look at Raven and know someday some tool is going to go head-over-heels, and I'll have to kill him. But thinking of Rae or Tina in a sexual manner makes me wanna hurl."

Leaning in, I whisper like it's a secret I don't want Rae's listening ears to overhear. "I hurt Tina's feelings, so now she hates my guts. We were hanging out like buds or... well, fucked up ex-step-relatives. We were going at it hot and heavy, and I freaked because I didn't freak. Next thing I knew, I was standing up, tearing the condom off, with my dick dripping a trail on the floor. I didn't even get to enjoy it. When I turned around with my shrinky dink, Tina was horrified thinking I lost my chub."

Devon leans back, issuing a deep belly laugh that's music to my ears. Hand clutching his stomach, Dev's eyes are glittering with sadistic delight. "That's..." heavy choked laughter. "That's why Tina's always twisting your nuts? You've got to tell her, dumbass."

"Fuck no!" I shout, outraged and blushing. "I ain't doing shit. I might as well cut my balls off and hand them to Tina. Humiliating."

"Yeah, it's better to let a beautiful woman with low self-esteem think her friend/half-assed relative went limp 'cuz she's gross."

"Tina thinks I think she's a whore, that's why," I grumble, and then flinch when Devon's glare pins me.

"I hate that word," he snarls. "Never say it again."

Rubbing my jaw where Dev cold-cocked me earlier, "I deserved that punch, bro. Ya wanna knee me in the nuts, too? I'll let ya."

"We're good," Dev mumbles, but he's trying not to smirk. Flowing fluidly to his feet without struggling– not even using his hands to propel himself up. The fucker is fast. Sitting. Blink. Standing.

Creepy.

Devon reaches down to tug my big ass up. I've never quite mastered all this height. Poor Weston, the kid grew seven inches in the past eight months. He walks around like a wobbly, newborn giraffe.

Always reading my mind, "Being short has its advantages. For one." Dev walks over to Rae and yanks her off the ground. Her giggle is adorable. "My center of gravity is lower, which is why you can never fight me and win. Two." He points at Weston. "Watch."

Like animals in the wild, West and Sage don't realize they're being watched. Wessie leans down, pecking a quick kiss to Sage's blushing cheek– a bit too close to the dude's lips for my comfort. Taking off like a rocket, Sage is across the cemetery and slipping inside a brand-spanking-new rich-bitch Lexus. Nebula Gray Pearl with a vanity plate: **GAY*SAGE**.

I hate that kid already.

Smirking, in a rare good mood, like Weston's budding love affair makes Devon happy, "If you're small, people think you're cute, and you get lots of hugs and kisses."

With a wild hair up my ass, I take off running at Weston. I sweep his feet out from underneath him and steal his football. "Asshole!" comes out warbled when he lands on his ass with a thud. "The fuck?"

"Your girlfriend is rich." I sneer, pissed off for some reason. "Is he your older sugar daddy?" Pacing around my baby brother, I toss the football between my palms. "He's too old for you, kid. Leave it alone. You'll get Sage's twink ass arrested if you're not careful."

Weston's glistening eyes give me pause. "Shit!" I hiss, forgetting I can never have the same type of relationship with the youngsters I have with Devon. "I was just yanking your chain–he's really cute."

As I apologize, I toss the ball between my palms. But from one toss to the next, I end up empty-handed. I stare at the ground in confusion as a cackle rumbles near my ear.

"Speed." Devon snickers. "Shorter means faster, you lumbering lummox!" Running at light-speed, Devon is halfway across the cemetery, football tucked underneath his arm, dodging tombstones like defensive linebackers. "KID!" he shouts, looking excited. "Keep-away! Keep away from Ren!"

It's laughable watching Weston try to get his ass off the ground. It takes both Rae and me to lift him back up. A naughty comment about how he's gonna crush Sage in every sex position is on the tip of my tongue, but I keep my yap shut.

"Thanks," West mumbles, not looking me in the eye. Rae takes off, trying to catch Devon's fast ass, leaving us alone. "We're not stupid," Weston says, looking as guilty as sad, instinctively knowing I don't like him fooling around with pocket-sized, rich cocksuckers.

No one is ever going to get me to admit why I have a debilitating fear over the type of sex Weston's going to have– I refuse to even think it. But sometimes that fear bubbles out my throat, sounding like bigotry when it's not.

Empathic Weston pats my shoulder, like he's reaching into my memories and understands it's not about Sage or him. "Kisses on the cheek are all Sage allows. Dev already read me the riot act, knowing all the laws."

"Won't be too long, will it?" I ask, being ignorant of the law.

Barking a humorless laugh that turns into a whimper. "Sage will be a junior at Berkeley before he can touch me legally."

"Seriously?" I grunt, shocked. I lift my hand to ruffle his hair, realizing he's a good two inches taller than me now. "You're shitting me, right? Kid, I was screwing my brains out at your age."

"It's about age groups. Under sixteen can do whatever the fuck they please with each other, as long as they aren't little kids–nobody gets into trouble because nobody can consent. Up to the day you hit eighteen, you can fool around with anyone over sixteen."

"So," I shrug, realizing by some miracle I never broke the law during my womanizing days. I pretty much just circled the waters of the girls in my grade and the one above me. "I suck at math."

"I'll still be fifteen when Sage hits eighteen." Blue eyes flicking away from mine, I can hear his gut-wrenching agony over being a month or two shy of the cutoff. "You didn't see Sage tonight, and if you did, it's because we're buds. Because until I turn sixteen, when Sage is a freshman in California, he'll be a child predator. After that, he'll get statutory rape, and you know how Dad is. He'll fucking do it, no matter what."

"To Opal's kid? No way!" I reach over and clasp Weston's shoulder, comforting him.

"Yeah, Dad will," my baby brother breathes out, and then he takes off running after Devon and Raven as they play keep-away with our football.

Laughing, running, looking healthy and alive, Devon plays with our baby brother and sister, as if he has no other place in the world he'd rather be. This Devon, the one tackling Raven, only to tickle her and then let her go, is the easy to love version. This Devon makes all the work of dealing with his bullshit worth it. I'd let my big brother torture me for life, just for a handful of moments like these.

"Kid!" I shout, charging across the grass, marveling how when Weston's finally on his feet, he's as graceful as dancer. I was good at football, but my height was my disadvantage because I never mastered it. I'd randomly trip over my feet– still do to this day. I have no regrets for letting the dream go. At fourteen, Weston blows my ass out of the water.

"You're gonna be a superstar!" I taunt, circling Weston as he makes an interception. "Your smarty-pants, richy-rich will be your hottest cheerleader when your ass runs out onto the field during your first Pro game."

CHAPTER ELEVEN

Devon Mason

It's the start to one of those good days that are guaranteed to become the worst fucking night of your life. Well, not the worst.

Been there. Done that.

I feel good, and I'm sober.

Doing the daily grind, and enjoying every second of it. I'm not even looking out for traffic violators I can manipulate as I make my way to FAHS. Chuckling to myself, I realize I'm like a schoolyard bully, stealing milk money from the wimpy kids. Except I'm stealing drugs from the bad guys, which makes me a bad guy in the eyes of the law. But I justify it since I'm using it as medicine, and it's not ending up in some kid's hand.

All's balanced.

I'm riding the calm before the storm, that feel-good time where I'm neither manic nor depressed. I'm hungry, sleepy, and can feel joy and pain. It's a greater rush than taking a toke too many of bud. I'm so mellow, I don't even care that this signals a descent into a dark, inescapable pit known as depression.

Head weaving to the beat, fingers tapping on the steering wheel, How to Destroy Angel's BBB flows from my parted lips. *"Get down. On the ground. Don't move. Make a sound. No more. No control. You do what you're told. Stand up. Sit back down. Your lies. Comes back around. Today. Patronized. Time's up. Close your eyes. Listen to the sound... of my... Big. Black. Boots."*

Driving on autopilot, I flick on my turning signal, entering the faculty parking lot of FAHS, avoiding squashing a gaggle of tweens. The static hum of my radio cuts into my buzz. Finger flicking out, I change the music. Expecting a dispatcher, "Chief Mason wears polka-dot jammies to bed," I chirp snarkily.

A long pause. "I sleep naked," comes deep and rough from the other end of the radio. "You've been listening to that electronic shit on my stereo again."

Ignoring the accusation. "S'up, Dad?"

"You only subject yourself to Jake Owen when you're pretending to listen to him for my benefit. Get your USB stick out of the port for the mobile laptop, ya dumbfuck."

My eyes betray my guilt, leveling on the port in the dashboard where my UBS stick is shoved. I don't bother parking in a parking spot– no police officers ever do. It's a benefit of the job. "I love Jake Owen," I say brightly. "Love me some country."

"Name one of his songs, and I'll let it go," Dad challenges me. I scramble to think of a title off the top of my head, and he starts humming Europe's The Final Countdown. I draw a blank. "Time's up, Dev."

"Hey, I better get to work," I utter quickly, dismissively.

"I'm your boss," Dad says wryly, a smile evident in his voice. "I don't care what shit you play in Colin and Kyle's cars. But your ear-bleeding bleating seeps into my ride and ruins its badass vibe. The Chief Mobile better make it back to the station in one piece. You have four hours at FAHS. Don't dick around."

"Next time I get radioed, I'm telling dispatch you read romance novels," I threaten, snickering.

"You go ahead and do that, Devon." Dad breathes heavily into the radio. Creepily. *Luke, I am your father.* "Don't forget, I'm your boss and your dad. You can't escape me. Don't dick around." He clicks off.

I slide out of the Chief Mobile, in a better mood than before. I love toying with Dad, because he likes it. Kids are shrieking, screaming insults at each other, and then giggling at some poor bullied child's reaction. Most couldn't tolerate this chaos. But after how I grew up with Mommy Dearest, Isis's volatile mood swings, then raising my siblings as if I created them, I enjoy my mornings at FAHS. It's one of the only places I make a difference. It's the only place I try, *try* to be the cop I was born and bred to be.

It's surreal. Five months into the job, three months at FAHS, and I still feel odd walking into the school wearing my uniform. When you enter a school, you automatically go back to the days you were a kid. It's harder when you're a few months shy of twenty-one and patrolling the kids who went to school with you.

Fairport Area Junior/Senior High School is a bad idea. We don't have thousands of kids in our area, so twelve-year-old seventh graders are dumped in with grown adult seniors. The major drawback for me, I've been out for almost four years, meaning there are still three grades of little assholes roaming these halls who were here when I was, and they don't listen to me for shit. I'm still Dev, not Officer Devon.

I leave the juniors and seniors alone for the most part—because they can kick my ass, and I can't carry a gun into the school. But after surveying the landscape for the past three months, I know who the problem children are. The '*adults*' have a lot of traffic violations from yours truly, and Colin since I sic him on football douchebags. The rest of the kids I try to help, figuring the others will get what's coming to them when Mommy and Daddy take their rides away.

The *Fabulous* Duo is holding up a section of lockers, which means my baby brother is somewhere nearby. If Ren was the cat's ass to the female population, then Weston is going to make billions doing magazine ads when he goes Pro. The female population will weep the day ol' Wessie comes out of the closet.

"Blink," I tease Sage, raising my hand to muss up his perfectly styled hair. Sage doesn't blink. He just keeps staring at Weston, who's being terrorized by Seth at the head of the hallway.

Balance.

I'm a bad cop.

I blame their crush on FAHS being Junior/Senior, otherwise, this would've never happened. I've kept Sage and Weston's secret for the past month. I'd do anything to ensure my baby brother's happiness.

Sage Fischer is the perfect opposite of West: tiny, androgynous, rich and cultured, and sarcastic and wicked. If Sage were a girl, he'd be the gorgeous cheerleader mean-girl. But since he's a gay kid in a conservative town, he's virtually friendless, and he's okay with that.

Bypassing Sage's perfect hair, I ruffle up the other half of the Fabulous Duo's. "Dev," Desiree chuckles, swatting my hand away. "It took forever to get my bun just right this morning."

Desiree is a third-generation waitress at the No-Name. She has all the *darlin', sweetie, sugar, hun, ma'am, and gorgeous* down pat. Desiree is destined to live a life of a service worker. I'm not insulting her; someday she may give the No-Name a name. When I graduated, she was a cute girl with brown pigtails. Now she's a grown woman. It makes me think of mortality, it does.

"I couldn't very well mess up Sage's hair, now could I?" I tease as I walk away, Desiree's laughter trailing me. Sage didn't even notice I came and went– damn love-struck kid.

"Dude, you look like a dumbass wearing sweats to school." Seth is taunting Weston, quickly flashing away before he gets swatted– by Violet. Weston doesn't fight. Ever. He has a gaggle of girls, Seth included, protecting his very large ass.

"I grew out of my jeans last week, and I can't afford to buy a new set of clothes every two months. When I stop growing, I'll stop wearing sweats to school. So deal." West bites out, some underlying animosity between the boys rearing its ugly head.

"Not a problem we'll ever face," Violet titters. Seeing the girl makes my breath wheeze out in shame. Violet is a cross between her sister and cousin, and I've fucked both girls over royally. Mustn't think of that now– got to keep the depression at bay to get through tonight first.

"Hello, baby brother." I knee Weston in the ass to get his attention. "Hello, future baby brother and sister," I say with a wave.

"You're in a strangely odd, good mood," Weston notes, sounding suspicious. But Seth and Violet don't notice. They just look embarrassed to be speaking with me at school, like talking to a cop will ruin their badass reputation.

The Homeroom warning bell rattles every kid in the school, making them scatter like cockroaches from light. I grab Seth before he can get away, putting him in a headlock and whispering in his ear. "Where's Tommy?"

Seth doesn't fight me; he relaxes. The kid can't wait to have big brothers, can't wait to get away from all the estrogen. He's also a little secret gatherer like his Uncle Robin. Nice thing to have when you're a cop– an informant.

"Tommy?" Now Seth sounds suspicious. "Is he in trouble?" In other words, he's not ratting out Tommy.

"Nope. Tommy's iPod was stolen, and it was in Evidence at the station. Just returning it, is all." I lie. I lie more than I tell the truth. I don't ever even think to tell the truth anymore. Lies. Always lies.

"Oh!" Seth chirps, pulling away from me. The final bell buzzes, and the kid's face falls.

"I'm the Truancy Officer, dickhead. You can't be late to homeroom if you're with me. C'mon." I tug him toward Mr. Dally's room. "You talk while I walk you to class."

No longer suspicious, Seth walks next to me and tells me what I want to know. "Tommy has Ms. Phillips for homeroom. But he's probably in the computer lab working on his robot project."

"Thanks, kid." I pat Seth on the shoulder, open the door to his classroom, and shove his ass inside. As I'm shutting him in, I give a happy wave to Mr. Dally, who waves back. All the teachers love me. They loved me when I was in school too.

Because I lie.

Sure as shit, Tommy's head is bent over a table, deft fingers working on a small circuit board. No monitor or teacher to be found, I slide into the chair next to him. He freezes instantly, realizes it's me, looks around for witnesses, and then thaws like ice cream on a hot summer's day.

Without speaking, Tommy tugs a pill bottle from his backpack, and when he hands it to me, he slips his payment out of my palm. I get up without a word myself, whistling as I exit the room to search out my next student.

Taryn Elsberry *was* a shy, pink Girl Scout a few years ago. Now she's a foul-mouthed, fierce, black-clad fourteen-year-old, hell-bent on terrorizing her mother. She's easy to locate… since she's terrorizing her mother. The demoness is screaming vile hatred at FAHS's music teacher. Mrs. Elsberry is a quintessential mother-figure with no backbone.

"You failed your pre-algebra test, Taryn." Elsberry's voice wavers. "You didn't even sign your own name. What's wrong with you?"

"Don't go there!" Taryn screams, picking up a desk, only to smash its feet back to the floor with an ear-splitting grating sound.

Do go there, Mrs. Elsberry. That is the question you should be asking a professional instead of ignoring the real issue. Your daughter didn't turn psycho because she got her period.

"Yoo-hoo," I sing while tapping on the doorjamb, stopping Taryn's tantrum before it starts. Wooden castanet held high over her head, preparing to smash it to smithereens to spite her mother, Taryn calms, and then gingerly places the musical instrument back on its shelf.

"Oh, thank God, Devon." Mrs. Elsberry sighs like I'm her savior. "You deal with her." Turning her back, Elsberry disappears from the room, sliding past me.

Deal with her? You cunt, you're her fucking mother.

Shutting us in alone in the music room, "C'mere," I breathe, curling my fingers to my palm in a *'get over here'* gesture.

The short, chubby, and irate teenage girl gives me a hug. I pat Taryn's shittily dyed black hair as she cries out her frustration against my shirt. "I brought you a gift." Huge watery green eyes stare up at me... with hope. Tear tracks smear the makeup making her pink skin white– so sad.

Plucking Tommy's ADHD meds from my pocket, I tuck them into Taryn's hoodie pouch. "Take the Adderall as was prescribed for Tommy. Okay?"

"Kay," Taryn sniffles, pulling away from me to examine her new meds– meds I've worked for three months to get Mrs. Elsberry to get her.

"No uppers or booze with this shit, girl," I warn. "Not only are you fucking yourself up now by burning, you'll kill yourself by mixing this shit together. You're depressed– I'm un-depressing you. You've been medicating yourself wrong."

Within the first week of walking the high school beat, I spotted Taryn as kindred. She has manic depressive tendencies already. Bipolar. She's depressed, and I don't mean where some dickhead hurt her feelings so she closed herself off. Clinically depressed... and smoking pot, drinking, and taking all sorts of downers, which only lowers her low. The girl has suicide by graduation tattooed on her forehead.

Taryn needs to be balanced.

I've done my damnedest to help Taryn where no one has ever helped me. Mrs. Elsberry. The guidance counselor. The superintendent.

Ignored.

Next up in my quest in *Save Taryn Elsberry,* Chief Mason by getting Taryn arrested for drugs. Last week, Dad got a wild hair up his ass about sending all the minors he arrests to rehab. There must be psychologists at rehab– a place beyond Mrs. Elsberry's, or even Reverend Braxton's, reach.

Enter Tommy Braxton. Tommy is a healthy boy with a religious zealot, fuckhead for a dad, who reads him the scariest bible scriptures at night. Tommy retaliates by acting out, because he's a teenage boy. The Baptist minister can't have anyone doubting his impeccable, perfectly religiously devout parenting skills, so he had Tommy diagnosed as ADHD as a copout.

Medicate my son, doctor, because clearly something is wrong with him, not my horrific parenting style.

Tommy doesn't need the Adderall, but he needs the cash to buy everything his father refuses him. What he really needs is no fear of Hellfire and Brimstone during breakfast, lunch, and dinner. I don't understand this version of God Reverend Braxton preaches, where He goes around striking down those who fart sideways or have an opinion or thought of their own.

The Adderall is all I could think of to keep Taryn from offing herself while I try my damnedest to get her the help she needs and deserves.

Pulling away, I ask, "You still got my cellphone number?"

Eyes burning a hole into the prescription label, Taryn says absentmindedly, "Yeah." Finally looking at me, "Thank you," sounding awed.

"Don't mention it." Really, don't mention it. I'll go to jail for 5-to-10. Cops don't fare well in the slammer. "You call me if you need me," I remind Taryn as I leave her alone in her mother's classroom.

I spend the next three hours holed up in a room the size of a storage closet off the main office. I've sent another set of requests about Taryn, all of which will go unheeded. I've argued with parents who swear their child's inability to drag its ass to school is the kid's fault. The last asshole, nutless wonder is now on my shit-list. He'll be hearing from me out on the road.

The static buzz of my radio grabs my attention before the caller speaks. Grabbing the mic off my shoulder hook, "Chief Mason reads historical romance while wearing polka-dot jammies."

Dead silence.

"Four pepperoni pizzas. Six boxes of various Little Debbie snack cakes. A case of snack-sized bags of chips– don't get the shit brands. We need Doritos, Cheetos, Funyuns, Sun Chips, Lays– the good shit. Pork Rinds. Beef Jerky. Snickers."

Laughing while shaking my head, I wind my way through the hallways. "Colin emptied the vending machine again, didn't he?"

"No shit." Dad grunts. "He's like a trash compactor. I want a large iced tea."

"What are the pizzas for?"

"I'm hungry." Dad clicks off without a goodbye. I'm in deep shit over the romance novel comment.

Every door opens to every classroom in the hallway I'm traversing when the bell rings. Pouring out in a wave of out-of-control hormones and awkwardness, they flow around me, leaving me a path. This uniform has its perks.

"You fucking faggot!" is shouted by some brain-dead Neanderthal, gaining my undivided attention. I breathe a sigh of relief that Weston or Sage is nowhere nearby. "Why don't you start prancing around as a girl? Maybe then I can pretend the lips wrapped around my cock aren't yours."

This homophobic bigot is the exact reason these assholes shouldn't be dumped in with the kids. The elementary school is on the other side of a shared parking lot, for shit's sake.

"I've seen your dick in the locker room, Joey," Maddox–Ren's replacement on the football team –is big enough, strong enough, and smart enough to take care of himself. Making a pinching motion with his fingertips, "Itty bitty dicky, Joey," he taunts. "There's a size-limit on this ride."

I keep on walking, refusing to get into the middle of something that is clearly buyer's remorse. Joey probably sucked Maddox off and is pissed he didn't get any in return. Even I can appreciate that Maddox has a future as Mr. January if Fairport ever makes a gay calendar. Let's hope Maddox gets out of this town before Auggie gets a hold of him.

Ren's a bit of a homophobe thanks to the shit that went down in that locker room, and I fear the worst of it is due to the missing parts of my memory of The Nightmare. Maddox is a good friend of Ren's, and he's never treated Weston differently because he's gay, but some insulting shit flows from Ren's mouth from time to time.

We all have our faults– even Mr. Perfect can't be perfect. The thought has me laughing to myself.

Whistling a jaunty tune, I make my way to the Chief Mobile, where I grab my Maglite, and then I take a little walk across the parking lot to the student's section.

I know every kid on the football team. It was Ren's job to keep the douchebags in line. Now that position falls to Maddox's capable hands. But in less than six months, Weston will join their ranks, and he's already practicing with them after school… and I can't have what I just heard being repeated near my baby brother.

Joey's piece of shit on four wheels is easy to locate with the Fairport Cougar's bumper stickers plastered all over it. An ego-stroking #23 is hand-painted on the center of the trunk.

Fairport's coach doesn't hand out numbers at random. Coach ranks you by your abilities at tryout versus those of your teammates. It's a sadistic ranking system. Even if you improve, it's a mark of shame as to how bad you once were. If those who come after you are worse, even if you improved, they are humiliated. Say you are #18 at tryout, but by all rights become a superstar, the next dude, no matter how great he is, becomes #19. Currently, there is only one guy with a number less than 10– Maddox.

Ren's number was #1. Langdon Stone, Ren's business partner at Wreck & Ruin, proudly had #2 retired when he graduated last spring. Maddox is #5. We've won state since Ren's sophomore year, with Maddox bringing it home this year.

Weston's already wearing Ren's jersey at practice, pissing off a lot of asshole players and parents. Next season, at fourteen and a freshman, Weston will be starting on the varsity team wearing his own jersey: Mason #1.

Joey's a second-string fumbler, so I do this without a thread of remorse.

"Oops." I sound shocked as the butt of my Maglite breaks out Joey's taillight, and then smashes the right one too. I don't give a shit about a simple fine– Joey's always on something, so the least he'll get is a DUI. Maybe I'm booking him a ticket to rehab, which eases my conscience for being a bad cop.

Slipping the flashlight back into my utility belt, I grab for my mic. "Dispatch," squawks when I press the switch.

"1-Sam-32." I wait for Nina to acknowledge my existence.

Sounding incredulous, "Junior Mason, is there actually an emergency at the school?"

"Patch me over to Leprechaun," I'm deadly serious.

"Don't let Colin hear you calling him that." Nina chuckles as she connects me.

"Dude, I'm hungry. Hurry up!" Colin's belly grumbling can be heard over the radio.

"I'll make it a meat lovers if you do me a favor. I need you to stop a bigot on a moving violation for me."

"Plate," is all Colin says, happy to pad his monthly quota with bullshit arrests.

"7-9-Adam-Nancy-Victor-2-Lincoln," I read off the dick's license plate number.

The combination of typing and chewing is all I can hear. "Joseph Daniels Sr.?"

"Only stop the car if Junior is driving," is my parting word.

"I want pizza—" is cut off with the flick of my finger.

CHAPTER TWELVE

Kieren Mason

"It's like you've been abducted by aliens, anally probed, and returned to Earth because you weren't found to be an intelligent life form." I kick Devon beneath the table yet again, and he doesn't as much as flinch.

Devon shows no signs of life: dark eyes heavily hooded, mouth slightly open as he breathes, cheeks as pale as milk, body motionless. He hasn't even roughed up his hair with our trademark Mason sign of frustration. Devon was in a fabulous mood this morning, but since he got home from work, he's been borderline catatonic.

"Can't you at least pretend to play cards, asshole?" I sort my hand, figuring out my next trick at Euchre. I grab for Devon's, determined to play his hand now too. We're losing miserably since Devon is refusing to play. His eyes flick in my direction, but that's the only move he makes– the only movement he's made in a solid hour.

"Excuse me," Willow says underneath her breath, quickly slipping from her chair. I watch her go, feeling like the biggest douchebag motherfucker on the planet. We had a good lunch together today, all the while I felt guilty for being tainted by Devon's secrets.

When I found out what Auggie did– what Devon probably had a hand in –by throwing Willow out of the Spook House, I was sickened. I wanted to kick Auggie's ass, but Devon literally beat me to the punch. I wasn't sure if Dev was punching Auggie for Willow, or because Devon secretly wished Auggie would beat him to death so he wouldn't have to do what needs to be done tonight.

If I can feel the suffocating pressure in the air, what is Devon experiencing? But, then again, Devon created this volatile situation in the first place.

My lunch with Willow was good and bad. Not only did I feel guilty, I felt that Devon might have been partially right. Willow flirted with me, chatted with me like I was her long-lost best bud. We had a great connection, and it was fun as shit. A non-date that was better than any date I'd ever been on– even made the No-Name Diner's food palatable.

If a girl was so in love with my brother, should she have the ability to flirt with me when I wasn't flirting with her? I was out of my depth in that situation, wanting Willow, but not wanting her until she and Devon had the ultimate of closures. I could tell whatever Willow had with Devon was lost. Not necessarily their friendship, but their relationship. It made me wonder if Willow would've ever dated Dev without Robin forcing Auggie into influencing Willow. My guess, they would've been good buds while Willow and I dated instead.

I want to hate Devon, but I understand how he's feeling tonight. He's a pawn not unlike the rest of us. Helpless. Powerless. Hopeless. Yet Devon is held accountable for his part. I can see the visible pain in his expression– this is literally *killing* him.

I want to hate Robin for putting us into this position in the first place, but I understand his pain as well. Robin was doing all he could to save us from ourselves. We were all on a path of destruction. While manipulative and sick, Rob is proving his love for us.

In a vicious cycle Devon would call *balance*, I want to hate Auggie for going after Willow, which forced Robin to take ruthless action. But in order to blame Auggie, I'd have to blame Aunt Isis. In order to blame Aunt Isis, I'd have to blame my cousin that was never born. The baby was innocent, and it set us all on a path of destruction.

You know what I'd rather do?

Get off this fucking blame-game-train, and move the hell on.

I just hope it doesn't all collapse after tonight, because I will not pick sides, not when it involves Devon versus Willow versus Essie. I love all three: my brother comes first. Essie is like family. Someday I hope Willow will be my family, and not because of Dad and Clover.

I want a real, adult relationship with Willow, but I can't if she won't overcome what's about to go down. How do you have an adult relationship with a girl who's stuck on behaving childishly? My biggest fear, Willow will perpetuate the cycle, and I can no longer live this chaotic, irrational, immature lifestyle.

Someone has to have the balls to step outside of the cycle, creating an imbalance, destroying this path of destruction we're set upon. Try as he might, Robin's failing. So the broken link in the chain is going to have to be me, and I won't do it by cerebrally fucking over my family members.

Honesty. Integrity. Loyalty. Laws of human nature and mankind. The Mason way.

So, now, I sit here at the Spook House among all the injured parties– Robin's way of twisting the knife deeply while glorifying in our resulting squirming. He wants us to see how our actions have affected those around us, how the pain we feel is mirrored in their eyes. I'm just not entirely sure Robin isn't enjoying it.

For hours, we were playing Euchre: Devon and me against Willow and Essie. Yeah, pure fucking torture, that.

Essie's gaze never leaves her cards, she only speaks when spoken to, and her eyes are bright red from suppressed tears– remorse and shame are bleeding out of her pores. Devon hasn't moved anything but his eyes, which keep flicking guiltily between Willow and Essie and me. I've spoken more than usual to compensate, which is an amazing feat since I usually never shut the fuck up. Willow is confused at our bizarre behavior.

Feeling frozen out, Willow makes her way to Rob, who pretends to console the girl he's been secretly playing for months.

"Dev," I growl from between clenched teeth. Kicking out with my foot, I bruise his shin– he still doesn't move anything but his creepy dark as coal eyeballs. "This isn't suspicious or anything."

Essie, red-rimmed eyes now filling with tears, "I can't take this for another second. I'm gonna puke." Bolting out of her chair, Essie's handbag gets caught up on the back of her chair. Struggling with her bag as she struggles not to cry, "I can't look at Willow without wanting to puke, not after what I did."

Unfreezing, "What *I* did," Devon's voice is deep and scratchy from disuse. "What *I* did," he repeats, stressing it.

"I gotta go." Essie croaks, wiping at her eyes with her knuckles. "Now."

Grabbing Essie's wrist with one hand while sliding his cellphone across the table, Devon proves he's not comatose. "I need Beth's cell number. Put yours in there, too."

Stunned, Essie stares at Devon's cellphone like it's going to bite her. "Please," my brother begs in a soft, intimate voice only Essie was meant to hear. With shaking hands, she picks it up, fingers barely able to punch in the number. After several failed attempts, Essie gets it right.

Trying to hand Dev's cell back, "Text yourself so you have my number," Devon orders Essie. I watch in utter disbelief as she continues to obey his commands.

They descend into some sort of trancelike conversation with their eyes. I look around to make sure Willow isn't witnessing it, only to find something more frightening. Isis is escorting Willow from the room, with Auggie and Robin looking floored.

Without saying goodbye, Essie yanks out of Devon's grip, fleeing the Spook House, Givenchy wafting in her wake.

"I told Aunt Isis earlier," Devon whispers when he notices me staring at the doorway Aunt Isis and Willow disappeared behind. "I couldn't do this to Willow without preparing her."

"What was that bullshit you were pulling all night? 'Cuz that sure as shit wasn't acting normal," I grit out between clenched teeth. "It wasn't your usual brooding cop bullshit where you don't speak. More like you were hibernating."

"Hold up," Devon gestures to me. "Robin!" he shouts boldly, gaining everyone's attention in the living room.

Rob prowls over without a care in the world. Rolling his eyes, he bows in perfect subservience. "Yes, Master Mason? How may I serve you?" flashing a shit-eating grin, devious enough to make Satan blush.

"Prick," Dev snarls. "You owe me one. Go comfort your cousin for making her stare at the girl she thinks she betrayed all fucking night long. You got your high off torturing us, made Auggie feel like the world's biggest douchebag, now clean up the mess you made."

"Oh, shit!" Rob rushes out of the house in a hurry.

I watch Rob in awe, surprised anything breaks into his pot-induced maniacal calm. "I was conserving energy for what's to come." Devon interrupts me from contemplating what Rob finds important— it's like nothing gets beneath Robin Prynne's skin. "I haven't had the best of days today."

"You were singing in the shower, whistling during breakfast, which you devoured for once, and then teasing Dad and Colin all damned day. You even pulled a prank on Kyle, and sent Nina a box of Little Debbie Oatmeal Cream Pies."

Devon just stares at me with dead eyes, like I should automatically understand how he could go from the happiest motherfucker on the planet, to a complete and total assmunch in less than a handful of hours.

Not answering me, Devon stands from his chair with precise, controlled movements. Conserving energy or pretending not to shake? Oddly sober, Devon's body is vibrating. Either he's jonesing for a hit of his drug of choice, or I'd say he was nervous or scared.

"I'll wait in the hallway for Aunt Isis to finish." Closing his eyes, Devon breathes to me, "Promise you'll take care of Willow after this. It's going to get messy. For once, I'm going to try to tell her as much truth as I can possibly stomach to speak. I love the girl, Ren. I don't want to hurt her, but I will without a second thought," he warns.

Drawing attention from the rest of Auggie's visitors, I tug Devon into the hallway for some privacy. "I'll take care of Willow," I promise.

"Good." Devon sighs in relief while surreptitiously wiping a betraying tear off his cheek. "We know Willow. She's going to go postal on Essie, and I can't be around that. If I see it, I may beat the living shit out of the girl, and that would solve nothing."

Devon leaves me to contemplate that petrifying confession as he stalks down the hallway toward the bathroom. I do know Willow, and she's not going to blame Devon for some illogical reason. She's going to hate Essie's guts. Violent, volatile, irrational, Willow will attack Essie at every turn.

This is the last of Devon I will see in a public setting for a long while, since he won't go near Willow unless coerced.

I'm always forced to take sides, but I still refuse to do so. Instead of worrying about what the future will hold, I'm going to be proactive. Robin is caring for Essie. I will care for Devon. That leaves a broken Willow. I'd love to be the one to pick up her pieces and put her back together again, but my brother will need me more tonight.

I slip back into the living room, finding a confused Auggie holding a conversation with Rory and Colin. His deep, jovial laughter sounds strained, as if he's sensing what's going down. Aunt Isis intercepts me before I get within ten feet of Auggie, signaling her part is finished, and Devon's has only just begun. With a kiss to my cheek and an arm squeeze around my waist, she leaves me to join Nina and Opal on the sofa.

I stand in the center of the living room, watching the conversations go on around me, as if it's just an ordinary night. The ladies are on the sofa, discussing soap of all things. The guys are huddled in the corner, laughing over some douche who broke two bar stools at Rush last night.

With a deep breath, I realize I better hurry the hell up, because I've been standing in the living room like a statue while my father stared at me like he was contemplating my mental health.

Two steps forward physically, fifty steps back emotionally, "Hey," I tug at Auggie's shirtsleeve to gain his attention. Swinging in my direction, his green eyes hold a wealth of suspicion.

"This is a first," Auggie grunts out. "You never address me unless you plan on insulting me. Are you going to punch me, too?"

"I get that. I do," I mumble, realizing I've been a *Grade A* asshole around Auggie since he hooked up with Willow last December. I laugh without humor and shake my head. "Sorry," I apologize for doing to Auggie over Willow what Devon's been doing to me over Essie. I never blamed Devon, but I've always blamed Auggie– for all of this.

Disbelieving, "Sure," Auggie mouths, and then turns back to his buds. They're laughing it up, calling out insults and jabs over some asshole who went to high school with them.

Fed up with Auggie's dismissive attitude, my hand grips the back of his neck and tugs. We're only two inches different in height, but the huge fucker weighs as much as an Army tank.

Looking over his shoulder at me with narrowed eyes and a face as red as his hair, "Ren?" It's a question and an unspoken warning that Auggie's about to annihilate me. But it's the clenched fists the size of frying pans that freak my ass out. I'm a big dude, but Augustus Kline is a *BIG DUDE*.

"Uncle Auggie," I say to cool him off. Our connection is something I forgot over the past four months since I've made his life a living hell. My grandfather emotionally adopted Auggie as his son, and my father sees Auggie as his brother. I've never known the man as anything other than Uncle Auggie.

I'm all about acting like an adult since I graduated, became celibate, and took over as co-owner of Wreck & Ruin with Stone. I finally recognize the parallels, and I understand my brother better in the process. I have to rise above all this bullshit, instead of making Auggie my scapegoat.

Swallowing my pride– a Mason tenet –I grovel lamely, "I'm sorry," and I mean it. "I'm sorry I've been an ass."

Nodding, Auggie hitches his chin toward the front door, silently asking me to go outside with him. If he wasn't looking at me like he was going to cuddle me to death, I'd be petrified we were going to the yard to duke it out.

I shuffle behind him, feet dragging as if I'm on a short journey to my execution. When I reach the front stoop, Auggie reaches behind me, grabbing the doorknob to shut us outside. I flinch, ready to piss my pants like Pissy Pants Robin.

"What'd Rob do now?" Auggie demands, leaning down to get into my face. His red curls are frizzed out, making him look like a mad scientist. "I'm not blind."

"It's not Rob." I lie but tell the truth at the same time. "Devon's breaking up with Willow right now, and I'll have to comfort him tonight."

"Keep Officer Hothead from doing something stupid, you mean?" is Auggie's immediate reply, and then he gets to thinking about what I just said. Furry eyebrows cinching together, "Why?" sounding mystified. "I was there the other night. Devon was…" Looking away from me, Adam's apple bobbing while he swallows convulsively. "Into it."

"I know he was," I say as if it doesn't bother me, and it doesn't. I wouldn't wish a nightmare of a sexual experience on anyone. I've had my fair share. I love my brother, and I love Willow enough to wish them a good experience together. "I'm more than good with that. But it's eating Devon alive– literally eating at him that he was into it."

"Ah…" Auggie turns away from me, stepping off the porch with one stride– 5 steps at a time. Tugging at his hair as if he was a blood-born Mason, Auggie paces around for a bit. "Choking on loyalty? I get that. I consume a couple hefty servings of guilt a day."

"So listen," I reach out to stop Auggie from pacing. It's freaking me out– he's the strong one, the level-headed one, the one with the good advice, even if he himself doesn't take it. "You need to make Willow feel better. Listen to her. Get her to understand Devon's not in a place to be with anyone right now."

"I can do that," Auggie says with determination, nodding his head in time with his words. "I can most certainly do that."

The Spook House's front door cracks open, sounding like a gun shot in the dark. Devon slinks out, looking shady as all hell, tears streaking down his cheeks. He doesn't even see us. Blindly, Dev lunges off the stoop and full-out runs away.

Auggie and I stare open-mouthed as Devon sprints down the center line of the street. "Well, kick me in the ass," Auggie purrs, and then it manifests into uncomfortable laughter. "That boy can run. Must've been training at the academy, 'cuz Dev was slow as shit a few years ago when he was running from my ass-whipping punishments."

The memory surfaces of Auggie overtaking Devon in about three strides, dropping his ass to the driveway, where Auggie literally spanked Devon for borrowing his truck without permission. That shit usually happened to me. I almost laugh, but the look on my brother's face when he exited the Spook House will haunt me for all time.

"I've got to go!" I shout over my shoulder, breaking into a run. When I get to the street, I stop and turn back. "Don't fuck her!" I bellow at Auggie. "Not only will I kill you, Aunt Isis will. She's standing in the front window right now." I point behind Auggie, where Aunt Isis is glowering with her arms crossed over her boobs. "She's supervising your fat ass."

Auggie doesn't look; I'm sure he has some kind of Isis-radar at this point. "Go," Auggie waves me off. "I'll behave, Rennie. GO!"

Assured, I lope off down the road at a steady pace. Dev is a fast fucker, I'll give him that. But I'm six-three, with a killer stride, and I run twice a damned day. Once in the morning with Weston for his football training, and once at night for my sanity. I pace myself, not wanting to catch up with Devon just yet.

None of your Business is our final destination.

CHAPTER THIRTEEN

Devon Mason

I run.

From Willow.

From the past.

But no matter how fast I run, I cannot escape myself. What I need to leave behind is playing out within my mind on an unavoidable vicious cycle on repeat.

I was cruel.

Vicious.

Unforgivable.

My words keep scrolling over and over again, warping until my voice sounds like the Devil Himself. Willow, I had to let her go, and I could see it in her eyes how she'd forgive me anything. Not only did she care for me, she was excusing my behavior because she thinks me a drug addict– someone unable to help themselves.

And that made me sick.

My labored breaths are in time with my footfalls, and since I'm running like a bat out of hell, I'm near hyperventilation levels. I'm blinded by the tears in my eyes. Tears I've long ago forgotten why they fall.

I'm the bad man. Evil. I just hurt a girl I care about because it was for her own good. My good intention doesn't make the words less painful, less wounding, or less debilitating.

I'm no better than Mom.

Worse.

I'm worse than Mom.

I'm worse than Mom because I was her only target– a target who deserved it. Dad, Ren, Rae, West, Aunt Isis, Auggie, Rob, Essie, and Willow… they don't deserve how I've treated them. Nothing they could ever do to me will ever displace the injustices I've dealt them.

Imbalanced.

Footfalls crunching on the gravel, I hadn't even realized my legs were carrying me here. "I. HATE. YOU!" I scream until the pressure behind my eyes builds, pushing against my eyeballs, throbbing the veins in my forehead, and pulsing in my veins.

Falling to my knees before **Camille Helena Jamison Mason**'s headstone, a rock sheers through my pants, slicing into my flesh but it doesn't hurt. I'm numb. I feel no pain except for the agony that's lit up my mind.

"Goddamned you! You ruined me! R-U-I-N-E-D!" I punch Mom's goddamned name. Jab after jab, I pound my fist into the granite slab until it glows red in the moonlight. I punch the only representation of her I have on earth, because I can't punch the woman in the flesh.

Blood drips hotly down my forearms, but I can't stop myself. "Like a cunt of a coward, you got away before I could make it balanced. Before I could tell you to get the fuck to Hell!"

Sapped of energy, I fall to my side, panting. No longer able to move, I can't stop the words from spilling. Croaking out in a hoarse voice, "You tainted me, warped me with your evil. Even if I hadn't contracted your disease, the way you treated me would've turned me into an evil bastard anyway."

Stealing from my energy reserves, I kick out– kick Mom. Kicking over and over again, I sob. "Everyone hates you, Mom. Loathes you. You were evil. Do you know what they think of me, Mom? They think I'm just like you. So that means they hate me, too. Do you know what, Mom?"

Rolling to my side, I wrap my arms around my torso. I breathe out to the vile woman, knowing she can't hear me all the way from Hell. "They're right."

CHAPTER FOURTEEN

Kieren Mason

Eyes closed against the horrific sight. Fists clenched at my sides. Body rigid as I lean against the Mason/Jamison monolith. The hardest thing I've had to do in my short, agonizing nineteen years, is allow Devon to release his pent-up pain– his pain directed at Mom.

I long to stop him, to the point every nerve in my body is signaling my brain to *MOVE!* Devon needs this, so I override my natural responses and wait him out. My brother's screams slice through the night. Every word is a sucker-punch to the nuts. Every word is proof of how we failed– not failed Mom.

Failed Devon.

I knew Mom was abusing Devon, and I said nothing. It wasn't normal. It wasn't *my* normal, but it was Devon's. Even when I was a little shit, I knew it wasn't right. Mom would lash out, systematically destroying my brother. We could blame it on mental illness, but there is a difference between an illness and vileness. Mental illness is unescapable, where you can't help it. But calculated attacks, manipulation, and abuse are not mental illness, no matter what fueled the urge. Mom used her sickness as a crutch to explain away the abuse.

Mom would target Devon when he was feeling good, and she'd destroy whatever made him smile, because she hated herself so much that she didn't want her firstborn to be happy either. Mom was jealous of Devon– we all could see it –and that is NOT mental illness.

That is abuse.

I knew Devon took it because if Mom wasn't giving it to him, she would have to give it to someone else– that someone else being me. Devon endured so I wouldn't have to, and I kept my mouth shut because he told me to. Sometimes keeping the secret is a bigger betrayal than breaking the promise and spilling it.

That secret has infected everything in our lives, made me Devon's bitch of an enabler. My brother took my punches, he suffered so we wouldn't, and he survived what those men did to protect me. My only debt of gratitude was to keep my mouth shut.

No more.

If I'd spoken out, told Dad how Mom treated Devon when no one was looking, Mom would've gotten help, or at least would've been taken out of our home. I kept that secret, so it's too late. I've enabled Devon's drug-use, because he deserves to escape the pain. As I watch Devon weep, I decide here and now, I will *not* keep this secret any longer. Devon needs help, not only with drugs but with the past.

As soon as I can deliver Devon to someone I trust, I'm talking to Dad.

We are brothers. But our paths were not the same, even if we were walking side-by-side, because Devon and I are separate entities who experience life differently. I'm not stronger. He's not weaker. We're just human.

Even in my new adult outlook, the outlook I've grabbed onto in order to survive, I still think Karma paid that bitch back three-fold.

Stomping over to Mom's grave, so Devon isn't startled, I work my mouth. Bending down at the waist, I spit on her headstone– my saliva mixing with Dev's blood. "You're right about one thing, brother. If I were a religious man, I'd guarantee Mom was burning in Hell. But you're wrong about everything else."

I drop to the ground to land on my ass. I make sure my back avoids Mom's stone, refusing to clean off my brother's spilt blood. We both need a visual of the invisible agony Devon feels because of Mom.

Listless, Dev's no longer *hibernating*. He's literally too exhausted to move. After tugging my brother's upper half into my lap, I stroke his hair as he looks up at me with bloodshot eyes filled with pain.

"You're wrong," I whisper. But then I think the better of it. Devon doesn't need a whisper. He needs a ballpeen hammer to the skull, forcing the truth into his mind. "YOU. ARE. NOT. LIKE. MOM." I bellow, my words floating back to us on an echo.

"Yes," Devon licks his lips, swallowing. "I. Am."

"I believe you think you are," I allow, realizing this is a losing battle. Devon believes he's Mom, so it's best if I don't badmouth the bitch anymore.

"I hurt Willow," Devon says so softly against my thigh, I have to bend down to hear him. "I was cruel."

A wince is torn from me when I notice how banged up Devon's hands are: swollen, purpling already, weeping blood from puffed up gashes– broken. The pain must be nauseating. "Mom was cruel for the sake of being cruel. The difference is your intent."

Turning his head to get a better look at me, I can see how angry Devon is at the world, but mostly himself. "Intent doesn't mean jackshit, Ren. Why you did something doesn't matter, nor does an apology." Voice small, sounding like a little boy, "It doesn't take it away. It still happened."

"Are you sorry, though? That's the difference. Mom was never sorry, even when she was apologizing. She liked to see you cry, Devon," I admit bitterly, seeing it in my mind's eye. "You didn't like hurting Willow," I say with great conviction. "I know you didn't."

"Willow forgave me the second it was out of my mouth. She would've accepted anything I did to her, and I couldn't live with that. So I had to be cruel to break her from me."

The sight of a single tear escaping Devon's right eye unmans me. It makes me realize I'd do anything to heal my big brother, even if I have to hurt him first. I understand what he's saying about Willow, more than he realizes, I suspect. Soon Devon will be on the same end of this situation. The betrayed side– the saved side.

"Sometimes it hurts to do the right thing, but it doesn't mean you're bad because of it. A bad person would've allowed Willow to stay, hurting her more and more every day, and they would've enjoyed it."

"I've hurt you, too," Devon whispers. He curls around my hip, bruised hands protected in my lap. "I was with Willow to hurt you."

"No." Again, I'm positive. "You did that to balance out the past. But it confused you more than anything." I chuckle wryly, but it turns sad. "I need to tell you this, bro. I don't care that you were with Willow, and I'll tell you why. You were her boyfriend, not me. Willow's not mine, and there are no guarantees she ever will be."

"I don't get you," Devon sound so confused that I huff a laugh.

"And I don't *want* to get you." I breathe out in a rush, fearing I'll insult my brother. "It petrifies me to know what goes on inside that mind of yours. I think it would give me nightmares for all eternity. So you go ahead and keep that shit locked up nice and tight, and I won't try to understand you."

Chuckling, Devon groans in pain against my leg. "Yeah, that's probably for the best, I think."

"No shit," I tease. "I know it's dark in there, bro. If you ever need a light, you know where to find me, right?"

"Right," Dev agrees to my unspoken offer. "I'm confused. I was with Willow, and I liked it. If I really loved Essie, I shouldn't have."

"Now that right there is hilarious." I hold down a struggling and pissed off Devon while I laugh heartily. "D-u-d-e! Calm yourself before you harm yourself," I laugh out. "I've fucked fifty-four girls, and while I might not have gotten off with them, it didn't mean I didn't love it. I just whacked like a lunatic the second I was alone."

Beyond confused, Dev gasps, "What?"

Still laughing, "Sex feels good, fool. Sex doesn't mean love. It's body parts touching, is all. Like shaking hands. You're not tearing out your beating heart and shoving it into the woman's chest, for Christ's sake. It's your dick into a cunt– repeat until cum spurts."

Devon finds the strength to taunt me, "You're totally doing it wrong. Neither girl was like a handshake."

"Well, that feeling is when you inject strong like, or even love into it. Remember my terror over Tina?" I laugh at myself, mortified by the memory. "Imagine how Auggie and Robin would feel if they had to wait for Aunt Isis to give it up again? After four years, they seem to have no issue messing around and separating it from love and loyalty."

"Someone needs to tell those asses the only people Aunt Isis would be jealous over is them doing each other, and no one else. She'd feel left out and want to join back in. Damn blockheads."

"Fuck," I murmur, awed. "You're a goddamned genius."

"That's not what my teachers said," Devon quickly retorts, and then changes the subject back to his shit. "It felt like I was cheating on Essie when I was with Willow," Devon admits, getting choked up.

"But you're not with Essie right now. I believe it would be difficult to deal with cheating on someone if you were in a committed relationship, and that only counts if you're *both* in a committed relationship," I stress, not Devon's imaginary relationship with Essie in his mind.

"I'm Essie's." Devon sounds so lost to love, it's ridiculous.

"Kill me if I ever sound like that," I beg. "Ya got to have the exclusive talk while dating for it to count. Or be engaged or married– that's a given. After that, that's cheating, bro. I think mentally it would be hard. But your dick has a brain of its own, and it's up to your big brain to tell it no. Loyalty outweighs the temptation, but it doesn't mean you won't still want other people."

I won't lie, I still love looking at Essie, even though she belongs to Devon. Look, *never* touch. I wouldn't touch Essie under penalty of death. The thought alone shrivels my dick. But there is a difference between your dick wanting and your mind needing. I don't give a shit what Willow looks like– she intrigues me. If it's attached to Willow, it makes me hot.

To quote my favorite daytime judge, *"Beauty fades. Dumb is forever."* If I plan on courting, winning, and keeping Willow forever, I better like her mind, because the outside package changes. Same with me– I won't be football-ready forever.

"I've never had a problem telling my dick to settle down. Opposite problem, actually," Dev grumbles, and I do my damnedest not to laugh again. "Not true. I went crazy on Essie the other night, same as how I felt when I was a teenager."

"Dev," I peer down at him, making sure he's paying attention. Beat up, exhausted, he's not suffering from ADHD. "I'm glad you had a good first time, even if it was with the wrong girl. Don't feel guilty. There was a reason it was with Willow, and it's not up to us to decipher why. I'm happy for you that it was good, and there's no shame in that. You and Willow deserved more than having a horrific experience."

"If I was selfless, I'd say the same to you about Essie." Devon's eyes flee mine, giving me a read on that scary-assed mind of his.

"Which means you wish we weren't a weeping, snotting, bawling mess while we banged? Hmm… Your growl has no punch when I'm holding you like a beaten puppy."

"Fuck you!" he spits, lashing out but looking all a fool.

"Don't kill me." I take a second to say a little prayer. "It wasn't all bad between Essie and me, okay? So if you kill me, Dad will be pissed."

Trying to sit up, but failing miserably, "What?"

"Dude, I was almost fourteen, rutting on the girl I'd been staring at for two years. I was inside her, touching those goddess tits of hers. It was quick because I was a virgin dumbass, who had to pull out. I ended up coming on her thigh while she jacked me off."

I freeze, preparing to be murdered. But all Devon does is stiffen up and say, "What? What about Essie?"

Odd reaction. "Um… I was a kid, and stupid, but not *that* stupid. I… um… used my fingers to finish the job. I figured it was a one-shot kind of deal. Being a blubbering mess was bad enough, so I made sure we both got something out of it."

Devon floors me, "Good."

"Good? What the fuck, man?" I half-shout, nearly shoving Devon off my lap. "You tried to murder my ass in my sleep… four separate times."

"It was only three times," Devon says dramatically, like there is a big difference between three versus four attempted murders plots. "Essie was supposed to lose her virginity in a good way, a way that didn't make her feel like a whore. So that was why I first tried to kill you," Devon rattles off without shame. "The other times: when she blew that first tool, and when Mike screwed her and she cried. Essie said yes, and hated every second of it. She was supposed to like it. I couldn't give it to her then, but before when I did, she loved it. Essie shouldn't have lost anything because of me."

"Bro." I sigh deeply. "You're a mental case, you know that, right?"

"I've been saying that for years," Devon says brightly, eyes shining up at me with pure happiness.

"You're creepy as fuck, dude!" My fingers search his skull, looking for head wounds. "Did you try to kill those idiots, too?"

"Maybe," is all he says. In the blink of an eye, my hand lashes out to slap him across the cheek. Smirking through the pulled hit, "Nah, I got the tool arrested for a DUI, but that was his fault for drinking and driving. I've left Mike alone– Essie said yes. It's on her that she hated it."

"Your demented version of balance," I mumble in appreciation. "Dang."

"I might need bail money in a few days," Devon says cryptically, but doesn't explain. "Have you ever had a bad sexual experience– an unwanted one?"

I freeze, unsure where this is headed. I've never told my brother what he's always wanted to know about the past, instinctively knowing if he was meant to know, he'd know– I wish I didn't know.

"What?" I slur, confused. But then I get a clue. "Essie was harmed? Is that why you'll need bail?" My fingers curl into fists at the thought alone.

Devon gets murderous over Essie not getting a fulfilling ride, how's he going to react over an uninvited one? Fuck bail money; Devon's going to need a lawyer and a judge in our back pocket.

Never giving me anything without getting payment first, "Answer the question," Dev demands.

"Yeah." My throat goes as dry as a desert. I know too many of Dev's secrets, and I've kept them all. I guess I should share another of mine. "I was a sophomore, and I'd just banged this really hot junior in the girl's bathroom. It's an intimacy thing for me, coming with someone. So I took a shower in the locker room while jerking off."

Snorting, "That's my favorite part, feeling them surrounding me, clenching on me– filling the girls up." Devon has the decency to flinch, thinking I'm going to deck him over that.

"You wore a condom, right?" I ask, voice wavering. I know how possessive Devon is, so I fear what he'd do on purpose.

Dev immediately answers, "With Willow, yeah– after the first time." But he changes the subject before I can kill him for not wearing a condom. Not that I did with Essie, either. But hey, I jizzed on her thigh, not inside her. "Jerking off in the shower?" he prompts, meaning nothing would've gotten him to pull out of Essie.

"You're a jackass." I snarl, lashing out because I don't want to voice this. "Shit. Fine." Deep breath. "So my forehead was leaning on the tile, spray hitting my neck, and I was jerking it while shooting, and some assmunch snuck up behind me and grabbed my dick."

"While you were coming?" Dev asks in a stiff voice filled with violent intent.

"Yeah," I admit, shuddering, feeling violated and humiliated all over again. "It was only a couple seconds, and I told Coach. Dad was brought in, lawyers– the schoolboard. It was kept quiet, and the janitor went to jail for three-to-five. But ever since, guys who like guys creep me out."

"Ren," Dev touches me with his broken hand. "Our baby brother is gay, remember?"

"Yeah, well... hard to forget when baby bro is a ho-bag. About two months ago, I was picking West up from practice, and I caught him pressing Maddox against the south wall in the locker room, sucking the dude's tongue down his throat while palming his package. I didn't say anything. I just went over to the stalls and puked up my lunch."

"Maddox? Whoa..." Devon sounds too impressed for my liking.

"Ho-bag," I repeat. "I didn't know about Sage until last night. But I recognized that rich-bitch Lexus. Maddox was riding around in it a few months ago. Gay Sage is a pimp."

Chuckling, and causing himself more pain, Devon finds my phobia of all things guy-on-guy hilarious. "I needed a good laugh," Devon thanks me. "West's Masonhood has finally kicked in. It's a wonder it took this long. I was thirteen and you were eleven. The kid is closing in on fifteen."

"Late bloomer sure is a randy sonofabitch! We need to spray him down with a hose. Stop it! It's not funny!" I snarl. "Weston's hand... was on... my buddy's... dick," I gasp out, feeling nauseous all over again. "Willingly, as the aggressor."

Dev rubs salt into the wound. "Weston's a lucky fucker. Both Maddox and Sage are prime pieces of ass to a gay guy."

"I wasn't worried over Maddox stealing Weston's innocence. Their asses will be cinched up nice and tight. But now with that prancing twink fairy, they have a willing victim."

"What?" Dev snorts. "Look at me, dumbass." When I refuse, Devon's bloody palm cups my cheek and turns my face back to his gaze. "Weston should have this experience, even if you had a bad one. But c'mon, did you seriously dub both those guys as tops? Your gay-dar sucks ass, literally."

"Maddox and Weston are all men," I mutter sheepishly.

"So what? Taking it doesn't make you a girl. Just ask Auggie," Dev challenges.

Shuddering, I sputter, "No fucking way," in denial.

"Soft and sinister Robin owns all exclusive rights to Auggie's mammoth ass– he's the only one who's ever been in there. Monster Auggie is the bottom in their relationship, and has only topped a few guys himself. Ya never know, Sage might shock you and be a top, or Weston a bottom– or both versatile, I don't know. It's not BDSM or who's manlier– it's who enjoys the intimacy of it." I can feel Devon shrugging against my leg, but I'm in utter disbelief. "How many straight dudes have we watched get pegged by their wives in the Playroom?"

"Shut up," I warn. "I'm gonna hurl. Ass is an exit only. Only mannish hand on my dick is my own." If Devon remembered The Nightmare, maybe he'd feel differently and wouldn't be laughing at me.

"Thanks for cheering me up, little brother," Devon teases me, somehow my dysfunction comforts him.

"Anytime," I say with a smile. "We good to go home?"

"We're good," Devon pauses, contemplates. "For now."

I pull my cellphone out of my pocket as Devon tries and fails to stand. I catch him around the waist and lower him back to the ground. We ain't walking back, that's for damned sure.

"You need to eat and sleep more," I warn.

Our conversation has Devon opening up to me more than usual. "It's not the drugs, Kieren. My mind keeps me awake, and my appetite is shit. The drugs usually help me eat, and then sleep. Ya know, the munchies? Imagine going through life as a homophobe surrounded by gay dudes; that's how I feel every day with nausea."

Stumped and terrified, I ask, "What's the cause?"

"Wish I knew," Devon answers, but I know he's lying to me. When he looks me in the eyes dead-to-rights, it's the ultimate sign he's lying. He challenges me to refute the lie. When he's telling the truth, he gets uncomfortable and looks away.

"Rae," I say into my cell. "We need a lift from None of your Business."

"Um…" comes groggily from the end of the line. "I only have my learners permit. You know that. You're the one teaching me how to drive."

"Shit," I hiss with feeling. "Dad home yet?"

"Yeah, Dad's using the kitchen table like a trough. It's kind of gross."

"You calling Dad a pig?" I snicker at Raven. "You're awesome, girl. But do you have the balls to say it to his face?"

"Hey, Dad?" Rae's voice calls in the distance. "Stop being a pig, and answer your middle son."

"Aunt-Isis-sized balls on that one," Devon adds.

"Yello," Dad says, sounding all chipper with a sharp edge of *pissed the fuck off.* "I've been stress-eating, waiting on your ass to call me. I had to beg Opal to pick me up after I ditched the Chief Mobile, just so I could drive your truck back home."

"Pick us up at the cemetery," I demand, and then hang up. I couldn't very well tell Dad what I wanted to say, not with a half-dead to the world Devon leaning against me, now could I?

CHAPTER FIFTEEN

Essie Prynne

I have nowhere to go.

When you're a small child, your home is your sanctuary. No matter what happened during the day, when you were at home with your parents, everything was normal and good. It was warm and comforting in their tiny nest– *home*. Your home, your parents, they were your *life*. My parents never fought, never grounded me, and I never lacked for anything, especially love.

Adulthood sucks the motherlode.

It's not like I can slink home with my tail tucked between my legs right now. When I left earlier tonight, Dad was ecstatic because Ginny sold our house in less than a week. Mom was upstairs packing. I'm happy for them, truly.

But what the fuck about me?

It was rather startling to realize William and Analiese Prynne weren't only Mom and Dad– they had hopes and dreams outside of anything pertaining to me. Will and Ana are human beings.

Where am I to go now that my sanctuary is no longer mine?

You don't realize when you're a child how nothing belongs to you, how fragile your hold on your life truly is. At any time, someone is in control of your destiny– they have the power to give and to take it away.

At twenty-one, it's time I became the power in my life. It's time I own my life– my nest, my home. It's high time I was in control of my destiny.

Sounds good, right? Strong? Empowering? Amazing? There are several problems with that solution. Without the means or knowhow, you're royally fucked.

If I'd known my parents had this dream for their retirement, I would've chosen a different path in life. I wouldn't have gone to school, burdening me with student loans. I wouldn't have bought a car on credit.

I'm working at a job to pay for the training I needed to have for the job. The circle is debilitating in this stage in my life. I have no money to live off of in order to meet the obligations of my debts. Yes, the future of the educated is brighter, but what about their present? Those who didn't educate themselves are years ahead of schedule– established –while I'm circling the drain as an adult-aged child.

Right now, I could give a flying fuck about the future. In the present, I'm motherfucking homeless, penniless, and terrified, and I may never get to meet the future at this rate.

I feel lower than dirt. I don't have much confidence in myself, knowing Mom and Dad still house, feed, and support me. They even pay for my goddamned cellphone, for Christ's sake. I want to be an independent woman, but every time I've tried to move out, I panicked.

Shit just got real, and really expensive.

With nowhere to go as I lick my wounds in shame, I hide out at my BFF's *apartment*. I love Bethany to pieces, because her future is bright, but her present sucks as badly as mine. Beth's imaginary independence is a plumbed bedroom over top of the Oman's garage. To be a brat, I've tortured Bethany with Hello Kitty paraphernalia because it made this space feel ironic and disturbingly like a child's bedroom.

Bethany will be closing in on retirement age before her student loans are paid off. There seems to be something off with that statement, doesn't it? You work your ass off to learn all you can before graduation to perform the job you were destined to do, only for it to take the life of your career to pay back for the training. How is that getting ahead?

I'm bitter, angry– at myself and everything else in my life – for all of us.

Huddled up on Bethany's Hello Kitty-covered, tiny twin bed, I scroll on *my* (parents') cellphone. I search the classifieds for another job and a shithole to hole up in.

Overqualified.

Underqualified.

Terrified.

As for the housing situation, I'll need three extra jobs and forget about sleeping, work the corner for fifty-cent blowjobs (since in Fairport, knob-bobbing is free from our loose-lipped denizens), and get about four roommates in my particular situation.

I've found a roommate, even if she doesn't realize it yet. As for the second job, I'll apply at every business in Fairport if I have to, and I have to. The salon doesn't open until nine a.m. I guess I know what I'll be doing from seven a.m. until opening– walking Fairport with my résumé, that's what.

I have a few weeks until the closing on my parents' house, and then I'm homeless.

Fuck… me…

"Does Devon suck in the sack that badly? You look like you killed someone's puppy." Rob scares the bejesus out of me. Heart rattling behind my ribs, I clutch my chest. "What am I doing here?" My grinning cousin reads my mind. "Checking up on you, Essie."

"I'm fine," rolls off my tongue on repeat. It's all I've been saying for the past twenty-four hours. I can't think about last night without simultaneously getting hot and cold. The few hours I was in Willow's presence made me want to hurl.

Rob shakes his head as he examines Bethany's doorknob. "Lock's broken," he notices, and thank goodness it was or else I wouldn't have gotten in here. "For a smarty pants, that's pretty fucking idiotic of Beth. Where's our playful puppy?"

"*Our* puppy?" My eyes enlarge as what Robin says sinks in. "Fuck," I breathe out in disappointment. "Not you, too. I'm gonna go vomit again." I surge across Beth's bed, and find my way to her toilet in less than two steps.

Laughing, Robin has the ability to simultaneously taunt me while looking embarrassed. "I'll do whatever I can to be around Auggie in that type of situation."

I'm not really sick. The nausea is a convergence of stress atop more stress. I lean forward and get a drink of tap water from Bethany's sink. Coming up for air, I wipe my mouth with the back of my hand. "Don't act like it's such a chore. Girlfriend's got some 'splainin' to do."

"Chore?" Robin leans against the door, contemplating. His chocolate brown eyebrows are tightly knitted together in concentration. "My time with Bethany is awkward to say the least. Not entirely enjoyable. But, damn, Beth's a great girl."

"Tell me something I don't already know," I mumble. Just to be nice, and to give myself an outlet, I buff the toothpaste residue off Beth's faucet with the cuff of my shirtsleeve. "I guess I'm more immature than I realized. I still can't wrap my brain around people having sex, especially all together with other people watching. I know that sounds dumb…"

"No, Ess." Rob crosses the space to pull me into a hug, and I sigh in relief. Home. "It's not immature. It's just how you feel. You're entitled. When I was your age, did I think for an instant I'd be running a den of iniquity? No fucking way. I was a randy sonofabitch, but I never touched anyone but Auggie and Isis. But shit happens, and that shit changes us. It's how we deal that determines whether or not that change was for the good or the bad."

"Do you regret?" I whisper against Rob's neck. My arms lock around his back, fingertips sinking in to find an anchor. I love hugging my cousin. Robin's small, not too much bigger than I am. He smells nice, like home. He's also warm and solid. Rob might not look it, but he's strong, stubborn, and resilient. He's a devious bastard, but that's the Prynne in him.

Squeezing me back as tightly as I'm squeezing him, Robin turns tough love on my ass. "No matter what Willow throws at you, Ess. No matter how far Devon falls. You'll never regret what you did with Devon. Don't start lying to yourself. I'm not here for hugs alone. I'm here for advice. Now, tell me when our pup will be home, 'cuz she shouldn't hear this shit unless you want to tell her yourself."

"Beth won't be back until after two at the earliest. She's at a study group at the university. It's an hour drive back." I pull away from Robin, not only taking strength from him, but from Bethany too. My best friend is an incredible person. Working full-time with me, going to school full-time an hour away. If Beth can spend two hours a day on the highway because she wants it that much, then I can get through this shit too.

I have problems, but my problems are no worse than anyone else's. I think it's high time I stop bitching and moaning, and actively solved them.

"I'm fine," I say strongly, and this time I even mean it. "Hit me with the advice, cousin. You're scary smart."

"Actually," Rob drawls out, eyes flicking around Bethany's place. "I can't stand being in here for another second, or else I won't be able to maintain wood next Thursday night. Hello Kitty is an instant boner deflator." Shuddering, "I'm gonna see this shit the next time I see Beth naked. What a pity."

Laughing uncomfortably, I swipe my hands together like I'm dusting them off. "Well, my work here is done. I personally created Robin Prynne Repellent– Hello Kitty to the rescue."

Hitting me upside the head with the side of his palm, Robin laughs evilly. "Let's walk and talk, Essie. I hate sitting still."

I quickly leave Bethany's apartment and traverse down the outside staircase. I walk down the driveway and head in the direction my feet take me. Robin follows at my side, deep in thought.

"Regret," he says as preamble, "Is a tricky bitch. To regret something and wish to change it, means you have to change everything it outwardly effected. So, no. I have no regrets. I have life lessons."

"Every day is an education," I agree as we walk side-by-side down the sidewalk. Like a dumbass, I realize where I'm headed– the Mason's. If Rob notices, he doesn't say so.

"Hindsight is also valuable. Like with me, if today's Robin Prynne could go back to the version of me from four years ago, I wouldn't have stopped Isis and Auggie's *creativity* that turned into a living nightmare. No, afterward, I would have tied Isis down on her bed and…" Rob turns to gaze at me, looking sheepish. Choosing his words wisely, "*Forced* Isis to take Auggie and me back into her body. But after four years, the fear has evolved into a full-out phobia."

Stopping in my tracks, "Isis doesn't have sex? She's the epitome of sex," I mutter, awed. "I always thought hot people fucked constantly."

"You're too cute," Rob chuckles, and I jolt like a bolt of lightning struck my ass. Not only does Rob use Devon's favorite descriptor, we're walking by the barely lit Mason residence.

As if summoned by our very presence, Malcolm ambles out of his house, looking wicked pissed. He gets into the family's pride and joy– John Mason's black as midnight, 1969 Chevy Camaro.

"I hate that car," Robin grumbles as Malcolm drives by us, tooting the horn and saluting on his way by.

"It's fucking awesome," I purr, getting wet just looking at it. "That car catches pussy for whoever the hell is driving it."

"Exactly," Robin pouts. "Mal wouldn't ever let me drive it."

"He lets Devon drive it everywhere." I hate how scratchy my voice sounds, like my throat is suddenly dry.

Shaking me, teasing me, "Simmer down, Ess. I take it the taste Dev gave you was addicting. Best keep your ass out of that car– we know how you fold the second a Mason traps you inside a vehicle. A Buick and a Volkswagen. You should've held out for the vintage Chevy, Ess. Tsk. Tsk."

"Hardy har har," I mock laugh. "Rae's learning to drive the pussy magnet. I wonder if it will repel or attract douchebags." I breathe, "Motherfucking badassed."

"I'm buying a new car," Rob says suddenly, like he's just now deciding. "Rory's Dodge Challenger is pretty sweet. But I'm thinking another SUV, in case I ever get a kid. I don't think I can pull off a Jeep. Maybe a Land Rover– they have great safety features."

"Since when did you turn into a Yuppie or go off-roading?" I say skeptically, mind blown over the fact that Robin Prynne has mannish wants and needs. "Speaking of kids, why doesn't Isis have sex? Doesn't Isis want you guys? I can't believe that. You and Auggie are opposites, but both um… pretty damned hot in your own right."

Rob slings his arm over my shoulder, grinning pleasantly. "Thank you. I'm glad you think I'm pretty, seeing as how we share a similar genetic code."

I shove his arm off, laughing. "Jackass."

"Isis wants us, all right. She will tease the hell out of us, bringing us to the brink. But if she thinks spunk's about to flow, she makes us put our pants back on. So frustrating," Rob rattles off like I understand what the hell he's talking about.

"Huh?" I grunt, happy to deal with someone else's shit for a change, so I can forget about my own.

"Isis lost our baby," Rob rasps, as if it's the first time he's ever said it aloud. I reach over to hold his hand, fingers wrapping tightly with his. "Auggie's baby. But mine too, just the same. Isis thinks she failed us, when it was just nature– the egg was fertilized while in her fallopian tube. It wouldn't have survived, and we didn't realize it until it hurt Isis."

"Oh, Robin!" I cry, suddenly realizing the world is huge, and my problems are so very small.

"Don't share this information around, okay? All the Masons know because Auggie told 'em, but that's it. My parents don't even know. There's no sense in our family mourning the loss of something they never knew existed."

"I understand. I won't tell a soul," I promise.

"Thank you," Robin sighs. "Isis pushed Auggie and me away, and we let her, thinking she'd snap out of it. But she never did. Hindsight, as I said. Instead of regret, I would've went back and made her snap out of it. We stood passively by while Isis destroyed us along with herself. Years later, I realize this, and I'm working my ass off to fix it."

"Um... so, is Isis scared of dick? I've had some bad experiences with that, but the fear is gone with someone you trust." I speak from experience, as in last night. I never once thought of that frat-boy-date-rapist.

"No, Isis is scared of being pregnant. She wants children badly, has since we were kids. She'd be a great mom." Robin gushes, and I can hear the love in his voice as if it were a physical entity. "But right now, she's more petrified of losing another baby, as if it's her fault somehow."

"Have you thought of the tough love approach? Just knock Isis up?" I stiffen, realizing what I'm suggesting. "Scratch that. I never said that. Rape is not the answer."

Tugging me to a stop, Robin turns a blindingly bright smile my way. "You're a genius. You make our family proud, Essie. You've officially became a Prynne tonight."

"What?" I gasp, terrified.

"Nothing." Robin does an about-face, and then leads me back from whence we came. "My advice is payment for yours, my dearest cousin."

Insulted, "I'm your only cousin!"

"Semantics," Rob tosses off my complaint. "I'm a plotter, and I've been thinking about you for some time. I feel partially responsible for most, if not all, of the shit Devon pulled over the past few months. So I'm going to give you point-by-point instructions to follow, got it?"

"Yes, Sensei," I groan.

"You're not moving to Florida. Uncle Will knew that when he asked. So don't fool yourself. Your parents want to screw all over their new house without you in it. It's reward for raising you for twenty-one years."

"I hate you sometimes," I whisper.

Hearing me anyway, Rob chuckles. "Sometimes? You have several options: Get your own place, which we all know you can't afford. You can move in with Mom and Dad, or move in with me. But since Willow will be after your head, it's not wise to cohabitate with her. But no matter what, you have a home because you are a Prynne."

"I don't want to be someone's obligation," I bite out fiercely.

Drawing me to a standstill, Rob grips my shoulders and shakes me. "You. Are. Not. An. Obligation. It's a joy to be around you, Essie. I really would welcome you into my home with open arms. If all else fails, you can bunk with Isis in my third of the loft over Rush. Isis is surprisingly an amazing roommate. Quiet and pretty to look at. A bit snoopy and bossy, though," Rob muses, obvious sadness over not having Isis living with him any longer.

"That's settled," Rob says, even though nothing was settled. "Willow. She's young, so everything is about her, even when it isn't. She's not going to take this well, Essie. You must be prepared to be patient. Never apologize, because you're not sorry and you shouldn't be. Just tell Willow you're sorry you hurt her, which is the truth."

I grab at my stomach again. "I think I'm going to be sick." I take a deep breath, waiting for the panic-induced nausea to abate. "I don't want to hurt Willow. I don't want her to know. Willow can kill me for all I care, because her being disappointed in me is a fate worse than death."

"Remember you said that while Willow tries to off your ass," Robin cautions. "Patience, Essie. No matter what Willow does, turn the other cheek. You were in the wrong, but that's not why. To defend yourself, to lash back, to hit her back, will only escalate it. Just let Willow scream, and hit, and rally against you, but don't you dare fucking flinch."

"I think that's actually excellent advice." I promise myself I'll take it.

"Don't sound so surprised." Rob is offended. We stop moving, and I'm shocked to see that we're standing beside my car at the end of Bethany's driveway. "Lastly, never forget you're a Prynne. We are a tenacious lot. We are stubborn. We never give up. If we want something, we get it."

Rob opens the door to my mom car, gesturing for me to crawl inside. "Thank you," I murmur as I settle into the seat. "Thank you for comforting me even though we both know I did this to myself."

Hanging onto the top of my door, Rob muses. "I'd say everyone makes mistakes, but this was an on purpose. When Willow finds out, I won't take sides, Essie. Because there are no sides to take. It was Devon's decision on who he wanted to be with, not Willow's. Someday, Willow will come to understand this."

"Or she won't," I fear.

"Or she won't," Robin agrees, shutting my car door. I reach forward to turn the ignition over. A sharp rasp of knuckles has me lowering my window. "Hester," Rob says in a commanding voice. "Devon needs help."

"I know," I breathe, voice quivering with panic.

"Our family will support you in all things, Essie, and we'll do it willingly and gladly. Dave and Mary Prynne won't let a stranger starve, nonetheless family. The only thing you should be concentrating on right now is getting Devon help." Robin says in parting, then walks over to his Explorer, leaving me to mull over everything he said.

CHAPTER SIXTEEN

Kieren Mason

Hand waving in front of Devon's face, I don't get as much as an eye twitch from him. "Hey, bro?" I snap my fingers next to his ear… and nothing. It's to the point I'm about to slap the prick. Sitting on the sofa since we deposited him there last night, Devon is catatonic. Wrapped hands resting on a pillow, Dev blinked out around the time Opal was tending to his wounds. Didn't even flinch or bitch about how bad the disinfectant stung.

Dev's not sleeping– he's hibernating.

Weston comes up behind me, and we gaze down at our big brother together. No doubt my worried expression is mirrored on West's face. "Are we going to run this morning?"

"Um… we better not," I decide leaving Devon would be a bad idea.

Every morning, like clockwork, we have a routine set into place. Weston and I run five miles, not only for his training and our health, but to clear our heads for the coming day. We do this again in the evening. While we're gone, it's hit or miss on whether or not Dad is home or not. Rae uses this time to hog the bathroom we all share. Devon performs his meticulous '*get ready for work*' routine, where he buffs his bullets and shines his flashlight. When we get back from our run, West takes a shower while Rae and I get breakfast handled. Then we go about our days: work and school.

Not this morning… Devon is spacing out instead of getting a mirror-shine on his badge. "Do you think he can hear us?" Weston whispers in my ear. "They say coma patients can hear."

"Dev can hear us," I say with absolute certainty. "He just doesn't give a shit about answering."

"Kitchen table," Dad's voice filters in from the kitchen, and then changes to a bellowed, "NOW!"

Weston and I are in the kitchen in a heartbeat, obviously Devon doesn't follow. Dad and Rae are already sitting at the table, a packet of paperwork spread out between them. I flow into my seat, wondering if I should make coffee and get the orange juice and milk for the kids.

"Family meeting time," Dad says with an authoritative air. No doubt worried and frustrated, he took it out on his hair. I'd laugh about his mussed up mess, but nothing is funny at the moment.

"We're sending Devon to rehab," I murmur, genius that I am deduces this from the admittance forms scattered across the tabletop. "But Dev's been sober for days." I gesture toward the living room. "Look at him."

"I know," Dad exhales, looking exhausted. "I met up with someone early this morning."

"It's only five-thirty right now," Rae points out, hating it when Dad pulls this shit. "Who?"

Sighing, tugging at his hair, Dad does the whole nine yards of frustrated Mason. "I just got back," he stresses to Rae. "It doesn't matter who. I'll call them concerned citizens. But they assured me, Devon is a drug addict."

"No shit," Weston and I say in unison, while Raven balks at the label.

"Raven." Dad reaches across the table to clasp her hand. "I know what you think is wrong with your brother, and they said you were right. You did great, baby girl. I took this paperwork with me and showed them the rehab center you picked out for Devon, and they said it was perfect."

Slumping to the table, Rae's crestfallen. "Then Dev doesn't need rehab at all. He's not a drug addict– he's sick."

"Wait? What?" My eyes flick between my dad and sister. "Explain what the fuck is going on. Now!"

Voice stiff, expression set in stone, Dad might as well have killed Santa Claus on Christmas Eve. "Devon admitted to our concerned citizens that he's bipolar."

"Oh, fuck." It's my turn to slump to the tabletop with an oomph. "I'm such a fucking moron. *I'm just like Mom. I'm just like Mom.* That's all Devon ever says, and I interpreted it wrong. I thought he meant he was evil and an insult to the human race."

"Ugh!" A grunt is pulled from my chest as Dad hits the back of my head with an open fist. "Sorry," I apologize lamely.

"This doesn't leave this table, got it?" Dad warns. "If I hear a whisper of this around town, one of you is getting beat down by dear ol' Dad."

"Okay," I say, a challenge thick in my voice. I rub the back of my noggin, realizing that was a pulled hit. Lord knows what a real punch would feel like.

"Yes, Daddy," Raven says like he's an idiot for asking.

"'Kay," Weston squeaks out– the sound is childish flowing from his man-sized mouth.

"My sources say that even if Devon *thinks* he's bipolar, we can't treat it until it's properly diagnosed. And since Devon has been medicating with street drugs, he's chemically dependent on them. So at best, Devon is a drug addict. At worst, he's a bipolar drug addict. We're going to help him."

"Let's truck Dev's ass to this place today, then." I look around for a phone number on the paperwork.

"I called them yesterday, along with a few other places. At the time, I thought I was just looking into rehab centers, not diagnostic centers. I'm initiating a new program for teen drug offenders, where they go to rehab instead of court. This place in Sedona agreed with my stance, and set me up with three places a few weeks from now. Their program is booked each cycle, and they offered three places every cycle– at our cost, of course."

Blue eyes huge, "Wow, Daddy," Raven's facial expression is pure awe. "I'm impressed."

"Me too!" Weston says excitedly, leaning halfway across the table to pat Dad on the shoulder. "Putting people in jail just breeds a better criminal."

Dad narrows tired eyes at Weston. "This is a cop family, kid," he warns. "That's what we do, arrest the criminals. It's not my problem whether or not they learn a damned thing while they are incarcerated. I save lives– those of the innocently targeted."

Deflated, Weston murmurs, "Sorry, Dad… but it is a good idea."

"*I* know," Dad stresses. "It's *my* idea."

Rae snorts, but quickly covers her mouth with a silencing palm. Dad manages to pull a '*STFU*' look as he speaks. "Devon has a few weeks furlough. I'll try to keep him busy at work, and off drugs."

"Daddy," Rae pipes in. "If Dev thinks he's medicating himself–" she gazes at a catatonic yet sober Devon frozen solid on our sofa. "Maybe you better let him take 'em."

Pointing at his chest, Dad raises both eyebrows to his hairline. "Chief. Of. Fairport. Police. As in the head cop for the county. Drugs are a crime." Pointing into the living room, "That drug addict, possible mental illness sufferer, is a fucking cop. Get it?"

"But, Daddy," Rae whines again, seeming desperate to be heard.

"Do you want to go live with Dave and Mary Prynne?" Dad glares at Weston and Raven. I keep my mouth glued shut for once, so I'm not lasered by his pissed off stare. "I'm not raising pacifists."

I turn to the side in my chair, using my forearm to fuse my mouth shut. I'm suffocating on the need to laugh. The intense look on Dad's face as he glares Rae and West down is the funniest fucking thing I've ever seen. I have to bite my tongue from saying, *"Dev would loooovvvveee living there. All the pot he could ever smoke, where a pint-sized female hell-bent on chopping off his nutsack will be beating the ever-loving hell out of his cheating dream girl."*

"What's a pacifist?" Weston grumbles, causing a giggle to bubble up Rae's throat.

"A jackass," Dad deadpans. "Jackasses who don't believe in the law."

"Mmm… kay." Weston doesn't have a clue. But I can tell the first chance he gets, he's Googling it.

"Masons," Dad levels us each with his intense stare. "We have one duty for the next few weeks. Keep Devon alive."

CHAPTER SEVENTEEN

Devon Mason

Utter darkness. When I try to express this depressive state of being, people who have never been there can't understand. Not that they are incapable, but that depression can't be explained.

When you fail a test, you get down on yourself. When your crush crushes you, you feel sad, like no one will ever love you. When you lose someone close to you, you miss them with a fierce ache.

People going through trying times will call themselves depressed, but that's not the case. Their emotions are being controlled by an outside force, and once removed or changed, they miraculously get better.

You try again, and succeed. You meet someone who sparks you, and you fall in love. You realize you will forever miss those who've passed on, but you fill your time with those who are still living.

When you get a splinter, you don't just sit there suffering while you watch it fester. You get a pair of tweezers and pull the splinter free of your flesh. Most people grab the tweezers. Those with depression, watch it fester, because they don't even notice the tweezers, let alone realize there is a solution to their problem. Depressed people don't even feel the splinter itself, not recognizing there is a problem at all, because this is our normal.

Being in agony *is* our normal. It's called depression.

Most people's problems are fixable– solvable. Healable. You move on, because, in actuality, you were never depressed. You were shouldering a burden, and when the weight subsided, the pressure was gone.

True depression is within your mind, and nothing will change it– heal it. There is no cause to resolve. There is no ache to soothe.

It. Just. Is.

Not only the words uttered, but the emotions behind them, filter through my fog. Only hope and light can chase the darkness away. *"Let's truck Dev's ass to this place today, then."*

After all I've done to Kieren, and he still wants me with him. Hope. I listen to their words as I come back to life. Using this burst of lucidity, I make plans.

I have a few weeks to get everything in order before they take me away. The addict in me is snarling, knowing this facility will murder him. The mental illness in me is screaming how we can't allow someone to pump us full of poison. But the son in me remembers Mom, remembers how wrong she was for not taking her medication.

The son wins out.

Three spots in rehab for those with mental and emotional difficulties. One spot for me. I personally have two spots to fill. *I* can finally help Taryn Elsberry. As a thank you for helping me with Taryn, I can get Tommy's brain unwashed, removing all the taint his bible-thumping father instilled in him through fear.

Hope always lights a path in the dark, long enough for you to recognize you either need to get help or need to take your medication. My family is getting me the help. I just have to stay lucid enough to get through these weeks without succumbing to the darkness– I need drugs.

The only thing that illuminates your state of mind is true purpose. I have a few weeks to fix the things I've broken. Apologies are worthless– words hold no true weight. Action always speaks louder than words.

1: Obtain uppers as medicine.

2: Get Taryn and Tommy arrested for drug possession.

3: Make Dad put T&T on the docket for rehab.

4: Interrogate Bethany.

5: Avenge Essie.

6: I'm a Mason.

"Masons, we have one duty for the next few weeks. Keep Devon alive."

In a fluid movement, I go from sitting motionless to fully standing in the living room. I need to eat– to fuel my body while I still can. I have a choice to make: take drugs that renders it impossible to eat or sleep, slowly draining my body from the inside out while keeping my mind alive, or do nothing and succumb to the darkness.

There is no choice, because I've never felt a dark this black before. It's descending quickly, worse than any other episode of depression I've suffered through before. I don't know if I can survive it this time. Drugs it is. Hopefully my body is strong enough to sustain the emaciation and sleep deprivation in my quest to keep my sanity.

I walk into the kitchen and start rutting around the refrigerator for protein: eggs, cheese, bacon and sausage. I pull out the cartons of milk and juice, forgoing coffee with its caffeine. I won't need any other stimulants in a few hours. Right now, I need solid sustenance.

Coke is my depression medicine of choice. In high school, I used Speed a lot. I've never been desperate enough to try Crack, Heroin, or Meth.

Yes, pot makes you giddy, where everything is so fucking funny and foggy. Alcohol gets you drunk, where you seem to be having a good time. It's a bullshit lie. They are depressants. The saying *cry in your beer* isn't just a saying– it's the truth. As the buzz abates, the darkness blankets you. Not only did you poison your body with chemicals, you're now worse off than before.

Depressants are my medication when I'm manic. I need something to make me manic when I'm depressed. It's not that complicated of a concept.

"What. The. Fuck?" Ren mutters as he avidly watches me prepare an omelet.

"You want one, too?" I offer, looking at my family as they surround the kitchen table, each and every one of them looks equally guilty and dazed.

I've never seen Dad move so quickly in all my life, as he scoops up the rehab papers to hide them out of my sight. Little does Dad know, I want to go. I'd wish I was going this morning, if it weren't for the things I have to get done first.

"How the fuck are you so… not hibernating," Ren stammers. With the look of utter disbelief on my brother's face, I'd laugh if I could muster the energy.

I grab a pan from the pot rack, and then dump a pound of bacon and a package of sausage links into it. I have a few thousand calories I have to eat while I still can.

I answer Ren's statement, "I've got shit to do." Spatula in hand, I turn to my family with a waning smile on my face. "Who wants breakfast?"

CHAPTER EIGHTEEN

Essie Prynne

Feeling dead to the world, "Let's get this day started, shall we?" I gesture for Bethany to unlock the front door of the salon, and switch the *Open* sign on.

Sitting on the counter, Bethany kicks me in the butt every time I walk by to collect my supplies. "You look like shit, girl. Ya gotta start getting some sleep." She kicks me again– this time on the back of the leg.

"It is what it is," I mumble, and continue on with my setup. "Are we going to have any customers today? Yesterday was a freakin' joke."

"Not if I don't open, we won't." Laughing at me while looking equally concerned, Bethany jumps off the counter and stalks to the front door.

I look like shit because I haven't slept in days, worry and stressors plaguing my mind. Last night was worse than the night before, not that I slept after my walk with Rob or before my secretive rendezvous with Malcolm.

I still cannot believe I outed Devon for his own good, as per Rob's instruction. I had to get Devon help, not for me because I need him or want him or sort of love him in the depths of my heart. The selfish part of me wanted to do it for my own benefit, wanting my best friend back. But the selfless part of me just needs Devon to be healed, whether or not I'm in his future.

Last night, being around Willow was murdering my soul. After what I'd done behind her back, it was the ultimate in punishments. I resolved never to get into that situation again– not the being around Willow, the doing something regretful to where you have to stare your indiscretion directly in the face.

Nothing's worth the pain you cause your victim and yourself, or the loss of sleep, or the inability to look yourself in the mirror, or the sensation of your impending doom. I've been jumping at shadows for days, waiting for Willow to find out and confront me, waiting for my family to find out and be disappointed in me.

It's not worth it.

I made a grave error, because even if Devon heals himself and finds his way back to me, our path was paved in deceit. Our first time, if I'm thinking positively, was tainted by how we betrayed another human being, someone we both love. No matter how much I mature, or how many years I may live, I will never escape that fact. If by some miracle, Devon and I have a happily ever after, I refuse to rewrite history with easy-to-swallow lies.

Devon cheated on Willow… with me. I accept this as truth. I won't let it wreck me, but I'll learn from it and move on.

Bethany leans out the front door, hands braced on the jamb, looking both directions down the block, and then she shuts the door again. Turning to me with worry etched across her pretty features, "Elma better do something about this bullshit before Salon goes under."

"Yeah, like how about naming this sinking ship," I snarl, thoroughly disgusted with my boss. "That might help."

Shaking her head, brunette ponytail swinging, "That's not going to do a damn thing. We had three customers yesterday. To be honest, Ess… I think I'm going to have to quit. I've got to find a better job, even if it's delivering newspapers."

Drained emotionally and physically, I slump to my ancient salon chair– only one of two. "I know. Me too," I breathe. "When I was a little girl, Mom would walk me down the street holding my hand, and I'd tug her into Salon just because it felt like home. I loved the cheesy pink décor, the chemical smell of perms and color treatments, and the whirl of the blow dryers. My favorite was squirming in the seat during a hair trim– the snip-snip sound near my ear made me quiver. I was meant for this job, Beth." The longing in my voice draws tears to my eyes.

Looking around Salon, I see it with fresh eyes, not the disillusioned eyes of a pretty princess. After two years of training in a high-tech, tricked-out environment, this place is dog shit. It hurts my feelings to think so little of the place I once loved– the place I'd love to revive.

Mauve vinyl commercial tiling. Peeling Pepto-Bismol pink wallpaper with poster-sized framed prints of hairstyles from the 1970s. There are only two hairdressing stations: salon chairs, hair washing basins, and the docking station for our supplies. There are only two hooded hair dryers– plastic and ancient, atop torn vinyl-padded chairs. A grouping of five white and pink chairs flank the door in front of the left window. In front of the right window is the front desk– laminated wood. The only upgrade is the pedicure station Elma bought when Bethany and I came to work for her, as a way to bring in extra income to Salon. There is one manicure station, but it's a joke.

The back room, which used to be for storage, is my domain. I personally bought, on credit, all the esthetician supplies: waxing warmers and the necessary supplies, electrolysis, facial, and laser equipment, and the patient table. Elma gets a percentage off everything I do in the backroom, but since I own it all and perform the job, it's like I'm paying her rent for the space and a commission… I'm still paying for all this shit myself. It's deducted from my bank account automatically, unlike my car payments. One sucks me dry, and the other puts money back into the bank account. I can walk to work, but I can't work without the tools of my trade.

Priorities.

"I know this was your dream, sweetie." Beth is always quick to comfort. "Elma's ruined this place. Upped the prices too high, never actually works herself– pays her girls squat, so they have to quit to survive. Without a name, without an image, what good is a salon without an identity and a good staff?"

"I *am* good staff," I grumble. "I'm certified in everything I could think was necessary. I go to the conferences and get continual training."

I was trained and certified by the best to wash, cut, color, straighten or perm, and style hair. I'm a certified esthetician: facials, microdermabrasion, laser hair removal, electrolysis, and waxing. I do manicures and pedicures. I'm the only person in the county people call for special occasions, such as weddings and proms, because I'm a professional cosmetician. I love to let out my creative side during makeovers. I will even accompany clients as a personal shopper, so they get the best wardrobe for their day. I'm qualified to wax, buff, and lacquer your skin, dress you, and style your hair and nails. I'm the ultimate employee, who gets paid squat.

Salon is always empty, so my commission is worse than minimum wage. Prom is once a year. Weddings are scattered throughout the year with a heavy wave in June. So I'm busy in

May and June. It's late March, ten months since I stockpiled funds, and I have bills to pay from my empty bank account.

"I applied to the No-Name this morning, so I can pay for all the equipment I bought through the school," I announce, causing Bethany to gasp in shock. "No, I'm not quitting Salon. No matter how much I'm being taken advantage of, I can't do that to my loyal cliental. I've already defaulted on the student loans and the car payment. I can't work at all if I they take my equipment back."

Eyes bulging, Beth mutters, "A second job?" Yeah, I will admit, until recently, I was the ultimate princess. My parents spoiled me rotten, and I'd only work a job I loved because it was my passion. Well, now I have to work another job to afford my current job, while still defaulting on the payments for my training of said job. Mindboggling.

"It's time I pull my own weight." I get up from my chair and approach the front desk. I survey the ledger and note there isn't a single appointment for the day. "Another day where we pray for walk-ins. Tomorrow is an empty slate as well."

Bethany hugs me from behind like a momma bear protecting her cub. I always feel cherished when my best friend hugs me. "I'm going to do us both a favor, girl." Beth quickly kisses my cheek as she pulls away. "I'm going home to study, leaving you here to pick up all the scraps."

Turning around, I look into Bethany's earnest eyes, "You need the money, too."

Shrugging, "Not as much as you. I'll always have Casa Hello Kitty, no matter what." I wince, getting the implications of what she's saying. The Omans will always be in that house, and Beth will always have a sanctuary to come home to. Grabbing for her bag, "Plus, my passion is helping people, not primping them. Not only am I helping you by making your share for the day one hundred percent, but I'm helping my future patients by getting my study on."

Pouting, I lean against the front desk, fingernails absentmindedly scraping at the peeling laminated wood. "It's so boring here without any clients and without you to entertain me. The day goes on for eons."

Smirking, "Jamison Reality has amazing Wi-Fi. My cell keeps picking it up from next door. Just think of all the browsing you could do."

"Password protected," I admit with a laugh. "I've tried to crack the bitch."

Hefting her bag onto her shoulder, Bethany makes her way toward the front door. "Ah, shucks! See ya later, Hester!"

"Bye," I grumble, sadder than I was when I walked into this depressing place. I stare down at the ledger, flipping the pages backward, calculating when the decline of appointments began– hoping to find a way to fix it.

Outside on the sidewalk, "Hey," Beth gets my attention by shouting at me and tapping on the window glass. "Shopping!"

Eyebrows scrunching together, I mumble, "Huh?"

"Ginny's password is *Shopping*!" Giggling like a little bitch, Bethany skips down the sidewalk to her car.

"Bullshit." I pull out my cellphone and connect to Ginny's Wi-Fi. I input Shopping as the password. "Well, shit," I say in awe when it connects. "I won't be too bored now. What to troll? What to browse? Dr. Phil should be my first stop, since Dr. Oman has left the building."

"Talking to yourself?" comes from a throaty voice, scaring the shit out of me. I jump, dropping my cellphone to clatter on the desktop. Eyes held wide, I stare up in horror at Isis and her two friends.

"Um… Hi! Sorry," I stammer out lamely– mortified. "Opal?" I lean to the right, trying to see around Isis's curvy form. "Bethany left for the day already. I thought your hair trim appointment was at the end of the week." Opal has a short, edgy style I taught Bethany– it looks rocking on Opal's tall, lithe form with her wispy white hair.

"It is," Isis answers for Opal. "We're here for pedicures. Girls' day," she says with false enthusiasm.

"Okay." Even to my own ears, I sound baffled. "We only have the one pedicure station." I blister bright red from embarrassment. "I'm sorry, but it will take a while for me to do all three of you, one at a time. Is that okay?"

A woman in her forties smiles sweetly at me, so I decide she's nice like Opal. "We're here for Isis." Rolling her vibrant blue eyes, "It's girls' day out, where we do as Isis says."

Huffing a laugh, I try to stem it and fail. I bite my lip as Isis glares at her un-named friend. Brave, Opal is snorting and holding her sides, she's laughing so hard. "It's true," Opal gasps out. "Isis made us come today, so we'll just sit and chat while you do your thing."

"Oh, thank God," I pray, hand clasped to my chest. "I just had a nightmare envisioned, of it taking me three hours to pamper you guys, and Isis getting really pissed off because she had to wait her turn."

"Ha-Ha," Isis mock laughs, but her vampy lips are curled up at the corners. "I'm the butt of the joke today, so it seems. This is Nina." Isis points at her friend. "Nina, this is Essie." Isis sounds suspiciously like I'm the butt of something today too, like she came in here specifically to point me out to Nina. "Opal, you guys have already met. Okay, introductions are complete."

"It's a pleasure to meet you, Nina." I lean around Isis to shake the woman's hand. "You have very thick hair," I compliment, and she turns a pretty shade of pink.

"I feel like you and I are kindred, Ms. Prynne," Nina purrs cryptically.

Blinking, "Okay," I drawl, creeped out. I wander over to the waiting area, and steal two chairs. It's not as if Salon will have anyone come in and need to sit in them anyway. To be nice, I place the chairs adjacent to the pedicure station, so Isis can chat with her girls while I do my thing.

"Do you sell any products?" Opal is gazing around, as if seeing the space with clear eyes for the first time too. I know Opal has this place imprinted in her memory. She gets her hair trimmed once a week as Bethany's payment for her services in the Playroom.

"We have a shelf of outdated shit I'd love to throw out." I growl, and then blush. "Sorry, I'm a bit of a disgruntled employee this morning. I just applied at the No-Name for a second job. Alice is retiring, and I was told I had first dibs. So now I'm looking for short-term work until then."

"Damn," all three women say in unison, but Nina continues on with, "Other than me and two other girls, everyone else at dispatch are volunteers."

"You'd be a beautiful Candy Striper at the hospital, but that's volunteering as well," Opal says, offering me a wan smile of apology.

With narrowed eyes, Isis grunts out, "Rush isn't hiring," meaning she's not hiring the likes of me.

Shrugging, "I'll find something, somewhere, to supplement my income... So yeah, everyone is too smart to buy any of the products we offer. I've wanted to buy new stuff for ages, but Elma ignores me."

"Shame." Opal's smile falls. "We're in sore need of a spa. The closest place is over an hour away, and they don't even offer massages or anything."

"Massages?" Nina snorts. "None here in town, you say?"

Ignoring her friends, Isis offers up her own suggestions as she toes off her stiletto boots and slides into the chair. "You should create a survey for the townsfolk to fill out, and pass around a petition to give to Elma."

"Fuck that noise." Nina's either stupid, stupid brave, or has a death wish. "Elma's seventy-four. Buy the old bitty out, and do what you want with the place."

"Good idea," Opal says brightly. "Then you could sell what you want, and I have some soaps that would be great in a spa."

Grumbling, frowning, "But still do the survey so you don't over-upgrade with shit Fairport doesn't need." Isis shifts in the massage chair, reaching for the remote to turn it to life.

"The survey is an excellent idea," I agree as I plunk my ass on the tiny stool on casters. "But, as for buying Elma out, I can barely afford the equipment I have in the back."

Arching a black, menacing eyebrow, "That's yours?" Isis sounds surprised.

"Yeah, once it's paid for, that is," I mumble, paling from worry, and then I blush from embarrassment– never show Isis your vulnerabilities.

Reaching to turn on the warm water in the foot bath, "Well, let's get you primped up, Isis–" the front door opening cuts off my words. "What the…"

Devon, fully clad in his police uniform, stands a few feet from us, looking expectantly at me.

Isis leans back in the chair, a satisfied smirk on her face, and the remote to the massage chair curled in her hand. She gets comfy, and I swear she whispers, "*'Bout time.*"

Slowly rising to my feet, I stammer, "What are you doing here, Dev? Did you need to speak to your aunt?" I glance over at Isis, who looks satisfied to wait for an eternity now.

I'd think this was a setup if it weren't for the fact that two of the three ladies, watching me with great interest I might add, frequent Salon at least once a week.

Scratching at his disastrous hair, Devon sheepishly says, "I need a cut, Ess."

"Ah… um…" Gape-mouthed, I stand here stammering, at a loss of what to do, as my eyes flick between Devon, his aunt, and my audience of two. "We seem short-staffed for once," I utter in obvious disbelief.

"I can wait," Isis offers selflessly, which startles the shit out of me.

Whipping around to face Isis, I gather up my Prynne courage– or stupidity, if you will. "What are you playing at?"

"You have to get back to work soon, don't ya, Dev?" Isis fiddles with the controls on the remote. "I, however, don't have to work until eight." With dramatic flair, Isis crosses her arms beneath her breasts, preparing to wait me out just so she can play witness to this awkward situation.

"What about them?" I point at an avidly watching Opal and Nina.

"I work odd hours," Opal says without shame. "And today is Nina's day off. We were just going to stalk around the Court House as a distraction, but Isis had a more interesting offer."

"Whatever," I grumble, stalking away. "You knew Devon was going to show up this morning, I'd bet my life on it." I grab a hold of Dev's wrist and tug him after me. I try to hide the waver in my voice, and fail since I'm so nervous. "Let's get you all fixed up. How would you like your hair styled?"

Devon flashes me a strained grin, like he's having a hard time with this himself, which means he wanted to do this without an audience too. "Surprise me."

"I could suck–"

A chorus of laughter spills from across the salon.

Turning feral, Devon snarls a warning. "Knock it the fuck off, or leave." I expect the ladies to volley back insults. Nina looks like she was physically struck. Opal looks mildly surprised. Isis, no surprise, she's amused.

"I feel like I'm in high school again," I mutter dramatically, rolling my eyes. I test the water spray, not wanting to scald Devon's scalp. "The mean girls are always watching, silently judging, and loudly baying their insults." I snap the cape, and then drape it over Devon's uniform.

Relaxing into the chair, Devon sighs, looking beyond exhausted. Laughing without humor, "Funny you should say that. I just left FAHS, and I'll be going back when I leave here."

I lower the chair with the foot hydraulics, and then lean Devon back against the basin. "Sounds like a nightmare," I mutter. "But then again, you probably love it."

"I know what you went through there, Ess," Devon says softly, so our listening ears can't hear over the spray of the water. "And I do love being the Truant Officer."

"Let's get you washed," I say more to myself than to Devon. "And pretend I don't have six eyes burning into my back."

I lean over Devon to reach for the shampoo, and his breath catches in his throat, causing mine to do the same. Swallowing thickly, Devon admits, "I live underneath a microscope, so I'm used to absolutely no privacy."

I don't know how to respond to that. Even if I did, I wouldn't with an audience. So I utter inane bullshit to distract myself. Fingers sliding through Devon's hair, I use the wand to thoroughly wet it. "You have amazing hair. I don't know if I ever told you that. I never forgot what it felt like between my fingers, and I've never felt another's like yours." Realizing what I just said, I breathe out with feeling, "Shit!"

Expecting titters, our audience is dead silent. Devon swallows again, his Adam's apple bobbing. "Have you never cut another Mason's hair?"

"It doesn't feel the same," I mumble. "If your hair was cut right, you'd have silky curls, versus Isis, Rae, and Malcolm's unruly hair. I'll try to get it right, but it might take a few cuts to train it to behave."

Devon doesn't make a sound, but I can tell he's silently laughing by the way his chest heaves. I find a rhythm as I wash, rinse, condition, and rinse Dev's hair. I try to ignore the fact that I even find his forehead perfectly interesting. I blink the disturbing thought away, and notice the state Devon's currently in.

Blotting Dev's hair dry with a towel, I lean down to whisper near his ear, "Why are your fingertips clenching the armrests, and why are you breathing heavily? Something wrong?"

Eyelids flip open, revealing blue eyes gone wild. I fear it's Devon's demons riding him, but he rasps out his malfunction. "Can I come back at lunch? I need to be alone with you for a few hours."

"Why?" I look away, closing my eyes as I try to reason this out. An internal struggle wages on as I fight with myself. I win and lose the battle. "We can't go there again, Devon," I whisper.

Gripping my chin, Devon makes me look at him. "I want to thank you, Essie. I know what you did early this morning."

Gasping, I pull away. I take several steps back, horrified. Voice shaking, the words are barely audible. "He promised not to tell. I told him you'd hate me."

Hand lashing out to clasp my wrist, Devon pulls me back to him. Tugging me down to his face, Devon breathes, "Dad didn't say who. Even though I didn't attend the family meeting discussing my mental health and future, I listened in anyway. I figured the only person who gave two shits about me enough to go to Dad was you."

Closing Devon out of my thoughts by shutting my eyes, I nod my affirmation.

"It's okay, Ess," Devon says softly. "I asked you for help, and you got it for me. I've tried for years, but I couldn't get the words to come out. I couldn't tell my family what was wrong with me. I just wanted to thank you is all."

Blinking away the tears, "You're welcome," comes out warbled. I have so many things I need to say, so of course nothing comes to mind.

I lean the chair to the upright position, and step on the hydraulics until Devon is at the correct height. "I'm not going to ask anything of you, Devon– nothing about me, anyway. No pressure, okay? I... I tried to get you help because I believe in you, not because I want something from you."

Dev reaches out to caress the back of my hand with a single fingertip. Voice barely rising above a whisper, "I know that, Ess. I may not be in my right mind, but even I help others just for their sake. The difference is, we're not strangers."

Wielding a comb and a pair of scissors, I say in warning, "Yeah, but for seven years you ignored my very existence. I cannot just go back to how it was when we were fourteen. Too much has happened. It's always zero-to-sixty with you. But right now, I need to flow slowly. No matter what insanity we experienced the other night, you had a girlfriend for over four months, my cousin, and I'm never going to be your frickin' rebound."

I yank the comb through Devon's unruly hair, getting caught on a snarl. I get violent with it, frustrated with myself more than

Devon. Upset with myself that I'm taking it out on him, I massage his scalp where I hurt it.

"I get that." Proving he doesn't, now that my hands are busy with his hair, he touches my hip instead– thumb feathering over my belly. "I'm kind of working on a timeline, Ess. I won't be stable enough to be around you for the next few weeks, then I'll be gone for sixty days. That's why I wanted to spend time with you today, because after this afternoon, I have to get to work."

"Work?" I take a deep breath to center myself, and release it in a rush. "I'm going to taper your hair up from the nape of your neck to the crown of your skull, and around to your temples. Then I'm going to trim off the dead ends on the top, leaving it to curl naturally. I'll shape your sideburns. Haven't you cut your hair since you got back from the academy?"

Smirking, Devon mouths, "*No,*" like he's a naughty little boy caught with his hand in the cookie jar. Stealing another cookie, Devon gets bolder, placing a hand on each of my hips, thumbs meeting in the center of my belly, with his fingers splayed on my ass.

"If you distract me too much, you're liable to get a Mohawk," I warn, eyes flicking to the sneaky thumbs that crept under my shirt and are now circling around my bellybutton. I ignore how the soothing sensation is causing my eyelids to droop heavily.

Slipping his thumbs beneath the waistband of my skinny jeans, "Then I'll proudly wear a Mohawk." Ignoring the ecstatic look of rapture on Dev's face, I get to combing and snipping. "Work– I have a few weeks to keep the darkness at bay, but that's at a price. I'm barely holding on right now, Essie. Being around you helps some– lights me up."

Fingertips freezing, my eyes shut from the desolation held within Devon's voice. With a sharp intake of breath, I unfreeze and begin trimming again.

"I have to find stronger medicine this afternoon," Devon admits he's on the hunt for the lethal shit. In the past, I pretended not to notice him hitting Aunt Mary up for '*medication*'. I ignored it because I've smoked enough of it myself. "So it won't be good for you to be around me. I have a lot of loose ends to tie up before I leave, and I wanted to have a normal few hours with you without tweaking out."

"Literally," I whisper, "Tweaking out, I take it."

Appearing ashamed, "Yeah, exactly." Trying again, "May we spend lunch together, please," he begs.

"Okay," I agree against my better judgment, meaning my judgment is shit when it comes to Devon Mason. "Almost done with the scissors, and then I won't be able to hear you over the buzz of the clippers."

Thank the heavens above.

I spend the next five minutes breathing through my nose as Devon just flat-out touches me any way he pleases. By the time I reach for the clippers to finish tapering his hair and shaping his sideburns, he's practically giving me a goddamned massage.

The whirl of the clippers blocks out the girls' quiet conversation and Devon's labored breathing– he's pretty much panting at this point. But it can't silence the thoughts rattling around in my head. Am I an enabler because I know what Devon's going to do this afternoon, and every day until he's shipped off to rehab? Am I an idiot for agreeing to lunch when I know food is not on the menu?

A hell yeah to both. I could use my lack of self-control around him as my only defense, but I know better. I'm insane is the only explanation.

"Nah," Devon breathes into my ear as I lean over him to holster the clippers on my station. No longer giving a shit who's looking and who's not, Devon pulls me down to him, hand gripping the back of my skull. Whispering against my cheek, "You're not insane. You know we won't have a chance like this for another three months or more, depending on how I am when I come back."

"Yeah, that's why," I grumble, wanting to feel ashamed of myself. I turn away with a motherfucking grin twisting my lips. I stand back up, and act offended. "You're a master manipulator, Officer Devon Mason. Get your ass out of my chair and look at your hair," I tease. "How do you like it?"

Gazing at himself in the mirror, Devon actually inspects every detail of his hair. Even distracted, I did the best of my abilities because it was for Devon. With a grave tone in his voice, "No one will ever cut my hair again but you," he promises, and it holds real weight– it feels like he's promising something else.

I stalk away, tears stinging my eyes. *I can't do this. I can't do this. I can't do this. I can't survive this fucking bullshit again. We were kids then, but now we're not. It means more as adults when before it was playacting. This is the real shit now. I can't fall for Devon's act as if it's true love. I can't allow him to wreck me. But I will, because I need to go to rehab.*

I'm addicted to Devon Johnathon Mason, and I'll be afflicted until death– mine.

"Hey," Devon comes right after me– relentless. He pulls me into a tight hug, gently rocking me back and forth. "It's okay, Essie. I can't promise everything will be good, but I'll try my hardest. It's okay," he murmurs repeatedly in a soothing manner.

"Sure," I gasp, trying not to break down.

Lunch = sex = Devon's way of saying goodbye to the present and hello to the future. I don't know if I'm ready for a life of zero-to-sixty in less than an instant.

A heavy palm presses my cheek to Devon's chest, where his steady heartbeat is soothing to my fragile nerves. My fingers clutch at his shoulders, tips twisting into the fabric of his jacket.

"You asked why I was breathing heavily," Devon whispers in my ear. "You asked why my fingers were clutching… now you know the answer," is a breath on the wind as he breezes out the door as quickly as he arrived.

Staring where Devon was standing just moments ago, I answer the question.

Fear.

Fear of the past, the present– the future. Fear of commitment and being alone. Fear of the unknown and the known. Fear of your emotions and what they cause you to do. Fear of regret, of pain, of happiness and love. Fear of surrendering to the fear and accepting your fate.

Fear is the ultimate paradox.

There is only one attribute that the Prynnes and Masons share in common– a commonality that keeps us on equal footing –courage. We're either too stupid or too stubborn to allow fear to freeze us. Sometimes it's a mistake, and sometimes it's life-altering, but we never turn away from a challenge.

I can do this, because I know no other path to walk. I do this because I must.

With a deep breath, I silence the need to sob and I smother the need to quiver. "Ladies." I walk back over to the three woman who witnessed a very private moment between Devon and me, which is exactly why they intruded in the first place.

I sit on my stool, tug Isis's feet into the footbath, and get to work. I listen to their conversation about everyday mundane things, and completely zone out. Isis's long talon poking me in the forehead is the only thing that gets through my inner musings.

This time Isis says it loud enough for my ears, "It's about time," and she's smiling brilliantly. With a start, I realize she wasn't speaking of Devon showing up at Salon on time. She was speaking of Devon coming after what I was so freely offering to give, because he's finally surrendered.

CHAPTER NINETEEN

Kieren Mason

Jackson's one edict was that the only thing we could listen to at the shop was Revolutionary Road. I started working at Wreck & Ruin was I was fifteen, in preparation to get my own set of wheels.

Grandpa John's car is Dad's beauty, but Dad pretty much handed it over to Devon when he turned sixteen. Like our house, the 1969 Chevy Camaro is the Mason household's car, not belonging to any individual. By the time I got my license, I knew I'd be competing with Dad and Devon for the keys, so I got smart.

I was walking home, since I was walking everywhere back then, and saw the *HELP WANTED* sign at Wreck & Ruin. It was the best, most life-altering, split decision of my life.

I thought I was earning some change so I could get a ride to bag more chicks, because I was sick of using my bipedal mode of transportation for picking up my next lay– pick them up in what? Put them where once I got them? Fuck them how if I had no car to do it in?

By the time I turned sixteen, I'd been inside of forty-three girls and their cars, trucks, vans, and even a camper or two.

Jackson was a wicked cool boss, except for the constant barrage of Revolutionary Road, both from the speaker system and his vocal cords. I was this-close to quitting when he handed me the keys to my F-150.

Some dumbass couldn't pay for the parts and labor on a brand-spanking-new engine and skipped out. Jackson tried to sue the asshole, but all he ended up with was the title to a vehicle worth only the price of the engine he put into it. Jackson handed me the keys and a bill for the parts, and told me to get it out of his sight.

I learned many valuable lessons that day: work is a commitment. If you respect your boss, they will respect you (if you have a good one, that is). Having a job is a privilege you should be thankful to have. A set of four wheels means more than getting laid– it's independence, and transportation to make more money, which leads to more independence. Through patience, I also learned that if you love and respect someone enough, you no longer hear Revolutionary Road when it's playing, even live in concert.

Almost four months ago, I actually cried when Jackson handed me another set of keys on New Year's Day. The keys to *my* Wreck & Ruin. Kieren Mason and Langdon Stone's Wreck & Ruin. I'm an honest to God business owner– and I didn't steal it. I earned the motherfucker through brain-bleeding mental taxation, sweat-inducing hard labor, and endless patience.

Now when I hear Revolutionary Road, I listen.

In my quest to get laid more, I earned a job, a surrogate father, a bro, and a set of wheels I not only used to drive my ass around but to plow snow to earn extra money. I learned a skillset and gained a profession, and through that, I found my future.

Life is funny that way, how you're walking down the street and you find your future where you least expect it. It just pops in with a cute hello and a perky wave, and it's always sporting a bouncing ponytail.

I wonder if Willow will ask me to lunch again today.

Pointing a finger to the center of my chest, "Shoot me." I growl and pull an imaginary trigger.

"Mason, pretty sure you didn't die the other fifty times you pulled the trigger... today alone." Stone's getting sick of my girly '*does she like me?*' tween crushing. In my quest to take my mind off the pile of dog shit going on at home, I've put all my energy in Willow. Doesn't help that Stone likes my girl. Not *like* likes. He sees Willow as a school bud now, which is odd yet comforting.

"I found the t-shirt in a small, but Weeping Willow's still gonna be swimming in it." Stone thrusts a bundle of black fabric into my arms. "I want to be around the day Willow meets my dad face-to-face."

"Fuck yeah!" Laughing, I turn in a circle while pointing. "Not that she can't see Jackson every time she visits."

In tribute to Jackson and Revolutionary Road and our new-found business ownership, Stone and I had all their album covers and several candid shots blown up into framed poster-sized prints. The service bays and the office are littered wall-to-wall with Jackson's mug.

"Maybe it's because I'm immune, but I don't get the appeal," Stone mumbles. "Mom was a roadie for a bunch of bands back in the day. It was like the eighties threw up in our house. I hate rock music, but more so, I cannot stand the sound of my father's voice at this point.

Stone stands in the center of the service bay, shrieking in a perfect rendition of Jackson on stage at the Calico. His violet eyes are pulsing, his long hair is swinging, and he looks and sounds exactly like his father.

When Stone's temper tantrum is over, I taunt him. "If you fail as a mechanic, you could so make a go of it in a Revolutionary Road cover band."

"Fuck. You. And the horse you rode in on, buddy boy." Stone stalks off, and it's as if Jackson's voice gets louder on the stereo system just to spite him.

Jackson's not dead and haunting us or anything— we really can't figure out how to turn the fucking music off. We swear some asshole is nearby controlling it via frequency waves or some shit. We rebuild cars, not gadgets.

Nope, after Jackson recuperated from his heart attack, he went cold turkey with the drugs, booze, deep-fat-fried food, caffeine, and nicotine. Only vice the forty-seven-year-old, semi-retired, rock star refused to give up was women. Jackson took off last week, not unusual and also why he hired me in the first place. He's getting stroked, sucked, and fucked by the hottest of 'em, I'm sure. Hot chicks love rock stars more than high school girls love a boy with a set of wheels.

The only thing remotely close to the pussy magnetization of a rock star is John Mason's Camaro, and that's pale by comparison. I hope Jackson and Willow never meet face-to-face because she has an odd obsession with the man, and the age gap won't mean shit to her. She already played in the big leagues with Auggie's old ass, and he's not a motherfucking rock star— literally a mother fucking rock star. Plus, even with my borderline homophobia, I can recognize that Jackson's still got that swagger going on.

"On my first real date with Willow, I'm using the Camaro." I inform Stone when he reappears after another bout of tantrums, this time on the speaker we can't seem to reach with every ladder we buy or rent. It's the speaker Revolutionary Road spills from day and night. We've even tried to the shoot the goddamned thing. We nicked it a bit, warping the sound, yet it miraculously healed itself in the middle of the night– with an upgraded smaller Bose system that is impossible to hit with our lousy aim.

When I became a business owner, I began to listen to Revolutionary Road again, remember? What I failed to mention is how before we were able to turn it off for sanity's sake. Jackson didn't give us Wreck & Ruin for free, you see.

The cost had a very steep price.

"Goddamn it! It's louder than before!" Stone drops to his knees, clutching his head, engaged in full-on theatrical mode. "Who the fuck are you, you cunt-licking cocksucker?"

"That's a bit of an oxymoron," Willow says matter-of-factly, as if appearing out of nowhere to stand next to me.

"Hi, Spanky!" I chirp brightly– too brightly for a dude. "It's only an oxymoron unless your name is Robin or Auggie. They both seem to qualify as cunt-licking cocksuckers."

I never pass up the chance to remind Willow how she screwed her brother's life-long boyfriend. It's gross, and as enlightened as I am about sex and who was there before me, it's still gross.

Ignoring my comment, Willow closes her eyes, sways to Jackson's crooning, and sings the chorus. "God, I could listen to this all day."

"NO!" Stone and I shout in unison, and sure as shit, the music cranks up another octave.

"Who. The. Fuck. Are. You?" Stone breaks, literally breaks. "I'm living in Hell," trails after him as he runs to his motorcycle. Within one heartbeat to the next, he's peeling out of the parking lot.

Revolutionary Road dims to mood music– much to Willow's annoyance and my delight. "What was that about?"

"Pretty sure Jackson's fucking with us remotely somehow. It only gets louder when Stone's in a bitchy mood. I think Jack's drilling the lyrics into Stone's head. I bet it would shut off if the son agreed to join the father on tour."

"Oh. My. God. Really?" Spanky's vibrating with excitement. Her big brown eyes are the size of saucers. "Like Lang would sing with Jackson… on stage?"

"Don't go there," I warn, hating how the girl is getting hot just by the thought. As if by magic, the music almost dips into silence as a way to reassure me that my girl is safe from the Stones. "Thanks, Jack," I say to the ceiling.

Smirking naughtily, looking too much like Rob for my tastes, "Hey, Jackson!" Willow waves into space. "Can you turn it up just an itty bit?" Jackson's gravelly deep voice returns to mood music, thrilling Willow. Jumping in thanks, "Whoop! Thank you, Jackson Stone!"

Tugging on her ponytail, "Spanky, you do realize it's probably some college kid like you who's a super-fan of RR, and Jackson's paying their tuition for fucking with us."

"You mean…" The wheels are spinning a 95mph and the RPMs are about to blow the engine in Willow's brain.

"Tech geek," I point out. "I think you're plenty smart, but we're talking Seth-level smart."

Face falling, "Oh," Willow gazes at the floor.

"But, that's just Stone's theory. I think it's actually Jackson watching us somewhere, because he wants to get to know his son better. He wanted Stone to join the family business in all aspects, dreaming of someday sharing a stage together."

Smiling, Willow pokes me in the ribs. "You're a romantic, Stud," she teases me.

I gesture at my chest with a palm, while popping an eyebrow. "Me? A romantic? You're shittin' me, right?"

"Yeah." Blushing a pretty pink high in her cheeks, I have to physically stop myself from molesting her. *Romantic? Try a predator.* Poking me again, "And I like that about you, Stud."

Ah, I get a clue. Willow likes me. She really, really *likes* me. I turn to the side, hiding my insta-grin from her. "So… I was wondering if you'd want to eat lunch with me again today," Willow finally asks what I'd tortured myself all morning over.

I stop myself from picking Willow up like a football and running toward the No-Name like it's the end zone and our booth will net me a touchdown. I just barely stop myself. "Yeah, I'd like that."

Looking at her feet again, Willow breathes, "Cool."

"Shit!" I throw my hands up in the air. "Stone took off on me, the asshole," I sound disappointed, but inside my mind, I'm beating my best bro with a tire iron on his pretty mug. Willow makes a move to leave– flee –but I grab her ponytail to tug her to a stop. "You want to eat with me?" I ask, willing to beg.

"Sure," she returns to perky levels. "I'd like that."

"Okay then. Awesome." Awkward. "Well, follow me this way." I head toward the office area, and just past that is the kitchen and bathroom. "Oomph." I grunt when Spanky jumps on my back.

"I need a lift." Spanky laughs into my ear, flirting with me big time, and I get a motherfucking clue.

How do you pick up the girl you really want? Let her come to you. Does it matter what you drive? No, because her favorite mode of transportation will always be your back. Who knew, I didn't need that F-150 after all.

I want to ask Willow how she's doing after what Devon pulled last night. I want to tell her about rehab and how we think Devon inherited the family curse. But those topics of conversation are off the discussion table. But then again, I'm glad they are. This makes this time about Willow and me. Not about Devon, or the family, or the past. Stress-free Willow and Ren time.

"How's work and school going?" I ask as I set Willow down on a chair in the kitchen. Not ready to cook yet, I sit down next to her.

"Good– great," Willow says brightly, but I can see the sadness lingering in her eyes. I long to tell her how strong I think she is, how this was for the best. "My new online system still has some bugs in it, but it's a helluva lot better than it was before I started at FCC. Revamped's profits have quadrupled thanks to yours truly."

I want to reach over for Willow's hand, but don't. The hell with it– I grab her hand and like it. I'm not stalking Willow. I'm touching her as a friend. "Thanks for helping Stone out with the books. The two of us were both pulling our hair out over it."

Silently laughing, always happy even when she's sad, Willow's exactly what I needed on a day like today. "Good thing." She pulls her hand from mine, only to reach up to muss up my hair. "You both have amazing hair."

"Hey, what did Auggie do with that Darth Vader I brought in four months ago," I ask, chuckling evilly.

Spanky snickers with me, like she knows what I was up to that day, when I know she doesn't have a clue. "Darth's on Auggie's desk in a special box– bolted down. It's in his line-of-sight at all times, and I can hear him chatting with Ol' Darth while he draws."

"Priceless." A bunch of memories inundate me.

"Stud." Willow pins me with her unflinching stare. "Spill the deets."

"Well…" I blush bright red. "See, Auggie was young and stupid, and I was just a little shit when I went into his room and stole all his action figures. With Isis and Devon's help, I kept Auggie's toys nice and safe for years and years, and he kept crying about them."

"Oh, that was mean." Willow gasps, a mixture of laughter and horror. "Poor Auggie." Again, she sounds a little bit evil like Robin, like she can appreciate the deviancy of the act.

"I needed some money to fix my 4-wheel drive, and I knew Auggie'd ante up. It was also a message. It took me five months to get into Revamped without getting my ass kicked to the curb, and that day I made it in unscathed."

"The message?" Willow prompts, instinctively knowing it's about her.

"Don't shoot the messenger," I say uncomfortably, sweating bullets. "I took Auggie's toys, and I was giving them back. He took my toy, and I was taking her back." I breathe the truth as I turn my head away, closing my eyes against whatever expression crosses Willow's face. "I've grown up a lot since then, Willow. I don't see you as a toy– I promise."

"Growing up… been there, doing that," Spanky mutters wryly. "I unwittingly thwarted your plan, because the toy was stupid and wandered back to Mr. Kline's toy box." She gives me the best apology she possibly could.

Smiling brightly, "That's okay, though. She's back to being my little buddy now." I tweak the tip of Spanky's nose. "So after I left with my cash, Auggie followed me, and beat me where no one could see. All the while he was sputtering about Darth Vader, and how I made him cry for losing something his mom's brother gave him when he was seven."

"Ah!" Willow cries, clutching her chest… and she calls me the romantic?

"So after Auggie beat the fuck out of me, he said thanks for keeping his toys safe and sound because he would've probably lost 'em on his own. He gave me a kiss and told me he loved me. Then he warned that if I ever hurt you, he'd kill me." I knock on the tabletop, and then stand– story complete. "Lunch?"

Willow tries to hide her sniffles, but she's doing a piss-poor job at it. I decide it's time for the gift I had Stone get for me.

"Arms up like I'm Chief Mason and you're robbing Wreck & Ruin," I order in a no-nonsense voice. Pulling my finger gun, I point it at Willow. "Freeze, you dirtbag motherfucker."

Laughing through her tears, Willow complies, putting her arms over her head. I tug her FCC sweatshirt over her head, muttering about how she must have one in every color. I snort at the Kool-Aid Man t-shirt she has on beneath. I feel up her back, remembering what she doesn't wear, and I don't want to get my nuts squashed for stripping her naked from the waist up. Her tank top strap is peaking out, so I'm safe to remove Mr. Kool-Aid Man.

I shouldn't get aroused by a thin tank top covered in tiny red cherries with green stems, but I do anyway. But it's the curve of Willow's neck and the little hairs that escaped her ponytail that I find the sexiest. I struggle not to attack the girl, knowing great things come to those who wait. Patience is a virtue when dealing with Willow Prynne.

I've been celibate for far too fucking long.

Dressing Spanky like she's a little kid, I tug her new t-shirt over her head, and step back to get a good look at her. "Perfect," I mutter. Willow looks like a hot mess, but now she looks like *my* hot mess.

"Oh. My. God. You rock so fucking hard." Spanky sputters as she stares down at her gift in awe– proudly wearing the original Wreck & Ruin t-shirt. Revolutionary Road's first album was titled Wreck & Ruin, so Jackson named the garage after it. Staring up at me through lashes thickened with tears, she smiles through the bitter-sweet. "Sam had one just like this."

With a small smile, I say, "Awesome," and knock on the table again. "Lunch? You're eating peanut butter and pickle, because it's my favorite. I hope you aren't like... healthy. 'Cuz we're also having Coke, chips, and snack cakes."

"My kind of lunch." Spanky shifts in her chair, still staring down in awe at her new t-shirt. I can see the memories playing out on her face.

I remember Sam well. Hell, Willow reminds me of Sam sometimes, which is impossible. Dad and Sam were buddies like Stone and me. There were many nights Dad and Sam sat out back in the lawn, even when it was snowing. Sam was the only thing that kept Dad engaged after Mom offed herself... and when we lost Sam, us kids were the only thing that kept Dad engaged with life.

Still teary-eyed, "Feed me, Seymour!"

I knock on the tabletop again, shaking my head in awe this time. "You're my kind of girl." And she is. Willow and I don't have to talk hearts and flowers and bitter misery because we just know what the other is feeling. An entire conversation about Sam passed between us in a heartbeat, and we moved on instead of dwelling in the past.

Devon was toxic to a girl like Willow, because they'd wallow in the misery together. Each of them needs a counterpart who's more interested in moving toward the future instead of always trying to move backward into the past. While I need someone to remind me to stop and pause instead of always surging forward into the unknown.

"What do you do at night? What do you do for fun?" Willow's asking me to hang out; I know she is.

I grab the Claussen's pickles and Coke from the fridge, and the Jif and Stroehmann's bread from the cupboard. I toss a few bags of chips onto the table, and a box of cupcakes quickly follows their arc of travel. "Watch TV and eat mass quantities of junk food. Why?"

"Well, I thought…" Sounding awkwardly sheepish, "I thought maybe since we both watch TV and eat junk food at night… that maybe we… that maybe we could just do it together at the same time in the same place."

"Sure." I play it cool while I make the girl a sandwich, when inside my belly's doing frickin' summersaults. "Since we're both doing it anyway already, that is."

CHAPTER TWENTY

Essie Prynne

I have a feeling Isis brought her friends in as an excuse to invade Salon for however long it was necessary until Devon graced us with his brooding presence. Since Dev showed early, I only had to primp Isis. After the pedicure, Isis gave me a tip and promptly left, but not before she gave me a piece of advice first.

"Beware of the black-haired Masons," Isis said cryptically. "They are difficult to love if you don't know what you're doing. Those blond, adorable punks are too sweet for their own good."

"You're a black-haired Mason," I reminded her.

"Exactly," Isis said with a feral smile. "I have two guys because neither of them is strong enough to love me by themselves. Even together, it's a struggle– until they are together-together, they will never be strong enough to love me the way I need."

I hated the way Isis's dark eyes lightened to stormy blue and filled with tears. "We're all working on that," I warned Isis– warned her Rob was doing a bang-up job on fixing their malfunctions. I'm pretty sure Auggie's just sitting on his ass and doing nothing until it's time to get in Robin's way.

Eyebrow raised, demanding I continue, but I kept my lips firmly locked. "Fine," Isis sighed, clearly annoyed I didn't obey her silent command. "You'll do just fine– you're a strong bitch like me. You go with your instincts and take what you want. Just remember, Devon will hurt you, and you have to be strong enough to survive."

"Thanks," I muttered sarcastically. "That didn't sound ominous at all… and so hope-filled."

Laughing, Isis gave me the advice she came to give. "Be quick to forgive, but guard your heart, and never forget."

Isis's advice keeps ringing in my ears as I do the first task Isis gave me, create a survey for the townsfolk to fill out. In the land where dreams are realized, my imagination, I become the owner of Salon. I rename it Primp, like I'm the style pimp of Fairport. In these dreams that will never manifest, everything on this list comes to fruition. Primp is a huge success, and I'm a happy pimp.

Of course none of that is going to happen, because it's 12:15 in the afternoon, and I've had exactly two customers today: one who paid me, and one who did not. Out of the thirty-five bucks Isis paid, I earned five, and then the five dollar tip. That's less than two dollars and fifty cents an hour. What is this, the 1970s? I wasn't even born yet.

My dream shrivels up and dies, so I stop my survey list, and log onto Jamison Reality's Wi-Fi to start another job search. I need something to tide me over until I can work the dinner rush at the No-Name. The gas station is looking for someone during the graveyard shift. I could work days at Salon, evenings at the No-Name, and when most people sleep, I could collect money from the dolts who buy gas with cash instead of using the machine on the pump.

I grab my survey again, putting *eyebrow shaping* on the list. My dream will not die, even if I have to pass out from sleep deprivation to make it come true. I didn't grow up to be the girliest girl, to study my damnedest for two years of my life, to owe the school my first born and my right hand in debt, just to sit down and die.

I'll get there. Someday.

Isis's advice finally clicks. *Forgive*: get over it, and dust your ass off after you stand back up. *Never forget*: use it to propel your ass forward, no matter the cost. *You'll do just fine. You're a strong bitch like me*: you'll keep Devon's ass alive, because you're too tenacious and stupid to ever give up.

~~Anal bleaching~~. Nah, too freaky for Fairport. *Anal bleaching*. Perfect for the Playroomers. *Brazilian Wax*. Perfect for everyone.

"What are you writing?" Devon scares the bejesus out of me. Leaning over the front desk, Devon studies my list of services. Grocery bags of food are swinging in each of his hands. Must be lunch is actually on the menu today.

Clutching my chest, pen ink dotting my blouse blue, I gasp out, "You're like a bat. Stomp or something when you enter."

Chuckling softly underneath his breath, "It's a good quality to have in a police officer. They actually train us to be silent so we can sneak up on criminals."

"Dude, you aced that shit, didn't you?" Dev nods his head yes, smirking. "You were always very graceful and surefooted," I compliment.

The besotted idiot that I am has always thought Devon was beautiful. His new haircut pushes him into devastatingly handsome. Looking at him, while he's looking at me like he's hungry and sad and loves me, makes me want to have his babies.

I'm screwed– in a good and a bad way.

"Hmm… let's see," Devon breathes near me, ticking my cheek. "I like this one… and this one…" Slim fingertips scanning my list, he's not making fun of me because he understands this is my dream. Clearing his throat, a blush burns brightly against his skin. "You have this one," he comments on the Brazilian Wax. "I really, really think you should put that one on there twice, 'cuz it's so…" Coughing into his hand. "Yeah, add some manscaping right there." Dev points to the end of the list. "Until you share a locker room with a bunch of burly cops, you won't realize how furry the fucktards are."

Manscaping. I think I might enjoy administering that particular service, and then gossiping about what I see. A snicker escapes my mouth as I finish the word with a flourish.

"You're bad," Devon teases me, reading my mind. "Just don't tell anyone about what's going on with my body."

"Promise," I bald-face lie, and Devon recognizes the liar in me because he's one too. What fun is girl-talk without the juicy shit? "What's all this?" I poke Devon's grocery bag.

Hefting the bags up onto the counter, Devon has a veritable feast. "I'm eating while I still can." He gives me a crooked, abashed smile. "I'd like to share a meal with you, if you'll join me."

Heart aching from the pain in Devon's voice, I say with a tear-thickened voice, "It will be my pleasure." I reach out to rub his forearm, jolting from the connection. I close my eyes, wondering how I'll get through the next few months, and what type of person Devon will be when he makes it to the other side.

"None of that." Dev warns, getting choked up. "Essie, I love you because you never let me go down that path." Taking a deep breath, he says in a rush, "I don't have to be back to the station until three o'clock. So I'd like to share those hours with you."

"That's a lot of food, Dev, but I doubt it will take us three hours to eat it," I tease. I get up from my stool, and prepare for our alone time. I flick the open sign off and lock the front door, then grab a piece of paper and a Sharpie.

Out to lunch.
Return after 3 p.m.
Thanks– Management.

After taping the note on the door, I turn to Devon. "Do you want to eat in my office? There isn't a wall of windows for people standing on the street to watch us."

I wave to Clover's mother-in-law as she narrows her eyes at Devon. Peggy has a hate-on for the Masons. Peggy and Pat stand on the sidewalk, shamelessly watching us, where they will tell everyone at church if they see something untoward.

Bitches.

Awesome bitches. I'm so going to grow up to be a little old church lady, making the lives of my children and grandchildren miserable for my own entertainment. Bullying hurts– I've been there and done that. But gossip just makes you realize everyone else's lives suck as badly as yours does. It's not about hate– it's about insecurity and finding a commonality between us. Bullying is about hate, there is a distinction.

Peggy– Margaret Webster is lonely and insecure, and I recognize in her what I hate about myself.

I grab Devon's hand and tug him toward the backroom. I might like to gossip with the best of 'em, but that doesn't mean I'm going to give Peggy and Pat any ammunition to lob at me on Sunday morning while we sit in the church pew.

Being a good girl with a bad girl reputation does have its advantages. They aren't shocked to see me lead Devon into the backroom, because they assume we're going to have sex, so the gossip won't be a high priority.

"Welcome to my lair." Arms spread wide, I grandly present my room. "Few enter, but they always return," I say with a snort, bungling up the quote. "So… yeah… this is all my shit. Well, after it's paid for, that is."

Salon's backroom is fairly good-sized, because it was meant to be partitioned off into office spaces. ~~Wisely~~ unwisely, I've spent all of my money in this room, in hopes of making my clients happy enough to grace me with their patronage again. The patient table is in the corner, on the same side of the door, so that if the door is opened by accident, nothing will be seen. I have a countertop set up with a cushioned chair behind a tri-fold screen for my clients to change behind. There is a station for all the necessities, as well as my microdermabrasion, electrolysis, and laser equipment. The table is multifunctional, able to be used as a massage table if Salon ever gets someone certified. Not me– I ran out of money for schooling, and they wouldn't give me any more aid with my defaulted loan.

For added comfort, I created a seating area with two cushioned chairs and a coffee table. It was in case my clients wanted to discuss their needs, or if they had friends they were comfortable to have in the room during their treatments.

The area is painted a soothing Caribbean Sea blue/green with billowing white panels on the walls to soften the sterile feel. I have a small stereo system set up that plays oceanic sounds, and I burn scented candles to compliment the design.

Currently, I have a several older women who love the facials and microdermabrasion, a handful of ladies who get waxed, and one who opted for the more permanent hair removal option– Isis has a hairy secret she keeps.

I try to get word out about my services, but with Salon in its current state, I fear it keeps potential clients at bay.

The day Elma gave me free-reign, she said, *"Do what you want in here, but it's your dime. Keep a ledger when you work on a client, and give me a thirty-five percent fee for using Salon."*

Elma's a hard woman to like. She's brusque, and never gives out a *good job,* or a *thank you,* or a *you're welcome.* But you always know where you stand with her since she tells you if she's upset, right when you upset her. As long as I follow Elma's rules, we're copasetic.

Salon is old-school, bare-bones because Elma is. She's a *hairdresser*, so she doesn't understand what I do, how I wish Salon was an all-inclusive day spa named Primp... and she doesn't want to know, either.

"Wow, Ess," Devon breathes out next to me, surveying my environment as I am.

Getting warm, feeling embarrassed– striped raw. "Gotta love Uncle Dave," I mutter as I take the bags from Devon's hands and place them on the coffee table.

Seeming curious, "Why's that?"

"The man does good work, and he works for free if you're family… and if you're not. As long as you help him and he gets to teach you something, he won't even make you pay for the materials."

"Gotta love Uncle Dave," Devon says with a wink.

I start removing containers from the bags, surprised since I thought Dev just grabbed some stuff at the store. Instead I find plastic containers filled with food he made from home.

Blushing, Dev looks more handsome than ever. "Clover's been teaching us to cook on the weekends. Rae's been practicing at home." Gesturing to the wide variety of casseroles, salads, and Prynne family recipes. "As you can see, Rae wants to make Clover proud."

Now that fucking chokes my ass up. "You better tell your sister that there is nothing she has to do to make Clover proud except to simply exist."

"I know." Devon sighs, slumping to the nearest chair. "I've told Rae that. Ren's told her that. But our mom didn't operate as a normal human being. It might take Rae a lifetime to trust Clover's unconditional mothering."

Not wanting to dive off the emotional deep-end, I change the subject. "I spy with my little eye," reaching for the container, "Clover's famous pasta salad. I love how she puts a Mediterranean twist on the traditional." I peel the lid off the container and grab a fork. "All mine." And my fork disappears from my hand. "What the?" I look around for my utensil while frowning.

"No eating until after." Devon points my fork at me– the thief. "It always makes you sleepy, and you won't want to fool around."

"Ah, so sex is on the menu," I say with a throaty laugh. "I'm starving, though. And just so you know, I can't cook for shit."

"I know." Devon grins at me knowingly. "I remember. You ought to join us on Saturday for a lesson… for the next decade," he teases.

"Ha-ha! No sex for you." I retaliate, perusing the coffee table for something I can eat like a cavewoman– with my hands.

The sound of something heavy hitting the floor draws my attention. I find Devon unbuttoning his uniform, with his duty belt resting by his feet. With obvious care, he folds his shirt and places it over his belt. Continuing on in this manner, never taking his eyes off me, Devon strips bare-assed naked.

Mouth gaping open, I simply stare in awe. The last time I saw Devon completely naked, he was a thirteen-year-old boy getting a vicious tongue lashing from his aunt. He was a scrawny kid, weighing no more than a hundred and ten pounds, and barely five and a half feet tall. I was a kid myself, so I didn't know the difference until later, but the boy hadn't been wielding much in the junk department either.

Standing before me today is a man. A well-honed body from hours and hours of physical activity. "You've grown." A whimper passes my parted lips. "A lot."

"Seems so." Shrugging, Dev acts like it's no big deal that he's standing here fully aroused. "I'm still too skinny." he points at the coffee table filled with food. "I'm bound to get skinnier in the next few weeks, but I'll put it back on in rehab. My um... mental state wouldn't ever let me eat as much as I needed."

At a loss of how to respond, "Yeah..." I ignore the protruding ribs in favor of the tight pecs and abs at my eye-level. I swallow thickly, knowing I'll never erase this sight from my memory– thank heavens.

"You've grown too," Dev murmurs while flashing me a naughty smirk. "We were short-changed the other night. It was dark out, and we had to do this clothed. I'd like to see you." He tacks on a begging, "Please."

"You're highly manipulative," I say pointedly, and Dev freezes. "But I like that about you, Officer Mason. It takes balls to go after what you really want." My gaze flicks south and widens in surprise. I raise an eyebrow– Dev's dick might be average, but the rumors of the Masons being like rabid rabbits on Viagra seems to hold true. His purple dick proudly juts out from his pelvis, with the biggest set of balls I've ever seen swinging beneath. "You've got that covered, eh?"

Flushing red, Devon actually looks bashful and slightly confused. "I have not heard that before. I don't go around dick measuring."

Leaning forward in my chair, I purr, "Judging by the blush working its way up to your hairline, there's a story behind that, Mr. Liar, Liar, Pants on Fire."

Laughing uncomfortably, Dev turns his back on me. I suck in a deep draw of air. "Your ass is your best feature." I lean forward further. "Jesus, I left nail marks all over your back and ass."

Rewarding me, "Every year on our birthdays, I force Ren to measure his dick, because if he ever grew bigger than me, I was going to cut it off in his sleep."

"You would've done it too," I mutter with absolute certainty. Devon thinks he would've done it, but he would've never gone through with it– I'm certain about that too. "Did Ren stop being the stud horse to all of Fairport's mares for a reason, Dev?" I tease.

"As of two months ago, Ren and I are identical in the junk department, right down to the centimeter. Balls, too." Devon turns around, challenging me to call him insane. But I refuse. I'm the girl who empathizes with Peggy because she's insecure. I get Devon more than he realizes.

"Well, then… Ren's grown some, too," I taunt myself. "Not my proudest moment, but not my worst either."

"I'm over it," Dev admits, surprising the hell out of me. "Recently. As in last night, I got over it. Ren told me some details that made it more palatable to swallow." I eye Devon, looking for Mr. Liar, Liar. But he's being open and honest– calm.

"Shit," I hiss. My body starts to shake, beginning at my fingers and toes and working through to the center of my body. "Double shit." I wonder if Ren has matching bruises to the ones on Dev's knuckles as a cost for *getting over it.*

"It's balanced now," Dev admits, and he looks like he wants to explain.

"No need," I stop him. "I agree. For right or wrong, it's over and done with. Balanced. Everybody involved was hurt– has hurt. Willow was collateral damage, and I wish she wasn't involved."

"Debatable," Devon grumbles, but doesn't continue. "That topic is off limits. You gonna give me shit about that, or are we good?"

I bark a sharp laugh, amused Devon is giving me attitude while standing bare-assed naked in my domain. I've made too many mistakes to judge anyone else. As I said, I like gossip because it makes me feel better about my past and present. I don't do it to judge who I'm talking shit about.

Leaning back in my chair, I cross my forearms over my breasts and eye Devon. "We're good. Just don't push it too far," I warn.

Isis said: *Be quick to forgive, but guard your heart, and never forget.*

I say: *don't be stupid. Unconditional goes both ways. Devon can push at my boundaries, but if he crosses them, he'll regret it.*

"I'm hungry." I whine, staring at the spread of food across my coffee table. I roll my eyes back up to a naked Devon, and he's on me in a heartbeat. Laughing, I try to fend him off. Devon's hands seem to be everywhere, tugging my blouse, unbuttoning it and my jeans. He even cops a feel or ten. "When did you turn into an octopus?" Breathlessly, I gasp out, "Hornier than fuck, junior high Devon is back with a vengeance."

Panting near my ear, Devon warns, "Wrong. That Devon is gone. Starving for Essie Devon has formed in his absence." I shriek when he tugs my shirt off, tossing it across the room. "No matter how much misery is on my mind, my need to be inside you chases the darkness away."

Startled, freezing, I allow Devon to remove the rest of my clothing. "Jesus, you ain't playing around. You're fucking serious."

Gripping my chin with his fingertips, Devon stares me down with disturbing intensity. "I'm insane, Essie, remember? When I get obsessed with something, nothing stands in my way. The only reason you were safe for the past seven years is because I didn't allow myself to have you. I have self-control in spades." The deep, dark tone in Devon's voice runs a shiver up my spine.

A smart woman should be petrified, but I never said I was smart. In fact, I'm pretty sure I said I wasn't. "Fuck," I whimper, and Devon takes that as permission. He slides off me, and then reaches down to lift me from my chair. Walking a few steps to the side, Devon takes us both down to the floor.

Settling me on the white carpeting, Devon reaches for one of the white towels and picks my ass up to ease it beneath me. Without preamble, he lies down on top of me and slides inside my body. We shudder, both of us equally shocked at how ready we were for the other.

Insanely intense, Devon thrusts as hard as humanly possible, making both of us grunt on impact. The only reason I don't slide several feet across the carpet is because of his strong hands gripping my shoulders, bruisingly so. Once he's satisfied that he has me, that he's penetrating me, he slows his ass down to a snail's pace.

Rolling his hips in a hypnotic wave, Devon stares down at me, refusing to blink. "I wonder where we'd be if I had a different mother, if the nightmare never came, if I never broke you, if I never got sick and addicted…"

"Don't go there," I warn, refusing to allow Devon to go backward. "It changes nothing. What happened, happened. Now is all that matters. If you're going to fuck me like you have something to prove, like you're trying to erase or escape the past, then my pussy's closed."

Devon stops moving, and I can see the emotions flashing rapidly across his face, like he's judging his emotional climate, determining whether or not what he's feeling is normal.

"I don't care that you use drugs as medication for your mental illness, making you a drug addict. I could give a shit less about you being bipolar, except that it petrifies you. I don't care that you screwed my cousin to get back at me, to get back at your brother, to get back at yourself– to get back at Willow for some reason. I can deal with all that because you're getting help, and you're going to get better. But what I cannot deal with is you being inside me while you're thinking about all of those things. Either be with me, only me, or don't be with me at all."

"I…" Devon's at a loss for words– good.

"I may be stupid, easily manipulated, and highly addicted to you. But one thing I'm not is a pushover. I warned you earlier not to push me, because I *will* push back."

Blinking, confused, Devon stammers, "No more zero-to-sixty? Ever?"

"Not right now, no," is my instantaneous reply.

"No more past." Devon nods his head as he speaks, his curls brushing against his forehead with the movement. "No more future talk. Only right now matters this afternoon," he tries on for size.

"Right now, yes," I confirm. "Okay? This afternoon is for both of us, and there is nothing to prove here, Dev. Just you and me. You were all about me during your haircut, but now you didn't even kiss me first like I'm a–"

Palm clasped over my mouth, Devon glares with bitter hatred burning from his eyes, but it's not directed at me. "If you ever speak that word in a non-professional sense, I will punch you in the cunt. Got it?"

Refusing to escalate this any further, I ask, "Are we good now?"

Devon can think his nightmare woke the illness that was lurking beneath the surface, but we've been here before. I was proficient at dealing with Devon's mercurial moods at a tender age.

Some women would be pissed at how Devon speaks to me. Some would be turned on, being arrogant enough to think they can heal the bad out of the boy with their *love,* which isn't fucking possible unless their pussy is a licensed psychiatrist.

All should be terrified, and I am, even if I pretend I'm not.

I'm just patient and calm, understanding why Devon's the way he is, but not allowing him to run me over in the process. Today isn't the first time I've told Devon not to push me. That's a code we started to use back when I was twelve and he began to manipulate me with a vengeance.

"We're good," Devon answers just as he did almost a decade ago. "We're better than good. I don't believe in apologies, so how about I prove it?"

"Do your worst," I challenge, playing with fire. Picking up the gauntlet, Devon does his best.

CHAPTER TWENTY-ONE

Devon Mason

Blinking away the discombobulating sensation of a manic episode colliding with the depression I'm barely holding at bay, I shake my head left and right, trying to clear my head.

"I'm an asshole." I laugh humorlessly as my lips descend to Essie's. The woman has never done anything remotely wrong enough to deserve the punishment of loving me.

Reading me, understanding me, Essie instinctively knows what's going on in my head. I hesitate, unsure if I'm selfish enough to accept her body when I should be shoving her away. That's why I always go for broke, taking her like a fiend. If I stop to think, I wouldn't act. Taking the choice out of my hands, Essie lifts her head and wraps her arms around my back, drawing my lips down to hers.

Lips opening on a moan, I experience the sweetest kiss of my life. It's not sweet because it's the kiss of innocence. It's the kiss of knowledge and experience and forgiveness and understanding, and most importantly– acceptance. It's the kiss a lucky man receives from his wife, every single day of his life.

I unhinge, and Essie takes me willingly. As long as it's about her, she deals with my octopus hands and my zero-to-sixty without complaint. Revels in it, actually.

Mouths fused together, our tongues remember the dance we taught each other. I think of nothing but Essie. A hazy film overlays the present with the past, but it's of similar scenes, proving the now is always better. I kiss Essie on the floor of her room at the salon, but in my mind I remember the thousands of kisses we shared in our childhood.

In our memories, it's always better than it was in actuality. But this is different, more intense, filled with things better left unsaid. I find my hope, my will to survive– the very thing my mother never found. I know with absolute certainty, I could spend the rest of my life kissing Essie, and each and every time would be better than the last.

"Devon," she moans my name. Her back arches up, pressing her body tightly against mine as I slowly roll my hips into her without breaking our lip-lock. Sharp nails bite into my ass, shooting sparks straight to the head of my cock.

"Fuck," I hiss, pulling free of her pussy. Panting, I try to get myself under control. "That was close." Gasping, I ignore how close it was– how my dick is dripping onto Essie's thigh.

"Revenge," she purrs, wiggling around beneath me.

"You're looking mighty proud of yourself," I tease Essie as she grins up at me. "No fair with the nails. You know how much I love that."

Flashing Essie a heated look, I palm both of her breasts, barely covering half of them. As I massage the part of Essie's body she loathes the most, the part that I've used as a visual aid every single time I've jerked off, it takes everything in me not to turn angry again– to stalk every fuck who's ever called such a sweet girl a whore.

I'll be the first in line to kick my own ass.

"Speaking of bigger…" My lips lower to capture her nipple, teeth sinking in slightly. Essie squeaks and tries to pull away. "Someone's been a good girl, drinking her milk and growing me such a perfect pair of titties. Are these my tits, Ess? Hmm?"

"Yeah," she agrees hesitantly, knowing when I'm feeling playful I'm not to be trusted.

"Guess I can do whatever I please to 'em, huh?" I receive a narrowed stare of suspicion, which makes me chuckle against her nipple. Just to keep Essie on her toes, I abandon her tits and head south.

I never want to be thought of as predictable. Essie starts giggling, as if she read my mind, or maybe my whisker stubble is tickling her belly. Teasing, going slowly versus usual, I nuzzle and kiss at her tummy and hip.

"Devon." Essie growls, getting frustrated with me. Her hips buck up, trying to herd me to her pussy. "You're killing me."

Rolling my eyes up to look at her, "You better advertise your services to the rest of the ladies of Fairport. Their men would pay hundreds for it. Who waxed you? I know you're not that flexible."

"Beth," Ess whispers like it's a secret, fingers seeking my hair to tug me down to her hair-free pussy. "Don't spontaneously erupt, but I do hers, too."

"Playroom-ready," I say with a snort. "Half the town's seen Bethany as a puppy. You should advertise Salon on her collar."

"Jackass." Essie swears at me, but not because I'm teasing her girl. She's frustrated. I love it when she's frustrated– she gets frisky. "Jesus Christ, I haven't had a mouth on me in years!"

Fingers wrapping around my curls, thighs spreading, Essie roughly shoves my face between her legs. All the while I laugh, experiencing a rare burst of pure happiness. Out of reflex, my tongue darts out for a taste, and then I dive in with a groan. Tonging her from asshole to clit, I swallow her cream down my throat as she continually creates it.

Gasping for breath, "You gave me that haircut so you could use it as a handle. Admit it," I taunt, trying to come up for air. But Essie has other ideas, allowing me no escape until she comes. Jaw aching, lips sucking, tongue flicking, Essie rides my face with her thighs pressing into my ears.

Out of practice after only doing this to the girl when I was a boy, this more demanding, adult Essie is a rush. I glorify in how she writhes against me, on how her wetness saturates my face to drip off my chin. Slipping two fingers deep inside her, I reach up with my other hand to violently twist and pull at her nipples.

In porn, the woman screams out like she's a banshee. "*I'm gonna come!*" Then she fake-moans and stares at the camera with blowjob lips. In reality, Essie grunts sharply while every muscle in her body locks up at once. Tearing my hair out at the roots, her nails dig into my scalp punishingly. Essie's thighs turn into a vise around my head as she grinds her cunt on my nose, lips, and chin, not giving a damn that's she suffocating me.

It's messy. It's sloppy. It's dirty. It's animalistic. It's real and raw, and it's 100% the Essie I've always known.

Laughing ecstatically, I wipe my face off on my forearm, and I'm still sopping wet. I lean back in wonder as Essie's body falls lax as quickly as it locked up. Laying on the floor is one satisfied woman wearing an even more satisfied smirk.

"You just ruined porn for me," I grumble, voice thick and scratchy from exertion. "I didn't think it was possible, but you're even more beautiful to me than you were when we were kids. I used to call you *my* pin-up girl, and I was the luckiest guy around."

Sprawled on the floor, arms raised above her head, showcasing her tits in the best possible way, one knee crooked and waving back and forth, giving glimpses of her glistening pussy, Essie stops and starts my heart.

Smiling secretly, as if she's thinking the naughtiest thoughts imaginable, "May I?" Essie's too relaxed to move anything but her finger. She points at my dick– my poor, throbbing dick that's drooling a string of pre-cum on my thigh.

"You want to?" I mutter in disbelief.

Essie *hated* giving me blowjobs after I *accidentally* came into her mouth once on purpose. After that, I had to beg. She'd give in eventually, but only after I got her off with my mouth first– sometimes two or three times.

After I broke her, Essie punished me by doing the one thing she refused to do to me, and she did it to every dick that did or didn't ask for it beforehand... and she hated every fucking minute of it, and so did I as I forced myself to watch as a sick form of self-punishment.

Self-punishment: when your inner sadist goes after your inner masochist, and your psyche is in pain and loving every disgusting second of it. Or is that the definition of insanity?

Shaking her head, Essie struggles to sit up on her ass. "I do. I want to see if I'll enjoy it."

Snorting, at both her answer and her inability to move. "The mechanics of it hasn't changed, Ess. It's still a blowjob, and it's the same dick– only bigger, as you've mentioned."

Finally overcoming her struggle to sit up, Essie floors me. Rasping out, "I've changed," in a serious tone, she grabs for my dick, and I fall to my ass in shock.

Crawling up my legs like a famished, gorgeous creature, Essie scares me to death. Her tongue juts out, missing my dickhead by inches, and I know she's testing her resolve. The hidden part of me does the same thing from time to time, meaning I'm right about two things: Essie's been forced before, as have I.

"You don't have to." I coax her to stop this insanity. "I can live without it. I'm just happy you let me inside your body– it doesn't matter where." Eyes held wide in fear, I stare at Essie's hand wrapped around the base of my willing and ready cock.

"What if I can't live without it?" Essie draws in a deep breath, as if she's going to say something else... and then deep throats me in a single swallow.

"Holy fuck!" I shout, hips jackknifing off the floor. I scramble backward awkwardly, but Essie stays with me. Her knees are resting on my thighs as she bends at the waist to worship at my cock. Gasping for breath, "You hate doing this... but, my God!" my voice breaks as I surrender. "Don't bite my dick off if I accidentally come, and this time it will be an accident."

Essie laughs around my dick, slurping me down her throat. "Don't do that... don't laugh. It vibrates on me. Jesus Fuck, is there a Dyson in your gut sucking me off?" Struggling to get away, "No! No... no. Stop laughing! It's gonna make me come."

Eyes rolling back in my head, I fall backward, and I don't even give two shits that I bang my skull on the floor. My fingers weave in Essie's silky hair, and this time I hold her against me instead of trying to yank her free of my cock. My hips rise and fall with her sucking motion as I do my damnedest not to come, because this is the first blowjob Essie's ever given where she's loved every single second of it.

Nutsack tightening up to my body, dick throbbing in warning, my spine bows, forcing me further down Essie's throat. Heeding my warning, she pulls free, only to crawl up my body and wiggle her pussy over my shaft.

"Jesus fuck!" My head hitches back, knocking against the floor. I release a whimper this time instead of scream. I'm too sated to move even though I haven't shot yet. The need to come is still intense, but my dick has greater opportunities to explore with Essie riding it. Behaving, it allows me the pleasure by holding out for a few more minutes.

Palms gripping Essie's tiny waist, my hips surge up to meet the slow, rhythmic roll of her body. I decide to permanently replace porn with belly dancing in my spank bank. The sway of her breasts hypnotizes me– I can look nowhere else.

"Someday I'm going to fuck your perfect tits while you suck my cockhead like my spunk is your favorite beverage." Essie's unusual reaction has me on the edge. "No laughing during sex... ever again. It's not funny, whether a blowjob or fucking, your laugh is potent insta-come."

Leaning forward, tits grazing my chest, Essie breathes into my ear. "Your laugh turns me into a pile of mush, completely susceptible to your manipulations. Pretend I didn't tell you that."

I raise my knees so Essie can't lean back again. Even though I loved the view, I thirst for the intimacy of her pressed to my chest even more. I wrap my arms around her, hands gripping her ass, and counterthrust with her rhythm.

I'm a cop, and cops talk as if everywhere is their dick-measuring locker room. It's not bad at the station because of Dad, but the academy was awful. Testosterone-fueled sexism that wove through the men like an infection. They talked shit about how they have to be in charge in the bedroom. How they only fuck– and only from behind or in a position where they are in total control. They had wives and girlfriends at the same time, and they thought a real man cheated on both. Their measure of a real man was by how many women they've screwed. They called every guy who was in love with their woman a pussy or a fag.

I'm a Mason, and we have a deep romantic streak, and I'm not ashamed to admit that. If I could change the past, I wouldn't have cheated on Essie with Willow. I wish I could proudly say I'd only ever been inside Essie. But I can't, so I make do with the knowledge that I've always been faithful in my heart.

I was rough with Essie earlier– on the cusp of an episode. But I enjoy slow, and I have no problem with Essie taking from me, being in charge. In fact, I prefer it, because it takes the stress off me over worrying about whether or not I'm doing it right. I've never touched Essie and not left her satisfied, even when I was a kid. That's why I finally let go of the past about Ren and Ess, knowing they both were satisfied.

I don't lose manhood points for cuddling Essie to my chest, for nuzzling at her cheek until she turns her face to mine so I can kiss her. Essie's wrapped around me, knees clutching my waist, arms under my armpits and around my shoulders with her fingertips curled in my hair. I love how Essie makes love to me, even if I don't think I deserve it.

Not as messy this time, the grunt and lock-up are unmistakable. I'm going to Hell for what I do next, so it's a good thing I don't believe in religion. I believe Hell's inside my psyche. I learned this the other night, and I'm not ashamed to admit I Googled it after. During sex, the grunt and lock-up accompanied Essie's pussy sucking my cock dry like a hungry mouth. I know what this is for now, and the bastard in me times my orgasm with hers to gain the optimum benefits of her clenching.

Fingertips gripping Essie's hips so forcefully I know she'll find bruises tomorrow, I thrust my hips up and pound her down on my cock, not allowing either of us to budge while we come.

Groaning together, we can't maintain a kiss. It's worse. The orgasm is more intense– painfully so –when you're doing it with a purpose. Spurt after spurt of unrelenting Mason seed floods Essie's clenching pussy. I know deep down I'm going to Hell, and I don't regret it for a second.

"Uh… uh… uh…" I grunt over and over, my body quaking with aftershocks. Essie falls to my chest, panting and gasping for air. "Nap with me for a minute," I breathe, coaxing her to stay with me, to keep me inside her body for a few moments more.

"You'll have to call the Fire Department to move me. It might be a while before I'm mobile again." Laughing, Essie's pussy does that thing again, where it clenches me with abandon.

In a sluggish voice, years of stress fade away, "Passing out now…"

Conceiving a kid is hard work, especially when you're praying to a god you don't believe in. *Please, God, give me a reason to hope.*

CHAPTER TWENTY-TWO

Essie Prynne

"Mmm… Raven's skills are improving." Fork pointing into the bowl as he speaks, "She'll make some beaten dude a good wife," Devon says while chewing thoughtfully. "This marinara trumps Ren's jarred shit hands-down."

Head cradled between Dev's shoulder and neck, I cuddle up to his side while he leans against the back of one of my cushioned chairs. We used the stack of towels for my clients as tiny blankets and huge napkins. I wasn't hungry after earlier, still drowsy and sated. Dev went gangbusters on everything he brought, eating days and days' worth of food in a single sitting.

"Beaten dude? Really? Wife?" I don't get angry at Dev's Cro-Magnon bullshit like another woman would. It's just Dev.

After tossing the plastic storage container and the fork onto the coffee table with a flourish, Devon wraps both arms around me and sighs deeply. "Beaten dude: Rae's never had a boyfriend, and when she does, he'll have to answer to Chief Mason and three over-protective brothers."

Laughter bubbles up my throat. "I'm glad I was an only child."

"You've had someone who's beyond over-protective watching out for you," Devon whispers near my ear. I shudder from the vibration and the implication. The boy who was kind and attentive while I gave him a haircut reappears. Dev's content to simply sit here and talk while stroking my skin.

"Wife: my sister is fascinated with Clover because she wants to be what she never had– she's learning, emulating. We didn't have a real mother, and that's bound to change a girl. Isis and Rae are just the same when it comes to this. They have an obsession with getting married and having babies. It's the men's job to make sure it's the right guy."

"Because they can't pick for themselves?" I turn so I can stare daggers at the side of Devon's face. "I think Isis has already chosen her guys, and don't say a bad word about Robbie."

"Hey, my brothers and I were young with Isis. But Dad put Auggie and Robin through the ringer. Where Ren is all brawn, Dad is all brains and guns," he mutters cryptically. Dev's chest rises and falls as he silently laughs over a memory I'll never experience.

"I don't want to ruin the mood, but I have to talk about something that's driving me crazy." I hesitate when Devon freezes beneath me, and then I go for broke. "It bothered me at first how you were with Willow, and I know you feel guilty and it's eating you alive. I just wish I could talk to Willow about it, ease her into it– make her feel better."

"Don't," Devon warns in a cold voice. "Don't go there, Hester."

Ignoring Devon, needing to be heard, "Willow doesn't have anyone but me for advice. I've sheltered the shit out of her– our entire family has. I couldn't even talk to her about Auggie because too much stuff from my past cropped up, and then I choked. But I know you, and I can explain."

"No," he says with finality, closing out the conversation.

"Yes," I utter defiantly. "Willow is my family. I'm her best friend. She doesn't have any other girls to talk to. I know it was awkward and scary with you. I also know there were good parts as well, and I'm okay with that."

"Essie, I'm trying to protect you here." Devon turns to the side, gripping my shoulders, and gives a sharp shake to wake me up. "You don't get it, do you? The reason Willow has no one to talk to is her own fucking fault. She is going to go violent on you like a rabid dog after its owner. She'll turn on you the first chance she gets."

"You can't know that," I mutter, sounding delusional.

"I *do* know that," Devon stresses. "Do you know why I was comfortable hanging out with Willow? Do you want to know?" Dev shakes me, making it look like I'm nodding my head yes. "Because it was like I was hanging out with myself. Do you know who Willow should be talking to right now? Violet."

"Huh?" I grunt out, confused.

"Don't play stupid, Hester." Manic Devon is back. "I swear the only people who don't know about Clover's secret are Willow and Ren. As an only child, it's about time you learned about the family dynamics between siblings. Rae just knows I'm going to boss her ass around and not give her an inch to hang herself. I protect her. I love her. I guide her. And that's what Willow has always done with Seth."

"Willow's always been obsessed with Seth," I mutter.

"Not obsessed– Willow's been Seth's big *sister*. Now, onto Weston for me, because Willow's been doing this to Seth, too. I was the first of us kids to hold my baby brother after he was born. One look into that trusting face, and I knew I'd give him anything he ever asked. I held and fed and bathed and played and read him stories at bedtime– we all were Weston's mother. To this day, I will do anything to ensure Weston's happiness, even if it's wrong."

"There isn't a soul alive who could be mean to West." I decide I better tack on, "And survive."

"Exactly," Dev says wryly. Turning to sit cross-legged, he moves me until we're sitting face-to-face. "Ren is my brother, my best friend– my partner. I love him as much as I hate him. Instinctively, Willow's been doing this with Violet since the beginning, but she hasn't got the love part down yet. It's pure jealousy. I can't stop myself from feeling it, and it was worse because it was Ren who betrayed me with you."

I go to stop him, putting my hand against his chest. "Devon, no–"

"No, you have to hear me, Essie. You see Willow as your little sister, and you love her and want to help her. But she's been beating the shit out of her actual little sister forever. What do you think she's going to do to you? I almost killed Ren in his sleep, and the only reason I didn't is because the love always overpowered the hate. Willow's not going to blame me– she's going to *kill* you," he warns.

"No... I... Willow will understand if I'm the one to tell her." Devon gives me a funny look filled with guilt.

"I think you're fucking nuts, Essie, and that's saying a lot coming from me." Dark eyes filled with sadness level on me. "Willow didn't give two shits about me romantically– we're friends, that's it. But she's going to give two shits about you. It wouldn't have mattered who you touched, she's going to make it about her and take it out on you... and I'm going to hate her, and want to kill her every time she opens her goddamned mouth to say something nasty to you."

I want to heed Devon's warning, and a large part of me believes him– trusts his judgment. But the part of me that has always been Willow's big sister can't rationalize Willow ever hating me.

"It took me almost six years to forgive Ren, and I didn't until last night. If you think an eighteen-year-old Willow is going to open her arms and hug you instead of punch you, you're a lunatic. It's all my fault, and I take responsibility for it, but you're going to be the one living with the consequences."

"I know it was wrong, but at the same time, I don't know what the big fucking deal is," I mutter, on the edge of tears. "Willow was going to break up with you– you weren't even really dating. She wants your damn brother. It's your decision to make, on who you want to be with."

"Doesn't matter," Devon mutters. "It won't matter. Willow and I are a lot alike." Smirking privately, "It's why Ren and I get along. It's why Willow will find her way to Ren. It's why you and Willow get along. It's why we found our way to each other. It's about balance. Friends and lovers have to balance each other out."

Staring down at my hands, I whisper, "Willow's going to hate me."

Laughing at my absurdity, "Willow already hated you. I was with her during your twenty-first birthday party. Asshole that I am, even *I* couldn't stop thinking about you, and that self-absorbed cunt didn't even remember. Until Willow grows up, you're dead to her."

Flinching, "You don't have to be so cruel," I whine.

Lifting my chin with a fingertip to make me look at him, "Being cruel would be to allow you to walk into the lion's mouth and let her crush you to death. If you went to Willow with blinders on and tried to have a heart-to-heart, it would hurt worse than knowing it was coming. If you love Willow, and I know you do, you're going to have to be strong and patient, and wait her out."

"I don't know if I can do that." I lower my head in defeat. "I'm going to want to apologize, and to defend myself, and to make her understand."

"Willow's incapable of hearing you right now." Devon's rumble of laughter brings my head back up. I narrow my eyes at him and he laughs harder. Face flushed, eyes bright, Devon's entertained in the extreme by the shit he dumped into my lap.

"Essie, the best advice I can give you is to pretend Willow's me. Use the tactics you've used to handle me on her."

"I'll try," I mumble, feeling lost and alone. I want to be happy with Devon, but I'm worried about him, worried about the present and the future. But it's hard to overcome the worry when I'm afraid I'll lose Willow forever.

"I'm sorry, Essie," Devon says in a deep voice filled with sympathy. "I never apologize to anyone for any reason. I don't believe in apologies because what's done is done– it's over and nothing will change it. But in this case, while I'm not sorry for what I did, or how I did it, or who I did it with, I'm sorry you're going to get hurt, and that's different."

"You don't need to apologize." I reach out to grab Devon's hand. "I was right there with you while *we* did it– *we* did it together, and *we*'re in this together. The same reason you apologized to me is why I must apologize to Willow."

"Yeah, well…" Devon stands up, and then looks down at me with eyes filled with intense sadness. "There is a difference, Essie."

Devon begins to dress and he never explains, so I do the same thing. That's how we work together. When he's done with a conversation, I don't fight him for more. I don't turn psycho-female and demand answers, and I expect the same respect in return.

Quietly, we work as a team to straighten up my room and put it back to rights. Obsessed about cleanliness in my work environment, I wipe everything down with disinfectant, even if we were nowhere near it.

Fully dressed, bags in hand, Devon stops me before I open the door to the salon. "The difference," he stresses, "Is that Willow will only blame *you*."

"Fuck me," is rolling off my tongue as I open the door. Eyes widening, I repeat, "Fuck me," for another reason entirely.

Salon is open for business, with Bethany curling Margaret Webster's hair with a curling iron. Elma is at the front desk, studying my list of improvements with a scowl on her face.

I swear to God, Devon turns into another person from one heartbeat to the next. He hitches up his pant leg, and then swaggers across the salon like a badassed, cocky motherfucker decked out in a police uniform. "Just grabbing some lunch together," he announces with his *'trust me, I'm a cop'* smile. He raises his bags as evidence of our innocence. I would be hilarious if it wasn't so fucking disturbing.

"It's three o'clock in the afternoon," Bethany deadpans, looking disappointed but not angry with me.

"Almost time for supper," Elma adds, still perusing my list of ideas.

"It sounds more like a nooner that turned into a three-hour tryst to me," Peggy says with a glare.

Feigning innocence while we all try to keep our composure, Devon turns into quite the thespian. Hand clasped to his chest, acting shocked, "Peggy, wherever did you hear such a word? Maybe I should start attending church, since the minister teaches such worldly concepts. But I don't think it's a good place for your grandchildren. Seth and Violet should never hear such a thing."

"Spreading it on a little thick, there, aren't ya?" I whisper out the side of my mouth at Devon. In reply, his grin turns up in wattage.

"Who do you think taught me that word?" Peggy says to whoever will listen.

"My guess?" Bethany saves the day. She puts the curling iron down and passes Peggy a hand mirror. "Looking good, Mrs. Webster."

Distracted from Devon, "Your guess?" Peggy asks Bethany as she fishes her payment out of her huge overnight-sized handbag, and then presses it into Beth's hand.

Tucking the money into her apron, "Lovely Violet swears like a pissed off pirate into his cups," Beth says with a straight face. "And she learned every word from Willow."

"Who learned every word from Clover," Elma adds, but this time she's smirking. "I always did love those Prynne girls."

"*Webster*," Peggy stresses, and then stomps out of Salon.

"That woman needs to get laid good and proper," Elma growls. "She's the most frustrated bitch I've ever seen. How Clover puts up with her shit is beyond me."

"Well," Devon interrupts my boss's diatribe on sex after fifty. "I was due back to work almost a half hour ago. Colin's going to put an APB out on his car if I don't get it back to the station."

"The car's not hard to find, boy," no nonsense Elma blurts out. "It's been hanging out at the curb for almost four hours, after sitting there earlier this morning. I suspect you'd be back again for *supper* if your dad didn't force your ass to do your job."

"It's rather hard to miss a Fairport Police Cruiser hanging out on Main, a block from the Courthouse," Bethany says drolly.

"I live across the street, ya know. There's no getting away from Salon for me." Elma looks beyond exhausted.

I charge forward, trying to defuse the situation. "I'm sorry, Elma. We didn't lose many customers, did we?"

"No." Elma rests her elbow on the counter, then lays her head in her palm. "Peggy pounded on my damn door to tattle like a child. I pretended I wasn't home, but she got louder. It's a good thing you locked the door to the backroom. Her hand was on the doorknob, twisting with all her might, and Peggy's mighty."

"And that would be when I showed up." Beth tosses me a look like I owe her one.

"I've got to go," Devon reminds me. "I'll see ya around, Ess."

"Okay." I choke up, knowing this is our anticlimactic *goodbye-for-now*.

"See ya," Devon says again, looking awkward and sheepish. He leans down, brushing his forehead against mine, pushing my face backward, then he feathers a soft kiss to my lips. "See ya," he whispers again as he pulls away.

On the verge of tears, "See ya," I parrot back. "Behave," I beg, hand reaching up to twist into his shirt, keeping him with me.

"No promises on that front." I expect a chuckle or an '*I'm kidding*' to follow, but he's being serious. "Here, read this when you're alone." Devon tucks a note folded into a tiny triangle into my palm, reminiscent of junior high. "See ya."

Gobsmacked, I just stare at the note in my hand instead of at Devon's back as he leaves me. I don't look back up until he's pulling the cruiser away from the curb.

"What the fuck was that?" Bethany flashes me a look of utter disbelief. "Didn't we just go through this shit less than seventy-two hours ago? Again? You're shittin' me, Ess."

I turn my back away from Beth and Elma, and just stare at the door to the backroom. What we did and said in there feels like an eternity ago.

I want to tell Bethany I need my best friend right now, not a therapist or a mother. She can't force me to scrub Devon off my skin and out of my body, and then hand me that evil pill again. I won't survive it this time.

"Leave the girl alone," Elma rushes to my defense, flooring me. My tears dry up in an instant. If this crotchety old woman gets it, then I'm not imagining it. "That boy manipulated our Essie."

"Yeah, but she didn't have to allow it," Beth grumbles.

"I manipulated him, too," I admit loudly, saying the words for the first time. "I always have."

Elma laughs, causing Bethany and me to turn to her in shock. In three years, we've never heard the woman laugh– not once. "The boy's a piece of work– a *hot* piece of work… What? I'm old, not dead." Elma's offended at our gape-mouthed expression. "But as long as the manipulation flows both ways, it'll work out just fine."

"It doesn't work that way," Bethany argues. "People need to respect each other."

"HA!" Elma scoffs. "This coming from a girl who's never been married. George and I were together for fifty-four years…" Pointing her middle finger in Beth's face. "And let me tell you something, missy. The only way someone can manipulate you is if you let 'em. Essie, here, she's wants whatever that Mason kid plants in her. Lay off and be her friend."

"It was just lunch," I mumble. I walk to the front door and tear my **Out to Lunch** sign down.

Elma barks a laugh while Bethany twists out, "Yeah, tell that to the bite mark on your neck and the *fucked hard* hairstyle you're rocking. Let's not forget how Devon just swaggered out of here like he scored the winning touchdown at the Super Bowl."

I turn to Bethany, tears in my eyes. "Don't judge, kay? If Rory had pulled up in his pussy magnet and yanked you inside, you would've went, no questions asked." Bethany tries to protest, but I cut her off. "And I would've been happy for you, and then held you when he crushed your heart."

Bethany walks toward me with her right hand held out. Confused, I take her hand. "Deal," Beth promises while we shake on it, and then she pulls me into a hug. "You'll always be my girl, even if you're stupid and smell like Devon."

Laughing through the tears, I squeeze Bethany back.

"What exactly is anal bleaching, and why are you offering it at the *Primp Day Spa*?" Elma asks, causing Bethany and me to bust out in hysterics.

CHAPTER TWENTY-THREE

Devon Mason

"Where were you all afternoon?" Dad interrogates me, but at least it's in private. He's not stupid, so he called my cellphone instead of using the police radio. My phone rang ten seconds after I reported my location to dispatch.

"I had shit to do." I grunt dismissively. "In other words, don't pressure me to answer something I'm not going to answer, something you already have the answer to. I'm in a horrible fucking mood."

Dad's sigh is amplified by the phone, stinging my ear, and I just know he's tearing his hair out at the roots over me. "And this is different than yesterday, or last week, or last year, how?"

"It's not," I grumble.

I'm sitting in Colin's car on County Route 5, just outside of Fairport's city limits. I'm in a dip, making me invisible to passing drivers. It's just after four in the afternoon– primetime. We, as in Fairport Police Department, get a kick out of finding little hidey holes that are fresh, and a big fucking surprise when we haul ass outta them to pull naughty drivers over. Eyes on the rearview mirror, I wait for approaching cars with my radar gun resting out my window.

"Well, I do know where you were, and I have a good idea of what you were doing, and who you were doing it with, so I'm just calling to ask how you're doing. You okay?"

I click the radar gun at a passing vehicle– a red Tahoe going four miles over the limit. No fun in that. "Not really," I mutter dryly. "I'd rather go back to around one o'clock this afternoon, and then freeze time. But since I'm not living in a fantasy world… not gonna fucking happen, Dad."

Treading lightly, because Dad is the master of pussy-footing around me, "Was it okay?"

"It wasn't the first time," I admit, feeling sort of cocky out of nowhere. "It was the fourth time, and each time was better than the last."

I'm a total bastard, and I get off on the shocked silence my confession brings. Right now, I'm sober and feel dead inside, so if shock-value makes me feels something, I'll take it. I smirk while clocking a Subaru at fifty-three miles per hour.

"Oh... When? How? And what happened with–"

"Shut the fuck up!" I warn, instantly turning rabid. "That topic is not to be discussed."

I know Dad so well, that the sound of his chair squeaking gives me a perfect visage of him sitting at his desk, elbows resting on the desktop, leaning his forehead on his palm. I exhaust him, and that makes me feel sick in the gut.

"So, you're not talking to anyone about Willow, or just me?"

"I'm sure you've already interrogated Ren, so you know he's keeping his mouth shut under penalty of death." A Prius pops into my mirror, and I don't even bother clocking it. They couldn't speed if they tried. "I killed it between Willow and me in a very permanent way, so that's over and we can all move on. As for talking to anyone, I'm not real big on that."

"Devon, please," Dad begs, and my eyes instantly tear up, which pisses my ass off.

"Everyone involved knows all they need to know." Breathing deeply, I blink a few times to push my reaction to Dad away. "Yes, I spoke to Ren... don't go sticking your nose into my shit."

"What are you doing tonight?"

I answer the questions he's actually asking. "I'm sober, have been for days. But don't get your hopes up. I'm not on the sobriety wagon, and I won't feel guilty when I dope up again, either. I plan on not being sober minutes after shift change, provided I find what I'm looking for, that is."

I miss whatever bullshit Dad replies with when an unmistakable Lexus comes into view. "Where are the kids?" I interrupt a barrage of screaming accusations.

"Sometimes I want to wring your goddamned neck," Dad growls. "The kids are wandering around somewhere. Why?"

"Gotta go." I pull the radar gun out of my window, and then turn over the ignition.

"Devon–"

"Speeder. Gotta go. I'll be careful, and I love you." I drop my phone into the passenger seat. Out of habit, the lights and sirens are flicked on before I even crank the wheel to get out of my hidey hole.

I have no clue whether or not Sage was speeding since I never clocked him, but I have to check something out for my own peace of mind. I know for a fact that he's speeding now, since after I pull out, he's long gone. Adrenalin pumping through my veins, I push my car to eighty-seven miles per hour before I spot his tail in the distance.

I'm not a police officer because it was required by Mason blood. I'm a cop because I'm damn good at it, and I love it. I may break more laws than I enforce, but that's because I'm a maniac by definition.

West's hot piece of ass is a little speeder. Sage Fischer has an expensive car that hugs curves at a fast rate of speed. Our squad cars are only a few years old, and they can beat just about every vehicle in the county, except for Rory's Challenger and our family car... and apparently, Gay Sage's Lexus.

I excelled in the academy during driving tactical maneuvers. I was the only idiot with a death wish who didn't care how fast he drove. I've wrecked a few times, but I learned from my mistakes. Sage has a faster, better car, but he's a newbie driver. I'm on his ass in less than a minute. His petrified expression glancing at me in his rearview mirror is priceless.

Sage is a good kid, and he pulls over even though he's breaking a law other than speeding. I go through the motions, pretending to go by the book. I talk into the mic without pressing the button, reciting GOLF-ALPHA-YANKEE-SIERRA-ALPHA-GOLF-ECHO as his license plate number. I slowly get out of my vehicle, palm on the butt of my gun as I approach the driver's side.

I rap on the window with my knuckles, and it's lowering before I even pull away. "Driver's license and registration, please," I order brusquely, like I don't know who I pulled over—like I always do. "Do you know why I pulled you over this afternoon, sir?" I flick my tablet open to transcribe whatever bullshit Sage is going to feed me.

"I... I..." Sage is stuttering as his license materializes in his shaking fingertips.

With a straight face, I lean into the window. "Don't piss your pants, buddy. I'm just fucking with ya." I wink at Weston, who's as white as a ghost.

"I thought you were Colin," West gasps out, clutching at the steering wheel. "I think I did piss my pants."

"I told you it was Dev!" Rae shouts from the backseat. "But your ass didn't believe me!"

Leaning my hip against the door, I ask, "So where y'all off to on a school night?"

Swallowing thickly, Sage is trying to get his beating heart under control. "Just driving around, listening to music. We can't really be seen in town."

"With a chaperone, I see," I point at my sister. "Good idea."

"We're not doing anything wrong," Weston grumbles, looking like a cock-blocked man, if I've ever seen one. "I'm being good."

"Not what I heard from Ren the other night," I mutter, thoroughly amused.

I bark a sharp laugh when Sage's tiny face whips to the side to glare West down. "*We*, as in Weston and I, have behaved," Sage stresses while staring at my brother. "So, I don't know what Ren said, but it wasn't about *me*."

Gulping, looking as guilty as sin, Weston chokes out a, "What?"

"Next time you're in the locker room, make sure it's empty and the door is locked. Ren's stomach isn't strong enough for such a sight," I tease.

"Oh," Sage draws out. "*That*. I knew about that already."

Rae leans between the seats, grinning like a villain. "I wanna know!"

Mortified, Sage and Weston shout in unison, "NO!"

"Well, kids, you have a good drive back to town with Raven interrogating you from the back seat."

"Christ," Weston snarls, banging his skull on the headrest three or four times.

I lean back into the window and get into Sage's perfect face. "Slow your ass down, pretty boy. I hit ninety before I caught up with ya. There's precious cargo in this car, and it's fragile–breakable. If you break it and survive, I break you. Got it?"

"Copacetic," Sage mutters, looking like he's about to piss his pants.

"Perfect," I purr while smiling as I lean back out. I pat Sage's car door and shout, "Have fun, kids!"

I laugh all the way back to the squad car. I can hear Raven lobbing questions left and right, and Weston answers them without shame. Baby boy has finally reached his Masonhood.

I sit in the car for a minute, waiting for the kids to drive off. I reach over and send a quick text to Dad because I know how he worries.

All's good. I'm headed back to the station.

I get an instantaneous reply. **I love you too, son.**

About a mile outside of town, a plume of smoke visualizes in my peripheral. I turn down the gravel drive to our local legend– Whitehall Hospital was abandoned almost forty years ago when they built a more modern hospital in a central location for the county. In that time span, the new hospital has been upgraded a few times, and here Whitehall sits untouched. Whitehall is the work of legends, ghost stories that keep generations of terrified children away.

In the parking lot, a pair of dumbasses torch a Volkswagen Beetle. Dumbass #1's hair matches the flames as he watches Dumbass #2 go balls to the wall on her own car. At a safe distance, I lean against the front bumper of the police cruiser and record the action with my cellphone. I'm sure Ren would get a kick out of watching this.

It would take a cold-hearted bastard not to get upset by the sight of Willow taking a maul to her flaming car hood– the very hood I made love to Essie on a few nights ago. I try to block out the emotions that are slowly filtering through the fog in my mind, but the darkness welcomes the anguish with open arms, and together they feed the depression.

I pretend I'm not crying, that I don't feel guilty, that I'm not going to miss Willow, that I never wanted her, or cared for her, or loved her. But I cannot lie to myself because the depression won't allow it. In a fog thicker than the black smoke fueled by burning plastic, rubber, and vinyl, the depression descends with a vengeance.

Heart hammering into my ribcage, lungs seizing, eyes leaking, I watch a wrecked Willow destroy her car with Auggie's help. Willow screams, descending into her own pit of despair. Madness takes over as she stares at her burning car with tears tracking down her face.

I want to be mad at Auggie, at Robin, at Kieren, at Essie, but I'm only angry with myself. I'm the one to blame. I gave them all power over me when I played their game by their rules. I should've never entered a vengeance quest that played into their hands. I should've told Robin, *"Fuck you. I'm not dating Willow. She's my friend, and I want her to stay that way."* I should've told Essie all those years ago, *"I love you, but I'll hurt you. It's your choice to suffer with me."* I shouldn't have forgiven Ren last night, because there was nothing to forgive– he did nothing wrong in the first place.

I allowed them to control me, and it spiraled out of control. We all need to grow the fuck up and move on. The biggest assholes amongst us need to grow up the most.

Auggie violently tugs Willow out of the burning car, where she was taking a reciprocating saw to the passenger seat. He tears the saw out of her hand, and tosses it to the ground. He hefts the girl over his shoulder and stalks over to his pickup truck. She's fighting him every step of the way. Her screams will haunt my nightmares until I draw my last breath.

Once Willow is safely belted into the seat, Auggie goes back for the tools of destruction, chucking them into the bed of his truck. He climbs in, and then drives off.

"You shouldn't play with fire," I call after Willow, even though she can't hear me. "You could've said no too. It's not all on me. You should've loved my brother enough to tell Auggie to fuck off, to not go after me and screw me. It's your fault too, little girl. Whether you admit it to yourself or not."

I unhook my radio mic from my shoulder. "We have a 503 in progress at Whitehall. Better call FFD. We have a code 2 vehicle fire."

I lean back against my car, watching flames from Hell invade Earth. "Well, it's going to be a long, miserable night now." The gas tank explodes with a large whoosh that vibrates the ground beneath my feet. Dryly, sarcastically, I continue to talk to myself. "Thanks, Willow. Thanks."

CHAPTER TWENTY-FOUR

Kieren Mason

I don't know why I'm so nervous. I never understood the term *butterflies in your stomach* before. Camille Mason sort of destroyed the excitement of the unknown and turned it into misery. Unless it involved bodily harm, and even then it would have to be like losing an appendage, I never got scared or nervous over anything. It's why I played ball so well. There was no such thing as pre-game jitters because I knew no one on the field was going to rape or murder me, or commit suicide in front of me. After the life I've lived, running plays on the field was easy.

It took a '**Wanna hang out???** ☺' to bring me to my knees.

It's not like it's a date or anything. I've been on hundreds of dates, all of which were a means to an end. And by that, I mean fucking in a car. It was never special, and more often than not, completely forgettable.

A simple night of hanging out on the sofa with Willow is terrifying me. Go figure. I can't imagine how I'd feel if it was a date, especially one ending with sex. I'd experience my first episode of erectile dysfunction, for sure.

With a deep breath, I rub my sweaty palms on my jeans, and then reach for the doorbell. A hollow, ominous gong rolls through the Spook House.

Jesus, I'm shaking.

The creak of the door is like a shot to my ass. "Hi," Willow greets me. She looks tired and sad, like she's been crying for hours. I decide it'd be rude to comment.

Aunt Isis taught me to keep my mouth shut on commenting about a lady's appearance, unless it's to say she looks nice. By taught, I mean she kicked me in the nuts for asking if she was gaining weight. I didn't mean she looked fat, even though she took it that way. I thought she looked healthy.

You know what's ruder? Not replying. "Hi," flows lamely from my lips. "Thanks for inviting me. The kids were off with their friends, Dad's still at the station, and Dev was on a call. I was all alone."

Willow flinches when I say my brother's name, and I add that to the long list of dos and don'ts. It would be easier if Willow would bring up their break-up. Technically, I'm here tonight as the buddy, since I don't know Willow's single.

Willow's smoky voice sounds even raspier than usual. "I didn't want to be alone, either." She steps to the side to allow me to enter. "Everyone's at Rush. The house is empty. Just you and me."

"Cool." I sound like a fucking dolt. "I brought some snacks. It's nothing much. Just grabbed them out of the cupboard before… yeah, before they were devoured."

Catching my slip-up, "The munchies will do that to ya… and food will disappear before your eyes when you have a resident drug addict."

Nope, Willow doesn't sound bitter at all. Not. At. All. This should be fun, and by fun, I mean torturous.

Willow just walks away without so much as a backward glance or a *follow me this way, Stud.* She's really upset tonight.

I shut and lock the door behind me, not knowing the Spook House's open-door policy. But if I had an eighty pound eighteen-year-old in here, I'd lock this monstrosity up tighter than a homophobe's asshole. And by homophobe's asshole, I mean mine.

I debate sitting in the living room and waiting for Willow to return, but what if she doesn't? I follow the sound of opening and closing cupboard doors, and find Willow rutting around in the kitchen like a hungry raccoon at a campground dumpster.

On the kitchen island is a growing supply of junk food. I toss my bags of chips and handful of candy bars on the pile. "Just curious…"

Willow's, "Yeah," comes muffled with her head in the refrigerator and her ass sticking out of it.

"Are we by chance reliving an afterschool special? Ya know, where the girls binge-eat while watching movies, they do a heart-to-heart conversation with loads of crying, and then the skinny one runs off to the bathroom to shove her finger down her throat and secretly puke."

Popping out of the fridge, arms loaded with soda and chocolate milk, "Huh? Are you asking if I'm bulimic, Stud?"

Thank God, I'm back to Stud again. "I hope you're not."

"I'm not," Willow reassures me. "Worse, I'm a fucking hog. Someday my metabolism will slow down and I'll weigh three hundred pounds and some change. But hopefully, I'll grow me some tits in the process."

I'm not sure how to respond to that as the buddy. I know how I want to respond to that, but I'm not going there. "Healthy's all I give a shit about," I settle on instead.

Plunking a quart of chocolate milk, three cans of orange pop, and a can of grape on the counter, Willow pulls off a patent-pending Auggie eyebrow raise. "No fucking way am I healthy, Stud."

I wait in awe as Willow pulls a supermarket basket from beneath the sink and starts filling it with junk food. "The stash in my room is gone. I have a mini-fridge so I don't have to come back down here every few minutes for a snack."

Petrified, my voice breaks, "We're going to your room?"

"Yeah, Stud." Willow snorts. "I won't molest you unless you want me to. But we sure as shit ain't sitting in the living room. That sofa sees more action than a whore's cunt. When Auggie and I came home tonight, Rob and Isis were making out, and Auggie just went in there and watched 'em. Fucking creeped my ass out. I haven't walked in there since."

The haunted look in Willow's eyes isn't from tonight. It's from a few nights ago, and the memory stars he-who-shall-remain-unmentioned. In one of his fits, Devon told me every single detail of what happened on that sofa, hoping to upset me.

If Willow's not going to bring it up, neither am I. I grab her supermarket basket to be a gentleman. "Lead the way, Spanky. I'll watch your ass as you go," slips out by accident, but I earn a giggle for my faux pas.

Looking over her shoulder as she traverses the kitchen steps to the second floor, "Only part of me worth watching." Willow reveals insecurities I didn't think she had.

Eyes glued to Willow's spankable ass every step she takes. "Ah, I remember your ass well on your birthday, Spanky." I growl before I can stop myself. "I remember how each of your cheeks fit perfectly in the palm of my hands, and how you groaned into my mouth when I squeezed them."

Opening the door to her room, Willow lets me into her world. "Ah, I remember that, too, Stud." Leaning into me as I walk by to set the basket on her bed, she whispers near my ear. "But I remember the sensation of my knee coming into contact with your nuts more so."

Ah, Willow's a psycho-flirt. "Spanky, I never figured you for a dirty girly." I put the basket on the bed, and then turn back to her. Her cheeks are pinked and a flush is creeping up her neck. "Do you know what else I remember?"

Standing in the middle of her bedroom, open door at her back, Willow puts her hands on her hips and stares me down. "I'm scared now. But go ahead and shock me," Willow challenges.

I cross about a dozen invisible boundaries. "I remember how you were close to coming for me. The little puff of a sound you made as you ground against my bulge, how you left behind a big wet spot on my jeans… and that was just at Rush. Let's not forget the Revolutionary Road concert."

Huge brown eyes bugging out, mouth gaping open like a blowjob queen, Willow stammers with her arms flailing about. "Hands down, Stud. *Hands down*, you win." She literally bows down to me while laughing. "Not my best moment, but clearly a memorable one."

"C'mon, ya got to at least add pleasurable to the list," I taunt, liking this naughty, easy to tease side of Willow.

"Oh, it was that in spades, Stud. In. Spades." Willow grabs the basket, then starts putting the stuff away. "So, I have a bunch of awesome shit saved up on the Hopper. Have you ever watched Game of Thrones? Rob's way into it, and keeps begging me to watch so we can discuss."

"I'm game," rolls off my tongue. "Weston wanted to watch it, but Rae wouldn't let him. Not sure what's up with that."

I wander around Willow's room, checking out her stuff. Everything is brand new, like she hasn't quite moved in yet. But it's definitely Willow's geeky style.

Willow snickers quietly as she loads the mini-fridge with pop and chocolate milk. "It's HBO. Rae shouldn't be watching it either."

"Rae's sixteen– she can handle it. If it's sex you're worried about with the show, from what I saw last month, that shouldn't be a problem for Weston."

"Ugh, gross." Willow's face twists up in revulsion. "The thought of Seth getting it on makes me puke in my mouth a little bit. Even though West is the youngest, he's full-grown looking and adorable, so I can swallow it."

"Trust me. It was gross to witness. The look on his face when he was... never mind what he was doing. I literally puked." I shudder and get sick to my stomach just remembering it. No one should see their baby brother molesting their football bro.

"Well, I'm going to go get my PJs on." Willow pulls back the covers on her bed, and it's like she kicked me in the junk again. I whimper in pain and divert my eyes from her cozy-looking sheets. "Take your shoes and socks off and get in. Just don't get any crumbs in my bedding. The shit was expensive."

Two minutes later... I'm still staring down at Willow's exposed bottom sheet in terror. She was my brother's girl a few days ago– she had sex with him a few days ago. I know she's not offering me that, but is she trying to torture me?

Only one way to find out. I kick my shoes off and tear my socks off. I climb into Willow's big bed and try not to freak out. It's so soft and cozy, and it smells like Willow. Surreal.

"I'm back," Willow warns, sticking her head out the bathroom door to peer into her bedroom, like she's checking to make sure I'm not misbehaving.

"Oh, God," I gulp when she walks out of the bathroom wearing the Wreck & Ruin t-shirt I gave her this afternoon, and nothing else but a pair of boy shorts. Shorts I'm pretty sure are her actual underwear.

Willow locks her bedroom door, grabs two sodas from the fridge and a bag of Cheetos off her dresser. She flicks the lights off, and then crawls into bed... with me.

"Just so we're clear," I rasp in a very deep voice. "I'm not your girlfriend. I will not paint your toenails unless I get to suck your toes first."

"Okay?" Willow laughs heartily.

"I'm not your guy friend who gives you advice on other dudes who want to fuck you," I warn.

"Pretty sure that won't come up, but yeah."

"If you ask, I'll give you bad advice on purpose."

Willow gasps, "Why?"

"Because I want to fuck you, like seriously wreck your pussy," I admit shamelessly.

"So I've gathered." Willow's voice is husky, like she's okay with the fact that I'm being lewd and blatantly honest.

I sober up and go for broke. "I'm crossing lines so you know where we stand, and I'll back off when I'm finished. I like you, Willow. I want to hang out with you– be your buddy. Your friend. Just know, someday, when you're ready, I want to take you on a real date, and I don't expect you to kiss me when I deliver you safe and sound to the Spook House's front door."

It's dark in Willow's room, because she hasn't turned the TV on yet. She's frozen next to me, speechless. But she isn't quiet. Willow is gasping for air, and I wait for her to get her emotions under control.

The TV glows to life, and I become worried that I ruined what I was building with Willow before it even started. She scrolls through the DVR, selects Game of Thrones, and then presses play on episode one.

When the HBO logo pops onto the screen, Willow breathes, "Okay." She accepts my conditions, and then tears open the Cheetos and begins crunching.

We spend the next few hours engrossed with violence, treachery, and a pair of incestuous twins. I'm the idiot who falls in love with a bunch of wolf puppies, and Willow teases the shit out of me because of it… and it was the best, most carefree two hours of my life.

CHAPTER TWENTY-FIVE

Devon Mason

I walk up to the front door of Rush, and it opens before I can reach the door handle. "You look like shit," Rory says while eyeing me over. "You here to see your aunt?"

"Nah…" I yawn, dead on my feet. But if I go to sleep, I might not wake up as I am now. I might end up staring at the ceiling for the rest of my life, eyes tracking all movement but not giving a shit otherwise.

The question is, does Dad want a drug addict son, or an institutionalized one? The climate of Fairport this evening screams Dad's keen on locking me up in a padded room for life, and that thought terrifies me.

A violent shiver starts at my feet and works its way up my spine. Tightening muscles are the preamble to vicious cramping. My stomach roils from a mix of hunger, fear, and withdrawal. I haven't had any pot in days, and no speed or coke in over a week, and my body is starting to shut down on me– not to mention my fucking mind. I need to shut off my emotions. All I feel is misery. Eyes open or closed, all I can see is Essie as she tried not to cry when I left her this afternoon. All I can hear is Willow's screams and my father's frustrated tirade over having such a piece of shit as his eldest son.

I'm suffocating. Black is creeping in along the edges of my vison. I'm fading out– the Devon everyone knows is dying.

Rory's strong hand grips my shoulder to keep me on my feet. "I can't let you in otherwise. You know the rules. Until you're twenty-one, you can only come on Saturday nights when your dad is here, or if you're visiting your aunt. That's it."

Swaying, half my mind is in the now, the other half is swimming through pure, unadulterated terror. Desperation causes me to behave as I feel on the inside, not as how I portray myself to the outside world. "Rory, I don't have time for this shit.

My day started out good yet sad, and then it turned into a living nightmare. I just need to get inside Rush for a few minutes, and then I'll leave."

Crossing his arms over his mammoth chest, "I can't. Sorry."

"I should have lied– why didn't I lie?" I mumble flatly, causing Rory to chuckle. "Truth?"

Leaning against the door, Rory's not budging for nothing. "Always."

"I can find worse shit on the streets than I can inside Rush. It's Auggie's domain, and it's clean as a virgin bride on her wedding night."

"I feel ya, and I know who you're looking for. Kurt ain't in there. I heard word you were after him. So, if I know, he knows."

"Jesus Christ," I snarl, tugging at my hair. "That cocksucker eluded me all fucking night. I'm not going to arrest him."

"Kurt's not worried about being arrested– he's worried about being jumped for his stash."

"Smart man," I grumble, because that was exactly what I was going to do. "I can't shake-down the dealers if Dad keeps arresting their suppliers, goddamnit!"

"You're going to have to go," Rory says calmly, but his patience is wearing thin. "It's a dead night anyway, with all the owners in house. You don't want to go in there looking like you do. Do you honestly think Malcolm didn't alert everyone to your evening plans, bud? If you want to get high, you shouldn't tell your dad beforehand."

"I was… I was just jerking his chain because he was smothering me. Motherfuck!" I shout to the night sky. "No wonder Fairport is dead tonight and all the cops are patrolling. FUCK!"

"You can talk to me, if ya want, bud," Rory offers sympathetically.

I like the guy, so I don't respond as nastily as I normally would. "I don't talk," I grunt. "Is Tina home?"

"Yeah, Tina's here. She was told to stay home, same with the rest of her… kind." I roll my eyes at Rory's inability to call Tina a whore, but that's not the kind he was talking about. Drug dealer.

Smirking evilly, "Ya gotta let me in to see Tina, Rory. Rules are rules. I can visit family all I want."

"Tina's not your family," Rory reminds me.

"Hmm…" I tap my chin. "I beg to differ. No one will ever dispute Auggie being my uncle, blood or not. Lisa, Auggie, and Tina were living in my house when I was born. Tina was sleeping in a crib beside me for a good year before Lisa found another man, and they kept coming back between men until Lisa married Patrick."

"Go get high, asshole." Rory snarls, stepping to the side to let me inside Rush. "It's your funeral."

It's the middle of the week and Rush is empty. Literally empty. They didn't even turn the sound system on, and the bartender is gone. Rory warned me about the owners being in house, but I assumed they'd be in their playpen. My aunt, Auggie, and Rob are sitting in a booth next to the hallway– the hallway I have to enter to go upstairs.

Fuck!

"Don't bother turning tail and running," Auggie's booming voice fills Rush. "We saw the Camaro enter the parking lot, jackass." My eyes flick around to the windowless warehouse-shaped nightclub. "Security cameras. Rory doesn't stand at the door like a dog awaiting its master."

"I warned you, but you didn't listen," Rory gloats on his way by me. "I'm calling it a night. Later." He waves to the wayward trio, and then he makes his way down the hallway to the hidden entrance to the staircase.

"Dad's been super busy tonight, I see." I laugh at Chief Mason's tenacity the entire time it takes me to walk across the club. "Is the town on lockdown? Curfew? All because Officer Devon Mason was jerking his old man's chain? Bit drastic, don't ya think?"

I approach the booth. Rob's avidly watching me, like I'm entertaining the fuck out of him. Aunt Isis has concern etched across her face. Auggie, he's furious: nostrils flaring, green eyes enflamed, fingers clenching the tabletop.

"Jerking his chain, or finally telling the truth? Why did you pay a visit to every single dealer in Fairport this evening?" Auggie interrogates me while his cohorts play witness.

"Why were all their suppliers sitting in the holding cell? It's like we're hosting a fucking drug dealer caucus down at the Courthouse tonight," I rattle off snidely. "It won't do any good. If anything, they're plotting together… and now there are no drugs to be found in this godforsaken stick-up-the-ass town!"

"Chief Mason believes Fairport should be a drug-free zone," Rob grumbles, looking guilty as all hell. I raise an eyebrow at what he said, but I don't comment about Mary and her gardening.

"Mayor Ross is very pleased with your father, Devon. You should feel proud that the Governor is going to give your department a commendation on a job well done." Auggie smirks, and I want to put my fist through his smug fucking face.

"I. Need. Drugs. Tonight." I seethe, barely keeping my shit together. "I'm going upstairs, and if you've emptied out Tina's stash again, I'm going to come back down here and kill you."

"Oh," Auggie barks out an arrogant laugh. "Look who's a badassed drug addict now. Are you looking to add another notch to your belt with my sister's name?" Auggie leans toward me, glaring. "You think you get a prize for screwing three pussies in less than a week since you lost your virginity, boy?"

"I hate your fucking guts," I grit out between clenched teeth. "I had to clean up your goddamned mess tonight. Did you tell your boyfriend how you helped his niece torch her car? Did you?" I smash my cellphone into Robin's hand. "Watch this."

It's a good thing Rob's on the opposite side of the booth from Auggie. Lunging halfway across the table, Isis catches Rob before he strangles Auggie to death.

"Have fun with that, assholes," I snarl. "I'm going upstairs now. To. Get. High." I walk two steps, and then turn back around to set Auggie straight. "Just because Tina's beautiful doesn't mean I want to fuck her," I say pointedly to Auggie. "You ought to look at my aunt if you don't know what I mean. Being hot doesn't automatically make you a whore, fuckface."

Rob's curled up in the corner of the booth, with Isis holding him hostage. My cellphone is gripped in his hand as he watches Willow come undone. He's wicked pissed, and not at me.

Handing my phone back, "I sent it to my cell. Thanks." In one fell swoop, Rob jumps onto the tabletop to get around Isis, smashes Auggie's hand with his boot, and then hops to the floor. "Don't come home tonight if you want to wake up breathing," Rob warns as he crosses to Rush's front door.

"Fuck you very much, druggie," Auggie growls at me. "I hate you, too. How about that?"

"How about that?" I mock. "How about that's fucking sick coming from my uncle. How about you grow the fuck up, Auggie? How about you treat my aunt with some goddamned respect?" I lean into Auggie's face, not caring that my death is mirrored in his eyes. "How. About. That?"

Silent, Auggie just stares at me, face twisted up as if he's taking a shit. I can see the wheels spinning in his head. If tonight was a night I felt my normal, I wouldn't say what comes out of my mouth next. "I don't hate you, Uncle Auggie. I hate what you do. I hate what *I* do. But I don't hate either one of us."

"Don't go upstairs, then," Auggie whispers sadly. "Please."

"I'm going upstairs to get high because I have to. You treat women like shit because you can. There is a difference." I turn and walk away. I can feel Auggie's eyes burning a hole into my back the entire time I stride down the hallway.

"Stay," Aunt Isis says to stop Auggie from dragging my ass out of Rush. "Dev's not lying for once. He has to do this."

Us dark-haired Masons have to stick together, and Dad is lumped in with the fair-of-hair and the faint-of-heart.

About halfway down the hallway, my destination reveals herself. Auggie's baby sister is a sight for sore eyes. Tall, curvy, blonde and blue-eyed, Willow once called Tina plastic. Tina's not fake– nothing on her is. She's cursed with beauty.

Tina Kline is Fairport's resident Barbie doll. A one-of-a-kind, drug-taking, sex-selling Barbie.

"Well, that went well." Tina flashes me a sympathetic smile. "Auggie's in a rare mood this evening, as is Mal."

"Had a visit from my dear ol' dad tonight, eh?" I lean in to peck a quick kiss to Tina's lips. It's not sexual in any way. It's inborn in us after years of watching Dad kiss every female on the lips in greeting. Tina kisses Auggie just the same as she does me. I really do see Tina as family, as my sister.

"Bad night, huh?" Tina says with a straight face, and then busts out laughing.

"Don't forget!" Auggie bellows at us just to be an ass.

Humor twisting into fury. "Motherfucker." With a bitch-glare, Tina screams down the hallway like a banshee. "Piss test in the morning, Augustus! Why don't you test Robin, while you're at it?"

"Shut the fuck up!" Auggie shouts back. "Get your ass upstairs before I pound you."

I wait for Tina to lead the way, because a part of me will always be a gentleman. "Are you gonna kiss your brother goodnight, or are you going to bite his face off?"

Stomping up the steps like a toddler instead of a grown woman, Tina growls, "This is me treating Auggie kindly after the shit he pulled earlier." Still in full-on tantrum mode, she enters her apartment, waits for me to follow, and then kicks the door shut. "No sense in locking the goddamned door since everyone and their brother has a cocksucking key."

Tina's apartment is about a quarter of the size of Aunt Isis's loft. There are four apartments above Rush. Half the space going to Aunt Isis, a quarter to Rory, and the last quarter is split into two efficiencies— one being Tina's place, and one is currently empty.

The space is tight but set up well: a small bathroom in one corner, a queen-sized bed, a seating area with a huge TV, and a tiny yet efficient kitchen. Tina's just one girl, so it's perfect for her. It's not as opulent as Aunt Isis's place, or as man-cave-ish as Rory's.

"You can't bitch too much," I state, feeling absolutely no need to pussy-foot around with Tina. I have no desire to put up with her tantrum, either. "I share a bedroom with my brother, and a bathroom with all my siblings. Don't bitch. It's free, it's decent, and may I remind you… it's *free*?"

"Yeah… yeah… yeah…" Tina grumbles, falling to sit on the couch. "I heard all that tonight already. It's free, but at what cost?"

I sit in a chair opposite Tina, and marvel over the fact that I'm one of the only people who gets her. Men and women take one look at the girl, and either want her or hate her on sight. Once they hear of her reputation for drugs and sex, they go after her with a vengeance. Last week, a rumor was floating around that Tina was molested as a kid because she seduced her abuser, and that's why she's a drug addict and a sex fiend.

Sitting across from me is a girl with a ponytail, wearing a pair of pajama pants with kittens and balls of yarn, a pink hoodie, and a pair of fuzzy boots. I want to protect Tina and kill every person who's ever bullied her. Auggie is first on my list.

"What do you mean? At what cost?" I don't like to talk shit through, but Tina has me curious. Plus, we aren't talking about me, which is a relief.

"First, I have something for you." Tina lobs a pill bottle at my head. On instinct, I catch it before it smashes into my forehead.

"You throw like a girl," I taunt. Eyes flicking to read the prescription bottle, I almost pass the hell out. "What the fuck? Where did you get this? Lithium? Huh?" I stammer, amazed to be holding something I've tried to get for months and couldn't find. It's what Mom was prescribed, but Mom's illness and mine are polar opposites. "How did you get it past the drug raid?"

"I didn't." She grabs a blanket off the back of the couch and wraps it around her shoulders, as if she's cold but not from the temperature. "Your dad, Auggie, and Officer McGregor," Tina sneers their names, "Came into my apartment like it's my gilded cage or prison cell, and searched every inch of it: knocked on all the walls, checked the toilet tank, even tore into every package of food I had– even the shit that was unopened. They dumped my mouthwash and my astringent facial wash down the sink. It was like being in a police state."

"I get what you mean about free having a cost," I mutter lamely, because I know my words cannot take the haunted look out of Tina's eyes.

"I… I can't take it anymore, Dev. The worse Auggie treats me, the more I want to take drugs just to spite him. When my brother looks at me, he doesn't see me. He either looks through me or at me with disgust. I can feel it in the air around him. I'm Auggie's obligation. He doesn't see me as a human being."

"That bastard loves you," I try to reassure Tina. "He's just as warped as the rest of us. More so, because he doesn't realize it."

"Well, even knowing that, it doesn't change anything. It doesn't take away the fact that my brother is the ring leader of my bullies. Auggie hates my guts for things I cannot change. He blames me for who my father is. He blames me for looking like Mom, saying I act like Mom, when that couldn't be farther from the truth."

"What is the truth?" It slips from my tongue before I can stop it. Usually Tina is as closed off as I am. What happened tonight must have hurt her badly.

Tina's sniffling, holding her eyes wide, but she doesn't cry. "Auggie happened– it's all about Auggie. I know no one but me pumps the drugs into my system. I know it's an excuse to use him as a reason to get high. But it doesn't take the pain away to be sober and misjudged. I was born, and Auggie treated me like shit because of who my father was. Blamed me."

"Wait–" I put my hand out. "What? You know who your dad is?"

Snorting in disgust. "I'm not some poor woe-is-me little girl with daddy issues. I met my father when I was fourteen, and I love him and he loves me, and Mom loves us both. I hear the rumors. I wasn't molested, or raped, or a succubus. I wasn't born a drug baby. We don't have addiction running in our veins, and we weren't born to be whores."

"You don't have daddy issues– you have Auggie issues," I say, understanding somewhat. "Who's your father?"

"No," Tina shakes her head, denying me. "I can't. Auggie would kill me if he caught wind that I breathed a word of this to anyone."

"Why? This guy is your dad, and it's your right to talk about him to anyone you damn well please," I snarl, smothering the urge to annihilate my uncle.

"Auggie met Dad briefly when Dad came back into Mom's life around the time I was conceived." Laughing bitterly, "My brother hated me before I was born. But now he loves and respects our father, but still hates my fucking guts– hates our mother's guts. What he doesn't get is that no one is to blame. It was just a bitch-slap from fate."

"I don't understand." It's my turn to shake my head to clear away the confusion. "I thought Auggie and you had different dads."

"Auggie met a giant red-headed man, and I was born less than a year later. I'm sure he figured that out, even if he was only seven at the time." This time, Tina wraps her blanket around her shoulders and allows the torrent to fall.

I give Tina privacy to cry without me staring at her in disbelief– I've never seen her cry before. I open my pill bottle, knowing how Taryn felt when I handed her the Adderall. Neither drug will fix us, because they aren't the right medications for what's wrong with us. As for me, I know it will take weeks for the Lithium to take effect, and I don't have weeks to suffer through while my moods try to stabilize, while I try to balance.

"I met my father when I was fourteen," Tina rasps, gaining my undivided attention. "I didn't learn the truth until I was fifteen– our dirty little secret. My mother wasn't molested, or raped, or abused either. She was heartbroken– that's why she ran away. The drugs always catch up to a runaway without a place to go. I unwittingly followed in her footsteps."

"I remember," I breathe, mind picturing Tina when she was younger. "I was doing drugs before you were. You were a little book worm."

"Auggie never saw me that way. I'm not stupid. I understand the phrase *what you fear, you create* better than anyone. Auggie shoved it down my throat how I'd turn into a drug addict whore, and I did."

"Why, though? Why did you allow Auggie to change you?"

"It wasn't Auggie," she answers immediately. "It was the truth about my father– the same man who ruined my mother. He didn't mean to, though. Fate's ultimate bitch-slap." Tina rubs her blanket on her face to wash away the tears. "Dad's not big and red-headed anymore. He's tall and thin because he sits at a desk all day. He has white hair because he's in his fifties now. He's not that thirty-year-old guy who Auggie met, so I didn't recognize him at first."

"How'd you figure it out?"

"You don't notice changes about someone if you're around them day-in and day-out, but once you're away from them and missing them… Mom was clean again, for good this time, and she moved us about a hundred miles from here. I missed Auggie terribly, and one day I heard him laugh, only it wasn't Auggie."

"Jesus," I hiss.

"So I confronted my mother, and she told me the truth. I finally figured out why Auggie hated me. So at fifteen, I ran away, and I followed the same path as my mother. Only it was worse, because I was the product of what made her go bad. I *was* bad to the core. So I went from being a straight A student, a virgin, and pure in every way, to a drug addict whore. Within a month, I was living on the streets, stealing to survive, and preyed upon. I couldn't see that I deserved anything better."

Tina gets up from the couch, and goes into the kitchen area to get a glass of water. "The Lithium was from Isis, by the way. Word-for-Word: *Tell Devon we'll fix the root of the problem. It's up to him to fight off what he's done to mask his illness.* Your family loves you, and like your problem, mine is in my genetic makeup too."

"I know you're not mentally ill," I state unequivocally. "You're the sanest person I know."

"Not everything's in the mind, Dev. Some of it's in the foundation of what makes us human beings, and there is no escaping it," Tina says ominously as she retakes her seat on the couch. "Devon, you can get clean, get therapy, and take your medication, and live a healthy, happy life."

"So can you," my voice breaks from desperation.

"I can get clean, but no amount of scrubbing will clean my blood," Tina says cryptically. "Auggie was a freak accident, and they didn't know until after. With me... *they knew*. Which in my brother's eyes makes me worse than him– makes him call our mother a whore because she had to have tempted and seduced our father with her body to get him to give in. Our existence couldn't be about love– something pure. It had to be evil, vile, nasty, because we are beasts– my brother and me."

"I don't want to know, do I?" I whisper faintly, scared shitless by the transformation that came over Tina. I've never seen anyone so enraged yet calm in my entire life.

"No, you don't," Tina warns. "Auggie hates me because he hates himself. I understand it, but it doesn't take the pain away like drugs do."

"What are you going to do?"

Tina floors me, "I'm leaving as soon as you leave."

"What? Auggie kicked you out?"

"No, Auggie can't stand looking at me, and I can't deal with it, so I'm getting out of his sight." Furious, Tina flicks tears off her cheeks with a fingertip. "It's not so much the whore comments, even though they sting. I could give a shit less how it bothers my brother that I enjoy sex. It's not how he calls me Druggie instead of Tina, either. It's how he looks at me that makes me sick to my stomach."

Unfathomable, I stare at Tina, knowing that if she was a Mason, even when she's at her worst, everything would still be unconditional. No matter what. "What did you do wrong?"

Tina glares at me, but she's not angry with me. "Nothing," she breathes. "I was born. Auggie was born. My father was born. My mother was born. While my parents have found a way to move on and deal– to heal –Auggie won't, and he won't let me either. So I'm getting the fuck away from him. Auggie is toxic to me. He makes me feel like shit. It's not an excuse to use drugs, but it's why I do it."

"You need to get help, Tina." I lean forward to squeeze her hand. "I'm getting help, and I want it. I'm working on a way to help a few other kids. I can get you help, too."

Sliding from her seat, Tina hugs me tightly. "Thank you, Devon. You're a good man, no matter who tells you otherwise. No matter what you think inside this fucked up brain of yours." Tina taps my temple, and we laugh together. "But I don't need your help. It's waiting for me at home. It's just up to me to take it when I'm ready."

"So you're going home?" I ask as Tina pulls away from me. Hope lights up in my body when she walks over by the door to sling a pink backpack over her shoulder. "Thank God."

Tina's smiling, but the expression on her face is wounded. "Can you believe this is the bag I used to run away with?" She pats the backpack while twisting a smirk. "I torture myself with it," she laughs, but it's infused with bitter hatred. "Auggie bought it for me for my first day of seventh grade, and it was filled with a bunch of goodies– markers, pens, and notebooks."

"See, Auggie can be sweet." I smile in remembrance of similar experiences with the man. "He loves you, Tina."

Tina nods her head. "I know. But Auggie hates himself more." She adjusts the backpack on her shoulder. "Two years later, it was filled with stolen shit: jewelry, pills, and small electronics. I was fifteen with a pink backpack– my innocent looks were lethal."

Huffing a laugh, "Tina, they still are. It's too bad some Hollywood assfuck didn't spot you first."

"Not my sort of life," she says flippantly. "I was mugging an older couple by knifepoint before they could get into their car. A cop spotted me, and I ran, and ran, and ran."

"Dude! Who?" The cop in me should be disgusted, but I can't seem to get the larger part of me to settle down. "Spill the rest."

My enthusiasm chases Tina's sadness away. "The cop eventually caught up with me in the woods. He was young, like, not just in age. Maybe early twenties," she says with a shrug. "But he was younger than me in life experience. I'd been living on the streets for about three months, and I wasn't the Tina I used to be. What Auggie feared the most, I created. I lost my virginity in the woods to a cop as a way to get out of trouble. The guy didn't know what hit him– I *wrecked* him. When he tried to arrest me, I told him I was fifteen and he'd see more time than I ever would. I walked away, just me and my backpack."

"Uh... Tina? Did this happen in Fairport? Please tell me it was somewhere else," I beg, knowing exactly who Tina fucked for life.

Ignoring my question. Tina pats her backpack again. "This was inches from me the whole time. It's been by my side, going down this broken road for seven years. My dad and I can burn it when I get home."

Horrified, I ask again. "So you're going home, then?"

Opening the door, Tina steps out into the hallway. "Not yet, but soon. See ya around, Dev," and then she's gone.

CHAPTER TWENTY-SIX

Essie Prynne

See, I'm a Prynne, and while we may be dainty and cute, we're made of sterner stuff. Prynnes by nature are stubborn and tenacious, yet playful and naughty. We're as equally kindhearted as we are vindictive.

You know those big, happy dogs with the loud bark that never bite? Yeah, well, that ain't a Prynne. We're those terriers–the ones whose bite is more vicious than its squeaky, obnoxious bark.

It's Saturday, nearly a week since my life was turned upside down. I could stay home and help my mother pack, feeling like shit because my parents are about to embark on a new adventure without me. I could stay home and fret and stew and not talk to my mother about what's truly disturbing me. I could keep my mouth shut…

But I'm a Prynne, and while we may be pacifists, we are not passive.

Willow has been AWOL from the family since Devon broke up with her. My instincts say she knows what I did, but I just can't believe Devon would do that to me. I asked to tell Willow the truth, and I plan on doing it today.

If we are stubborn, than Clover is the queen of all of us. No one is stupid enough not to attend a family-mandated cooking lesson. Every Saturday Clover teaches her children and Malcolm's children how to fend for themselves: cooking, cleaning, etiquette and manners, even household maintenance and budgeting. Now that I'm on my own (will be very shortly), I need to learn all those things too. Clover invited me, so I'm going to go.

Willow will have to be there, and I will have to look her in the eye. Prynnes have huge, motherfucking metaphorical balls, and I'm going to need them this afternoon to get through this.

I haven't heard from Devon– not a single word, smoke signal, or even seen him around town. But I didn't expect to either. Not after his note.

Essie,

Here are the facts. Heed them.

1: I love you. I always will

2: I'm irreparably broken. Don't believe for one second #1 can heal #2. No amount of love, trust, and understanding can fix me on a cellular level. I'm mentally ill, and I will be until the day I die.

3: I'm a drug addict, and even if I get clean, I'll always be a drug addict. My chemical imbalance made me seek out chemicals, which made me become dependent. If/when I get clean, I'll never be clean. I will have to take medication until the day that I die, because if I don't, I will die by my own hand.

4: I will hurt you. I don't want to hurt you, but I will just the same. I may or may not even regret it afterward. It's inevitable.

5: I will never be normal. I will never have a content life because of fact #2. It's impossible. I will simply exist. Ginny assures me my thoughts on this might change over time with proper medication. But I wasn't around my grammy enough to compare her to my mother. The life behind me, in front of me, is a long stretch of misery.

6: My children will always carry this part of me inside them. No matter how cute, or smart, or kind, or precious they may be, they will have my illness lying dormant, and they will pass it on to their children, and their children's children.

7: While fact #1 is resolute, there are no guarantees I will be nice to you. In fact, it's guaranteed that I won't be. I will, however, take care of you in all the other ways that I can. I will say things, do things, and behave in such a manner that will disgust you, hurt you, and make you wonder what you've done wrong.

8: You've done nothing wrong. It's me. All me.

9: I lie. I will always lie, because of #2. Never forget #8.

10: I'm afraid. No, I'm petrified. I don't want to be the way I am, and I don't want to face it. The only way to get help is to acknowledge it, and I can't bring myself to say the words. Because by acknowledging it as fact, is to make it reality.

11: Don't push me, but don't let me push you either.

I know you love me as much as I love you, Ess. But I can't do to you, what my mother did to my father, to me, to my siblings.

Dad didn't realize. He was duped into thinking he was getting a woman like my grandmother– someone who could function. Someone who could love him in return. I don't know where I fall on the severity scale because of #10. But I will know sooner rather than later.

I refuse to do to you what my mother unwittingly did to my father. So, take the time to think this over until I get back from Sedona. If you decide you can live with #1 – #11, then I can live with the fact that you love me.

–Dev.

After shoving the note back into my pocket, with a deep breath, I open Clover's door. I don't bother knocking for two reasons. One, all of the Prynne houses have an open-door policy. We're family– these homes belong to all of us. Two, Clover specifically invited me. Heart hammering in my chest, palms sweating, I have to do the right thing, even if everyone will hate me because of it. I'll pull Willow to the side and tell her the truth, knowing if things get out of hand, she'll have a support system at her side and none of them will let her kill me.

The instant my feet hit the living room floor, I know I've made an epic mistake.

Willow knows.

Seth's wide eyes take me, begging me to back up, but I don't listen. I'm not a coward. Stupid? Hell yes, I am. A coward? No, I'm too stupid to be a coward.

Seth backs away, yet manages to trap me at the entrance to the kitchen. The only person who looks happy to see me is Clover. With Ren bleeding pity, Devon acting spineless, and Raven and Weston looking back and forth between us all.

Then there's Willow, who's charging forward like an enraged bull. "Get out!" bellows from her mouth, ponytail swinging like the head of an axe.

Standing my ground, I need to get this over with. To not speak my piece means we have to go through this over and over again until there is closure. I step forward, hands raised to ward Willow off.

"I need to explain," I try to get out, but Willow won't let me say anything.

"Leave," she hisses, brown eyes burning with rage. "Don't set foot over this threshold again, or next door, or Revamped, or the Spook House, or Wreck & Ruin. If I frequent it, you're no longer welcome there."

In this instant, I learn everyone will betray you. If they will cheat with you, they will cheat on you– in all ways. See rule #9. Devon always lies. Lies about everything.

I also learn another valuable lesson: there is no such thing as unconditional. I accept everyone for who they are, yet they don't accept me. These people, my family and the kids I've known since they were born, they are going to stand by and allow Willow to annihilate me.

Devon's words ring in my ears the entire time I face down my cousins and the Mason kids. All these people who used to love me turn on me. All I wanted to do was take responsibility for my part in what happened.

Devon won't look at me. Maybe he's ashamed of himself, or maybe he's ashamed of me. I stare at him, willing him to explain– all the bastard does is stare down at his feet. My gut clenches, muscles twisting as my heart breaks and the ground beneath my feet shifts and wavers, or maybe I'm just on the edge of fainting.

After the past few days, I thought we were past this shit. I feel fourteen all over again. Left in the school hallway after Devon called me a whore and turned his back on me. After he walked away from me and gave me the cold shoulder and the silent treatment for nearly seven years.

Masons don't marry whores.

Devon had warned me all those years ago, and he tested me over the past few days. A test I failed. I finally proved Devon right, along with every other person who has ever called me a whore.

If they will cheat with you, they will cheat on you. Now Devon knows I'm nothing more than a worthless whore with big tits and a dead-end life, and he'll never be able to trust me again.

My biggest mistake was my inability to tell Devon no.

Past tense. Was. I'll have no problems saying no from this moment forth.

"You told her?" Lip quivering, tears stinging my eyes, nothing has ever hurt this much before. Soul deep, as if something vital in me is shifting. Now my sense of self matches the views of every person who's ever thought negatively of me.

I want to beg Devon to explain, to tell me I'm wrong and he didn't betray me yet again. But I have to swallow down my self-pity, because no doubt I hurt Willow just as badly. While I deserve how I feel, my cousin doesn't.

Willing Devon to look at me, "How could you? You promised not to tell."

Willow sputters as she stalks my way, shaking her head in utter disgust. "Oh… Oh… that is fucking rich, coming from *you* of all people." My eyes narrow as she grabs something off the countertop. "Since the shirt I made you four years ago is long gone, this will have to suffice."

Mind spinning, I try to figure out what Willow is talking about. My feet are frozen to the linoleum as I notice Willow popping the lid off a marker with her front teeth.

Still frozen in shock, breath seized within my lungs, my eyes held wide and tear-filled, I allow myself to be subjected to Willow carving an *A* in the center of my forehead in permanent marker.

The ink burns– it's cloying smell stings my nostrils just as much as my eyes. The tip jabs into the sensitive skin of my forehead, bruisingly so. It doesn't glide smoothly– the marker skips as Willow carves the universal sign of adultery into my flesh.

Branded. Long after the visual reminder wears away, this moment will be permanently etched into my psyche, essentially changing who I am from this moment forth.

No one moves to intervene, not even Clover. Whether she birthed Willow or not, Clover has been like a big sister to me since I was born. There aren't many Prynnes, so we're very close. But then there is Devon, who doesn't even bother to watch.

My young cousin is confused, and his innocence hurts me even more. Seth asks Weston a bizarre question, "The anarchy symbol?" But perhaps he's trying to diffuse the situation. One would hope someone was on her side, but this situation is hopeless.

"Dipshit, you need to pay closer attention in English class," Violet hisses. "More importantly, you need to pay attention to your family history. Essie just earned her right to be named after her namesake– Hester Prynne."

"So fucking rich." I'm Willow's sole focus right now, brown eyes burning with murderous intent. "You are accusing him–" she points at Devon, who now has the audacity of looking up, but only at Willow "–of betraying your trust. Are you fucking kidding me? You, who betrayed me, expected Devon, who betrayed me, not to betray you? You deserve each other."

Dazed, I just stare at Willow as sparks of bitter hatred shine from her eyes. There is no way this level of loathing started with what I did with Devon a few nights ago. No way, no how. There is more to this story, but fuck if I know what.

"Leave," Violet orders, causing me to break my staring contest with Willow. "This is our house, and you're no longer welcome. I don't know why Willow isn't kicking Devon out, but there must be a reason. I can't kick Devon's ass. But you're family, and family is fair game. I have no issue with punching a bitch out."

It's never the man's fault. Not ever. Women always blame other women for anything that happens. I was targeted in school by every girl whose boyfriend looked at me, no matter how many layers of clothing I wore. Instead of my family taking mine and Willow's side, everyone takes Devon's side by blaming me, and we all swallow it as if they're only taking Willow's side.

Devon can stay, the mastermind of all of this, but I'm shoved out of one of the places I call home.

Everything is conditional– everything has a price. As long as I was useful to them, drove their asses wherever they wanted to go, cut and styled their hair so they'd look good in school, listened to their problems and gave them advice from my own experiences, I was being a good cousin.

The only thing I received was a feeling of belonging because we have the same blood flowing in our veins. I asked nothing from them, while all they did was take and take some more.

I can see it– I'm dead to them. Just like that. Conditionally.

Then there's Devon. All he ever did was ask of me, use me, and he lets me dangle over the precipice and doesn't offer me a hand up. If anything, his failure to look at me is no different than pushing me off the ledge.

Frozen, all I can do is watch in horror as Violet's violence is displayed in Technicolor. I'm unable to even flinch as Violet's elbow flies back as if in slow-motion, yet none of us are quick enough to stop her– not that anyone even tries to protect me.

The pain is immediate and excruciating, radiating through my eye socket, across my cheek, and down along my jawline. My ear rings, a discombobulating sound. Then the burning sting begins– first hot, then a chilly iciness.

Humiliation hurts worse than the physical violence. The betrayal of no one stepping in hurts the most. Knowing, as I run out of a house I've called my own since I was a toddler, they will congratulate Violet and comfort Willow because I'm the villain… that is the worst feeling of all.

Running to a stop at the sidewalk in front of Clover's house, I'm at a loss of where to go. No tears fall because I'm in a state of shock. There are no options open to me. None.

Slowly creeping in, panic eclipses all other emotions warring in my mind. Not only did I just lose Devon, knowing I never had him to begin with, I also lost a best friend who never treated me as a friend. But what's worst of all, I lost that sense of belonging.

Family.

Prynne in name only, but no longer welcome just when my parents are abandoning me, I walk down the sidewalk toward destinations unknown.

CHAPTER TWENTY-SEVEN

Kieren Mason

Even after everything, Devon still comes first with me. I just blatantly lied to everyone as if I didn't already know what happened between Devon and Essie. I lied because I knew Willow would never forgive me, would judge me forever, and Devon allowed me to lie. But what was the worst, was how no one blamed Devon, or even asked him to leave. Willow is inside Clover's kitchen with Devon right this second, as if nothing bad had happened between them.

My soul feels tainted more and more every day, the stress on my shoulders is beginning to be too much to bear. Willow is innocent in all of this, as am I, but we contributed to the problem as a whole. Willow needs to take a long look in the mirror. I'm crazy for the girl, but I can't stand by and watch someone be abused, especially someone who was manipulated into being an accomplice.

Devon used Essie as a scapegoat, and Willow not only stood by and allowed it, she swallowed it. I feel sick for doing the same.

Someone has to think of the girl who was just assaulted in more ways than one. Running down the front walk, "Essie!" I call out, looking first right, then left down the sidewalk. Essie's car is in the shop, so I know she's on foot. Assuming she's either going home or going to Bethany's, I jog that direction down the sidewalk.

Sitting on her front porch as always, Peggy Webster points me in the right direction, shaking her head in disgust. "Your brother needs to be castrated."

"Thanks!" I shout to the old bitty who judges everyone for everything. It comes as a bit of a surprise how she's not judging Essie. I guess years do give wisdom, because the old bat is the only one blaming the right guy instead of the injured party.

"Essie!" I call out again when I catch sight of her hunched shoulders. "Wait up!" She doesn't even acknowledge that she hears me, pace never slowing or speeding up. "Hey?" I call out as my hand lands on her shoulder. "Hey."

Blank eyes stare up at me, their blue vivaciousness is now lifeless, and there is no ignoring the giant, black **A** riding her forehead. "I have to be at work soon." Essie doesn't pull away from me, but she doesn't stop walking either.

"Salon's closed on Saturday afternoons, as always," I mutter, confused. "Essie, wait." Tugging her to a stop, she rocks slightly like she's not steady on her feet. "I can't even begin to imagine how you're feeling right now."

"I deserve it," is all she says in reply, then begins walking again.

"Can we just talk about it for a minute? Please," I beg, confused as Essie walks past her house. "I don't want you thinking it was your fault. How Willow treated you was wrong, but exactly how I expected her to act. Violet? Clover better spank her ass is all I can say."

"My shift at the No-Name starts in less than an hour– I gotta be fifteen minutes early to restock the tables, and I gotta get dressed before that," Essie rambles. "Then there's covering up my eventual black eye and scouring off the A on my forehead. Not gonna get many tips looking like this."

"Since when do you work at the diner?" Mind spinning, it's like I've been levitated from our world and placed in the Twilight Zone. "Did you quit working at Salon?"

"No," is all Essie mutters in reply. Her foot catches on a crack between two sidewalk slabs, and I quickly reach out to grab her elbow. "I'm picking up random night shifts at the gas station too."

"Why?" My hand clenches, fingers wrapping tightly around Essie's upper arm. It's like she's a different person than the one I knew last week. Right now, she reminds me of Devon when he sits on the sofa and stares off into space. She's just as closed off, refusing to tell me anything.

"Because I make less than three bucks an hour at Salon on a good day. Who can live off twenty-five bucks a day? Even living with my parents, it's not enough to pay the bills I do have. Joys of working a service job that is sustained by customer gratuities."

I make more in an hour than Essie makes in a day?

What?

"You're shitting me, right?" My head hitches to the side, and I look at Essie– truly look at her. I always felt Essie and I were kindred, seeing Willow and Devon more alike. But right now, all I see is desperation and panic written across Essie's face, and it utterly terrifies me.

"The tips and wages at the diner are better than at Salon. Irony– one job anyone can do, and the other I needed a formal education and licensing."

"I never really realized where the money was going when I was paying fifteen bucks for a haircut that took twenty minutes."

"In a big salon, there is money to be made. In a small town salon, it may only take me twenty minutes to cut your hair, but there are no guarantees I have two more customers to fill that hour. I literally get a cut of the haircut, with the rest going to Elma to pay for the costs of doing business."

"People need to tip you more money then," I mutter lamely.

"Those tips are a godsend, but it would be gross to require someone who also doesn't make much money to over-tip me just because I make squat. It's a haircut. Just because Salon doesn't do much business doesn't mean that haircut should cost four times what it's worth."

"So that's why you're working at the No-Name now?"

"Yeah, that's why. My car is in the shop, but it's probably already been repossessed from there. I'm weeks away from prom and wedding season, which means my savings dried up months ago. I have to pay for my equipment first and my student loans second. But I also have to bank up enough money to be able to afford a security deposit, first and last month's rent, and utility deposits in the next few weeks. Not to mention I own nothing to use once I get a place. Not gonna happen, but I'm trying the best that I can."

"Essie, what's going on with you? What are you talking about?"

Looking at me incredulously, one manicured eyebrow reaches her hairline, causing the A in the middle of her forehead to wrinkle. "Did you just miss what happened back there? That was my world imploding. Didn't you hear it or see it? Do you want me to do a rehash?"

"Willow will get over it, and the shit with Devon is because he's Devon." Yet again, I find myself making excuses– for everyone. "I get that you and Devon pulled a shit move on

Willow. But the girl was not into Devon, no matter how much she protests that fact. She was flirting with me something fierce, and I know when a woman is flirting with intent."

"You think I don't know that?" Essie's voice cracks. "You think we all don't see it? Willow's been hung up on you since forever. So when I try to play matchmaker, she throws it in both of our faces by screwing around with Auggie– then Devon. Now, in a roundabout way, she'll latch onto you. But she's gonna call me all sorts of hellish names, make my life a living nightmare, and I'll deserve feeling like the whore she calls me. It was my choice to be with Devon, so I'll suffer the consequences, hypocrisy be damned."

"I'm just– I'm at a loss."

"I was naïve," Essie murmurs just as the No-Name Diner comes into focus. "I didn't realize Devon had told Willow what we did when he broke up with her. I truly thought I could talk to her– my bad. But I have bigger problems than Willow's temper tantrums, Violet's violence, and Devon being Devon."

"Like what? Why are you working so much?" I tug the door to the No-Name open, and Essie walks in ahead of me. The place is suffering from the lull between lunch and supper, no doubt it looks busy as all heck compared to Salon though. Essie doesn't push me off, even when I follow her through the diner, down the hallway, and into the employee restroom.

The place is tight quarters, with just a single toilet, sink, and a bar bolted to the wall to hang clothing, with a few shelves tacked to the wall for handbags and personal belongings.

I realize Essie is more upset than she's letting on as she strips out of her blouse and shorts, right down to her panties and bra. It's not fair that I watch, but I can't stop myself. Essie's creamy tits are overflowing the lacey fabric, and half of her round ass cheeks are peeking out the bottom of a matching pair of panties as she bends to step out of her shorts. I'm simultaneously relieved and disappointed as she tugs a pink and white uniform over her head.

I'm a man, I'll never deny that fact, and my body reacts accordingly. I wish it didn't, but it does. I would never ruin our friendship by going there again, especially with how distraught Essie is, but I can appreciate something I find gorgeous. What makes it worse, and probably earns Essie more tips, is the fact that the uniform is like a second skin on her curvy body, highlighting just how luscious her tits and ass and tiny waist truly are.

There will always be sexual tension between us. How could there not be when we've slept together? But it will forever be overshadowed by our friendship. I truly love the girl as a human being. Part of me knows it's because she's Devon's, and right now I'm taking care of Essie because he can't, and part of me knows it's because Devon and I have the same taste in women.

Mason men are bizarrely attracted to Prynne women, even though they come in all shapes and sizes and a variety of attitudes.

"Eyes up here," Essie warns, grabbing for a white, fuzzy sweater to tug on over top of her uniform. She covers herself, no doubt wearing it while working to keep the men from ogling her and the women from punishing her through a lack of tips. Watching Essie tie a white scarf around her neck to cover what little of her cleavage is showing, when I've never seen any of the waitresses in the No-Name wear one, it gives me a new appreciation for the struggle women go through. How we men see them as a piece of flesh for our pleasure, and how other women judge them for our reactions to something they have no control over.

"Do you get hot wearing that while working?" stumbles from between my parted lips. "Sorry for staring– you took me by surprise, is all. Ya know… seeing you in your underwear."

"Forgiven," Essie replies, and I know she means it. "Sometimes I feel faint from how hot I get wearing this sweater." Essie reaches for a polka dot bag off one of the shelves, and then she walks up to the sink. She talks to me while fishing around, looking for something specific. "Waitressing is never easy, and this place has no air conditioning. But it's a helluva lot hotter when a teenage girl dumps scorching coffee on my chest because her boyfriend is staring at my tits and ass."

Fists clenching at my sides, I growl, "You're joking, right?"

"No, I'm not." The scent of fingernail polish remover wrinkles my nose, and I find Essie applying the caustic shit to her forehead. I wince in sympathy. "Do you want to hear the punchline?" I breathe a sigh of relief that the marker is coming off, but it's leaving a red welt behind instead. "They weren't even sitting at one of my tables.

"The girl stomped over to me while I was waiting on another table, and pitched an entire cup of hot coffee on my chest, splattering a little kid as I passed him his chocolate milk. She shouted at me during the dinner rush, how I was trying to steal her man so he'd take care of me, because the only thing I was good at was selling my body for tips. She pegged me wrong, like I was in desperate need of a man and not educated with three jobs. But she was right in her whore estimation of me.

"I never spoke to her boyfriend, looked at her boyfriend, or acknowledged the fact that his eyes were glued to my body like I was a porn magazine and he was alone in his bedroom with a vat of hand lotion. I felt violated by him and assaulted by her, but I was to blame because I inherited my mother's big tits and my father's petite body."

"Shit, Essie. That's just…" Slumping against the wall in the small bathroom, I'm at a loss. "Disgusting. I almost feel like I should apologize for how I see you, for enjoying how you look– for looking at you as I do, for thinking about you when I do."

"There's a difference, Ren." Essie turns to me with a red mark shaped like Italy on her forehead and a shiner blooming under her right eye. "When you look at me, I feel flattered and wanted, because you know me and like me on a personal level. It'd be about *us*– coming together. When they look at me, they see a whore they can use to get off on, even if it's in their spank bank. They feel entitled to me– to envision what I look like without clothing –and I have no right to say no. I'm not a human being with feelings and hopes and dreams. I'm a series of holes they can penetrate and brag to their friends about.

"They don't want to come together with me and make it about us. They want to get off *on* me. Their stupid girlfriends are jealous, not realizing it's not me who will ultimately destroy their relationship, but the misogynistic asshat they chose to sleep with."

Not sure how to reply, since I'm sure it will lead to the elephant in the room we're ignoring, I change the subject. "How ya gonna cover up that little gift from Violent Violet?"

"I'm a cosmetologist, Ren," Essie teases me, and I fear for the fallout when reality finally hits. "Watch and learn." She turns back to the mirror, makeup bag in hand.

"Essie?" Ever so slowly, I approach her from behind and rest my palm on her shoulder. "You weren't Devon's other woman, no matter how much you believe it. You were his *only* woman.

Spanky and Dev were over, and they both knew it. She's going to hang onto that because she has to be angry about something at all times. Instead of Dave and Mary with a political or environmental agenda, it's Willow hating someone for some reason."

"It's because she lost Sam," Essie breathes, makeup brush stilling in the air. "I know Willow better than anyone, even if she never bothered to learn who I truly am." Eyes gazing downward, causing her lashes to create half-moon shadows on her cheeks, Essie looks beautifully destroyed. "I'm sorry– about everything. That's all I wanted to say to Willow."

"I'm sorry too, Ess." I step back to give her space and privacy, because I know she needs it. "So sorry."

"I just–" Essie's hand falls lax, tube of whatever type of makeup landing in the sink. "I never told Willow about Devon and me because she was so young when it happened– still a child. I just turned fourteen when he called me a whore and turned his back on me. Then when you and I hooked up–"

"Not our proudest moment," I interject. "Memorable, though," causes Essie to blush.

"Definitely memorable. But it wasn't something you share with your baby cousin who looked up to you like a big sister. It's not something you tell them when they have a crush on the kid you deflowered. Just saying... I wanted Willow to look up to me, see something in me I don't even see in myself. The problem with that was that no matter how much Willow said we were best friends, she never truly knew who I was because I was hiding the negative side of me from her."

"Spanky's not perfect," I remind Essie.

"I know. No one is." Essie sighs, turns her head left and right as she looks in the mirror, and then faces me. "Will I do?"

"You'll do," I mutter with a smirk. Essie will more than do. "You amaze me. I have no idea how you covered up a shiner and a mark that looked like a misfortunate make-out session left you with a hickey on your forehead."

"That's why you don't kiss virgins, Ren. Shoulda learned that by now, seeing as you've been with all of them in Fairport."

"A-ha-ha," I mock laugh, knowing she's just jerking my chain, but it's too close to the truth. As I said, Essie and I are closer in personality than most would believe. We feel the same about our torrid sexual history– shame. We were having sex to chase our demons, not because it felt good.

"Essie?" My voice shifts back to serious. "Why are you working here? Your parents–"

"Are moving, already sold the house, and I have to be out by the closing date."

A whole new level of worry falls on my overburdened shoulders. "Does Devon know?"

"Devon had one agenda in mind, so that's what we did. Didn't leave much time for me to talk about myself, ya know?"

"Yeah." I snort, disgusted but not surprised. "Devon kind of has a one-track mind… taking, thinking, and worrying about himself."

"I can't hate him," Essie admits like it's a shameful secret.

"I know. Same here– so what are you going to do about your parents?"

"I can either move with them, when they know I won't, which was their way of being nice by asking but secretly hoping I wouldn't go with them. I don't blame them for wanting a life outside of parenting me. My other option *was* moving in with a Prynne, which Robin assured me was okay. But Willow just banned me from everyone who would shelter me. So now I have until the closing to make enough bank to support myself."

"I'll help you any way I can, Essie." Reaching forward, I cup her face, finger trailing lightly on the swelling her bang-up makeup job couldn't cover. "All you have to do is ask. We're friends for life. Unconditionally."

Essie's face twists with agony, then the tears spring from the corners of her eyes. By the time her bottom lip is quivering and a sob is spilling from her mouth, I've pulled her into my arms and pressed her head to my chest.

"What'd I say wrong?" Hands rubbing her back, I try to soothe her.

"Nothing," Essie gasps. "You said exactly what I needed to hear, and you actually meant it. Ren, you meant it."

The bathroom door opening has me gazing over my shoulder at the intruder. A bigger teenage girl, wearing the same uniform as Essie, peers inside at us. It takes me a moment to place her.

"Desiree?" She's only a few years younger than me, so I vaguely remember her from school. I think she's a junior now. If I remember right, she's best buddies with Weston's *friend*. Sage.

"Hey, Ren– you okay, Essie?" Desiree squeezes in with us, hands hovering in the air, wanting to make it all go away. "Do you want me to cover you?"

"No, hun." Essie pulls away, and I miss holding her. I'm not comparing apples and oranges, but Willow never acts like she needs anyone. As a man, the urge to protect and provide is ingrained. As a Mason, the need is exacerbated. Right now, taking care of Devon's woman, I felt briefly like a grown man for once.

Scrubbing at her face with the backs of her palms, but managing not to mess up her makeup, Essie prepares herself for battle. "I'm good. Let's feed the hungry denizens of Fairport."

"I'm gonna stick around and have a bite to eat." I try to be sneaky, but Essie sees through how I'm trying to keep an eye on her to make sure she's truly okay. "Missed the cooking lesson, after all." Hamming it up, I rub my belly. "I'm starving for some fried food."

"Well, you came to the right place, Ren!" Desiree tugs me out of the bathroom, giving Essie some privacy. As soon as the door shuts, the girl is on me. "What'd you do?"

"Nothing," I defend myself, insulted. Seriously, I'm the cleanup crew. Always. "I was being Essie's friend, okay?"

"Okay," Desiree allows, noticing how genuinely concerned I am for Essie. "Did you call Bethany?"

"I plan on it. But I'll wait around here until Beth arrives."

"Good." The girl tugs me down the hallway and into the diner proper. My ass meets a booth bench. "You got Facebook on your cellphone?"

"Yeah, why?" Confused, I look up to the girl, trying to figure out what the hell is going on. A menu is shoved into my open hand. "I'm a grown man, ya know? I don't need to be on Facebook like it's my lifeblood."

"You've haven't even been outta school for a whole year yet, Ren." Desiree rolls her eyes. "You ought to be on there as much as possible because your sister is in my class."

"What's that supposed to mean?"

The menu is wrenched out of my hands. "What do you want to order? Hurry up."

"Don't plan on much of a tip," I growl, not liking this forceful side of the little girl I used to know. "Just dump some fried food on a plate and bring me a vat of ranch."

"Coke?" Desiree asks, being impatient. I nod in reply. "Get on Facebook. Then you best call Bethany for backup."

"Jesus Christ!" I cry out, having a bad feeling about this. I fish my cell from my back pocket, only to discover my battery is dead. Shaking my head in disgust, I shove it back into my pocket.

"Why aren't you looking?" Desiree demands as she plunks a flat fountain soda on the table in front of me.

"My battery is dead," I grumble, embarrassed. To distract myself, I grab a handful of napkins and use the overflow of flat Coke to scrub up the table. No-Name isn't exactly known for its cleanliness or its food.

"Figures." Desiree snorts, stalking off to the counter, where most of the patrons are lined up on stools. She hauls a kid off a stool, and then drags him back to me.

"Shoot me," I whisper underneath my breath when Weston's too perfect little buddy is shoved on the other side of the booth. At least the kid looks terrified– there is that.

"Show Ren," Desiree demands, and then goes back to work like business as usual, just as Essie flows from the hallway into the dining room. I watch her go about filling salt and pepper shakers.

"Allow me to formally introduce myself," the kid's voice is cultured, and ten times deeper than I imagined it to be. Looking at his tiny frame, with even tinier taut muscles, perfectly styled white-blond hair, and a shirt that probably cost as much as all four tires on my Ford, I hate the kid on principle.

"I never figured your mother came from money," pops out without my permission.

"The Sages of Massachusetts may have money, but that's because we never spend it. It gets reinvested in other rich assholes' political careers or squirreled away for a rainy day, but never spent on a Sage."

"Wait–" I put a hand up to stop him because the kid looks like a talker– a very condescending one. "I thought your first name was Sage."

"Don't strain your brain muscle." Gray-blue eyes glare at me with thinly veiled resentment. "Opal Sage married Byron Fischer, and that is where I came into the equation. They're divorced now, which is how we came to live in Fairport instead of Boston. The Sages are assholes."

"I'm so glad we agree on something," I mutter, never breaking the kid's stare.

Lips twisting up at the corners, my annoyance amuses the little fuckface. "Allow me to introduce myself." He has the balls to reach across the booth and present his hand for a shake. My hand is in his out of habit. "I'm Sage Fischer. I'm gay, and I'm a liberal."

"The fuck?" Pulling away, I wipe my palm off on my pants.

"You don't like me very much. I can see how unsettled you are by me. Because I'm gay. Because I'm rich. Because your brother wants me. Maybe because I'm small and pretty enough, I ping your girl-radar. I'm *not* a girl, so don't let that twist your tighty whities in a wad. Nothing about me is feminine in nature. None of that has anything to do with me, and everything to do with whatever you've got playing out inside your own head."

"I have nothing playing out in my head," I defend myself, even if my homophobia is threatening to rise. Then I realize the kid has a point. So what if the queer janitor sexually assaulted me in the locker room? Sage didn't. I love my brother enough to try to not view his sexual preferences as anything but normal, but it's going to be hard to forget what it felt like when that guy's grubby hand wrapped around my dick just as I started to come.

Shuddering, I push the evil, vile thoughts away.

"My family has money, so what? It's not like I get to spend it. I'll be educated and dressed to look the part of cultured doctors' grandson and son from two highly political families. But that doesn't change your life, does it?"

"I-I-I–" stammering, all I can do is become tongue-tied by this thumb-sized, little prick. Sage is right, but that doesn't change the fact that he truly is condescending. A commotion near the counter has both of our heads turning.

"What's wrong, sugar? Hmm… you can put out for everyone else, but you got a problem with me?" A fifty-year-old man is harassing Essie, with Desiree tugging Essie behind the counter. "No tip for you," he threatens.

Essie's expression is devoid of all life as she goes about filling ketchup into red squeeze bottles. "What the hell was that shit?" I snarl, and thankfully Sage fills me in.

"Just a regular day at the No-Name." If I'm pissed, Sage is feral. "My guess, the old guy grabbed Essie's ass. Sometimes they spank 'em, sometimes they grab so much their fingers try to wiggle where they don't belong. The dresses are for their protection, because a pair of pants would mean fingers could wedge in places they shouldn't go. The men never have the balls to actually lift the dress up and fish under it, versus trying to go *through* it."

"Are you just trying to get me fired up?" I stare across the table at the kid, but the sickened expression on his chiseled face tells me otherwise.

"Wish I was." Sighing, Sage folds his hands in his lap, but he doesn't look down at them like I would. Nope, Sage stares right back at me, holding my gaze with the supreme confidence of a dictator.

"I spend most of my time here making sure Desiree's okay. The older the guy, the worse they act. There are some seventy-year-old local men who pull the girls into their laps, expecting them to giggle while they take their orders. Loving the way their asses feel mashed against their crotch. They pat their behinds, and send them on their merry way back to the kitchen, or when they pay, they accidentally brush against their breasts. The girls have no way of drawing attention to it without making a commotion."

"That's just–"

"That's just how it is while we have the current owner," Sage stresses. "Desiree– she's a great girl. Feisty and quick-witted."

"I'm assuming she wouldn't survive being your friend otherwise," I mutter sardonically, causing Sage to laugh. Goddamn it, I wish I hadn't heard the sound, because no doubt it drives Weston to distraction. High and operatic, completely at odds with his deep yet raspy voice.

"I only surround myself with amazing, highly intelligent life forms." Sage raises his eyebrow, waiting for me to mention my baby brother, but I refuse to just to mess with his head. Mr. Clean Wessie and this uptight prick probably get along famously.

"My girl is still a minor, yet those misogynistic old bastards don't care. They're just playing around, they say. Just joking, they say. They say the girls love the attention. One guy holds on to the money and tells Desiree to beg for it, tugging it out of her hands every time she tries to reach for it. This is an everyday occurrence. My smoking hot, gay ass keeps them away for the most part, because I terrify them on so many levels."

"Huh?" is all I've got as I stare at Sage, realizing I reluctantly like him. "You sit at the counter the whole time Desiree works, don't you?"

"Yeah, I do. When she's not working, I hang out with your brother and sister. That's my life unless I'm spending the weekend with the Sages."

"Thank you," I mutter, surprised the words flow from my mouth.

"I'm not doing it for you." Sage doesn't take praise well. "Ya know what's worse than old men groping girls? Teenage girls. Now, I don't want to have to do this, because I've gotten to know Essie over the past week. I even let her style my flawless hair." The kid preens like a peacock displaying its feathers. "Here."

A top-of-the-line, ridiculously expensive cellphone is pressed into my hand. Gazing down, I notice it's opened to the Facebook app, and I'm suddenly thankful I hadn't eaten anything today.

Hand shaking, I bring the phone closer to my face, finding it impossible that I'm seeing what I'm seeing.

"I have one year left of the cesspool known as high school, but this terrifies me," Sage is murmuring while I glare in disbelief at the screen. "I thought this shit didn't follow you out into the real world. Essie's what? Twenty-two? Twenty-one, maybe? She's been out of school for almost four years, right? Bullying…"

Zoning out, I don't hear anything else the kid has to say.

Violet Webster tagged Willow Prynne, Essie Prynne, and Devon Mason in a status update: **Would anyone ever screw their cousin's boyfriend while riding in their cousin's car? No? Well, Fairport's whore with the big tits did just that. If you see Essie swaying her fat ass around town, say hello to the whore. #AisForAdultery.**

Over two hundred likes and almost fifty shares, not counting the horrific comments. "Jesus Christ," I snarl, tossing the phone back to the kid. "You staying 'til the shift change?"

"Yes, I am, Hoss." Sage tucks his phone into the pocket of his ridiculously expensive shirt. "I'd suggest you go find the source and delete the post. I've already recruited as many people as possible to report the post, including your brothers and sister. At least Seth was furious over it. He even reported his own sister."

"I can't believe Willow condoned this." At a loss, I rise to my feet, ignoring Sage's knowing smirk.

"Teenage girls are worse than overly dramatic gays, and I would know since spiteful is my middle name." Sage raises a manicured eyebrow. "If you like Willow, I'd suggest you convince her to act classy instead of trashy. Violet is a lost cause, trying so hard to be a violent badass that she's lost her prim and proper ways– I go to school with her, so I'd know."

My order is placed in front of me, but Desiree doesn't utter a single word. With a fingertip, I push the fried surprise Sage's way, and then I begin digging out my wallet.

"Aww… thank you. But wish you would've ordered some habanero raspberry dipping sauce instead of a vat of ranch." Taking a bite of a mozzarella stick, Sage chews thoroughly while I place enough cash on the table to cover my meal and a hefty tip. "Ironic how no one cares that Essie didn't screw herself. Devon had a dick in that, ya know? Yet no one says a single word about him."

"Yeah, that's how it always is."

"I'd say I'm glad I'm gay." Sage takes a sip of my flat Coke, then winces. "But society always dubs one of us as the girl and pushes the blame off onto them. Who do you think that would be, Kieren?" Sage gestures to his petite body, and I know how he feels after being in the shadows of a big brother who could do no wrong as a way to make up for the fact that our mother thought he could do no right.

"I'll take care of it," I mutter as my goodbye, but I'm not so sure I can fix the damage that's already been done.

CHAPTER TWENTY-EIGHT

Essie Prynne

You can only do what you can do, I repeat to myself over and over again as I work. It's not without a struggle to ignore the way my breath catches in my throat, or the burning sting of tears in my eyes, or the throbbing bruise hidden beneath three layers of makeup, or the chemical burn searing its way through my flesh to my brain.

It's next to impossible to ignore having my female patrons glare at me like they can still see the A on my forehead, like I'm about to straddle their man's cock and ride all the way home. Then there's the leering eyes of the males trying to use x-ray vision to see through the clothing hiding my body, like they have knowledge of what a bad girl is like and I fit the bill to a T. The whispering is the worst, because they make sure I can hear what they have to say about *me*– someone they don't know, about events they don't understand. I'm just tonight's entertainment for them.

If there are women or children at the table, I barely get a tip. If it's just men, I get three or four times what is socially acceptable, and the irony is that it's the respectable men who do this. The men who leer and snicker when I approach, they give no tip because I didn't live up to their expectations by flirting and selling myself for a few extra quarters. A few women have actually looked at me sympathetically– one patted my hand while she paid, no doubt having been in my shoes a time or two. What made me feel like I could survive this is the fact that she had to be in her seventies.

Isis and Opal's friend, Nina, was in here with Jackson Stone, and she gave me a hug while he paid for their supper.

Not everyone is an asshole, but I feel no less shame because of it.

Devon didn't fuck himself, but I should've told him to go do so. I'm at fault for whatever I get in return. I just didn't expect every person in the No-Name to know what Devon and I had done together. I want to rally against everyone and ask why only I have to take responsibility, or why it even matters.

Responsibility for what, exactly? Having sex with a friend? We're adults, not kids in junior high, so I find this attention given to my sex parts rather disgusting. A guy gets a pat on the back, while a girl gets the scarlet letter inked on her forehead.

What happens between two people should stay between those same two people. We were consenting adults who have known each other since pre-K. Semantics– Willow and Devon hadn't broken up yet, but were over nonetheless. So why did Willow have the right to dictate what Devon did with his body like she had ownership of it? If a man told a woman what she was or wasn't allowed to do with her own body, to the point he sicced others on her, he would be called an abuser. In reverse, it's just a right on the girlfriend's part.

If I ever had a boyfriend, even though that's not going to happen now, I wouldn't feel entitled to boss him around like he's a child. Devon made the choice, and Willow is acting like the spurned woman while she flirts with Devon's brother.

Why does Willow get to play the victim card, with Devon as the martyr, and me as the whorish villainess?

Every tale has to have a nemesis, and I guess I'll act the part. But I'm no longer a kid in school without a care in the world, where drama is created to give the illusion we have a complex life. I have more important problems than my own family members smearing my name across town and Facebook. Emotions be damned, I've got work to do, or I'll be living on the street once my parents' house closes with the buyers.

One of my old classmates is sitting at the counter by himself, and to say it's been awkward would be an understatement. "You need a warmup, Cody?" Coffee carafe poised and at the ready over a cup, his palm is flattened over the rim to stop me.

"I'm good." Cody smiles, pulling a few bills from his wallet. Standing from the stool at the counter, he leans into me a bit. "You still doing what you did in high school?" he asks.

"What?" I gasp, confused.

"What time's your shift over?" The question has ice water running through my veins. "What about a break? Wanna meet me out in my car? Ya know, for a little bit of mouth action?"

I'd love to say I keep my composure, but what else do I have to lose.

"I could pretend I don't know what the fuck you're getting at, Cody. You're treating me like I'm some bitch with low self-esteem, daddy issues, and no education. I'm working this job because I need money, not because I'm pining away for some man to take care of me. This routine only works on that type of girl, because my type just thinks you sound like a douchebag."

"Oh, c'mon, Hester." Cody grins, like he's God's gift and women should fall to their knees and service him.

"C'mon, Cody, right back at ya, asshole," I snarl. "I'm sure as hell not gonna go suck you off to get you off, while I only get a jaw-ache. What's in it for me? And I don't mean because I should be getting paid for it. If you want your dick taken care of, why don't you try to actually give a shit about the woman you want to use?"

"Don't be that way." Cody shoulder bumps me, nearly knocking me off my feet, but he acts like he's being playful. "You used to do all the guys in school."

"I'll repeat. What. Would. Be. In. It. For. Me? Abso-fucking-lutely nothing, that's what. So why should you get off while I get used? Think next time you ask some poor woman to suck your toddler-size junk, what do you have to offer *her*?"

"Cunt," Cody snarls, pushing off the counter, and then stalking away. Only he doesn't get far because a small but furious middle-age man places a palm on Cody's chest to stop him.

"Dad?" I quicken my pace forward to stop whatever is about to go down. My dad isn't a big guy, and he's about as passive as they come, but he's here defending his baby girl, and my heart feels like it's going to explode.

"I'd give you a lecture about how Essie is my daughter. How she's somebody's granddaughter, daughter, niece, cousin, and friend. I could say that in hopes you'd think twice about treating a woman like shit, all because you wouldn't want your own mother or sister treated that way. But I think that's a bullshit argument, as if Essie is only important because she belongs to other people. How about you treat Essie with respect because she's a person– *a human being.* That's why."

"Maybe you should've raised your daughter better," Cody snarls, but Dad doesn't let him go by.

"Maybe your parents should have raised a son who didn't think he was entitled to use a girl. Girls don't screw themselves."

"Don't talk about my parents." Cody's palms slam into my dad's chest, but Will Prynne doesn't move an inch.

"What we celebrate as men shouldn't be used as a weapon against women, think about that." Dad steps to the side to let Cody pass. "Someday you're going to have a wife and children, and I want you to remember how you treated *my* daughter. I'd say I want you to imagine some man treating your wife and daughter this way. But I'd rather you think about how you'd feel if someone treated *you* like this. Powerless. Degraded. Subhuman."

"I wouldn't let anyone treat me like that."

"Bully for you being a big, strapping male propositioning a girl who's half your size. That makes you the asshole, doesn't it? You're not the biggest person in this town. I'm sure I could find someone to teach you a lesson. Big red-headed fella who likes guys and girls. Maybe you've heard of him–"

"Dad?" I caution, knowing Auggie wouldn't lift a finger for me ever again. "Don't go there."

Gesturing to the door, "Go forth and try not to repopulate the earth with narrow-minded sons and browbeaten daughters who will be prey for someone else's narrow-minded son."

Ass landing on a stool, my legs have given up the good fight after the day I've had. My shift is nearly over after suffering through the dinner rush and the slow trickling of late night eaters and post-party munchers.

"I truly fear for the education Fairport High School provides, if Cody is considered one of their brightest." Will Prynne can be a condescending asshole if the agenda fits. Willow came by her attitude naturally, from both sides of her family. It's one of the reasons I love her so much, because she felt like home, reminding me of my dad.

"Fairport High had nothing to do with it," I mutter, emotionally and physically exhausted. "I'm pretty sure it has to do with the fact that there are two types of girls. Good girls who are ignored in school because they don't cater to boys, and bad girls who do… and they're only bad because they make those boys seem more important than they are. Boys like Cody are a dime a dozen, and they should mean nothing to all girls until they prove their worth, not the other way around."

"That's my girl." Dad smiles, reaching out to touch the swelling on my cheek, fingertips lingering so he doesn't cause pain.

"What are you doing here, Dad?"

"Cody's behavior solidified my stance. There was no way in hell I was going to let you walk home, Hester." Dad steps closer, not caring that everyone in the No-Name is eavesdropping. It's not like all of my business isn't being shared all over Facebook to Hell and back, by my own family.

"I don't know if I want to be trapped in a car with my angry and disappointed father, even if it's only for three minutes." Sighing, I've never loved the man more, even if he doesn't like who I am anymore.

"Essie," Dad whispers softly. "Meet me out by the car after you change– *please*."

"Okay, Daddy," I breathe back, ignoring the tears in my voice and the stream of them rolling down my cheeks.

I debate between lingering and changing as quickly as humanly possible, but in the end, I'm too exhausted to do anything that isn't on autopilot. I'm surprised when I hit the parking lot to find Dad leaning against the hood of the car, just staring off into space, when I assumed he'd be waiting in the driver's seat for me.

Will Prynne was the baby, with Uncle Dave nearly twenty years older. Uncle Dave carried on the family business of Prynne Renovations, whereas Dad was allowed to run off and chase his own dreams. Not as passive as his big brother, Dad joined the corporate world. Watching Dad retire in his early fifties truly made me think an education was the way to go. What Dad failed to tell me was it mattered what you chose as an occupation.

I didn't choose the primp life– the primp life chose me, even if that means I'll be broke.

To say I was spoiled would be an understatement. As the only kid to the baby of the family and a stay-at-home mom, I was given anything my heart desired. Not that I didn't appreciate it. It just allowed me to gain a need for the finer things in life. So this new development of taking care of myself is a hard pill to swallow. The only thing Dad refused to pay for was my education and my equipment, simply because the late Dave Prynne Senior never paid a dime of Dad's. But I know if I'd asked, Dad would've paid off my car note. But I didn't want to ask, because

I'm not a shitty human being who leeches anything off her parents that isn't bare essentials for survival.

Stepping forward, I whisper, "Dad?" to gain his attention. A sob is torn from my throat at the sight of his arms opening wide to welcome me home. Flying into them, burying my face against his chest, I finally feel safe after a day and night where everything felt like it was an attack on my person.

"Shh… there… there. Let it out, Essie," Dad murmurs, patting my back. "Everything's going to be okay. I promise. You're just going through growing pains."

"I'm a little old for growing pains." I laugh through the tears.

"Not for this kind, you're not," Dad replies, humor thick in his voice. "You're going to be fine, because you're a Prynne."

"You're not mad at me?" I squeak out in surprise.

"Why would I be?" Dad leans back, pulling me away from his chest so he can gaze down at me. "You didn't do anything wrong."

After snorting, I force out between gritted teeth, "Tell that to Willow."

"You're an adult. Devon is an adult. You chose to have sex with one another. That is not about Willow." Dad pulls me back at arm's length and looks deep into my eyes. "You're my daughter, and that's all I give a shit about."

"Dad?" Lips twisting into a smirk, I think the guy has lost his ever-loving mind. "That's sweet and all, but really crappy advice. Willow is your niece and I cheated on her with her boyfriend."

"There's a difference between a teenager playacting a relationship, and actual adults connecting on a human level. I'm not discussing right or wrong with you, Hester. I'm simply telling you I don't give a shit because you're my daughter, and you're what I care about."

"Thank you," is an exhausted whisper from my lips. Knees barely supporting me, Dad helps me into the car.

"No one in the family is taking sides, Essie." Dad brings up the one thing I dreaded the most. "Adultery, even though I would not dub what you did as such, is a very adult notion. However, one cannot claim to be an adult if they engage in marking up their cousin's face with a Sharpie, or allow others to punch her and then defame her on Facebook. So you can't commit adultery against someone who is essentially behaving as the child we think her to be. I love Willow unconditionally, but I will not stand by while she abuses you, no matter what you did to provoke it."

"I take responsibility for my actions," I stammer as Dad pulls into our driveway. We live one street over from Clover's and Dave and Mary's side-by-side houses. By one street over, I mean the back of our properties are butted up against one another. It's only three streets over to the Spook House. Instead of feeling safe, I feel suffocated by guilt and shame.

"The punishment must fit the crime, and you aren't a criminal. Matters of the heart should never be punished, only forgiven." Holding my elbow to guide me to the house, Dad stops in the middle of the front walk. "Don't ever tell Dave I said this," he whispers conspiratorially. "But there's a big difference between taking responsibility for your actions and allowing your victim to become your victimizer."

"Don't be a doormat, Essie," I remind myself to put that into practice where Devon is concerned. "As much as we love to say we Prynnes are passive, we're a vicious lot. I know this firsthand. A lot of what Uncle Dave does is more passive-aggressive than passive."

"That's my girl," Dad sings as we enter the house. "And here's my other favorite girl." He brightens when Mom greets us in the living room. "Brought her home safe and sound and no worse for wear."

"With the exception of Miss Violet's handiwork, I see," Mom murmurs while gripping my chin between her fingertips, turning my face left and right. "No doubt you've got it concealed with your magic makeup."

Eyes casting down, I spot my gray, fluffy kitty weaving her way around the newel post, and all I want to do is lie in bed while listening to Fluffernutter purr my troubles away.

"You're not taking my cat," blurts out before I can stop it. "Shit, you are, aren't you?"

"You could always come with us," Mom tries again. But I'm pretty sure this is just a nicety. She might mean it a little bit, because no doubt they're going to miss their only daughter. But I know they secretly want to be rid of me and my shitty problems, so they can finally honeymoon for the rests of their lives.

I'm not selfish enough to cling onto them and follow them to Florida. It's easier to think of them abandoning me, than for me to feel like a third wheel for the rest of my life.

"I just want to lie down now." As if walking through quicksand, I make my way to the staircase with Fluffernutter following in my wake. "Thanks for the ride home, Dad, and for sticking up for me against Cody. Never fear that I have daddy issues, because you're the best dad a girl could ever wish for."

"What happened with Cody?" Mom interrogates Dad, just as I knew she would, which is why I said it. I wanted to buy myself some privacy before Mom attempts to mother me.

Ambling up to my bedroom, I slip inside and go directly to my vanity. Sitting down, I gaze around at the room that won't be mine for much longer. This frilly pink world has been all I've ever known for over twenty-one years. Everything in it is something I've picked out, yet I am powerless to keep its safety mine.

Next I look in the mirror, asking myself if it's written on my features to be the type of person I am. Devon's comment on how big tits make a person a whore, and how Masons never marry whores, has always ridden beside me through life. I know when people look at the sharp, razor cut on my chin-length, brown hair, they assume I'm a person who only cares about looks. This is compounded when they hear my profession, as if I'm an empty-headed girl who only cares about the pretty things in life. When the real reason I do what I do is because I want everyone to feel comfortable in their own skin.

It's not about me. I do it for them, because I know what it's like to feel inadequate.

Sighing in resignation, with a shaking hand, I grab for a moist toilette to scrub the makeup off my face.

"Let me do that, hun." Mom snuck up on me. Her hands cup my shoulders, spinning me around on my vanity stool. "I'll be careful around your eye and forehead."

"Thank you," I murmur, knowing I don't deserve the kindness.

Damp cloth swathing across my face, my mom stares down at me, and I'm yet again struck at how amazing she is. I could go on and on about how the woman in her early forties looks closer to my age, but what she looks like isn't a portrayal of who she truly is. Most daughters disregard what their mothers have to say. But I'm not one of them, because Mom's advice was wrought through experience. Mom's kind. Soft. Motherly. Nonjudgmental. Understanding.

"I've cheated on people."

A little bit warped.

"I was cheated on first. But I never saw it as cheating, Essie. Cheating is what happens in a committed relationship, where you're partners, whether married or not. It's not during the in between state of childhood and adulthood."

"I don't understand," I murmur, trying not to shake my head left and right as Mom wipes the makeup from my face.

"I've always told you how a boy will have to break your heart before you're smart enough to recognize the one who won't. I stand by that. I dated a kid named Joshua all through high school. We were still dating after graduation."

"Joshua Freeman?" The guy and his family lives down the block– I used to babysit his sons when they were littler. Jeez, Mom's a masochist.

"Yeah." Mom's lips twist slightly, trying to keep her fond smile private. "We were going on dates to the movies and dinner, talking on the phone and taking walks. Of course we were screwing, but that's beside the point. One day he met a girl and tried to explain how he felt differently about her than he did for me."

"Oh, Mom," I cry out, arm wrapping around her waist, trying to comfort her.

"We'd been together for over four years, so I was heartbroken to say the least. Devastated, actually. Back then, I didn't understand, but I do now. I felt like he did this horrible thing *to me*. But later, I met a guy at college and we began dating– dated the whole way through. Then I did the same thing to Ben that Joshua did to me."

"What? Come again?"

"I realized what Josh and I had was friendship. He didn't cheat on me because we weren't a couple– partners. What I had with Ben was also friendship, even if I knew I was going to cause him pain. When I started working as the assistant to your father's business partner, which is how I met Will Prynne in the first place, I was able to recognize the man who wouldn't break my heart. Not only that, Will set the goddamn thing on fire."

Laughing, gibberish babbles out my lips. "Dad? *My* dad? My *tiny* dad?"

"Oh, yeah," Mom purrs, causing me to smile. My parents have always been batshit cray-cray for each other. "Even knowing how much it hurt to be pushed aside by another, I couldn't stop myself from hurting Ben the same way. There is such a thing as being loyal to a person at the expense of being disloyal to yourself. It's not selfish, nor is it cheating, to honor your feelings. No one can dictate your emotions or how physical chemistry affects you. No one does this on purpose.

"If you're not committed, you're looking for the right one, even if you're dating someone else. It's a fact of life. I was just too young to realize this when I was with Josh and Ben, but I learned it when I met Will.

"If Josh and I had been right for one another, we would've married long before we broke up. Same with Ben and me. We weren't right, and that's why we were dragging our feet. It wasn't cheating– we were friends who dated and had sex, but that's it. Josh broke it off when he met Kara, and I broke it off with Ben when I met Will. I'm glad I didn't bend to society's pressure to get hitched to a man so I could leave my dad's home. You have to find yourself, and know exactly who you are and what you want, before you can give yourself to another human being. I wasn't ready with Josh and Ben, but I was when I met Will."

"Mom, in a roundabout way, I think I actually understand what you're saying, and I even agree with you. I'm not just saying that to clear my conscience, either."

"At twenty-one, with the things I know you've been through, even if you've never told me to spare my feelings, I knew you'd understand." Mom's words have me looking away in shame. "At eighteen, Willow is incapable of understanding. Give her a few months to see if what she's building with Kieren is real, for her to recognize what she had with Devon was false. Her pride might not let her admit it to you, but she won't be out for your blood anymore."

"I still need to apologize to her, because I hurt because I hurt her," I admit.

"Essie." Mom tugs my chin so I'll look at her. "You can keep saying the same thing over and over again, but if the person isn't receptive to hearing it, they won't. Willow is going to be too busy justifying why she feels what she feels the entire time you're speaking. She's going to be thinking of nasty rebuttals instead of hearing you. This is just how it's going to be. So the best thing you can do is keep your mouth shut, stay away from her without neglecting your ties to the family, and wait until she grows up.

"If you don't, you'll be the target for every bit of anger and frustration Willow feels, even if you're not the culprit. You'll be the safe zone– the person who loves Willow unconditionally. The one who can take it, sticks it out, and doesn't leave her. There is no such thing as taking it while waiting for forgiveness– it's called abuse. I won't allow my daughter to be abused, but I also won't let you teach Willow how to be an abuser."

"You don't think Willow has a right to be angry?" Eyebrows scrunching in confusion, I stare at my mother's reflection in the mirror.

"Of course Willow does, but not for the reasons you think. It's not your fault that what Willow and Devon had together didn't work out– their lack of chemistry and connection. Love can't be forced, nor can it be demanded or controlled. If one in the couple isn't feeling it, they shouldn't be trapped in fear because whoever they fall for next will be targeted on Facebook."

I want to hear Mom, but there's a negative dialogue playing out in my head. One that says I'm a bad person. But then I realize that actually acts in my favor, because it proves Mom's point. I'm too busy wallowing in what's inside my head to hear her. The same holds true with Willow. Whatever she has going on inside her head will infect whatever I try to say or do to make reparations, and none of it will have a damn thing to do with me.

"Essie?" Mom grips my chin, forcing me to look in the mirror. Moving my face left and right, she highlights the red splotch on my forehead from the chemical burn and the blue-black bruise forming just beneath my eye on my cheek bone. "These are not marks because you hurt Willow. The burn and the bruise are a sign of unleashed aggression and frustration because Devon didn't love and want Willow back, even if she didn't want or love him herself."

"I don't understand why you see Willow like this?"

"To understand the daughter is to have known the father. I won't pussyfoot around. I know you know Sam was Willow's dad. Sam was a great guy. Jovial and giving. But he treated Clover like a goddamn rat-bastard, taking all of his frustrations out on her because he could. I see this in all three of his children. Does it make them bad people? No. It just means they need to recognize it and filter it into something productive versus destructive. If they don't, we're going to have two bitches and a prick trying to railroad everyone in this family, and that isn't fair to any of us."

Tears pricking my eyes, I nod my head up and down while sniffling. "I'd always wondered about Clover and Sam."

"Sam loved Clover more than life itself, just as Willow loves you. But the closest people get the brunt of the force when it comes to people like them. I won't allow you to take the hits, nor will I allow you to teach Willow that it's okay to behave that way. Even if you hurt Willow, this behavior is unacceptable. Do I make myself clear, young lady? You are not a verbal or physical punching bag."

"I get it– I do."

"Get undressed and into your nightgown," Mom orders, and I obey. I can feel her eyes on my body the entire time, so I try to shield myself while disrobing. "Essie, for every person who disrespects you, there are thousands who will respect you. Don't let the views of a handful of people affect how you view yourself."

"That's all well and good, Mom–" I tug my nightgown over my head, and I breathe deeply in relief because I'm finally covered. "Until you're trying to fight off some guy who won't take no for an answer, or have to ignore glares and whispered words."

"Essie? If someone with a flawed body was being made fun of, you'd step in. Just because the disrespectful person likes what they see, that doesn't make it any less bullying." Mom walks over to my bed, and then whips the covers back. "Get in."

Doing as I'm told, I crawl in between my sheets and sigh in bliss as my body shapes itself to the bed I've used since I left the crib. Mom gets in behind me, curling protectively around my body.

"About Devon–"

"Shit!" I hiss with feeling, heart hammering against the inside of my chest.

"I'm not saying I told you so, or you reap what you sow, and any of that other horseshit. Obviously there is something between the two of you that is undeniable. All I want to say is how you can't hold him accountable for what he's pulling right now, because he's not in his right mind."

"So I'm supposed to what? Just accept it? You don't want me to allow Willow to abuse me, even if we all can agree I deserve it to a certain extent. You want me to see the people who try to take advantage of me as bullies. But it's okay if Devon plays fiddler with my heartstrings? What the fuck, Mom."

Chuckling into my ear, Mom's arm wraps around my belly, pulling me closer to her chest. "Oh, I don't want you accepting anything from Officer Douchebag. All I was saying… you can forgive once he's altered his ways. You can forgive, but you should never forget. You have to protect yourself, but at the same time you have to let it go. Because what Devon does has nothing to do with you, even if he's doing it to you. Same with Willow. Same with what Devon and you did to Willow. I don't know if Devon is your future or not, but don't let his actions taint how you feel about yourself."

"I'll try," but I make no promises.

"Good luck with that." Mom chuckles evilly. "If your dad was a bipolar addict, I would've been fucked. Because I don't have the ability to tell him no, no matter what he wants from me. So that, my daughter, is why no one in our family is upset with you, disappointed in you, or angry with you. We all get it. We've been there before– Willow and Violet, they'll have the joy of learning this lesson someday, and we'll stick by them while they flounder."

CHAPTER TWENTY-NINE

Devon Mason

Filled with indecision, I pace back and forth across the street from Essie's house. Stalker? You bet. There's so much to say, but I don't have the words to say them. If I didn't already feel depressed, like the pits of Hell are opening up to welcome me home, seeing the total destruction of Essie this afternoon would have done it.

I'd love to say Willow and Violet were spared from my wrath today by the simple fact they will be my stepsisters someday, but that's a bullshit lie. I was nearly catatonic with not giving a shit about breathing at the time, to the point I couldn't muster up the energy to save Essie. Which only makes me feel that much worse.

It took snorting several bumps of coke for me to make my way here. It was a hard-earned high, forcing me to drive several hours away from Chief Mason's stranglehold on the criminal element in Fairport.

The addict in me realizes how I took the time, energy, and effort to waste five hours of my time chasing a high, when I couldn't be bothered to step in and stop the aftermath I'd caused. The guy who has loved Essie since grade school hates the addict, but he knows he can't survive without him.

As the coke felt like it melted into my brain, the addictive euphoria and thrumming energy was like coming up for air after drowning in a sea of despair. A part of me acknowledges that the drug addict is talking, but another part knows it's the only way to chase the darkness away.

Everything is heightened, as if I can hear a fly's wings cutting a path through the air, or even feel the air itself brushing against my face. Dilated eyes dart in every direction, picking up things I miss when I'm numb. Pacing, hands shaking for an entirely different reason than they were this morning, I'm forced to stop every once and a while when the sneezing fits hit me.

"You just going to stalk around like a creeper, or are you going to knock on my front door?" Will Prynne scares the piss out of me. Bad enough my heart was already racing.

"You're going to give me a heart attack," I mutter, loping across the street to meet him.

"The coke will do that first," Will mutters wryly. Laidback and easy-going, I know Essie's dad is making fun of me, but I can't really fault him for it.

"Is Essie okay?" squeaks out, my voice pitching higher than I expected.

"You could come in and find out, ya know?" Will sits on the top step to his porch, still wearing a pair of slacks and a long-sleeved shirt from working today. "No matter what happens, I'll never keep you from my daughter."

"I know– but maybe you should." Stepping closer, I still stay out of arm's reach.

"Hester's a grown woman. I'm not going to stunt her by treating her like a child."

Suddenly I experience verbal vomit. "I want to see Essie, but I think it's best if she doesn't see me– for her sake. I didn't want what happened today to happen, and I want to apologize. But I'm not in a good place, and I don't want to burden Essie with it. So I'm trying to stay away, but I don't want her to think I abandoned her either."

Tilting his head to the side, Will just gazes at me for what feels like hours. A bug under a microscope, waiting for the sun to fry it. "I believe that you believe what you say," he says at length. "Would you like to know a surefire way to make sure Essie knows you didn't abandon her?"

"Yes," I breathe, too much hope in my voice for my liking, as I step closer to Will. "Manic. Depressed. High. Up or down, I never want Essie to think I've abandoned her."

"Get help," is all Will says, eyes still boring into me.

"I am. Dad found a place in Arizona, and I wanted to go immediately. But they were booked up, so now it could be weeks, maybe even months until I can go. I'm trying my hardest to do the right thing."

"Which is why you were pacing across the street while staring at my daughter's bedroom window at nearly midnight, instead of knocking on my door?"

"Yes, Will." Tugging at my hair, I walk in a circle. The energy is intensifying. My skin is crawling with the need to… "It's for the best if I leave Essie alone, like last time."

Run!

Muscles coiled, I bound forward, headed right down the middle of the street. I can breathe deeper the faster I go, burning off the excess energy coursing through my veins. My mind feels clear, but I don't know if it's an illusion or reality.

My mind is focused on two things: protect Essie and get Tommy and Taryn help too.

Sweat dripping down my face, I blink to clear my vision, only to discover I'm at Bethany's door. Testing the knob, I twist and find myself inside her tiny apartment.

"What the–" Bethany whips her head around as she sits at her child-size desk, brown ponytail swinging in an arch behind her. "Devon, are you okay? What did you do? Is Essie okay?" flows rapidly as she rises to her feet.

"Nothing you don't already know," I mutter, shutting the door behind me. My shoulders curl inward, skeeved out by the Hello Kitty paraphernalia all over the place. "Essie is fine. She's at home with her parents. I just talked to Will and he seems content, so that means Essie is good too."

"Okay." Bethany slowly lowers herself back into her chair. "What can I do for you?" Looking away, her snort ricochets like a gunshot in the dark. "This is beyond awkward. A little over a week ago, I had to watch you defile my best friend, and I was powerless to stop it. Now you waltz right into my place without knocking."

"You should lock your door," I say without shame. "Trust me when I say both Essie and I wanted to do what we did, even if it was a catastrophic idea."

"Glad we agree on something." Beth's place is so small, while sitting at her desk, she leans backward to grab a bottle of water from her mini-fridge. I ignore the creepy Hello Kitty microwave smiling at me. "Here!"

A bottle of water is lobbed at my face. Energized by coke, my reflexes are quick enough to make sure I don't have a shiner to match Essie's. "Thanks." I drain the entire bottle in a few gulps. "Thirstier than I expected, I guess."

Another bottle flies through the air, this one I miss. Bouncing off my chest, it falls to the floor with a dull thud. Shrugging, I retrieve it and drain it too.

"Thanks," I mutter dryly. "I need something to occupy my time between now and rehab… and by occupy, I mean I need something to be obsessed about enough to keep me from doing other stupid shit. So I need you to tell me what happened to Essie."

Voice innocent, Beth won't look at me as she speaks. "Who says anything happened to Essie."

"Goddamnit!" I lob the empty bottle at her head. "Don't play games with me, Bethany. We've known each other since preschool. I know when you're being evasive."

"Don't throw things at me." Beth pouts, tossing the bottle in her Hello Kitty trashcan.

"You threw two bottles at me–" the audacity.

"Not out of anger."

"No, out of frustration." I plop down to sit on the foot of Beth's bed, inches from her. "Don't be evasive. I've had enough therapists to know the lingo and to recognize what you're doing. Answer the question. Essie obviously had something bad happen to her, and I want the details."

"Devon." Bethany looks me straight in the eyes with tears springing from hers. "I can't. I'm sorry. I can't. Not only because Essie wouldn't want you to know, but you're not in the right frame of mind to make good choices. Okay?"

"No, it's not okay," I snarl, fisting the blanket resting beneath my fingertips. "What is up with this Hello Kitty shit?" I drop the blanket like the sight of it burns me. "Beth, I need to be distracted."

Looking heavenward, Beth sighs. "Fine… we both know she never had a good sexual experience during high school, and I know you paid them all back by having Colin arrest them for this or that. But frat parties are a different beast. The person who harmed Essie has been taken care of, and that's all you need to know. She's dealing with it, some days better than others. But it was the powerlessness and humiliation that hurts the worst. That and the fact that she blames it on how she looks, not how we raise boys to think they can take from girls what the girls aren't willing to give."

Breathing deeply, seeing nothing but the crimson tide of rage, my mind plays snippets of my past. Mom held down in the middle of our living room, with Kieren tied to the chair next to me. Mom's sharp cries of pain as men took from her what she never would've willingly given them. Over and over and over again, they took until they drained what little life was left in Mom's tainted soul.

That happened to Essie. *My* Essie.

Yet another reason I've failed.

"Details. Now," I demand, making sure Bethany knows I will not leave here until she tells me what I came here to know.

Eyes closed, I know Beth is counting in her head. "It was rush week. Everyone was abuzz at cosmetology school about the endless parties our sister college would be hosting. Essie and I went to a few, and each one was more out of control than the last. I could blame what happened on how we had too much to drink, how we were dressed or how we looked, or I could say we were stupid for going somewhere that put us in danger. But we were at a party with our peers, and they shouldn't take advantage. They should be raised better than to think they have a right to anyone's body. But a mob mentality descended, and that's why I will lock my own children up if they ever try to go to a frat party. Son or daughter.

"There was an energy in the air infecting everyone, making it so they lost all sense of right or wrong. Riding that energy was fear, a fear the frat boys were consuming. The pledges found girls in the crowd, and the only consent they needed was how the girl was in the house. Like setting foot into the party meant you were free meat. Crowds watched, as girls who were so drunk or high they couldn't even walk, let alone say yes or no, were tossed in the yard and taken from behind like dogs."

In a flash, I find myself bent over Bethany's toilet, retching up bile because I haven't eaten in days. Imagination too vivid with coke and rage coursing through my veins, I'm transported to a place and time I've never been, only I'm inside Essie's skin. Knees pressing into the earth, only it's carpet abrading my flesh, not the lush softness of grass.

On the heels of that vision is another nightmare, only it was once my reality. A reality where normalcy is replaced by the worst of mankind. Where a single man would never do what he does when in a group.

Animals.

Separate, they behave.

Together, they're depraved.

"You like watching your momma get pounded, boy? Dontcha?" Strong hands caress my shoulders, a fingertip skims along my jawline, forcing me to watch a man rut so violently on my mother, I see a red wash on her thighs. *"There's too many of us for just little ol' momma. She's only got enough holes for two. How old are ya, boy?"*

"Answer him!" the second of three men demands as he kneels over my mother's face, causing her to choke on the body part thrusting down her throat. *"Answer him or the little one will be put to good use."*

"Fourteen!" I shout, voice breaking with terror. *"I'll be fourteen next week."*

"Pick– you or your brother?" the third man forces me to make an impossible decision.

"Me!" I scream without hesitation, ignoring how Ren begs me to make the other choice.

"Devon?" Bethany shakes me from what has to have been a repressed memory, a secret Ren's always kept– from everyone, especially from me. "Hey, Dev? You okay?" Beth's bony arms slide around my shoulders, and I'm too fried not to take the comfort that's being offered. After wiping my mouth with a wet washcloth, she helps me sit back on the bed. *"Right now,"* Beth stresses. "Right now everyone you love and care for is safe and sound. I promise."

Bethany says exactly what I needed to hear.

"What happened to the frat boys?" is whispered against her breast as it cradles me softly. "What happened?"

"I called 911, as did about fifty others. Most were drawn to the evil energy weaving its way through the crowd, but those unaffected called for help. Essie threw up about a minute into it, and it pissed the guy off. So he kicked her away and one of his frat buddies tossed him another girl to take– just tossed a girl like she meant nothing. When the cops showed up, they arrested just about everyone. Took statements. The victims were taken to the hospital for rape kits."

"Essie?"

"No, the guy was banging another unwilling victim, so they overlooked Essie, which is what she wanted. I tried to get her to come forward, and a few of the cops just knew. One look at her, and they just *knew*. But she wouldn't give in."

Feeling like my balls were just shorn off, I sob against Bethany's chest, soaking up all the comfort she can provide. Arms wrapped around her, I twist my fingers into the back of her shirt. I ignore the rhythmic tapping of what I know is her fingertips on her cellphone.

"One of the guys there that night– one of the pledges. He wouldn't participate. He was so changed by what happened, by witnessing the cops coming to the rescue, he quit school and enrolled in the police academy. His new wife was one of the victims."

"Who? Why are you telling me that?" I nestle closer, needing Beth's warmth and support.

"I was drunk, and I couldn't protect Essie or myself. I suffer from a heavy dose of survivor's guilt over this, which is why my educational path veered off course as well. But if you ever need any details from a person who was stone, cold sober, all you have to do is ask your partner."

"What?" I gasp, voice breaking. "Kyle?" Bethany nods her head yes, chin brushing the top of my head. "Oh, God. Poor Renee."

"Yes, poor Renee, who was Essie's replacement, and not at all drunk. Poor Renee, and Essie, and Holly, and Christine, and Dori, and Shawna, and every girl and boy or woman and man, who every single day is preyed upon by predators and their peers, friends, and family members who are supposed to protect them. *That* is why I changed, and why I will do the job I was created to do."

Firm hands cup my armpits and tug me free from Bethany's embrace. I'd freak out if I didn't recognize them immediately. "C'mon, bro. Let's get you home– Beth, get a real lock on your door."

Gazing up at my brother, I show him that I just got a glimpse of the truth, and I realize he never wanted me to know because it was better for all of us that I didn't. But what was the cost for Kieren to keep such a dark secret?

"Not tonight," Ren begs. "Let's go home and get some sleep. Please."

Nodding, too emotionally raw and mentally and physically exhausted to stand on my own, Ren helps me walk down to the car. I don't pass out, but I drift off into my happy place. A place where everything is muted gray, with no stimulation of any kind. I call this place Balance.

Blinking out of my catatonic state, I find myself being lowered to my bed. No doubt I walked in here on my own, like a sleepwalker, which is how I spend most of my days and nights, never truly in the moment. For an instant, I almost beg Ren to join me. But then I remember I'm the big brother who was supposed to protect him, not the other way around.

Less than two years apart in age, Kieren can read me better than an identical twin can read their other half. Sliding into bed behind me, Ren curls around my body, protecting me from the big, bad world… and then I begin to cry.

CHAPTER THIRTY

Kieren Mason

"Hi!" comes brightly from the Spook House's front door. I fall into Willow's smile, losing sight of everything else. After years of chasing after curvaceous women, somehow I'm drawn to the girl wearing a Kool-Aid Man t-shirt and torn jeans, with a pair of old Chucks covered in skulls with the medium of Sharpie. "You're early."

"I always am," I tease with a wink. "Which is why you're already ready." Reaching forward, I drag a thumb across Willow's bottom lip, flirting while acknowledging the lipstick she's wearing to impress me. "Hi, right back atcha, Spanky."

We're at the halfway mark from the time we signed Devon up for rehab to when they will finally admit him. A few weeks turned into six. Three weeks down, three weeks to go. But I refuse to voice the dull thud throbbing at the back of my mind while in Willow's presence. We don't speak of Devon or Essie, or the fact that we know Clover and Dad are messing around behind our backs.

Willow is my distraction, as I am hers. Our time together is just about us. It's about having fun and getting to know one another, without letting anything, and I mean *anything*, interfere or interrupt the few hours a week we carve out just for ourselves.

"I've never been on a real date." Willow blushes, bringing out the smattering of freckles on her face. I swear to God, she looks just like Seth right now, and that's not genetically possible because it's the Webster features that are the commonality right now, not the Prynne features.

"I've been on a lot of dates," I pull no punches. "But none of them have felt *real*… do you have everything you need?"

Willow raises her hands above her head, and then turns in a circle. "I seem to be fully clothed." Then she pats her back pockets, causing her bubble butt to jiggle. I step from foot-to-foot, hoping to unkink my dick as it tries to rise. "Got my cash, my license, and my cell. We're good to go."

"Just used to women like Isis, Rae, and Aunt Ginny," I mutter, blushing. "I swear they could live out of their purses."

"Mom's got a purse like that– big enough to shove Seth in there." Willow's taunting laughter flows as she skips down the sidewalk. "Clover and I still get in trouble for touching that fucking bag. You'd swear there were nuclear launch codes in her wallet, not a few fives and ones, and probably a coupon for rolling papers."

Mary Prynne is the only drug grower in Fairport Dad won't arrest, much to our amusement and his frustration.

Skidding to a stop, Willow looks at me over her shoulder, brown eyes popping wide. "We're..." she stammers, voice hitching as her hand glides down the body of my car. "We're taking the pussy magnet?" With a loud whoop, Willow jumps in place a few times, then runs to the driver's side. "I'm driving."

"Hey!" I shout, chasing Willow down, thankful my stride is three times longer than hers. "Nope. No can do. This is a date, and the man drives *his* car."

"Your car? Pfft..." Willow gets in, shuts the door in my face, locks it, and then straps in. The ignition is turning over before I admit defeat and shuffle over to the passenger side. When I get in, Willow continues. "This is Chief Mason's hot ride, not yours. So you can share the wealth, Stud."

"Don't wreck it," I warn, terrified. "It's been in the family for over forty years. Grandpa John owned this car before my dad was even born. Weston's supposed to learn to drive it next. It's a family tradition. All Masons learn to drive using the pussy magnet."

"I'm a good driver, been doing it since I was eleven." Willow's confession is even more terrifying than her driving my car. "The adventures Seth and I used to get into." Leaning into me, she whispers conspiratorially, "If I had a kid who acted like me, I would've beat them senseless just as Clover beat me." Laughing carefree, Willow picks up speed. "Remind me never to have kids– KARMA!" she shouts, high on life. "Where we going, Stud?"

Leaning back against the seat with a wicked smile twisting my lips, I just murmur, "Just drive, and drive fast."

Willow drives like the wind, and I've never felt more free. Together, it's like nothing can touch us.

I made reservations at a popular restaurant three towns over from Fairport. Whereas I dressed up for the occasion, a pair of khakis and a polo, Willow refused to bend.

"I don't care if they stare," Willow's voice pitches high as we wait at the hostess station. "This is who I am."

"I like you just the way you are." Insanity, the need to touch Willow has my fingers curling to meet my palms. Thank goodness the hostess saves me from making a fool out of myself. "Mason. We have a reservation for two at seven tonight."

The well-dressed woman's eyes flick back and forth between Willow and me. No doubt I look spiffy like a college student, and the actual student looks like she's in middle school, which I think is why Willow dressed as she did. There is nothing that's going to make her look older than the simple act of time.

"Follow me," the hostess murmurs, and I know we're going to get the shittiest table in the house.

"Watch this." Willow elbows me, eyes cutting in the direction of the slowly walking hostess, as if we'll get lost walking to the table. "We're either going to be seated near the kitchen doors or the bathroom. Not that I care, 'cuz we'll just get our food all the quicker."

Willow's not-so whispered words have the hostess changing direction to seat us near the side windows overlooking a nearby park.

Sharing a smirk, we accept a menu while the hostess quickly prattles off the specials. "You are a devious minx, Ms. Prynne– I like that about you. I like that a lot."

Smiling mischievously, now Willow reminds me of Robin. It's like she's a chimera. As freaky as it is, we'll never have a dull moment together.

"I know bitches like her," Willow offers as example. "It's called reverse psychology. Too bad she's too stupid to realize it. Hmm…" she opens her menu, perusing the options. "You having spaghetti?"

"Ha!" my sharp bark of laughter has all eyes lasering in on us. "I had spaghetti four times out of the last seven days."

"I know. You better stop weaseling your way outta Clover's cooking class, 'cuz I'm a girl who loves to eat." Willow purrs– the naughty, naughty girl –and my heart starts galloping out of control.

All of my other dates were just a formality to get the girl into my truck afterward. With Willow tonight, I know we won't be having sex or even sharing a kiss at the Spook House's front door.

The lack of pressure, and the ability to just be friends who are having a good time getting to know one another, it's something special I've never experienced before. Carefree. Priceless. Without expectation and demand.

"We need meat." Willow's appetite never fails to amaze me, which is why I picked a steakhouse. Mass quantities of food are on the menu, not because she'll owe me at the end of the night, but because I love sharing a meal with her. "Let's pick out two entrees we'd both want to eat, and then share. Yay or nay?"

"Hell, yay." Smirking, I spy a porterhouse with my name on it, but also the pork loin with balsamic glaze. "How we doing this, anyway? I don't want to call out what I want, only to have you agree with me when you don't."

"Oh, I'm not like you, Stud." Willow's lips curl in a knowing smirk. "I'm not selfless at all. I know at least one of my choices will be on the menu for tonight. But I'd like to know how well we know the other. So let's type out our choices in a text, and then send them at the same time."

"Win-win," I murmur, quickly typing out everything, including how I want garlic smashed potatoes and sautéed green beans. At the last second, I realize I better give a temperature for my steak. Medium is a good middle ground, I think. "Ready?" Willow nods. "Sending."

My text alert vibrates my hand.

Spanky: *Stud, we're ordering what you want, because we both know I'll eat anything. Thank you for taking me out tonight.*

"You're not getting choked up over that, are you?" Willow teases me, but she's simultaneously smiling and blushing. "Clover feeds me good. Robin loves to cook too. Auggie is a giant man who has to eat nonstop. I'm nothing if not well-fed. Since I moved to the Spook House, I've gone up a dress-size."

"Spanky, pick something out," I practically whine, causing her to reach across the table to take my hand.

"You cook all the meals in your house– the least I can do is let you pick out what we eat tonight." After a squeeze, Willow releases my hand and leans back in her seat. "I'll pick dessert and after dinner entertainment. Fair?"

"More than fair," I murmur just as the waitress arrives. I order for the both of us without hesitation. I can tell the waitress was standing nearby eavesdropping, because she's extra sweet to us and not looking like we can't afford this place or don't deserve to be here.

Always comfortable around each other, like we've been best friends forever, even with the sexual tension riding the air, Willow and I chat without any uncomfortable silences. She's chatting animatedly about one of her professors when our meal arrives.

"So Stone is totally calling out our economics professor— he's such a tool." Willow accepts the pork loin with a thank you to the waitress. "I should reiterate. Professor Kirkland is the tool, not Stone. But I'm sure Kirkland didn't appreciate being called a daft lummox by one of his students. We all knew Kirkland was wrong– Google search doesn't lie."

"Oh, of course everything on the internet is gospel," I tease, portioning the steak and sides into two. Then we awkwardly make our trade.

"It is when you're talking math." Insert patented eye roll here. "Ermahgerd," Willow moans when the steak hit her mouth. "Best fucking food ever."

I take a few moments to appreciate the blissed out expression on Willow's face. As wrong of me as it is to wonder… I pop chub, just knowing that's the same noise she'd make during sex– while I feed her mouth my cock.

"Stud?" Willow interrupts my thoughts. "Eat your food." She taps her fork on the edge of my plate. "Trust me– it's way better than the sex you're thinking about right now."

"I highly doubt that," I murmur, taking a bite of steak. Eyes closing, I wonder if we should get a doggie bag so Clover can replicate the recipe. But then I realize we have two people eating one steak, and there won't be a bite left to share. "We need to have sex that's as good as this steak."

"We should have ordered two steaks, because this pork loin is dry," Willow mutters, looking disappointed. "But if your reputation lives up to the nickname I gave you, I don't doubt for a second having sex with you would be better than this steak."

"Keep talking like that, and I won't have enough blood to fuel my brain, Spanky." My words sound teasing, but there's an edge of threat to them.

Our first date, which we're both ignoring because Essie was with us, involved Willow getting off on me in the hallway at

Rush. Well, off enough to leave my pants sopping wet and me with a serious case of bruised blue balls from her kneeing me. Our next date, which was actually a group date to see Revolutionary Road, where Willow was supposedly with Devon, led to more grinding action and her tiny hand cupping my crotch like she was slapping her ownership stamp on it. For the past three weeks, we've spent at least two hours together every night before bedtime, watching shows and movies. Every night, the sexual tension is so thick we could choke on it, and I know the second I leave, Willow's rubbing one out.

Fuck.

We finish our meal in companionable silence, enjoying every morsel while ignoring the elephant in the room. We can keep pretending we're twelve-year-olds who are buddies, but eventually one of us is going to snap and make the first move– I'm hoping that will be Willow. It's not that I don't want her, but after feeling like a goddamn predator, I want to be preyed upon for a change.

After dinner, I ask Willow if she wants to drive us back, but she declines, telling me to take her to Revamped. Confused, I have no idea why she'd want to go to work at this hour, but I do as I'm told.

"Am I dropping you off here for the night, or do you want me to come in with you?" My voice trails off with obvious confusion.

"C'mon, Stud!" Willow jumps out of my car, then jogs over to the front door, keys in hand. "I said I got to pick the after dinner entertainment, and I want to play some old school shoot 'em up."

"I think I'm in love with you," flows out before I can stop it, and Willow's laugh tells me she thinks I'm joking. Yanking me into Revamped, I'm always floored at the nostalgia of the place. Revamped reminds me of every grandmother's house you've ever been in, mixed with a geeky teenage boy's bedroom.

Revamped is one of my favorite places on Earth– obviously Willow's too.

With practiced ease, Willow has the N64 booted up to the ancient console television set, and we're crowded together on a yellow sofa with broken down cushions.

"Don't get mad at me if I spring wood over Joanna Dark's naughty black catsuit. I'm a man– I can't help it if cartoon sexiness gets me hot and bothered."

"Comic-Con is going to be a blast with you," Willow teases me. "Even I will agree she's the sexiest video game heroine. It's why Auggie makes us play as Elvis."

"Oh, God– don't do that while I'm around." I shudder in revulsion of the short avatar with the huge noggin. "Don't ruin the game for me."

"Teams? Or do you want a hundred minions coming after both of us?" Willow's face glows from the light cast off the TV, and it takes everything in me not to grab her face and kiss the ever-loving hell out of her. I'd like to think she wants it, but the only way I'll know for sure is when she finally kisses me again.

Patience is a virtue that is infuriating right now.

"Teams, with helper minions. King of the hill."

"Oh, Stud," Willow purrs, getting up slightly to sit on her calves so we're closer in height. "You're going down."

"Winner gets to pick tomorrow night's show selection." I throw out there, not caring either way, but figuring the competition will add an extra level of fun.

"You're on, mister!" Willow mock-punches me in the bicep, always copping a feel before she pulls away, and it never fails to bring a smile to my face.

The next few hours, Willow and I spend it by verbally razzing one another while physically attacking the other's avatar. Leaning into one another, bodies doing all they can to come into contact, we laugh and have a good time.

Innocent fun, and it's exactly what we both needed. Besides being stressed about school and how off Violet and Clover have been around her, Willow and I share the same stressors: Clover and my dad are sneaking around behind our backs for some reason, Devon's constant need to pull us in while driving us away while we wait for his impending rehab visit, and Essie's life imploding, even if Willow pretends she doesn't care. It's all been too much to handle.

We need these few stolen hours to feel normal, to put ourselves first, and to carve a little slice out of this life to call our own. My worries will come back the moment I'm away from Willow, just like I know hers will do the same.

Tonight was the best date I've ever had. Even when we're old and gray, I'm not going to forget a single second of it. Judging by the breathy kiss to my cheek, which came a little too close to my mouth to be considered platonic, and the way Willow rubbed her body on mine before she pulled away to say goodnight, it was memorable for her too.

CHAPTER THIRTY-ONE

Devon Mason

The water stain on the ceiling above my bed has anchored me to life for the past few days. Lying in bed, the only gumption I can harness is poured into staring at the stain above my head.

The nightmares are back– have been since that revelation at Bethany's place weeks ago. I know no more now than I did then, but too much for me to handle nevertheless. I experience all of it up to that specific point, and I can take a wild guess what happened next– the very thing Ren helped me cover up. Then the memories fast-forward to where Ren is gnawing at the duct tape holding him hostage in one of our dining chairs, and I'm sitting there with fresh tape, because clearly I had been removed from my chair during the blackout. Dad rushing in to save the day always fills me with shame– always has. But only now do I understand why. Shame over how he'd know what happened to me, no doubt.

No wonder my mother killed herself. I don't know which is worse, the sons watching the mother, or the mother and youngest son watching the eldest son. Watching Mom be degraded and tortured was bad enough. In a way, I'm glad I volunteered for whatever I volunteered for, because I don't think I could've survived with the memory of Ren being harmed playing out in my head.

It gives me a new appreciation over what Ren has been through– watching and feeling guilt is worse than experiencing and feeling shame.

The memories bombard me whether I'm awake or asleep, and I wonder how deep my issues go.

Am I only bipolar? Am I even bipolar? Or am I suffering from some sort of repressed PTSD?

One things for sure, I am a drug addict.

I'll admit it since my rock bottom has finally materialized. It's pretty damn bad when my fellow police officers have to pass me drugs to keep my head out of the nearest toilet and the tremors at bay. Nothing like going through withdrawal weeks before rehab, because your old man locked out the town's drug suppliers.

I have no idea where Colin and Kyle get the steady stream of coke and heroin– yes, I've upgraded to harder shit since it's impossible to find what I'm looking for when I need it, so I take whatever I can get my hands on. It's probably one of the only reasons I'm still breathing, besides this water stain on my ceiling.

Once you've gotten this hooked, it's no longer about willpower. You truly need a professional to be your guide, because withdrawals are no joke. My body and brain are now hotwired to the drugs, and the withdrawal symptoms are my body's way of fighting to survive without them.

When I say I need them, I don't mean I want them. I *need* them to survive.

While lying here for the past few days, I've thought of nothing and everything. I miss Essie, and I imagine her going about her day, her infectious personality as she cuts hair and serves patrons. It's been over a month since I saw her last, barely avoiding her while I work. But I've tried, for her sake.

But mostly as I've laid here, even when Ren dragged me to the bathroom to clean the vomit and urine from my body as West cleaned and changed my sheets, I've thought exclusively of Mom.

Over the years since Camille Mason killed herself, everyone always says how selfish Mom was, or they ask what they could've done to prevent it. If I had the words, I'd console them by telling them it wasn't their fault, because there was absolutely nothing they could've done to change the outcome.

Mom wasn't thinking of Dad, or me, or Kieren, or even Raven and Weston. She had no thoughts of Aunt Ginny. Mom wasn't being selfish by not thinking of those who loved her most, because she was being consumed by the darkness as her memories assaulted her as if life was her version of eternal damnation.

Ending her life allowed Mom to dwell in the darkness, only there would be silence accompanying her instead of constant, swirling chaos.

As I've laid here, going through withdrawal, knowing I don't deserve this level of Hell as I puke on myself, I've forgiven myself while simultaneously forgiving Mom.

"Son?" Dad's voice barely breaches the darkness because I'm too focused on the dot on the ceiling and my private thoughts, as a way to block out how badly my body spasms like I'm hooked up to a car battery.

A calloused hand cups my cheek, and I know my will to live is still strong, because I find myself leaning into the touch.

"I think you need to go to work." Dad's voice breaks, and I want to tell him he's making no sense. "No more days off between now and Arizona… no more days off."

Then it clicks– Dad's words register. Since I wasn't scheduled to work for over three days in a row, I've laid on my bed to rot in my state of withdrawal. Dad knows someone is feeding me medicine to keep me alive and well at work.

Now when I say I need drugs, he'll believe me. Maybe.

"I hurt–" is all I can manage to say, terrified I'll bite my own tongue off as my teeth clatter.

Large hands begin rubbing my arms, trying to soothe muscles that are hooked up to a brain that is misfiring. In my peripheral, I see Dad's youngest minions performing my ritual with my uniform and belt. Weston's eye for detail misses nothing, while Raven takes delicate care with my service weapon– delicate care to remove the round from the chamber and slip the clip into the pouch of her hoodie.

Staring up at my father, I see the moment when his brain clicks over from Fairport Chief of Police to Dad. The wheels are spinning, no doubt wondering if it's still enabling if he gives me drugs to stop the pain.

At least at rehab, he won't have to witness it– Dad can pretend it's not happening. At least at rehab, Ren won't be throwing me in the shower so I can get washed while pissing on myself, because I'm too weak to hold my own dick. At least Weston won't have to wash my sheets, clean out my puke bucket, or the spots on the floor where I missed it.

Ren's not with us right now because he's spending a few hours escaping the dark reality of having a drug addict for a brother. There isn't a cell in my body that's jealous– I want him to reach serenity, even better if it's with Willow.

Dad signals for Weston and Raven to leave, then he dresses me because I'm incapable. It's not a matter of being depressed anymore. I don't know the last time I ate anything, so my body is shutting down. Not that I'd keep it down if I had. The only reason I have anything to puke up or piss out is because everyone in my family forces liquids down my throat, sometimes meal replacement shakes that come up as quickly as they went down.

Sitting up while leaning against the wall for support, my stomach roils for another reason entirely. My dad shouldn't have to pull my socks on and tie my shoes for me like I'm a child or invalid, but he does it nonetheless.

"You have a visitor who's going to spend some time with you before you make your way back to work." I'm at a loss, because I can't even talk, let alone become mobile.

Dad rises to his feet, then stares down at me with tears glinting in his eyes. "I'll be at work when you arrive. Ren's with Willow, and the kids are going to have a sleepover with Seth and Violet tonight. You do what you need to do."

Vertigo hits me as I'm lifted from the bed as if I weigh next to nothing. It takes all the strength I have left not to vomit on Dad's shoulder as he carries me. Waves crash over me as I live through the spasm of my throat clenching and releasing to trigger my gag reflex. I swallow it down for as long as I'm able.

Laying on my side in the cool grass of our front lawn, I don't even have the strength to lift my head. Powerful surges expel a small amount of bile and the last of the water I drank earlier. Panting on the ground, a pair of paint-splattered deck shoes come into my line of sight.

"The nausea will be gone momentarily," Robin's nasal voice pounds loud in my ears. "I promise, Malcolm. Your boy will be eating in no time."

"I'll believe it when I see it," Dad grumbles, kneeling down next to me to touch my forehead.

"You'll believe it, and you'll be the first one in line to vote to make marijuana legal in Massachusetts, should our politicians ever get their heads out of the asses of pharmaceutical companies."

"Not now, Rob." Dad sighs, brushing hair off my forehead. "Let's get you in Rob's Explorer." The rush of being picked up isn't as violent this time, so I manage not to trash Dad's uniform while he buckles me into the passenger seat. The door shuts, but thankfully the window is down.

Closing my eyes, I press my face into the night air, letting the cool breeze cleanse me.

"No more of this cold-turkey bullshit," Robin snarls at Dad as he hops into the driver's seat. "Dev has a cocktail of chemical dependencies in him, working in tandem and against each other, added on top of that is mental illness and probably PTSD. This boy needs medical detox."

"I get that now." Dad slumps against the SUV, looking almost as fatigued as I feel. "This is nothing like I read up on."

"That rehab center would've told you this was fucking fatal, Malcolm. People can die doing it this way– either from the withdrawal symptoms themselves or suicide. Is there even a drug Devon has never taken? What isn't he hooked on? It's not a matter of willpower– his brain is no longer the same, not that it was ever wired like yours in the first place."

"No figh–" I try and fail to get *no fighting* to come out, but I lose steam.

"I'll deliver your son back to you at the Batcave. But you have to do your part of pushing food down his throat, hydrating him, and turning a blind eye when he does what he needs to do. Got it?"

"I'm doing the best that I can." Dad pushes off from the car, looking half crazed out of his mind.

"Devon needed to go into detox at a facility around here while you waited for his spot to open up in Arizona. I trust the place you're sending him, but six weeks was too long of a wait."

"What am I supposed to do in the next ten days?" Dad yanks at his hair, and I want to promise him I'll be good so he won't worry.

"Pray to the god you don't believe in," is Robin's parting shot as he drives away.

My stomach lurches from the movement– the heaviest wave of vertigo crashing over me. A bucket is shoved into my lap, right under my slumped chin. Eyes slipping shut to stop the sensation, I'm able to get my body under control.

"C'mon, Devon," Robin coaxes, when I hadn't realized we'd stopped moving. "I can't carry you," he nearly whines. "And I can't go get help, seeing as I'm here to drug up a police officer right on fucking Main Street."

"'Kay," I mutter listlessly, as I slide from my seat. My feet hit the ground, but my knees give out, unable to support my weight.

"Here we go," Robin breathes near my ear as his arm hooks around my waist. Pressed tightly to his side, I do my best to stay upright as we walk from the car to the entrance to his studio.

I want to tell Robin thank you first, and then I want to tell him how I've never been in here. But he already knows, seeing as how no one, including Aunt Isis, is allowed inside Robin's creative space.

Eyes fuzzy, cloth-draped canvases resting on easels look like prehistoric dinosaurs roaming in the wild. The smell of paint thinner wrinkles my nose, but not as much as the greasy scent of takeout burgers and fries.

Unceremoniously dumped on an antique sofa, which was obviously a Spook House reject, I flail about to keep myself from falling to the floor.

"Sorry," Rob mutters, but he sounds anything but. "I'm a painter, not a people mover." With a hollow thud, my bucket is placed between my feet on the floor. "First up is Mary Prynne's finest anti-nausea medication. Followed by that, God willing, is sustenance. Unless you're spasming on me, or trying to off yourself, we're going to keep the uppers away from you, because what goes up, must come waaaayyy, waaaayyy down."

Dropping to sit next to me on the sofa, Robin reaches forward to drag the coffee table closer. Then the bag of takeout is set next to my bucket.

"I know you're probably wondering why I'm helping you– I would be, anyway." Hitting the coffee table with the side of his fist, Rob hits a mechanism that has the tabletop popping up to reveal what's hidden beneath.

Holy shit.

"I see myself as your uncle, even though Isis and I will never marry. I've known you since you were born. As Isis's favorite, she carried you everywhere. Even after Raven was born, Isis loved you best." Leaning into me, Robin whispers like it's a secret. "Your sister is not the cheeriest of people. Hard to fawn all over her when she'd rather go hide."

All I can do is grunt in agreement.

"Not that I don't love Rae– but an introvert isn't who you drag around town for shits 'n' giggles when you're a teenager. So Isis loved you best. She knew you best too. We can all agree you had Undercover Cop Mason as a dad until that tragic night, and finally got Dad afterward when he became Chief Mason."

Fingers hovering over the good shit– Coke. Heroin. Speed. Pharmaceuticals –Robin selects a baggie of bud instead. Now I understand where Isis got the lithium.

"I'm not a drug dealer." Robin has the audacity to look insulted. "I'm also not a user. You can thank Tina for all of this but Mom's weed. I bypassed Auggie and went straight to the source– Patrick Kline. As you know, Lisa's husband is a drug and alcohol counselor. Unethical as it may be, this is a *keep Devon alive until rehab* care package."

If I wasn't so listless, I'd attack the contents of the coffee table. As it is, new symptoms are arising. I'm salivating so badly, I can't swallow it quickly enough. My skin is twitchy and enflamed, like fire ants are marching to battle across it.

"As I was saying," Robin murmurs as he prepares a bong. "Isis knew you best, which meant I knew you pretty dang good, and Malcolm didn't really get to know you until *afterward*," he stresses. "So we, Isis and I, noticed a profound difference in you and Ren. We both know there is more to your issues than *Mommy beat me because she was bipolar, I'm pretty sure I inherited her mental illness, and I have PTSD from traumatic events.*

"Your dad chose to ignore it until it was time for you to be sexually active. Meanwhile, Ren was fucking a swath through Fairport. The opposite reactions were similar to the same thing Essie was going through. How she went from playing hoover to being a nun. Don't worry, my cousin told me, so you listening isn't breaking a confidence."

To add insult to injury, Rob takes a hit in front of me, and then relaxes on the sofa like it's no big fucking deal. My stomach grumbles as if I'm starving– I am, but the addict in me isn't wanting food.

If pot is all Robin's willing to share, hurry the fuck up with it. I'm dying here.

"I like this." Robin sighs, all relaxed and replete. "You not being a prick back to me is a welcome change. I almost want to delay giving you a hit because it's so pleasant. See, you and Raven do have a similar personality, except for the fact that you'll actually engage me."

Held hostage by a sadist, and I mean that in the literal sense. Everyone assumes it's Isis doing the damage.

Dave Prynne is a master builder of BDSM equipment, all of it belonging to Robin Prynne.

Summoning strength, I try and fail to reach forward.

"The fatigue and listlessness are a real bitch, ain't they?" Rob taunts me. "Should've thought of that after coming down from a coke bender, where you lost your appetite. Only to go into withdrawals where it's impossible to keep anything down. You can only live so long without eating, ya know?"

Robin finally puts me out of my misery by placing the bong against my mouth, following by lighting the bowl.

Try as I might, I can't find the strength to inhale deep enough. Struggling, I'm panting so hard the smoke fills the air instead of my lungs.

"Well, shit." Robin takes the bong from me, only to torture me by taking another hit instead. Whimpering in pain, all I can do is watch. A small hand cups my forehead while the other takes control of my chin. Then a mouth gets closer and closer to mine, until Robin is doing a parody of mouth-to-mouth, only he's forcing smoke into my lungs.

Struggling through the irrational panic, I breathe as deeply as I can, but end up having a coughing fit like a fucking noob. Sputtering, the convulsions affect all of the muscles in my torso. Before I can catch my breath, Robin's mouth is back with another hit.

We go through this process over and over again until Robin's satisfied I've had enough to combat the nausea and actually keep some food down.

Floaty, fading away, I whisper in a thready voice, "God, I've missed this."

"Being able to talk now that your teeth aren't chattering, or the rush of being high?" Robin asks conversationally as he grabs the fast food takeout bag. Humming to himself, he reaches in and extracts a big, juicy burger.

With my mouth watering for the first time in over a week, I actually try to reach for the food.

Robin takes a big, honking bite out of the burger, then purrs. "Mmm... so tasty. Yum." Then he precedes to eat the entire fucking burger in front of me. "So good." His hand comes out of the bag with a fistful of fries, which he shoves into his mouth.

"Sadist," spills from my tingling lips.

"Oh, you want some?" Robin thrusts a fry in my mouth, and I try to take a bite before he snatches it away. "Nope. This was my munchie surprise. I have something special for you, baby boy."

Out of the bottom of the bag comes a plastic container with a fork snapped on its lid. Robin hums to himself as he dismantles the lunch container, then presents me with my meal.

"Rice?" I practically sob, wanting to reach down Rob's gullet and fist the burger he just ate.

"I'm being nice, Dev– honest." Robin puts a forkful into my mouth. "You'll thank me later when you're not puking your guts up. Your belly has been empty for far too long, so we're going to go slow, allowing you to digest the food. I have other tasty morsels specifically made for you."

"Joy," I grumble, but my head is craning to reach for the fork.

"From now until rehab, you've got to promise me you'll keep eating and stop going cold turkey. Just smoke to keep up your appetite and the nausea at bay, and don't do the hard shit unless you really fucking need it. Promise."

I'm held hostage by the sadist again, only this time it's my food he won't give me.

"I promise." I'm rewarded with food for the next few hours, and I actually thank Rob a billion times when he drops me off at the police station, with my care package on my person.

CHAPTER THIRTY-TWO

Essie Prynne

Working with tears clouding my vision is similar to having my hair hanging in my eyes. My hair is tucked back by a headband, thanks to the fact that Mom throws a fit when I work around the house with it veiling my face. There's nothing to be done about the tears, though. There's no magic solution for heartbreak.

I can't pinpoint what's poking at my frayed nerves, because everything seems to have me wavering on the cusp of viciously lashing out or bawling hysterically. Slumped to the floor, I'm holding a Revolutionary Road concert stub I found discarded beneath my dresser, tears dampening the yellowed paper.

"Oh, hun." Mom's been hovering for the past two days as we pack up the house– we've been packing for five weeks, but for some reason she's been watching me closely the past few days.

Maybe my bizarre mood swings are scaring Mom, because they sure as hell are scaring the piss out of me. Maybe it's because it's the crack of dawn, and she found me wearing my sheep pajamas while crying uncontrollably as I hold the remnant of Willow's and my friendship in the palm of my hand.

"I thought it was bad after Willow's birthday," I murmur to myself, knowing Mom's listening anyway. "But I understood."

Willow cut me off after I tried to hook her and Ren up. It felt like I lost a limb, never hearing from her, never having my texts and calls answered. But I was happy for Willow, and proud she was trying to get her life together. When she started renovating the Spook House and going to school, I watched from afar as she grew up. I pretended it didn't hurt as Devon gave Willow what he never gave me.

Friendship. Support. Comfort. His time.

Masons don't marry whores, and I was terrified for both Ren and me that Willow would end up with Devon. Willow's considered a good girl, and apparently I'm not. I kept my mouth shut, hurting in private silence as Devon supported Willow, all the while Willow forgot I existed.

I thought that was bad but survivable, but being Willow's enemy is worse. I see her around town, at church, at the Sunday supper table. Oh, she glares at me with self-righteous indignation, like she's challenging me to say something so she can lash out and hurt me. She doesn't speak to me, but she makes quips that are obviously pointed directly at me. It's the gossip that hurts the worst, and I don't even know if Willow's responsible for it– a hunch tells me she is.

Everyone knows what happened from Willow's skewed point of view. Willow and Devon were the loves of each other's lives, and I swooped in with my mammoth tits and seduced him away from her. Just a one-night-stand, because I'm not worth more than that. Even though they broke up, Willow and Devon are still the best of friends, with it bringing Willow and Kieren closer together. Meanwhile, I'm Fairport's Delilah.

That's all a bullshit lie Willow's telling herself and the town, but I've kept my mouth shut on the truth– my way of trying to keep what little dignity I have left. Between Facebook and the townsfolk sneering at me, it's been insufferable.

Violet even started a Facebook event, trying to get everyone to treat me so horribly I'll move away to Florida with my parents. But I refuse to hide and act as if I have anything to be ashamed of.

I did a shit thing– so what? Sex with a consenting adult isn't a crime. Should it ruin my life forever because Willow didn't get to break up with Devon first? It's hypocritical that Ren and Devon and Auggie, and whoever else Willow licked, is off-limits for life because she wanted them. On the flip side, if Auggie said Willow couldn't date someone ten years from now, Willow would throw a shit-fit. It's none of Willow's business what they do– the men are the only ones who dictate what happens to their bodies.

I didn't do it alone, and Willow isn't innocent in any of this. The entire county and all of Willow's Facebook-reach are calling me a whore for having sex with my childhood boyfriend, after not touching anyone else in years. Meanwhile, in a handful of months, good girl Willow messed around with Ren, Auggie, back to Ren while with Devon, probably Auggie in there again somewhere, then Devon, now back to Ren. Willow's acting like a teenager, so I won't judge her. What she does is her business, but she can't compare her teenage drama to my adult issues, because then it becomes my business when my private shit is spread worldwide.

Ostracized. Abandoned. Bullied. So much for the unconditional love of family and a best friend.

The adults in my family are walking around on eggshells, trying to pretend nothing is going on between me and Clover's kids. Willow obviously has the support of the twins. With Seth turning into a misogynistic little puke, he's worse than Violet has been to me.

There wasn't any main event that had me changing, but just a series of painful digs that had me say fuck it all. It's been over five weeks since the shit hit the fan. I haven't seen Devon– not even a glance around town, which means he's actively avoiding me. What hurts the worst, Devon isn't avoiding Willow. Devon isn't having a smear campaign leveled against him.

Devon has his own shit he's dealing with, so I'm not going irrational female on his ass and blaming him. I won't let Willow's behavior drive a bigger wedge between Dev and me. If I raged and pointed out the hypocrisy, I'd stress Devon out more... so I've just faded to the background in my own life.

Other than Sundays with church and supper, I avoid my entire family. I'm not the center of their universe, and they all have things they're struggling with. Kieren tries to keep in touch with me, but I push him away. I won't take his calls, answer his texts, or do anything but act cordial when he's in the diner. Just as I won't let Willow become a wedge between Devon and me, I refuse to be one between Willow and Kieren. Kieren's my friend, and I love him like a brother, but I've closed him out to protect his friendship with Willow.

Willow sees everything I do as ammunition, so I removed the gun from her hands. She can hate me, but she's not going to use me anymore.

Use me.

They all used me, used me up, then threw me away.

Salon is doing so poorly, Elma changed the hours of operation to fit my other work schedules. We're only open from ten in the morning until one in the afternoon, for regular clients who do their errands in the morning or on their lunch break. It's by appointment-only with five-day notice, because I need to be able to let my other jobs know whether I can work my shifts or not. If there are no appointments scheduled that day, we don't open at all. For those who can't come during weekly business hours, we're open on Saturday afternoons for three hours, for both appointment and walk-ins.

Elma's in her mid-seventies, a widow with no kids, and I can tell she's ready to call it quits and retire. The status of Salon has me weepy as fuck, but combined with the other shit, I find myself crying for no explicable reason.

Shuffling between Salon, the No-Name, and the Quick Stop, work is a good distraction. My car was repossessed, but I just let the bank have it. My credit has tanked, but the Toyota wasn't worth what I owed, especially with the repair bills added on top. It's Fairport– I can walk to work and I have nowhere else to go since I can't afford fun. Only plus was that I canceled my car insurance, saving me a couple hundred bucks a month.

Beth and I don't have much time for one another anymore, but it's not the same as what Willow did to me over the winter. Between finals and putting all of her attention on her thesis, Beth still finds time to check in with me several times a day. We may not see each other every day, but an '*I'm thinking of you*' text goes a long way to keep our friendship alive.

Banking up money for an apartment isn't going too well since my wages are now being garnished for defaulted student loans. I'm just biding my time before the bank does the same for the Corolla. To add insult to injury, they won't just let me pay the note off– they want impound fees too. The car doesn't even run– it can rust to dust for all I care.

Sure, all this bullshit stress I'm experiencing is my fault– the bank owes me nothing. It's all my poor choices coming back to bite me in the ass. I've learned from my mistakes, and I'm trying to right the wrongs, but that doesn't mean an '*I told you so*' or '*You're an idiot*' or '*You're a whore*' is helpful or inspiring when you're floundering in life.

"Did you just wake up?" Mom crouches next to me, warm palm curling around my shoulder. "Or have you been up all night again?"

"I just–" eyeing the mess I've made around me, my dresser drawers are lying on the floor, with their contents vomiting all over the place. "Have you ever just… woken up out of a dead sleep, and you have to get the hell out of bed or you'll explode?" I try to explain why I'm up two hours before my alarm goes off, cleaning out my drawers to decide what to pack and what will go to a consignment shop.

"It's called an anxiety attack, Essie." Mom flows to the floor, folding her legs to sit beside me. She's already dressed for another day of packing herself, with a cup of coffee cradled in her hand. "Are you sure you won't go with us?"

"We've talked that to death," I grumble, reaching forward to quickly hide the ticket stub that had me mourning the loss of a friendship I'm unsure was ever real. "Drop it, okay?"

Chuckling lightly, Mom lifts her mug to her lips, blowing softly to cool her coffee down. "Your father and I aren't like we were when we first got married." More laughter, like she's thinking naughty thoughts. "Trust me when I say we won't be christening every surface in our new house... maybe on the weekend, after some wine–"

"Just stop," I beg, stomach twisting in on itself, with my throat convulsing like I'm going to upchuck. Ignoring my physical discomfort, I glare at my racy underthings. Burn it. Burn it all to hell.

Sipping coffee with one hand, Mom rubs my back with the other. "Those are lovely," she gestures to the lace bootie shorts I'm holding. "As a parent, your children don't stop being your children at the age of eighteen. You're not a burden. We know how much we're going to miss you, so don't think for an instant that we're not contemplating kidnaping you and forcing you to come with us. We didn't have you to not want you with us always."

"Dad's retired after working hard, and you're going to be volunteering your time. You guys deserve a life where my shit isn't splattering your happiness." Balling the panties in my fist, I chuck the pair into the garbage bag destined for Craigslist. Maybe one of the Playroomers will get off on buying The Whore of Fairport's unmentionables.

"I'm going to miss you." Mom curls over my back, resting her chin on my shoulder. "I *already* miss you, and you've been home more than ever lately."

"Having no social life does that to a girl," I mutter underneath my breath, hating how the tears renew their quest to dehydrate me.

Pulling away, I can feel Mom's disappointment and sadness like a physical force beating at my flesh. "You're a vibrant young woman, and it kills me to see you hurting so much." Mom reaches into the bag and extracts the lacy panties, placing them on the miniscule pile of what I'm keeping. She pats them in place, silently telling me I'm keeping them.

I'm downsizing, and not just because I'm selling everything that isn't nailed down. Homeless, I'll be living out of a bag as I crash with whomever will take me. If I find an apartment, I can't even afford an efficiency, so there's nothing I can keep anyway. Hell, I'm not above sneaking into Salon and sleeping in my room in the back. If it wasn't for Elma living across the street, I'd try to get away with it.

I eavesdropped on Mom and Dad with Aunt Mary and Uncle Dave last night. Clover and Malcolm are secretly getting married and moving into the pink monstrosity across from the Spook House. They have a lot of work to do before Devon gets back from rehab, with Ginny selling their houses too.

All the houses I called home during my childhood will belong to other families. All the memories stored at the Masons will fade away with time. The endless Sunday suppers at Aunt Mary's will cease to be our family tradition. The ability to run over to Clover's and hide will be no more. My entire identity as William and Analiese Prynne's daughter is being rewritten as I learn how to be an adult. No more nest– safe haven.

Not only am I losing the comfort, I'm being pushed from the nest without knowing how to fly. Everyone is moving on– moving forward. But, then there is me, the whorish Essie is perpetually being propelled ten steps back. I'm not an idiot, but I have no idea how to stop the inertia of my downward spiral.

I overheard my parents and aunt and uncle discussing options for both me and them. When your baby brother by nearly two decades is retiring, and you had to un-retire yourself because your son-in-law died, it's time to reevaluate. Since I'm not moving with my parents, Uncle Dave and Aunt Mary will be taking over the room that was to be mine during the winter months, and everyone is forcing Robin to do Uncle Dave's job at Prynne Renovations.

I'm genuinely happy for everyone, even if the stress and terror has me lunging to my feet, thanking God that I grew up spoiled enough to have an en suite bathroom. Hand gripping the lid, my head meets the seat just in time for me to pray to the porcelain god.

Retching, my stomach muscles clench as my throat contracts in a torturous rhythm. Dying on the inside and out, I wipe my mouth on one of the happy sheep printed on my pajama top sleeve.

"See," Mom purrs, but I can hear the amusement riding her voice. A hand smooths my hair back in a rhythmic pattern. "There's a reason I hammered it into you to wear your hair away from your face." Laughing softly, "Your stomach acid would've ruined your funky dye-job."

"Funny, Mom." Struggling, I reach forward for the hand towel draped over my sink. Mom's taller by half a foot, so she beats me to it, being kind enough to dampen it before handing it to me.

"Feeling better?" Mom rests the back of her hand against my forehead in a mothering gesture as old as the test of time.

"I don't have a fever," I grumble none too kindly, but instantly feel bad for turning bitchy. After flushing the toilet, I crawl away on my knees, then collapse against the sink vanity. Wrapping my arms around my legs, I hide my face against my knees.

"I'll admit I'm drowning," I whisper like it's a secret. "I've seen enough Dr. Phil to know my stress is manifesting into anxiety, which is making me unable to sleep and eat, leaving me physically sick."

"Yeah," Mom breathes so quietly, I struggle to hear the loaded word. "Sure– *stress.*"

"Hey, my BFF is a psych major, for shit's sake." With rough movements, I scrub the hell out of my face with the damp hand towel. "I know what I'm talking about here. Firsthand knowledge is a bitch."

"I'm stressed just watching you stress out." Mom tugs me to my feet in a fluid movement, then drags me back into my bedroom. My pretty princess bedroom looks like a tornado hit, with the furniture already gone to new homes of happy Craigslisters. Ordinarily, Mom would plunk me down on my vanity stool to give me a lecture. Poof. No more vanity or stool for a fuck-up like me.

Everything I own is in piles on the floor, lining the walls. Other than my mattress, my dresser is going to a new home this afternoon. A mom and dad of a young girl bought my princess bedroom set, patient enough to grab it piecemeal as I packed. A few college kids bought the rest of the random shit over the past week.

Mom follows my gaze to the leaning towers of DVDs lining the wall, all are being gifted to Bethany. Her family doesn't waste a dime, because they don't have two nickels to rub together. They only have basic cable and shoddy DSL, so everyone buys Beth DVDs as a treat. I might need the money, but my best friend needs an escape more. Plus, we can share custody of the television series, maybe while splitting a carton of ice cream while cuddled underneath a Hello Kitty blanket.

"Bethany's on her way here." The compassion in Mom's voice draws my attention, but not nearly as her bizarre words do.

"What?" Eyes narrowed, my voice cracks. "Why? It's only six in the morning."

"How long have you been up?" Mom asks again. "Have you peed this morning yet?"

"Jesus, Mom." I struggle to stand from my mattress as it rests on the floor, missing my fucking bedframe. "Why?" Our heads turn, listening to the tap of Beth's feet on the stair treads.

Reaching out to me, "Answer me. Please," Mom begs.

It's not the request– it's the compassion that fuels my response. "You're scaring me." Voice breaking. "Why? Why do you keep asking me that?" Heart beating out of control, I can feel it pounding on the underside of my breast. Sweat beads on my forehead, dampening my hair.

"I was only up for about a half hour before you wandered into my bedroom. It was like an invisible force propelled me out of bed and showed me that goddamn concert ticket hiding beneath my dresser."

Tears obscuring my vision, my eyes flick up to see Beth leaning against the doorjamb to my bedroom. Blinking to clear my eyes, a trembling starts as I register how upset Bethany is. Terrified. Pained. For me.

"Hey," Bethany breathes as she walks into my room, headed directly for me. One of her arms is tucked behind her back, hiding something. "Did I get here in time? It's best straight away."

"Yeah." Mom's whispered word is filled with tears, and it confuses me.

"What's going on? Why are you here?" I rapid fire questions at Beth and my mother at the same time. "I thought you had study group at the university today."

"Sorry, Ana– there's no easing into it for Essie." Beth grabs my hand, tugging me back into my bathroom. "Pop a squat." An impossibly strong hand is pressing on my shoulder, barely giving me time to yank my pajama bottoms down before my ass lands on the toilet.

This time it's Mom camping out on the doorjamb, every emotion playing out on her features is directed toward me. "I've been too much of a coward for the past few days," Mom whispers in shame, and I move to rise from the toilet so I can comfort her.

"Sit," is snapped in my direction. "Ana's not the one we're worried about here." Bethany's hand materialized from behind her back, showing she has a small paper bag clutched in her fist. All of my focus narrows to a pinprick as I watch Beth fish out an oblong box from the bag.

In a whoosh, all the oxygen flees my body, causing me to slump backward to rest on the toilet tank. Eyes wide and unblinking, I try to formulate words but nothing flows.

"Get the timer ready on your cell, Ana." Beth is in authoritative, caretaker-mode. Fingertip digging into the top of the box, she tears into the cardboard. A heartbeat later, a foil-wrapped wand materializes in her hand. With a sharp rip, the wand is freed and shoved into my palm. "I'm not gonna hold it while you piss on it, girlfriend."

"I've never–"

"All women instinctively know the drill," Beth mutters patiently. "I know you don't have a shy bladder, so get to tinkling on the absorbent tip. Count to ten. Pull it out. Put the cap on it. Then hand it back to me."

Mortified. Humiliated. Petrified. Disbelieving. With a shaking hand, I awkwardly grasp the pregnancy test. Shifting slightly on the toilet, I have to tug my pajama bottoms down farther so I can spread my legs more. Laughing hysterically, I mumble to myself. "It was spreading my legs that got me into this situation in the first place."

"While you're pissing and waiting–" Beth folds her arms over her tits, staring down at me in a parental sort of way. Laughing more, I realize no one has ever called Beth a whore because of her curvy body. Tits and ass perfect, with a lot of extra flesh that never settles on her tiny waist, Beth is a guy's wet dream. She's also sexually experienced– more than I ever will be in a lifetime. For fuck sake, Beth's field of study is the psychology of sexuality. Yet everyone treats her with respect because her intelligence overpowers the size of her tits.

Something about me screams use me, abuse me– rape me. I'm a worthless, vapid whore.

"Essie," Beth cautions, no doubt hearing my silent thoughts. "While you're pissing and waiting, I want you to remember how you felt when I put the Plan-B in your palm." Arms unfolding, leaning down, Beth grips my shoulder. "You. Can. Do. This."

So I do it.

"You gave her Plan-B?" Mom sounds shocked, and it confuses me, until she continues. "And Essie didn't take it?" Mom's eyes close in defeat, then flash back open as the sound of my pee tinkling hits her ears.

Hunched over awkwardly with my hand between my legs, I end up pissing on my thumb in the process. "… Seven… Eight… Nine… Ten." Sighing, I pull the test away from my body while still peeing. I try to cap it without my pissy thumb contaminating it. I ignore what Bethany does with the test while I finish up my business and wash my hands.

Leaning with my hands braced on the edge of the sink, I stare into the mirror. With my hair pulled back from my face, I look young, like a little kid, which is why I got that trendy hairstyle in the first place. Too young to have a kid.

Leaning my forehead against the mirror, I sigh in defeat. I don't even need to know what the test says– I know. I hadn't thought about it since I was with Devon last. Not one single thought on whether or not I could be pregnant. Even with me puking nonstop for the past three days, I just thought it was stress. The dizziness was from not eating or sleeping. The mood swings were from the bullying, not an influx of hormones.

"Stupid. Stupid." I bang my head against the mirror lightly. "Stupid. You're a stupid girl. A stupid, stupid whore."

Mom's hand yanks me from the mirror just as a beeping sounds from her cellphone. "You're my daughter–"

"Your child's mother," Bethany simultaneously cuts Mom off while giving us the results. Mom's sharp intake of breath is eclipsed by Bethany's lecture. "No matter what, you are what you do, how you act, and who you are. You're not how people perceive you or treat you."

"Easier said than done," I mutter, slumping to land ass-first on the toilet seat. "Jesus Christ, what have I done?" I stare at my hands like they hold the secrets of the universe. "I'm struggling to take care of myself." Eyes flicking up, I beg and plead for help. "What do I do, Mom?"

Mom shrugs one shoulder, tears glistening in her eyes, but it's the curve of her lips that confuses the piss out of me. "You're pregnant– you eat, sleep, and take care of yourself, in order to grow your baby. That's all you have to do. You can either come with us to Florida, or you stay with Aunt Mary."

"I can't do either," I gasp, on the edge of hyperventilating. "Willow–"

"Doesn't factor into this," Mom cuts me off. "So what? You're pregnant. You're twenty-one, with job skills and degrees, and a support system who will have your back. You're not the first woman to be sucked in by an idiot, and you won't be the last. There are probably thirty girls across this country who're in your situation, who in the past minute just found out they're pregnant after a stupid *on purpose*, and they're dealing. So you'll deal."

"It was like a fantasy," I admit in a voice so hoarse I can barely hear myself speak. "It was foggy with anti-reality. I'm not stupid. I know how babies are made, and so does Dev. But, in this fantasy, where we were different people, it was unavoidable. I honestly hadn't thought about it once since."

Head in hands, I stare at my bathroom tile, knowing I won't be living here much longer. So much change. The comfort and pleasure Devon gave me over a few hours in time means nothing compared to the pile of shit it created. I was already sitting at rock bottom, now this…

"Fuck!" I jerk forward to stand up, then squeeze past a stunned stupid Bethany and a surprisingly amused Mom. "How do I do this?" Voice warbling on a sob, "How?"

"Hey." Beth tries to hug me, but I sidestep her.

Mom's craftier than Beth, she hooks her arm around my waist, then forces me to sit on my mattress. "Devon's family loves Devon. Your family loves you. A child is never a tragedy, no matter how they are conceived. With all that love, your child is wanted, even if it's not convenient–"

"And hella irresponsible," Beth whispers, but Mom and I both hear her anyway. "Glad I tossed your mousy ballet flats. Lord knows what those sneaker babies would've looked like."

Beth and I share a snort, confusing my mom. But Mom's not stupid, so she still looks amused– happy even.

"That–" Beth reaches down to palm my belly. "–is going to be a cute little shit. Probably be a little asshole. Psycho, but cute as fuck."

"I'm so telling your future patients that you use the term psycho." Laughing to myself, I crawl off my mattress, landing on my ass, then rut around my keep pile. Balling the fabric in my palm, I launch the panties at Mom. Beth's too curvy for some of my clothes, but Mom and I are the same shape, with Mom taller than me by half a foot. "I have no use for sexy panties, now that my ass is gonna grow. Might as well wear those around your new house on Saturday nights while drinking wine."

Smirking, Mom plays along by holding the lacy bootie shorts up to her hips, then sways side to side. I wasn't being serious, needing some comic relief, so I pretend Mom doesn't pocket them for later use.

Stepping over me, Mom leans down to dig around in the drawer I haven't sorted yet, coming out with a matching bralette to the panties– I always buy underthings in sets. The bra disappears wherever the panties had gone.

Awed and confused, I stare at the mess on the floor before me. Mom's knees come into view first as she crouches down. "I know you're worried that Dad and I will be disappointed in you." Mom's fingertips clench my chin, then tug until I look her in the eye. "We're proud of you."

An animalistic sound of agony is released from my throat as I break away. Scrambling, I launch myself to my feet, then find myself leaning against the wall, all the way across my bedroom.

"Essie." Mom sighs heavily, already exhausted by me at six in the morning.

"I told her." Beth's sheepish voice has my eyes flicking in her direction, but she won't look at me. "I told Ana how Devon was behaving." Whispering softer and softer, "I told her every detail."

"Why?" I breathe back, surprised that I don't feel betrayed.

"Your dad and I had to be prepared." Mom slowly approaches me like I'm an injured animal. "We knew about the car ride and the lunch incident just after it happened. Your dad even spoke to Devon a few weeks back when he came to stalk you from a far."

"What?" I step away from the wall, shocked. "Devon was here?"

Mom ignores the hope in my voice. "I remember what happened when you were kids and Devon tried to have sex with you. Only this time Bethany feared he accomplished it. So I had to be on the lookout for symptoms. Beth and I waited a few days to make sure you weren't just sick with a stomach bug."

"Why aren't you mad at me?!" I shout at my mother. Heart beating a mile a minute, I can feel the rush of blood through my veins. My body flashes with a cold sweat, dampening my pajama top. My breathing becomes labored, to the point I'm gasping. Turning to Beth, I shout. "Why aren't you telling me *I told you so*?!"

"Essie, I–"

"Listen to me," this time Mom cuts Bethany off. Stalking toward me, my mother clasps my shoulders in her palms, holding me in place. She forces me to hold her gaze. "I am *proud* of you, and so is your father."

"Are you insane?!" The incredulity is thick in my voice as I wrench my gaze from my mother, flicking over to stare at Beth for some backup. "I'm knocked up by my cousin's boyfriend."

Beth just shakes her head at me, looking sadder than sad.

"Hester." Mom tries again to catch my undivided attention. "At any time, Dad and I could've written a check to pay off your car, then have it towed to get it repaired. We could've paid your loans off– your equipment too. You could've laid down and done nothing to help yourself as Salon crumbles and your reputation darkens. But none of that happened. You proved your worth by not asking for help, by getting not one but three jobs, and you've walked around with your shoulders back and your head held high with dignity."

"I feel really dignified right now," I grumble, swallowing back the need to puke my guts up. My mind shifts, coming to terms with the fact that it's not stress. Morning sickness. I have a little person telling me he's with me. I'm not alone. He needs me to sleep– to eat –and he'll offer me unconditional love in return for growing him.

Floored, my body loses all strength, but I don't hit the carpet. A mother is always a mother, no matter how old her child may be. Almost fainting, mine manages to grab me by the armpits with her impressive, mom-fueled strength before I slump to the floor.

I'm a mother.

Breathing deeply, it takes a few seconds, but my body regains its ability to support me and the baby on its own.

Palms shifting from my pits to curl around my cheeks, Mom cradles my face. "I'm happy," is whispered like a secret. "I always wanted a big family. But the curse of being a Prynne is that our family will always be small."

"Mom." Heart racing, the implications of what Mom is saying hit me hard. It took my grandparents seventeen years to have a second child, which is why there's such a huge gap between Uncle Dave and Dad. There's seven years between Clover and Robin. Mom just hit menopause, but that's not why I'm an only child. It took years before I was conceived because Dad shot a ton of blanks. We all hoped there would be another miracle before Mom got too old, just like it did when Grandma had Dad and Mary had Robin... but it never happened, and now it's too late.

Fearing the curse now weighs heavily on Robin.

"All it takes is a Mason being in the same room with the one they want." Beth lightens the mood, knowing about the Prynne curse, with the added bonus of knowing the Playroomers' deepest secrets. "Isis avoids penetration for a reason. Rob's scared, but he shouldn't be, not with Isis being a Mason."

Laughing heartily, Mom's face is vibrant with wry amusement. "Clover." Palm pressed to the stitch in her side, Mom bends at the waist. "It's wrong to gossip, but Uncle Dave and your Dad have been placing bets. They already figured you were pregnant, and were placing odds on Clover and Malcolm."

"Willow," Bethany interjects. "She's playing with fire."

"She's on the shot," I mutter with relief. "Like clockwork–Violet too."

"Birth control fails," Bethany's cerebral side rears its ugly head, knowing every statistic when it comes to this because of her thesis.

"It's true." Mom's face is flushed, glowing like she's pregnant. How bad did she want to be a grandma? "Clover was on birth control when the twins were conceived. Sam spent too much time with Malcolm, making him more virile via contact with the ultimate Mason breeder."

"Mom!" I chastise, flabbergasted.

Mom's undaunted by my outburst. "As I said, Will and Dave have been laughing it up as the Mason men stalk our girls, saying the curse has been broken."

"Lunatics," Bethany blurts out. Squatting, she starts sorting through the mess I have on the floor. It takes her seconds to make choices I mulled over for hours. In less than a minute, she empties an entire drawer into three piles.

"You girls do not want to know what Will said the other night." Mom's eyes track Bethany's movements, then she flashes forward to steal another bralette she wants for herself. "Irony. Dave and Will think it would be proper punishment if Willow found herself knocked up after calling you a whore. Only difference, you know who the father of your baby is, and Willow would have to visit Maury Povich for a paternity test."

"Jesus– fuck." Dropping, I land ass-first on my mattress. "I may be pissed at Willow, but that's just cruel."

"Rob inherited his sadistic personality from somewhere– your dad and uncle are twisted." Beth doesn't sound surprised in the least. "Isis said the same thing to me last week. She's all about female empowerment, and Willow's been pissing her off. If it wasn't for the fact that it would hurt Isis if Auggie was the father, or Essie if Devon was the father, it would be rather ironic."

"Subject change, because the thought of our kids being siblings is too…" Lying back on the mattress, I shudder in revulsion. "We can't share a baby daddy, because Willow would be the epitome of parental alienation."

"I wish my niece no ill will." Mom settles on the mattress next to me, while Bethany continues to sort what's left in my room. I don't fail to notice the covetous glances she's giving the stacks of DVDs.

Mom wants my unmentionables, and Bethany needs entertainment… and I need my head examined.

"I love Willow– Lord knows I do." Mom sighs dramatically. "She's grown up so much recently, but she still needs someone to beat the living shit out of her."

"You are aware Ren calls Willow Spanky, right?" Bethany chuckles sadistically. "Auggie started it."

"Fuck," Mom grunts. "Someone needs to spank her harder."

"Ha! The ruler… I'm going to be a rabid momma like you," I murmur with affection, reaching over to squeeze her hand. "I understand Willow, Mom. She's hurting, and she's always vicious when she's in pain. I hurt her, and I take full responsibility for it."

"Facebook and the townsfolk are uncalled for, yet no one is taking Willow to task for her behavior." Mom shifts slightly, deciding to help Bethany sort my stuff, which makes me feel stupid that I'm not doing it myself. "It should've stayed within our family and your group of friends– that's it."

"I'm going to have to talk to Willow soon," Beth announces, getting closer and closer to the DVDs. "Ren collared me last week, confused as to why Isis was throwing a fit over Willow. Willow and Ren have formed boundaries about Essie and Devon, and she's been good around him. So Ren couldn't believe that Willow was the instigator with Facebook, writing it off as Violet being a teenager and sticking her nose where it doesn't belong."

"I think that too." With a shrug, I start bagging up the piles of name-brand clothing I'm taking to the consignment shop. The rest I'll sell in lots on Craigslist and online yard sale sites. "Willow's hurt, but she's not cruel."

"You're delusional." Giving up all pretenses, Bethany drags a box over and starts loading up her loot. I pretend I don't see a slinky nightie hiding in the bottom of the box.

"Dave showed Clover the Facebook posts." Mom distracts Beth by gesturing for her to open a garbage bag for me to fill, then she tosses the nightie's matching robe in with the DVDs. "Violet's been treating you better, hasn't she? Because I'm pretty sure Clover beat her ass and gave her a lesson in feminism."

"You're right." Cocking my head to the side, I think about the past few days, how Violet hasn't been lobbing insults at me when I see her. On my hands and knees, I start stuffing a pile of sweaters into the bag Beth's holding open. "Good thing too, because in a week or so, I'll be shoved up her ass."

Mom turns misty with tears, no doubt she's been ignoring the reason we're bagging up my belongings in the first place. "I think this situation will be enlightening for Violet. This way she can see both sides, Willow versus you, where neither of you were right nor wrong. Maybe she won't make similar mistakes."

"Violet's smart enough to think for herself." Beth blushes when she spots the robe in her box. "We're talking around the elephant in the room..." she trails off, going back to alphabetizing the DVDs in her box.

"I'm not going to throw another layer of stress on Devon," I warn, glaring both my mother and best friend down. "I'll let him know when he gets back from rehab, but not before. This pregnancy isn't a trap."

"I know the boy isn't capable of marriage yet." Now it's my mom sounding delusional– there is no *yet* for us. "But he needs to know sooner rather than later."

"You're supposed to be tight-lipped during the first trimester anyway." Standing, I survey my room, happy to note everything but what I'm keeping is boxed or bagged up. I decide to start tugging the bags out into the hallway. "What if I miscarry, hmm? The last thing Devon needs to know is that he was going to be a dad but I lost his kid."

"I was there." Beth yanks the bag out of my hands, then tosses it into the hallway like it weighs nothing. "No lifting a damn thing, idiot." Going for another bag, "Devon needs something to hold onto. Hope. A future. If you don't tell him, I will."

"I just…" Stomach twisting, and this time I know it's not from morning sickness, it takes everything in me not to upchuck. "Let me think about it, okay? Last I heard, they were waiting to learn when Devon could be placed in Sedona. It takes nine months to have a baby, and this shit with Devon is more important."

"Who would've thought my spoiled daughter would grow up to be a martyr," Mom muses, the calm before the storm.

"Me?" I point a manicured finger at my chest. "A martyr?"

"Yeah." Mom turns to face me, anger etched across her features. "This family only has space for one martyr, and Clover filled the position nineteen years ago."

"What the hell is that supposed to mean?"

"I didn't struggle to get pregnant for six years to have my daughter lose her fucking voice." Now Mom's pointing at me with a fierceness she hardly ever exhibits. She's a happy-go-lucky, bubbly, mothering type of woman. "The fertility tests, then the fertility treatments, then the IVF. I didn't do all that for my daughter to pull a Clover."

Hand automatically going to my belly, I prove I'm my mother's daughter. "This kid is *mine*. You sure the hell ain't raising it for me."

"That's not what I meant." Mom stomps across my room, grabs a garbage bag and tears it down the middle, clothes spewing everywhere. "You're not spoiled– you're loved." Pointing down at the designer clothing I bagged up to sell, "You earned these, buying them with your own money, or your dad and

I gave them to you as gifts. You don't see them as a status symbol, or a way to get attention– you just love and appreciate them. Your voice. I didn't go through all that shit to watch you struggle."

"You hear what everyone says about me." Throwing my hands in the air, I'm so flabbergasted tears are streaming down my cheeks. "I'm just a vapid, party girl who can't keep her legs closed. I sure as shit am not going to give them any more ammunition."

Face twisting up in agony, Mom looks on the verge of crying herself. "We all stood by and watched the Clover we loved disappear. She was perfectly flawed the way she was formed. After she got pregnant with Willow, she lived the mistake and is still paying for it. But Willow wasn't a mistake, and neither is your baby. Clover lost her voice, and all we could do is stand by in silence."

"I'm not Clover," I protest. "She's stronger than me."

"That!" Bethany stomps away, giving my mom the floor, because the woman is sucking in air like she's about to explode.

"I'm not pussy-footing around with you, Hester." Mom points her finger directly into my face "No repeating that history. If Clover and Sam would've given in, Willow would have been raised by them– they would have gotten therapy for their marriage and would've been happy together. Clover's been bearing that cross for nineteen years. Not going to let you do the same bullshit."

I can't help it, head kicked back, I laugh to the ceiling. "There are no parallels whatsoever. You're losing it, Mom." Wiping tears off my face with the back of my hands, I don't know if they're from amusement or shame.

"We all make decisions, but that doesn't mean something you say yes to today will still be a yes tomorrow. We're not signing our souls away with blood when we make a decision. When Willow was four, Clover and Sam got married. Clover had it in her head that because she made a decision, she had to stick to it. Willow should've been returned to her parents, and we wouldn't be liars today."

"No one would argue that, Mom. But what does that have to do with my situation?"

"When I was nineteen, everyone in this town thought Joshua and I were going to get married. If Josh and I stuck by our decisions, continued dating, I'd be Ana Freeman right now, and there'd be no Essie– no Craig and Tyler."

"What?" Bethany steps away from the wall, Mom's odd conversations switch-up confusing her too.

Mom just rolls with it. "Clover was sixteen when she decided to give Willow up to Dave and Mary. For her to be held to that decision for the rest of her life..." Mom sighs, looking defeated for me. "My point. Emotions change. We grow up, and we grow apart. If Josh had ignored what he felt for Meredith out of a sense of misguided loyalty to me, all because he and I had dated for four years, he would've missed out on the love of his life and I would've never met Will."

"Ana's telling you not to be a martyr, girlfriend." Of course, Bethany gets it, and I still don't. Proof positive I'm too shallow for my own good.

Finger pointing at my chest, "You will *not* apologize to Willow again. Do you hear me?" Mom looks on the verge of shaking some sense into me. "You owe her nothing, and neither does Devon. Just because they dated for a few weeks doesn't mean Willow owns Devon."

"It was still a pretty shitty thing to do, Mom." Snorting, I think of all the sermons Mom must've zoned out on.

"You apologized." With a swipe of her hand, "Done! Over. In the past. If you could go back in time and erase it, Willow still wouldn't let you forget it. So I'm not going to allow you to martyr yourself for life. Cut your arm off and hand it to her, still won't change it, will it?"

"Willow's more the type to *pull* my arm off for me–"

"I've told you over and over again, you need heartbreak to recognize the real shit."

"Real shit, all right," Bethany mutters wryly, trying hard not to laugh.

"Beth, you need to listen to me." Now Mom has her sights set on my best friend too. "People live in mediocrity every day and don't recognize it until they live for real." Then she pins me in her stare. "Essie, Devon fucking you in that car was the realest thing either of you has ever done."

"Holy shit." Bethany comes to stand next to me. "Where is your mom going with this?"

"No clue– total Analiese Prynne moment we're having here. She'll circle back eventually."

"I was no virgin bride." Mom's voice is filled with pride. "But I can tell you this, if you end up with your childhood sweetheart, there's a good chance it won't be fireworks. If I hadn't met Will, I would've settled for mediocrity, and never realized there was more out there for me. If I had stuck to the decisions I made, I would've missed out. Willow and Devon would be miserably together forever."

"I see where you're going with this." Beth plays interpreter, because sometimes Mom goes off on a tangent, and nothing adds up. "Decisions based on emotions may change, and you're not a bad person for listening to your emotions. Devon and Willow weren't working out, so they shouldn't stay together just because they said they'd date. Devon's allowed to change his mind. Willow's allowed to go after Ren if she wants him. And Essie isn't to blame for Devon wanting her, when there is no blame or shame in that. Love and lust can't be dictated or controlled. So Essie needs to stop playing the martyr."

"Thank you." Mom bows her head, closing her eyes. "So for you to act like you need to repent for life, lose your voice, all because you had sex with some guy Willow said she owned… that's pretty fucking insulting. Devon is a human being, and he can make his own decisions."

"I'm not losing my voice." I scoff, thoroughly offended. "I'm trying to be responsible. Pay my bills. Not make more shitty choices while suffering the cost of the ones I've already made. I'm trying to grow up. I can't play princess for life, making people pretty."

"Essie," Beth breathes softly, hand slipping into mine, giving a squeeze of comfort and pity. "It's like my best friend was replaced with a body-double."

"You light up a room when you walk into it, but you've dimmed since Willow's birthday. Dimmed to where you no longer cast light at all."

"It's true," Beth pipes in.

"Being an extrovert isn't synonymous with shallow, just as being an introvert doesn't equate being intelligent. Just because someone is quiet doesn't mean they're contemplating the meaning of life. Being a social butterfly isn't a bad thing. It doesn't make you any less intelligent. Gossiping doesn't mean you're an asshole. Talking about politics doesn't make you deep–"

"Usually that's a sign of a pretentious assmunch," Beth interjects, shuddering. "If you have to advertise your intelligence, most likely you're a moron. I'm debating on continuing my education past the master's program– the fact that I'd rather watch contouring YouTube tutorials doesn't make me any less intelligent. I get enough posturing at school. I want to relax and enjoy myself– I miss that Essie."

"*Me too!*" Mom's face twists up in misery. "I miss Essie fixing her hair, wearing nice clothes, and doing her makeup. I miss drinking coffee and gossiping. Martyr Mary Jane has descended upon this house."

"Mom." Taking a deep breath, I close my eyes and try to put my thoughts into words. "What I do is worthless. Being pretty means nothing. I *am* shallow– vapid. Who gives a fuck if I can paint a face and cut hair? I'm making no difference in this world."

"Oh, Essie." Bethany tries to give me a hug, but Mom intercepts her.

"No." Mom pushes Beth back to her side of my bedroom. "I finally had my baby." Now it's Mom's turn to cry, only her tears are silent, and they're killing me. "I had this pink, happy baby. I don't give a fuck if in this politically correct culture everything is supposed to be gender neutral, as if pink is inherently evil. Being girly is frowned upon and made fun of. You organically gravitated to pretty princess–"

"I didn't say I didn't *like* it." I roll my eyes at Mom's theatrics. "Just that there's no value in it."

Blue eyes narrowing, Mom's sick of my shit. "You *will* quit the job at the gas station. You *will* cut your hours back at the No-Name. You *will* get your ass back to Salon where you belong."

"I'll starve!" Clutching my stomach, I glare at my mother. "There's a baby in here! A. Baby. I can't quit!" Tearing my eyes away, I whisper underneath my breath. "I need to kill Devon for this."

"The world is a different place, Essie. We're all still trying to play by the rules of our parents, but the American dream is dead. There's a reason both of you girls still live at home. Twenty years ago, a kid could move out at eighteen and afford it– that kid would've only been working at the gas station, and nowhere else."

"I need a time machine," I mutter begrudgingly. "I'd never go to cosmetology school– I'd never invest in all that equipment.

I'd go be a plumber or something useful. Clogged toilets are universal– we can live without eyebrow shaping."

"How old will you be when your student loans are paid off, Bethany?" Mom waits patiently, confident this will somehow prove her point.

Shrugging, face twisted up in contemplation, "Forty-five, maybe? That's for my master's. If I continue on... I may be dead before my student loans are paid off."

"That's fucking disgusting," I snarl, mind's eye seeing the deductions from my paycheck. "You'll pay it off by retirement. I'll only be twenty-eight when mine's paid off."

"It's gross, but it's my reality." Bethany shrugs flippantly. "Unless Essie finds us a cheap place, they'll have to carry me out of my parents' garage in a pine box– and I feel no shame in that."

"I can't leech off anyone anymore," I mutter to myself. Hearing all those horrid things people say about me is bad enough, I can't give them more ammunition.

"I don't care what people think, Essie." Beth reaches out, imploring me to see her side of things. "I'm working *and* working my ass off studying. I'm not lazy– it costs my parents nothing for me to stay above the garage, but it would cost more than I have to rent a place. I'll never make much money, and I'm okay with that. I took this path to help people, because I wanted to go to work and not feel like it was a *job*."

"I'll probably be calling you Dr. Oman someday, Beth." Defeated, I drop to sit on the edge of my mattress. "Of course you have nothing to be ashamed about, you're amazing."

"Essie?" Mom calls to get my attention, and I take notice that she's moved to stand in front of me, looking down in disapproval. "You're my daughter, and I refuse to watch you struggle– that'd make me a downright shitty mom. I won't allow you to think poorly of yourself, nor will I allow anyone else to do it to you. Would you let anyone harm your baby?" She answers her own question. "No. So don't allow anyone to harm your baby's mother, including you."

"I'm just being realistic, Mom." We all ignore how I sound like I'm whining.

Smile fond, "Even when you were a toddler, you loved Salon. You'd tug my hand while we walked by, or you'd do that grabby wave from your stroller." Mom mimics the hand movement, causing Bethany to chuckle. "I'm not going to let you lose that– I'm not going to let you forget who you are to fit into society's tiny boxes. Just ask Clover someday. Ask her how no matter how much she changed, it was never good enough for Sam, because who she was originally was the person he wanted her to be– the person he missed. The person he blamed himself for losing."

"Oh," I murmur, staring down at the decimation of my bedroom, and all my pretty things. "That's why you keep bringing up Sam and Clover."

"Yes." Mom looks down at me with tears in her eyes. "Devon loves you. It's raw, and a bit insane, but it's love. He loved this version of you–" Mom gestures around my room. "If he comes back from rehab to find a younger version of Clover… Devon needs brightness in his life to combat the darkness– quit snuffing out your own flame."

"What am I supposed to do then?" I toss my hands in the air in utter defeat. "Tell me!"

Crouching, Mom gets to my level. "You go back to Salon– you talk to Elma. You advertise all those amazing things you know how to do–"

"Everyone's broke, Mom." Sighing, I slump my shoulders. "They don't have money enough to eat– *I'd know*. Jesus Christ, look at me floundering. I couldn't afford a manicure, so how can I ask them to pay me for one?"

"The economy sucks," Mom agrees, but she's not giving in. "Just as Bethany will be counseling people, you'll be giving them confidence. As a people, we've lost ourselves into bitterness. We sit at home, getting fatter, wasting money on vices instead of paying the mountain of bills causing the stress, because we feel like shit inside and out. We turn to the negative. Give a person a new outlook, and they'll have the confidence to get that new job, to find that new guy." Mom pulls the panty set from her back pocket. "To feel sexy enough to spark life back into their marriage. You say you're vapid, and I say you're necessary. The world needs beauty to inspire and cause hope. We lose if all we do is work to eat, so we can shit it back out."

"I love your mom." Bethany laughs, looking inspired. "She's right. It's like an infection. You playing martyr won't change the past. I *need* to talk about girly shit with you, or else it's all work, work, work for me. I am a woman, and I'm not going to apologize for it."

"You can be sexy and still be a good person, Essie." Mom stands back up, then looks back down at me, eyebrow raised because I never wore actual pajamas until recently– always flirty nighties, even as a kid. "You're a beautiful person, inside and out. Love is not earned– it's resolute. You deserve respect because you're a human being."

"Well, that's quite the exit," I mutter, baffled, as my mother charges out of my bedroom like her ass is on fire. I turn to my lurking BFF. "Was this a pre-planned intervention?"

The sadistic chuckle is answer enough. "I've known you were pregnant for almost a month," Beth admits, looking sheepish.

Grabbing a handful of clothing, I toss it out of a pure frustration. "How?"

"Our cycles have always been synced." We share a chuckle, because I know where she's headed with this. "There was no ice cream, Bugles, and Diet Coke, Nicholas Sparks binge-watching session last month."

"Bitch," I mutter with affection, hitting Bethany upside the head with a pair of panties.

"I know you are, but what am I?" she murmurs back, smirking.

"Stay classy, Dr. Oman– stay classy. Or should I call you Dr. Essex?"

"Bitch!" The panties are lobbed back at me, hitting me in the side of the face.

"Rory and Bethany, sitting on the sidewalk, fighting over chalk… first comes love, then comes marriage… oh, look! Here comes Essie with a baby carriage." We both snicker at my bastardization of the children's song. Sighing a heavy breath, I look back up to my best friend in the whole wide world. "What am I gonna do, Beth?"

Reaching over, she squeezes my hand. "We'll get through this. Together."

A soft sniffle reaches my ears, and I look up to find my mom standing in the doorway, watching with love shining from her eyes. "I'm going to miss you girls so much. We may have to stay summers up here when Dave and Mary come back." Striding forward, she drops a tablet and pen into my lap. "We have work to do, ladies. We have to redo all these bags, because Essie's keeping some pretty things."

"Mom," I growl, getting even more annoyed. "I'm going to be living out of a duffle bag until I get settled somewhere."

"You think me stupid." Mom accuses, narrowed eyes seeing right through me. "Dressing like a librarian isn't going to change how the town views you. Wearing sweaters year-round won't hide your boobs." Being poked with a finger proves they are indeed tender. "We know they're hiding in there anyway, so you may as well show 'em off."

"I think they look bigger." Hiding her laughter, Bethany coughs into her hand. "Essie, they're just jealous. Fuck 'em."

"Not literally, hun," Mom interjects, proving she's either a comedian or thinks me stupid. "I'm going to wear this pantie set and feel good about myself. You snuck that nightie in Bethany's DVD box. Don't be a hypocrite by wanting us to feel sexy while thinking you shouldn't."

Rolling my eyes, I know there's no winning against my mom. I'm just thankful she dropped the whole moving to Florida with her campaign. "What's this for?" I wiggle the tablet in her line of sight.

"While Bethany and I sort through your clothes–" Mom pauses to give me a loaded look. "Because you can't be objective –you're going to write a list of goals. Short term, as in this week, this month, and next month. Long term, as in three months from now. There's no planning further in advance than that, because Lord knows… then I want you to write down all the ways Salon could generate revenue."

"This is a waste of time," I grumble, staring down at the notebook with eyes gone blurry from tears. Tears caused from the warmth of knowing I do have people who love me unconditionally, and they will always have my back. No matter what.

CHAPTER THIRTY-THREE

Devon Mason

"Nice digs," I mutter sarcastically as I slip into the house Tina's holing up in. The abandoned squat house is crumbling into the ground, long ago being taken off the market because of its condition. The irony is that it's directly across the street from Rush. In Fairport, no one wanted to live near a club. "Nice view—betcha wish you'd never bitched about how small the loft was."

"You're such a prick when you're jonesing for your next hit." Tina peeks out the door, making sure no one saw me enter. After firmly closing it behind her, she leans against it, as if fearing Auggie can *feel* her near him.

Sighing, I can't look Tina in the eye— I can't look anyone in the eye, because the way they see me is reflected back. With Tina, it's even harder. She knows me almost better than anyone. She knows my darkest secrets, because I spill them when I'm high out of my mind. We literally shared a crib. Then when Lisa would drag Tina back to us at random intervals, she'd crawl into my bed to chase my nightmares away.

I ignore the tall blonde staring into my soul in lieu of checking out the place. Wandering around, I snort at how low we've fallen. A cop from a cop family, yet I'm standing in squat waiting for a drug dealer to show up. Then there's Tina, the granddaughter of a Pastor Kline and the stepdaughter of a drug and alcohol counselor. Too bad I'm not sure either one of us has hit rock bottom yet.

The ceilings have so much water-damage, the wallpaper is peeling off the walls, and the carpet is rotting away. I chuckle at how one side of the couch is a few inches shorter than the other— missing half its feet, there's a stack of ancient phonebooks propping it up the best it can. There's a strong musty odor that rankles my nose, making it hard to take a deep breath, but the reason I'm here outweighs the discomfort.

Itching at my forearms, I ignore the bloody marks I leave behind. I've taken so many different types of drugs lately, my body has no idea how to process it all. Dad's cleaned up our county too well. I would've been better off sticking to one drug, but there wasn't enough to keep me supplied, so I've been taking whatever I can get my hands on. The more I take, the more I want. If I hadn't run dry, I wouldn't be mobile right now.

"You're not sleeping here, are you?" Tina's wellbeing overpowers my insane needs. "God, you'll probably catch something just breathing the air."

"I've stayed in worse," Tina mutters brusquely, using her palms to propel her off the door. It takes my mind a while to notice Tina's sober. "You look like death warmed over, Dev." She reaches to give me a hug, but I pull away before we make contact. I feel worse when she flashes me a look of understanding. I love hugs, and I like hugging Tina, that's why I don't want her touching me.

Filthy, right down to the blood roaring through my veins.

"Any way you can get your stepdad to send me another care package?" Shifty, my eyes track over every surface in the living room, looking for Tina's stash. The things I've done in the past few weeks... will haunt me for as long as I live. At this rate, it won't be much longer.

"Rob wasn't supposed to give it to you." Tina sighs heavily, yanking a blanket from a basket resting near the couch. She wraps herself up, then settles on the leaning plaid sofa. Even though it's nearly ninety outside, the house is so damp there's a chill seeping into my bones. "And Patrick isn't my stepdad."

Blinking, I wonder if I'm so high my ears don't work right anymore. "Um, Patrick is married to your mom, so that makes him your stepdad." Wandering, I pretend I'm not hunting for Tina's stash. There's no honor between addicts. Fingertips searching through a basket, I find a bunch of knitting bullshit– this must've been an elderly woman's home.

"Weathersby is his mother's maiden name." Tina watches me, knowing exactly what I'm up to. "There aren't any drugs in the house, you dumb shit. It's why we're waiting on Kurt to show up."

"What does Patrick's last name have a goddamn thing to do with him not being your stepdad?" Angry, I stomp across the room, tugging at my thinning hair, then drop to the sofa in a huff. The dang thing shifts, knocking the stack of phonebooks over.

The force propels me to the side, until I'm squishing Tina into the armrest.

Growling audibly, Tina shoves my ass onto the floor. With quick movements, she jumps to her feet, then kneels down. Picking up the end of the sofa, she puts the phonebooks back to rights. Body cannibalizing itself from the inside out, I muster the strength to move in the time it takes Tina to fix the sofa and sit back down on it. Feeling her glaring at the side of my face, I sit as gingerly as possible, not to upset all of her hard work.

Fingers tapping on my thigh, I focus on my ravaged nails, noticing the darkness of blood staining them. "And, when exactly will Kurt be gracing us with his presence?"

"Jesus Christ, Devon." Tina wants to slug me, I can tell, but she doesn't feel like fixing the couch again. "You have no idea what I've had to do to get you more shit. It was bad enough begging my dad for it."

"Ha!" A rare smirk curls my lips. "You admit Patrick is your stepdad."

"No, Patrick is my *dad*," she stresses. "And I have to fuck Kurt for you, asshole."

With too much information at once, I find myself standing, and I don't remember moving. Skin doing its infamous creepy-crawly sensation, I need to move. I haven't slept in so long, and I can't sit still for more than a few minutes at a time.

"Get up!" I order, voice hostile. With newfound strength, I tug Tina off the couch, then kick the dang thing backward. "Use your brain, Tina– phonebooks?" Movements on autopilot, I don't remember reaching for my Maglite, but I find it clutched in my hand as I knock the feet off the sofa with killing blows.

"You have no idea how disturbing you look right now." Tina keeps backing up, going toward the door. Escape. "A tweaker wearing a police officer uniform– thank God someone with a few working brain cells took your gun away."

"Hey!" I shout, experiencing another time lapse. Tina's behind me, hand tearing the Maglite from my grip.

"You've killed it– stop." Slowly taking the weapon away, as if not to startle me, Tina unarms me. "You're not getting this back, because someone has to protect you from yourself."

"I fixed the fucking problem, didn't I?" Defensive, I snarl in Tina's face, then kick the sofa back upright. It bounces several times, the floor reverberating under our feet, before it comes to rest. I flop down, a plume of dust mites and mold spores filling the air. "Ungrateful bitch."

"You're such a joy, Devon Mason." Tina reclaims her blanket, then sits next to me. "I have no idea how Dad can handle dealing with drug addicts around the clock, and I am one. Being around you the past few weeks, it's been my version of rehab. I don't want to become you."

"Don't be a cunt," I snarl, baring my teeth. "Just get me what I want, and I'll get the fuck out of your hair."

"If I didn't love you…" Tina trails off, no doubt on the verge of cutting me lose like everyone else has. I've been a vicious bastard lately, unable to stop myself from tearing people down. The need to lash out is sometimes stronger than my need to get high.

I've never felt closer to Mom than I do right now.

"As soon as your ass is headed to Sedona, I'm going home– I can't take living like this anymore. I'm admitting defeat."

"I don't know why the fuck you left in the first place. Why you followed your mother back to my house, followed her with all those guys, when you should've just stayed at home with your grandparents and Toby."

Laughing sardonically, Tina shows her own dark side. "Pastor Kline is pitied for having a train wreck of a daughter, and revered by his wife and congregation. *Pfft!*" She pulls her cellphone out to check a text message. "Dad and Mom forgave Grandpa and their lives got better. I wrecked my own uncle when Toby ran away with me a few months ago, but he's better off where he ended up. I don't know which I need to do– stay away or go home. Obviously staying away isn't working for me."

"How is Toby?" Tina's been in my life for always. My grandfather found Lisa and Auggie in a house no different than this one, then brought them home. Dad said Grandpa was shocked to find out Lisa had run away from her Methodist family. After Grandpa died, Lisa found out she was pregnant with Tina, and the cycle of Dad shuffling them back and forth between Pastor Kline's and our house began. I've visited Tina's grandparents a lot, and they seem like nice, forgiving people. Lisa has a little brother who's a few years younger than Tina and me. Sure, it's odd that Auggie and Tina's uncle is younger than them, but it's not uncommon. Look at the age-gap between Dave and Will Prynne…

Last I heard, Toby was being shipped off to Boston University School of Theology.

"When I figured out Patrick was my dad, not my stepdad, obviously Toby was the first person I told." Looking away, Tina's hiding something from me. "A few months ago, Toby and I got on the first available bus leaving the station. Toby's faith got bent by what Grandpa caused my parents to do– when he found out his own truth. So we got high, got on a bus, ended up in Dominion, New York. Found ourselves at some club called Restraint because it reminded me of Rush, and Toby got himself into some trouble. Like a coward, I left him there, ran back home with my tail between my legs. Toby's better off where he is, working as a personal assistant to some bigshot named Dexter Hayes. Then Auggie came barreling in, kidnapped me from Mom and Dad, then locked me in the loft above Rush– this is my escape from the gilded cage of hate."

"Just spit it out," I order while scratching the piss out of my thigh. I've been doing it so much lately, my trousers are getting threadbare and the skin beneath is bruised. It's why my fingernails are such a wreck. It's a compulsion– I can't stop. "I probably won't remember anyway."

"You just want me to occupy you while we wait for Kurt." Laughing to herself, Tina checks her cellphone again. "Pastor Geoff Kline likes to diddle young women in his congregation."

Gripping my empty stomach, I let out a braying, wheezy laugh. "What the hell is wrong with your grandmother? She's like the quintessential Pastor's wife, doting and disillusioned mother, and cookie-baking grandmother. I always loved dropping your ass back home, just so I could hang around Carol Kline."

"You're such an asshole." Now that the sofa won't collapse, Tina has no problem balling up her fist and pounding me in the chest. "I'm not talking about my parents with you, but I'll tell you about Toby because it's common knowledge."

"Tina, really? You don't want me to know your secrets?" I shift on the sofa to stare her down. "You're the one I called last night when I broke into a dealer's house–"

"Because you're a fucking moron!" A tiny fist punches me in the chest again. "Some cop you are. You ought to have learned not to break a window and climb into a guy's house when he leads a life of crime. Seriously, windows smashing create noise. You didn't expect him to shoot at your skinny ass?"

"Fucker chased after me for a good mile, too." Laughing at the insanity my life has turned into, I remember the look on Tina's face when she found me hiding in a dumpster outside of Rush last night. "If I hadn't just stole a few bumps of coke from the guy, I wouldn't have made it ten feet. If only Dad hadn't taken my gun from me."

"Thank fuck for small favors." Tina sounds horrified. "There's a reason I begged Kurt to meet us when all of Fairport County is on alert."

"I'm rather proud of my role in the eradication of Fairport's criminal element–"

"They're petrified of you stealing their product, not being arrested by you. God!" Tina tugs her blanket tighter around her small shoulders. "You make me long for the boringness of sobriety. I've lived on the streets, and even I haven't sank as low as you."

"I excel at everything I do," I deadpan, then my mood shifts yet again. "Where the fuck is Kurt?!" Fist pounding my thigh, I land a mind-clearing punch directly over the worst of the bruising. The pain pushes away the fire ant sensation crawling over my skin.

"Fine," Tina spits, yanking her cellphone back out. "I'll keep pestering him. You do realize Kurt is Ren's age, right? He's dealing for his dad– the guy your dad arrested last week. They aren't selling to you for a reason, and it's not because they want you to sober up. They want you to hurt."

"Yeah, I get the dichotomy of the fucked up situation I'm currently in, which is why you're my go-between."

"You think they don't know that?" Tina snorts. "We shared a fucking address for half hour lives, idiot."

Ironic laughter spills from my throat, "If I know you so well, then why won't you share your secrets with me? Keep my mind off the fact that I'm getting impatient."

"Toby isn't my grandmother's kid," Tina blurts out. "Grandpa was fucking around with a young girl in his congregation. When Toby was a few days old, the girl's parents dropped the baby off and left town."

"Sinful," I slur, chuckling. "That right there is why I'm an atheist. Religion pushers are the biggest sinners, using God as an excuse to do bad things."

"Yeah, you'd know all about sin," Tina mutters flatly. "No one believed Pastor Kline would do something like that, so swallowing that Toby was Carol Kline's kid was easy. Too bad our family believed it too."

"No wonder Toby ditched seminary school– don't blame the kid." Tugging the blanket, I try to get Tina to look at me. "It's your grandfather's sin, so don't look so ashamed."

"Yeah, well... the sins of the father are visited upon the son." Tina stands up, flinging the blanket to the sofa. "In my case, the sins of the father are visited upon the son and daughter, then visited upon their son and daughter."

"What?" I drawl, drug-addled mind trying to reason out Tina's cryptic words.

"Shame is written in my DNA." Walking across the living room toward the front door, Tina looks at me over her shoulder. "I'm filthy in a way that can't be scrubbed off– born a sinner, where no amount of redemption will allow me to pass unto Heaven."

"You don't honestly believe that bullshit, do you?" Snickering, I choke on a snort, but then stop when I notice the tears staining Tina's cheeks.

With a shrug and a slight shake of her head, Tina opens the front door. "I have to pay Kurt, so don't go into the back of the house until we come out."

"Tina?" I lunge to my feet. "Don't do *that* for me."

"It won't be the first time, or the last time." Tina flashes me a smile reminiscent of our shared childhood, and my conscience slams into me. "I have no skills, no job– no worth outside of getting guys off. Besides, Kurt was a virgin when I hooked up with him, and we've only been doing each other. It's not as whorish as it sounds."

Gathering strength to argue with Tina, I'm cut off by the front door opening wider. In walks a guy who looks like he goes to college with Willow and Langdon– maybe he does. As short as me, but geeky with glasses and a Marvel T-shirt, Kurt doesn't look like he does drugs, let alone sells them. He's probably his father's pride and joy– biggest earner, by his ability to fit in with drug-hungry college kids.

Kurt gives me a passing glance of disdain, eyes immediately returning to the object of his desires. "Hey, babe– sorry I'm late. I had to lie to Dad and say I was making a sale at FCC."

"Give Dev his shit." Tina abruptly stalks across the room, trying to hide the fact that she's embarrassed I'm witnessing this. "I'm going to need some for after."

"'Kay, babe." Kurt swaggers his dinky ass across the living room, hard-on tenting his khakis. This guy wouldn't be getting laid if it wasn't for me.

"Tina?" I call out, stalking past Kurt, even if half of me is struggling because he has what I need. Tugging her into what used to be a kitchen before plumbing scavengers tore it to the wall studs, "I can just jump this asshole, and then we'll get out of here."

"Dev." Palm resting over my chest, Tina's fingers curl into my t-shirt. "Kurt and I sell as a team for his dad. We hit the colleges and shopping centers as Barbie and The Geek. We're selling the fantasy that drug users can be beautiful and intelligent. Kurt doesn't use, but I do. If we jump Junior, Senior will kill all three of us." Hand falling away, "I don't mind– I need the release in more ways than one."

"You can't live like this." I try to tug Tina back to me as she pulls away.

"I won't be– I'll be going home as soon as your ass is in Sedona. While you fight your demons, I'll be leaving mine behind." Then she disappears into the back of the house.

Kurt peels himself away from the wall, having listened to every word we said. "Your shit is on the couch." Noticing the concern I have for Tina outweighs the addict's need crawling in my veins, he puts me out of my misery. "Tina and I are friends, Dev– I'm not going to hurt her." Walking away, Kurt's whispered words flutter back to me. "*She's going to ruin me.*"

At a crossroads, half of me wants to barge in there and tear Kurt off Tina– knowing Tina, she's probably the initiator –the other half of me is stronger, pulling me back to the sofa. Feet moving on their own volition, time ceases to have meaning.

"Meth," escapes my numb lips, no doubt Kurt's dad is giving me a big *fuck you* after all the shit I've pulled in the past few months, after Dad shutting down his operation time and time again. I've never used meth, because something about it seems so low. I've been working my way through the drug alphabet, graduating to heroin these past few weeks. But meth?

Reaching forward, mind spinning with indecision, body begging for the cocktail of chemicals my brain will release in my blood the instant the drug makes its way inside me. At least there won't be any witnesses to my downward spiral. Using drugs is more intimate than sex– just like years and years of abstinence and my own hand, I only get high by myself.

Devon and the addict struggle for what feels like hours, tearing me apart in the process. A vibration from my back pocket helps me swim back into the light. After a deep breath, I clear my throat, trying to mimic the voice I used to have.

Devon Mason: Consummate actor. Liar. Addict. Insane.

"Yes?" I answer with a levity I don't feel, too jittery to even read the caller ID.

"Hey, Dev," Beth's voice sounds far away, like she's whispering. Or guilty, my mind supplies. No, the guilt I hear is all mine. "How are you? Any news on when you're going to Sedona.

The swift change in my mood has a whiplash effect on my body. Physically jerking as if struck, I swallow down the rage. Always those questions. I no longer have any privacy. I bite back the need to scream at Beth how it's none of her fucking business.

"What do you want?" is the most polite thing I can muster to say, but my voice has changed back to its new normal– the version of me that terrifies my family, to the point I no longer speak.

"I need to talk to you, Dev." If Beth is afraid of how I sound, she doesn't show it. "Can you meet me at the swing set at nine tonight?"

Swing set? Beth and Essie may still be those same kids, but I sure as fuck am not. There's no returning to our childhood meeting place– the place where three kids became best friends who were together every day until The Nightmare manifested.

"No," I blurt out harshly, knowing I'll be floating in the sky by then. "I'm busy."

"Devon, please," Bethany begs, and it has my suspicions rising.

"I can't face Essie, Beth." Gripping my cellphone in my fisted hand so hard, I almost crack the screen. "I'm staying away for her own good. I don't even want you to see me as I am right now."

"Essie's not coming." Beth speaks with false lightness, so I know she's liar. A liar can spot another of our kind. "Rory's been sniffing around me, but you know I can't give him the time of day until Auggie releases me from our contract."

Beth needed entrance into the Playroom, so she offered up her body in order to pick Auggie's brain. Win-win. Yeah, there's no way in hell Rory will ever share, especially with Auggie.

"Best just wait until your thesis is completed." I stare down at the meth waiting for me, shocked that I'm holding a coherent conversation in its presence. Salivating, I lean closer, losing track of time.

"Rory's not taking no for an answer." Beth laughs a sound I've heard all my life– in this, I know she's telling the truth. I relax some, trusting her. "You know Auggie better than anyone, so just meet me tonight."

The dead silence has me pulling my cellphone away from my ear to stare at the screen as it shows the call has ended. "Confident, ain't she?" I mutter to the meth like it's another entity in the living room. "Sure, Beth is dealing with Rory, but we both know this is about Essie."

Eyes narrowed, focusing solely on my next high, I don't need excuses or reasons to take my next hit. I don't lie to myself. This isn't about medicating a mental illness anymore. In my quest for light, the beast sunk its talons in me. There's no keeping the shadowy darkness away, because I've welcomed it with open arms.

I'm a drug addict, and I need no other excuse to use. The sweats go away, the shakes even out, and the fire ants licking at my skin quiet in the face of my decision to chase the high.

I don't fight it.

I surrender to the addict.

CHAPTER THIRTY-FOUR

Kieren Mason

Our family is seated around the table, eating spaghetti again. Devon's seat is empty, not that I'm surprised. I saw him this morning when he was slinking out of the house like a shadow, after coming home smelling like a dumpster last night. In a way, it's like we can all breathe deeply without Devon in our face, sitting across the table. We can ignore the fact that he's not eating, never resting unless he's sleeping something off. With the problem not staring us in the face, offering us a direct challenge, we're able to relax and forget, even for all of three minutes in a row.

There's a chaotic, disruptive energy Devon releases when he's in the house. It makes it difficult to relax, let alone think straight. Even though I hate what Dev is doing to himself and the family, I can't help but fear how Devon must feel on the inside to be able to put that much negative energy out into the world.

I miss Devon– I want my best friend back.

Stabbing a piece of garlic bread with a fork, I get my share before Weston inhales it. "Gimme the agenda," I order, needing to know where everyone will be, because I need to know if it's safe to escape with Willow for two or three hours tonight.

Unable to help himself, Dad reaches over to squeeze my neck, thick fingers working out the kinks. The more stressed he is, the more he touches as a coping mechanism. After a few more squeezes, where my eyes close in bliss, Dad goes back to shoveling in spaghetti.

"Rae and I are going out," Weston announces, acting all shady.

Sage.

"Where?" Dad can never turn off his inner cop. "Who will you be with? How long will you be gone? What time will you be home?"

"Daddy!" Raven laughs, covering for Weston, who's looking guiltier by the second and blushing like a little bitch. "Don't worry about us. We're too smart to repeat the fool mistakes you've all done."

My baby sister points her fork at me, cackling, then steals my garlic bread.

Lunging forward, I try to retrieve it, but the entire piece disappears in Weston's mouth, leaving Rae and me groaning in disappointment. That boy loves garlic bread– apparently kissing isn't on his agenda tonight.

Too easy, Dad smiles, thinking Rae an angel. Technically Rae isn't up to no good– not-so-innocent Wessie is. Dad has blinders on when it comes to his kids, no one will ever deny that fact.

"Good news," Dad announces, smiling blindingly. "The admissions director from Sedona called me just as I was leaving work tonight. We have three spots ready and waiting. If we can just keep Devon secured over the weekend, we'll be golden."

"Thank fuck," I murmur as I slump to the table. I notice Weston and Rae have done the same thing. It's like the relief had all of our muscles relaxing at once. "I can't wait to get off this crazy train."

"Go!" Dad reaches back over to give my neck a few more squeezes. "You go on– I know you need to spend some time with Willow. I'll clean up and let the kids go do whatever they're hiding from me."

"But what are you hiding from us?" I call Dad out for acting shady too.

Pulling a Rae, Dad makes fun of himself and us. "I'm too smart to repeat fool mistakes. Get going– skedaddle."

"You don't have to ask me twice." My laughter follows me down the hallway, happy Weston ate my garlic bread. There won't be any kissing tonight, but I don't want to stink for Willow's benefit.

The entire drive over to the Spook House, I'm bursting to share Dad's news, but then I get deflated as reality descends. Willow and I have topics we *can't* touch. We both need an escape from life, even if it's just a few hours a week. Honestly, I don't know how I would've survived the past five or six weeks without

Willow and I entertaining each other. So no matter how deflated I am that I can't talk about anything pertaining to Devon or Essie, the payoff is worth the cost.

As always, the front door cracks open as I jog up the sidewalk, with Willow's face the first thing I see. "Hiya, Stud!" Smile wide, Willow's greeting makes all the stress melt away. "How's it hanging?"

"To the left," I answer honestly. "And probably a bit too sweaty for your liking."

Big eyes shining bright, Willow's laughter erases all the bad thoughts I had today. Leading the way, she prattles on about already fetching our evening snacks and how the Hopper is locked and loaded for our viewing pleasure.

We may be keeping everything in the friend-zone while learning what makes the other tick, but I'm still a man. Eyes glued, I watch as Willow's ass jiggles the entire way up the staircase. It takes everything in me not to reach out and grab a healthy handful or give a playful swat. The fact that she no longer wears jeans around me isn't helping. Willow always greets me in a pair of lounge pants, which she strips off down to her undershorts before she crawls into bed next to me.

The delicious sight no longer has me hanging left– no longer hanging at all. Suppressing a groan, I surreptitiously adjust myself, only to be caught by Robin waiting to descend the stairs. "Shit," I hiss, mind reeling to think up a good excuse. I'd rather say I have crabs than admit the truth.

Palm landing in the center of my chest, Rob stops me in my tracks, excellent for erection-deflation. "Ren will be right with ya," he calls to Willow, who turns to see what's keeping me.

"Okay," Willow says with a shrug, slipping into her bedroom. Then her face pops out, smirking. "Don't keep me waiting– gotta get my Jax fix."

"I'm not a fan of Sons of Anarchy." Rob's fingers curl into my t-shirt, dragging me in the opposite direction of Willow's bedroom. "She's a Prynne– we are notorious eavesdroppers."

Bypassing his own bedroom, Rob pulls me into one I've never been in before, probably because Willow's ear is pressed to the wall she shares with his room. "Listen," I stammer, eyes flicking around in discomfort. "Let's hurry this up, because I don't want Auggie kicking my ass for being in here."

There's no other way to describe the room other than to say it epitomizes Augustus Kline. The ginormous bedframe is rough-hewn lumber and metal covered by a medieval tapestry instead of a comforter. The walls are covered with life-sized sketches of dragons dwarfing castles. But it's the seven-by-four-foot oil painting that has my breath catching in my lungs– it's like Auggie and my aunt's eyes are boring into my soul, more lifelike than in reality.

Robin's otherworldly talent is only overshadowed by his obsession with his wayward lovers, but his manipulation screams the loudest. Rob makes Auggie sleep in that bed with a life-sized portrait of himself and Isis staring back at him.

Leaning down to flip through a sketchbook resting on the nightstand, "Pussy," Robin mutters out the corner of his mouth at me. "Hmm… that right there is gorgeous." Fingertip tapping on a sketch, he makes a pleased sound in the back of his throat. "I'll see if I can duplicate it in another medium."

"What. Do. You. Want. Robin?" Impatient for my Willow time, I interrupt whatever the hell he's up to. Sadist that he is, he fucking makes me wait until he's done flipping through Auggie's newest sketches. "Hey, does that door lead into your bedroom?"

Chuckling as he snaps the sketchpad shut, Robin turns to me with a shit-eating grin plastered on his face as an answer. Then his expression shuts down, terrifying me. Everyone thinks Robin is the masochist in their relationship, which is a rumor he started. Rob even lied to Willow's face about it, calling himself a pain slut. He is a pain slut– a slut for causing pain… and Isis doesn't factor into this equation.

It's all about perception, and no one sees my beautiful aunt, beastly Auggie, or the effeminate Robin accurately. Rob's the balls and brains of this operation, and he's utterly terrifying.

I don't see a springtime omen of a bird when I look at Robin– a ferret, weasel, and snake in the form of a cuddly bunny.

"Enjoy yourself tonight, Ren." Robin pats my shoulder affectionately. I don't doubt the freak loves me, but that doesn't mean he won't pull me out like I'm a trump card in his own personal deck of cards. "But I need you to be home around ten tonight. Okay?"

Heart beating uncontrollably, "Why?" I mutter with suspicion. "What do you know that I don't?"

"Everything." Robin barks a sharp laugh. "Tonight, you will be home at ten, then tomorrow you will go to Essie. I don't want to hear any bullshit from you about Willow. Willow is your girlfriend, but don't turn your back on Essie– she's been your friend for far too long for you to ditch her."

"Essie won't talk to me," I whine out in frustration, fists balled at my sides. "No matter what I try. She has Beth."

Ignoring my outburst, "Beth's going to be a bit distracted by Rory for the rest of her life." As always, Robin knows all the gossip. "You're going to flash those dimples and blue peepers at Willow, and you're going to get her to forgive Essie. Enjoy tonight, because these topics are back on your conversational table."

"Wait, Robin!" I shout in a panic as he heads toward the door to the right of the creepy portrait. "What's going on?"

Turning to face me, one foot in his own bedroom with the rest of his body in Auggie's, the sudden sheen covering his eyes scares the piss out of me. "It's a good thing you and Willow have really gotten to know one another– *truly*. But Essie needs you, and she needs Willow. The three of you need each other, and Devon's gonna need a united front when he returns or he's destined for the grave."

The door shuts between us. Gulping the lump down in my throat, I blink a few times. When the door reopens, Robin's voice carries, but he doesn't reappear. "If your charm won't win Willow over, guilt her into being selfless enough to forgive Essie. There's a reason you idiots swapped back and forth– you're woven together for life. I'm not fucking around. If you three aren't solid when Devon comes home, he won't survive it."

The sound of the door slamming shut between us reverberates in my head the entire walk to Willow's bedroom. Half my brain is trying to figure out Robin, which is an impossible task, while the other half is wondering what I can and can't tell Willow– she's going to ask, and I'm not going to lie, then our night will fucking suck.

Willow's door is cracked open, and before I enter, I can already feel her confusion wafting out. Robin's parting shot was said from his bedroom for a reason– he made sure Willow heard it as she eavesdropped.

"Hey." Willow won't look at me, and doesn't even bother hiding her confusion. Arms folded over her tiny breasts, she stares at the ground dejectedly. No matter whose point of view you look at this situation from, it's painful. Willow's hurt. Essie's hurt.

I'm collateral damage.

"I can't not talk about my brother anymore," I mutter bluntly, looking Willow dead-to-rights. I won't back down and act sheepish. "This is the final weekend of Devon's drug rampage, then he's off to Arizona for help. Devon's my brother and my best friend, and that's something I *need* to share with my girlfriend."

Sniffling, Willow doesn't say anything, which is actually a good sign. As long as she's not screaming or erupting into a violent fit, she's hearing me.

"Just the important shit," I amend. "Not going to shove your nose in it. But it's not fair to me that I have to shoulder this burden, then not have anyone who will support me."

Walking across the room, Willow reaches out to take my hand. Squeezing slightly, she surprises me. "I've prayed for Devon every single night, and sometimes during the day when he pops into my head. I'm relieved for you and your family that he's going to be somewhere safe where he can't hurt himself anymore. If he hurts, you hurt… I hurt… Essie hurts. Rob's right, but I'm not ready for Essie yet."

"Okay." And just like that, it's over. There's no theatrics or arguing, because that can't exist in the face of the black and white truth. I'll always tell Willow the truth as I see it, just as I'll always tell her how I feel, even if it hurts. You can't argue over that.

Tugging my hand, Willow pulls me to the bed. "We have time for two episodes tonight, then you better get home." Releasing my hand, I don't feel like I'm losing her. It's like whatever walls we erected around ourselves have disintegrated. "I trust you, but don't shove Essie on me."

After toeing off my sneakers and socks, I crawl between Willow's sheets. "Are these new?"

"Yeah," Willow murmurs while she flicks the lock on her bedroom door. She grabs a handful of snacks and two sodas on her way back.

"Cool," I mutter lamely about the sugar skulls staring at me from the purple sheets. More like creepy.

Laughing, a bag of Cool Ranch Doritos is lobbed at my chest, with a bag of Snickers following. Willow strips off her pajama bottoms, then quickly slips into bed before I can get a peek at her underwear. "I know they're creeping your ass out, Stud. It's why I bought them."

"You evil, evil girl," I tease, accepting the Orange Crush Willow hands me. "Press play– you gotta get your Jax fix while I drool over their rides."

We spend a good hour munching on snacks, yelling at the TV, then getting in a heated debate over the plot and characters. We're so involved with one another, nothing else in the world exists. By the time we're halfway through the night's second episode, we're both blissfully sated in everything but our lust.

There's always this heat riding the air, and we stopped ignoring it weeks ago. As an unwritten rule, we acknowledge its existence but we don't act on it. Willow and I are always handsy– she giggles when I tickle her for an excuse to touch her tits and ass. Willow's always asking how my dick is doing– she kneed me at Rush, grabbed me at Calico, and randomly palms me at the Spook House. We always make sure the other knows we want them, even if we're not ready for hardcore fuckage.

Except tonight feels different, like there's an undeniable charge building in the air.

About a minute ago, I stopped paying attention to what's happening on Sons of Anarchy, more interested in watching Willow watch Jax get it on. Voice deep as he groans, Willow is wiggling around on the bed like she's being tickled.

Biting my lip, I try not to release a knowing chuckle. The pressure building in my balls is bad enough, but then Willow subconsciously cuddles up to my side, leg wrapping around my thigh. The volume pitches louder, and I sigh in relief that it goes to commercial break. The only problem is that Willow doesn't seem to notice.

I try not to move, even breathe, in fear Willow will stop. Face tucked in the crook of my neck, she wiggles around the mattress, pressing her crotch against my thigh. Rocking back and forth, Willow releases these barely audible grunts from the back of her throat.

Fingers curling with need, I'm so fucking hard right now I think I'm going to die. All the other times I pushed Willow too far, too quickly, like back in the hallway at Rush. I'm never going to make that same mistake again. Lying in Willow's bed, I give her whatever she's willing to take, and nothing more.

Fingertips walking up my chest, "Stud," is a breathy moan, almost sounding like she's asking for permission.

So I do the only thing I can. "Spanky," I answer in a rough rasp. Mirroring everything Willow does to me, I reach out to touch her chest, fingertip hitting a pebbled nipple as if it was my target.

Shuddering, Willow flows up my body, legs straddling my hips. We don't kiss. We don't talk. As she begins rutting in a rocking motion, the notch between her thighs fitting perfectly over my bulge, I can't stop my arms from wrapping around her.

"Ren," is a breathy moan directly into my ear. Willow must've been hot and bothered all night, because in less than a minute, she's moving faster, rhythm jerky.

No sound flows from my lips, but that doesn't mean this isn't the most intense yet unexpected sexual experience of my life. Pitching my self-restraint, my hands grip Willow's delectable ass, fingertips biting in. Grinding hard, Willow's fat ass jiggles against my palms, and I swear to God, I'm going to come with her.

After what happened to Devon during The Nightmare, the thought of ever letting go enough to get off with someone else is unthinkable. I trusted Essie, but ended up bawling. I freaked out with Tina. Until Willow's birthday, I honestly didn't think I'd be able to be that intimate with another person. But Willow had me going fucking nuts in seconds, same with at the Revolutionary Road concert.

For a self-proclaimed slut, I haven't had sex in over a year, and it's been killing me to be around Willow and not be *inside* her. Patience is a virtue most rewarded.

Arching my back, I flex my hips, adding more friction for the both of us. I don't even give a fuck that my jeans are rubbing my cock raw. It'll be a constant reminder of how hot Willow sounds, how right she feels grinding against me.

Faster and faster, Willow's rocking so hard she's breathing in one continuous moan. Things get dicey from here on out, like if Willow wasn't seconds from popping off, she'd have my fly torn open and be riding my dick in a heartbeat.

Turning wild, Willow's teeth sink into the flesh where my neck meets my shoulder, her fingernails dig into my chest, and her crotch is about to start a fire between us. Saying fuck it all, I slip my hands beneath her shorts and grip her bare ass in my palms. Thrusting up, I grind her down on me, then slap her ass as hard as her shorts will allow.

The thwack is loud, echoing, but not nearly as sharp as the grunt Willow releases as she comes for me. Muscles locking up tight, Willow turns to stone against me, then the writhing starts. Through it all, I let go enough to come for the first time with another person, at the same fucking time. Stunned, no sounds flows from my throat, but I just keep pumping and pumping out jizz in my pants. The coolness puts out the fire, but then the telltale sting of a brush burn starts.

I'm going to be hurting something fierce, but it'll be worth it.

Shuddering, Willow embraces me with her arms and legs, holding me as tightly as humanly possible. Whimpering, she buries her face against the side of my neck, damp breath stinging the bite mark she gave me.

Holding Willow back, I know we're never going to talk what just happened, but we don't need to. Our bodies are speaking volumes.

Jesus, if this is what dry-humping feels like with Willow... sex is going to change life as I know it.

A Taco Bell commercial was playing as we got off– I'll never be able to eat a taco or drive by a Taco Bell without getting a hard-on from here on out. Spanky sex is my new Fourth Meal.

CHAPTER THIRTY-FIVE

Essie Prynne

With the house almost packed up, the movers are set to arrive to load everything we own into a tractor trailer tomorrow, including some of my aunt and uncle's belongings. My parents will be leaving Fairport in a few days, so they're staying with Aunt Mary and Uncle Dave, as I will be indefinitely. It's selfish to say, but I don't want them to leave right now. The timing couldn't be worse. But, at the same time, I get it. I'll deal.

Proving she's the best friend on the planet, Bethany didn't drive up to the university today. She stuck with me through thick and thin, helped packed up my stuff, waited with me for the last of the Craigslisters, and then helped me hock my shit at the consignment shops. Afterward, we went apartment hunting… total bust.

The last apartment we visited– only one we could afford – was a one bedroom efficiency in a building that ought to be condemned. Beth and I made plans to go back tomorrow with the money, but we both know that's never going to happen. Beth proved her point that our being roomies wasn't an option– we can't afford it, and I can't fit on her twin bed in the plumbed bedroom. I'd rather sleep in the same room with Willow, not caring if she was ignoring me or screaming at me like a chain-smoking alarm clock, than pay that smarmy assmunch a nickel in rent.

There's a definite *ending* sensation riding the air tonight, like life as we know it will cease to exist. Beth asked me to meet her at the swing sets at nine– in order to end this, we have to meet where it all began. She's been distant lately, preoccupied, and I have a feeling Rory got underneath her skin and is not letting her make excuses anymore.

If I was hooked on Devon growing up, Bethany was addicted to Rory. They were next door neighbors, with Rory nearly

Auggie's age– Rory was Auggie, Isis, and Rob's junior sidekick. Since Bethany was so young, Rory held her at arm's length once he wasn't a little shit himself. Their sidewalk chalk days turned into Bethany sunbathing in the front lawn– in the cold months too –trying and failing to get Rory's attention.

Now that Beth's a grown woman, Rory's attention is caught. Only problem is that Beth wants to concentrate on her schooling and is struggling with a deal she made with the devil– Auggie. We all know Rory isn't going to share.

Call it best-friend-radar, if you will, but I have a sneaking suspicion Beth has something to tell me tonight at the swing sets.

With the elementary school playground coming into view, my cellphone vibrates my boob. After pulling it out of my bra, "Clover?" I rasp in surprise.

"Hey, Ess–" Clover sounds breathless. "Why is my parents' house locked up tight? I even went to the backdoor, but I can't get in. I can hear them in there laughing."

Chuckling, a vision of my parents and Clover's sitting at the Prynne supper table flashes through my mind. "They're plotting in there," I answer without thought. "It's cute. They kicked me out too."

"Plotting what?" Clover's voice breaks, always fearing the worst. She treats Uncle Dave and Aunt Mary like they're fragile, when they're the most formidable yet entertaining people I know.

"I have no clue." I lie– no way in hell am I spilling. I have the feeling Clover doesn't realize Malcolm's been plotting with her parents for a few months. I was kicked out of their house tonight because I was caught snooping in on their conversation. No way does Clover know Dave and Mary are selling their house, moving in with my parents for the winters, and living with her and Malcolm during the summers, because she doesn't even know Malcolm bought her a house in the first place.

Dealing with Willow is bad enough, I'm not inciting the mother lioness.

Pretty sure even sneaky Robin doesn't realize he'll have a new job description as the owner and operator of Prynne Renovations. Our folks taught us everything we know, and now we underestimate them. The parents are sick of their children's shit, and they're fixing us up and letting us go.

"It must be about me," Clover muses, no doubt the direction of her thoughts is dead accurate. "Hmm… come visit me tomorrow– my house is always open to you, no matter what, Essie."

"Thank you," I whisper, heart hurting. "I love you."

"I love you too– bye!"

In a few weeks, it'll be four years since I graduated, so it's bittersweet to be walking across the high school parking lot, with my destination the little school playground. A lot of good and bad went down at FAHS. Smiling privately, I welcome the warmth and push out the cold.

Skipping over to the bank of swing sets that only has three seats, I marvel how in a few short years, the baby in my belly will be sitting here too. Maybe he'll make friends with a brooding little boy and a rainbow-colored little girl, just like I did when I was in preschool. Hopefully the cycle will stop, and my baby's friends will have his back well after graduation.

Sweet, carefree laughter and a few tears fill my ears from memory's past. Smiling, I kick with my feet to get the swing to arc. The creaking sound is a soothing balm as wind whips my hair– flying.

I have no idea what I'm going to do, even knowing my place with Aunt Mary and Uncle Dave is temporary, because they're selling their house too. But I have faith that I'll figure something out.

The *right* something is what Mom and Bethany were trying to get me to see, not the desperate, poor choices of a cornered animal, fearing what others think.

I won't rent that cesspool of an apartment, because that would be taking twenty steps back, all because I fear giving Willow and the townsfolk ammunition against me. Asking for and receiving help doesn't make you weak– it makes you human. The knowledge I learned at school, no matter the cost and inconvenience, is a blessing not a curse– what I learned can never be taken away from me. I won't apologize to Willow again until she can *hear* me. My baby will *never* be a mistake, nor will I see the good and bad times I spent with Devon as one either.

"Hey," Bethany's voice sounds far away as she approaches, sheepish even.

"Hey," I echo as she sits in the swing next to me. Beth doesn't start pushing with her feet– she just sways a few inches back and forth like a pendulum, so I rip the bandage off. "You're with Rory now, and between school and him, you're scared I'll see it as abandonment."

Chuckling sardonically, Beth shakes her head left and right. "Close," she murmurs, sounding amused yet terrified. "I'll *never* abandon you, Essie." She reaches over to rest her hand atop mine where it's clasping the swing.

"*I know*," I stress. "I may be going through a bunch of shit, but I'd rather help you with yours."

"Rory isn't taking no for an answer, and not listening that I have things that I can't do if he's around. He says he can slay all my dragons. I need to concentrate on my studies. I'm trying for my master's, then I may continue on. My thesis is important to me, and that means I have to have Auggie and the Playroom to accomplish that. But I can't tell him these things, because I'm borderline ashamed of it."

After Willow's birthday, I freaked out a bit about Auggie and his playpen of iniquity. When I heard about how Willow lost her virginity, I was livid and terrified for her. I felt guilty I couldn't protect her– I *still* think I should've protected Willow. At Rob's insistence, I let Devon go for Willow, as penance and a way to keep Auggie away from her. I confided all of that to Beth, and she finally told me the truth– the depths she was willing to sink in her quest to write the thesis of a lifetime.

"You have nothing to be ashamed of, Beth." Flipping my hand around, I curl my fingers with hers, then squeeze. "Rory can slay all your dragons, and he'll give you space to accomplish your dreams. God, Bethany– Rory's a keeper."

"I don't feel like an independent woman right now," Beth grumbles, angry at herself. "Why do I get so… hot thinking about Rory solving all my problems? It's so anti-feminism. But Rory's so big and buff, with these mammoth shoulder to carry my burdens. He's older, more experienced and set in life. Feminism flies right out the window in the face of emotion, lust, safety, and security."

Snorting, I can't help but laugh. "Jesus, girl. I'm like a perpetual damsel in distress, so I get it. I want to slay my own dragons, but even I can admit it's nice to have someone who gives two shits that wants to help. It's probably written in our DNA somewhere– no matter how independent we may be, it's still fucking hot to see a man stand up and be a man."

Chuckling, Bethany doesn't surprise me with what she says next. "That's in my thesis too, part of human sexuality. Wanting him still makes me feel like I'm turning my back on women everywhere, giving us a bad name."

"Your happiness is all I give a shit about, girlfriend." I reach over to swat Beth's ass, causing her swing to arc. "With your doctorate, write a paper on the evolution of primal human needs affecting the modern woman. If we don't mate, the human race dies."

"Rory wants…" Bethany trails off, whispering like she's scared it will hurt my feelings. "He wants to pay my tuition and have me move in with him."

I may need a white knight to ride in and save the day, but I won't begrudge Bethany one when she doesn't need saving. "You want it, but fear it will make you look like his whore?"

"Yes," she breathes in shame.

"I'm assuming a man like Rory isn't asking to shack up– rings and legal binding agreements. Like you said, he's older and established in life. He's ready for a family, I suspect. It's a partnership. If you think this makes you look like a whore, then every woman on this planet is one just because she has sex with her significant other. If that's the definition of feminism, then why is it degrading to women?"

"You need to remember that, Essie," Beth levels at me. "The only people who are whores are paid for sex, and that doesn't make them bad people. If I can give into Rory, then you have to stop living that label."

"I'm trying," I whisper the truth. Something about knowing I'll never be alone again is helping me deal. Even if Bethany were to be whisked away by Rory, I wouldn't be sitting here alone. My baby's inside me, keeping me company– loving me simply because I exist so he can too. My flaws mean nothing to this baby.

"You promised!" cuts through the night, voice so distorted I hardly recognize it. Bethany and I are on our feet before the words even register in with our brains, swings hitting us in the back of our thighs. "You promised you wouldn't bring her– I told you I didn't want to see her!"

Gutted, I grip my stomach as Devon shrieks at us from the shadows. "I don't want to see Essie! I don't. I don't. I don't. I don't. I! DON'T!"

Lunging forward on wobbly legs, Devon comes into view. Completely out of his mind, he's bellowing while tugging at his hair. Illuminated by the streetlight, Devon's clothing is hanging off an emaciated and filthy body, with greasy hair spiked in wild clumps. Pupils blown, eyes glazed with a combination of drugs and lunacy, Devon's face is covered in scratches, like he's tried to tear his flesh from bone.

"Essie," Beth cautions, placing her forearm across my chest to keep me from stepping forward. "Look at his fingernails."

Eyes flicking on Beth's order, it's hard to ignore the dark stain of dried blood coating Devon's fingers, and the fresh wash of red beading along his torn and stubby nailbeds.

It's been nearly six weeks since I've laid eyes on Devon Mason, and if it wasn't for the fact that he's screaming a litany at us, I wouldn't have recognized him, not even his voice. Weakened by the sight, I slump backward, having faith the swing will be where it ought to be.

"He needs help now," I breathe. "He's not going to survive much longer." Closing my eyes, I tune Devon out– he's been shouting for several minutes, none of it making much sense. It won't be long before someone calls 911 to report it.

Love is unconditional, and God knows I'll love Devon even after I'm in the grave. But while Devon shouts obscenities at me, saying horrific things about me that I already feel during my darkest hours, I realize I have to love myself unconditionally too.

Because I love me– because I love our baby –because I love Devon, I let him go.

By blocking out Devon, I fail to hear Bethany talking right back at him. The rage-fueled tone is unmistakable, but the words are jumbled. That is until one sentence registers…

"Get rid of IT!" hits my ears with life-altering force.

Standing from the swing, I turn to walk away, not bothering to stop my childhood best friends from verbally and physically assaulting one another. After growing up as a Prynne, where half the family are scrappers and the other half are pacifists, I've never been in a fight.

Dad's advice follows me as I walk home, to the background soundtrack of my best friends slaughtering each other. *If you hit someone, expect to be hit back. If you hit back, expect to be beaten… don't stop to defend yourself if you have the ability to walk away.*

I love my baby more than Devon, more than Bethany, so I take care of myself by not getting into the middle of *that*.

Footstep after footstep, I make my way back to my old house, knowing it's an empty husk of my childhood. I fear for

Beth, but she obviously set this up. I told her Devon wasn't ready– I wasn't ready to tell him. Too much stress on a person who is already fractured...

Beth said Devon needed hope.

Beth said Devon always wanted a child with me, which is the hope he needed to get him through the coming days...

What I didn't expect is the pure loathing pouring out of Devon– bitter hatred directed solely at me.

In the past, Devon shouted at me in the middle of a packed hallway at FAHS– *Masons don't marry whores!*

That moment has burdened me for over seven years, but I let the label fall away as I walk away.

In the present, Devon shouted the worst thing another human being can say to another...

"Get rid of IT!"

There is no getting rid of *it*– there's only getting rid of Devon. No less than one hundred times, Devon screamed for me to get away from him.

No fear in that, because I don't want Devon anywhere near me.

No tears, no guilt, I feel nothing but pride over how I handled myself as I step into my house and make my way up to my empty bedroom. I'm not being selfish or unsympathetic by walking away. People like Devon drain everyone around them dry. I won't let him kill me as a side-effect of his slow-suicide. An empty husk can't grow and support a baby.

Devon's family is helping him, but now he has to accept the help for himself.

CHAPTER THIRTY-SIX

Kieren Mason

Robin said to be home by ten, so like a good boy I was home by nine-thirty. I've long ago showered, slathered my sore cock with ointment, and put on some sweats. It's now almost midnight, and I'm starting to think Robin Prynne is losing his touch.

Working on restocking Wreck & Ruin's inventory on my laptop, I'm sitting at the kitchen table with a two-liter of Dr. Pepper and an entire pan of brownies. "I'm gonna get fat," I grumble wryly as I take another bite. "Too young to be sitting here, waiting for my kids to get home."

Lost in the mindless task of imputing item numbers on my supplier's website, I barely notice Weston slipping through the kitchen like a ghost. Eyes flicking up, I connect with my baby sister– frozen like a bunny rabbit caught in the act, she doesn't have the balls to run by me.

"It's a school night," I remind Rae as she grips the backdoor like a lifeline. "Even if it wasn't, you're still two hours past your weekend curfew."

"Don't blame me." Rae unfreezes, shuts the door, then slumps in her usual seat at the table. With a fingertip, I push the pan of brownies in her direction. We both jump when the door to the bathroom slams with force.

"What's up with him?" I hitch a finger over my shoulder, in the general direction of Weston throwing himself in the bathroom. "Why were you so late?"

"Sage–" my fierce growling cuts Rae off. "Sage is an amazing person, Ren. It's West who's turned into an asshole. He might not show that side of himself to you and Dad, but he's got a bit of all of us in him."

"What exactly does that mean?" After double-checking everything is safely in my online cart, I shut my laptop. "Do I have to worry about another one of you assholes? Devon hasn't been home in almost twenty-four hours– I don't have time for this shit."

"I'm good." Rae puts up her hands, showing she's unarmed and innocent, then she dives into the brownies. "Sage is teaching me to drive."

"No!" I point in her face. "That's illegal because the twink isn't an adult yet, and it's *my* job to teach you. Don't be so impatient."

"Ren," Rae sighs dramatically, obviously frustrated. "It's Dad's job to teach me to drive. And you're right, you don't have time for this shit. I was trying to lessen your burden by taking care of Weston while getting something out of it. Plus…" she giggles manically. "I get to drive Sage's car."

"It is a sweet ride," I mutter begrudgingly. "So what's up with the door slamming?" As if on cue, Weston glides into the kitchen, headed straight for the refrigerator. He's relaxed and acting like himself, and I begin to fear we'll have more than one bipolar Mason on our hands– we learned our lesson with Devon.

"Mmm…" Weston makes yummy food noises as he wanders away with a container of pasta salad clutched to his chest, no fork in sight. "Night!" flows in from the hallway, all chipper.

"I can't take it," I plead, slumping to lean on the tabletop. "I can't take this shit, Raven. Am I in Hell? Or am I so insane I didn't realize I resided in an asylum until now?"

Giggling while chomping on a brownie, Rae reaches over to snag my Dr. Pepper. After a gulping swallow, she can finally respond. "I have three brothers and a dad... Weston's not nuts– he's horny and being cock-blocked by his boyfriend."

"Oh, Wessie just jerked it and now he's hungry." Washing my palms over my face, embarrassed laughter bubbles up my throat. "God, Sage can't graduate fast enough."

"Sage is amazing," Rae repeats, and I want to strangler the traitor. "West is the problem. Sage only lets West kiss him on the cheek, and he won't return the favor. But sometimes Weston steals an actual kiss and Sage shuts his ass down."

"Really?" I murmur in awe– the self-restraint that kid must have.

"Really," Rae stresses, giggling. "It's like my baby brother turns into The Hulk– I'm waiting for West to turn green and tear off his clothes. He gets *mad*, then stomps off and punches a wall."

"Poor kid–"

"I know. I feel so bad for Sage," Rae sympathizes, getting it all wrong. "After West calms down, Sage lectures him about how his behavior is the exact reason they can't date."

"All those hormones." Shuddering, I remember how it felt, and I'm so thankful I don't have to go through that irrational bullshit again. "If a patronizing little shit was talking down to me, I'd want to punch a wall too."

"It's not like that." Rae climbs to her feet, then starts rutting around in the fridge. Pulling a gallon of milk out, Rae tests that it's still sealed. The girl knows we all drink from the container, and she won't touch it if our lips have been on it.

"I don't see the attraction." Mind avoiding the pitfalls that always have my fear making me say inappropriate things, I focus on the facts. "They don't have anything in common."

"They do," comes from the fridge as Rae forages around. A small bottle of chocolate milk is placed on the table, Rae's fist not releasing it, because she knows I'll snatch it up and drain it. Not letting go, she grabs a couple brownies, tossing them on a napkin for portability.

"Sage loves to *debate*." Rae means argue. "Weston gives as good as he takes. Hell, they even get going on politics. Half the shit goes over my head, but I don't feel bad since they're unnaturally smart."

"Sometimes I forget how quick that brain is in Wessie's head, because he's so good at football." Now I feel like shit for not seeing my baby brother clearly. "I think that's why he gravitated toward Seth at first."

"Lord," Rae growls, tucking her chocolate milk in the crook of her elbow. Taking her brownies, she says over her shoulder, "Hell is Sage and Seth debating anything. Separately, those boys are awesome. Together–" Rae disappears from my sight, but her voice flows down the hallway. "KILL ME!"

I'm still chuckling at my baby sister's dramatics when the backdoor explodes inward. I'm moving before my mind catches up with me. "Don't come in here!" I scream down the hallway at the kids. "Go into Dad's room and stay put."

Twin sets of spooked eyes glow at me from the depths of the hallway, and I breathe deeply when I hear the snap of Dad's door shutting. I want them as far away from Devon as I can get them, because seeing and hearing this version of Devon would give them nightmares.

"Shit!" I hiss underneath my breath, eyes glued to the horror movie version of my big brother. "I don't know what to do... what do I do?"

Devon won't look at me, but the energy he's giving off is a billion times stronger than ever before– I'm choking on his presence. It's been twenty-four-hours since I set sight of him, but Devon looks like he's aged a decade since.

"You're bleeding– you stink." Standing from the table, all I can do is stare at the frozen form of Devon standing where the backdoor used to be.

"No matter what I do, it won't go away," Devon whispers, but this is my translation, because he's slurring his words so badly I don't recognize his voice. "And I've done some bad shit tonight."

Eyes closing, I breathe deeply, not sure which version of Devon I'm going to get– all are equally terrifying. Nose wrinkling, I can't ignore how my brother smells like all the body functions combined. Swallowing convulsively, I fight the need to retch.

"He touched..." Devon trails off as he tears his rotten t-shirt off, flopping it on the floor. I see nothing but the bruises and scratch marks covering his chest and arms, but it's the track marks in his inner elbows that has panic roaring in my veins.

"You're doing heroin?" I choke on disgust.

"Meth-smeth." Dev chuckles at his disturbing rhyme, toeing off his sneakers, destroyed jeans following. Everything on Devon's body needs to meet fire. Pointing down at his t-shirt, he bursts out crying, "That's not my jizz!"

Muttering in horror, "What happened?" all I can do is stare at my naked brother– he's so skinny, all the bones in his skeleton are visible. His flesh is covered in scratches, marks, and bruises.

Devon's close to death. Mouth opening, I start to tell him it's time to go to Sedona. "We got a call earlier today–"

"I need to eat." Devon stumbles across the kitchen, jeans hooked on his ankle, foot dragging them behind him. Struggling to free himself, Devon falls to the floor, bouncing on his ass. "I win!" is a shouted mix of hysterical crying and laughing.

"I need to get strong for Essie... I told Beth I didn't want her to see me– didn't want her to see me this way. Need to eat so I don't look like this anymore, so she can see me again. Need to see Essie... need to see her."

"Devon?" I call out, wanting to touch him— *to help him* —but too terrified to touch him, knowing he'll push me away. "You saw Essie tonight? Is she okay?"

"Need to eat… need to eat…" Devon turns into a broken record as he stumbles to his feet, then falls against the fridge. "Need to eat," warps as he struggles to open the fridge. Then he attacks the contents.

Body and mind conflicted, my body tries to move forward to stop Devon, but my mind propels me backward at a safe distance.

"I. Need. To. Eat!" Devon screams bloody murder, hands curved around the handles of a casserole dish. Raising the dish above his head, "I told her to get rid of *it*!"

Smash!

In an explosion, the casserole dish lands on the floor, shards flying like shrapnel. Devon's body gets peppered with cuts, but the sting doesn't stop him.

Dish after dish is torn from the refrigerator, held over his head, then smashed with immense force. "*I tainted Essie,*" is followed by a guttural groan. "I tainted her and the baby. She has to get rid of it— it's filled with my crazy and drugs. Drugs. DRUGS!"

Self-preservation vanishing, I lunge forward, grabbing my brother. Hands wrapped around his bony shoulders, I shake him vigorously. "Your sperm doesn't carry drugs." It may carry the crazy gene, but so does mine. "It's the mother who makes drug babies because she grows the baby." I try to reason with Devon, but he refuses to hear me.

The mournful sobs start. "I want our baby." Then my brother falls against my chest, reeking of sickness and body fluids. "I ruined us— I told her I didn't want her to see me like this." Turning away from me, "I need to eat."

Devon looks at the destruction he's caused, tears cleansing the filth from his face. "I ruined the food." Dropping to his knees, red flowing from glass shards gouging into his shins, Devon picks up a piece of chicken and cradles it in his palms. "I'm not hungry anymore."

Lifting the chicken, Devon leans down and takes a big bite out of it. "I have to eat." Horrified, I watch as blood spurts from his tongue. "Tastes like chicken." Devon laughs at himself, mutilated fingers probing his mouth for the piece of glass that cut him. The chicken splats to the floor, followed by the tinkling of glass. "All done." Patting his concave belly, "All filled up now."

"I'm never going to unsee this moment," I whisper beneath my breath, horrified beyond belief. I must be in shock, because my emotions have flat-lined and my mind can't process a solid thought.

"I remember everything," Devon admits, blood slipping out the corner of his mouth. "The one... the one didn't want Mom– didn't like girls."

THAT!

"Listen to me, Devon." With fingertips biting into his skin, he doesn't even feel me as I shake him roughly with desperation. "You're gonna be okay– we're gonna get you help. We already have your flight arranged."

Devon looks up at me, and for a split-second I see my brother lurking in the depths of his eyes. Holding onto that hope, I continue. "We're gonna get you help, get you better, then you can see Essie. Okay? You leave in three days. Ya only gotta hold out three more days– just stay here with me where it's safe."

"Three days?" Devon's gaunt face lights up like Christmas, then he lunges to his feet like that single bite of chicken, which he never swallowed, invigorated him. "I have a lot to do in three days. Gotta go get Tommy and Taryn."

"Devon!" I call out, struggling to get to my feet. Slipping and sliding through the food and glass, my shins and palms get cut to bits. "Devon, come back here!"

"I'll see you in three days!" is the last thing Devon says as he disappears out the broken backdoor and into the night. Stark-raving mad. Higher than any high before. Bare naked, dripping blood.

"Devon!" voice cracking from the force, the petrifying quality in my voice will ring in my ears for all the days to come.

"Go," is a hoarse whisper, and I turn to find Weston holding Rae, her face pressed to his chest so she can't see anything. Face blank, Weston grew up a decade in the last minute. "Follow Dev." With a deep breath, Weston pulls Rae away, then turns back to me. "We'll clean up– you bring Devon home."

"I never wanted..." gasping for air, I can't get the words out. Our kitchen looks like a crime scene, and I know exactly what a crime scene looks like. Blood, the food the guts– even the glass tinted red looks familiar. The indescribable emotions are just the same too.

I feel like Dad now, with Weston and Raven being brave as they stand behind me, just as Devon and I stood behind Dad in the aftermath of The Nightmare. We cleaned the kitchen, the living room, the bedroom and bathroom, while Dad ran off to make sure there were no more of them. Then we took care of our lifeless Mom.

The parallels are staggering.

Devon remembered– Devon remembered why I'll always keep his secrets, even if it hurts us both. Not once have I ever told a soul, barely ever think about it. But Dad somehow knew, fatherly instinct maybe. People think Dad's a pervert for taking us to the Playroom, but he did because he knew– knew I kept a secret that only I remembered. A secret that's destroyed my brother.

"One hour, no more." Panting, I race from the kitchen, headed right out the backdoor and into the night after my destructive and destroyed brother.

CHAPTER THIRTY-SEVEN

Essie Prynne

"I hear her parents are moving," is whispered fiercely behind me as I sit in a booth at the No-Name. It's after my shift, and I just wanted a few minutes of peace to form a game plan for my future. I'm homeless now, with our house empty, and there's too much excitement at Aunt Mary's for me to think straight.

"They're going to Florida." The other woman isn't even trying to sound like she doesn't want me to overhear. She's talking loud enough that she's intruding on half the diner's conversations.

"Yeah, because they're ashamed by their daughter's loose reputation." Both women share a snort at my expense. "The whole family is trash– that Willow is no better. I heard a rumor that Clover is shacking up with Chief Mason."

Jesus Christ, I've been through enough bullshit in the past few month– these grown bitches should know better than to judge what they can't understand. It's none of their goddamn business. There's no peace or escape to be found. Anywhere.

I *need* my own place.

"They were raised like heathens." They share a conspiratorial laugh. "Mary grows and sells marijuana– so gross. Then they have the nerve to show up to church. Chief Mason must be crooked to put up with it."

"Look at Junior Mason– he's on a countywide crime spree right now. It's been nonstop 911 calls, and they have an APB out."

"What'd he do?" There's a juicy quality to the lady's voice that makes me want to lunge over the booth and choke the shit out of her.

"You mean other than screwing the slut waitress?"

Furious, I move to stand, but a small hand pushes me back in my seat. "Not worth it," Sage murmurs as he flows into the booth bench opposite me. "Just ignore them."

"Easier said than done." Demoralized, I flip my notebook shut, no longer motivated to get anything done.

"Once you've been called every slur these ignoramuses can come up with, it starts to fade into background noise." Shifting slightly in the booth so he can see most of the restaurant, he pulls out a paperback and begins to read. Spine destroyed, the cover is hidden, as is the title and author.

After thirty seconds, curiosity killed the cat. "What are you reading? I always see your head in a book, or you're engrossed with your Kindle."

"Fairport has a good library and an even naughtier librarian with great taste in smut… I'm bored, and you're still here. Let's share secrets, my bitch twin." Sage flips around, grinning, then tosses the book in the middle of the table. Biting back a laugh, I stare down at the rippled torso of a dude wearing a kilt. "I *love* smut. Hot dudes and smut."

"Who doesn't love hot dudes and smut?"

"Straight males and lesbians," Sage supplies without missing a beat. "I secretly write naughty fanfiction on an X-rated site. Grandfather wants me to go into politics, so I decided I'd taint my future by writing the nastiest shit imaginable. Dark. Incest. Non-consensual gangbangs. Cocks and balls every-fucking-where. Under my given name."

"Jesus, Sage." Sucking in air, I huff a laugh of pure amazement. "You never fail to shock the piss out of me."

"That's my goal in life." Sage snatches up his paperback, then hides it beside his leg in the booth. He's confident, but not confident enough to give the townsfolk any more ammunition. "So… don't take this as an insult—"

"Which means you're going to insult me," I mutter wryly.

Sage's resulting laughter has an addictive quality, causing me to smile for the first time in days. He really is a pretentious ass, but endearing just the same. "I couldn't help but see what you were working on."

"Which means you were snooping," I point out, tapping the cover of my notebook.

Perfect eyebrow raised in challenge, "From one bitch to another, I feel no shame."

"I like you— you're my type of people." We share a grin.

"Like seeks like, which is what I want to talk to you about." Reaching forward, Sage steals my notebook, then flips it open to the page I was working on. "So I have to drive down to Boston every weekend to appease a custody agreement."

Impressed beyond belief, "Which is probably how you managed to snag that Lexus."

"Oh, yes," Sage murmurs with pride, voice holding a wealth of arrogance. "When I came out, my mom came out too in support of me. The conservative Christian lifestyle was slowing killing us. So Mom found a place that was far enough away from Boston that our family wouldn't pop in nonstop, but close enough that shuffling me back and forth wouldn't take forever. She also needed a hospital nearby that would hire her– Fairport fit the bill."

"You must hate it here." Shaking my head in awe, if it wasn't for the roots I have tying me to this place, I'd fit in a metropolis area better.

"The culture is better in Boston, but the family is there, so I'll take the ignorance of Fairport any day... back to the Lexus. Dad would drive up here every weekend, but he wanted to stay *here* for the weekend, trying to win Mom back."

"Eww," I grumble in disgust, flinching.

"You don't know the half of it– Dad's older than my grandfather. They're colleagues, which is how Mom met Dad. Anyway, I earned that Lexus, because that meant the Sages and Fischers would stay the hell away from Fairport."

"Nice," I drawl out, really liking this kid. As long as Desiree is working, Sage is here. A few times I had to work when his girl didn't, Sage popped in to keep me company anyway.

"Which brings me full circle." With slanted precision, Sage's handwriting is impeccable as he begins a list of his own in my notebook. "Clearly I'm prissy." The boy gestures to his designer clothing, then the haircut that must've cost a couple hundred bucks for a trim.

"I like prissy." Pointing to the fact that I contoured and did a blow-out of my hair today to make myself feel better and cover the signs of no sleep and too much crying. "I'm prissy too."

"Like seeks like," Sage repeats. "The douche dicks me around, cancels appointments, and acts like he's a rock star. He doesn't deserve any more of my money. I'd rather spend it here in town. So you need to tell me what's going on with Salon."

"Sage," I caution, trying to keep my voice even. "You have money, but no one else does. You can't support a salon on a monthly trim."

"Monthly? Pfft," Sage scoffs. "I said I was prissy, not high-maintenance. Try bi-weekly trim, weekly eyebrow-shaping and manicure. *Slash*," Sage rolls his eyes. "Who the fuck names their kid Slash? Clearly the douche made that up– told you he thinks himself a rock star. Slash won't meet my needs."

"Okay, so you can't support a salon by popping in once a week, and the rest of the town is broke."

"Having money and spending money is not the same thing. Conservative Christians, remember? Grandfather hoards money, shoves it up his ass, and doesn't shit it out until the coal turns to diamonds."

"Oh, my God!" Palm covering my mouth, I laugh harder than I have in months. "Where have you been all my life?"

"Waiting to turn eighteen when all parental legal rights to my person expires." Sage pauses to add a few more things to his list. "I have impeccable style, but I'm only allowed so many articles of clothing– money is no object as long as it's quality. Same goes with looking good at all times to entice hospital donors. The Lexus was a bribe."

"Where are you going with this?" Sage and my mom better never be in the same place at the same time, or the time-space continuum will implode.

"I don't have diamonds stored up my ass– my family has money, not me. I get bribed to behave. I worry over grades to get scholarships, because Grandfather won't pay for an English degree. A life of eating ramen and driving a thirty-year-old Lexus until it disintegrates from the rust. The same bullshit rules apply to me– am I pretty enough?"

"What?" I grunt in confusion, and Sage passes my notebook back to me as explanation.

Sage Fischer: Hair. Eyebrows. Nails.

Raven Mason: Rats nest hair. Facial hair– electrolysis or laser treatments, at the very least wax her entire body.

Violet Webster: Use your girl as the 'after' example.

Taryn Elsberry: Personal shopper to find her clothing that fits her bodacious figure. Cut & Dye job. Makeup tutorial.

Seth Webster: Take your boy to the store and avoid the little boy's clothing section.

Desiree Merit: Let her play dress-up in your closet once and a while, and teach her how to contour.

Tommy Braxton: Get that kid a haircut that will show off his face and brighten his eyes.

The list goes on and on... "What's this?"

"You keep saying the town is broke, but we're not talking billions of dollars here. The high school is teeming with potential clients. For twenty bucks a month of their allowance, you'd be changing their lives. Like Tommy, with a haircut that would show off that face, he'd be getting laid nonstop. Then you have Rae– I love the girl –but she is bullied over her body hair every fucking day in gym class."

"Oh, Rae," I cry out, clasping my chest. "I didn't know."

"Get 'em while they're young." For someone who says they hate politics and corporate America, Sage sure does have a head for business. "Salon catered to little old ladies. Change it up– we're the ones with the buying power now."

"Wow." Eyes held wide, I gaze down at the dozens and dozens of entries Sage made. "I need to thank you for snooping on what I was working on."

"On your next shift, I'll make you a list of all the adults. I have nothing but time on my hands while I sit in here observing their lack of style." Eyes bugging out slightly as the front door jingles with a new arrival, "The intolerant Mason arrives."

"Intolerant Mason?" my voice pitches high.

"Sympathizer Mason. Intolerant Mason, who'd make a great character in a Gay-for-You novel. Then there's Intolerant Mason's younger, hotter, smarter, more athletic, gay brother–"

"Ren," I guess, chuckling. "I wouldn't call him intolerant."

Sage slides from the booth. "Intolerant Mason must be here to see you," is murmured a split-second before a set of soft lips nuzzles at my cheek. "God, I wish hot guys would greet me like that."

"How are you?" Ren kisses my cheek, then pulls away. Giving the boy a wide-birth, "Sage," he mutters quietly as he slips into the booth Sage just abruptly exited.

"Kieren Mason," Sage says brightly, voice quivering from intimidation. "It's always a pleasure to see you."

"You too," Ren says in dismissal, which has me rethinking how I thought him tolerant. "Hot guys do greet you like that–

Weston's always getting caught kissing your cheek. Keep it out of the public eye," he warns.

"I try." Sage scurries away, when he normally sashays everywhere. Perhaps looking at Ren gives Sage an inkling on what Weston will look like when he's a grown man, and it makes Sage hot under the collar.

"What's your deal with Sage?" I tuck the notebook on my lap for safekeeping. "He's awesome."

"He's too old for my brother," Ren mumbles gruffly.

"Something tells me Weston's the initiator in the relationship," I mutter wryly.

"All those damn Mason hormones flowing in his veins, except he's going to be worse than I ever was. I'm thankful he's gay."

"Why?"

"Weston has no sexual hang-ups like I did, and look at the damage I did to the female population of FAHS. There's probably like only five gay kids in the area, keeping Weston from turning into a slut."

"This must be the slut and whore booth." I tease us both, truly finding it humorous now. I'm not a whore, no matter how many people say it to my face and behind my back. Since I got no sleep last night, I've been exploring the parallels in our quad-relationship.

Kieren and I are the male and female representations of the same type of person, whereas Devon and Willow are. I love Willow just as much as Ren loves Devon, so it's no wonder we're hooked on them. We get each other, as do Devon and Willow. We're just going to have to let bygones be bygones and swallow the hurt and jealousy if we're going to make this work.

Snapping out of my thoughts, I find Ren scowling at me, joke falling flat. "You look like hell, Ren." Now that Sage isn't sucking up all the attention, I take a really good look at Ren. He's aged a decade since last night, and I don't mean that he's no longer young and gorgeous.

It's the eyes– their depths are ancient.

"Are you coming off your shift?" Ren tilts his chin at the fact that I'm not in my uniform.

"Yeah." Chuckling at the absurdity, "I have nowhere else to go. Most people would get the hell out of their place of employment, fearing more work would be asked of them."

"Let's get out of here, then." Ren mutters brusquely. Not waiting for a reply, he reaches over to grab my hand, then yanks me from the booth. Walking through the diner hand-in-hand gets varying reactions out of our observers.

Once we hit the sidewalk, Ren doesn't release me, tugging me to his truck idling at the curb. "I just need to escape for a bit— I haven't even been to work today yet."

Crawling into the truck cab, I mull Ren's words over, considering it's the middle of the afternoon.

CHAPTER THIRTY-EIGHT

Kieren Mason

"Thanks for hanging out with me." I try to hide the exhaustion in my voice as we pull away from the curb. "I haven't sat still since last night."

"Are you okay?" The concern in Essie's voice is the exact reason I decided to go to her. It wasn't Robin's insistence last night– I needed to be around someone who got it, didn't want anything from me, and wouldn't pressure me to feel any differently than I do. "Maybe you ought to go home and go to bed. Take some time for yourself."

"There are ghosts haunting that house," I murmur underneath my breath, hoping she doesn't hear me. I've been home twice since the middle of the night, and each time it was like being thrust into a horror film. Didn't matter which room I was in, memories play out as if was happening in reality. I can still hear Devon's screams ringing in my mind– maybe always will.

But I can't go into that without breaking down, not even with Essie, so I play it off. "If I go home, there's always something I need to do. If I sat down to watch TV or to take a nap, I'd feel guilty, or I'd get interrupted when one of the kids came home."

"Jesus, Ren." Essie reaches over to squeeze my hand that's gripping the stick-shift. *This* is what I needed. Comfort without a cost. "Is Willow at school right now?" She treads lightly, not even having to voice what she's really asking.

A long time ago, I stopped playing games, and I'm not going to play them now either. "I needed to hang with you," I answer in all honesty, truck finding its destination without any directions from me.

"Ren?" Essie releases an uncomfortable laugh, eyes flicking around the scenery. We're pulled up a few hundred yard on an old logging road on the outskirts of Fairport. "We will *never* go down that road again."

Figurative and literal road... the road where we lost our virginity.

Laughing while scrubbing a palm roughly against the back of my neck, my face flushes hot. "I'm not an idiot, I won't pretend to be offended that you don't want to have a repeat. But the truck drove itself here on its own– honest."

"I trust you," Essie says, when anyone else would've said *I believe you.*

After unhooking my seatbelt, I shift to the side on the bench seat, facing Essie so we can talk. "You and I need to be solid, more than ever."

"Shit," Essie hisses, face quickly turning to look away from me. "I haven't told anyone at all. Mom and Beth were with me, then Beth trapped me by telling Devon. I don't want this to get out until I'm ready. I need to go to the doctor to get it confirmed, for Christ's sake."

"You said you trusted me," I remind Essie. Reaching over, I play with a strand of her hair to get her to look at me. "Are you okay?"

"Are *you*?" Essie stresses, bugging her eyes out. "If you know, that means you saw Devon after I did. Is he at home? Is that why you don't want to go back there?"

Pulling away, I lean against the steering wheel, gazing out at the trees like they'll give me the answers to the questions I didn't even know I was asking. "I don't want to talk about Devon yet."

"Same here," Essie grumbles, staring at those same trees, seeking those same answers.

"We have to be solid," I repeat. "Dad's hiding it, but I know he's up to something with Clover. Willow and I both know, but we're playing along. So I know the way we've been living is about to end– *has* to end. I'm looking forward to it. But that means we have to get a game plan."

"We?" Essie hugs that dang notebook to her chest, not getting it. She's been carrying it around for days, and the town gossips have theories– all wrong. I know Essie better than Devon or Willow does, because they tend to wallow in their own shit and forget others have shit too.

"I'm at a crossroads with Willow." Sucking in a big gulp of air, I can't believe I admitted that. "I can't talk to anyone. Devon's *our* wreck, so it's not fair if we voice any problems we're having to each other. Dad's busy with work, with Devon, with the kids, with Clover. He has too much on his plate. Then there's the kids– I can't confide in them because I'm supposed to be raising them. I can't talk to Willow about Willow."

"If there's two people on this planet who understand Willow and Devon the most, it's us." Essie unhooks her seatbelt and turns to sit crossed-legged on the bench seat, notebook clutched like a teddy bear. "Go ahead."

Willow would see this as a betrayal– I know it.

"This is like the foundation, ya know?" Fuck it! "That's the reason I was okay with not talking about Devon and you. Six weeks of getting to know how the other ticks, just having fun– nothing too serious. Without a solid foundation, you're just fucking. I've done enough fucking to last a lifetime."

"Willow's not the type of girl to just mess around." Essie proves she knows my girl best. "She's young and her insecurities get the best of her."

"That's the problem. *Right now–*" Huffing and huffing, I can't seem to catch my breath. "I have to be the strong one at all times, but sometimes I need someone to support me. But Willow and I aren't in that place right now, because what I need to do will push her away from me."

"What do you need to do?" Suspiciously sounds like when we were in this place before, where Essie promised she'd help me no matter what.

"Crossroads– Jesus, I can't believe I'm going to admit this." Huff. Huff. "There are things I will never compromise on, and if Willow can't accept that, than it won't matter if we love each other or not."

"You don't trust her yet." Essie's voice, combined with the way her eyebrows knit together, informs me she's not pleased with my admission. No matter what Willow does to Essie, I know Essie's on her cousin's side. "What're your hard limits?"

"I don't give a fuck who was inside who and when. I wasn't mad at Willow when she was fooling around with Auggie or Devon. I was pissed in general. Furious I was being drawn into something, taking my control away. I understand what Rob was doing– I do. But I hated being a pawn, being silenced, when if someone had just spoken up, we'd be where we are now, but without as many casualties."

"I remember when I was in junior high, and I'd hear gossip trickling down from the older kids. Who was or wasn't a virgin anymore." Essie throws me off, and I have no idea where she's headed with this. "Younger than that, when a girl started her period, the ones who hadn't yet made fun of her."

"You're losing me here, Ess." Chuckling, I realize she reminds me of her mother, and no woman wants to hear that.

"Willow's that girl– the one who hasn't grown up yet. Some women never do in this regard. The mentality. '*Eww, did you hear how Jennifer did it with Chad last weekend?*'" Essie mimics, in a squeaky cheerleader voice. "All girls go through that when they're young, but we usually grow out of it. Like my period comment. I was ten and had to hide it, but when they found out, they were like savages."

Realizing I'm not picking up what she's putting down, Essie laughs at herself, face reddening. "That's why you can't trust Willow yet– why I couldn't trust her with my secrets. It's this irrational need to judge what she doesn't understand, and I'm not making fun of her. Willow's fearless, intoxicating, exciting– Willow breathes life into mine."

"Preaching to the choir," I mutter wryly.

"It's hard to open up to someone who will judge you when all you need is a shoulder to cry on. Jesus, I already feel like shit, guilty and ashamed– I need a hug, not a punch to the face and a list of all my faults."

"Shit needs to be let go. If someone is sorry for real, let it go. If they aren't, let them go. End of the story. Life's simpler that way. Willow knows better than to say this shit in front of me, but I'm not stupid."

"Honestly, I'm not sure she'll ever lose the mindset of how there's an odometer on crotches. She'll always be jealous of those who came before her, even if it's none of her business."

"*That* is it. *That* is why I'm sitting with you right now." Heart twisting, I feel like a scumbag, like I'm betraying Willow by talking behind her back, but I have to get it out. "When I hear that type of talk out of her mouth, it makes me feel like shit."

"I *love* Willow," Essie stresses, reaching out to squeeze my knee. "But while she's spewing I'm a whore for breaking the sister-code because I was with you, she's insulting *you*."

"Yes." Nodding in jerky starts and stops, I try to put my thoughts into words. "When Willow's attacking you, calling you a whore, when you've only been with me and Devon–" the pause is subconscious on my part, knowing she's been with others, but pretty sure it wasn't consensual. "But Willow's saying this with such venom right in front of me, when I've been with almost sixty people."

"So if two people makes me the whore of Babylon, then you're wondering what Willow thinks of you?" Essie guesses correctly. "She's not– she's ignoring that fact. She's comparing herself to other women, and men don't factor into it."

"That's my hard limit. I can't be with someone who can't see how hurtful they're being. After my mom– after Devon. It's abusive. Devon's going to need forgiveness and compassion. He can't be made to bleed for the rest of his life, because he won't survive it."

"So tell her," Essie blurts out, like I haven't already thought of that.

"Yeah, and then she'd scream bloody murder at me, blame me, and then freeze me out." Fingers curling, I clutch the steering wheel. "I love her, Essie. I love hanging around her when it's just us. But when she's being vicious to the most important people in my world, I can't live like that."

"Don't." Essie peels my fingers from wheel, rubbing the blood back into my white knuckles. "Tell her. Ren–" She grabs my chin, forcing me to look at her. "*Tell. Her.* Willow won't grow up unless we require more of her. Two of my biggest regrets are not telling her about you and me, and about me and Devon. You're right, if only I'd spoken up."

"Yeah, but Willow wouldn't have understood," I mutter lamely.

"Then that's on her– me not telling her is on *me*." Dropping her hand, Essie takes a big breath. "Willow is insecure and terrified, so she acts like an asshole because it's easier than being rejected or hurt."

"That's no excuse!" I hiss through my teeth. After last night, never again. "I can't live like that. She should tell people she's hurt, not act like an asshole. I don't like how she hits people, either."

"Require more of her– *tell her*." Essie's face twists, like she's sick of repeating herself. "I've been with Willow since she took her first breath, and her biggest problem is that everyone walks around on eggshells when it comes to her. Why do you think Auggie was able to manipulate her? He fucking told her to knock her shit off."

Slumping back in my seat, I think about that for a moment, mind replaying the past few weeks. Even last night, Willow held back until I took control, then she lost control.

"Unlike Auggie, you're tactful and want her to be happy. You won't dish her shit back to her. You'll be compassionate with your words, understanding, but you'll have to make her realize you won't budge."

"Last night, I decided I couldn't do it anymore–"

"Same here." Essie chuckles sardonically. "I walked away while Bethany and Devon were fighting. Not just screaming at each other, but pounding the living shit out of one another. I walked away. I was scared for them both and was contemplating calling your dad. But do you want to know what Beth said to me when she caught up to me three minutes later?"

Head jerking up, my eyes connect with Essie's. "What?"

"We're–" Essie points between us "–the problem. If we don't like something, we put up with it. Mom would call us martyrs. But Beth calls us enablers. They couldn't behave this way if we didn't allow it. So I'm never going to apologize to Willow again. If she'll ever speak to me, I'll explain the difference of back then versus now. Until then, I'll love Willow from afar and try my damnedest not to turn bitter, resentful, or take her negativity to heart."

Robin's words ring in my mind. "The three most important people in Devon's life have to be solid when he comes home."

Wheezing a sobbing sound, Essie looks away from me and talks to the window. "If he even makes it to Arizona."

"If you were anyone else, I'd tell you a bullshit lie to comfort you right now, but both of us saw him last night." I have to release it to the world. "There's more going on with Devon than you realize. He remembered what happened the night Mom was raped. He came into the house last night and totally fucking lost it, and I don't know how a person comes back from that."

"It was hours later before I registered half of what he said." Essie's voice is filled with horror. "I'll never break his trust by saying it out loud."

Yeah, Essie knows– that's a relief.

"Hey." I tug at Essie's arm, trying to draw her into a hug, but she won't budge. "While Devon was smashing the contents of the fridge all over the kitchen floor… while he was eating glass and calling it chicken… just before he ran out of the house buck-ass naked… the only lucid thing he could talk about was you. It wasn't that he didn't want to see you, it was that he didn't want you to see him like that– same reason I didn't want the kids to see him. One of the last things he said to me was that he wanted your baby. He was terrified drugs and mental illness tainted your baby, and he couldn't live with the guilt."

"That's why I let him go." Essie turns to me, eyes watery with tears. "I let him go– walked away. The version of Devon who loves me would hate if the version he is now hurt me… so I walked away and didn't look back."

"I'm not as strong as you– I ran after him, Essie. I ran and ran, and didn't stop running until I picked you up. And after I drop you off, I'll run after him *still*." Head in hands, I bite back a sob. "What happened last night will haunt me for the rest of my life. I can't unsee it." Choking. Suffocating. Huffing in air at a rapid rate, I try with all my might not to cry– I haven't cried in so long, because I'm the one who always wipes away the tears…

"C'mere," Essie murmurs, tugging me against her chest, arms wrapping around my back to squeeze me tightly. The smell of her perfume transports me in the past almost a decade ago, to my happy place.

Home.

"I miss him– I miss my best friend," I gasp against the side of Essie's neck, holding onto her like she's a lifeline. "Even when Devon's in the same room with me– it's *not* him."

"Let it out." Essie whispers words of comfort while rocking me back and forth, and I do let it out. I let it all out. I say words I probably shouldn't, all the while bawling my goddamn eyes out.

Essie holds a part of Devon, the part I miss and want back. Before The Nightmare, when Mom was still alive, it was *us*. Back then, I never made friends of my own, because I didn't need to. Devon loved me– I was his favorite person. Unlike most big brothers, he shared his friends, he was proud to call me his baby brother, and his friends genuinely liked me back. I didn't trail after them, pestering for attention, because I was standing right beside Devon the entire time.

Essie was with us more than she wasn't. She made Devon laugh, even after Mom had hurt his feelings. She'd talk to me like I was an adult. She'd brush Raven's hair and help Weston with his K'nex. Essie treated us like family, because she wanted to be a part of ours.

Being around Essie returns me to an innocent time when I was happy, and I won't give that up for Willow– I can't.

"I miss him too." Essie sobs against the top of my head, palms cupping my neck to hold me closer. "I miss him so goddamn much it was easier to let him go than to look at the stranger he's become– I had to walk away."

Being understood is a comfort. Wrapping Essie as tightly to my body as I can, I feel like Devon's with us, because Essie loves my brother as much as I do– the good *and* the bad. My brother grows inside Essie, so even if we lose him forever, the best part of him will live on.

CHAPTER THIRTY-NINE

Essie Prynne

Once the tears had dried, Ren started to get antsy, needing to check in with his dad to see if any more 911 calls had come in because of Devon– Malcolm has the whole county on alert. In a few short days, Devon's off to Sedona, but we have to find him first in order to get him there.

"You need to go to Willow," I order Ren as we drive back into Fairport.

Ignoring me, "Where do you want me to drop you off?" We sit at the red light, with Ren's hand hovering over the turning signal. "Is your car at the No-Name?"

"Salon," flows out of my mouth without thought, and a warming sensation overpowers me– it felt right, so I'm going with it. "I'm using the money I made from selling my stuff to get my car out of hock tomorrow. So beware, I'll be dropping the piece of shit off at Wreck & Ruin, and I'll be expecting a family discount."

"Free of charge, then?" Ren beams at me, knowing there's no way in hell I'll allow that, but he's secretly hoping I will.

"I was thinking more along the lines of parts and labor." My heart starts kicking as we roll down Main Street, getting closer to Salon.

"Compromise," Ren cautions in a serious tone as he pulls up to the curb. "Parts, and I'll eat the labor because I need to keep busy and feel useful."

"Compromise." I bite back a smile. "Parts, but only if you go directly to Willow. No running all over Fairport looking for Devon. If your dad hears anything, he'll call you. Go to Willow– just escape by being together."

"But you don't have someone you can escape with." The heart-wrenching tone in Ren's voice would bring me to my knees if I wasn't already seated.

Clutching my notebook even tighter to my chest, "I got something better– a plan." Reaching over, I hold out my hand for a shake. "Do we have a deal? Parts and Willow?"

"Deal," Ren mutters begrudgingly, using my hand to pull me into a tight hug. Squeezing, fingers clench against my back. "But I'm not talking to Willow until after Devon is gone– I can only concentrate on one badly behaving idiot at a time."

"Give Willow more credit than that, Ren," I caution as I pull away, mildly insulted for Willow. "I was wrong, and Willow was wrong. I didn't realize by not opening up to her, I was broadcasting that I didn't trust her. I'll never make that mistake with anyone else. You're doing the same thing."

"I don't want to fight with Willow." Ren shudders, eyes drooping with exhaustion, and I get it. "It's easier to keep the peace."

"It's a false peace," I warn. "Treat Willow like the woman she should be, or you're the one turning her into the child you don't like."

"Deep," Ren mutters roughly, proving I hit my target. Then he pokes me in the forehead for being a pretentious assmunch. "Right now I need a girl who'll entertain me with snacks, mindless TV shows, and orgasms."

"Well, I know where you can find a girl like that…" Huffing a laugh underneath my breath, I turn to hop out of Ren's truck, but he reaches for me again.

Pulling me into another hug, Ren whispers against my cheek. "You said you'd always be there for me, and you've never broken it. I promised I'd always be there for you. I'm going to man up– Willow and you will be solid again."

"Why do you think I let her treat me like shit?" I move to give Ren a kiss goodbye on the cheek, but he intercepts my lips instead. The kiss is only affectionate, but lasts a second longer than it should. Smiling brightly, "I'm too amazing to hate."

Ren's laughter follows me out of the truck, and I can still hear it inside my head as he drives off to go visit Willow, probably with a detour to the Courthouse first.

Notebook clutched to my chest with one hand, I wiggle the keys to Salon out of my pocket with the other. I feel good– right. I realize it's a bizarre reaction, but once I made the decision, the stress melted away and was replaced with excitement.

If Beth can let go enough to allow Rory to whisk her away to Vegas to become Mrs. Rory Essex, than I can latch onto my dream and make it reality. Chuckling, I realize they're probably getting hitched right now– *wow*. Unreal.

Standing in the middle of the sidewalk, gazing in wonder at the façade of Salon, I remember… I remember tugging my mom up the sidewalk, pressing my face against the large window in the front, and finding my place in the world.

Life is about worth, not money. I've been thinking of money, not worth. People used to barter, because they each had a skill or a product the other needed, and no money exchanged hands. Value. People saw family as a unit, where each person performed a duty and created a fulfilling life.

We've been so driven by money, we've lost our worth.

My mom worked before I was born, then after trying to have me for so long, she became a stay-at-home-mom. Her worth didn't diminish because she wasn't bringing money into the home. If anything, her worth in our family was invaluable because we needed her.

While I've fretted and stewed, trying to amass as much money as possible, I was taking ten steps back in progress because I feared how the town gossips would perceive me. That fear almost forced me to take an apartment I couldn't afford, where I would go backward every month, until I was forced to vacate and land on a relative's couch, where I'd be worse off than I am now. Only much worse for both me and Salon, because I would've taken a bunch of jobs at the cost of Salon losing relevance in the town.

Elma had set the hours of operation to fit *my* schedule. The more people who came here to find it closed, they'd go elsewhere– an elsewhere they'd frequent from here on out.

Uncle Dave was pointblank with me. He looked me straight in the eye and told me the truth. I work hard, I'm not lazy, and I'm trying my best, so I'm not using them. Whether I stayed with him or not, that room would still exist, those utilities would still be used and paid, and the food on the table would still be eaten by me, because it wasn't called the Prynne table for nothing. Even if I was in my own place, they'd miss me if I didn't eat with them. With me in their home, Uncle Dave is out nothing, but we gain each other's company, especially now with my parents leaving. Clover hunted me down this morning to thank me, because she didn't have to worry about her parents as much with me there.

It took watching Devon, hearing reports around town of how devastated Malcolm and Kieren were, that finally had me listening and hearing both my mother and Uncle Dave. There is a difference between struggling, asking for help, and receiving, versus not helping yourself, taking, and using. One adds value to a family, and the other subtracts.

Staring at the pink awning, seeing the wear and tear, and how faded the word *Salon* is printed across the canvas, I won't let my bullheadedness devalue Salon because I wasn't here when she needed me.

I *am* Salon.

I was a toddler when I fell in love. I was only thirteen when I started working here, washing hair and sweeping up clippings– not because I needed money, but because it was my dream. I have a lot to offer people, and I have a lot of people who I can count on. One hand washes the other, without money ever exchanging hands. I know carpenters, mechanics, artists, number-crunchers, and bakers and soap-makers.

Sage made me realize there is another Essie in this town somewhere, someone who will love Salon as much as I do. Someone who needs to be mentored, and through them, we'll keep the dream alive.

Key in the lock, with a twist, the door opens and I'm hit with the scent of product. Like an artist with paint, my medium is product. It speeds my heart and rushes blood through my veins. The roar of the dryers, the heat of the irons, the scents of straighteners and dyes. The artist's finished product is on canvas, whereas mine is on the living and breathing.

To silence Salon, to allow the air to grow stagnant…

My profession isn't vapid– it's valid. A pair of scissors in my hand will transform the downtrodden who slumped their way into Salon. After I'm through, they walk out with their shoulders back and a smile on their face, feeling confident and good about themselves.

The stress and fear had me forgetting my purpose. Bethany will be a therapist whose patients sit on a couch. A bartender's patients sit on a stool. Mine sit in a salon chair. I listen to my clients– *hear them* –make them feel special when they return because I *remember*, care enough to ask how they're doing, if their lives have improved. They leave Salon feeling good on the inside, looking great on the outside, and feeling relaxed from the scalp massage and the gossipy venting session.

I'd forgotten.

Placing my notebook on the counter, I crack it open to a new page. Mom gave this to me yesterday morning, hard to believe, but I added pages and pages since– the notebook is half-filled with ideas on how to bring life back to Salon, and the people who are going to help me do it.

"Girl, you've got a gossip fire storm brewing." Elma's voice flows from the front door as she enters– no doubt she watched Kieren drive up and drop me off from her front windows across the street.

"I'm guessing I don't want to know." My mood doesn't sour for once, not in the face of my troubles with Devon, or the poor way the town views me.

The fact that Elma's laughing terrifies me. Maybe it's because I'm used to Robin, and find Willow's antics humorous and a comfort, but Elma's demented personality has always felt like home.

The Italian emigrant only has a slight accent after nearly sixty years on US soil. A true hairdresser, refusing to show off her grays– hair so black it looks as dark and wet as spilled ink, with penciled in eyebrows and visible lip liner. She's perfected the permed bouffant combo on our aging denizens. Elma's not a fan of adhering to societal standards, which is why I love the old bat so much.

All of Elma's clients come in for the gossip and a style, where they leave with a hairnet on to keep it perfect– they never take the hairnet off, sleeping in it and not washing their hair for the entire week until they come back– and they always come back with a fresh batch of gossip.

Still chuckling, Elma pulls up a stool to the counter, and sits her generous ass down. "Word of advice, since you're so opposed to being the town's best source of entertainment."

"I haven't done anything," I whine, frustrated. With a forceful smack, I slam the appointment book on the counter. "What now? I can tell you're dying to tell me."

"I would be bored without you, Hester." Elma's voice is light and amused, but I can tell she has genuine affection for me. "You know me, I love gossip. The more the merrier, but you don't like the spotlight glaring at you. So perhaps you shouldn't accept kisses from yet another Mason during the pre-dinner rush at the diner, then give kisses while sitting in a truck on Main Street."

"For fuck's sake!" For added dramatics, I pick the appointment book back up, just so I can smack it down again. "It was affection– Jesus, I wasn't fucking him. Willow's going to skin me alive."

"Hester, girl." Elma rubs my back as I stand next to her at the counter. "The first thing I learned when Charlie brought me here… was how the American people are so sexually repressed, they make everything about sex while denigrating it."

"Tell me about it," I grumble. "I'm living proof of that shit."

"Europe is not like this." Elma sighs, and I hope she's gearing up for story time. Another perk of my job– everyone is so busy, they never listen anymore, and our histories are dying. But I'm lucky enough to have all these people telling me tidbits of their special moments from the past.

"I have a large family. I'm the oldest of a brother and three sisters. I just saw on the cover of The Inquisitor, a young actress being called a child molester for taking a picture of her kissing her toddler on the lips and posting it on Instagram."

"You haven't been getting on the internet again, have you?" I shudder, remembering all the trouble she got into last time.

"No… no…" Elma whispers, getting softer and softer. "Well, some." Snickering evilly, she switches back to memory lane. "Where I'm from, we kissed everyone on the lips, the cheeks, gave hugs, and it wasn't sexual. I know Kieren was kissing you like that. But I also know Fairport."

"How has Malcolm gotten away with kissing Isis and Rae without being called a pervert?" I mutter to myself, thinking the man has a gossip-reflecting shield around him. Even Devon's antics aren't blowing up as much as they should.

"Charlie brought me here, introduced me to my new sister-in-law, and I did the unthinkable–"

"Punched her?" I raise an eyebrow, waiting. There's a reason I haven't gone insane at Salon while there was no work to be done, Elma is entertaining. "Insulted her?"

"I kissed her." Elma grimaces at the memory. "Just a quick peck to the lips in greeting to my new sister, barely made contact with the air between us. I was excited to have someone other than Charlie to welcome me after coming from such a large family… and the bitch acted like I tried to rape her."

"She *didn't*," I mutter, completely floor. Dragging my stool over, I plunk my ass on it. "After Charlie dragged you all the way from Italy, and that's the welcome you got?"

"We never did get along." Elma flashes me a sadistic grin and a wink. "I was younger than you are now, in a simpler time– talk about a culture shock."

"I always wanted to ask." But I was too terrified of pissing you off, goes unvoiced. "Why did you marry Charlie? Fairport sucks, but its roots are dug in deep with me. I couldn't imagine coming here voluntarily and leaving that big family behind."

Laughing hardily, Elma slaps me on the back. "Oh, Hester, how I'll miss you when I'm gone... It was sixty years ago– if you wanted to get out of your father's house or have sex, you got married to the first person who could support you. Antiquated, but nonetheless true."

"So Charlie popped up and whisked you away?" voice dreamy, I romanticize Elma and Charlie's early life like it's out of a Nicholas Sparks movie.

"No, girl– I was engaged twice before Charlie. The first one was a dud, and the second one was because he wasn't financially ready to take a wife. Loved Niko with all my heart, but I had wanderlust. Charlie was on leave and was eating in my family's café. He was instantly taken with me, promised he'd show me the world."

"And he did?"

"For a bit." Elma's enthusiasm dims, and it hurts my heart. "We got married, spent a week in bed, and then traveled around Europe for a month or so. I was excited after hearing all about how amazing America was– like forbidden fruit, I had to have it, so I went with Charlie. But he had to go back to the Army, so he brought me here to his sister, then left me."

Palm over my heart, I gasp in shock. "The sister you tried to kiss?"

"The very one," Elma says with a shrug. "It was about ten years of Charlie popping in and out of my life randomly. I got sick of waiting, none of the promises were kept. I'd left my family behind– *Niko behind* –because of a case of wanderlust, real lust, the need to get out of my papà's house, and the thrill of saying I was coming to America. I was barely eighteen. Stupid."

"What'd you do?"

Elma just waves her hand around us, gesturing to Salon. "Made my own life. I wasn't going to wait around for the man. I also wasn't stupid– soldiers on leave screw around. I established a life, tried to save up enough money to visit my family again, and opened Salon. Charlie retired from the military when he was in his late thirties, then worked at the hardware store. It wasn't the exciting life I'd bought into. Stupid."

Knowing Charlie passed away a good decade ago, I have to ask. "Did you ever go back?"

"Twice." Elma looks away, hiding the tears glistening in her eyes, then clears her throat. "Twenty years ago, we found out my sister had lung cancer." Turning farther away from me, she whispers, "The sister who married Niko."

"Jesus," I breathe in shock.

"I loved my sister– loved Niko. They were very happy together. We almost lost Stella, it was a very trying time. The cancer came back several times, each time quieter and less severe than the initial time, so it was shocking when it finally claimed her three years ago. I went back to take care of her the first time. I was there for almost a year– closed Salon. Then again for her funeral while you were away at school."

Not having a sister to call my own, I picture Willow, Violet, or even Rae, and I can't imagine watching them suffer for nearly two decades. "Wow... so your sister took your fiancé," I tease by being inappropriate.

Elma barks a sharp laugh of surprise, grinning through the tears. "There's a reason why I treat you like my own– you remind me of me."

"I don't know if you should insult yourself like that," I taunt, truly joking around.

"Girl." Elma levels me with a potent look of compassion and understanding. All these years, I've seen my mentor in a loving yet terrified way, scared to ask Elma about herself. She'd feed me bits and pieces as a moral to help me with my problems. She never said to me, *I told you so*. She used snippets of her own life as the lesson. Today is no different.

Elma knows how to handle me because she's walked in the same shoes sixty years before me.

"I'm going to issue a warning, tell you my tale, then give you advice–"

"S. O. P." I interrupt to be a brat.

After snorting, Elma makes a *tsk-tsk* sound. "Be mindful around Kieren."

"I know, Willow's going to kill me."

"That's not what I mean," Elma utters in a grave voice. "Be careful, and I'll tell you why... Stress and grief muddies the waters with affection and lust and love, and it turns it into a potent cocktail that can repair or destroy relationships."

"I'm never–" taking a deep breath, I begin to shake. "I will *never* go there with Ren."

"Again, you mean?" Elma points out, causing me to flinch as if struck. "I'm not judging, Hester. I'm trying to tell you something, and you need to listen. Once you go there, it's easier to revisit, especially when you add grief into the mix."

"We're not grieving anyone, Elma." Covering my face with my palms, I try to keep my emotions in check. "Don't be so morbid. I need hope right now. Devon is going to make it."

"Grief for the *living*," Elma stresses. "I loved Niko, and I was young and dumb when I left him. He moved onto my sister because we shared the same traits he fell in love with, and it made him miss me less."

"Yeah," flows out on a wavering breath. "I can see that."

"My sister was dying. It was months and months of watching Stella waste away to a husk with no humanity or dignity. She was lost– gone. Niko and I were taking care of her around the clock, draining ourselves of the will to live. We were watching Stella *die*."

Sob lodged in my throat, I cover my mouth with the back of my hand. "Please don't go any further."

"It was killing us, like those zombies on that show kids are watching nowadays. Stella was draining us of life, and our lack of hope was killing her… I won't go into detail, but you know where I'm headed. In our grief, in the face of watching Stella die, we wanted to feel close to her, so we sought each other out for comfort. It wasn't about lust or love– it was about Stella. She felt more alive when we were together, than when we were with her, then that transferred over to when we were with her. We were alive, we gave her hope, and she got better."

"Did you ever tell your sister?" Heart in my throat, I'm horrified.

"Yes," is a simple admission, but the emotions behind it are staggering. "There's nothing black and white when it comes to these things, Hester. Stella loved us, and I think she knew all along, and was happy we found succor from the pain she was causing us. The next time she came out of remission, Stella begged me to come to her and I refused."

"Why?" I gasp, shocked.

"I was a married woman back then– I could rationalize the why, romanticize it, but it was still wrong. I cheated. It didn't make me a bad person, but I wasn't going there again. The second bout of cancer was mild compared to the first, and I was relieved I didn't go to her. The third was even milder, so Stella didn't ask me to come and I didn't think to come… and that time it took her rapidly. Like the blink of an eye– she was strong one day, dying the next, and passed before my plane landed."

"Do you feel guilty? I mean, about Niko, not missing her passing."

"No to both. Stella, Niko, and I came to terms with it, and that's all that matters." Taking a deep breath, Elma looks away from me. "We were together at her funeral, and it was hard to deny– my family knew. Old lady or not, the body may age, but the need is still there– the need to connect and comfort."

"What are you going to do?"

"First, I'm going to give you the advice, then I'm going to tell you what *you're* going to do. Don't be worrying your pretty head about this old bag of bones."

"Bones?" I chuckle, Elma is a voluptuous woman. No wonder Charlie snagged her and Niko could never forget her.

"I know it's been hard for you with all the gossip, but you have to know most women nearing forty and older sympathize with you. We've lived long enough to get it."

Snorting, "I find that hard to believe."

"It's true, Hester. It's true. We've lived the hypocrisy– we've lived with the pain and shame caused by jealous women. Women who haven't lived enough life to make difficult choices, no matter how old they may be. But you can't put yourself in harm's way anymore."

"What do you mean?"

"Danger lies ahead if you find yourself alone with Kieren Mason. I saw both of you today, and it was the look of two people who were communing. Your makeup is covered with tear tracks, girl. The way you interacted. Kissed you goodbye– on the mouth. You *are* Americans."

"We will never go there," I stress, yet again, same as I did with Ren.

"You're grieving for the living. You've already gone there for the same reason before. Willow is raging because she's hurt. Kieren Mason has not committed to your cousin yet. You and he know each other, love each other, and get each other, and it would be easy to fall into that trap."

"I won't," I snarl. "I've learned my lesson."

"I'm not judging, nor did I say it was wrong. But it's not what you want, so I'm giving you advice. I've lived eighty years, my dear. I'm not stupid anymore. I have no children of my own. When I took you in, it became my lot in life to make sure you aren't stupid either."

"What do I do?"

"I know all the gossip, girl. All of it. Willow isn't upset about you and Devon."

"The hell she isn't."

"She's not. It's all about Kieren, and not your quick tryst in the car. Willow's always looked up to you, wanted to be like you. It's the dynamic of sisters– *I'd know*. Mine took my fiancé to prove she was as good as me. Gossip, as I said. Willow thinks Kieren puts you first, and that's why she doesn't cause a stink when he's around, knowing he'd choose you over her."

"Yeah, but not because of what Willow thinks," I vehemently deny. "Because it was Ren *and* me. Not just *me*. Ren feels responsible. And that's bullshit about me coming first. Ren and I put Devon and Willow first!"

Smirking like she has a secret, Elma chuckles. "I know, but someone ought to tell the girl that. She's going nuts because of it. You and Kieren put Willow and Devon first. Even off his rocker and higher than a kite, Devon manages to put you, all of his family, and Willow first. Someone ought to tell Willow that so the girl would loosen up."

"Willow has trust issue," I mutter, not liking Elma making fun of her. "I'd love to tell her, but she won't let me."

"Just stay away from meaningful talks with Kieren Mason. The boy looks at you, and I know he has a backup plan. If it doesn't work out with Willow… if Devon's too broken. I'm not saying you're his backup choice. But he is a man, and if you ask him, I doubt he'd deny it."

"Kieren is not *in* love with me," I snarl.

"I didn't say he was, but I also didn't say he couldn't find his way there easy enough." Elma reaches over to pat my back, mimicking the soothing of my ruffled feathers. "You know those boys love similar traits in you and Willow, just as it was with Niko with Stella and me. I suggest you push Kieren to seek

Willow out for his intimate, soul-connecting conversational needs. Trust me, that's how Niko got me. Over and over again. Learn from this old lady."

"Did Niko do it on purpose? Didn't he love your sister?"

"No, not on purpose." I have no idea why, but Elma finds that question hilarious. "Yes, he loved my sister with all of his heart. They were happy together. But love and happiness don't erase lust and need. He still wanted me, just as I wanted him. It's the lifetime curse of having sex with someone you're connected to with mind, body, and spirit. It's why I refused to go back there, because once we went there, he didn't want to stop. He begs me to come home."

"Why haven't you?"

"Because you're not ready for me to leave yet, my girl." Elma pats my cheek condescendingly. "Someone has to keep you from being stupid."

CHAPTER FORTY

Kieren Mason

Dad shoved my ass out of the Batcave, saying my fretting was distracting the piss out of him, so I'm off to hold up my end of the bargain with Essie. I feel lighter after releasing all those pent-up emotions. I have to be strong at home to help everyone else deal, and it felt good to know someone would be there for me.

As I pull up out front of the Spook House, I notice the **For Sale** sign in the front yard of the Pink Taco Hut is gone. I begin to wonder what fool bought such a big house, but then Dad's bizarre behavior trickles in. I count the amount of bodies that would have to fit into a house should Dad manage to snag Clover.

Good Lord, Dad bought himself a house.

There's no way in hell Devon could heal being smashed in a house with four teenagers, living directly across from the Spook House. Dad and Clover and their kids deserve a normal life. If Dad can buy a house, maybe I can too. I've been working for four years, one of which was fulltime, and I haven't had to pay regular bills. I have collateral with Wreck & Ruin.

Devon will need constant monitoring in a calm environment. We've shared a room for nineteen years, we could cohabitate in an entire house. Essie's pretty much homeless right now, with Devon's baby on the way. Then there's the joke Auggie's made of his life by having Willow live in his house, and he wonders why Isis won't move in. If I convince Willow Devon needs her, that I need her, that Essie needs her, I could get her ass out of the Spook House and my aunt where she belongs.

Taking a page out of Essie's notebook, I plan. Wiggling around in my seat, I snag my cellphone out of my back pocket, then quickly scroll to find my other aunt's number.

"Ren?" Ginny sounds breathless. "Are you okay?"

"I'm sitting outside of Dad's new house, and I have a plan." My comment is met with dead silence. "Willow and I aren't idiots, Aunt Gin– jeez. We're just playing along, pretending we don't know Dad, Clover, and the kids are keeping us in the dark."

"I don't want to have to lie to you." Ginny sighs, then speaks softly to someone else. "I'm hosting an open house right now, Ren. So this has to be quick."

"I think I have the solution to solve all of our problems."

"This will be good." Ginny chuckles. "Fine, what do you want to know?"

"Who all's moving into the Pink Taco Hut?"

"Clover knows nothing of this," Ginny warns. "So you can't tell your dad you know, and you sure as shit can't tell Willow. Your dad is slowly easing Clover into it. "

"I'll promise you anything if you help me."

"–No, the house doesn't have stainless steel appliances or double sinks in the baths." Ginny's voice is professional yet irritated. There's the sound of a door closing, then the background chatter disappears. "Sorry, Ren. These people expect a two-hundred-thousand dollar home for seventy."

Laughing, I'm not an idiot. I know whatever I can buy will be a piece of shit. "I'm surprised they don't want granite and crown molding."

"It's like a never-ending episode of House Hunters, Fairport edition– same ridiculous, impossible demands for their budgets." Ginny giggles at her own joke. "Malcolm and Dave have been conspiring," she admits, voice warbling with worry. "It's time for Clover to let go and enjoy life. So I'm listing your house and Clover's to pay for the pink monstrosity. Then I'm listing Dave's for his retirement."

"Essie's out of yet another place?" I gasp in shock, feeling sick to my stomach. I was laying all my shit at her feet this afternoon, when she need me instead.

"Dave and Mary will be splitting their time with Essie's parents and Clover and Malcolm– your dad thought that would calm Clover down. Essie's welcome, I'm sure."

"I need you to find me a house," I blurt out.

"What?!" Ginny squawks.

"You heard me." I chuckle sardonically. "Ain't no way in hell I'm living in the Pink Taco Hut with four teenagers, Clover and Dad, Dave and Mary, and Essie. Fuck no– Devon would go nuts."

"The boy's already nuts." Not a hint of humor leaks into Ginny's tone. "Okay, I'll see what I can do. But you have to tell me who the house is for. Just you? You know your dad wants you shoved up his ass."

"Dad's getting an enema," I tease, chuckling. "I'm going to take care of Devon so Dad can concentrate on the kids and Clover, and Essie and Willow are going to help me."

"Do *they* know that?" Ginny huffs an uncomfortable laugh. "You are aware of the gossip going around, right? This will add fuel to the fire."

"I don't give a shit." Yanking my keys from the ignition, I feel resolute and calm with the decision. "Work your magic and find me a house– Devon and I should be able to afford it. I'll drain his account for the down payment if I have to."

"You can do that?" Ginny sounds impressed.

"Dev's been a drug addict for years, Aunt Gin. Dad made it so Dev's direct deposits flowed into my bank account so he couldn't buy drugs. I have every cent Devon's ever earned as a cop."

"Jesus," Ginny hisses. "Okay, I'll find you a house." The sound of a door opening is followed by rapid fire questions. "Shit– gotta go. Love ya!"

"Love you, too." Slipping from my truck, I tuck my phone into my back pocket. The sound of cheering and smack talk filters into my ears from the Spook House's backyard. Instead of making my way up the walk to the front door, I curve around the ginormous building to see what's the ruckus.

A grin spreads my lips and warmth fills my heart– we *needed* this. The Spook House's backyard is the venue for a soccer game. Auggie and Weston are acting as goalies, the goals are trees connected by clothesline rope. Facing off, Auggie's side is Willow and the twins, with Weston's Rob, Isis, and Rae.

With Robin flowing like water around Willow, Auggie dives to catch the ball, but ends up landing on his chest with the ball flying into the clothesline rope. "Eat that!" Rob points down at Auggie, trailing a taunting laugh while dancing a jig.

"Ugh!" Rob grunts as Auggie's big paw hooks on his ankle, dragging his ass down to the grass. Game forgotten, the fools wrestle around, mock hitting each other while laughing.

"Hey!" Rae spots me, then runs over. "Ren's here. Let's play Ladder Ball!"

Snagging my baby sister around the waist, I pepper raspberries to her face. "No. Hell to the no."

"Why?" Willow's voice flows breathy, causing me to take a good look at her. She was having fun when I walked up, but now an awkwardness settles over us, and I begin to wonder about Aunt Ginny's gossip comment.

Isis raises an eyebrow– the subtle movement is an entire conversation between us. "Five minute timeout while we figure out a way to even out the teams."

"I can call a buddy," Weston's eager voice warbles slightly, causing Rae and me to share a snort.

"I'll call," Rae volunteers to summon Sage. "See who else we can round up, since Ren won't let us play Ladder Ball." With a push by my baby sister, I'm shoved toward Willow.

"He's not allowed on Rob's team," I warn, knowing the lithe, quick creatures will decimate the other team.

"Who?" Rob perks up from biting the hand palming his face– Auggie's.

"Sage," comes from multiple sources, including from me.

"Sage isn't on my team," Rob mutters wryly, having to bring sexual orientation into it. "But I'm sure we could kick ass together in soccer. I used to play for Fairport High."

Wandering away, I head in Willow's direction, but she's focusing on Seth like her life depends on it. "Git!" I order, smooshing the kid's cheeks, making him squishy faced. "Need to talk to Willow for a sec."

"What's up with Ladder Ball?" Willow's muttering, hesitant to follow me deeper into the yard, away from everyone.

"I suck," I admit without shame. Pulling on Willow's ponytail, I'm happy to see her. I feel slightly guilty over what I spoke to Essie about, but the venting helped, as did the advice.

"I find *that* hard to believe." Willow won't look me in the eye– she's emotionally exhausted, as are the rest of us, which is why I don't want to wade through relationship bullshit. I want to play, to have fun– to forget.

Escape.

Escape, even if it's only for a few minutes where I don't worry about Devon.

"It's true," I murmur softly, tugging Willow's ponytail until she has to look at me. "After our cooking lesson tomorrow, we'll play. I'll make a fool of myself, just so you can laugh at me."

The nonresponse speaks volumes, so I take that advice and use it.

"I spent an hour with Essie this afternoon to talk about Devon–" holding my palm out, I stop Willow before she can say anything. The perturbed look she gives me is hilarious. "You're too cute with your mouth hanging open in speechlessness."

"Ass!" is accompanied with a palm swatting me in the chest. Face falling, Willow rolls her eyes up to meet mine. "I understand. Essie's… she's easy to talk to, fun, and pretty. She's built–" Words getting softer and softer, Willow mutters underneath her breath, "Like a porn star."

"Aww, you say the sweetest things about the girl you're pissed at," I tease, yanking her ponytail harder. Allowing the chocolate strands to fall through my fingertips, I try to think of a way to say this without sounding like an ass.

"Essie's hot," I answer with all honesty. "I'm attracted to her. But you don't see me getting insanely jealous because you want Jax Teller. You joke around with me about Lagertha on The Vikings when I get hard watching her."

"That's fantasy." Willow raises her hand, then waves it in an arc. "Essie's everywhere."

"I appreciate her– she's my friend." Looking down at Willow, I try to get a read on her emotions, but she's giving me a calm face. I get a clue. "I'm not a bad person, Willow. I'm not going to ditch my friends because you're having a tiff about *me*. You're too close to cut Essie out of your life. You'll be back together again, and I'm not going to make it worse."

"Make it worse how?" Willow challenges. "By kissing her?"

Snorting, I can't help but grin. "For Devon. For my family." Running my finger up Willow's chest, I swirl around where her heart lies. "For *you*. You'll feel guilty later if you force everyone to push Essie away as a showing of loyalty toward you. So I'm not going to do it. You're family– family sticks together."

"I heard you and Rob last night," Willow admits. "I don't see what Essie has to do with this at all. Why does she have to be involved with Devon's recovery?"

"That's between you and Essie– *talk to her*," I repeat Essie's earlier words. "Better yet, listen when she's talking to you."

"I don't want to deal with this right now," Willow growls.

"I ought to spank the bitterness outta you, Spanky." Stilling my swirling above her heart, I glide over her breast, up her throat, and then wrap my palm around the nape of her neck. Pulling Willow toward me, I rest my lips beneath her ear.

"I didn't kiss Essie like this." Mouth parted, I suck lightly on Willow's throat, causing her to fall against my chest. "I kissed her like a sister." Willow's snort has me chuckling. "Okay, I'll admit I'm a man, but I'm a loyal one. I haven't touched anyone since we graduated high school."

"A year ago?" Willow gasps in surprise, fingers curling against my chest.

"I said I was loyal, and I meant it. Loyal to myself, my beliefs and wants, and I'm not going to ruin this between us." Jolting in surprise, I bite back a moan as Willow's palm glides down my chest, hesitating over my bulge, then comes to a rest on my hip. "Why do you do that all the time?"

Willow freezes against me, embarrassment and mortification making her unable to answer.

Wrapping my hand around Willow's, I curve her palm around my bulge, holding it in place. I ignore the way I'm throbbing beneath her touch, and bite my lip against the hiss readying to erupt because of the stinging brush burn.

"If you're doing this because you want to touch me, do it," I growl in a husky voice. "Do it all the damn time. But if you're doing it to see if you turn me on, that's not right. Don't test me—*trust me*. Trust what I say and what I show you."

Backing Willow up farther, I skirt us around a tree, hiding us from view of our families. "Trust this." Hand flowing down Willow's back, I cup her ass in my palm, squeezing. Cock jumping under her hand, she has to feel how badly I want her.

"I trust you," Willow gulps out, suddenly breathless and pliant. As she steps away from me, her hand falls away from my crotch. "I don't want to play soccer anymore. Let's go binge-watch."

Laughing, I give Willow's ass a firm swat, causing her to jump. Slipping both hands around her ass, I yank her to me roughly. With a grunt of surprise, Willow hangs in my hands, trusting me. Lifting, I press her front to mine, not only passing her test, I prove just how much I want to *binge-watch*.

"C'mon!" Rob shouts from across the yard. "You can fool around later."

"Leave 'em be." Auggie sounds satisfied, which is what has me stepping away from Willow to take her hand.

"I'm on Rob's team," I announce, suddenly feeling competitive.

Laughter just as satisfied, Willow's either getting off on my jealous streak, or my competitive one. "You're going down, Stud– going down."

CHAPTER FORTY-ONE

Essie Prynne

Romanticizing the epic love story of Elma and Niko, I can't figure out why she wouldn't book the next flight back to Italy to be with him and her family. "Why haven't you?"

"Because you're not ready for me to leave yet, my girl." Elma pats my cheek condescendingly. "Someone has to keep you from being stupid."

"Ugh!" Speechless and insulted, all I can do is stare at my mentor while she laughs back at me.

"Girl, what's that notebook you keep carrying around." Elma doesn't wait for permission, she just snatches it up and opens it. Knowing her since I was a toddler, and working for her since I was thirteen, I expect nothing less than her snoopy highhandedness.

"I-I-I–" stammering, I fear Elma thinking I'm stupider than she originally thought.

"There's so many rumors flying around about this notebook after everyone saw you carrying it around. Then you sat at the No-Name before and after your shift, head in this book. List of guys you've been carnal with. Kill list." Elma tries to snort while laughing, but ends up choking instead. "The size and quality of the manhood you've encountered. Everyone wants a peek in here, especially after the vibrant Mr. Fischer was seen writing in it."

"A kill list?" I drawl dramatically. "What the hell is wrong with you people?"

"We're bored." Elma chuckles, smirking, as she reads the entries Sage wrote earlier. "I like this kid– you need to get his ass in here and primp him."

Primp?

Whimpering, I fear Elma will turn to the pages where I'm balancing out how it's possible to turn Elma's Salon into *my* Primp. I'm petrified I'll end up offending Elma.

"Robin, eh?" A dyed black eyebrow raises high when she spots my plan on funding. "I get that people think he's pretty, but he's not at all the metrosexual type."

"No, but he's the type of family I have," I mutter, befuddled that Elma's finding the contents of my notebook amusing instead of insulting.

"What type's that?"

"Since no sane bank will give me a loan, Robin's the type who has disposable income and loves me."

"Can't have enough of those types in your life." Elma chuckles outright as she reads my business plan, and doesn't bother whispering, "*Stupid girl*– so, you want to buy out my lease of Salon, do you?"

"Yes, ma'am." Swallowing thickly, I try to wet my mouth enough to speak. "I respect what you've built, but I think you should retire and spend the rest of your days with Niko and your family. I couldn't imagine life without mine, and you deserve it after all you've given up."

"Hmm…" Elma taps a pen to her chin thinking. "Perhaps I would enjoy being surrounded by generations of my nieces and nephews." Pen scratching on a random page in my notebook, Elma pushes it toward me. "I'll stay on until the first of the year, teaching you all I know for the next six months. How about this amount?"

$41, 983. 57

Gap-mouthed, I stare down at what it will take to chase my dream. "That's it? To buy out your entire business and supplies?"

"Well, you'll still have to pay the rent on the building. But Jessup gave me a life lease with fixed rent I pay yearly– I'll make sure the same applies to you. His choice is an empty building on Main Street, with businesses coming in and out but never staying. He knows it's more advantageous to keep the rent low and have a tenet in place, than to have his building sit empty for months or years at a time. It's bad for our local economy, and his fire insurance increases if it's empty."

"I have a lot to learn." Voice breaking, fear creeps in. "I have no money, and I don't know if I can convince Robin to take a chance on me, especially since I'm living off family as it is. I'm a bad risk for him to take."

Shifting down, Elma reaches underneath the counter for the locked box she keeps out of sight. Fishing a key from around her neck, she opens it.

Curiosity getting the better of me, I lean forward for a better look. In all of my years at Salon, I've never seen what's in the lockbox. Out of respect, I've never tried to jimmy the lock open either. A few bundles of cash are pushed to the side, a glimpse of Elma's old-school beautician license from eons ago, then a notebook similar to the one I've been toting around is pulled from the box.

"Check this one out, girl." Elma flips to the first page of the notebook, and I gasp in shock.

Entry after entry of the activities in my backroom, with the total price of the transactions and the commission Elma was paid. Pages and pages are filled, because most of the revenue Salon was bringing in came from my esthetician services.

Gut twisting, I fear Elma didn't trust me. "Never once did I go behind your back. If I charged a price, I gave you your cut." Eyes scrolling the pages, I can't believe how much work I've done in the past two years.

"I know, girl– I know." Elma pats my back. "If you'd tried to jip me, my trust would've been broken. But the outcome would've been the same. You should check out the total amount you paid me for the use of the backroom." Elma quickly flips to the back page, her meticulous accounting the total.

$41, 983. 57

"What? I don't understand," rambling, the words just fall out of my mouth. Eyes flicking between the price she wrote in my notebook and the total I paid her written in hers. "What's this mean?"

"A savings account of sorts." Elma sounds sheepish, tan skin blushing. "Perhaps a test to see if you deserved it. You didn't owe me anything for using the backroom, Hester, because it drew in more clientele. No young woman has money to start their own business, so I'm doing for you what my mentor did for me, and what you'll do someday for another young woman."

Speaking on a broken sob, "I don't deserve this. Why would you do this for me?"

"You *earned* it– you unknowingly *paid* for it. Why?" Elma leans back in her chair, tears glistening in her eyes. "Because I know what it's like to be a woman, one who makes mistakes and is judged for them. Mistakes I made at seventeen still haunt me at eighty. You'd asked why I hardly went back to Italy, because I was ostracized for leaving my fiancé behind and chasing the

America dream with a handsome stranger… I'm going back now that those who judged me are dead."

"Oh, Elma!" With my hand pressed to my heart, I feel for the woman.

"I was uneducated, could barely speak English, living with a woman who resented me, and left by the man I was stupid enough to follow here. I walked into Salon, and the older woman running the place took me in, even with the negative gossip floating around about me. She took a chance, and I earned the life I deserved. It doesn't matter that the people gave me a reputation I didn't deserve– I proved who I was by how I behaved."

"I just… I don't know what to say."

"There's nothing you need to say, because you're walking in my shoes. I know how you feel, girl. Exactly how you feel. Only you're lucky enough to have family who supports you. As soon as I think you're ready, I'm going back to mine. I told you older women understand because we've been there– I want you to promise me when you see a girl like yourself, you'll take her in as your own and teach her she's worthy simply for existing."

Leaping off my stool, my arms wrap around Elma, clasping her comforting weight to my chest. *"Thank you. Thank you. Thank you."* I whisper rapidly with tears streaming down my face. "Thank you for believing in me."

Clearing her throat, Elma tugs me away, then pats my hand in a *there-there* fashion. "When you have the ability to help, it makes you an asshole when you don't. Pay it forward, that's all I ask."

"I will," I gasp, shocked. "Holy shit!"

Life is changing for all of us. Mom and Dad are moving. Malcolm is trying to convince Clover to give him a chance. Devon will be getting the help he should've had years ago. Beth finally gave in to Rory. Willow and Ren are together.

Sure, I may be homeless with a baby in my belly, and Willow's still not speaking to me. But with Primp at the tip of my fingers, it's the foundation I need for a better life. Willow will come around eventually, or she won't, and I accept I can't force her to forgive me.

Happiness isn't money or being half of a couple. Sometimes happiness comes in the form of achievement– having a dream and doing all you can to reach it.

ONE MONTH LATER...

CHAPTER FORTY-TWO

Devon Mason

"Are you still having trouble sleeping?" The mothering yet no-nonsense Ms. Amelia is genuinely concerned for me. "If you're not sleeping regularly, the center won't sign-off on your family visit."

Sighing, I wash a palm over my face, barely avoiding the Mason hair-tug. The first three therapists, their pens would fly over their notepads when I'd do that. I raise a finger, asking for a minute to get my thoughts in order. I haven't been a model patient over the past three weeks. After I mentally woke up in the middle of detox, I've been fighting my nature.

Stubborn, I don't like to be controlled. After raising myself, being in charge of my siblings and using Dad's guilt against him, I'm used to getting my own way. Here in Sedona, that shit doesn't fly. If I thought I was manipulative... the therapists here are sociopaths and sadists.

Ms. Amelia is lucky number seven– I drove all the other therapists before her away, seeing right to the heart of their manipulative bullshit. They didn't care about my welfare. They were getting off on controlling me. The more I fought, the brighter the glint in their eye became.

They wanted to break me, not *heal* me.

Even now, weeks out of detox, weeks on a drug cocktail of mood stabilizers, I recognize how paranoid that belief makes me seem. As a cop, I have to trust my gut. That's not instability– that's the voice no one should ever ignore.

Instinct.

Ms. Amelia is *my* therapist, even if the center doesn't believe so. I have sessions with four others on a weekly basis– one every single day. Dr. Delaney is the worst of the worst. The harder I fought him, the more he enjoyed our war. I play the bullshit game with him now, by telling him what he wants to hear, not what I need to voice.

I've lost count of all the people who want to drill inside my head, especially with group therapy sessions. Not counting the orderlies who count my pills, smell my shit, and hover over my shoulder while watching me eat. There isn't a second of my day or night where I'm alone, even inside my private thoughts.

The control, the lack of autonomy is harder to handle than the need to get high to forget. With this hell hanging over my head for life, I'll never take another drug again, even sleeping pills.

I need my freedom.

I need to think.

I *need* privacy.

Besides *Bipolar*, Ms. Amelia gave me another label. *Ambivert*. I need to be around people, but I also need to be alone, so this mental institution fronting as a rehab is hell on earth for me.

Even knowing there are only five more weeks to go, my heart still races at the thought of going through this every single minute of those weeks. The sweats are reminiscent of detox– the nausea of having someone count my every shit, piss, shower, sleep, and breath taken… my humanity has been taken from me, leaving me as an object who can fight back, one the sadists here long to break.

The punishment fits the crime.

"I want to get better," I admit, the rightness ringing in my voice. "I know I will never be what society thinks is normal. I just want to be *me*."

"Devon." Ms. Amelia sighs, leaning forward as if she wants to pat my hand. What I like about her is that she's the type of woman I wished I would've had as a mom. She also doesn't write anything down on a notepad. She keeps no record of anything I say. She has a steel-trap of a memory. What I say to her never leaves this room, never leaves her head to spew out her mouth. Ms. Amelia is my confessor, a compassionate person who is as ethical as good.

"I'm not pulling the same bullshit as everyone else around here." Ms. Amelia snorts, which is why I chose her as the one I trust. "I want to lie right now to get my way– tell you a bunch of bullshit about how I'm sleeping so I can see my family."

"But you won't." Ms. Amelia steeples her fingers in her usual thinking pose. "I understand why you won't take the sleeping pills Dr. Delaney prescribed, but perhaps we should revisit the discussion."

"No!" I say adamantly, the first stirring of anger erupting in my voice. Ms. Amelia doesn't even flinch, which is why I trust the woman. We have to walk around here as zombies, our mood stabilizers numbing us out. But I've since learned it's not the medication that causes that effect on the residents.

Fear.

Locked in a facility surrounded by a killing sun, I'm not allowed to disagree, voice an independent thought, or show any high or low emotions. If I do, I'll be drugged into compliance. Most of the patients welcome the escape, but that's not why I'm here. I'm sober, I'm thinking clearly, and I intend to stay in that state of being. No high. No low. Since I need my mood stabilizers at the accurate level, the only honest thing I tell Dr. Delaney is how I'm feeling, because he's the one who prescribes my meds.

I may not show it, but I *feel*. Everything.

"I understand." Ms. Amelia fails to stop herself this time— a gentle hand rests atop mine, giving a squeeze of reassurance. "Believe me, I do. You fear any addictive substance. But without sleep, you can't think rationally."

"I sleep," I blurt out, never able to sensor myself around her like I am with everyone else. Eyes flicking around rapidly, nerves rubbed raw, I find comfort in the sameness of Ms. Amelia's office— everything looks the same around here. Phony tranquility. "I welcome sleep. I even welcome the nightmares. But they wake me up. Keep me awake."

"Nightmares?" Ms. Amelia shifts in her seat. Clarity has me seeing everything in a heightened way: Any noise sounds loud. All movement seems harsh, instead of fluid. Scents are either pleasant or cloying. An accidental bump has the reaction of being slapped. A fingertip touching me out of kindness has the impact of a full-body hug. "Will you ever be ready to voice them aloud?"

"No," I admit, feeling no shame in denying everyone something that should be private. Private between my mother, my brother, and our attackers. "But it's not just that... it's everything I did before I came here. The things I blocked out— blacked out. I remember them, and it—"

"It?" Ms. Amelia generally doesn't push, but she can tell I need her to right now.

"*Hurts*." Voice breaking, a single tear escapes the corner of my eye. I haven't cried since I set foot onto this baked desert. "The guilt is eating me alive– makes me sick."

"Makes you want to get high?"

"No!" Breathless, my heart beats out of control. With a fist to my chest, I try to control my reaction. "No." Shaking my head rapidly over and over again. "The cravings aren't worth it."

"Worth what?"

"I'm sober now." I do the finger-raise-thing to get a minute to put my thoughts into words before Ms. Amelia can speak to coax me when I'm not ready. "The impact I have on everyone around me... I could escape the pain by the sweet kiss of a needle biting into my arm."

Ms. Amelia's eyebrow raising by the intoxicated quality of my voice has me pausing. After a few heartbeats, I continue. "The escape will make it worse. For them. For *me*. I'd have to go through this hell again, and I don't have another in me. The choice is life or death, and I'm *not* my mother."

Ms. Amelia has to look away from me, with the edge of her jaw and the slope of her cheek the only visible to me. "Good," flows hoarsely from her throat. The tear she releases informs me she's walked in my shoes before I did, and that's no doubt the reason I was drawn to the older woman.

Wise eyes flick to connect with me, and we commune for a few moments, sharing our similar pain. The reasons we sought drugs don't matter in the face of all those we hurt during the journey. It's their pain that stops me now that I'm sober enough to recognize it.

"I'm a drug addict," I admit without hesitation, unlike the first week I spent here. During detox, I kept screaming for my medicine until I didn't have the strength to scream anymore. For the week afterward, I used every manipulation in my arsenal, blaming the past and bipolarism for my need to get high. Worn down by my loss of autonomy, combined with journaling my evil deeds, during group therapy I admitted I was a drug addict.

"But I'm a people user too," rolls off my tongue for the first time. "I'm no different than anyone else here, patient or staff. I want control. Anyway I can get it. Since I can't control how my body functions, I used drugs because I could guarantee their reaction."

Looking away sharply, Ms. Amelia whispers, "Don't let that define you, just reel it in when you recognize how you're falling into those destructive patterns."

"That's why I won't use my manipulative powers on anyone here," I mutter wryly. We're all cut from the same cloth– the patients and the staff. The patients are learning to cope. The staff are better at lying to themselves, to everyone else, and faking their way through life.

Ms. Amelia fought her way from patient to staff, which is why she's not faking anything. There are a handful of others like her, who are here to help. But the rest are just better sociopaths than the patients. They're so broken, they use our pain as a gauge of their normalcy to make themselves feel better about their own life choices.

Sanity is an illusion– everyone on this planet is fucked up in their own way.

"Devon," Ms. Amelia chastises me gently, no doubt reading my amusement accurately– I'm a dark bastard. "I know you refuse to voice your inner demons, but have you been keeping a journal to let it out?"

Laughing without humor, I scrub my palms over my face again, wanting to rub it raw. I can never cleanse the filth away– can never be punished for all of my sins. "Yes, I'm writing in my journal." Looking my therapist in the eyes, I make a promise. "If you're lying about how my journal is sacred, and anyone reads it, I will kill you. Do you understand?"

A sly smile curling her lips, Ms. Amelia is amused by my reaction. Dr. Delaney would've called in the four thugs he calls orderlies to shoot me up with a tranquilizer, then strap me in my bed for a long timeout for my runaway mouth.

"Your very *human* reactions are a gift to me." Chuckling lightly, Ms. Amelia knows damn well I was being serious. "I'm so used to brain-dead patients who are terrified to be real with me. I won't judge you for telling me how you really feel."

"Answer my question," I demand, fingers clenching my thighs.

Laughing harder, "The sharing of a journal is a very intimate experience for the writer. Its contents are yours, and no one on our staff will violate that oath. When you get home…" she trails off, smirking. "I suggest you share it with someone, or lock it in a safe and throw away the key if you wish to keep it, or sacrifice it by fire."

"I wrote what happened to me to let it go," I admit hesitantly, knowing it will *never* truly be gone. "My secrets aren't just mine, so I don't think I should share it."

"Share it with your brother," Ms. Amelia suggests, eager to set sights on Kieren. She promised to leave my family alone during their visit, but will get her due when they come to fetch me from this hell.

"Shit!" Hissing through clenched teeth, I clamp my eyes tightly, trying my damnedest to keep the tears at bay. Only Ren would get that reaction out of me. I miss him the most– *owe* him the most.

"You can let it out." Ms. Amelia's voice sounds far away, hollow beneath the thudding of my heartbeat. "You *should* let it out, so I can truly help you heal…"

Kieren and I lock eyes, blocking out the pain-filled moans and the red. All I see is red. Red washing over my mother as her screams died away. The only anchor I have is my brother. The brother I failed to protect. The mother I failed.

All night, I felt guilty yet proud over what had happened with Essie, and pissed at Aunt Isis for stopping me. Blinded by rage as I was duct taped to a kitchen chair, my first thought was how I was thankful Aunt Isis showed up to stop me, because she was so furious at me, she took my baby brother and sister with her.

Ren's strong enough to survive this. I don't think my mother is, and I'm not sure about me. But there was no way in hell Raven and Weston would've had a snowball's chance in hell after tonight had they been home.

Holding tighter, Ren and I focus on one another, trying hard to ignore the fucker with the cascading tear tattoos gliding down his cheek from the corner of his eye. I've watched enough movies and bled Dad dry of scary, real stories, to know what those tears mean. Stories I never thought would become our reality.

Holding tighter yet, the garbled, choking sound Mom's making hits my ears– sputtering for breath around a cock. Ren's eyes bulge impossibly wide, terrified out of his mind. We concentrate on looking at each other to block out what's happening to Mom. My brother's innocent, but I'm not. I don't need to see it to know what's happening.

"Cunt!" *We both flinch at the sharp sound of flesh hitting flesh. I can tell Ren thinks the man slapped Mom, but I know*

better... he used his cock, not a fist. "Watch the teeth– Jesus Christ, Juarez. Stop thrusting so hard. You're forcing this bitch to bite me."

This afternoon, Essie, Ren, West, and Rae played Monopoly with me in the same spot Mom's now being viciously gang-banged by actual fucking gangbangers. The disturbing part of me is that I'm numb to what they're doing to Mom. But the rage is building because they're destroying my happy place with my family.

The sickest part of me sees this as a fitting punishment for all my mother's ever done to me, for infecting me with her disease, for never taking care of the family she made. The even sicker part of me is glad these fuckers only wanted to humiliate Mom by forcing us to watch.

"Switch with me," is a sharp demand, lashing out to cause Ren to flinch. "Sick of fucking a hole that bites back."

Amused, masculine laughter has me nearly pissing my pants– the guy who painted Mom red. It's not the violent things that hurt me the worst, knowing nothing but that with my mother. It's the softer things that hurt the worst. Juarez isn't violent, doing everything in slow-motion.

Voice twisting my guts, "Skank's nice and wet for you now." Turning to the side so I miss puking on myself, I bow my head as violent convulsions overpower me. A puddle of vomit grows at the side of my chair. Ren makes impatient, pleading sounds in the back of his throat, scared for me but also needing me to look at him– anchor him.

Skank's nice and wet for you now... earlier, Juarez bitched how Mom was too tight and too dry, so he took his sweet time loosening her up– with a knife. The wet is red.

Ren missed that. Raging, I was the first one duct taped to a chair, placed front and center. Juarez hurt Mom while Ren was being strapped in while still in the kitchen. Cascading Tears Tattoo carried Ren into the living room, chair and all. Juarez was already raping Mom by then, with Cocksuck suffocating her.

Cascading Tears has been babysitting us while his friends hurt Mom, getting off on our reactions.

Turning my head sharply to the side, I rub my mouth on my shoulder to wipe the puke away. I've lost track of how many times I've puked so far, only snotty shit coming up now. At least

Cascading Tears didn't tape my mouth shut like he did Ren's, or I would've drowned.

Eyes latching back onto my brothers, we both ignore the dying sounds Mom's making, while pretending to ignore Juarez and Cocksuck grunting as they hurt her. Cascading Tears keeps ducking his head, bending down, and chuckling as he tries to get into our line of sight.

"Those two–" Tears points at Mom. "Didn't have much fun in lock-up." Chuckling sinisterly, he gets off on the fact that Ren and I react by quickly looking at the gang-rape, then back at him.

Ren's staring in dawning horror at the tattoos, while I find them a comfort. This torture can't last forever. "And you did?" I ask, balls so big I can never keep my mouth shut. Maybe they'll kill me sooner. Hopefully they do Ren first, so he won't have to suffer through watching me and Mom die.

"I reigned in prison," Tears gloats, coming to kneel between us by our feet, now that we're his captive audience. "Don't have much use for pussy. Plenty of willing and unwilling ass in prison– reward, threat, punishment."

Eyeing Tears, I take him in. Six feet of tattooed, tanned skin stretched tight over bulging muscles. Cascading Tears is the reward, threat, and punishment all rolled into one. He had nothing to fear in prison, but his smaller, straight partners apparently did.

Bravado thick in my voice, I try to hide the quiver. "What's your name?" Balls– I have 'em. I need to know what to call the guy I'm going to wish I never met, because I understand the look he's giving me because I gave the same one to Essie earlier today.

I'm banking on him wanting willing over unwilling, because he has no reason to punish Ren.

"Alejandro– Ale." Crouching lower, Ale only has eyes for me. "Juarez and Stephen will wear themselves out soon. Guy can only come so many times, ya know?"

Eyes getting bigger, Ren is babbling something beneath the tape. "Ren– don't," I warn to stop him, knowing it's too late.

"This one looks like your mom." Ale hitches his thumb over his shoulder where the pitiful moaning is flowing, then he flutters Ren's blond hair. "But you–" Ale looks me dead in the eyes, and I can see the loathing he feels for my father. "Is your name Malcolm Mason Junior?"

"No," I answer without hesitation. I'm his target because of my father, same reason Mom's Juarez and Stephen's. "Devon."

"Brothers in Blue are their own type of gang." Ale continues to stare at me unflinchingly. "But I thought that was Irish? Your names aren't. Scottish? English? It's bizarre after being locked up with everyone but."

Baffled, the words flow without thought. "We're the lowlife scum who escaped starvation and indentured servitude– mixed bastards with a strong heritage." Shuddering, I hear my dad speaking John Mason's words about how we are men, men who have a say in all aspects of our lives. If I don't have control of the situation, bend it until I have enough to survive.

I can't live with Ren being hurt, so I'll shade him until I'm all Alejandro sees.

"Scum, you say?" Ale chuckles, finding me entertaining. "Boy, you have no idea what you're talking about." Sobering, he levels me with a look of utter hatred. "You plan on following in your pop's footsteps?"

"I don't plan on surviving the night," I deadpan, causing Ale to laugh harder. Mom's torture pauses long enough for Ale to relay what I said. Worse is hearing Juarez and Stephen laugh as they push Mom harder than before.

"Until tonight, did you plan on following dear old pop by becoming a brother in blue?" Words light, I can tell my answer will impact what happens next. I'm a liar, but for some reason I can't seem to find the strength to lie, even to myself.

Holding Ale's gaze, I utter with conviction, "Yes."

Without looking away from me, voice as tight as his strained lips, "And the pretty boy?"

"No." I do lie this time, because I don't know if Ren wants to be a cop or not, but I know it means something to Ale. "Football."

"Hmm…" Ale purrs, tasting my words while staring at my brother. "You'll survive this night, boys. The dead can't carry messages that need to be heard. Malcolm Mason has to know who hurt him and why."

I say nothing. Ren can't speak. My mother only has the ability to make involuntary noises from deep within her chest. Ale's friends are too busy to keep up with our conversation.

"There's something about you..." Ale laughs, the sound edged with annoyance. "There's a vibe I get from you, like you're a little punk. An asshole. Controlling. Worse than your dad."

Smirking, I can't help myself because I know it will piss Ale off enough not to notice Ren anymore. "The real man of the house?"

"That." Alejandro narrows his eyes, thinking. "How old are both of you?"

"Fourteen," I say without hesitation, because to say thirteen is to split hairs. "Eleven." Even though Ren turned twelve months ago. Let Ale believe Ren is big for his age, with me being small for mine.

Sadistic amusement in his voice, "Can he get wood yet?"

My "No" is so instantaneous that Alejandro has to believe me. "No, not yet– we make fun of him for being a late-bloomer compared to the rest of the Masons."

"An arrogant asshole." Lips spreading into a smirk, Ale's going to enjoy breaking me. "Reward. Threat–"

"Punishment."

"You're a scary motherfucker for a sheltered, little white boy, aren't you?"

"The only things you said that were accurate were scary white boy." Real fury fuels words that Ale thinks are pure bravado. "The bitch your buddies are torturing has tortured me for fourteen years." Shrugging, I act like I don't care, but it's killing me. "Sheltered?"

Alejandro jerks backward by the edge of rage warping my laughter. "This is my family– my house. My brother. My mother. If I wasn't taped to this chair... did you forget what happened in the kitchen?"

Alejandro couldn't contain me– all three of them barely got me into the chair after I went for the knife block. Size means dick when you're insane with terror and the need to protect your family.

Swallowing thickly, Ale knows ways of controlling me now. "Reward. Threat. Punishment. You have a choice. You do as I say, or I'll do your brother."

"Nworw-umph!" Ren's chair legs slam against the floor as he struggles. The tape pulls at his wrists, skin reddening.

Fearing what will happen if he doesn't stop, "Kieren!" I shout, using my voice to lash out since I can't touch him. "Knock it off. I'm your big brother."

"Kieren?" Alejandro laughs, sounding shocked, even after we did a genealogy lesson. "No shit?"

"Mmworugh–" Ren tries and fails to communicate with his lips fused shut with duct tape, but at least he stops struggling.

"What do you want?" I give in, not giving a shit about me or Mom. Ren. I'll do whatever I have to do for Ren, and Ale knows it.

"I'm bored." Big man with the scary death-total tattoos pouts. "Juarez and Stephen are having all the fun. But I know you'll play with me."

"Don't!" I order, knowing my brother is gearing up again. Ren's taller than me, bigger than me, but younger than me. At least Ren looks his age while taped to a chair with tears streaming down his cheeks, innocent eyes the size of saucers.

The only time I cried tonight was when the paring knife was torn from my hand– out of pure frustration. The knife that was used on Mom to make her wet– my punishment for not behaving. Lesson learned.

"Get it over with." Voice weak and thready, I slump to the back of the chair. The urge to puke has left me, but I'm sweating enough to dehydrate. Pretty sure my heart will never beat normally ever again.

If we survive, none of us will be normal after this.

With a taunting laugh trailing him, Ale swaggers over to the scene of the gang-bang to fetch the paring knife. Earlier today, Ren used it to cut up an onion for spaghetti, now it's red with Mom's blood– blood from her... area. Lord knows what my contribution will be.

Juarez and Stephen never hit my mother or tied her up. Mom gave up the second they came into this house, with Ren and me trying to fight them off to save her. I ignore how she's slumped to her belly, cheek resting against the carpet. This wasn't about Mom– it was about sending a message. Mom's nightgown is still in one piece because all they needed was somewhere to stick their dicks. They're fully clothed, with their flies open. Stephen's taking his turn. Juarez's limp junk is stained red as he sits on the coffee table where we played Monopoly earlier.

Alejandro said they couldn't get it up over and over again– at least I won't have to take on all three of them.

Ren's chair pounds on the floor as he renews his struggles, sounds more like what Mom was making earlier flow from his throat. It takes everything in me not to struggle too, to tear at the tape on my wrists. Not to run away or fight, but so I can reach out to comfort my little brother.

"Shh... it's okay." Voice low, lips not moving, only Ren can hear me. "No matter what happens, I'll keep you safe."

The look Ren flashes me speaks volumes– it's worse watching than experiencing. The guilt. The shame. I already feel guilty that I didn't take Mom's place, because I'd be strong enough to not break until their cocks couldn't rise anymore. Mom wasn't– she was already broken.

"I'm sorry," I whisper as Alejandro approaches me, knife drawn. Ren moans a sound I never wanted to hear. "Close your eyes– focus on something in the room and don't look away from it. It's what I always do when Mom's rampaging on me."

Quickly looking away from Ale, I make sure my brother is doing as he was told. "Trust me– do it." All well and good, except Ren chooses me to focus on. "Shit! Look away!" I yell in a panic, voice breaking.

Alejandro and his friends won't break me, but Ren can. "Look! Away!"

Knife in hand, Ale crouches by my chair. Lowered until we're eye-level, he presses the tip of the blade to the tape binding my wrist to the wooden armrest. "Deal?"

"Anything," I blurt out, still feeling Ren's goddamn eyes on the side of my face. It's like he's punishing himself by forcing himself not to look away from what's going to happen to me.

"If you can get off before I do–"

"What?!" I squawk, heart fluttering so fast I fear it will explode. "You expect me to get off, let alone get hard. With that– " I point to Juarez watching me, with Stephen seconds away from tapping out. "Happening in front of me."

"If you can't, I won't care if your brother's too little to get hard– I'll do worse to him."

Huffing in large gasps of air, I'm on the edge of hyperventilating. "What do you want?"

"Just a blowjob," Alejandro mutters nonchalantly, like it's no big deal. "Jerk yourself off at the same time."

"I'm not that fucking coordinated!" I snarl, baring my teeth.

"Better hope the boy doesn't bite like his momma." Stephen pulls out of Mom, cock slick with cum and blood. I pray he can't get it up again while swallowing the need to puke. I'd suck

Alejandro for the rest of my life, as long as that meant nothing that touched my mother touches me.

"Devon won't," Ale says with certainty. "If you don't get off before me, I'll fuck baby boy's ass. Deal?"

With a nod, my wrists are cut free to the background soundtrack of Ren losing his shit.

"Did you go through with it?" Ms. Amelia's voice draws me to the present. With horror, I realize I was speaking aloud, not reliving the past. "Is that why your father included yours and your brother's sexual issues in the admissions packet?"

Laughing without humor, I nod my head up and down, hair whipping me in the cheeks. "You think?" Hiding my face behind my palms, I admit the truth. "Yeah, I went through with it. I didn't remember it until recently. I mean, I *knew*. I just didn't allow myself to think it."

"It all makes so much sense now," Ms. Amelia muses, sounding surprised I opened up to her.

"To me too." Chuckling darkly, I think of all the shit I pulled in recent months. It wasn't all because I was bipolar or a drug addict. "I had fresh tape on my wrists when Dad came home. His eyes missed nothing– it's why he's such a good cop. Stephen and Juarez watched Alejandro and me, then all three of them searched our house.

"My mouth wasn't taped shut for a reason– I thought it was because I was puking." I flash Ms. Amelia a loaded look. "After they left us alone, I leaned over to pull the tape off Ren's mouth, trying to get a corner with my front teeth. I succeeded obviously, because Dad came home just as we were gnawing at our own wrists."

"Devon, this explains so much– it will help us treat you more effectively."

"Tamp down your enthusiasm," I mutter dryly. "I know all this shit, but it doesn't change anything. Dad never asked, but between the tape and the fact that Ren and I went nuts when it came to sex. Ren's obviously homophobic now– which is painful with a gay baby brother –and he fucked anything with a pulse and a pussy, but couldn't come."

"Because you were forced to do that–"

"No shit, Amelia," I snarl. "I already told you that we both know why– Ren and me. I couldn't get *hard*. At all. Only revenge got the blood flowing. Ren couldn't get off unless he was by himself. I don't need a degree to diagnose that shit, and neither did Dad. Why do you think he made us go to the Playroom? Why do you think he put up with me?"

"Your father loves you," Ms. Amelia says with a conviction I already feel. "Kurt–"

Head hitching backward, I laugh my first real laugh in months. "Oh, my God. I'm so fucking ashamed with what I did to Kurt. He's the first apology note I wrote, and the only one I sent."

"I'm surprised you're speaking of him, when this was another off-limits topic." Ms. Amelia does walk on eggshells with me, but only certain eggshells. "Your brother added his own notes to your admissions packet, minus anything that happened during the assault."

"Well…" I choke on a laugh. "I only remember bits and pieces where Ren was concerned. But tearing off my clothes, smashing food on the floor, eating glass, and crying about giving head tends to stick with a guy. I have no idea what Ren put in his notes, but I'm sure it involved how he was chasing my naked ass down the sidewalk, screaming for all the neighborhood to hear about how I sucked someone off, with me shouting Kurt's name back."

Turning away abruptly, Ms. Amelia's heavy chest heaves like she's trying hard not to laugh but failing, so she goes for being silent instead. "Something along those lines," she mutters wryly. "It's not funny–"

"Yes, it is." I grin at my therapist. "It really is."

"In retrospect, it truly is." Ms. Amelia allows herself a hearty laugh at my expense, and I join her instead of feeling insulted. "What happened? Why was Kurt the only one you mailed the letter?"

"It was… enlightening." I try very hard not to be thrust back into the past. "I can't blame any of it on being high. I learned I'm as straight as straight can get, but can understand how someone who isn't feels. Um… yeah, Kurt learned he loved a guy sucking his cock."

"Could you get any higher?" With me sitting on the broken couch, Tina stands before me, looking down at me like a disapproving parent. "How'd you get the shiner and cut on your cheek?"

"There's no getting high enough to forget Essie's pregnant with Damien." Eyes fluttering shut, the weight of the lids too

much to bear, I notice Tina brought friends. I tried so hard, but now I don't give a shit.

"I assume it's yours since you're naming the kid after the devil," Tina mutters wryly, completely sober. "Congratulations, Dad. I did as you asked–" Gesturing behind her at Taryn and Tommy. "Rounded up Satan's spawn and Jesus's disciple."

"And Kurt." I smile brightly, wanting what the man has to offer.

"I'm not good with this." Kurt pipes up from behind Tina. "This isn't what I signed off on, Tina, and you can't fuck me enough to make up for how shitty this is making me feel."

"I need to get high in order to put up with Devon." With a huff, Tina drops to sit on the sofa next to me. "Devon has cash– I only fuck you because I want to."

"I'm a virgin," Taryn squeaks like we didn't already know that, then hides behind the taller yet slimmer Tommy. The boy is a good one– protective. Not that Kurt would ever force either one of them to pay up in anything other than cash.

"No shit, baby Manson." Tina laughs a mean girl cackle. "It's not that you're chubby that's keeping you pure. It's the vibe of how you're going to kill the boys afterward, like a black widow spider."

"I don't like you," Taryn snarls, gearing up to throw a fit. "You have no idea what it's like because you're goddamn perfect." Tommy flinches at the blasphemy.

"Perfect?" Tina looks at me, mouth gaping open. "Perfect? Pfft..."

Not having the energy, "Tommy, make sure Taryn is comfortable," flows from my numb lips. "Order a pizza, hang out in here– don't get high until I tell you to."

"Okay, Dev." Tommy's voice quivers like he's scared of me– or scared for me. "I'll do anything you say because I can't live this way."

"Why them?" Kurt's eyes drink in my wayward students. "I don't get it. They're not addicts."

"Malcolm's rehab is more of a looney bin." Tina answers for me. "But is any drug addict actually sane? My drug counselor dad would say we have issues."

Tommy tries to answer for himself. "My father is a preacher–"

"Deprogrammed?" Kurt looks at the kid with respect. "I saw a documentary on that a few weeks ago." Turning to Taryn, "What about you, sweetheart?"

"A budding me," I answer for Taryn, not trusting a polite response because she's turning purple after being called sweetheart. Mustn't insult the drug dealer in the room. "She's bipolar, and I'm waiting for Mrs. Elsberry to pray it away with Reverend Braxton."

Tommy and Taryn relax, finding me hilarious, but my comment has Tina and Kurt looking at me sideways. "What? I'm a good guy," I protest. "A high one, but a good one nonetheless."

Fingers outlining the wounds on my face, "How'd you get the black eye and fingernail scratches?" Tina asks again, refusing to let it go. Realizing I'm tight-lipped due to my captive audience, "Go to my bedroom in the back of the house and take a nap or something. Kurt will get us a few pizzas in a few."

"I'm not your bitch!" Kurt whisper-shouts, suddenly furious at the dynamic he shares with his drug-dealing partner in crime.

"Yes, you are." Tina waits until Tommy and Taryn leave the room. "Who went Rocky on your ass?"

"Beth," blurts out my numb lips. "She tricked me into seeing Essie, took me by surprise. I was high out of my mind, and I said some shit out of fear. Shouldn't tell a guy he's going to be a dad in an ambush."

"So she beat you up?" Kurt stands before me this time, only he looks concerned instead of disappointed like Tina did earlier. "That's not cool, man."

"I deserved it," I mutter, tears prickling at my eyes. I fucked our baby up. "I need more."

"I need cash," Kurt volleys back, brooking no room for argument.

Eyes hitching in Tina's direction, I know I need enough for me, for her, and a few hits for the kids so they're high when I leak our location. "We need to negotiate in private."

"What?" Tina swats my chest with the back of her hand, offended beyond belief. "What the fuck, Devon?"

"Enough," I snarl, struggling to stand. Kurt reaches down to help me to my feet. "Been beat up by enough girls tonight. Hit my daily quota, you'll have to wait until tomorrow to take your frustrations out on me."

Bouncing off the hallway walls, I lead Kurt to the bathroom I found earlier. At least this piece of shit Tina's camped out in has electricity and flowing water. Once inside the bathroom, I turn on the faucet to block us out in case Tina gets too curious. Leaning against the door, I check Kurt out.

The guy can't be much older than Ren. He must be a disappointment to his dad. The older Kurt is a rough dude, bald as a cue ball with a ratty goatee hanging to his chest. He's a drug dealer I pay without complaint, never extorting from him because I'm a cop. His son looks like a tiny geek who ought to be sitting in a classroom somewhere, not passing out baggies for cash.

"You don't look like a drug dealer," I slur, eyelids winning the fight against my vision. Eyes closed or not, I know damned well the guy is wearing a polo shirt.

"I am against my will." Kurt folds his arms over his bony chest. "Dad's making me work off all the child support he gave Mom."

"What?" I bark out, furious for him.

"Only the money that wasn't used on me, which was most of it." The resentment in Kurt's voice is so thick I almost choke on it for him. "You want your kid, right? You're not going to blame Essie?"

Eyes stinging, I don't dare open them. "Yeah, I love my kid– I'm terrified my drugged-out jizz fucked it up."

"Biology doesn't work that way," Kurt explains, but I don't dare believe him. "I go to school with your ex... or is Willow your brother's girl? I don't know which. Anyway, I'm can only go to community college because I have to work off Mom's debt with Dad."

"What are you going to study?" I ask out of pure curiosity. "If... If we could get the charges to stick on your dad, would you do it? Would you be free of the debt enough to go to school wherever you want?"

"Fuck," Kurt gasps, bending at the waist in shock. "He'd kill me– pre-med. I want to go to med school."

"After this is all over, talk to my dad," I offer sincerely. "He'll get you what you need as long as you have something to make it stick... but–"

"But not until I get you high for the next few days?" Kurt mutters wryly.

"Yeah, that." Chuckling at the ridiculousness, I slide down the bathroom door to land on my ass. "You're the world's worst drug dealer, you know that, right?" Wiggling around, I try to get the roll of cash out of my pocket, but it's wedged in there nice and tight. "Gimme whatever you got– I have to keep Tina and me high, plus a bit for the kids, until I let the Batcave know where I am."

"Trust me." Kurt reaches down, grabs the wad out of my hand, then begins counting. "You don't have enough to afford all I have on me, and you're too high to jump me."

"Clearly," I mutter, then start laughing like a crazy man. "I can't take you on and win, not after the whooping Bethany gave me."

Kurt ignores me, pockets my cash, then begins plucking baggies out of secret compartments in his jacket. Reminds me of Willow's old, puffy jacket, with how she could hide her stash without it being seen or felt, even during a hug.

"That's it?" I whine, glaring at the baggies lining the edge of the sink. "That's not enough for me, let alone for them. What else you got?"

"Cash?" Kurt holds out his hand. "Your badge means squat to me right now, and Tina already screwed me for you yesterday."

"Don't talk about her like that." I growl, getting frustrated and anxious. What I have in me is wearing off. Each high is lasting less time than the last. "Tina's like a sister to me."

"Jesus, Dev." Kurt slumps to sit on the edge of the bathtub. "Tina's the one Dad forced to show me the ropes." The way Kurt stresses ropes, I know he means drug dealing and sex. "She's the only girl I've touched because it freaked me out when I realized she'd been doing my dad."

"Eww…" I grimace in revulsion. "No offense, but your dad is disgusting."

Face twisted, Kurt looks like he's going to puke. "The man gets a lot of pussy."

"I'll blow you," I blurt out. Mouth going wide, I clamp my eyes shut. "I've done it before. Oh, my God, why can't I shut up?"

"You're high," Kurt offers as a logical explanation, but his voice is tight.

Eyes flicking open, I look at Kurt with surprise. The guy's pupils are blown like he's been mainlining drugs all day like I have been. Sliding to my knees, I wiggle closer to Kurt, knowing I can exploit this situation.

"I'm straight, but willing." Voice husky, I reach for his jacket. "You give me what's in here, I'll give you a blowjob and you can keep the cash."

"Devon." Kurt jerks away from me, looking ashamed. "I'm not a whore, and neither are you. Tina never fucked me for payment."

Even in the midst of a drug craze, the Nightmare is battering at my mind. "This isn't just about you, or the drugs. I've got to do this, and I can tell you want it." Before I can blink, I realize my hand is cupping the bulge in Kurt's jeans, fingers kneading.

"I'm not gay," Kurt sputters, but he doesn't fling my hand away.

"You're something," I negotiate.

"Bi," is his reply, but I take it as Kurt agreeing to our bargain.

Refusing to allow Kurt to not do as I want, "Gimme your jacket, then unzip your fly." I concentrate on the feel of nylon slipping between my fingers as I take possession of all the drugs, ignoring how the past is overlapping the present.

"I won't freak out on you," I say more to myself than to Kurt. "If I do anything strange to myself, it's not about you."

"Is it because you're high?" Kurt sounds uncertain, voice quivering.

"No, not because I'm high." Even drugged out of my mind, I can read his body language. "Sitting on the edge of the tub, or standing, it doesn't matter to me."

"I've never done this before." Kurt lifts his hips as he unzips, opting to sit on the tub.

With a deep breath, I stare down at his dick— it's a helluva lot smaller than Alejandro's. Pinker. Cleaner. Younger. Innocent. Safe. "Got sucked off in general, or by another dude?"

"Both." Kurt's voice breaks, but his cock hitching toward me is more telling.

"I'm in control here," I mutter underneath my breath. "This is my choice. Alejandro won't own me anymore."

"Who's Alejandro?"

"Doesn't matter— he's dead." My mouth swallowing Kurt cuts off the million questions the guy was about to ask me.

"Did you freak out?" Ms. Amelia's question draws me back into the present.

"Not in the way you'd think." Coughing, I try to clear my throat. "I was in control the entire time. Kurt is too nice– too innocent."

"Do you feel like you took advantage of Kurt?"

"Yes," I whisper like it's a secret, which is why his was the only note I sent.

"How old is he?"

"Nineteen."

"And you're only twenty," Ms. Amelia points out.

"Twenty-one next week," I remind her. "But it was because Kurt was innocent. I took advantage by giving him his first blowjob in exchange for his drug stash."

"Did Kurt enjoy it?"

Laughing, I just rub the back of my neck in answer.

"You said you didn't freak out in the way you thought I would assume. What did you mean by that, Devon?"

"I wanted to… I wanted to reenact what I did with Alejandro. Ya know, exorcise my demons, so to speak."

"*Wanted to*? But you didn't?"

"*Couldn't*," I stress. "I've felt nothing but shame over what happened between Ale and me– I didn't want to get off, but I *had* to. With Kurt, it really was funny because it was so awkward. Truthfully, if he'll forgive me, I want to be his friend when I go back home."

"Kurt wrote you back, Devon." Ms. Amelia reaches for an envelope on her desk. "Dr. Delaney gave this to me earlier today, asking if I was willing to read it, because he knows how you don't trust him."

"Read it?"

"In-coming mail must be read in case there's anything that could interfere with your progress." Ms. Amelia hands me the envelope. "I don't need to read it after hearing about Kurt. He won't hurt you."

Staring down at the heavy envelope, I gape in awe at the Boston University address. Toby– Auggie and Tina's baby uncle –was set to go there until Hurricane Tina hit Massachusetts. "Good. If Tina couldn't fuck Kurt up… if his dad couldn't fuck him up, I know I didn't."

"I'm more worried about your reaction than Kurt's. What did you mean by saying you wanted to reenact your past?"

Ms. Amelia rewarded me with Kurt's letter, proved her loyalty by not opening it first, so I owe her the truth in return. "I tried to jerk off while I did it, but it wasn't the same. I couldn't get hard."

"Was it upsetting that you couldn't get hard?"

"No," I answer in all honesty. "It was a relief. Kurt wasn't Alejandro. It was a different situation. I was in control, and I enjoyed it... until–" Head hitching backward, I laugh so hard Ms. Amelia can't help but join me even though she has no idea why. "No power-trip can get me to swallow. I ruined my fucking shirt."

Laughing with me, Ms. Amelia gives me information I'm sure wasn't meant for me to ever hear. "Kieren added that to his notes. How you kept saying you had jizz on you while you stripped naked. He was terrified for you."

"Honestly." Rubbing at the back of my neck, I chuckle. "If I hadn't been high, if I hadn't whored myself out, if it hadn't been about erasing Alejandro as the only guy, I would've enjoyed it. I liked the control– the power. It did nothing for me, couldn't get hard, but it was like... mentally arousing."

"That's what freaked you out?" Ms. Amelia fishes. "That makes a ton of sense. How do you feel about it now?"

Holding Kurt's letter like a talisman, "I've made peace with it, I guess. But it freaked me out in other ways. After how I was raised, I had this one woman, one man mentality. Like I could only ever love one woman, only be attracted to her, and if I lusted after anyone else, I didn't love her enough."

"Willow?" Ms. Amelia guesses right. An outsider would interpret her question wrong, but we've mastered shorthand conversations.

"Yeah, Willow." If anyone else asked me, I'd get defensive. I won't lash out like I would with Ren or Dad, but I freeze up and turn silent. But this is Ms. Amelia, and she needs to know me inside and out, so she can tell Dr. Delaney how to tweak my prescriptions.

"After Alejandro–" I decide to say his name instead of saying the Nightmare. Ale did it to me, and he shouldn't have power over me. "I couldn't get hard. What happened with Willow, I convinced myself it was about revenge, not that I truly wanted her or loved her."

"Did you?"

Nodding my head, I finally admit what Ren tried to yank out of me time and time again, and he was okay with it. I know damned well he knows because he feels the same way about Essie.

Conflicted.

"I was in love with Willow– I fucking wanted her. I'm in love with Essie, and I want her so badly that there's nothing that could possibly happen to me that would change how I feel. But I've hurt them both so much, I can't look in the goddamn mirror."

"Why?"

"I can accept that I mentally got off on sucking a dude, that maybe I might need to do that in the future. The need to feel in control because I feel powerless about everything else. I can accept that this fairytale I had built about only having sex with my wife is gone. But I can't accept how I destroyed Willow and Essie's friendship, when nothing could ever tear Ren and me apart– it's not fair, and I make myself sick."

"Their friendship is about them and has absolutely nothing to do with you."

"Yeah, Dr. Delaney loves talking about them *every-fucking-session*," I spit out, seething, unable to contain my stronger emotions. "He knows I won't share with him."

"Just because Dr. Delaney is your doctor, doesn't make him immune to being prideful. You're a challenge for him. This is exactly why our patients have multiple doctors and counselors, to make sure all facets are covered. Also why we deal with nutrition, fitness, and spirituality too."

"I get it– in theory. But that doesn't mean I have to like it. You know me and how I like to feel in control."

"There's a difference between feeling and *being* in control, Devon." Ms. Amelia looks me straight in the eye and blows my mind. "Have you been masturbating?"

"You don't know?" I go on the defensive, when ordinarily I'm an open book for Amelia. "I thought jerking off would be categorized with the rest of my body functions, with the data cataloged for future reference."

"It is," Ms. Amelia cedes. "But I thought's I'd ask, because I refuse to break your trust by looking at the daily reports."

Falling back into destructive patterns, "I bet Delaney looks," I draw out, smirking.

"Devon," is a chastisement. "We don't compile the data to get off on it. It's important. So, please, answer my question truthfully and stop deflecting."

"When I'm talking to you, sometimes I forget you're a therapist because you remind me so much of my Aunt Ginny. Then you go and say shit like that to remind me."

"I'm flattered, Devon– truly. Virginia Jamison sounded like a highly intelligent woman, judging by the notes she included in your admissions packet. Your grandmother and mother's mental histories were included, as well as their medical records."

"Nice, got the whole dang family involved."

"And half of your town," Ms. Amelia mutters wryly. "You're well-loved, Devon. Everyone wants the best for you."

She really knows how to cut to the quick. With a deep breath, I answer her uncomfortable question. "No, I'm not masturbating."

"Why not? Is it like before? You said you couldn't get aroused with Kurt."

"Ha-ha, no." Snorting, I formulate my thoughts into words. "I'm not broken or anything. I'm just stressed out and don't feel like jerking off with an audience jotting down how long I lasted and how big my load was."

"We don't…" Ms. Amelia trails off, but her blush calls her a liar. "You do realize it's a stress-reliever."

"No shit, really?" I mock-gasp in surprise. "I honestly don't have the desire. But I do lie in bed, *with a hard-on*."

"What do you think about?"

"Normal stuff, I guess." Blushing, I want to shy away from answering. But I trust Ms. Amelia enough to realize my answer must be important. "Past experiences. Stuff I want to do… Essie mostly, sometimes Willow. Even Kurt pops in there sometimes, but not him. How I felt during, I guess. I'm not broken. I'm not punishing myself. I just don't feel like doing it as I examine what I want and why I want it after being so narrow in my view of it."

"Your uncle–" Ms. Amelia pauses, pulls a tablet off her desk, then scans it. "Augustus Kline– Tina's brother?" She raises an eyebrow at our odd, non-blooded familial relationship. "Augustus Kline expressed that you were highly judgmental when it came to sex, how this represses you."

"Oh, you need to dive into that fucker's head for thirty seconds, then try to say that with a straight face." Chuckling, I realize Bethany may be good for Auggie, thesis be damned. Ms. Amelia is a comfort, because what makes her a good therapist reminds me of why Bethany used to be my best friend.

"Being here has given me nothing but time… sucking off Kurt was enlightening. Admitting I wanted Willow has helped. The journaling. The fantasizing without jerking off. Being sober. Being even. I know myself better now, and I will admit I was a judgmental prick who wasn't very compassionate about other people's bizarre needs."

"Good." Ms. Amelia looks relieved, and I realize she was truly worried I was freaking out about Alejandro and Kurt. "Next time we talk, it's time we began discussing your mother."

"Fuck, Amelia," I gasp breathlessly. "I give you an inch, you take a goddamn mile."

"I'll make a deal with you– two deals." Ms. Amelia smiles brightly, knowing she has me. Leaning forward, she pats my knee. "If you open up about your mother, I'll tell Delaney to sign-off on your family visitation."

"Okay," I breathe out in a rush, relieved.

"*But–*" Ms. Amelia raises a brow in my direction, knowing how I operate. "If you don't half-ass it and actually let me in, I'll arrange a lunch between you, Taryn, and Tommy."

"You bitch," I mutter in appreciation. "You win. *You win.*"

"Never forget, Mr. Mason." Ms. Amelia smirks at me. "There is a difference between feeling and being in control."

"Shit," I hiss, frustrated. "I need to *be* in control, especially when I'm stuck in a place that ought to be in a dystopian novel. Anarchy!"

Laughing heartily, Ms. Amelia truly is a remarkable woman. "Make the most of being here, Devon, because we're not teaching you how to feel in control– we're teaching you how to *be* in control." Rising from her seat, she gesture to the door. "Go forth and do yoga."

"I'd rather go masturbate," I deadpan, hearing Ms. Amelia's laughter as I cross the desert hot walkways toward to my session with Leo.

CHAPTER FORTY-THREE

Willow Prynne

Bouncing down the back staircase to the kitchen, I do what I always do. Pretend I'm not pissed the fuck off. I paste a smile on my face, just in case someone is milling around. Everyone is lying to me, and it's grating on my last nerve.

Clover's acting so sheepish, I'm about to just scream **I know!** But there must be a method to her madness, so I've tried to let it go as everyone I know lies directly to my face. Do they think me stupid?

I feel so goddamn paranoid.

The only time I let the anger go is when it's just Ren and me– we forget the world. But that's not a healthy way to live, using my boyfriend as my newest escape. Can't drink. Can't toke up. Can't scream bloody murder in the faces of those who've wronged me without looking like a spiteful, little bitch.

God! I can see it from their point of view, but they're not seeing it from mine. Silence ascends the staircase, so I light up a cig before I hit the backdoor. The nicotine hits my veins before I land on the bottom step, instantly calming my nerves.

"Willow," Auggie chastises me from his seat at the kitchen island, causing me to release a girly meep– cigarette landing on the tile floor with a single bounce.

After bending down to pick it up, I give a cursory glance at the filter, then take a deep drag. "I'm ten feet from the backdoor."

"And you couldn't wait?" Auggie looks up at me, spoon filled with Lucky Charms clutched in his giant paw. "The fact that you couldn't is quite telling."

"I'm not in the mood for you today," I snarl. Leaning against the sink, I reach back to flick ash into the basin. At least the kitchen window is open, and the screen door is letting fresh air in.

"Wake up on the wrong side of the bed?" Auggie arches his fuzzy brow while pouring more cereal into his bowl. The beast can go through a box in a single sitting.

"Do you want me to lie?" I blow smoke rings just to be a dick, but Auggie doesn't find me amusing.

"I'd prefer if you didn't," is said from around a mouthful of cereal. "Is that all you're having for breakfast?

I toss the pack of Marlboros and the lighter on the counter, then reach into the fridge to grab a Coke. "Breakfast of champions– nicotine, caffeine, and sugar." With the flick of my finger, I crack the can open.

With narrowed eyes, Auggie and I hold a staring contest, all the while I smoke and he chews. "I tried to visit my parents last night, but Robin turned me away at the front door. He said Essie was in there, but I didn't care. Then I tried to visit Clover, and *Seth* turned me away."

"Oh!" The spoon disappears into Auggie's big mouth. I wait him out while he chews, and the motherfucker reloads his mouth so he doesn't have to talk.

"You said you preferred if I didn't lie," I remind Auggie. "*I know.*"

"Oh," is a soft murmur as he stares down at the pink milk swirling around his bowl. Auggie does the spoon routine again.

"You were supposed to be my mentor, Mr. Kline. Yet now you've lost the ability to speak." I take a big gulp of Coke, finding enjoyment in the bubbles stinging my tongue. "I feel so betrayed right now. By everyone. I'm a ball of rage."

"Don't make a habit of smoking in here, Willow." Completely dismissing me, Auggie tucks the cereal box closed instead of eating the entire box like usual. "Maybe eat a PopTart or something."

"Auggie?" I bark out, then take a deep drag as he stares up at me. "Do you have any idea how you're making me feel right now?"

"Loyalty is a wicked mistress, Willow." Auggie goes about cleaning up after himself, saying no more. When he makes a move to flee the kitchen, I step in his path. "You feel betrayed, and it's understandable. But I feel so goddamn torn right now– so torn it's easier for Robin and Seth to turn you away at the door instead of look you in the eye."

"Clover needs to tell me." Gasping, I try to stop the tears from coming. "I can't live like this. I know you know. I know everyone fucking knows."

"Ren doesn't," Auggie interrupts me.

"I told him."

"Oh," is all Auggie can say.

"I needed someone to talk to, someone who puts me first, even if it's a lie."

"What's that supposed to mean?"

"I know Ren puts Devon and Essie first– I'm just the girl he fucks."

"Willow." Sighing deeply, Auggie grabs a hold of my arms, big fingers curling. "I'm sorry." Eyes closing, "You've known for a few weeks, and it's driving you nuts. Imagine how Clover feels right now. I said it was about divided loyalty. Clover needs to do this on her own time. It's about you, but it's not."

Jerking out of Auggie's grip, I stalk away, then slump to a stool at the island. "I get so sick of hearing people say that to me. *My* boyfriend fucked *my* cousin in *my* car, but it wasn't about *me*. I'm not supposed to be upset because I was going to break up with him anyway, like that erases it. The fact that it hurt me doesn't matter. My entire family and half the town has lied to my face for nearly nineteen years, but I'm not to take ownership in how much it hurts me, because the pain belongs to Clover. Do you hear yourself?"

"Do you hear yourself?" Auggie leans his elbows on the island, directly across from me. Looking at me with compassion and understanding, I know Auggie's hurting for me. "*I'm sorry for everything.*"

Huffing in gasps of air, I'm close to suffocating on a sob. "I need someone to understand," I whine. "Someone who puts me first and gives a shit."

"You're blinded by your pain, going around hurting others and not realizing it. We all let you get away with it because we feel guilty. That was the major reason all the bullshit that happened eight months ago happened."

"Here I thought that was you throwing a tantrum." Reaching back, I grab my smokes and lighter. I don't give a shit if it pisses Auggie off or not, I light up another one.

"Life isn't a competition. We're allowed to love as many people as humanly possible without it taking away the love we feel for you. Kieren does put you first, but you're tied up there with his family. Ren's loyal– if he pushed Essie and Devon away to prove he loved you, he wouldn't be the man you love, now would he?"

"I just–"

"You say you're a ball of rage, how do you think Clover feels? She's terrified over how you'll react. I suggest you do nothing but tell her you love her. The guilt that woman feels– she's not the Clover I knew when I was a boy. That Clover reminded me of *you*."

"I can't wrap my head around what you're saying, Auggie."

"*Try*," he begs, leaning farther over the island. With his fingertips, he flicks the cigarette out of my mouth, then he stomps it into the tile. "Clover lost her husband– and I know this is where you scream how Sam was your father *–too bad*. I'm talking about Clover right now, *not you*. She lost her husband, has been raising her children, and is terrified her oldest will hate her for life. Added to all that, she's grieving as she moves on with Malcolm. Imagine how scary it must be for her to take that leap of faith, to move on, to move on with another man. A man with too many kids– kids who are at each other's throats. Then throw a pregnant Essie into the mix."

"*I get it*," I stress, the rage filling me until its vibration is all I feel.

"No, you don't." Auggie reaches up to smooth my hair away from my face, a look of affection written across his expression. "You're young, and no one blames you for feeling as you do. But you're not innocent in all of this."

"What the fuck, Auggie?" With the back of my hand, I fling his away. "What have I done to any of you?"

"Hold on to that self-righteous indignation, little girl. Its fire will keep you warm at night after you push us all away." Auggie doesn't even blink as I flinch back as if he struck me with an open fist. "You fuck up, we still love you. If we fuck up, you want us to bleed for life. You're pissed at your cousin for messing around with your *ex*-boyfriend, but you fucked me in front of Robin."

"Are we gonna go *there* right now? Yes, we are," I snarl. "I didn't know!" I shout in outrage, so angry I can only manage to breathe in jerky stops and starts. "I didn't know! That's on you."

"Doesn't matter, does it?" Auggie is calm in the face of my rage. "We're not talking about me– we're talking about you. Ignorance isn't bliss, and I won't let you become a hypocrite.

You still did it. You watched Isis kiss me, then later that night you had no issue with me touching you– after you nearly fucked Ren in the hallway at Rush, then tried to blame him when there was no blame to be had. You wanted Ren– full stop. You wanted me, even though you knew about Isis and Rob. You didn't say no."

"I couldn't," I murmur, mind spinning.

"Did I rape you, Willow?" Auggie tilts his head, looking like a hawk sighting prey. "Every step we took was your choice. When you told me to back off, I did. Then there was Devon– you didn't say no. This was why Ren was so wicked pissed at you– you were supposed to say no, but you said yes. Yes." Auggie's throat opens, bellowing the single word until it sinks beneath my skin. "*YES!*"

"I was confused. I…" shaking my head, I try to clear the fog that has descended. "I did what I thought everyone wanted me to do."

"Excuses are for children, Willow."

"Harsh," I rasp, pained soul deep.

"If you can't give Clover the benefit of the doubt for choices she made at sixteen when it dealt with creating a life– *your life* – then you can't make excuses for choices you made at eighteen when it was only about having sex. Clover's was life or death. Yours mean nothing in the greater scheme of things."

"It meant something to me," I mutter hollowly, feeling gutted and put in my place.

"You know that's not what I fucking meant." Reaching across the counter, Auggie grabs my wrist, then yanks me roughly. "It always takes two, but you keep going around like you have no blame. But what you don't seem to realize, there is no blame to be had. It's just sex. It's just love. You keep equating it as if we got married, or had a kid, or killed someone– nothing is permanent besides death. People change. We fall out of lust or love, and we're allowed to bow out of a relationship."

"Don't trivialize how I feel, goddamn you!"

"I'm not, but you're blowing it out of proportion for some reason, dwelling in your self-created misery. We all did what we did, and it changed us. So we deal and move the fuck on, Willow."

"What am I supposed to do, Auggie?"

"Move the fuck on, Willow." He releases my wrist so quickly, I almost fall off the stool. "We know you're hurt. We know we hurt you. It's fucking unfair, but life isn't fair. Grow the fuck up– you're not the only one with issues. We get it, you're like a goddamn broken record. But what you seem to forget is how you've hurt us too. We've moved on, but you won't. *You won't.*"

The doorbell gonging has me jumping off the stool. Wide-eyed, I stare at Auggie while bleeding shame and confusion.

"Don't." Auggie snaps his fingers in front of my face, snapping me out of it. "You made choices, not mistakes– just the same as we have. They've shaped you into the incredible woman you are. Move on." Leaving the room, he shouts over his shoulder. "I suggest you remember everything I said while you deal with your guests."

"My guests?" I watch in horror, eyes narrowing as Auggie swings the front door open to reveal Kieren and Essie. Eyes watering, bottom lip quivering, I don't have the strength to cover up my pain with anger.

No one gets it. It's not about Clover giving me up for adoption to my grandparents. It's not about Essie losing her virginity to Kieren, or having sex with Devon in my car. It's the lies. Lies. Lies. *LIES!*

Lies break promises, loyalty, and trust. Lies ruin lives.

Is it so hard to tell the goddamn truth?

Sucking in air, I try hard not to cry as I stare at Essie down the length of the hallway. The two most influential women in my life will always be Clover and Essie. The woman I believed to be my sister is actually my mother, and the woman who is my cousin but I saw her as my sister.

Scuffing my sneakers as I do my walk of shame, I can't look anyone in the eye. It's worse because I feel cornered. This must be an intervention of some sort.

"Do you want a drink, or something to eat, or something– anything?" *Bone marrow? A blood donation? An egg? Forget a piece of my liver or a lung– they're probably too damaged.*

Refusing to look at anyone, I play the mistress of the house. Until Isis reigns at the Spook House, the duty falls upon my shoulders when Robin isn't present. Mary Prynne and Clover Webster would be disappointed in me if I didn't at least offer snacks. Clover would probably go whip up a five-course breakfast.

I catch Kieren and Essie sharing a look, like they're not sure how to answer. "Some water?" I turn on my heels to head back to the kitchen. "I need some. I'll meet you in the living room, unless Auggie soiled it again."

"Monster," Auggie growls, embarrassed. "That is *not* how it sounds."

"I don't know what other way that could possibly sound." Kieren's amusement relaxes me, but Essie's giggle has my guts clenching.

"One blowjob. In the kitchen. Almost nine months ago before we even moved in here…" Auggie doesn't appreciate my payback for handing me a new asshole this morning. "That's the only time, dammit! So now when she catches me kissing Robin anywhere in the house, she says it's soiled."

"Wait– not with Rob, right?" Essie sounds horrified.

"You'd have to fumigate the entire fucking place if that's the case." Ren volleys back and forth with Auggie, both of them releasing that devastating man laugh. "Nina?"

"Of course." Auggie sounds proud. "Since we closed the Playroom, Rob said he'd cut my balls off it I touched anyone but him or Isis. So I'm a bit testy."

"Don't you mean testes?" Ren knows how to make my cousin giggle with crude, middle school humor– damn him all to hell.

Auggie finds me hiding like a coward, leaning against the counter next to the refrigerator, hugging an armful of cold water bottles.

Large palm cupping my cheek, he kisses my forehead. Words vibrating against my flesh, "I'm proud of you for behaving like my Good Girl."

Snorting, I roll my eyes. "You emotionally exhausted me with your attack, which was your plan. Zombiefied."

"I did that because I love you." Pulling away, Auggie kisses the tip of my nose, then shoves me out of the kitchen. "It's in your best interests to just listen. Trust Mr. Kline."

"Famous last words," I mutter underneath my breath as I shuffle down the hallway. Auggie doesn't follow me into the living room, so I guess his portion of this shitty journey has ended.

I find Ren and Essie sitting side-by-side on the sofa I refuse to touch. I wanted to kill it with fire, but Auggie's partial to it.

Sighing, it really is too bad they look so good together. If they had a kid, it would grow up to be a model.

"Since Auggie isn't joining us, I guess we have an extra water," I say in a rush, voice warbling. I place a bottle in front of Ren, then one in front of Essie. I double-fist the others as I take my seat on the coffee table.

Seriously, I'm never touching that sofa again.

"So…" I trail off, wanting to laugh at how formal I'm being. Last night, Ren and I screwed in the half bath while we waited for the pizza guy, then we each ate a pizza while leaning over the kitchen island. Less than twelve hours later…

We all pause to unscrew the caps on our water bottles, then take tiny sips, like we need to wet our mouths for the verbal battle to come. "Do I really sound like a broken record?" I ask Kieren in a no-bullshit voice.

"What are you talking about?" Eyebrows knitted in confusion, Ren tries and fails to silently communicate with his eyes.

"Something Auggie said, is all…" Taking a deep breath, I let the words roll out. "I try to behave. Obviously I don't necessarily always accomplish it."

Essie and I share a private grin, then quickly dart our eyes away.

The last time I saw Essie, I was refusing to apologize for trying to beat the shit out of her. There's a fading scratch mark on her perfect cheek. My scalp gives a subtle warning throb where I'm missing a chunk of hair– Clover tore it out when she yanked me off Essie.

Well-earned battle wounds.

"There's a ton of things I don't say." Gesturing at Ren, "And I know if I don't keep my mouth shut, you'll drop me in a heartbeat."

"That's not–" Ren tries to deny it, but Essie cuts him off.

"It's the look on your face," she explains. "Not anything you say. Dev always looked at Ren that way. It's louder than any words you could scream."

"Oh," I huff, sounding just like Auggie did earlier. "I can't help that, now can I? Kinda involuntary."

"I didn't say you were a broken record." Essie looks at me like she used to, no longer that pitiful, apologetic pout, and it makes me miss her so goddamn much my heart throbs. "It's only when we come face-to-face that you erupt, so I've stayed out of your way the best I could."

"Auggie browbeat me before you got here, so I'm too exhausted for that." A sardonic chuckle escapes my mouth before I can stop it.

Uncomfortable silence descends, and I have no idea why they're here. Ren and I have clear-cut boundaries we abide by. We hang around Wreck & Ruin, since Langdon Stone and I didn't sign up for summer courses. Then we binge-watch while stuffing our faces, followed by various sexual activities to ease our stress. Ren and I are about escapism, with no talk of anything important. It's too shallow, and we both want more, but we're both too terrified to move forward.

Essie's in the way– I'm at fault, though. I can admit it.

The grandfather clock clicking makes me feel like a Jeopardy contestant.

"I try to say how I'm feeling, but someone always cuts me off with how it doesn't matter." I speak down at the water bottle in my hands, since I can't look either one of them in the eye. "Everyone else has issues, and I'm just trying to figure out when mine will be as important as theirs."

"You had no problem expressing yourself a couple days ago." The venom in Kieren's voice draws me up short.

"Ren, don't," Essie orders, placing a hand on Ren's thigh. "Don't go there."

Ren goes there– "You're right. You keep your mouth shut around me, so I assumed that's how you were with everyone. I didn't want to believe it. But Violet called me while you were fighting with Essie, so I could listen to you guys go for each other's throats."

"Oh, that explains it." Ren's been different with me the past two nights. Doesn't speak. Isn't playful. Doesn't want to watch TV, but shovels in as much food as he can. Fucks me quickly, like he has something to prove, then leaves. "I guess that's why you're here."

Essie realizes something before I do. Kieren's about to lose his shit, and I've never seen him do that before. "Ren, don't–"

"You know what?" Ren shifts on the sofa, face warped with anger. "I've got to get this out. What happens here today will determine what happens between me and you." Movements rapid, Ren points between us. "I heard some shit that really fucking insulted me– shit that was said in front of the twins. *The twins*," he stresses. "This time next week, they'll be my stepbrother and stepsister."

"I–"

"No!" Ren barks, pointing in my face. "In front of Clover. My *stepmother*. Goddamn it, no more. I fucking mean it."

"Okay." Tears prickling my eyes, I concede immediately. Upsetting Ren isn't worth it, not even if I have to bottle up how I'm feeling.

"Devon and I are private men." Actual pain is riding Kieren's voice. "With the shit we've gone through… our sex lives are *private*. We may joke around with Auggie because he's Auggie, but that's it. I don't give two shits if you girls want to do locker room talk, because that's gonna happen between me and Dev. But when I heard you both shouting about Devon and me in front of Clover and the twins… I thought I was going to be sick."

Vision clouded with tears, I stare down in shock to see Essie and I are gripping each other's hand.

"I wasn't going to make this about me and you today, but… this possessive shit has got to stop. I lived through it with Devon, and I can't do it with you too. It's a slap in the face to hear you girls screaming about the sister-code, like just because you called dibs I lose my right to say who I want."

Squeezing my hand, Essie forces me to meet her gaze, and the same comforting, blue eyes as Clover's shines back at me. Essie knows where Ren's headed, and she doesn't like it one bit.

"Kieren," I try to interrupt his tirade, but it's like once he's started, he can't stop.

"Willow," Kieren says sharply to gain my undivided attention. "Even if we get married, you don't own me. If I decide to cheat on you, I will. It's my right as a human being to decide what I do with my body. There's no sister-code or bro-code. If your facial expressions are involuntary, so is my looking at someone I find attractive– hating every girl I look at isn't going to change anything. Acting possessive and jealous is only going to suffocate me. It's not flattering– it's insulting. But it boils down to trust. If you really *knew me*, you'd know I'd never cheat on you. You'd *trust* me."

"Ren." With her free hand, Essie grips Kieren's chin, tugging him to look at her. "Jealousy and possessiveness aren't about you– it's about Willow. Everyone has insecurities, and Devon did a number on her."

Involuntarily, my hand squeezes Essie's tightly. She flips her hand around, lacing her fingers with mine. We're in this together, no matter what. Unbidden, the fucking tears start streaming down my cheeks.

"I don't give a shit," Kieren mutters to Essie, then turns to glare at me in open defiance. "Willow, this is a hard limit for me. I tell you I want you. I show you I want you. Trust me. Believe me– don't make me *prove* I want you." He stares at me, unmoved by my tears. "I won't play mind games. After how I grew up, I can't handle anything but stability. Take it, or leave me."

"Take it," flows without hesitation from my tear-dampened lips. "I'll try, but I can't promise I won't fuck up from time to time."

Hardness softening from his face, Kieren looks relieved. "I have one other hard limit. Devon's a given."

"Essie." I already fucking knew that. It hurts, but I knew it. Breath hitching, I nearly choke on a sob.

"It's not what you think, Willow," Ren murmurs sadly. "I love Essie because she's Essie. But you put your hands on her, and I can't live with that. No matter how much I may love you, I can't... I just can't. It reminds me too much of my mom, how she'd hit Dev."

Hand moving to cup Essie's tiny belly, Ren rubs in a possessive circle, like the baby in there belongs to him. "My niece or nephew is a defenseless bundle of cells right now– fragile. Because of Dev and Essie, it's a part of both of us." Ren gestures between us.

"I know– I'm so fucking ashamed of myself." Sobbing silently, tears fly as I nod up and down rapidly. "I'm so sorry."

"My other hard limit is physical violence. If you hit anyone ever again, outside of defending yourself or sport, I'm going to hit you," Kieren threatens. "I mean, punch you the fuck out so you can see what it's like. Never again. Use your goddamn words. It's not cute. It's not badass. It's abusive and irrational."

Snorting through a sob, Essie starts to laugh in short bursts. "Oh, my God. Prynnes say they're pacifists, but we're bloodthirsty... am I hearing Ren right?"

Covering my face with my palms, I giggle through the tears. "If I fuck up and hit someone, go ahead and clobber me."

"Kieren Mason just became a man," Essie murmurs in awe.

"This–" Ren gestures between Essie and me. "Stops. Today. It doesn't matter how many people we've had sex with, or when, or why, or how often. When I heard you guys fighting over tallies, calling each other sluts and whores, I almost broke my fucking phone. I've had a lot of sex and it doesn't have a goddamn thing to do with either of you– it's none of your business. I don't regret it, and I never will. But since I've been with ten times more people than both of you combined, all I feel is judged."

"No!" I can't help but reach out to Kieren. Cradling his hand to my chest, my words are pleading. "No, I'm not judging you."

"It's different for girls," Essie tries to explain. "The guys aren't even in the equation."

"I don't give a shit, Essie." Ren pulls his hand away from me, like I'm the one who pissed him off. "You two are going to be the biggest feminine influences in this baby's life, and I don't want that bullshit infecting it. No more jealousy. No more comparison. No more lashing out in violent fits of rage."

"Don't we get a say in anything," I voice for both Essie and myself.

"No," Ren shuts me down immediately. "My brother and his kid are all I give a shit about right now. If I have to, I'll give up what I have growing with you, Willow. It's life or death, and stability is the only thing that's going to help Devon survive."

"So everyone's supposed to stay silent for life, because how they feel doesn't fucking matter?"

Eyes bulging from his skull, Kieren turns into a stranger. Bellowing with the frustrated rage I feel, "It. Is. NOT. About. You. Willow!" His words hit me in the face from an inch away as he crowds me, the force of it nearly knocking me off the coffee table.

In the blink of an eye, Auggie's tearing Kieren away to pin him to the wall, and Essie's tugging me into her lap, her sobs shaking us both. But I'm not going to stay silent this time.

Charging to my feet, I bellow right back at my boyfriend. "I'll trust you. I won't hit anyone. But what I won't do is stay silent." All the pent-up rage and agony pours out my throat in a stream of violence. "How. I. Fucking. Feel. Matters. Goddamn you!"

With Auggie holding him back, Kieren unleashes his own verbal assault. "I don't give a shit if Devon fucked a thousand members of your family in your car, or if you spread your legs for every member of the Playroom. Grow the fuck up, Willow! We've got a life growing in this room, and I'm visiting my brother in a goddamn mental facility tomorrow!"

"Hey." Auggie's voice is low and soothing as he rubs circles against Kieren's chest. "Back off, okay? Calm down."

"I can't take it." Pacing, I yank at my hair as tears drench my t-shirt. "I can't take it. No one lets me get it out. Always stopping me, making assumptions, putting words in my mouth, thinking they know me so well I don't need to speak ever again. No one gives a shit about what I feel, because everything else is always going to be more important."

"I care," Essie's whispered words are soft but hit with force. "I care– it was me caring too much about how you felt that got us into this mess. I'm not assuming anything, so tell me."

Sobbing silently, I palm my forehead and just stare at the ceiling. "I have a boyfriend I can't talk to, so we ended up here right now. I've got a best friend I miss so goddamn much it's killing me, but she's a stranger."

"I'm right here." Essie's fingers wrap around my wrist, tugging me back to the coffee table, forcing me to talk face-to-face with her. Auggie keeps a shocked Kieren over by the wall. "Tell me how you feel."

"It's the lies." Essie nods, understanding. "I miss you, but I feel like I don't know you. I mean, I miss the person I thought you were, but that's not who you truly are."

Essie sucks in a big gulp of air and releases it in a hissing sound. "Fuck."

Snorting, I couldn't agree more. "This has nothing to do with who we've fucked," I mutter bluntly. "What I thought was reality has crashed, and now I feel like shit. Horrible. A lot of it has to do with Clover, but most of it's on me. But I'm blaming you because you didn't tell me the truth."

"How so?" Essie hands me a bottle of water, since I could barely choke the words out of my raw throat.

I take a sip as an excuse to figure out what I want to say. "This has nothing to do with Ren– he can keep staring at your tits. *I* stare at your tits." Gesturing to Essie's chest, I can't help but turn speechless. "Pregnancy has only improved you."

"Thanks," Essie mutters dryly, not impressed. "I think."

"It's about Devon, but not how everyone automatically assumes. My bitching about the sister-code is my own guilt, but it's your fault. I've learned a lot in the past eight months." Eyes flicking up, I meet Auggie's concerned gaze. "Mr. Kline is *never* right. If only you would've told me how you felt about Devon, I would've just been his friend. *I* broke the fucking code, not you!"

Turning away abruptly, I can't look anyone in the eye. Huffing in air, I try to stop the sobs from releasing, but the tears flow anyway. "I feel like I don't know you. One of the most important things in a person's life, and you kept it from me. Now I feel like shit, like I was smearing Devon in your face, kissing him in front of you. I make myself sick."

"On your birthday." Essie flashes me a private smile only I will understand. "You should've accepted the real gift I was giving you." I don't miss how Essie's eyes dart to Kieren.

"I know. Believe me, I do."

Essie reaches for my hands, taking both in hers. "My turn to explain. No bullshit. All truth. Will you listen?"

"Okay," I mutter meekly.

"Everyone needs one person who looks up to them, makes them feel important. Like they matter." Essie pauses to make sure I understand how she understands why I've been so frustrated at being silenced. "You were that person for me, and I didn't want to break the fantasy.

"I was too young to mess around with Devon, but I was addicted to his brand of crazy. He made me feel important. If I was young, you were a baby, and I couldn't talk about oral sex, masturbation, and *I'll only put the tip in* with a child."

Sucking in a breath to speak, Essie halts me with a raised fingertip.

"That's not an insult. You really were an actual child at the time. But then Devon turned on me, changed how I viewed myself, and I needed you more than ever. My boyfriend– *my best friend* –called me a whore in the middle of a packed hallway in front of most of the school, and it changed me. I started working for Elma because it kept me from doing something drastic, and I forgot Devon even existed.

"Then what happened with Ren happened, and I no longer just felt like a whore. God, the last thing I ever wanted you to know was *that*." Essie stares down at our hands. "Zip forward a billion years later, Devon's acting like a human being and you're no longer fucking around with the PedoBear in this room–"

"Hey, now!" Auggie warns, but there's laughter riding his tone.

"You know how you keep saying your feelings don't matter? In that second, mine didn't. Seeing you and Devon happy was more important than anything I wanted– that's all I wanted. So I kept my mouth shut, because I wanted you to have what I never did."

"I wish you hadn't kept your mouth shut." The regret and shame are so thick I can barely look in the mirror. "Everything would've been different."

"I didn't realize that until today." Essie leans back, then looks me dead in the eyes. "I know you and I will never be the same, because we're no longer the same people we were last year. I know it's going to take a lot of work, but I'm willing to try to become adult friends, if you are."

"I'll try, but it's going to be hard." Voice quivering, I pull my hands away to hug myself. "It hurts."

"I know how you're feeling right now, Willow, because we're feeling the exact same way." Standing from the sofa, Essie looks down at me. "Never doubt that." Turning to Kieren, "You two need to be alone right now, maybe go discuss our living situation. I need to go talk to Robin."

"C'mon." Auggie steps away from the wall, eyeing Ren for a heartbeat or two. "Rob's up in Isis's room, getting it ready for you."

Busying myself with the discarded water bottles, I ignore Kieren because I feel ashamed over how we screamed at each other. It's not right. I'm so used to fighting it out, I don't know how to *use my goddamn words*.

Even now, the rage is riding beneath the surface, because I'm so frustrated I can barely breathe. Every time I try to use my words, someone is cutting me off, telling me there are worse problems in the world, and I should just let it go and move on. How do I move on if I'm not allowed to voice what's wrong in the first place?

If I wasn't stifled, Essie and I might've attempted to work this bullshit out months ago. But everyone around me kept telling me to shut up and deal with it, assuming I was upset about her being with Devon. By the time I'd see Essie face-to-face, the frustration had built up to violent levels, and I couldn't hold back the torrent of pain that spilled out my mouth. In the moment, the hows and whys didn't matter to me, because Essie and Devon still did something wrong, and no one seemed to give a shit.

That's why I told Kieren I refuse to keep my mouth shut and go with the flow for the rest of my life. I *know* it's not about me– that's not what I'm trying to express. Devon would've been helped a decade ago if anyone would've held him accountable for his actions. If someone other than Clover tried to do that with me when I was growing up, I wouldn't have majored in pot-smoking and binge-drinking. If Essie would've opened up to me, she wouldn't have been a blowjob queen in high school. So, now, when I see a problem, I try to address it immediately, but everyone tells me to shut the fuck up like I'm a pestering tattletale.

Devon and Essie fucking in my car while Kieren spilled their mutual nightmare was not normal, rational behavior. Yes, the fact that we hadn't broken up was important, because people don't do that shit to those they love. They get closure first. Instead of everyone telling me to shut the fuck up, they should've heard me and gotten Devon help weeks sooner.

As I enter the kitchen, Kieren follows me a few feet behind like a stormy shadow. I've never seen him act like that before. It's been a few months of not talking about anything of any importance, and we're both bottling it up. The main reason I don't talk to Kieren is because I understand he's under a ton of pressure, and I don't want to dump my shit in his lap.

I know my problems aren't Kieren's problems, so I keep my trap shut. But, at the same time, it motherfucking hurts that we can't talk to each other about things that are important. What's the sense of having a boyfriend if you're too scared to open up in fear he'll scream how what you have to say isn't important.

In uncomfortable silence, I can feel Kieren watching me as I pour the water from the bottles into the houseplants lining the kitchen window sill. I'm not going to dump it down the drain, and I'm not going to drink it.

After tossing the bottles in the recycling, I turn to face Kieren. Refusing to back down, I don't cower. I look my boyfriend in the eyes, because I won't feel ashamed for feeling as I feel.

"I have something I need to show you." Kieren's not backing down either. Eyes pinning me in place, he curls his fingertips in a come-hither motion. "C'mere. Hop on."

"Hop on?" Eyebrows scrunching together in the center of my forehead, I just gape as Ren turns to give me his back, then crouches slightly.

"Hop on– I'll give you a ride to our destination."

Baffled, I do what I want to do. Striding across the kitchen, I jump on Kieren's back, releasing a relieved laugh as I move. Arms and legs wrapped tightly around my boyfriend, I hitch a ride to wherever the hell he wants to take me.

CHAPTER FORTY-FOUR

Kieren Mason

Feeling like a dick, I hoist Willow up onto my back, then stride down the hallway toward the front door. I've got to get out of the Spook House, because my words are echoing hollowly around the place.

Such a dick...

"Get the knob for me, Spanky." Voice light and teasing, I turn to the side to give her access. Once the door's open, I walk us through it, then pause for her to close it behind us. Stalking down the front walk, with Willow bouncing against my back, I decide I better stop being a dick.

"I... uh– I'm stressed out about seeing Dev tomorrow." Stammering, I step out onto the sidewalk. Willow doesn't respond, and I hate it. It hadn't dawned on me that she was quiet because she feared I wouldn't like her if she spoke– at least that was one of the things I took away from our shouting match.

Willow and I both pretend we don't see Dad lurking in the backyard of the Pink Taco Hut. Idiots think they're fooling us. Weeks ago, Dad asked if he could tell me something important, but he said I couldn't tell Willow. So I told him no just to mess with his head.

Everyone thinks Willow and I are morons who can't see what's going on right in front of our faces, so I kind of get where Willow's coming from with her outburst.

Dick.

Tugging on Willow's arm, I swing her around to face me, then make sure she lands on her feet. One of the most startling things about Willow is how she reminds me of one of the brown-eyed Precious Moments figurines Grammy Maeve used to collect.

I may have talked a big game back there in the living room, but it was all bullshit. One second of looking into Willow's huge eyes, and I begin spiraling down until I'm fucking lost, which is terrifying.

"Dick or not, I'm not going to apologize for what I said back there." Placing my hands on Willow's shoulders, I make sure she can't get away from me. "I think we both needed to say our piece."

My words are met with silence and watery eyes filled with steely determination. Willow's not going to back down, and neither am I, so this phony bullshit we've been pulling has to stop.

It's quite possible Willow's pissed enough to give me the silent treatment– a specialty of Devon's that he passed down to Raven.

Sliding my palms up the column of Willow's throat, she jerks slightly, as if afraid I'm going to wring her neck. As I cup her face in my hands, she relaxes. "I do care about how you feel, and I want to hear your opinions. I do need you to tell me what you want from me, because I'm not a mind-reader."

"But we're not like that," Willow whispers, and I hate how her bottom lip quivers.

"Not at first– no…" I draw out, trying to buy time as I figure how to explain what I mean. "At first, everything was crazy. All the drama. I just wanted to get to know you through having fun– be your friend. Build a stable foundation for later. Lusting after somebody is hot as fuck, but if you can't talk to 'em…"

"I didn't think I could talk to you." You know what's worse than falling into those giant eyes? Having Willow close them on me– shut me out.

"*Ohhh…* I heard you loud and clear." A dark chuckle escapes my mouth as Willow glares at me, all because I got her to look at me again. "I don't want to get into anything deep in the middle of the sidewalk, not with Dad hiding against the side of the Pink Taco Hut so he can eavesdrop all stealth-like. But I just wanted you to know that when I get back from Arizona, I want us to have a different kind of relationship."

"That's terrifying." Willow takes the words right out of my mouth.

Hands dropping, I want to kiss Willow but not with an audience. I can feel the residents of the Spook House staring at us from the upstairs windows… then there's sneaky Dad. The Playroom wasn't my thing. Outside of holding hands and flirty cuddling, I'm not much into PDA, especially in front of relatives. I don't kiss and tell, either– with Dev as the exception.

"I have a surprise, so hop back on." Feeling lighter without the weight of stress on my shoulders, I present Willow my back.

Willow's able to giggle, even though it comes out kind of strange sounding because of her raspy, smoky voice. The sound has me grinning as she hangs onto me like a spider monkey.

"Cleaning out the pipes," Willow says near my ear, vibrating words causing me to shudder. I take off down the block with her bouncing on my back. "Clover calls what we just did cleaning out the pipes."

"Why?" We've both put on a few pounds in the past few weeks, so it's a good thing the new house is only a block down the street.

"Our old pastor wouldn't marry Sam and Clover without premarital counseling. He said it was healthy to blow up and let it out, instead of stewing over it. The Prynnes and Websters operate differently than most. We fight, but it's over the second it's over. Done. I've been trying to do that, but no one would let me."

"The Masons sulk and let it eat them alive," I admit, seeing Willow's point. Then I realize Grandpa John tried to instill the same shit in us. "Dad and Auggie would wrestle in the yard, then take a walk, and they'd be laughing together when they got back."

"I'm not allowed to hit anyone, remember?" Willow thinks I drop her because of her asinine comment. Chuckling, I smooth Willow's hair away from her face, surprised to see it's not in a ponytail.

"Spanky?" Ducking my head, I rub the tip of our noses together. "Pound whomever you want, just as long as they're not pregnant, the next generation of Masons, or the children we make together."

Willow's sharp gasp of surprise has me grinning. She seriously has no fucking clue how much she's sunk into my soul– there's no getting away from Willow for me. Permanent. If I lost her, she'd be my phantom limb.

"C'mon." Grabbing for her hand, I tug Willow up the sidewalk to the new house. "Home. Sweet. Home… for now."

"What?" Mouth gaping, Willow's eyes dart between the Jamison Reality **SOLD** sign and the outside of the house. "I don't understand."

"This is me being highhanded," I admit, voice warbling with worry. "Essie's my insider with the goings on inside our families." I miss Willow's reaction as I bend down to poke the four-digit code into the key box hooked on the front doorknob. Aunt Ginny knows how to make shit easy for herself, so she doesn't have to run around with a billion freaking keys.

"Some things I don't know how to tell you, so I don't." Turning, I lean against the door, because I don't want to say this inside the house. "I understand, Willow."

"Understand what?" She's so confused, I want to wrap her in my arms and squeeze the shit out of her.

"I understand why people have been avoiding you, and I understand how it's making you feel. That's one of the major reasons why we've only been having fun together."

"Because we need the escape." This girl breaks my heart.

"Yeah," I breathe, feeling gutted for everyone involved. "It has to get worse before it can get better, and we've yet to start crawling out of the shit pile."

"I feel like whatever you're going to tell me is gonna hurt," Willow mutters slowly, refusing to let me look away.

"Well, it's actually pretty fucking awesome." My voice pitches high with excitement I can't contain. "But I know Essie is a sore subject for you. I know you feel like I pick her over you, like I'm hanging out with her behind your back."

"No," Willow denies, shaking her head. "You do it blatantly in front of my face. It hurts, but I don't say anything because I do have the ability to use higher reasoning and logic."

The girl is still stinging over earlier.

"By the time I get back from Arizona, your houses won't be yours anymore, neither will mine." Understanding dawns, causing Willow's lips to do that quivery thing again– I can't take the tears. "Your mom and dad, Clover, my dad, and our siblings will be moving into the Pink Taco Hut. It's why Rob was showing Essie Isis's room."

"Essie's moving into the Spook House?" is jerked from Willow's mouth so quickly it shocks her. There's still venom lacing her voice, but it's going to be awhile before that sting goes away– a long while.

"*I'm* moving into the Spook House." Here I am, being a dick again. "*With you.*"

"I don't get to ask you?!" Flabbergasted, Willow lifts her arms like she wants to fly away, or punch me, then flops them back down. "You didn't ask me!"

"If I said anything, you would've asked me anyway. If I asked, you would've said yes."

"That's not!" Willow turns in a circle, then faces me again. "UGH! That's not the point, Kieren. Jesus, I get Essie moving in, dammit! No matter how pissed I'm at her, she's family. Between you, Rob, and Clover, one of you would flay me alive if I didn't let her stay at the Spook House. But–"

"But what?"

"But you and me…" Huffing in large gulps of air, Willow's trying her damnedest not to implode, or maybe explode on me after I said I'd hit her back and knock her ass out. "That's a big fucking deal, Ren. Those are milestones a girl likes to go through. I already missed my goddamn prom-moment. I may not be a girly fucking girl, but don't take away moving in with my boyfriend too."

Getting a big motherfucking clue, I lunge forward, grab Willow and sling her in my arms. Stepping forward, I struggle to get the key in the lock. Swinging the door open, I carry Willow over the threshold like she's my bride.

Kicking the door closed behind us, I lean down to kiss Willow. Drinking her down, I suck in her gasps of surprise. Frozen in my arms, Willow doesn't respond to my kiss because she's freaking out.

"There's a reason I didn't ask to use the Spook House as a layover, Spanky." Arms ready to give out, I set Willow on her feet. "I'm not moving into the Spook House with you, so I didn't ask, because I'm asking you to move out of the Spook House and move in here with me."

"I-I-I– what?" Eyes flicking around the shit-tastic living room, Willow centers back on me. "Oh."

"*Oh, she says*," I tease in a light voice, heart beating wildly because I fear she'll pick the house she renovated over me. "Aunt Ginny bought this house for Devon– a land contract. Dev's going to need a stable environment, and he's going to need support. But there's no way he'd handle the chaos of the Pink Taco Hut or the Spook House."

"This is Devon and Essie's house, isn't it?" Willow catches on quickly. "Because of the baby? And you want us to babysit all three of them?"

Chuckling, *I love you* almost slips free, but I'm not ready to say that out loud yet. Instead, I reach over to clasp the back of her neck with my palm, then drag her lips up to mine. The kiss is quick, the smacking sound echoes around the empty room.

"I *want* you to live with me, but I *need* to be here for my brother," I stress. "We all need each other right now, Willow– we do. Plus, look on the bright side."

"There's a bright side?" Willow mutters sardonically as she looks around our shithole.

"There is." Gesturing around the place, I can't help but laugh at the pinched look Willow flashes me. "You get free reign on renovating another house."

Eyes wider than I've ever seen them before, Willow purrs, "OOOHHHH…"

"You are– my favorite person in the whole wide world," I ramble quickly, instead of those three little words that mean so much but I find too intense to deal with. "Think of it as practice for when you and I get to buy our dream house."

"Keep talking like that, Mr. Mason, and you can give me a billion hard limits and I won't give a shit." Willow's lost in thought, no doubt making lists. "What's my budget?"

I take that as a yes. I don't know if Willow's agreeing because she wants to be with me, or because she wants to get her hands on this house, but I really don't care, because I get to be with her either way.

Missing the ponytail I use to tug Willow around by, I grab her hand instead. "We'll deal with that later– let's look around."

Eyes glazed with a calculating light, Willow drags two fingertips over every surface she comes into contact with, making comments on what needs to be done. "Are we able to start now?"

"This house is in escrow." I follow behind Willow as she scratches a fingernail on the painted window sill over the kitchen sink. "It's complicated. Aunt Ginny is buying it from the seller, then Devon has to sign a bunch of paperwork with Aunt Ginny. So it's like the house is being bought twice in a matter of weeks. Aunt Ginny can't finalize everything until after Dev gets home. But the sellers know Aunt Ginny personally, so they're okay with things like painting until Aunt Ginny owns it outright. Nothing major, though."

"That sucks." Willow sighs, slumping against the uneven countertop.

"Why?" Crowding in her personal space, I pluck Willow off the floor and deposit her on the countertop, then wedge my hips between her thighs. "Listen, I know we're moving really fast, and I should've asked you in a more romantic way–"

"*Really?*" Willow chuckles, but it holds a pissed off edge. "You think?"

"I'm a dick," I mutter underneath my breath while rolling my eyes. "So I get it if you want to stay in your house with Rob and Auggie. I wouldn't want to move into this shithole after living there. I know you feel possessive of the Spook House, because it's *your* baby... and it's gonna be drama-filled here–"

"You're really selling me here, Ren," Willow teases, hands slowly rising to land on my hips. I'm ashamed to admit I get a bit droopy-eyed when she starts digging her fingers in a massaging rhythm. "I love a challenge. But that's not why I was worried about the closing date."

"Why, then?" Taking her affectionate touch as permission, because I've always used Willow initiating as a guide as to whether or not my touch is welcome, I let my hands wander wherever they want. Tits. Usually her ass, but she's sitting on it.

It's Willow's turn to roll her eyes at me. "The closing date is good and bad. The good, I think Devon needs this." She reaches up with little force to tear the cupboard door off. Laughing, she tosses it into the middle of the kitchen with a loud bang to the floor. "I know people still see me as a tantrum-throwing child–"

"I don't–"

"*You so do.*" Willow's eyes dart away from mine, but not before I see tears glistening. "You really do, and so does everyone else. The old Willow would've thrown tantrums over Essie and Devon, so everyone assumed I would do it now, not giving me a chance to speak my piece. But working at the Spook House helped me, gave me a purpose, and when it was completed, I was a different person than when I started. Devon needs that– I'll help, but he has to do most of it himself."

Getting a big motherfucking clue, "You're right," pops out of my mouth.

"Don't underestimate Devon when he comes home, Ren." Voice deepening with concern Willow stops petting my stomach because it's distracting me. "That's why I got so pissed back at the Spook House. You've already decided how what you need and want, what I need and want, doesn't matter, because we have to put Devon first. You're going to walk around on eggshells, but that means you're not requiring enough of Devon. You'll take his pride away when he needs it the most."

"How do you know that's how he'll feel?" With confusion thick in my voice, my eyebrows scrunch together. "I couldn't imagine what it would be like to have someone take care of me for five minutes, to put me first. Seems like it would feel good."

"Yes, *it does*." Willow's hands sneak beneath my t-shirt, then her fingers begin massaging me again. "But it has the opposite effect on someone who's always been babied. That was my problem. That *is* Devon's problem. I'm not a spiteful, little bitch anymore, no matter if everyone else sees me that way. Devon needs to find a purpose, not be babysat. If he falls off the wagon, he does. Suffocating him will only make him do it that much quicker– *I'd know*."

"First of all–" I reach up to tug Willow's hair playfully, but she releases a pain-filled sound that has me freezing in my tracks.

"Ponytails make good handholds to yank me out of a fight." Eyes flicking away in shame, Willow refuses to look at me, and I get a clue. "War injury. Be happy I don't have PTSD. First of all?"

"You like to make jokes when you're upset." Willow shrugs at my observation. "First of all, I don't think you're a spiteful, little bitch. You work harder than anyone I know– I like *you*, Spanky. So just talk to me from now on."

"I'll try, if you'll listen."

"And I'll try not to suffocate Devon, but it's gonna be hard after catering to his every whim since I was born." Placing a fingertip against Willow's lips, I silence her, which is ironic after I told her to talk to me when she needed to. Laughing, I realize I've been doing that to her constantly for weeks. Censoring. Silencing.

"So you'll show Devon how to fix his own house while we try to live around the mess?"

"That's the good and bad I was talking about, Ren. Essie needs to pick out what she wants in her own house, but she can't be in here while the paint is being stripped– it might be lead-based." Ah, that explains why Willow was scratching at the window sill earlier. "The paint fumes. I'd suggest I get started on that as soon as possible. When you get time, I need you to bring Essie here—"

"Why don't you—"

"Don't push me, Ren." Willow uses a momma voice that brooks no room for argument. "You bring Essie here and ask her what colors she wants in which rooms, then give me a list. I'll work on that while we wait for the closing. After Dev gets back, we'll take care of the major shit before we move in, because Essie can't be around toxic chemicals."

"Rob and Auggie said we could stay for as long as we need." Gripping Willow's hips, I lift her off the countertop and plunk her feet on the floor, then I continue our tour. "This place has three bedrooms. The master has an attached bathroom, and there's a three-quarter-bath in the hallway, whatever the hell that means. It's Aunt Ginny realtor-speak."

"It means it only has a shower." Willow groans, annoyed. "I'll be visiting my old room at the Spook House once in a while when I need to take a good, long soak, I guess… they wanted me to move out, didn't they?"

The desolation in Willow's voice guts me. "Auggie told me to move in when he was acting nutty. It felt like he was trying to push me away when he had the Playroomers invade my renovation. Then he kicked me out. I love the Spook House, but there's been this vibe, like I'm invading their space and they want me to leave."

Voice soft, heart breaking, I lead her into our future bedroom. "Willow, no—"

"I get it." Willow pulls away from me to scope out the room. She tries to open the closet door, but it gets stuck. With force, she opens it, but the accordion door comes off in her hands. Setting it gingerly on the floor, she looks as lost and broken down as the door.

"Auggie gave me the riot act this morning before you showed up. Reality check. Isis must hate me. Robbie's going nuts, wanting Isis to move into her bedroom, but she won't. I just now realized *I'm* the reason why… and you knew that, didn't you?"

"Hey, now." Resting my hands on Willow's shoulders, I try to think of a way to comfort her, but the truth hurts.

Staring sightlessly into the depths of the closet, Willow's words are hollow— numb. "I get it." She shrugs out from beneath my hands, but I can hear the sniffle she tries to hide. "Someday I'll have my own place, and I won't feel beholden to someone else. Like they can pull the rug out from beneath my feet. Growing up, my parents could've kicked me out at any time because I was a little cunt-bag. Auggie can kick me out for *any* reason. I don't feel safe and secure. I've felt like that for months– after Auggie kicked me out, the Spook House hasn't felt like my home... and no matter how much work I put into this house, it will never be *my* home."

Arms sliding around her chest, I draw Willow's back to my front, enveloping her tightly. "*That*, I do get. Someday, Spanky– someday. For me too."

Moisture dampens my forearm, but I don't call attention to it as Willow cries in earnest. "I love being around you, Kieren. I feel like myself, like nothing else matters. I want to live with you– it's not because I want to escape where I'm not wanted, or because I get to fix another house. I like how I feel when I'm around you, and I'm so goddamn sorry that you think I judge you– I don't."

This. This is what it feels like to connect to someone. Not fucking in cars because the girl thinks I'm hot. Not walking on eggshells with Devon one minute, connecting with him for another, then waiting for him to explode in the next. This isn't the escapism of ignoring our problems. This is actually sorting them out and repairing what's broken, just like we'll do with this house. This is why you don't censor your girlfriend, because you'll miss out on the most important thing a person needs– having a voice and being heard.

This is why Willow was screaming bloody murder at me in the Spook House living room. She needs this, and so do I.

For once, I talk about something that matters, and I take a leap of faith that Willow will listen.

Holding her tightly, I no longer ignore the tears splattering against my arm– I acknowledge them by making sure this isn't one-sided anymore. "I know you're not judging me, Willow. But I've been in both yours and Essie's shoes. So, while I get where you're both coming from, when you say things about Essie, I feel like you're saying them about me."

"I'm not, though." Willow tries to turn in my arms, but I don't let her. I need to say this, but I don't have the balls to do it while looking her in the eyes.

"Devon." Voice rough, I have to cough to clear my throat. "Devon was very upset after he found out about Essie and me losing our virginity. He made me pay for it in more ways than one. He made me feel shame and guilt, when I was just a little kid. Today, I see it as nothing but a fond memory and a learning experience. But Devon made my life a living hell. So when I saw the Facebook posts, when I heard your fight with Essie, it brought that all back to me again. The shame. The guilt. The feeling of humiliation. The worst was knowing I hurt my brother, so it was painful to watch you hurt your cousin, knowing you'd regret it later. I knew exactly how Essie felt going through it all, but I also knew how you felt. I just felt sick while being tugged back and forth in the middle."

"I need to say something before you say anything else," Willow interrupts. I want to be pissed off, but this is supposed to be give-and-take, so I let it go. "I knew nothing of the Facebook bullshit– I don't use it for anything but Revamped's business account and helping Stone with Wreck & Ruin's page. I had an account in junior high, and I thought I'd deactivated it. Violet was tagging my old account in her posts. Clover found out from Robbie, and we were all lectured to within an inch of our lives– *in front of Essie*. Jesus, Violet's only fourteen." Willow shrugs it off. "But I will agree that I've been a cunt about some of the shit with Essie. I was hurt, but that's no excuse."

"Okay," I whisper, thankful that my gut-instinct was right. I kept saying I didn't think Willow would do that, but no one believed me. The *old* Willow would've done it, but she's not the person *I* know. "You also need to understand something else. We all understand– Essie and me, even Devon. We've all been the asshole and the injured party, you included."

"Auggie browbeat that into me this morning." Willow shudders in what I assume is shame– shame I wish she didn't feel. "There's nothing anyone can say to me that will make me believe what Essie and Devon did was right, and I don't mean the sex. I mean the timing– that was wrong. I wish someone would acknowledge that at least. But I was so blind, I didn't realize Devon and I were hurting you and Essie while we were together– didn't realize I was hurting Robbie and Isis during Auggie's and my short-lived whatever you wanna call that godawful disaster."

Rotating Willow, I turn her to face me. I allow the intensity to flow in, instead of pushing it away and turning everything we do into a game. I let myself *feel* things for Willow. "Thank you for talking to me," I mutter in a small voice.

"Thank you for listening to me," is her even softer reply. Tiny arms wrap around my waist, tugging me closer. Willow gets on her tippy toes, leaning up to kiss me. "I'm going to miss you something fierce while you're gone this week."

"No, you won't," I tease, bullshitting. "You'll work nonstop to keep busy."

"True." Willow grins up at me, but it wilts into sadness. "I'm putting a fork in whatever's going on with Clover. Auggie warned me it's happening tomorrow, but I don't know what to do... don't know how I feel about it."

Making a poor attempt at stopping the flood, my thumbs quickly swipe at Willow's tears, but they're unrelenting. "If my mom was still alive... the angry part of me wants to rage against her." A twisted flash of memory, featuring Devon beating Mom's gravestone until it was marred red with his blood, has my stomach twisting in knots.

"What would you do?" Willow stares up at me like my answer will influence how she reacts to Clover, and I feel about ten feet tall because of it.

Huffing in a deep breath, I try my damnedest not to cry, because this type of shit is just too raw– too real. Too intense. Shrugging, ignoring the sniffling sound coming from my own nose, "I'd just hug her. Tell Mom I loved her, then tell her I was sorry."

"Shit!" Willow turns her head away, chest releasing a sob.

I change the subject, because we can't shift gears from playmates to soulmates in a matter of minutes– it's too much. But I still turn sappy. "I'm gonna miss you this week."

"No, you won't," Willow mimics me, then giggles that raspy, smoky sound that never fails to get me hard. "Give Devon a hug for me... and let him know– let him know I'm taking care of everything on the home front while you guys are gone. I have to help Dad with some plumbing problem at the Pink Taco Hut, but I'll find the time to drag Essie's flat ass over here to pick out paint colors."

Head hitching backward, I release a laugh so loud I feel like an idiot. "I knew you would– I knew you couldn't stop yourself." Still laughing, I lean down to kiss Willow, putting every emotion I feel for her into the way my lips move against hers. "You're my absolute, most favoritest person in the whole wide world."

Holding me tight, kissing me back with a ferocity that takes my breath away, somehow Willow knew my silly words meant I love you.

CHAPTER FORTY-FIVE

Devon Mason

"Delaney, do you have any idea what this is like?" Panting, I try my hardest to take deep breaths, but there's something about this prick that rubs me the wrong way. Dr. Delaney's office isn't like all the rest– it's cold, sterile. Intimidating. Never thought I'd miss the colors of baked earth and foliage as much as I do right now.

Trying my damnedest to center myself, I fear what will happen if I don't. Dad, Ren, and the kids are due here tomorrow. The cost of the flights won't matter to a puke like Delaney. If I don't do what he wants, he'll turn them away at the gate to hell.

"Of course I do, Devon." Delaney always looks me in the eye, even when he's writing in his insufferable notebook. The fifty-something doctor doesn't look like he's seen a second of adversity in his lifetime.

"I'm trying my best to keep even around you," I admit it's a struggle. "But meeting with you first thing after having an orderly watch me swallow my meds, then probe around my mouth with a latex-tasting finger… then have another watch me eat my yogurt, boiled egg, and fruit. I feel so–"

"Dehumanized?" Delaney supplies. "I am your doctor, Devon. My personal life will never enter our conversations. If I'm to remain professional at all times, even a second can't be about me. I know Amelia isn't as strict as I am, but there is a reason."

"A doctorate versus a master's degree?" I mutter just to be an asshole. "Don't discount Ms. Amelia because she didn't go to school as long as you."

"I'm a *medical doctor*," Delaney stresses, but doesn't slip his cool demeanor. "Don't pit us against one another, Devon. It's not going to work. We function as a team, Amelia and I."

"Doubtful," I mutter begrudgingly, finally earning a reaction out of Delaney.

A snort. Uptight, silver-haired Delaney snorts.

Hell freezes over, the asshole chuckles. "What is said between you and Amelia is private." I hate the way my therapist's name intimately wraps around his tongue. "What is said between you and me is shared with Amelia. Do you trust Amelia's judgment?"

"Yes," I mutter emphatically without hesitation.

"Good." Delaney sits up straighter in his leather chair, which is hard to believe because he already looked like a stick was shoved up his ass and into his spine. "Today you will be discussing your mother with Amelia, and I will be observing."

"No," is an instant denial as my emotional control slips. "I don't trust you."

"Devon, you just said you trusted Amelia." Delaney leans forward, somehow lending me control over my emotions because he can sense I'm about to go off the rails. Every nerve in my body is raw all the time, with the slightest thing setting me off. "If you trust Amelia, then you must trust me. Today I will monitor your session."

"Why?" is barely audible from my tight lips.

"Your family will be with us for several days, breaking into your fifth week here. I must observe your session with Amelia because it will impact how much freedom you receive with them. Whether there is any one-on-one alone time, or if Amelia or myself must be present. This will also help me gauge whether or not your current mood stabilizer cocktail is functioning. This is science, but of the mind, and it will take all eight weeks or more to get it right."

"Or more?" I coax, because none of the doctors or therapists ever hint at what comes next. All saying those conversations are held until week six or seven.

"I've been in constant contact with your new psychiatrist in Massachusetts, along with the local therapist who will be handling your three weekly sessions. Then there is the vetting of which NA group you should attend."

"You're a controlling bastard, aren't you?" I mutter snidely through gritted teeth. It takes a lot of mental effort not to press my stubby fingernails into my thighs.

"I have to be, Devon." Nothing ruffles Delaney's feathers. "You have two choices to make in the next minute. One, either allow me to monitor your session with Amelia, or lose your privileges to the family visit. Your father will still meet with your team, with all of your data given to him, but he won't see you in person–"

"*You bastard*," I snarl in awe.

"Two, do you wish to have your session in my office, or Amelia's? I realize many patients find hers to be more comforting."

Challenge thrown down. Challenge accepted. "Here," is a spontaneous reaction to the controlling doctor. "Now."

"Good." I may have imagined it, but I thought I heard relief riding Delaney's voice.

"I still don't trust you," I warn, not happy at all. I won't half-ass it, because I want to see Taryn and Tommy, but I won't be as open as I would have been.

Sighing, Delaney stands from his chair. Looking down at me with icy blue eyes, I can tell I frustrate the piss out of the man. "Do you ever wonder why you call Amelia Ms. Amelia?"

"Because you think you deserve the honorific because you're a doctor," I mutter at Delaney's back as he walks over to his office door. "A way to lower Ms. Amelia because she's a woman. You won't even give her the respect of using her surname."

Turning slightly, Delaney looks at me over his shoulder as his hand rests on the doorknob. "Hmm… or perhaps her surname is Delaney."

My mouth is still gaping open as Ms. Amelia enters the office. If I wasn't so shocked, I'd feel betrayed. Fit and handsome, I figured the doctor would have a trophy wife stashed at home, not a wife his age, who works in his field, and quintessentially looks like a mom. They probably have perfect kids my age, ones who go to Harvard. Ms. Amelia bakes them cookie care packages when Delaney passive-aggressively calls them disappointments.

"Delaney?" Ms. Amelia's irate voice breaks into my gawking. "Honestly? You told Devon." Sighing, she takes over Delaney's leather chair opposite me. "Your pride will be the death of you."

"Devon baited me." If I didn't know any better, I'd say Delaney was pouting. "He frustrates me so badly, I want to punch myself in the face. We've never treated a patient together– I just don't get why Devon is the first after twenty years."

"Because Devon reminds me of you," shuts off both Delaney's whining and the verbal vomit readying to spew from my lips.

After mulling that over for a moment, "Huh," is a huff of agreement from me, one Delaney makes at the same time.

"You seem agitated today, Devon," Ms. Amelia observes after Delaney and I settle down.

"You think?"

Goddamn eyebrow raise.

Dr. Delaney = feeling in control.

Ms. Amelia = being in control.

There is a difference.

"I thought you'd be excited to see your family tomorrow," Ms. Amelia uses as a segue into whatever direction she's trying to take me.

Eyes refusing to meet my doctor's or my therapist's, I focus on a glass paperweight resting on the desk. I have no idea how they made it, but a lifelike purple flower blooms inside the glass bubble.

"It's a Corning Glass paperweight," Delaney breaks into my contemplation.

"It's… interesting," I stumble over my wording because I could stare at it all day and still not make heads or tails how the artist created it.

"Thank you." Delaney sounds pleased with himself. Reaching over, he fetches it from his desk, then plops its heavy weight into my palm. "It's from my hometown– Corning, New York."

Fingers wrapping around the cool bubble, I relax. "I'm terrified." I answer with honesty I only reserve for Ms. Amelia, even with Delaney listening in. He's her husband– she obviously trusts him.

"Why? Your father and brother haven't changed." As promised, Ms. Amelia takes point, with Delaney sitting quietly next to me on the leather sofa. He doesn't even have his notebook out.

"I've changed," I mutter with a shrug. "I don't know what's expected of me."

"Nothing," Ms. Amelia soothes my greatest fear. "They expect nothing. This is your journey, and they're merely the passengers. You take the lead on how your interactions will go, and they will follow."

"I don't… I don't want them to treat me as if I'm as fragile as glass," I admit what's truly been bothering me. "I want them to have expectations of me, and to hold me to them."

"That paperweight could kill a man." The ferocity in Ms. Amelia's voice surprises the hell out of me. "It's a beautiful decoration. It's useful to hold paper down when the windows are open. But there is nothing fragile about this glass, just as there is nothing fragile about you."

Tearing up, the words spew with abandon. "I miss my mother– no one knew her like I did. There's a bond that formed between us. The abuser and her victim. As sick as it sounds, I loved her more because of it."

"That's not uncommon." Ms. Amelia is treading carefully, scared to push me because Delaney is here. I can tell by the way the man slumped against the sofa cushion that I shocked him by saying what I did.

"I resent Dad and Ren. They hate her, and she didn't even abuse them. But I love her, and she hurt me continually for fourteen years. It's not fair how they could let her go, and I can't."

"Toxic dynamics are never fair– never logical." Ms. Amelia always gives just enough of a response to coax more out of me.

"Neither is love," flows from beside me. "Does your brother speak of your mother badly?"

I'm being tag-teamed now, much to Ms. Amelia's horror.

"Badly?" I huff a laugh as my answer.

"That's an emotional response to pain." Delaney's the one who replies. "There's a thin line between love and hate, because there is no line. Hate is passionate. If you truly didn't like someone, the emotional response is indifference. If Kieren says bad things about your mother, then she's still causing him pain– he still loves her. Misses her. Is angry with her."

"Shit," I hiss, heart fluttering wildly inside my chest. "I have a feeling you're going to gloat by saying I should've been opening up to you all along, aren't you?"

"You said it, not me." Delaney shrugs. "When you're deep in pain, it's difficult to see anything from another's perspective. I have the sneaking suspicion that you're at the cusp of doing this on your own, seeing your mother with clear eyes. But you've yet to look at your father and brother that way."

Gape-mouthed, I flounder as I stare at Ms. Amelia for help.

"Have you written about your mother in your journal?" Ms. Amelia waits patiently for an answer I don't have to give. "Give it over."

"How do you know it's on me?"

The husband and wife duo chuckles in response, both knowing mood stabilizers won't change the fact that I'm a paranoid shit.

"Fine." Pulling my shirt up, I yank my journal from its hiding spot near my hip, always using my boxers' waistband to hold it securely in place. Thumbing through the journal, I find an entry I'm comfortable sharing, then I hand the book to Ms. Amelia for safekeeping.

I feel so angry all the time, and I can't let it out. No matter what, it always circles back to Mom. We're all to blame for Mom's suicide. Aunt Ginny always said Grammy was high-functioning, but everyone with bipolar disorder is different. But I can see Mom sitting on the couch like it was yesterday– a lifeless husk. That wasn't normal, even for someone with a mental illness. Mom wasn't capable of taking care of herself, so why do we all blame her for not taking care of us kids?

If only we'd required more out of her. "It's just Camille, leave her alone," they'd say. They were saying the same shit about me before I came here. Everyone requires more out of me here, and I give it.

They were lazy. It was easier to ignore the problem than to fix it.

I'm to blame for my mother abusing me. I should have told Dad. But it felt almost as good as it hurt to share the intimate secret with Mom, like we were in it together and no one else was special enough to be included. She'd hit me. I'd cry. She'd hold me and tell me she loved me. Mom never told Ren, Rae, or West she loved them... never told Dad either.

Every day for fourteen years, Mom was treated as if she didn't exist. But in our abuse, we both existed with equal importance. If the victim tells the truth, the abuse stops, then the abuser ceases to exist. You can't have one without the other. I remember begging Ren not to tell Dad, because I didn't want it to end. Mom made me feel special in the most heinous of ways.

Mom told me goodbye, but no one else. To this day, I feel a level of self-importance because of it. I didn't believe her at the time, because she told me goodbye dozens of times over the years, but I wasn't surprised when I heard the gunshot.

Kieren is brutal when he talks about Mom. Dad doesn't do it, but I can tell he wants to say the same shit too. Ren means what he says, and it makes me sick. They didn't see Mom as a human being. I know what it's like after being reduced to nothing here, where I'm taken care of instead of living life.

If I wasn't so stubborn, I'd have no pride left, then I'd truly be broken.

When I'd scream how I was just like Mom, it was a culmination of many things. Bipolarism. The dark personality. The abuse, manipulation– the user of people. But also the Nightmare. I had a small taste compared to what Mom experienced. I can't imagine what it would've been like if I'd been swallowed by the darkness when it happened.

They call Mom a coward, but I don't.

When the men barged into our house, I felt helpless– powerless. I fought back because I was defending my mother and brother, never thinking of myself whatsoever. Then the defeat settled in. When I saw a chance to protect Ren, I took it. The entire time I felt shame because I couldn't protect them, but rage was along for the ride.

Rage at Mom for not protecting us, rage I assumed Ren felt toward me.

Mom didn't fight, didn't even struggle. She just gave up and gave herself to them.

But being here, working through all this bullshit, I see it in a different light.

Mom wasn't defeated– she was doing all she could to protect her children, in the only way she knew how. She kept two of our three attackers occupied, as they cut and raped her repeatedly in front of her oldest children. She didn't even pass out until Dad arrived.

It wasn't defeat that had me bargaining with Alejandro to save Kieren– it was cunning calculation in order to save the youngest of us. I couldn't fight him, so I gave in to him. No different than Mom sacrificing herself to save us.

In the aftermath, people's thoughts were so loud, they didn't see Mom as a victim. "Why didn't you protect your children?" "Why didn't you fight back?" Their judgments were thought so loudly they were written on the air for Mom to see.

I had but a taste of the guilt and shame my mother must have felt, and everyone just let her be, without compassion or sympathy. "Camille is such a victim!" "Camille ought to be happy now that she has a reason to wallow around and act depressed." "Camille deserved it!" They never saw her as a person, before or after her death.

I miss Mom. I both loved and hated her because I understood her. If I'd been older, I would've tried to help her– save her.

I feel the guiltiest because I'm here today– alive and in a place that is helping me, a place Mom should've been in way before the Nightmare happened.

I resent Dad and Ren because they loved me more than they loved Mom– loved me enough to help me, when they didn't lift a finger to help Mom.

There's no value on life. Whether it be a vegetating housewife, a drug addict cop, or a young, confused girl in high school, we all deserve to be treated with the same level of humanity and respect. We are not our occupations or what we contribute to society– we are human beings.

I'm angry at my mother because I'm angry at myself for not saving her, but I'm angriest that my family valued my life above hers.

"I see you understand more than most." Ms. Amelia passes my journal back to me for safekeeping. Taking a leap of faith, I hand my most prized possession to Delaney, instead of acting paranoid by shoving it back into my pants. "Even the subtlest of nuances that I missed."

CHAPTER FORTY-SIX

Willow Prynne

"You're now ready for the torch." Dad hits the striker, sparking the torch to life, then hands the torch to me. Enthralled, I stare at the flame for a second before heating the pipe from beneath. "You'll feel a bit of a sucking pop when it gets hot– the pipe sliding in farther. Yeah… that. Now melt the solder to fuse them together. Make sure everything is covered, or it'll leak."

"Like this?" Always been a daddy's girl, no matter which daddy I was trying to please. I was probably the only kid who couldn't wait until the weekend so I could go to the jobsite with Dad and Sam. I'd follow them around as their little helper monkey, handing them tools and picking up messes. It always hurts when I realize Seth missed out on that because Sam died right when Seth would've been taken to work with his dad– *our* dad.

I wasn't sure how I'd react when Clover finally told me the truth. I'd been carrying it around for so long, I was scared I'd blow up like I used to. I'm trying to be a better person– a grown up. But sometimes I can't help but act like a spoiled brat.

While we made Devon's birthday cake, I could feel the rage simmering beneath the surface, where anything could make me go off. I started going off the rails as Clover was telling me, but her panic attack hit, utterly terrifying me. So I took Auggie's and Ren's advice, figuring if they agreed on something, it must be right. I called Clover *Mom* and told her I loved her…

Then I left, because looking at me was creating a physical reaction in Clover. Panic attack. I feel shitty for two reasons. One, just looking at me made my mom physically sick. Two, she was so upset, she couldn't breathe.

When I'm stressed, I want to seek out shit that will help me forget like I always did– toke up a bowl or grab a fifth of 99 Berries. Devon may have been lying to me for nearly a year, but I'm not breaking the promise I made him or myself, and I'm going to help him when he gets home. So I sought my new coping mechanism. Work.

"You're doing better than expected," Dad murmurs near my ear. We're crouched in the Pink Taco Hut's basement, replacing all the copper piping Oliver Zypher stripped a few nights ago. Ozzy's been staying with Mom and Dad, as has Essie. It's like a freaking halfway house over there right now– pregnant women and convict orphans. I've been barred from entering my own house for over two weeks. Not that it's mine anymore... not with all of our lives changing dramatically overnight. It's hard to handle.

"I'm not stupid." Rolling my eyes, I twist the valve to the torch, extinguishing it. "I've known, but was waiting Clover out."

"I knew you'd be okay." Dad pats me on the back, then takes the torch from my hand. My empty palm is filled with a fitting next, followed by a scrubby cloth. "Clean the fitting until it shines– the solder won't stick otherwise."

"What do I call you?" I concentrate on the scratchy sound of polishing the copper, ignoring how my heart is beating a rapid tattoo against the inside of my chest. I know the world doesn't revolve around me, but the people I thought were my parents are actually my grandparents. The woman I thought was my sister is my mother. The man I've mourned for too many years wasn't my brother-in-law. Sam was my daddy.

"If you don't call me Dad..." he trails off, handing me the flux. "You may as well tear my nuts off, because I'm the one who raised you. If I ever hear you call Mom anything but Mom, I'm going to have Clover beat your ass."

Relieved, a chuckle flows up my throat. "Thanks, Dad– I needed that."

"Paint the flux on the fitting." Dad hands me a brush. "It's up to you what you want to call Clover– it's between you and Clover, but it's only up to *you* what *you* call her. Okay?"

"Thank you." Tears sting my eyes as I repeat the torch process.

I haven't felt like anyone was on my side. Not one step of the way have I felt like someone had my back. In order for me to feel vindicated, it would be at the expense of Clover and Essie. It wasn't a test my family failed because they didn't pick me over them. I just needed to feel secure in this family, like my feelings mattered. But everyone told me to get over it and move on, without dealing with *it* first.

I understand Clover's not able to give me what I need, and I accept that. Which is why I left when she figured I'd berate her and make her feel like shit.

Dad's making me feel how I needed to feel right now– like I had a choice. A voice. He's not beating a dead horse by talking it out. He's teaching me a trade so I will feel worthy. Dad understands how I can't feel what I don't, and can't help how I do.

Dad still wants to be *my* dad.

"Very good, Willow– *very good.*" Taking the torch from me, he hands me another fitting. "We'll make a jack-of-all-trades out of you yet." Releasing a raspy laugh, one that sounds just like mine, Dad gestures to the ginormous basement. "Now, repeat that a billion times, and we'll have water flowing upstairs in no time."

"By *in no time*, you mean like midnight tonight, if we work nonstop," I mutter, rolling my eyes.

"Practice makes perfect." Dad grins at me, tape-measure armed and at the ready. He measures the next expanse between fittings, then cuts the length of copper pipe for me to fit.

"Hey, Ozzy!" I shout, voice echoing across the cavernous basement. "How long did it take you to chop all this down?"

I remember Ozzy from school– the kid was a sophomore when I graduated. He was a cute little bugger with a big mop of dark curls. He had a growth spurt, and it did him wonders. God, poor Essie having to hang around with him… Ozzy's hot enough to make me melt a little bit, and I've got Ren keeping me bothered. He's still a baby, not yet eighteen.

Bizarrely, Ozzy reminds me a bit of Devon, and not just the dark hair and killer eyes. Quiet. Reserved. Too intelligent for his own good. A little bit damaged in an intoxicating way. All of us are suckers for the bad boy with the good heart. Thank God I fell for the good guy with a selfless heart– the bad boy did a number on me.

"Not fast enough, apparently," rumbles from the dark depths. "I got caught, didn't I?"

"By Violet." Dad huffs in a laugh, then coughs because of the fumes the flux is giving off. "Oliver's a good kid– good at blending into the background. He takes orders well, does a good job. A quick study."

"Ozzy!" I shout loudly again, projecting. "Sure wish replacing the copper was as fast as chopping it down." Turning to Dad, I grumble underneath my breath because I like playing with the water-sealer goop. "You ought to be teaching him how to fit pipe, not how to waterproof a basement."

"Today of all days, I think you and I needed some father-daughter time, don't you?" Dad doesn't say any more, doesn't move to hug me or anything else affectionate. He hands me the torch again– Dave Prynne's version of *I love you*.

I prefer Dad's way to how clingy the Masons are. It's taken a bit of patience not to get skeeved out with how handsy Kieren is all the time. Devon wasn't like that– he's a hugger, one amazing hug goodbye per visit. Part of me loves how Ren can't keep his hands off me, but I couldn't imagine one of my parents being fused to my body at all times. Whether it's a slap, a shout, or a pat on the back, they all mean the same thing to a Prynne– we're in each other's blood, we don't need any more reassurance than that.

Which is why Kieren didn't understand Essie's and my fight. If we wouldn't have gotten interrupted, physical violence aside, we would've gotten it out of our systems and moved on. Not being able to fight it out fucked us up. It's the Prynne way.

Releasing a sadistic chuckle, realization hits. "Dad, Clover… how the hell is Clover gonna deal with Malcolm?" Shuddering, I envision Malcolm touching Clover whenever she's in arm's reach. The woman isn't frigid, but like the rest of us, she sure as shit isn't used to it. It's been overwhelming for me, and Ren is nowhere near as clingy as Malcolm.

"Malcolm's been breaking Clover in." God love Dad, Robbie inherited his personality. Blunt. Naughty and mischievous. Diabolical. Selfless and protective. "Clover's been a bit frazzled lately. But I suspect the week Malcolm is gone will help some. She'll miss what she can't have, then crave it."

Kieren's still in the air, flying over the entire United States. I'd do anything to talk to him right now. We had to bleed a little bit to truly connect– the Prynne way. After our fight yesterday morning, we looked at the house, parted ways for the rest of the day, then spent the night together. I feel closer to Ren than ever– like adults, instead of playacting a relationship.

"Clover had a panic attack– that's why I left her alone." Voice cracking, I remember how Clover looked, how terrified I felt, how I'll see it in my worst nightmares for life. "Seeing me was making it worse."

"Not her first." Dad goes about business, as if it's no big deal his daughter was going off the rails. "Better be her last. I suspect Malcolm won't be able to handle seeing Clover like that, not after how his first wife was."

"Christ," I snarl, emotions hitting a breaking point. "I need a break." Crawling to my feet, I swipe the dust off my behind. "Hey, Ozzy!" I call across the basement as I make my way to the Bilco door steps. "Do you smoke?"

"Don't get the boy started." Dad answers me instead, and I hear nary a grunt from Ozzy. "Don't ask him if he needs a drink or a snack, because the fella will lie straight to your face because he doesn't want to be a bother."

"Translated…" I locate my smokes and lighter near the bottom step. "Bring the fellas a drink and a snack, little woman."

"You may not believe it, but you remind me of who your mother used to be." Dad looks so sad, my heart breaks for our family. "You all have parts of me in you, and I miss seeing that reflected in my daughter."

"I'll yank that stick out of Clover's ass," I promise. "Then I'll have my real mother back– your daughter."

"That's a good girl."

I leave Dad and Ozzy working while I make my escape. Anyone who values an escape while at work smokes. I smoked on and off while partying in school, but pot was my life back then. I had to keep some vices: cigarettes, caffeine, and sugar. It bugs the piss out of Auggie, and Clover has asthma, so I'm down to four smokes a day, outside so it doesn't linger and stick to my clothes and hair. I'm slowly weening myself off, but I need something to use as an excuse to escape when shit gets too real.

Smoking ensures a few minutes that belong solely to me, where I can think and just be myself. Not sure what I'll replace smoking with, and I won't stop until I find out.

Camping on the side of the Pink Taco Hut, I nurse my cigarette while staring across the street at the Spook House. I love that goddamn house. A part of me will always yearn to possess it. All the blood, sweat, and tears I put into it, and it's not even mine. But I got the better part of the bargain– the Spook House made me a better person.

Someday I want to own a big ol' house. I'd love to return it to its former glory, put it on the Historical Society list, and have people traipse through to appreciate all the hard work I've done. It'd feel like an achievement– a measure of my worth.

Someday.

Until then, pissed off and hurt by them or not, I'll put all my energy and effort into making Devon and Essie's little house the house of their dreams, all the while mourning what I've lost.

Groaning because my break's over, I take one final drag down to the filter, all the while staring at the Spook House. Going to miss it. Miss what it represents, but not miss the pain it caused everyone.

I regret nothing, because I wouldn't be this version of me today if I rewrote even a single moment of my history. I like this me, flaws and all, including cigarette breath and bratty tantrums when no one listens to me. I wouldn't even bring Sam back, no matter how much I miss him, because I know Malcolm is going to bring the very best, most flawed, amazing version of Clover back out, and that is the mother I wish to know.

Dragging the cooler out of the bed of the truck, I rest it on the lowered tailgate. I wonder if Dad would be willing to give me his truck while he plays snowbird for the winter. Now that I'm moving out of the Spook House, I won't have access to Robbie's Explorer or Auggie's truck, and Ren will take his truck to Wreck & Ruin. Dad's truck is a Prynne Renovation work truck, filled with toolboxes loaded for bear and a handy ladder rack. I could do a lot of home improvements out of this truck.

Robbie will probably get it– I'd be a better choice for budding foreman, even if Robbie is floating the business financially.

As I dig around the cooler for our drinks, ice feeling refreshing on my overheated flesh, I decide I want to buy my own truck. I work several jobs, and I already have the next few semesters of tuition banked. I'm sure I'll have to pay a quarter of all the bills in Dev's house, but that can't be all that much.

Feeling lighter, I palm a Coke in each hand after tucking Dad's iced tea in the crook of my arm. "I'm gonna buy me a truck. A truck with a ladder rack and tool boxes."

"Hmm… interesting first major purchase for a girl." Clover's voice has Dad's iced tea bottle bouncing on the sidewalk. Before I can grab it, Robbie's catlike reflexes is catching it.

"It's definitely more Willow's speed." Robbie steals the Cokes, fearing for their longevity. "I'd offer to help you pick it out, but you better take Ren with you instead. If anyone knows trucks, it's a mechanic."

"I could take Stone," I mutter to distract myself from Clover's presence.

"Nah, Langdon Stone's the brain behind the operation, not the man doing all the work." Robbie and I share a grin over the truth.

Awkwardness descends, and a sheepish Clover and I wait for Robbie to fix it.

"Well, this isn't uncomfortable, or anything…" Robbie looks between us with his eyebrows pinched. "We come bearing food."

That's all I needed to hear– I'm down for that. "Oh, let me carry it." Clover smothers a laugh as I grab the tote filled with something that smells yummy. "Am I allowed in the house, or do I need to eat on the lawn? I'm not taking food into that dungeon you call a basement."

"My house is your house, as always, Sapling." Worry, fear, and affection bleed from Clover's voice. Just like with Dad, Clover's saying *I love you* without actually saying it.

"Better get a screen door for the front," I mutter over my shoulder as I carry my loot up to the porch. "Any house of mine needs a door that slams shut behind me to announce my arrival."

Smiling blindingly, no doubt relieved I'm not mad at her, Clover knows my silly words mean *I love you too, Mom.* "Rob, fetch the men from the basement, will ya?"

"I'm always someone's bitch." Robbie sighs dramatically, stomping through the house to the basement stairs, instead of going around the back and down via the Bilco door.

"Always a bridesmaid, never a bride," I mutter sarcastically as I plunk the food on the counter. "Nice place you got here, Clover. I'd love to get my hands on it. First things first, you've got to change the color. Godawful pink? Do you know what they call it?"

"Pink Taco Hut." Clover shrugs, relaxing in intervals as I prove I'm okay by acting as sarcastic and pain-in-the-ass-ish as usual. "Why?"

"I've died and gone to heaven– you made a batch of enchiladas." I hold the baking dish like it's a gift from above. I'm starve-gutted since no one would let me inside to sit at the Prynne supper table. "You do know what a pink taco is, don't you?"

"No." Clover goes into hostess-mode, arranging plates and flatware.

"Dad said you used to be like me, and I promised to bring that woman back to him." I just gape at how innocent she truly is. "No one related to the pervert known as Robin Prynne should ever be ignorant on the term pink taco."

"Hey!" Robbie shouts, stomping on the top step from the basement, popping out a door underneath the main staircase to the upper floors. "I'm proud to be a pervert."

"What's a pink taco?" Clover asks, looking nothing but curious and innocent as she dishes up rolled tortillas filled with chicken and cheesy goodness.

"A pussy, sis." Robbie says with a straight face, stealing the plate of food I was reaching for. He swats my hand away, staring me down when I pout. "I made this, I'll have you know."

"A pink taco is a pussy?" The way Clover says this has us busting a gut, just in time for Dad and Ozzy to overhear. Clover's face burns bright red, and it only gets brighter as Dad, Robbie, and I share the same laugh, with Ozzy blushing even redder.

"I'm calling a house painter as soon as possible." Clover's lips curl up at the corners, then she's laughing at herself. "Willow, please tell me there's nothing wrong with the color blue."

"No!" We all shout at once, with Rob the loudest. "The Pink Taco Hut shall forever remain pink!"

All of my family isn't present, but the next few hours are pure bliss. Mom and Essie enlisted the twins' help in packing, and Clover and I both got texts as soon as the Masons landed in Arizona safe and sound. We spend the time it takes to devour a giant pan of enchiladas and polish off a strawberry pie, getting a game plan for the next week. Minor repairs. The moving of three houses into one. A POD is being delivered in the morning for the things Essie kept from her parents, plus Dev and Ren's stuff, all waiting to go into Dev's place once it closes. We make plans for a yard sale and what's going to Revamped to pawn off on the townsfolk.

This is what I'm good at, work and getting shit done, to the point I can't focus on why I'm supposed to be angry or how much I'm missing Kieren.

I'd feared and anticipated this day for a long time– the day Clover told me she was my birth mother, that Sam was my daddy, and the twins my baby sister and brother. All the stress made it feel anticlimactic, for which I'm thankful. I wouldn't trade anything in the world for this moment, being with my family, making happy plans for the future, so I let all the hurt go and latch onto whatever's coming my way with both hands and my Prynne stubborn determination.

CHAPTER FORTY-SEVEN

Devon Mason

Shaking in the hundred-degree, constant sunshine, my leg goes up and down and my fingers tap irregular beats on the picnic table. I fucked up during my first visit with Dad, Ren, and the kids yesterday afternoon. I was stressed out and feeling raw, and it was too much to handle, especially with it being my twenty-first birthday.

There was a ton of bullshit spinning around in my head, and I feared Delaney wouldn't allow me to see them again during their visit because of my bad behavior. As the head of the center, I was escorted to Delaney's office before my family even made it off the grounds. But Delaney surprised me by giving me advice and upping the unsupervised visit from a half hour to a full hour.

You initiate. You give the hug, and you pull away first. You bring up what subjects you want to discuss. If something is said that you can't handle, change the subject. You are in control here, Devon. They only want to be near you– they understand why it has to be on your terms. If you need quiet, sit together in silence. If it gets to be too much, walk away and don't fear insulting them. They know you love them.

Dad's hug yesterday was too much, after no one touching me for nearly five weeks. My skin is hyper-sensitive now. Other than having an orderly prod along the inside of my mouth to make sure I swallowed my meds, and the random hand pat from Ms. Amelia, Ren yanking up my t-shirt to check out my stomach put me in a tailspin. I'm not going to tell them, and I'm going to suffer through it, because I want them to touch me, even if I can't handle it yet.

The cake Willow and Clover made gave me the shits after not having processed sugar in ages. I'd seriously kill for a burger, and I don't care how long I have to sit on the john afterward– it would be worth it. When I get home, I'm going to get fucking fat after being deprived.

Sucking in deep breaths, I try not to move my chest too much because it would be obvious I'm on the edge of breaking down. That's one thing the patients learn early on– how to hide the stronger reactions. We're always being watched, even if they say it's unsupervised. I can sense someone watching, and it isn't Leo the yoga instructor pretending to soak up some rays a few yards from the picnic table. I can't tell if it's Ms. Amelia or Delaney, but I have a sneaking suspicion they're together and watching from the shadows of the meditation pavilion.

I acknowledge I'm a paranoid shit, but my instincts are always accurate.

The patient arrivals are staggered for a reason. We arrive in groups of five, because we need specialized care, with different needs being met during the specific weeks. The staggering ensures we all get the same level of care. I know Taryn is somewhere in the main building waiting for Ms. Elsberry to visit, with her doctor and therapist hiding nearby. Same with Tommy and Reverend Braxton– they're in the nondenominational temple. I haven't seen the kids yet, but I was promised a lunch with them during week seven, because they know we'll be going home together and Taryn will especially need my support.

Index finger picking up speed, I can hear Weston and Rae's chatter before I catch sight of them. One. Two. In. One. Two. Out. I school my breathing, knowing I'm being watched, but also because I need to be in control of my emotions. I can't allow outside stimuli to affect me.

One. Two. In. One. Two. Out.

Standing from the picnic table, I watch my family, with only Dad and Ren spotting me with their hawk-like gaze. "Hi!" Raising my palm, I give a little wave and smile as they approach. Skin quivering over my muscles, I can't handle the onslaught of affection coming my way.

I'm in control.

Knowing the Delaneys are watching, it gives me strength I didn't know I had. Shocking Dad silent and immobile, I grab a hold of his wrists so he can't hug me, then I tug downward until we're face-to-face. Pecking a quick kiss to his cheek, I hope he's happy because that's all I've got in me to give.

Looking melty, all the stress flows out of Dad's muscles, so I know I did good. "Is the hotel okay?" I go for bullshit, small talk.

Moving over to Weston, I ruffle up the kid's hair. Somehow understanding, the kid flows with it. "Yeah, the pool is frickin' sweet!" My baby brother is so healthy and strong– happy. Everything I've gone through will be worth it, as long as this kid has a good life.

"When you go pro, the first thing you should get yourself is a pool." We all talk smack like that to the kid, but now I realize how much pressure he's under.

The contemplative expression on Weston's too young face informs me that is his plan, but he's scared he'll fail. "Yeah, I like that idea."

"No!" Rae whines. "You're gonna buy me a hot tub."

"Go visit Aunt Ginny," Weston snaps back, when I've never heard him raise his voice before. Trouble in paradise for my baby siblings.

Rae flinches, and it's a knee-jerk reaction on my part to tug her into a hug. "C'mere," I murmur into her ear, really squeezing her. I've always given good hugs, and I was scared I'd lost it. "This is nice, hugging someone the exact same size as me– it's like hugging myself."

Weston's vicious dig forgotten, Rae giggles and squeezes me back. "The big brutes like to act all intimidating."

Pulling away, I catch sight of Dad and Ren rolling their eyes. "What am I, chopped liver?" Ren gestures at himself when I don't make a move to touch him.

"I–" lips fluttering, I try to be nice with my request, because my brand of bluntness leads me to using people by forcing them to comply. "I would like to spend today with Ren– *alone*."

"Devon?" Dad moves to stand in front of me, gazing down with disappointment and a heavy dose of hurt. "I miss you."

"I know, Dad." Deep breath. "I know." Reaching forward, I rest my hand on Dad's chest to stop him from touching me, but also to soothe his ruffled feathers. "Tomorrow. Just you and me, okay? Our last day will be all of us."

"I'm good." West puts his palms out, reading my expression accurately. "I'm not getting bent out of shape. I get it."

"Daddy," Rae coaxes, tugging on Dad's hand. "Leave 'em be."

Eyes closed, I try to express myself instead of lashing out. "It's hard because you need things from me I can't give you right now." Eyes opening, I connect with Dad. "I'm feeling a bit raw, edgy. I haven't been touched or touched anyone in *weeks*, so let Ren desensitize me so I can be around you."

"I won't touch you." Dad steps back, palms raised, which was exactly what I wanted to avoid.

"Maybe I want you to, okay?" Deep breath. "It doesn't have to make sense, just roll with it."

"Okay." Dad's hurt but trying his damnedest not to show it. So I tug on his wrist again to give him a kiss on the cheek. When I pull away, he's smiling at me. The man needs a dozen sessions with Delaney over his need for constant displays of affection.

"It's only forty-five-minutes, so just go hang out in the meditation pavilion– there's an indoor koi pond in there."

"And no sun," Rae stresses, pale nose already pinking.

"Exactly," I mutter with a smile. "We'll meet you in there a few minutes before our time is up."

Ren and I wait in silence as our family disappears into the building a few hundred feet from me. I wait a heartbeat more, going on a hunch. Sure as shit, Ms. Amelia steps from the shadowed side of the building to follow them inside. Smirking, I raise two fingers in a salute to Delaney, knowing I'm not a paranoid shit.

"What are you…" Ren trails off, thinking me crazy.

"My doctor is hanging out like a bat in the belfry." Chuckling, I fist Ren's t-shirt and yank him until his feet start moving. "Let's walk, bro. I can't sit still long."

"Outside?" Ren sounds aghast while pulling his shirt away from his chest, fluttering the fabric to fan his heated skin. "Isn't there any air-conditioning around here?"

"I'm used to it," I mutter with a shrug.

"You have a helluva fucking tan, bro." Ren looks at me with appreciation shining from his eyes. "Dayum!"

"There's no cold water," I blurt out, so fucking ecstatic to hold a regular conversation with someone without walking on eggshells. We're discouraged from forming relationships with our fellow patients because anyone with a shred of empathy will take on everyone else's problems and not work on their own. Other than Ms. Amelia, it's all been regimented bullshit.

"What?" Ren squawks, and I don't know whether it's because he's shocked over my admission, or because a lizard just scurried up the stone-paver pathway.

"Back home, ya know how we have to run the hot water for a minute until the cold water in the pipes is drained?"

"Yeah," Ren mutters absentmindedly, looking like he's been dropped on an alien planet. "Hate brushing my teeth with icy water."

"Yeah, there's no such thing as a cold water tank." Chuckling, I remember scalding myself a time or two. "I have to let the water run a few minutes, because what's in the pipes has heated to a billion fucking degrees."

"You're shitting me." Ren shoves his palm against my chest, looking floored. "Right?"

"Not a billion degrees, but definitely a hundred fucking degrees– there's no such thing as a cold shower around here."

"Probably ought to have signed you up last winter, eh?" Ren turns contemplative, so I have to steer the conversation.

"I'm sorry I freaked out yesterday," I blurt out before my brother can say anything. "It felt like I was being buried, so I had to get away."

"We brought up no-no subjects." The guilt in Ren's voice kills me.

"Listen." Gripping Ren's t-shirt in my fist, I wheel him around and plunk him down on one of the convenient benches scattered around everywhere. "I can't talk about important shit while walking, but I can't sit long. It's a tic I've picked up."

Eyebrows scrunching together in the center of his forehead, I can tell I'm entering a territory Ren's never going to understand. "Tic?"

"I'm filled with this nervous energy, always have been. It took the doctors a few weeks to separate it from the drug addiction and bipolarism. It's just me, like how athletic you, Dad, and Weston are. I have to have an outlet, like tapping my finger, or scrubbing at the back of my neck, or yanking at my hair, or standing abruptly and walking it off."

"Like Weston's restless leg syndrome?" Ren is trying so hard to understand, I could hug him.

"Yeah, just like that– like my skin is gonna crawl off my flesh if I don't move. So don't freak out if I start wigging out a bit when we're talking."

"We don't have to talk."

"Yes, we do– I need it." Turning to the side to face my brother, I tuck my leg underneath my ass. *I'm sorry.*

"What?" Panic etches across Ren's features. "Why? Don't!"

Using my thumbnail, I start peeling at my index fingernail. With a deep breath, I look my brother in the eye and spill. "I'm sorry for not protecting you—"

"Don't—" Ren is cut off by my palm smothering his mouth.

"You *will* listen," I order. "You won't reply until I get home. I want you to think about what I'm saying for a long time, okay?"

After waiting a few seconds to make sure Ren keeps his trap shut, I drop my hand. "I have a lot to say, and I don't have a lot of time to say it. It's the reason why I never mailed the notes I wrote to you guys. You deserve to hear it from my lips while I look you in the eye."

"Okay." Ren slumps to the back of the bench, defeated.

"I'm mad at you," I finally admit the truth. "So fucking furious."

Eyes widening, "What?" Ren breathes out in shock.

"You have to make me a goddamn promise before I say anything else," I demand, then realize I'm falling back into how I used to act. After a second, where I check in with how I'm reacting, I realize this is part of my core personality and not a damn thing to do with being mental.

"The second you see Weston, or Raven, or my kid, or your own… your grandkids, nieces or nephews… any kid or adult act like I did, you get them help immediately." Gasping for air, I try to calm myself down.

"I… I–I don't understand," Ren stammers, obviously confused.

"With Grammy and Aunt Ginny, what happened with Mom should've never gone down. What happened with me shouldn't have either. I'm not blaming you or Dad— I'm trying to get you to see the truth. We have a history of mental illness in our family, and no one should be left behind. The quicker it's diagnosed and properly treated, the outlook for a fulfilling life is greater."

"I kept your secrets because you made me promise," Ren whispers, looking more horrified than he sounds.

"I said I wasn't blaming you— I'm apologizing for putting you in that situation. I'm also begging you to help anyone in need, no matter what promises they make you give."

"What about Raven?" Voice quivering, Ren's truly worried about our baby sister. "She's so dark all the time."

"That's her personality— she's fine." I've never felt more positive about anything before. "She's a teenager, leave her be. But I'm more worried about Weston's transformation."

Laughing sardonically, Ren rubs his tummy. "Kid– the kid is horny and being cock-blocked."

"Yeah, but why's he being nasty to Rae?" I mutter in confusion, understanding how hormones make a guy go off the rails.

Ren's words are nearly lost in his laughter. "Rae's the cock-block."

"Oh!" Eyes widening, I chuckle too. Sobering, the verbal vomit spews. "I'm sorry about all the shit with Essie and Willow– suffocating you with a pillow, choking you... fucking your girlfriend."

The only reaction Ren gives me is a smirk, like I don't have to voice any of that because he already knows. "My doctor forced me to admit I wanted Willow. It wasn't about revenge."

"No shit." Ren snorts.

"I regret it– wish I'd never touched Willow like that."

"Just so we're clear." Ren flashes me a pointed look. "I don't regret touching Essie, and I'd rather you didn't regret touching Willow."

"It's complicated," I mutter, feeling an inch big.

"I repeat– *no shit.*" A huge grin spreads across my brother's face, and it scares the piss out of me. "I know I freaked you out by telling you about the house, but I want to know why."

Deep breath. "My biggest regret is how Willow and Essie's friendship was my collateral damage." Turning sharply, I stare my brother down. "You can't put Willow in a house with Essie and me, shoving her nose in what we did. That's not fair.... I can't– I can't stand by and keep my shit in check if Willow's targeting Essie all the time. I can't. It's unhealthy."

"We're good." Ren reaches over to squeeze my neck a few times, massaging the tension away. "Your girl is doing good, so is your kid. Essie's been hanging around Clover and Mary a lot, but mostly Rob and Dave."

"What?" voice pitching high with confusion, I try to reason that out. "Why?"

"Essie froze me out for a while before and after you left, worried about how Willow would react, but I didn't give up. So we're good now. She loves telling me stories about how Clover treats Dave like an invalid. After taking care of his family for seventy years, he gets off on being mothered. Clover brings him food, puts his socks on his feet, combs his hair, makes him comfy and gives him fresh newspapers. But the minute Clover leaves, Dave's back to being the man of the house, working manual labor and giving advice. Essie finds it hilarious."

"She's living with Dave and Mary?" I coax for more info, since no one will tell me anything here. "What about Beth?"

Ren's laughter is so infectious, I don't worry about what he has to tell me. "Beth and Rory eloped. They're living in the loft above Rush."

"Wow." Blinking rapidly, I realize I missed a lot while living in a drug haze.

"Essie will be staying with Dave and Mary for few more days– she's loosened up and has been enjoying their company."

"A few more days? Is your house ready or something?"

"No." Ren pauses, and I know he's trying to figure out if he should tell me everything or not. "Listen, while we're here, there's been a lot of shit going down back home. Clover told Willow the truth. They've been packing up our house, Dave and Mary's, Clover's, and everyone will be moving into the Pink Taco Hut on Sunday, with the rest of us at the Spook House. Dad and Clover are getting married Monday morning at the Courthouse."

"*Jesus.*" It takes a few seconds for me to realize I'm scrubbing at the back of my neck, anxiety ratcheting up to toxic level. "Your house?"

"It's in escrow." Pausing again, I fear what else my brother has to tell me. "It's not *my* house."

"What do you mean?"

"It's Aunt Ginny's." Ren shrugs like it's no big deal. "No credit equals a shitty credit score. Then there's Essie…" My brother laughs like he finds my future wife's predicament cute. "Anyway, no matter how big of a down payment we could swing, we'd be paying interest for twenty-some years on a thirty-year mortgage, just so we could have a smaller monthly payment. Ginny bought the house outright and is going to do a land contract with you. Interest-free for all of us."

"*With me?*" Try as I might, I can't wrap my mind around that.

"It's your house." Ren cuffs me in the shoulder, smiling widely. "Willow and I will help with your payments and shit until everyone is on their feet and we can afford our own house."

"Babysitting me, you mean?"

"No shit." Ren chuckles at how I can still get pissed off, no matter how many meds I have streaming in my veins. "We've always lived together, so what's the big fucking deal? It will help Dad sleep at night–"

"Leave us alone, you mean?"

"Exactly." Ren couldn't be prouder of himself if he tried.

Fury turning to concern, "What about Willow and Essie?"

"There's some kinks, but we're working it out." Ren turns sheepish, and I struggle to figure out how to scrub the back of my neck and itch my thigh at the same time. "Essie's good– she gets it. Willow's a work-in-progress, but I'm hopeful."

"You've told them?"

"I'm not a fucking idiot, Dev– of course I told 'em." Ren grimaces, so it must've not been a fun conversation. "The four of us need each other for different reason, okay?"

"Are you still looking at Essie like you want to fuck her?" I blurt out, sounding like my old self. Ren just smirks at me in answer. "That's not cool, dumbass. Willow's– I hurt Willow in ways no one should be hurt. I said shit that probably fucked her up."

"Made her an insecure mess?" Ren glares at me pointedly. "Yeah, it's been fun navigating the landmines you planted, but we're fucking nonstop–"

"You are?" I mutter in awe. "Is it any good?"

Now I have Ren yanking his own hair out. "Fuck, I don't know if you're a masochist or a sadist."

"Both," I answer honestly. "If there's two extremes of anything, I'm always both."

"Noted," Ren mutters with narrowed eyes. "It's good. It's been a lot of fun. We've been avoiding I love yous and deep, meaningful conversations because I can't trust Willow until she forgives Essie." Refusing to look me in the eye, Ren whispers so quietly I have to lean forward. "Sometimes it gets too intense so I pull back and make Willow laugh."

"Huh?" I grunt, mulling that over. "Maybe someday I'll know what fun feels like. It's always been terrifying and intense for me. Wait–" Blushing, I don't know if I should say it. "What I did with Kurt was for fun. Awkwardly hilarious."

"No. no. no… nononononono…" Ren whispers while cupping his palms over his ears. "Don't wanna know. My brother would never do that willingly."

"Pretty sure one of your brothers is being a nasty puke because he's not allowed to do *that*," I tease. "Seriously, though. It helped me let go of Alejandro."

Shuddering, Ren is rendered speechless.

"Kieren?" I call to get his attention, because his eyes are glazed over in horror. "You need to talk to someone before I come home. But, what I need the most–" Sighing heavily, I let it out. "I know the world doesn't revolve around me, but I've worked so hard to get where I am today and I won't allow anything to jeopardize it. If Willow and Essie aren't getting along in *my* house, I'll kick everyone out for my sanity's sake."

"Even if I have to lock them in a goddamn room until they work their shit out, I promise Willow and Essie will be best friends again." Ren levels me with a look. "My future depends on it too."

"Do you forgive me?" voice sounding small, like a terrified child. "For everything?"

Gripping the front of my throat, Ren's palm is hot against my flesh. "Do you forgive me?" He gives me a bit of a shake, trying to rattle the answer out of me.

"We're good."

"We're good." Ren smiles slyly. "Now where's my fucking hug?"

CHAPTER FORTY-EIGHT

Willow Prynne

Over the past few weeks, we've been allowing life to sweep us by. Devon will be home tonight. It seems like yesterday since he left for rehab. But at the same time, it feels like forever and a day ago. So much has happened. Life has hit an even keel because we can't have chaos swirling around Devon now that he's coming home.

Everyone is settled in at the Pink Taco Hut, with the Spook House welcoming Essie as if she'd always been there. Rob seems happier to have us both with him, like a bit of our old home is in his new one. It's the same reason Auggie's been happier with Ren staying with us, or maybe it's because Isis is around more often now, visiting everyone at the two houses. So clannish– I can't wait for a house to call my own, yet they all love being shoved up each other's asses. Poor Clover, but she's rolling with it.

Essie and I are no longer avoiding one another, but we don't seek each other out unless absolutely necessary. We're too busy, with both of us working nonstop. There's hurt on both sides, and only best friends have the ammunition to make snippy, side remarks meant to wound. I'm trying my best to not do that shit anymore, but a few insults slip out before I can stop them– playful insults that never used to wound Essie when we were BFFs, but maybe they always did and she just hid it well.

Malcolm and Kieren left for Arizona to pick up Devon, needing to speak with his team on the dos and don'ts of his recovery, but they'll all be home tonight. I'm at a standstill at Devon's house. The closing isn't until the end of the week, because Dev needs to sign paperwork for the land contract agreement with Ginny. The passing of a house between three parties takes a lot of time, red-tape, and legal mumbo-jumbo I don't understand. The previous owners and Ginny allowed me to paint every room and do anything that involved toxic chemicals or vapors, so it would be aired out when Essie moves in. The rest of the stuff, I'm waiting on Devon to help so he can take ownership in his own house, with Essie decorating it. Acting just like my dad– the house isn't mine, but I'll help for free as long as I'm showing them how to fix it for themselves. If they plan on being lazy, with me doing all the work, I'm out.

Clover and I are just winging it. Somedays we're too sarcastic to each other, and it feels like we're undoing all the work we've put in. Other days, we're sappy, bawling and hugging each other while spewing our feelings. We're never going to have a mother-daughter relationship like we have with Mom, so we're finding our own path.

Today, I feel oddly like a girl without a purpose. No home improvements to be done until Devon gets here. No Kieren to goof off with because he's on his way to Arizona. No Wreck & Ruin because Stone is off to a Revolutionary Road concert with his dad. Jackson Stone– who I've yet to catch in person –he's forcing Stone to learn the family business. Dad's having one-on-one guy-time with Ozzy, since Malcolm isn't around dominating the guy's time. Revamped is closed for the day, because Auggie's being an adult and having every property he owns appraised. I have no idea why he's worried about his assets, but Robbie's been a giddy shit lately, so I assume it's connected.

With nothing better to do, I decide to go bother the residents of the Pink Taco Hut, since I saw Essie crossing the street from my bedroom window a few minutes ago. Idle hands are the devil's playground and all that jazz, I've got to keep busy or bad habits start screaming for attention.

I tiptoe on the porch, loving how I freak everyone out when I sneak in. I've been trying to get Clover to let me install a screen door, since a house is not a home without a screen door banging to announce my arrival.

Words flowing outside, I can't help but eavesdrop– alright, I purposefully eavesdrop. I am related to Robin Prynne, after all. "God, I thought morning sickness sucked." A nasty part of me secretly gets off on Essie being uncomfortable, but the part that loves her smoothers it. An added plus, I know I'm going to love that baby as if it were my own. "I'm not very big. I just feel so bloated, like my skin is gonna burst. It makes bending impossible."

Leaning on the doorjamb, I fold my arms over my chest and watch my family interact. "That right there," Rae grumbles, pointing at Essie's swollen midsection, "is the best birth control on the planet."

Rae's changed over the past few weeks, now that we share Clover. Hard to believe the girl is my stepsister– Ren is my *stepbrother*. Rae's always quiet, hiding in the background, but when it's just a handful of people she trusts, she comes out of her shell and truly glows. The girl has good instincts, and she feels comforted with Essie around, which rubs me both right and wrong. Rae isn't comfortable with me around. But then again, Rae's known Essie since she was a tiny girl– wish I would've known that major piece of information last year.

"I can't believe Dad is letting you get on the shot," Violet says, sounding amazed. If Rae is stepping into the spotlight, my violent sister is stepping out of it. Still girly and posh, Violet seems more introspective lately, which worries me some. I'm not sure how I feel about her calling Malcolm Dad. What about Sam? It's the same reason I won't call Clover Mom, or call my grandparents anything but Mom and Dad. They raised me and deserve the honorific. Sam shouldn't be forgotten, even if Malcolm is an amazing stepfather.

The mischievous Prynne comes out of Violet, the part that some find insulting and hard to swallow. "Now I can't tease you about how great it was not to worry about starting my period in gym class and staining my white shorts."

"Ahahahaa…" Essie mock laughs, and I bite back one of my own. I'll never forget how mortified Essie was when it happened to her. She was so jealous when I was put on the shot once my period started. "Remind me never to share in girl talk with you, ya little narc. Most mortifying moment of my life. I was only twelve."

"I told Daddy that it wasn't about sex," Rae answers Violet's earlier remark. "Seeing as how you'll be a fifty-year-old virgin with a herd of cats."

"Bitch," Violet blurts out, but she's smirking. The girls remind me of Essie and me back in the day, age-gap included. "You so did not say that to him."

Rae grins back, which is out of the ordinary for her. "Nah, I told him the truth. I didn't bleach my moustache for the last two weeks, and then I cried, telling Daddy it was his horrible genetics that were making me a sideshow freak. I bartered for birth control, hoping for laser treatments."

Violet finishes Rae's sentences as if Rae is her twin. "But Dad's more worried about your new fascination with Ozzy, so that was a no-go. F-A-I-L!"

"I know, right? Sucks. I really wanted those laser treatments," Rae grumbles.

Last year, Ren told me about how he had to beat the shit out of a boy for calling Rae the bearded lady. Isis is gorgeous, and Rae looks just like her aunt, but the bullying and her introverted ways have made her dress in dark-colored, grubby clothing, in order to fade into the background.

Looking utterly defeated, Rae mumbles, "If it gets bad enough, I'll trade in my '*whatever fund*' for them."

If it gets bad enough, I'll give Rae *my* 'whatever fund' to help her pay for treatments. I was saving it for a down payment on a new truck. I'm covering my own tuition, and I'm not a princess, fairytale wedding sort of girl. Whatever's left over will go toward a down payment on a house. But I'd give it up if it meant Rae didn't feel she had to hide in the shadows to avoid being humiliated.

"Clover?" The look on Essie's face is so sympathetic, I can't help but melt because of it. No doubt Rae will be on Essie's table, no payment expected. I can see Essie's wheels spinning, then see as she thinks better than to bring it up without asking Malcolm in private. "I'm only twenty-one, but when in the fuck did this shit change? Five, six years ago, this was not on my mind."

"Maybe Mom should've taken you on girls' day before now. You coulda used the protection." Violet so bluntly puts it– atta girl, my baby sister. "Now, instead of the shot, you're gonna have a doctor listen to your baby's heartbeat. The shit just got real, cousin."

"No shit," I mutter too loudly, drawing attention to me lurking in the doorway.

"I'm going to install a screen door for you to smash into the wall so I'll hear you coming. This ghostly routine freaks my ass out." Clover grins at me, knowing damned well I want to play carpenter, but she's the one not giving in.

It's a little, mischievous game we play. What's a bit of fun banter between mother and daughter as an ice breaker?

"Girls' day? Little late for that, Essie." The words flow, as does the snicker, without a thought from me. Instantly I feel bad, because this isn't like old times between Essie and me, where we'd tease each other but didn't mean anything by it. "Sorry," I mutter, coughing into my hand.

"Are you coming with us, too?" Beaming, Violet skips over to me, always happy to have me around now that we have a solid sister relationship and I treat her right. "It sucked last time, just me and Mom. I didn't have anyone to grin and bear it while I got stuck."

All the blood flows out of my body as my heart ceases to beat. I sway on my feet, suddenly dizzy. "Last time?" is a weak rasp as a cold sweat sheens my body. Mental calculations take place. When I'd gone to the clinic last, I'd been a different person back then.

Shit!

"Yeah, you didn't go with us. I was sad that you were so grown up you were going by yourself." Violet issues the patented Prynne pout. "I felt abandoned."

Horrified, all I can do is look to Clover for help. Instead of seeing reassurance shining back at me, my mom ass-plants on the sofa. "Mom?" croaks out, voice warbling with terror. Finally my heart starts beating, but it's too rapid. My body goes from swaying on my feet to buzzing with its own vibration. "What... what happens if you miss a course? Aren't you supposed to start your period?"

Eyes closed, Clover's words pool dread in my belly. "You'll share my appointment with me. Essie can go with the girls for their shots." Rising from the sofa, she walks across the living room as if treading through quicksand. "C'mon girls. Let's start our girls' day," Clover says, sounding chipper yet strained.

"What's wrong, Mom?" Looking back and forth between us, Violet sounds as petrified as I feel. "Willow?"

Mind clearing slightly, I come to find my fingernails engaged in a death-grip with the doorframe. Body swaying, I'm scared I'm going to faint.

"All's good," Essie steps in because Clover and I are incapable.

"Sure," Rae mutters, not sounding convinced. "I wouldn't call it '*good*'. More like a catastrophe. Fuck those laser treatments– I'm buying a hysterectomy. That will even protect me against immaculate conception."

"No," I mutter in denial. "No." No girl can remain in denial when their mother practically picks her up to lead her to the car.

With Essie driving, and Rae riding shotgun, I'm tucked between my mom and my sister, shaking so violently they are keeping me from shattering apart.

Mind doing calculations, "Three months ago I missed my shot, right?"

"Right," Violet squeezes my hand tightly. "Ninety days ago today."

"Essie?!" I practically shout, my question obvious.

Blue eyes held impossibly wide, Essie gapes at me in the rearview mirror, only fear for me etched on her expression. No '*I told you so*' or '*serves you right*' like I deserve after treating her like shit for months.

"Ninety days is twelve weeks. I'm fourteen weeks. It's not impossible, but highly unlikely it would be Devon's. It would take a bit for you to ovulate again. If anything, you'd be fertile about now, not back then. There's a higher chance you're *not* pregnant."

"So if I am…" I trail off, thinking of how Ren would react. Ren's so goddamn selfless, even by some nightmare brought to life, where I was pregnant with Devon's kid, Ren would love it just as much as his own. "It should be Ren's, but what if it's not? We need chaos-free. *Fuck!*"

"At least it can't be Auggie's." Violet shines on the bright spot, but she says it in a way where I'd swear it was Robbie sitting next to me. The diabolical girl is both worried and excited by the drama. "Kinda ironic after bitching about Essie. We may need Maury Povich."

"Dr. Phil," Essie breathes, not looking amused. "V, don't harass Willow right now. None of us can take it."

"Drive faster," Rae mutters in a panic. "I need that shot now. There's possibly three pregnant women in this car, and it's a contagion. I'm only sixteen, and there's a hot boy living in our house. I accidently brushed up against Ozzy in the hallway earlier, and he was only wearing a pair of sweat pants."

"*Nice*," Violet murmurs in appreciation. "You need to pay better attention in biology, girlfriend– it doesn't work that way. I avoid the bathtub drains after the boys get out of the shower. You just know they're doing nasty things in there. I always spray the entire tub with bleach, let it sit for five minutes, rinse, then take my shower."

"That's what's taking so long in there?" Rae sounds shocked. "I just thought you were being a selfish bitch by hogging the bathroom."

My predicament momentarily forgotten, I home in on Clover. "Mom?"

"Either I'm menopausal in my mid-thirties…" Clover shudders next to me. "Or Masons reproduce like bunnies."

"Oh, no!" Rae cries out, palming the dashboard as Essie pulls into the clinic. "*I'm a Mason.*"

"Oh, shush!" Violet hits Rae in the back of the head. "You're an atheist. Did you suddenly find God and become The Virgin Mary. Shut it– we've got bigger fish to fry here."

"Everyone calm down." My once crazy cousin turns into the only adult in the car, because even Clover has spaced out. "Prynnes are hard to impregnate."

"The Prynne *men* are close to infertile," Clover sparks to life. "I got knocked up with Willow after one time– the twins while on the pill. If I'm not pregnant with Malcolm's kid, I don't know what that man's been trying to do for the past three months."

"Oh, you're pregnant." Essie chuckles mischievously while pulling the keys out of the ignition. "Rae, you're fine. But I'm worried about Willow right now. So let's get inside. She can take my appointment, and I'll wait until my ultrasound next month."

"Willow will go with me– you go with the girls. Hold hands, grit teeth when stuck, bond as sisters." Clover flows from the car, then yanks my immobile behind after her. "We'll be okay."

The adult in me disappears, and my mommy has to take over for me. Clover pushes me into a seat in the waiting room, with Violet and Rae flanking me, then goes off to check-in for herself and her three daughters. Essie shows she's more adult than the rest of us, checking herself in at the counter.

Slumped forward, with Violet and Raven chatting to one another over top of my bent head, I glance around the waiting room. A mix of sick kids, coughing and sneezing until we'll all end up on death's door, with a few shady looking young woman clearly waiting for the clinic's gynecological services– they don't want to be here any more than I do.

"Mrs. Mason. Ms. Willow Prynne." A nurse calls from the open doorway, making sure I know she means me and not Essie. On heavy feet, I amble toward the woman like I'm going to the gallows. "Your mother said it was okay to share an appointment. Is this okay, or do you wish to speak to the doctor in private."

Nice ethics in this place– I like this nurse. The old bitty who used to be the nurse around here never gave Violet or me a choice, and she was super judgy. All three of us had to go in together, with Clover hearing all the answers to the usual embarrassing questions.

"There's nothing she doesn't already know," I mumble, following the nurse through the hallway, with Clover bringing up the rear. I'm handed a cup, which feels too light in my numb hand.

"You know the drill." The nurse winks at me, because I go through this routine every visit before getting the shot– the pregnancy test. No doubt, if I'm negative, I'll be getting stuck– thank fuck. But what if it's positive?

Shit!

There's a reason Clover's with me, instead of me doing this routine with my sisters– she's scared I'm pregnant too.

After we both do the pee-in-a-cup-business, we're escorted to the examine room, with me being told to sit on the table, with Clover sitting in a chair. After the nurse asks a few questions of both of us, she leaves, then Clover hops up on the table to sit right next to me.

"We're going to be okay," is the last thing we say for a very long time. The clinic is busy, and it could take a while before we're seen by the doctor.

My mind spins, but the shaking never lessens. In order to protect myself, I start wondering what it would be like. Not being pregnant or childbirth, because I want no part of that uncomfortable business. But what it would be like to share a kid with Kieren. He'd be an amazing father, and I know he wants children someday. We could fast-forward through this insecure, unsure portion of our relationship, where neither one of us knows what's up from down. I'm in love with Ren, can see myself spending forever with him, and I know he feels the same way. But neither of us has the confidence to tell the other. This would either fast-track that or destroy what we're building.

For about a half hour, I use in-depth fantasies to build a life with Kieren Mason, experiencing what the future could hold. In the beginning, it was about desensitizing myself to reality. But I realize along the journey, I want this for all the right and wrong reasons, and I begin to understand my cousin more than I ever had.

Cupping what could or could not be inside my belly, I laugh at how ridiculous I've been. Irresponsible and judgmental, while calling everyone else out on their bullshit– bullshit that was none of my business.

"I never understood the definition of irony." My words cause Clover to release a disturbingly painful bark of sharp laughter. "I was always using it wrong... but now I know."

"But now you know." Laughing harder, Clover's losing it, and I need her to be strong so I won't fall apart. "Now I bet you wished you hadn't called Essie an irresponsible whore. Not that you're a whore– just that you thought Essie being pregnant made her one."

"I'm not pregnant," I deny, voice breaking. Half of me is hoping I'm not, while the other half is wishing I am, but the whole of me is terrified. "What do you find so funny?"

Still laughing manically, "I've got a joke for you. Ready?" Clover pauses heavily, so I shrug in reply. "A mother and daughter are sitting in their doctor's office, waiting for their piss to be tested. One could be a new mother and a grandmother at the age of fucking thirty-five. That, my daughter, is the very definition of irony."

"I don't see why that's ironic," I mumble, confused by how odd Clover's behaving.

"Because I worked my entire life to give you a different life than the one I led." Gesturing around the doctor's office, "And yet, look where we are. Ironic."

"Like mother, like daughter," I whisper, tears finally making an appearance. "This isn't fair," I whimper, sounding like a child, when I could be carrying a child. Shaking, I doubt I've ever been this terrified in my whole entire life. Every nerve in my body is vibrating in fear. My teeth are chattering.

Somehow understanding exactly how I feel in this moment, because we wouldn't be sitting here if she didn't, Clover takes my hand, squeezing tightly. "It's life. It's not fair. Life is in the driver's seat– we are merely its passengers."

Whipping my head up, the door cracking open draws my complete attention. "Mrs. Mason? Ms. Prynne?" Dr. Gilmore announces her arrival while staring down at a sheet of paper within a folder. Clover and I share a terrified look as the doctor says, "I have your test results."

Shuddering violently, I'm on the verge of fainting. Clover wraps her arm around me, lending me strength. "Dr. Gilmore, please tell my daughter before she passes out on me."

"Oh, sorry!" Dr. Gilmore is a woman in her fifties, the same doctor I've had for most of my life. She drags a stool over by hooking her ankle on it, then sits in front of us. "Sometimes I forget how scary or exciting this is, after doing this day in and day out since I was in my late twenties."

Clover and I just stare at Dr. Gilmore, as she smiles brightly. "I think someone needs this." She produces the birth control shot as her answer. "You know the procedure, Willow. When you're ready for children, we'll discuss the proper way of going off birth control."

Slumping in shock, I can't feel my hands or feet, so Clover helps the doctor prepare me for the shot. "Everything will be okay," Clover whispers in my ear, rubbing her hands up and down my shoulders and arms. "You'll have a child when you're ready. Just let this be a lesson. No matter how responsible you are, shit happens, and it's not fair to judge other women when you've been there yourself. Never look down on another girl again, not for sex or pregnancy or any reason at all, while excusing the boy for the same actions."

"Yes, Mom." I wince sharply as the needle bites into my flesh. Adrenaline rushing from my veins leaves me crashing– emotionally, mentally, and physically.

"Clover." Dr. Gilmore turns to my mother. "I assume you already know what comes next after going through this twice before. Undress, then hop on the table. I have to examine you."

Clover does as she's told, leaving me in the chair she was originally sitting in. Peeking around the folding divider she's undressing behind, she orders the doctor around. "Dr. Gilmore, could you go get my girls before we get started. I'd like them to see this part– best birth control on the planet. I need Essie to take Willow somewhere to talk."

"Why?" I utter, just now realizing I'm bawling hysterically, not sure if it's in relief or mourning over the fantasy I built up over the past hour.

The doctor leaves the room silently, somehow knowing what's going on when I don't. Clover reappears wearing a paper examination gown to cover her nakedness.

"You need Essie right now, Sapling." Clover reaches over to clear my cheeks with her thumb. "I'm not abandoning you right now, but I need to take care of my baby." Her words have the truth kicking me in the ass.

"Jesus, I'll almost be twenty with a baby sibling. Gross–"

"What did I say about making judgments?" Clover raises an eyebrow, chastising me. "Devon will be hitting twenty-two by the time the kid is born, with a kid of his own. But that's what happens when you have a set of kids in your late teens, and another when you're a mature adult."

"Point taken and heard." Standing on wobbly legs, I sniffle to clear my nose. "I don't know why I'm so upset right now." The tears will *not* stop. My breath keeps hitching. Instead of shaking, I feel like my body's so light I'm going to keel over.

Clover just looks at me with sympathy and pity etched across her features, somehow knowing how I feel when I don't. She's saved from saying anything by Violet charging into the examination room. "Who's pregnant? Oh, my God, what's going on? Why is Willow crying? She never cries. Is someone dying?"

A laughing Clover takes control of Violet, while also managing to keep Raven from hiding in the corner out of sight and out of mind. "You guys are going to have a baby brother or sister, and I want you to be with me the first time we hear the heartbeat."

Clover looks over everyone's heads, spotting Essie in the doorway. A silent conversation flows between them, one I'll never understand, causing Essie to head in my direction.

"Way too many people in a small room– Dr. Gilmore doesn't even fit in here. C'mon, Willow, let's go to Salon. We'll get the footbath in the pedicure station warmed up for their girls' day. Will you help me?"

"Okay," I mumble numbly, with a bizarre thought hitting me out of nowhere. "How are we getting to Salon?"

"We'll walk, silly." Essie wraps her arm around my shoulders, which is nice and comforting since we're the same height. "It's not that far. Since my car met the big trash compactor in the sky, my only means of transportation has been bipedal."

Essie and I have been sharing Robbie's Explorer, since he just bought a swanky Land Rover. By sharing, I mean Essie only uses it if I'm home and not going anywhere. Most of the time, I'm not home, so the Explorer is with me. Ren's been driving

Essie to and from Salon. The few nights a week Essie works at the No-Name, Sage Fischer picks her up– the boy loves the opportunity to stare at the Pink Taco Hut with longing, because Weston usually finds a reason to hang in the front lawn shirtless when Essie's being picked up for work.

I was there when Kieren and Stone told Essie it would cost more to get her car running than what it was worth. Essie cried when Ren hooked her Toyota to the back of a tow truck, headed to the junkyard. Now I'm crying, and not for a car. I cried when I lost my car too– when I torched it. When I killed it with fire because of Essie and Devon… the anger tries to erupt to erase whatever keeps the tears spilling from my eyes. But then I remember the words of wisdom Clover just hit me with. I was almost in a position where I could've been pregnant with Kieren's kid because I was irresponsible… worse, it could've been Devon's baby.

I know Essie's not at fault, but I still want to blame her. But it's difficult to do when her arm is slung over my shoulder, while she chatters a never-ending stream of nothingness while walking me down the sidewalk. At least Essie knows who her baby's daddy is– that's more than I would've known.

Irony. Throwing stones and living in glass houses– I have no room to judge.

"Why can't I stop crying?" Blinking back the tears, I finally take notice that Essie's unlocking Salon like she owns the place.

"Get in here first." Essie tugs me into the shop, then shuts and locks the door behind us. I'm shoved into the massaging pedicure chair, with the remote thrust into my hand, followed by a packet of tissues.

Essie leaves me to look around while she pulls the shades on the huge front windows. I don't ever remember there being shades, which makes me notice other things. "It looks different in here."

"Is different nice?" Essie smiles, tears shining in her eyes, but there's pride lingering there too. "I'm going for a day-spa vibe."

Blinking repeatedly, I gaze around to see that Salon is a different place entirely. I haven't been in here since Essie was a teenager working after school, with Elma ordering her around. It used to be puke-pink with framed posters of out-of-date hairstyles from the eighties. The shelf of expired hair products that were covered in dust has been replaced with a new unit filled with girly soaps and scrubs. There's now three pedicure stations on one side, three styling stations on the other, still only one hair-washing basin near the door to the backroom, with three tables set up in the center of the salon for manicures.

"Wow, it looks like a real salon– hey, isn't that your parents' sofa?" Laughing, I realize the cozy waiting area looks suspiciously like Aunt Ana's living room. Gone are the ripped, pink vinyl-covered chairs and the pressboard coffee table littered with style guides from the eighties.

"Uncle Dave repainted the place about a month ago." Essie's beaming with pride. "We bartered for a year's worth of free haircuts. Rob painted the mural over there– a lifetime worth of haircuts…" she trails off on a giggle, the infectious sound I've missed for months.

"Robbie's work is high-end," I mutter in awe at the lifelike rendering of Essie in her own environment. "I don't understand. What about Elma?"

"On January first, Salon will be renamed Primp." Essie sits on a brand new stool, then leans forward with difficulty due to her budding belly. She begins filling the footbath with warm water. "The new stations are courtesy of Isis. Right now it's just me, with Elma cutting hair until she retires. Beth comes in when I have a bunch of appointments in case there are walk-ins. I'm on the lookout for a teenager or two to mentor. If business picks up, I'll post an ad for licensed help."

Still confused, the words spill from my mouth, flowing faster than the water in the basin beneath my feet. "I don't understand. What's going on? What did Isis get out of it?"

"Rae's not the only one with excess body hair. Isis has been my best customer. We've tried waxing, but it gave her ingrown hairs. We've tried the laser, and she was a great candidate with her pale skin and dark hair, but it didn't work. *At all*. If anything, it made it worse. We're now trying electrolysis. Since I'm already paying off the esthetician equipment, the new salon stuff was purchased by bartering a lifetime of hair-removal for Isis Mason… and that hair is hella stubborn."

"Lost your biggest customer?" I have no idea why Essie's being nice to me after months of me being a cunt. She slips my flip-flops off my feet, then places first one foot, then the other, in the warm water.

"Yeah, but gained an upgrade to my salon, so I say it's an amazing deal." Essie squirts something that smells amazing into the water. "I can empathize with Isis and Rae, so I'll do whatever I can to ease their embarrassment. People can be cruel."

"Essie," I gasp out as a sob. Then the waterworks spring from nowhere. "Primp is yours, isn't it? You own this now?" Huffing in big swallows of air, I feel close to suffocating. "I'm proud of you, but I feel like shit. I own nothing, not even my own car. But now you have a business to call your own. A house. Devon," is torn from me, but the next is what hurts the worst. "*A baby.*"

"You little brat," Essie cries out, flying off her stool to land nearly on top of me, smothering me in a hug. "You're a few years younger than me, and I'm not insulting you by saying that. I was homeless a few weeks ago, with no car, a dead-end job, a drug addict's baby in my belly, and a mountain of debt... with my cousins doing a helluva smear campaign across town. Life takes time. You have to earn it. It's not instantaneous. It's not sunshine and rainbows for me, but I'm trying my damnedest."

"Why am I so upset?" Clutching Essie to me, I can't stop sobbing.

Tightening her arms around me, Essie seems stronger than I remember– more formidable. "I could tell you completely forgot about getting the shot, so it took you by surprise. It's easy for me to know how you're feeling right now. A lot of relief, I suspect, but a ton of grief over losing something you never had but wished you did."

"I didn't– I didn't think I wanted a kid," I gasp out, struggling to understand why I feel such gripping agony instead of relief. "But it feels like I lost a tiny towheaded Kieren, and it's killing me."

"Ren will make some cute babies," Essie teases me, trying to lighten my dark mood.

"Our babies could've grown up together, played together– been as close as siblings." The '*might've been siblings*' goes without saying. "But that's not happening now."

"It will in the future. Shh..." Essie rocks me back and forth like a mother would her child, and I've never felt so young in my entire life. "I understand– it's okay. Maybe now you can see why I wasn't going crazy over being pregnant. Devon needed something to hang onto. Hope. It's why I didn't want to tell him

I was pregnant until he came home, but Beth took that out of my hands. I feared if I lost the baby, he wouldn't recover from it."

"Please," I beg, fingernails biting into Essie's back. "Don't ever tell Ren about what happened today– please."

"This is between you and me, girlfriend." Releasing me, Essie glances up at the clock. "Someday you'll have a couple kids. When you and Kieren are ready. This is more of a blessing than a curse. You and Ren will be stronger, your lives more settled, and it will be better for your children if you wait."

"But what… but what if–" I struggle to voice my biggest fear as Essie crosses the salon to unlock the door and pull up the shades. "What if I can't have kids? Shouldn't I have gotten pregnant? Ren and I have been going at it like rabbits, and I wasn't on birth control like I thought I was."

"Willow," Essie sighs my name, making me feel even younger. She flips the lighted sign on, signaling the salon is open for business. "Everyone is different, but you don't start ovulating the instant your shot wears off. It takes time for a cycle to right itself. Don't be freaking out because you're scared you won't be able to have kids."

"But what if I can't?" I whine, tears renewing. "I couldn't imagine any of Malcolm's kids not wanting a bunch of kids to smoother. What if I can't? Will Kieren leave me?"

"You're only eighteen–" Essie puts her hand up to stop me, a grin pulling at her lips. "No more half-year bullshit once you become an adult, Willow. The day you turn nineteen is the day I call you nineteen. This is an illogical reaction to anxiety, and I won't put up with it."

"When did you get so firm?" I ask just as the door dings open. My family pours in, laughing and smiling. But they instantly go on alert when they notice the tension between Essie and me and the tears still staining my cheeks.

"Since I've been going to therapy. Since I've been dealing with the fact that I have to be strong for my baby, because my baby will have a father who may or may not be here for us. Since I knew I had to be firm in order to stop Devon from self-destructing. I don't give a shit if you don't want to be my friend anymore, Willow– I won't let anyone in my family act like an asshat."

"Asshat?" Head jerking backward into the padded headrest, I glare at Essie.

"Yeah, an asshat." Essie murmurs a few requests to the girls, telling them to pick out paint colors, then plant their asses in a seat. "I let you break down because I understood. Then I comforted you with the truth. Now it's time for you to get your ass outta that chair and let your pregnant mother sit down."

"Bossy," I grumble, taking my feet out of the footbath. Clover half-hugs me as she slips into the chair. We're not huggers most of the time, but the Masons are wearing off on us. She keeps her mouth shut, realizing Essie's making headway with me.

"Think of it as practice for when I'm a mother." Essie points at the stool next to hers. "Sit. I've given you enough pedicures, you know the procedure. Do Rae's tootsies."

Rae's dark blue eyes turn to saucers, as uncomfortable with me touching her as I am. Lips curling slightly, I try to put her at ease because she is my stepsister, and someday she may be my sister-in-law. No matter what, we'll always be in each other's lives, and it's time I got to know the girl.

"Don't worry." I wink at Rae while smirking at Essie. "This isn't as difficult as it looks– even a monkey could do it. I know what I'm doing, just ask Essie how many times I've done her toes."

"Just don't ask Willow for makeup or fashion advice." Essie banters back, sitting shoulder-to-shoulder with me while she works on Clover and I work on Rae. Violet's silently waiting her turn, playing a game on her cellphone while the chair massages her back.

"Bitch," I mutter with affection, splashing Essie from the footbath.

Turning to the side, we face one another, sharing a grin. "Right back atcha, girlfriend.

CHAPTER FORTY-NINE

Devon Mason

"So this was your room?" Kieren's presence is creeping me out, like he's invading my space– a space that's no longer mine. After sharing a room with Ren my entire life, then bunking at the academy in a barracks, this room was an empty paradise. I was told it's the size of a dorm room, but it feels larger because we aren't allowed to share private spaces with other patients to avoid unhealthy contact. My space had the usual things, but it's painted a warm yellow, instead of clinical white.

"Some lucky person will be moving in here in the next couple of hours." I think over my words, secretly smiling to myself. A feral animal, it took about a week before I regained a piece of my humanity. Eight weeks later, I'm still more zombie than human. "More accurately, an unlucky person, not realizing the hell they're about to go through."

"Aren't you glad you're being sprung from this joint?" My brother takes my suitcase from me, passing it off to an orderly who will stow it in Dad's rental car. Another orderly escorts us to Dr. Delaney's office, where Dad is going through the process for my release.

Terrified, I don't answer Ren, because I fear how I'd reply.

I'm left with only a backpack filled with stuff I've gone without for eight weeks. Independence and the ability to seek information: My wallet filled with identification and money. My cellphone, which has been factory reset against past horrors– text messages and images –with only numbers of family, coworkers, and close friends added to the contact list. My cell is loaded with a billion alarms to alert me when to take my meds, when to eat, when to sleep– a babysitter because everyone knows I'm incapable at this point. My tablet, loaded with inspirational and motivational materials to keep me even on the flight home.

Two items of hope are tucked in the backpack: a picture of Essie that Ren snapped with my cellphone before flying out here this morning. I cried when I saw her belly, fucking bawled. Ren handed me my badge, letting me know as long as I try, I still have good in me. Being a police officer is my beacon of hope. As long as I don't get in my own way, I can help others as a form of repayment and redemption.

Yesterday, my half-hour lunch with Taryn and Tommy helped me more than the other two-thousand-six-hundred-eighty-eight half-hours I've spent at the center. All it took was a simple *thank you* to remove all the guilt I felt. Taryn and Tommy don't see their teams as changing their lives, like I do mine. They see me as the hero who got them the help they needed.

Since we're being sprung at the same time, Dad volunteered to bring us all home, because Mrs. Elsberry and Reverend Braxton are destitute after paying the cost of the center and all the cross-country flights. As Fairport Chief of Police, they gave him the authority to sign the release paperwork at the center.

Dad and Ren are going to be mad at me, but I'm going to sit on the flight home with Taryn and Tommy. I need them just as much as they need me. We're raw right now, hypersensitive to our surroundings. As much as my family loves me, missed me, they can never understand. They'll try, but some situations you have to experience to truly empathize with, or else it's just guessing.

As an addict diagnosed with rapid-cycling Bipolar I Disorder and PTSD, there is no room for guessing in my lifestyle. From here on out, I have to have stability– a world with a black and white routine with no room for interpretation. Spontaneity is a sign my cocktail of mood stabilizers isn't working properly. For most, it's called fun, but for me it's called going off the rails. What society would consider boring is what I need to be able to stay even. Only those going through this will truly understand.

Tommy Braxton is suffering from Religious Trauma Syndrome. Reverend Braxton's constant hellfire and brimstone affected Tommy on a mental level, causing severe anxiety, compulsive disorders, and the inability to make his own decisions after being controlled. Tommy was here to learn how to take control of his own life, to trust his instincts, and to have a voice. I felt paranoid until Tommy explained how deeply '*God is always watching*' terrified yet violated him. He's going home to his older sister, who understands but wasn't harmed in the way he was by their father's constant control in the name of God.

Taryn Elsberry was diagnosed with Bipolar II Disorder, as well as severe hormonal imbalances. She and I will be the only people in Fairport who will ever truly know what we're going through. Since she's still a minor, I've been tasked with driving her to our weekly group therapy sessions. Even if the girl moves away, she'll always be in my life.

Kieren keeps tossing concerned looks in my direction as we follow the orderly to Dr. Delaney's office. After eight weeks of this routine, I think nothing of constant silence. We were here to think, not react. I highly doubt I'll ever be able to participate in small talk again. I don't know if I've changed, or if I'm now who I was always meant to become.

Since I can literally feel Ren wigging out on me, I reach over to rest my palm in the center of his back. As my brother's muscles relax beneath my touch, so do I.

After being segregated, only being around others during group sessions, I'm more sensitive to the moods around me. Dr. Delaney said I've always been this way, which made me feel *off*. In the silence, I learned the flavor of my own moods. Now I'm able to separate how I'm feeling versus those around me.

My brother keeps looking at me from the corner of his eye, like he doesn't recognize me. I know me, and I know Ren, but the two have never met, not even a month ago.

"I'm just preparing myself," I speak softly while scratching lightly at Ren's back. "It's going to be a shock to my system– all those people in the airport, then being packed on a long flight."

"Dad's making sure everyone's staying away, told 'em you'll want to see them one-on-one over a few days."

"Good," is all I reply as we enter the corridor leading to Dr. Delaney's office.

"The Spook House is pretty quiet. Auggie and Rob are like ghosts, usually found in the kitchen when they're not in the attic or their rooms. Willow and Essie are always working, or over at the Pink Taco Hut. So we're headed there, and who you see and where you go will be up to you."

The orderly stops, waiting. "Thank you," I say to both the staff member and my brother. Hand dropping away from Ren's back, I enter the office first. Muscles locking up, I fear Dad will attack me with a bear hug. Earlier, Ren was brought to me while Dad had been led here.

I've always been able to read body language, but now I feel more adept at it. Dad's a quick study, knowing fast movements and physical touches feel like an attack. His fingers curl into fists, but I know it's not out of aggression. Before Dad stands his son, and it's killing him not to reach out and touch me to reassure himself we're okay.

"Hey, Dad." Waving lamely, I walk across the office toward him, ignoring Dr. Delaney and Ms. Amelia. Remembering from last month, Dad leans down slightly, offering up his cheek. Instead of kissing him, I simply lean my cheek against his, enjoying the closeness without feeling trapped and accosted. "Thank you... for everything."

After passing Ren my backpack, I test my resolve by hooking my arms around Dad's shoulders, pulling him down into a hug. There is a difference. When I'm hugged, usually I'm the smaller person, with my arms wrapped around their chest. I can no longer handle the sensation of my arms being trapped, of arms circling me, of a taller person hovering over me. With me being the hugger, I'm in control. With my arms on top, I have the freedom of movement.

It's the small things that make the greatest difference.

Struggling with his own emotions, Dad's on the verge of breaking down, so I decide it's time to get this shit-show on the road. "Delaneys, what do you need from me?"

Instead of ignoring the emotions as I always have, I allow them to flow over me. The sight of tears glistening in Ms. Amelia's eyes has a feeling of immense pride swelling within me. I'm one of her best achievements, hers and her husband's. Once I opened up to Delaney, the last thirty days have been when I've experienced the most growth. I know Amelia's going to miss me, but the tears are because day-one Devon is not the same person as day-sixty Devon.

"Please, everyone have a seat." Ms. Amelia gestures to my dad and brother. The Delaneys and I take our usual seats, with Dad sharing the sofa next to me. Ren sits on the arm of the sofa next to dad, instinctively knowing not to pin me down between them. The plane ride home is going to kill Taryn, Tommy, and me.

"I've already discussed the rest of your progress with your father," Delaney says from his position at his desk. "I personally met with Thomas Braxton and Taryn Elsberry's team. I've given Chief Mason their release packets– as well as yours."

"I would like to speak with Kieren while you continue speaking with Delaney, if you don't mind, Devon." Ms. Amelia is treading carefully. "*In private*, if you're not comfortable with me speaking in front of your father."

Empathy kicking, I find my hand wrapped around my dad's, squeezing tightly, because what I'm about to say will rankle. Kieren and I are private– it's none of Dad's business, and I don't want him to ever shoulder this burden.

"Ren, Ms. Amelia is going to take you to her office, okay?" My brother knows it's in the form of a question, but it's actually an order. I may have discovered new personality traits in the solace, but I'm still me.

"Okay." Ren stands from the sofa, hand squeezing Dad's shoulder, because the man is frozen solid next to me. "This won't take long, will it? I don't want us to miss our flight."

"No, Kieren." Ms. Amelia's lips curl up in a genuine, comforting smile of a mother. "I just need to discuss a few things with you since you'll be living with your brother."

Delaney and I hold eye-contact while his wife and my brother leave the office, with my father stewing beside me. Once the door is closed at my back, closing the three of us in together, Delaney sparks to life.

"Devon, I think it would help your father if you were to voice your fears." Fingers steepling, Delaney is asking exactly what he asked me earlier this morning, only requesting I repeat it for my father's benefit, so I don't get too bent out of shape.

Sighing, I look down to where my hand is being cupped between my dad's warm palms. "Devon." It's a chastisement– I know that sharp yet coaxing tone well. "Eye contact, please. You have to own what you're feeling, and you mustn't hide from it."

Trying again, this time I take a deep breath and meet Dad's eyes. "I'm not the same as I was." I try to voice how I've changed but not why. "I'm raw right now. My normal used to be foggy, with no clarity. But now everything is too bright, too loud, overpowering, to the point it's startling.

"I don't expect anyone to make changes in their lives for me, so I fear seeing the pity. I fear you walking on eggshells, or doing everything for me because you don't think I can handle it. I need to gradually go about life, not be caged for my safety."

"Chief Mason?" Delaney calls out after several long moments of silence, causing Dad's gaze to snap from mine. "Just as every human being, Devon needs to have a purpose, to have goals, to learn from failure and find pride in achievements. He's terrified you won't trust him, to the point you won't allow him to live his own life."

"I am trying so very hard," Dad murmurs, keeping his tone even, when anyone with eyes could see how distressed he is. "I vow not to add any stress or undue pressure to my son."

"*That*," I point out, tugging my hand out from between Dad's. "That's the problem. After I acclimate at home– give me a week or two so it's not so overpowering after being in solitude for months –I don't want you to bottle up what you want to say to me. I don't want you to hold back, refusing to come to me if you need something from me. I *need* you to treat me like your son, not a drug addicted mental patient and you're my caregiver."

"I'm so over my head right now," Dad stammers, close to tears, and it kills me to see such a strong man rendered motionless and speechless, like I've broken him.

"Chief Mason," Dr. Delaney tries again. "Devon is telling you want he needs from you. What he's saying is he doesn't want you to treat him differently than you treat anyone else. You will never be a negative influence in his life, so you asking him to do his job as his boss will not send him into a tailspin where he seeks drugs."

"Whatever I do from this day forth is *my* fault." I fist a hand over my chest, thumping. "I'm thinking clearly, making my own decisions. *I am in control*. If I fuck up, it's on *me*. Treat me as a human being, not an inanimate object."

Gasping for breath, I try with all my might not to release my pain over Mom. I don't blame Dad for Mom's inability to maintain her regimen, remembering the screaming fights where he had to shove the pills in her mouth, but I do blame him for not hospitalizing her. I see my mom sitting on the sofa, a shell of a human being, and I don't want Dad to treat me as he did his wife.

Once I've calmed, I begin again. "Do you see what I did there, Dad?" Turning on the sofa, I completely face him, looking him straight in the eyes. "I recognized how my emotions were getting out of control, I recognized why I felt as I did, then I reigned it in. Once emotions are involved, a conversation turns into a confrontation, where nothing will be solved. Do you see how I'm strong enough now?"

"Chief Mason, our goal for Devon is not for him to suppress how he feels, or to drug away his emotions. Our goal is for Devon to accept how he feels, understand what triggered the emotion, then work through it in a healthy way. At any time, if Devon feels a conversation is too high with emotion, he will walk away. You holding a conversation with your son will not harm his recovery, because we've given him the tools. Now we must trust him to wield them properly."

"How will I–" Dad keeps one eye trained on me while he speaks to Delaney, fearing I'll think he's talking about me like I'm not in the room. "How will I know when to seek help for Devon? How will I know what behavior is out of the ordinary."

"That is one of the things my wife is speaking with Kieren about right now, knowledge he will share with their partners." Unlike Dad, Delaney doesn't care if I feel he's treating me like a piece of furniture. "Give it two weeks to a month to learn Devon's routine, including moods. Make sure he's still meeting with his psychiatrist, his therapist, attending NA, and attending the bipolar group therapy sessions. If Devon does anything out of the ordinary, or fails to maintain his drug regimen or go to his sessions, contact his psychiatrist immediately, and the doctor will contact me."

"I don't want to feel as if I'm policing my adult son." Dad's eyes dart in my direction, looking hella sheepish. "I want to trust him, but that can only go so far after everything."

"There is trust, then there is turning a blind eye." Delaney points out, voice amused. "Don't be blind– Devon knows what to expect from you. He only wants you to expect more out of him, to treat him as a productive member of your family, and to help him should he fail."

"Is my son always going to be so…" Dad's at a loss for words.

"No," Delaney answers the question I understood. "Just as you feel things strongly. Had a bad day at work, one of your kids is being stubborn, you're hurt because your wife said something that upset you… Devon's mood stabilizers alter his brain chemistry, trying to right the wayward way his brain is firing. Before it was his brain affecting his emotions, now life will affect his mood. Being upset or angry is not the same as a manic or depressive episode."

Horror etches across Dad's face. "Will those still happen?"

"Yes, but not as often. We will adjust Devon's medications over a longer period of time. Sixty days of intense treatment was just to set a baseline. But the episodes won't be as intense, and Devon has the tools to seek appropriate help when the time comes, which is why we have a team in place near your hometown."

"Dad, I'm going to be okay." I reach over to take his hand, knowing he needs the reassurance of physical touch. "I want this– I *needed* it. Between the past and inheriting a mental illness, I can admit being high exacerbated it. It wasn't medicine."

"That's a common trap that's easy to fall into." Delaney tries to comfort me, which is unusual. "We're a diagnostic center. Our rehabilitation facility is based on psychiatric issues, because most often, there are underlying issues hidden beneath the addiction."

A knock on the door startles me and Dad, but Delaney looks unaffected. "Come in," he calls out, and Ms. Amelia peeks her head in the door.

"Not to interrupt, but we can't keep them any longer or they'll miss their flight." Ms. Amelia opens the door all the way, revealing she's with Kieren, Taryn, and Tommy. "Plus, we have five new arrivals coming within the hour."

"Very well then, Amelia." Delaney is fighting a smirk as he stands from his desk. "Word of advice: Everything is going to be overwhelming. Don't feel guilty for seeking solace, for telling people you care about that you can't be around them just yet. You need to desensitize yourself to social situations slowly."

"Thank you, Dr. Delaney." I stand, offering the man my hand, and he seems surprised by the gesture. After an uncomfortable handshake, where we promise to keep in touch– and Delaney means it –I hug Ms. Amelia goodbye, both of us a bit teary-eyed. Sixty days of intense therapy has bonded me to the couple, almost as if they're my surrogate parents. We'll keep in touch, I don't doubt that for a second.

CHAPTER FIFTY

Kieren Mason

This has been one of the most bizarre, never-ending days of my entire existence, fourteen hours of which has been spent sitting on an airplane. Nothing like roundtrip from Massachusetts to Arizona, and back… On. The. Same. Day.

Devon is not the brother I knew. I'd expected the guy I'd met a month ago. Instead I faced a stranger who acts either afraid of me, or pissed at me, and I'm pretty sure it's a combination of both.

Devon won't touch me. He doesn't speak to me. My brother doesn't ask anything of me, just as Ms. Amelia predicted. Our session wasn't about Devon at all. The therapist focused on me, calling me out for being an enabler. Not for what I've done in the past, or will do in the future, but for how it will affect me in the present.

Ms. Amelia told me I'm someone who needs to be needed, and it created an unhealthy dynamic between my brother and me. Now that Devon won't allow anyone to cater to his every whim, I'm the one who's going to feel left without a purpose, as will my dad. But Dad has a family of his own to make him feel like a man, whereas all I have is Devon.

I spent the seven hour flight home mulling this over, and my mind immediately lit on Essie versus Willow. Willow's never needed me– she hasn't from the start. So I've held her off at arm's length, refusing to tell her how I feel. All the while, I've tried to come to Essie's rescue, tried to be her shoulder to cry on, even told her I'd raise her baby as if it were my own, but she refused me time and time again. I was frustrated, but assumed I could take care of Devon when he got home instead, buying him a house and everything.

The Devon who told Dad he was going to sit with Tommy and Taryn on our return flight, did so without guilt in the face of Dad pouting. My brother, the confident stranger, he didn't speak a single word during the entire flight, and neither did his companions. The three of them had noise-cancelling headphones on, pens flying like mad in their journals.

I felt useless, not needed, unnecessary, but it took seeing Dad pout to realize Ms. Amelia was right. I'm an enabler, needing to be needed, to the point I could see how I'd subconsciously sabotage Devon like I did our entire lives. So while my brother was in his own world, Dad and I discussed this unhealthy dynamic. We decided to let Devon go at the risk of our own manhood, because it wasn't fair that we'd been emasculating Devon up until this point.

Understanding why I feel as I do isn't helping matters as I watch my brother say goodbye to Taryn. We dropped Tommy off first, and Devon had to go inspect Stacey Baxter's apartment before he'd let the kid out of his sight. Now we're at Mrs. Elsberry's home, sitting in the driveway, while Devon says goodbye to the girl.

It feels voyeuristic and too intimate, as Dad and I watch Devon and Taryn. They don't touch, but their conversation is intense, and it leaves me feeling strangely jealous of their connection.

"This is going to take some getting used to," I mutter in the quiet of the car. Dad's reply is a gruff scoff– he's having a hard time letting go of the enabler role. I'd texted Willow a long list of instructions while Dad drove us home from the airport. I learned some interesting news that will have Dad feeling better, which is why I'm not being pissy with him for acting like a rotten shit.

"Does my son even love me anymore?" Despondent and pouty, Dad's driving me nuts. I learned my enabler ways from him, after he got all clingy because he lost his mom when Aunt Isis was born. Aunt Isis has never put up with it, telling Dad off or simply palming his forehead and shoving. I'm Dad's counterpart, feeding his tactile addiction without complaint. So an added layer of jealousy piles on, because Dad doesn't need me as he yearns for Devon.

Devon slips into the backseat, silent as a ghost. "Thanks." He's so courteous and formal now. "I'm ready to go home." As bossy as ever, more so maybe. It's the confidence– it's oozing out of his pores. Devon knows what he wants, and is clear-headed enough to get it. It's utterly terrifying how in control he seems. I'm just waiting for Devon to snap.

"Dad." Dev leans forward between Dad and me, palm resting on the center console of Robin's new ride. We all wouldn't fit in my pickup truck, and we sure as shit couldn't drive the Chief Mobile to the airport. After telling Willow my hard limit was jealousy, I'm jealous of everything tonight, including Robin for having a sweet ride.

"Listen, I'm gonna tell you goodbye when we park." Devon's telling Dad, not asking for permission. "I want to see the kids, but I can't after all the people in the airport. First thing tomorrow I'll be over to visit– tell Clover we're all coming for breakfast."

Chuckling underneath my breath, I watch Dad's expression shift through a dozen emotions. Devon's smooth, man– *smooth*. Dad was about to fly off the handle, but that bit about breakfast and Clover had Dad melting. The man loves nothing more than to have us shoved up his ass, all at the same time. The promise of his favorite activity has Dad forgetting all about feeling rejected.

Devon's a better manipulator than ever, because he genuinely means what he's saying now.

Their goodbye is awkward to watch, because I can see how much anxiety it causes my brother to give Dad the affection he so desperately needs.

Ms. Amelia explained why this is happening, why my brother turned into this no-touch creature. The shit with Alejandro is fresh in Devon's head, like it just happened a few months ago when he remembered. She explained that Dev shouldn't have any issue with anyone in the family his size or smaller. Right now, Devon's instinct is to get far away from a threat, and we're big dudes compared to him. Given time and familiarity, Devon should have no trouble getting back to touching us as before, but he'll always be skittish of strangers.

Hearing Ms. Amelia say Alejandro's name almost dropped me to my knees, so I can't imagine how Devon must feel right now. Raw. Since I get it, I'll play by Dev's rules. But, for some reason, the jealousy is only getting stronger with every person my brother touches and speaks to, while he continues to deny me.

It was supposed to be Devon and me against the world.

"It's so strange." Devon sneaks up on me, causing me to jump. Laughing sinisterly, just like he used to, Dev takes his suitcase from my hand. At least some things don't change– my brother is still a creepy fucker. God, how I've missed him. "I mean, I'm home in Fairport. But I'll never go home again, never set foot into our house. I thought I could handle it."

"Are you going to be okay?" Jesus, did I just sound perky when I asked that? I'm so eager to help, I suddenly want Devon to have a problem I can fix, or a wound I can heal, or a hurt I can soothe. Maybe I'm the mental one.

"I'll deal." Devon shoulders his backpack and hefts his suitcase, then strides up the front walk to the Spook House with purpose. "Change is scary, but this is a good scary. I can't wait to see the new house tomorrow."

I can handle confident but silent, bossy Devon, because he reminds me of the sadistic version who used to try to suffocate me in my sleep. But when Dev mixes happy into the emotional pool, I get a bit freaked out. This is what a normal Devon would've been like, versus the brother who was all over the place during my entire life.

"Hey, I'm home," Devon calls as he opens the front door. My text to Willow was to warn her about the no-touch policy in effect. Hopefully she relayed the message, because if the household rushes him…

Worried, I take the steps two at a time, and nearly bump into my brother's back as he enters the house. First person I see is Robin, giving a wave from the entrance to the living room, but not moving to steal a hug. Devon releases an honest to God laugh. It's so dang happy, it draws tears to my eyes.

Auggie is affectionately shoulder-bumped out of the way so Devon can get at Willow, who happens to look spooked for being targeted right off the bat. Dev full-on hugs my girlfriend, kissing her on the cheek, and I'm so goddamn jealous I can taste it.

Jealous because I want that full-contact hug– how sick is that shit? The Devon from last month never gave me a hug, either. I'm the only one who's been denied.

Devon's whispering in Willow's ear, causing her to rumble a smokey laugh. As he pulls away, he kisses my girlfriend's cheek again. "Go on now." My brother releases that man laugh all the men in my family have. I feel like a proud parent watching their toddler perform a new trick– Devon never laughed like that before.

Everything about my brother is suddenly intriguing.

Willow walks the few feet separating us far too slowly for my liking, but I don't meet her halfway. I'm not big on public displays of affection, so I can't wait to get her alone. It's awkward as all hell with our family filling the foyer, but I yank my girlfriend into my arms and kiss the shit out of her because I missed her that much– missed the familiar, missed how Willow makes me feel.

Eyes closed in comfort, Willow fits perfectly against me as I snuggle her close. "What'd he whisper to you?" I'm too curious for my own good. Willow giggles in response, struggling to get out of my arms.

"Dev told me to stop making you jealous, and get over here to put you out of your misery," Willow teases me. No doubt, to listening ears, this conversation sounds completely different. But Willow and I both know the context in which Devon meant, and it's creepy when examined. But I can't help it, can I?

"Is that all he said?" It seemed like Devon said more than that, and I can tell he did by the way Willow turns away sheepishly when I ask. On the verge of interrogating my girlfriend, we're both distracted by Essie and Devon.

They're facing off, with Essie all the way up the hallway at the mouth of the kitchen. Essie looks surprised yet terrified, and I have no idea what expression is on my brother's face because his back is to me. After a good minute or two, where no one moves, let alone breathes, Devon cuts the distance between them in three strides.

Essie doesn't get a hug, she gets consumed. It's not a dramatic, romantic embrace. I'd thought Devon's goodbye to Taryn felt too intimate, but I was wrong. Choking back sobs of my own, I watch as my brother buries his face in the side of Essie's neck, his rapid speech a continual buzzing sound.

Willow and I share a loaded look, both of us seeking out Auggie and Rob. The sound of Devon bawling into the side of Essie's neck has my heart twisting, Willow tearing up, and Auggie and Rob fleeing for the living room. I don't know if they left to give Devon privacy while he cries, or because they couldn't handle witnessing it.

Willow's palm slips into mine, when generally she's not a touchy-feeling kind of girl, so I'm taken aback by her initiating it. Squeezing her hand, I'm thankful for the strength she's lending me, because watching my brother and Essie is making me feel light-headed and wobbly from the stress of it all.

After what feels like a decade, where I begin to wonder why Willow's forcing me to witness this, Devon pulls away from

Essie. Wiping the tears off his face with the backs of his hands, my brother turns to me with a smile.

"Ready to go to bed?"

"Huh?" is a grunt of confusion. I look over my shoulder to see if Devon's speaking to someone behind me, but it's the dang closed door back there.

Devon snorts, a sound I'm as familiar with as his breathing– he's still my brother after all. "I asked Willow if I could kick her out of her bed tonight…"

"Oh!" Turning to Willow with my eyebrows scrunched together, I try to get a read on the situation.

"Go!" Willow palms my back, shoving me down the hallway toward Devon. "Go on now– I have free reign of this entire house. I'll be okay. May camp out on the sofa."

Blinking rapidly in confusion, I catch sight of Essie taking the stairs as quickly as her short legs will allow. After a few seconds, the sound of her bedroom door clicking shut filters down to hit my ears. At the same time, Willow disappeared in the living room with Auggie and Rob, leaving Devon and me alone.

"You sure you don't want to spend some time with Essie?" I mutter at Devon's back as he bends down to fetch his backpack and suitcase.

"Are you sure you don't want to spend some time with Willow?" he volleys back, acting like the Devon I used to know, relaxing me some.

"I'm not the one who hasn't seen my girl in sixty days," I remind Devon. "I woke up with Willow this morning, remember?"

"Essie understands," is Devon's answer, when I wished I understood what was going through his head. "It's so wild being back here," he muses as he walks up the stairs. Feeling magnetized to my brother, my feet follow him, taking me along for the ride. "The last time I was here…" he trails off, headed straight for Willow's and my bedroom.

If Devon's going to bring it up, does it mean it's okay for me to comment on it? Probably not. Confused and creeped out, I enter my bedroom, seeing it with the eyes I had sixty days ago, but I bite my tongue.

"Last time I was in here…" Devon fingers the clay figure I'd made him in shop class years ago. Smiling, he puts it back on the dresser. "Thank you for keeping it safe." He begins rutting around in his suitcase for something.

"Last time you were in here?" I prompt, curious to see if Devon will go *there*.

"Last time I was in this room…" Devon continues rutting around in his suitcase, distracting me. "You were holding me down while Rob beat my face to a bloody pulp."

Devon went there– he *really* went there.

"I'm glad to see you're not suffering from an Invasion of the Body Snatchers," I tease, toeing off my sneakers. It's the light ribbing between brothers, and I'm terrified our relationship won't be that way anymore.

Devon's laughter is intoxicating as he goes about unpacking his toiletry bag and a pair of pajama pants from his suitcase. It's a comfort to see he's still as anal retentive about his belongings as before. He used to spend an hour on his uniform and utility belt every day before and after work.

"I'm not– when I look back to who I used to be…" Devon's words are cut off as he begins stripping in front of me. We're brothers, it's no big deal, especially when I spent my teen years in a locker room. Unbidden, I check him out, happy to see how healthy and tan he looks, versus how I last saw him in this room when he was on death's door.

"It's like thinking in the third-person. I take full responsibility for my actions, recognize that I did them. But it's so bizarre, because who I am today would never pull that shit. So I have a difficult time fusing who I used to be with who I am now."

"Like separate entities?" I decide I better get ready for bed too.

"Mmm-hmm…" Dev murmurs as he folds his clothing, then stacks it on top of Willow's hamper. "It feels better in here with your stuff too. I was a bit concerned I wouldn't feel comfortable if it felt like before. I needed the familiarity of home, but home doesn't exist anymore."

Ah! That's a big motherfucking clue as to why Devon's in here with me right now. My heart expands in my chest, to the point I fear it's going to explode. Deciding to piss and brush my teeth later, I crawl into bed, too curious to see what Devon's going to do next.

Stripped down to his boxers, Devon materializes a journal– it was literally attached at his hip. Eyes darting around wildly, Devon kneels on the floor next to Willow's side of the bed, then the mattress moves. When my brother pops back to his feet, the journal is nowhere in sight.

I decide it's best not to comment on that odd behavior as Devon strips out of his boxers and dons a pair of pajama pants.

"I have nightmares now." Devon continues to do unnecessary tasks, trying to waste time. "After sleeping alone for a few months in total isolation, I couldn't just crawl in Essie's bed. Besides, I've never spent the night with her. Too much, too soon."

"So that's why you're in here with me?" The jealousy shit is for the birds. I thought Devon wanted to be around me, but maybe it's because I'm the lesser of two evils.

Devon ignores my question, walks around to my side of the bed, then hands me a heavy object. "Delaney had one similar to this on his desk." I roll the glass paperweight between my palms, looking at the colorful design spiraling inside. "Because I liked it so much, he bought me one as a belated birthday gift."

"It's amazing," I murmur, half awed and half wondering if gift-giving between a doctor and patient is ethical. "How's it made?"

"Delaney's brother is a glassblower– he showed me a video on YouTube. I ordered one for Auggie and Rob for housing us, because I thought they'd appreciate the artistry of it."

Everyone is getting hugs and gifts, and I'm over here feeling sorry for myself. Devon takes the paperweight from my hands, then gingerly sets it next to the clay figurine I made him.

"This is yours– mine's in my bag, all soothing yellows and blues. I thought you'd like the reds spirals. Plus I know Willow loves red too."

Heart beating out of control, I nearly choke on my words. "Wow, thanks– I love it."

"You're welcome." So formal, the new version of my brother. Devon crawls into bed with me, then clicks off Willow's retro lamp. Frozen solid, the sound of my brother moving around the sheets has gooseflesh beading on my skin.

"The nightmares…" Devon scoots closer to me, until I can feel his body heat. "I didn't want to scare Essie, and I didn't want to be scared myself. I thought if I was with you, the familiarity of you, I'd feel safe."

"Safe is good?" I ask like a moron, tongue slurring my words.

"Ren." Devon's sadistic chuckle has me shivering. Then a hand wraps around my wrist, pulling me from the edge of the bed. "You're going to fall to the floor in the middle of the night– I'm not going to bite."

No, but you'll freak out if I touch you.

Before the thought forms into verbal vomit, Devon's wrapping my arm around his waist, scooting up against me as the little spoon. Eyes held wide in the dark, my entire body thrums with shock.

"Wait a minute–" I'm pissed, but I don't push him out of bed. This is the calculating, punishing Devon I know. "You wouldn't hug me, not last month or today! But you're cuddling with me now?"

"You deserve it after thinking I was terrified of you." Devon's laughter echoes around the bedroom. "Dad freaks me out, like he's going to need things from me I can't give him yet. But you... you've never asked anything of me, always giving to me instead. I'm in here with you because you're my home."

Just like Dad, I'm a sucker for Devon's manipulations. But it's worse than ever, the emotional extortion, because my brother means the shit he's saying.

It takes a long time before sleep descends. But after the long, stressful day, the sound of Devon's even breathing takes me under. A while later, I'm startled awake. I have no idea how long we'd been asleep, but the sound of my brother's sobs murders a piece of my soul. Devon spews his sins, guilt keeping him from resting, and all I can do is support him. The devastation simultaneously makes me feel useless and useful.

CHAPTER FIFTY-ONE

Essie Prynne

Curled up in a ginormous bed with my laptop and a notebook filled with lists, I distract myself by helping Beth out tonight. "Dayum, girl!" Bethany's voice sounds tinny via Skype. "I cannot get over Isis's room. Pan the camera around for me, will ya?"

Doing as requested, I giggle as I pause on the disturbing murals Robin painted on the walls. "I'd much rather look at your place– I've never been in Rory's loft." Moving the laptop a bit more, I show off the black vampires-esque furnishings dripping with crimson accents.

"It's now Rory's *and* my loft," Beth corrects me. "Those paintings are something else, but the shit in that room was definitely picked out by Auggie. I've been in Isis's loft, and it's nothing like this. It's sedate and economical."

"You should see Auggie's room– it looks like a Nordic god is sitting on a throne in there."

"I've seen it." The miniature version of Beth shudders on my laptop screen. "I bet Rob's room is bare-bones and efficient."

"You'd bet right." We share a giggle at my diabolical cousin's expense. "After knowing Isis when I was a kid, and seeing the fools in this house trip over themselves, everything they do is wrong if they're trying to get Isis back."

"I know that more than anyone." Beth's been mum's the word when it comes to the object of her thesis. She acted sheepish around Auggie for a few weeks after she got back from Vegas. But Willow pulled me to the side last week, tattling about how Auggie had been taking both Beth and Rory up to the attic to visit the Playroom. Bethany and I may be best friends, but I instinctively know that topic is none of my goddamn business.

Beth will tell me when she wants to tell me, until then... I change the subject. "Well, girl. Is there anyone you don't want me to invite?"

"Essie, you shouldn't be doing this right now." Rory's giant torso passes behind Bethany as she sits at her desk, a hint to keep this conversation PG-13. "How's Devon doing?"

"Well, he's holed up with Ren in Willow's bedroom–"

"Is Willow in there too?" Rory's horrified voice echoes.

Chuckling at his reaction, I put Rory out of his misery. "No, she was in the living room with Rob and Auggie last I saw her. I think she's going to camp out on the sofa."

"Willow *hates* that sofa." Rory is apparently part of this conversation now, and privy to things even I don't know. He is best buds with Isis, so maybe that's where he's getting his inside information. I love a man who can gossip.

"If you're going to join us, bub, sit down next to your wife," I chastise. "Your torso is a work of art, but I feel skeeved out chatting with it." Rory's masculine face comes into view, cheeks flaming red with a blush. "Devon will want to see you both in a few days, so don't be surprised if he makes you feel uncomfortable with the apologies he'll offer."

Now it's my turn to apologize. I feel bad for being relieved that Ren is taking care of Devon tonight, but the shit Dev was saying to me was too hard to handle. He's feeling raw and exposed, overstimulated, and he managed to make me feel the same way within a matter of seconds.

"I'm super curious to see Devon." Rory pulls up a chair, flashing me a view of his ass. Track pants do amazing things to the male anatomy. Beth sticks her tongue out at me for checking out her husband's assets.

Utterly shameless, I shrug and grin. There's a reason Ren and I get along so well together– we're the male and female versions of the same personality. We're appreciating, not leering.

Rory's blushing face comes into view next to Beth, no doubt knowing I was checking him out. "I can't think of anyone I don't want to invite. I've already posted a notice that Rush would be closed for a private party."

"Don't you think it's a little late for us to have a wedding reception?" Beth turns to look at her husband. "I don't want our friends and family feeling like we're begging for gifts."

"Beth." I learn forward, filling the camera with my face. "As your very best friend, when you eloped, I lost the honor of being your maid of honor. That was not cool, so don't take this away from me. I'm planning your freaking reception, and you're going to like it or lump it, because we want to celebrate your union."

"I think it's awesome." Rory shares a grin with me. He's been feeding me lists of things he thinks Bethany would want. Our girl is too selfless, and she needs to feel as special as we think she is.

"You should be concentrating on Dev right now–"

Rory's scoff cuts Bethany off. "This is fun. Everyone needs fun right now."

"You have two choices, girlfriend. Either you tell us who you want to invite, what you want as decorations, and what food you want to serve, or you just show up at the time we chose and have people think our ideas were yours."

"Bitch!" Bethany hisses, but she's grinning.

"Hey, that's what I call Essie too!" Willow's mischievous cackle startles me as she slips into the bedroom. "Whatcha doing?" Striding over to the bed, Willow curls over the back of the laptop, giving Rory and Beth an upside down view of her face. "Hi!"

"Nice outfit," I mutter, trying hard not to laugh. Willow's wearing a Wonder Woman t-shirt and a pair of pink shorts with frolicking bunnies hopping around. Her clothing style is as contradictory as her personality.

"Thanks." Crawling across the mattress, Willow plunks her behind right next to me, then waves at the screen. "I was too cowardly to enter my bedroom, so I grabbed whatever I could find in the dryer. It was either these shorts or a pair of jeans."

"Good choice." Beth laughs, but Willow doesn't seem to find it insulting, like she would with me. Knowing Beth, she's not making fun of Willow anyway.

"So… what are we doing?" Willow picks up my notepad, and scans the list. "Oh, can I help?"

"How bored are you?" Rory leans forward like he can see Willow better.

"Desperately." Willow rolls her eyes heavenward. "I'd be glued to my TV about now. Since it's Devon invading my bed, and I refuse to touch that sofa–"

"Told you!" Rory shouts, pointing at us through the screen.

"–Essie's going to be hospitable and ask me in for a slumber party."

"Isis is going to love *that*," Beth murmurs softly out the side of her mouth to Rory, but the mic picks it up anyway. "The sacred bedroom, remember the fight she had with Rob over letting Essie sleep in there?"

"Who do you think ordered me in here?" Willow flashes a shit-eating grin. "The woman stormed into the house, took one look at me playing Connect-Four with Robbie, and told me to get my ass out of her sight."

Wincing for Willow, I reach over to rub her back. "That's not nice."

"We just got done dealing with Isis before we logged-on." Rory's face twists in indecision, but he can't help but spill. "She turned the house-lights up, pushed the DJ out of his booth, and used his mic to tell everyone to get the fuck out of Rush."

"Even I had to help do damage control by passing out drink vouchers at the door." Beth raises an eyebrow in my direction, but Willow ends up thinking it's for her.

"You know what we should do?" Willow's voice pitches high with excitement. "I should grab those jeans, then Essie and I can hijack Robbie's ride. We could go to Rush and do this in person. Yeah? I can bring snacks."

"Sounds fun to me," I mutter with a shrug, knowing we should ask instead of invite ourselves.

"Since Rory has an unexpected night off..." Beth trails off, and Rory's cheeks turn bright red.

"Oh..." Willow winks exaggeratedly. "Gotcha."

"How about we make plans for tomorrow night?" I peek to the side at Willow. The girl loves to work, but she sure as hell doesn't give two shits about party planning. "Just us girls?"

"Hey, I run a club for shit's sake." Nothing like a big, hot dude pouting to make a girl melt into a puddle of arousal– poor Beth is reaching forward to slam her laptop shut on us. "I want to help."

"You have to work," Beth points out, wanting to keep her husband to herself. Rory's a bit of a harmless flirt, so three girls and Rory isn't a wise idea. "We were going to stock the new inventory of Opal's soaps tomorrow. If Willow wants to join us, she can stop into Salon."

"Primp," Willow says with pride. "I'm going to take Devon to the new house tomorrow and get his help with some stuff, but I doubt he'll have much stamina to work long. So I'll steal some baked goods from Clover after breakfast, and we'll have a treat while we plan your reception."

"Girly." Rory leans closer to the screen, no doubt remembering how insulting he was to Willow when he first met her on her birthday. It was unintentional and for her own good, but it stung Willow bad. "I've heard good things about your work ethic, but don't you have an off switch? How packed is your schedule tomorrow?"

Instead of blushing from the attention, Willow pales. "It's best if I keep myself busy with no downtime." Looking sheepish, maybe ashamed, my cousin meets my eyes. "Keep that in mind with Devon, okay? Keep him busy. Tasks with obtainable goals."

"Duly noted," I murmur, sharing a look of complete understanding with my cousin. This morning shifted something in our relationship for us. Holding a woman while she cries will do that– it feels the same, but it's not. We're starting an adult friendship now.

"It's been fun, girls." Rory flashes us a panty-melting grin. "But it's Mr. and Mrs. Essex sleepover time."

Willow and I both bend like idiots to see what's going on in their apartment as Beth slowly closes her laptop. Bethany's giggle is the last thing we hear.

"Rory's nicer than I remember." Willow's face is still pale, but her cheeks are pinking slightly. "I remember him flirting with you."

"Rory's a flirt– it's why he does so well at his job." After shutting my laptop, I stow it in Isis's antique armoire. "He doesn't mean anything by it. He's super outgoing and friendly, but his heart belongs to Bethany."

"Beth's awesome too." Willow flips my notepad shut, then tosses it onto the nightstand. "They make a cute couple."

"*You* and Ren make a cute couple too." I tug at Willow's ponytail because she's entering a headspace that is never healthy– *for m*e. If Willow gets upset, I'll become an easy target who'll never fight back, one who will love her no matter what.

"I still look like a dang kid." Willow plucks at her jammie bottoms. "I got these in the little girl section because they fit. Guys like girls who look like you and Bethany."

"Beth and I look nothing alike," I point out, terrified of the direction this conversation is headed, especially since we're sharing this room tonight.

"Just womanly, ya know?" Turning sheepish, Willow looks away from me. "Yeah, I get how I have a chip on my shoulder about my looks. I know you're going to say I'm almost three years younger than you, and it's my perception that had you looking older at this age. Yes, I know Kieren is hot for me." Trailing off quieter and quieter with every word, "But he appreciates all women."

"That's not a bad thing, Willow. It's not." Shifting on the mattress until Willow and I are face-to-face, I get real with the girl. "You always said you'd trust my boy advice. Trust this– Kieren is a keeper. He may appreciate how a woman looks, but he doesn't want to screw her. It's no different than when we check out a guy. The only difference is you have self-image issues. Don't be a hypocrite."

Chewing on her bottom lip, Willow mulls that over for a minute or two. Then she smiles brightly, tugging up her t-shirt. "I'm getting a pot-gut on me. Look!"

"You are probably the only woman in recorded history who is excited about that." Chuckling, I reach out to pinch an inch of Willow's belly. Then I poke her in the gut to get her to squee like the Pillsbury Dough Boy.

"Part of the reason I wanted to be pregnant was so I'd look more feminine." Eyes downcast, Willow tugs her shirt back into place. "I'll settle for getting chubby."

Growling in frustration, I palm Willow's shoulders, then shove. Sitting astride her hips on the mattress, I glare down at my cousin. "A baby is a human being put on this earth for life, not a quick pass to some tits." I snarl into her face. "Don't do unhealthy shit, you stupid bitch. If you're hungry, eat. If you're not, don't. Quit making up these excuses in your head– you have no more cravings."

"The hell I don't!" Willow shouts in outrage, struggling beneath me, but I've got a good thirty pounds on the girl now. Pot-gut or not, she hasn't hit triple-digits yet.

"You don't." After grabbing for Willow's wrists to catch her fluttering hands, I shove them beneath my knees so she can't hit me. "If Auggie hadn't intervened, you would've had a full-blown addiction to alcohol, like you do with cigarettes now."

"I still want to drink," Willow mumbles, looking dejected. "I'd kill for a toke of Mom's finest."

"You want a drink and a hit for the same reason we all do– to escape. You're not a drunk, but you could've turned into one.

There's a huge difference between you and Devon. Your problems are self-created."

"So these tits aren't flat, and I don't look like a ten-year-old boy?"

"So what?!" I shout, fed the hell up with Willow's theatrics. I hope to God I'm not having a girl, because I couldn't survive the teenage years. "You're only eighteen years old, Willow. You're a baby. I developed early because of my mom's genetics, and you're developing late because of the Prynne genetics. Stop getting bent out of shape, and quit comparing yourself to everyone else."

"It's hard not to when my boyfriend is looking at your tits like he wants to motorboat them!"

To be a total bitch, I squeeze my boobs together to make them look bigger. Willow bucks beneath me, trying to gently topple me to the mattress. At least she's learning.

"Ren's a guy." I roll my eyes. "Not all guys are like that, but Ren's type is. Get over yourself. The father of my baby greeted you first, hugged you first, actually kissed you when he didn't kiss me, and I'm not upset over it."

Now *that* admission totally threw my cousin for a loop. "Why aren't you upset? I'd be fucking furious."

"We're not the same people, Willow. I think differently than you." I release her hands from beneath my knees, but I don't get off her thighs. "I have no idea where Devon and I stand. We're not together, but we're going to be parents. I'm not saying there isn't a possibility, but I've got more important things to worry about, and I'm happier for worrying about them instead. Looks mean jack, little girl."

"Don't call me that!" Willow renews her struggles, but is so dang gentle about it, she doesn't budge me an inch.

"Little girls play high school games by comparing themselves to other women. They never grow up, no matter how old they may be. Like Ren, I can appreciate something about every person I see, and not in a sexual way. We all have body flaws, so no person on this planet is ugly unless their soul is black."

Willow stares up at me with the biggest brown eyes I've ever seen– the watery glint only adds to their effect. "I think you're a beautiful person, Willow, no matter how shitty you feel about yourself. So when I call you a little girl, it's because you're still thinking like one, while acting like an adult."

"You can't tell me it doesn't bother you that we've both screwed a pair of brothers." Willow glares up at me in defiance and challenge, but beneath that is regret. She wants it to bug me because it bugs her.

"No, it doesn't," I answer truthfully. "Devon and Kieren are amazing people. I love you to the point that I was so fucking happy you and Devon were together, because you got the opportunity to lose your virginity for real, with someone you cared about, while in a real relationship. I wanted to de-nut Auggie so badly for what he'd done with you."

"I don't get why you're not fucking furious with me," Willow grits out between clenched teeth, and I begin to wonder if this is how Devon treated Kieren all those years. It's like explaining color to the blind.

"Because I don't count what Ren and I did as losing our virginities, Willow. I don't count what you and Auggie did, either. I don't count getting date-raped as losing it, either."

"What?" Willow gasps, and I realize I said more than I should.

Sighing, I stare at the ceiling as Willow rubs at my thighs. "Devon and I did everything but when we were too young to understand. Then the awkwardness with Ren. Dev hurt me *bad*, Willow. It's why I know whatever he said to you when you broke up did a number on you too. I get it."

Willow's eyes are held wide with dawning horror. "I remember how bizarre you were acting when you started dragging me to parties."

"I started dragging you to parties so I'd behave," I admit for the first time. "It was wrong of me, but you were my safety net, the one I measured myself against. Long before then, I was at a party, just after Devon annihilated me. It was like we were challenging each other, which is why I refuse to play games now. He was challenging me to keep going, and I was asking him to prove he loved me by forcing me to stop."

"Devon didn't stop you?"

"No." Head bowed, I close Willow out by shutting my eyes. "The couple minutes with Ren didn't count, Willow– it didn't. Not to me, anyway. My second time didn't count either. I was so drunk, I couldn't consent, even though I said yes. I don't blame the guy. Truly, I don't. He was drunk too. He would've stopped if I said no, but I was punishing myself because Devon didn't say stop. The guy wasn't a mind-reader, so it's not fair to blame him. I take responsibility for my actions. We need to teach boys *and* girls about what it means to consent... the next time I had sex, I was raped."

"Essie," Willow breathes sharply, springing up to wrap her arms around my shoulders. "Why didn't you tell me? Are you okay?" Running her hands up and down my arms, Willow acts like she's looking for physical wounds.

"I was ashamed– I didn't want you to know." Shrugging, I swallow a sob before it can erupt. "There's always the shame, Willow. *Always*."

"It wasn't your fault, Essie. It wasn't."

"I know, but it doesn't matter," I mutter flippantly. "The date-rape, I consider that as neither of us being able to consent to the other. Just because he was the guy and I was the girl, it didn't make him guilty by default. I said yes, I touched him, he touched me back– that was verbal and physical confirmation. But both of us were too drunk to think clearly. Can't really say a guy date-raped me when I was riding his lap, using the excuse of being drunk because of buyer's remorse. So I feel shame in that, because what if the guy looks back and realizes I couldn't consent? That would fuck a person up."

"No wonder I make such a big deal about sex," Willow mutters underneath her breath. "Now I see why Auggie opened the Playroom. It was black and white with no room for interpretation."

"That's exactly why," I reply, thinking over all Beth had told me about the Playroom. "At the frat party, I wasn't drunk. I'd given a guy a blowjob because I needed a hit of feeling like shit. Every guy there thought that gave them permission to touch me, even if I said no. But that didn't matter either, because they were raping girls who hadn't touched anyone that night."

"My God, did they get arrested? When did this happen? Are the other girls okay? Are you okay?" The Willow I used to know erupts– the cousin I've always seen as my little sister.

"It was while I was away at cosmetology school. Beth and I went to a frat party. Part of me will always blame myself for going to that party. In theory, I should be able to walk down the street naked and not be touched if I don't want to be. But there is also self-preservation. I wouldn't walk around with hundred dollar bills taped to my body and not expect someone to rob me. They shouldn't rob me, but that doesn't mean they won't, so I still need to take personal responsibility for my own safety. I've had a hard time finding a happy medium where I don't blame myself or feel ashamed."

"It wouldn't have happened to *you*, if you hadn't gone to the party," Willow stresses. "But it still would've happened to the rest of the girls. You staying home would've protected you, but it wouldn't have stopped those fuckers from being rapists."

"I know. I get it." I flash Willow a sheepish smile. "Most of the time. But this is why I don't get all bent out of shape when Ren looks at me. I know the difference between appreciating how I look, like how Rob stares at paintings, or Auggie covets action figures, or you swoon when you hear Revolutionary Road, versus leering with intent to take what isn't given. I *know* the difference."

Sliding off Willow's thighs, I'm too raw to touch her while talking. I suddenly realize this is how Devon feels nonstop now. Open. Exposed.

"I won't lie– it hurt me when you were with Devon, but I was happy for both of you because I love you. I wanted you guys to have what I'd never experienced."

"Jesus Christ!" Willow bellows, hands covering her face. "All those times I called you a whore."

"There's always two sides, Willow– remember that." Fingers curling around her wrists, I tug Willow's palms away from her face. "What you have with Ren is real. No matter what Devon said to you in the past, it's anti-reality. I acted like a whore because I allowed Devon to make me feel like one. Don't let Devon's dark words infect what you have with Kieren. The guy is head over heels in love with you– his eyes follow you. He wants you, no matter if you're skinny or pudgy. Don't let the insecurities win, because I'm proof positive that will only make you lose."

"I know– believe me, I do." Willow scrambles to sit cross-legged on the mattress. "Kieren's jealousy hard limit is based on my insecurities. If I trusted him, I wouldn't feel insecure about how he feels about me. But it's a hard habit to break."

"You're trying." I fix Willow's ponytail, then wipe at her eyes. "Most women are insecure until the day they die, and it infects every relationship they have, friends and family too. Ask Beth, it's what she's studying."

"If Beth says it, it's gospel." Out of context, the words sound sarcastic, but Willow's tone is genuine.

I used to feel jealous that Willow and Beth would like each other more than they'd like me. Taking a page from Ren's playbook, I realize I'm harming all three of us. Willow needs a strong, female influence like Bethany. The day they both realize binge-watching crappy TV shows is their mutual hobby, will be the day I have to start watching television.

"I want you to help me plan Beth's party, okay?" Rubbing the back of my hand underneath my nose, I snot all over myself.

"It actually does sound like fun." Willow scoots off the foot of the bed. "The guys will be shoved up each other's asses after missing one another for a few months. Might be good if I find people who aren't related to me—"

"Hey!" I jump off the bed, stalking after Willow as she enters the Jack-and-Jill bathroom I share with Auggie. Sounds odd, but technically this is Isis's bedroom. Auggie's room is flanked by Isis's and Rob's, with Rob having the master bedroom with attached bath. "I'm related to you, and you *are* my friend."

Releasing a raspy laugh, Willow reaches for a washcloth, then hands it to me. "Blow your nose and wash your face, you filthy slut."

In retaliation, I swat Willow in the boob. Then I clean up my face while Willow snoops in Auggie's shit.

"Men are so fucking bizarre." Willow holds up Auggie's body wash, wiggling the bottle. "Dark Forest? It sounds like it's formulated for serial killers."

"Oh, my God," I gasp out, holding my hand over my mouth. I'm always quick and quiet in the bathroom, knowing Auggie might jiggle the doorknob at any moment as he tries to get in here.

"But, then again, all of our girly stuff makes it sound like we shit glitter." Willow's on a roll, and I have a hard time keeping my ass quiet. My toiletry bag is attacked next. "Summer's Eve, really? *Labia*, not vagina, because I know how pissy you get when I call the outside bits a vag... vag wash called Summer's Eve? Pfft! I'd rather use the serial killer shit."

"Stop!" Giggling, I snatch my body wash from Willow's grasp.

"The smell of murdered trees, cut down by a guy with a full bush of chest hair." Willow's voice deepens, taking on the cadence of Auggie's. "Manly men smell like freshly dug graves sprinkled with the blood of deflowered virgins."

We both erupt into a giggle fit.

"STOP!" flows from Auggie's bedroom.

Willow and I find ourselves wrapped tightly together, shaking from the intensity of that singular word screamed from Isis's throat. We stare at each other, wide-eyed, fearing for our lives.

"How the fuck did this happen?!"

Eyes connecting, we realize we're not in trouble. Isis is in Auggie's bedroom, screaming at someone. It only takes a heartbeat before Willow spots the problem. Pointing, she gestures to Auggie's cracked door. If Willow hadn't distracted me earlier, I would've noticed. It's the first thing I do, lock the inside of Auggie's door before I drop trou. That's our system– Auggie's and mine, and I just broke our trust.

Gaze connected with mine, Willow tilts her chin in invitation. A rapid shake of my head is my reply. An eyebrow pops up, asking again. Gossip whore that I am, I can't resist nodding in agreement.

Without disconnecting our hug, we shuffle a few feet to the cracked door, then peek inside Auggie's bedroom. Being smarter than the average bear, Willow's arm shoots out to flick the light off so we can see better.

"Rob would be so proud," I breathe into Willow's ear. Her silent laughter vibrates both of us.

Rob's sitting in Auggie's ginormous wooden throne in the corner of the room, with a satisfied smirk flirting along his lips. I swear the God, the devious bastard knows we're watching. On second thought, I know Rob knows we are, and I'm pretty sure that wooden chair is his, not Auggie's. No man would look that comfortable in another man's throne.

Auggie's a slumped mountain at the foot of his bed, with his back to us. "Isis, this doesn't make any goddamn sense. Something might ail you. Maybe we better go to the emergency room. Opal's working tonight, and she took amazing care of you last time."

Isis was pacing between the foot of the bed and that ridiculous chair, but Auggie's words froze her in place. Going from immobile to lunacy, Isis screams like a feral banshee. "I'm not fucking crazy, Augustus!"

"C'mon, Ice!" Auggie lunges to his feet, totally losing his shit. Yet Robin watches on with amusement. "No dick has gotten near your pussy in four years! I get that you think you're fucking special, but you're not the goddamn Virgin Mary!"

Willow and I stare at each other, eyes wide, silent laughter spilling out our parted lips. "We better warn Rae that Masons do get impregnated by Immaculate Conception."

"Shut up," I hiss silently at Willow, body vibrating with the need to make noise. "You're killing me."

"There's no fucking way." Auggie falls to land on his bed. "No. Fucking. Way. You need to go to the doctor. Something's wrong with you."

"Here ya go, fucker!" A stick is lobbed through the air, with the trajectory Auggie's forehead. The pregnancy test bounces, then lands in his lap. "Nothing's wrong with me, except for the fact that I'm knocked up, haven't had sex, and have no clue whose kid is in my gut."

"Jesus. Christ." Willow and I mouth at one another. It takes me a second, but then I notice Rob. Willow checks in next. A heartbeat later, Auggie and Isis whip their heads in Rob's direction.

"What. Did. You. Do?" They mutter in unison, murder flashing in their eyes.

"I did what had to be done." Rob lazes in the chair, one leg thrown over the armrest, looking like a conquering villain. "You're both terrified after losing our baby. You've both ruined our lives for the past four years. You've fucked anything that had a heartbeat, including my own niece– Willow was the last fucking straw, Auggie. I did what had to be done."

"What did you do?" Isis's voice breaks, and tears spill from my eyes for her.

"I righted the past." Rob shifts in the chair, placing both feet on the carpet. "You wanted to be a mother, and we wanted to be fathers... so I made you pregnant."

"How?" Auggie's voice is loaded with betrayal, but it's the awe that rings the loudest.

"Doesn't matter– I did what needed to be done." Rob shrugs nonchalantly. "I was able to do it without triggering Isis's anxiety, knowing once she was pregnant, the fear would evaporate and she'd touch us again. I was successful in my endeavors, and you two should thank me."

"Thank you?!" Isis screams, picking up the discarded pregnancy test. "I should cut one of your goddamn nuts off and shove it down Auggie's throat, because your balls are too big and Auggie's aren't big enough."

"Are you calling me a coward?" Auggie mutters conversationally, which means he's on the verge of punching Isis in the face.

"Children," Rob intervenes. "We mustn't fight– think of the child."

"How?" Isis repeats Auggie's question, while he asks a new one. "Who?"

Robin waves his hands in their direction, sinister laughter echoing around the room. "I'm a diabolical bastard, but I'm not suicidal. If I'm going to impregnate a woman against her will, I sure as shit am not going to use my own sperm."

Sharing a mortified look, still wrapped in each other's arms, Willow and I back away from the door. Just as we're readying to close the door to my side of the bathroom, Rob's ecstatic voice fills the room.

"Congratulations, Auggie and Isis– I'm so happy to announce you're going to be the proud parents of a red-haired, irrational child!"

"Rob can't know that," I blabber, shocked out of my mind. As soon as Willow and I are back in the bedroom, I lock the door to the bathroom, putting an extra layer of soundproofing between us. "We've got to get the fuck out of this lunatic asylum, sooner rather than later."

Pacing in front of the bed, face as white as a ghost, Willow starts chewing on the ends of her hair. "I agree… and not just because of Devon. That was so wrong– I feel violated for Isis."

"I feel partially responsible," I admit, remembering a conversation I had with Rob many months ago. "Rob said he was willing to do anything to get his life back."

"Just stop." Willow turns into the adult version of herself in the middle of a crisis. "They've been fucked up since birth, and they've tried taking countless others with them. I love them. I love this house. But tomorrow, I'm going to walk through your new house with Devon and see what needs to be done immediately in order for us to move in. Then I need you and Ren to get your asses there, because we're moving from this shit-show starting tomorrow– I'm not sleeping another night here."

Numbness dissipating, I fetch my list. "Beth's party planning can wait a few days. What do we need to do? There's no way I can sleep tonight, so let's make an itinerary."

"Should we wake the guys?" Willow stops her pacing, then looks at me like I know what I'm doing. I don't, so I wing it.

"No, let them sleep." I grab my pen and begin writing. "We need to prove we're good in a crisis, that you and I can come together and get this shit done, without running to the men like damsels in distress."

"But I think Ren likes running to your rescue." Willow raises an eyebrow, skeeving me out because it reminds me of Auggie.

Shuddering, I mutter, "Too bad. Ren will need his rest because he's moving furniture tomorrow... first things first, Sunday breakfast at Clover's–"

"Great place to find help!" Willow grins, then begins searching for another pen. "Dad, Ozzy, Devon, and I will work on the house, while you and Ren direct the four little shits."

Pointing my pen at Willow, my tone brooks no room for argument. "No Auggie or Robin."

"Fuck no." Willow's not immune to being skeeved out either, judging by the way her entire body shudders in a wave from her toes to the top of her ponytail. "No Malcolm or Clover. Let the kids burn off some energy."

"Sit," I order, because Willow's hyper vibe is giving me the shakes. "Let's map this shit out."

"Get to writing, bitch." Voice surly, Willow winks at me.

CHAPTER FIFTY-TWO

Devon Mason

Waking in Massachusetts when my body is on Arizona time is a real bitch, especially when my life depends on structure and routine. "Now I know the definition of jetlag. The three-hour time difference means I slept too late here, but my body shouldn't be awake yet. My med schedule is gonna be fucked since I need to take some with food."

Crawling out of bed, I find Ren whispering at the cracked door. My brother has always been an early riser, so he must've stayed quiet doing things in the room while I slept.

"Hey, sleepyhead." Ren grins at me, but it looks strained. Through the crack, I can see Essie's painted toes and Willow's flip-flops– they leaned away to be unseen, but forgot to move their feet.

"Let 'em in." I stalk over to the door, not caring that I'm only wearing a pair of pajama pants. Everyone here has seen the show. "Good morning, ladies."

"Oh!" Essie falls into the room, hand combing at her messy hair. "Hi!"

"I need some duds." Willow ignores us by stalking over to her dresser. "Cool paperweight."

"Thanks," I mutter, not looking away from Essie. "What's up? I can sense this type of shit now that I'm not drugged out of my skull." I don't touch her, but I want to. We need to talk, take it slow, not fuck it up. "You're freaking out about something."

"I'm gonna go get dressed." Willow squeezes past me, then disappears into the bathroom.

"Clover's in heaven." Ren ignores my earlier question. "Breakfast is almost ready, so you better get a move on, Dev."

"Okay." With one last look at Essie, I stalk over to my suitcase. As I dig around, I wonder what happened to all of my shit. Where is it? I don't want to live out of a suitcase for too long, not when it would cause my anxiety to bloom. "Formal or causal? I'm not used to wearing anything with zippers and buttons, and I don't feel like dealing with it today."

"Wear whatever, bro." Ren chuckles, smirking at me. Then he reaches into my suitcase to grab a pair of loose sweat pants. "Wear these and a t-shirt. I'm not changing what I have on."

With a cursory glance, I notice Ren's in a pair of shorts, then my eyes light on Essie. She's wearing a sundress, one she just tugged on. It doesn't have anything but her boobs holding the dang scrap of fabric up, and I experience a twinge of pure lust for the first time in months. The need is instantly dampened because it terrifies me. I never did jerk off like Ms. Amelia warned me, lying and saying I did. I was too scared, fearing Alejandro would rear his goddamn head, which is exactly why my therapist wanted me to do it in a controlled environment.

Essie and Ren chat about what's on today's agenda while I step out of my pajama pants. Having no shame, I'm buck-ass naked as I fish out a pair of boxers from my suitcase. It's not like everyone in this house hasn't seen me naked. Last time I was in this room, high out of my skull, I was stalking around naked like a raving lunatic. Now I do it to prove a level of comfort and trust.

Bending to pull up my boxers, a sharp gasp has my attention snapping to Essie. Raising an eyebrow, "What?" I mutter, confused at the peculiar look on the girl's face.

Ren answers for Essie, releasing a laugh that has her shivering. "Yeah, I think I'm going to go help Spanky get dressed. Be back in three minutes," he warns before slipping into the bathroom.

After tugging on my pants, I'm magnetized to Essie. "What? I can tell something's wrong. I can *feel* it in the air."

Essie just shakes her head in answer, hair swinging around her jawline. I know she's trying very hard not to stress me out, which I appreciate, but it also pisses me off.

"Hey." Unable to stop myself, I pull Essie into a hug, settling her cheek against my bare chest. "I'm not fragile. I can handle anything you need to tell me."

Shuddering against me, I don't know if Essie is laughing, or crying, or cold, but I do know I like her in my arms. I thought it would be difficult to touch her, but it's as easy as breathing and just as addictive as my vices.

There's love and lust, and hurt and shame, and it's all balled up into a need so strong I don't know how to handle it. I push away from the fear, and simply hug Essie. I am a tactile creature after the way I was raised, but a bit more impartial than my father. Some people I need to touch, while others I hug out of obligation.

A happy sound rumbles in the back of my throat as my hands rub up and down Essie's arms. So much bare skin with this sundress, I'm so tempted to tug it down to spill her breasts out. I need skin-on-skin contact, and not in a sexual way. I just want to lie on the bed with Essie, holding each other, in a stronger way than I needed Ren last night.

My brother made me feel safe enough to sleep. Essie makes me feel like a man because I'd be the one making her feel safe. There is a big difference, but both are necessary to my survival right now.

"We're moving to our new house today." Following my lead, Essie's fingertips knead into the muscles running along my spine. Shuddering against her, I snuggle closer. "Ginny owns the house, and you can sign the paperwork when she's ready. But it would make more sense not to get into a routine here, then ditch it, only to need to make another routine at the new house. May as well cut out this layover at the Spook House."

"Something happened last night, I take it?" Rumbling a laugh, I nuzzle Essie's ear with the tip of my nose. "You don't have to tell me right now, but I'm not stupid."

Freezing in my embrace, Essie's fingernails indent the flesh of my hips. "After breakfast, we were going to explain, but we don't have time right now."

"I understand," I whisper, and I truly do. "Just hold me for another minute, okay?" Burying my face against the side of Essie's neck, I doubt she has any idea how much this means to me. She should hate me after how I left things– what I said and did at the park when Beth told me Essie was pregnant... I hate the person I used to be because of it.

The narcissistic version of myself acknowledges how there is nothing Essie wouldn't forgive me for, while the stronger part makes sure I'll never use her or hurt her again on purpose. I can't promise I'll never hurt her, because life hurts and shit happens out of our control. But I'll make sure I never do it on purpose, because I love her and never want to make her bleed for me again.

Warm deep down to my soul, in a heat that has nothing to do with the sun, hard and throbbing, without fear of nightmares brought to life, my hands take on a mind of their own. I can't get enough of Essie– touching, squeezing, pulling, gripping. Hungry,

I haven't touched Essie like this since I put a baby in her belly, over three months ago. It's not sexual, but it is.

Essie's laughter is infectious, drawing a chuckle from my chest. "What?" My lips murmur against the side of her neck, causing her to shiver. "What's so funny?"

"You're... ah–" Essie trails off, pulling away from me. Without her clouding all my senses, I feel Willow and Ren at my back, exiting the bathroom.

"Last time I saw you..." Willow steps around us, grabbing her cellphone off the dresser. "You looked like shit."

"I know." I step away, grabbing for my t-shirt. After slipping it on, I slide my feet into a pair of sneakers, then I shrug my backpack over one shoulder. I'll never go anywhere without my meds and cellphone alarms. "Delaney forced me to look at the pictures you took for the first three weeks of my stay."

Trying to cover her blush with a smirk, Willow's eyes drink me in from my sneakers to my shaggy hair. "Then stop playing an idiot. You know exactly why Essie's all tongue-tied around your naked ass. You want me to say it?"

"Say what?" My eyebrows scrunch in confusion– I truly have no idea what the hell Willow's getting at. Wanting to jot this moment down, I go fetch my journal from underneath the mattress, then tuck it into my waistband, covering it with my t-shirt.

"No longer looking like you stepped out of a death camp, all tan and shit..." Willow smirks, blush still tinting her cheeks. "Yeah, I get it now." She walks past me, then whispers something in Essie's ear. Both of them erupt into naughty giggles.

"What?" I ask my brother, stalking after them as they jog down the stairs. "Hey!" I yank Ren back before he follows them to the front door. "Explain."

"Spanky's always jealous over me checking out Essie, when we all know it's involuntary on my part." Ren's grin stretches across his face. "I don't mind getting a taste of my own medicine, since it's teaching her a lesson."

"What lesson?" We walk side-by-side down the front walk, across the street, then up the sidewalk to the Pink Taco Hut.

After rolling his eyes, Ren chucks me in the shoulder. "The girls think you look hot, dumbass." My brother leaves me stunned on the front steps of my dad's new home.

Refusing to mull that bullshit over, I hesitate as I enter the house. I've never set foot in here, but I know it's packed wall-to-wall with family members who want to see me, judge me, determine if I'm *better*, not realizing there's no cure for what ails me. There's no getting better from addiction or mental illness– it's an everyday struggle, not a choice, or something a pill can erase. They're well-meaning, and love me, but they're also trying too damn hard.

Wandering through the huge house toward the loud voices, I find everyone scooting close together to fit around the dining room table. They ignore me to give me time to acclimate, which I appreciate, but it only makes it worse. They're trying to appear calm, but I can feel they're anything but.

Drawing in a deep breath of relief, I squeeze into the chair between Ren and Essie, smiling as everyone pretends to ignore me. No bombardment of hugs and kisses. No unanswerable questions. No pointing out how I look healthy, have a tan, need a haircut…

I love my family.

Dad's sitting at the head of the table, blatantly ignoring me, as he showers kisses along Clover's neck. Across the table from me, Seth is rolling his eyes at his mom, with Weston reaching past both Violet and Ozzy to jab the kid in the side for being a dumb-shit. Ozzy's cozied up between Seth and Violet, silent as I remember him in school. We both tilt our heads in acknowledgement, but don't speak. Violet's talking loudly across the table, teasing Willow. Dave and Mary are at the other end of the table, looking proud as hell of their family, especially of the foul-mouthed banter coming from their granddaughters.

The version of me I left dead and buried back in Arizona on week five, he would've thrown himself because everyone isn't fawning all over him, dropping what they're doing, and making him feel special as the center of attention. That person I no longer recognize as me, as I said to Ren about thinking in the third-person. I know that's how I used to act, but who I am today can't wrap my mind around it. I like sitting back, observing my family, getting to know them again– see them with fresh eyes, clear of mental illness and the taint of addiction.

Smirking to myself, glorifying in the comforting weight of my brother's arm pressing into my shoulder, I scoop food onto my plate as the dishes are passed around. I don't take from every platter, fearing the wicked belly ache to come. But then I realize several of the dishes are bland, nutrient-rich foods meant for me. Smiling in thanks at Clover, she winks back at me.

Growling at the greasy bacon and slab of scrapple on Essie's plate, I salivate. "I'll have to work my way up to that," I whisper in her ear, loving how she shivers for me. Eyes flicking to my plate, Essie shakes her head at the fruit, scrambled egg whites, and dry toast.

"Adventurous," Essie teases, smirking as she passes me a saucer with three pieces of turkey bacon I assume were cooked just for me. "Willow and Ren are little hogs now, so it won't be long before you're not as sensitive to fats and sugar."

"Shit yeah." Ren bumps against my shoulder, laughing. "I'm joining whatever workout regimen you've got going on, starting tomorrow. Weston no longer runs with me–"

West jabs his tongue out at us from across the table, then shovels in a large forkful of pancakes.

"Little shit has friends he'd rather jog with, ain't got no time for his big brother no more." Ren pats his gut. "Now that you're back..." he trails off.

"Yeah, sure– I gotta stick to a routine, so that works for me. I don't mind jogging alone, helps me think. But I tend to slag a bit if no one is pacing me."

"I don't do physical activity," Willow announces to the table. "Don't ask me to go jogging, do yoga, meditate, or whatever new craze is flashing through Fairport."

"Only woman I know who is proud of her pot-gut," Essie grumbles underneath her breath.

"I work nonstop– that's good enough." Willow reaches across Ren's plate to drop a mini-muffin onto mine. "It's bran, I assume it's for you. Grabbed it by mistake, thinking it was cinnamon raisin."

An angry storm cloud enters the dining room, and I feel my baby sister before I see her. She doesn't speak, but the maelstrom of emotions are suffocating.

Delaney explained family dynamics to me, how there is a black sheep in every family, no matter what. This is a fluid thing, jumping from host to host as the family matures. There isn't a family on the planet devoid of a *problem child*, and all the blame and frustration gets dumped at this person's feet. It isn't the individual's fault, no matter how it seems. The family taints this person, creates a balance of good and evil– you can't have one without the other. In a quest to be right, someone has to be wrong, and the family dynamic will subconsciously create the problem child for the sake of balance.

After Mom, this passed to Ren, then it passed to me. In Clover's family, it was Willow, then it was Seth acting like a prick. It tried to jump to Essie, but it didn't stick. Now, I can see how it's struggling to find a host between Weston and Raven, for completely different reasons.

The break I took from our family gave me the ability to see it from the outside looking in. It's not the same family I left, blending two dynamics into one. Since I'm not an active participant yet, I can see what Delaney, Ms. Amelia, and probably what Bethany sees when they look around.

A part of me is relieved I'm no longer the scape goat, but the stronger part aches for my baby sister as she stands behind her chair looking lost. Dressed in a black hoodie and torn jeans, Rae's hair is in a messy bun like she doesn't care how she looks anymore. My baby sister is a beautiful person, inside and out, but she's trying very hard to fade into the background. By trying not to be noticed, she's making herself a target for bullying because of how scruffy she's looking.

"You started without me." Rae's words are pouting, but there's rage flashing in her eyes. No doubt she knew when breakfast was, but was testing everyone to see if they'd wait for her. I pulled that toxic tactic in the past. "You're in my chair." Not getting the attention she seeks, Rae swats Violet upside the head."

"What?" Violet brushes Rae off, then goes back to chatting with Ozzy.

"You're in my chair," Rae says again, louder this time, drawing the attention of everyone at the table.

"What's it matter?" Violet twists in her seat to pin Rae down with a glare. "Just sit down and eat before it gets cold. Mom and Grandma didn't work their asses off in the kitchen to have to sit here and listen to you bitch."

Eyes flicking all around the table, I wait for someone to intervene, but Dad has always had us sort out our own shit.

"You're in my chair," Rae whines, clearly frustrated. "Sitting next to my brother." She looks around the table, her seat last on that side, with Mary at the end and Willow sitting across from her. "This is your family– mine's down there."

"Jesus Christ, Raven!" Violet loses her temper. "We're all family. You're not going to talk anyway." Making a show of it, she thrusts her plate down past Weston to land on Rae's empty place setting, then shoves out of her seat. "If you sat your ass in your seat, you'd still be sitting next to your brother– you're just pissy because you want to sit next to Ozzy too."

Ozzy's eyes slip shut, straining at the corners, with his fist clenching his fork. Poor guy looks like he's about to upchuck everything he ate this morning. This must happen all the time.

"Girls," Dad cautions, voice brooking no room for argument. "Just sit and eat. Please don't start anything, today of all days. Let's just break bread and enjoy Devon's company and the baby news."

"Baby news?" I look around, hoping someone will answer me, but my normally silent sister is stealing the show.

"GAWD! Why do you have to embarrass me?!" Raven grabs the back of the chair, lifting it slightly, then slams the feet back to the floor.

"You're embarrassing yourself and making everyone, especially Ozzy, uncomfortable." Violet grabs for her plate, but Rae tears it out of her hands. "Knock it off– what's your malfunction?"

"Rae," Weston tries to stop the fight, like always, but it doesn't help any.

"Why did you have to bring Ozzy into it?" Betrayal breaks Rae's voice. "I told you to stop sitting next to him, always smothering him."

"*I'm* smothering him?" Violet points at her chest. "I'm just trying to get to know the guy."

Enraged, Raven clutches Violet's plate in her hand, looking on the verge of smashing it. "I called dibs first!"

"Oh, Christ!" whispers from all the mouths on our side of the table, with Ren releasing an honest to God snarl. "I hate that cocksucking bullshit."

"Rae," Violet mutters in a calm tone. "I'm not boy-crazy. I could give a shit less about guys. I'm trying to be Ozzy's friend, because he lives with us and I want him to feel welcome. You're the one making it into something it isn't."

"I warned you!"

"Son?" Dad directs at Ozzy, that singular word holding a punch.

Eyes still closed, Ozzy is obviously distraught. "Don't ruin this for me, Rae," he pleads. The fork falls from his fist to land with a crashing sound on his plate. "I'm starting senior year, and I'm not emancipated. I need Dave and Malcolm. *Don't ruins this–* don't make Malcolm think there's something going on when there isn't."

With dawning horror, I watch my sister tear up, drop Violet's plate back on the table, then run from the room.

"Well, don't look at me– I'm not going after her." Violet retrieves her plate, then takes a bite of her pancakes. "She's been driving me bat-shit for weeks. Imagine sharing a room with someone you want to smother in their sleep with a pillow."

Snorting, Ren and I share a look of perfect understanding.

"I'm…" Dad's flabbergasted and so out of his league after raising boys.

Looking around, everyone with Prynne blood is tucking into their food, completely unfazed. Us Masons, we're confused. Poor Ozzy, he's just staring down at his plate, utterly silent and immobile, looking lost and terrified.

In perfect sync, both Ren and Essie elbow me in the ribs to fix it. Dave and Mary look entertained. Dad looks on the verge of freaking out. I discover what the baby news is by the green tinge to Clover's face and the way she's cupping her belly– damn, Dad needs to keep it in his pants. The youngsters are following Violet's lead by scarfing up their food, because she's their alpha bitch.

My group is waiting for me to fix it– the drug addict, mental patient. Like Violet, I'm their alpha, so I have to take the lead.

Dad has enough to deal with, so I decide on a divide and conquer plan of attack. The youngsters can learn from our recent mistakes. "Violet, go up to your room– Essie and Willow are going to give you and Raven a lecture on why Ren is seething over the dibs comment."

"Dibs is fucking stupid," Violet mutters around a mouthful of pancakes. "I don't need a lecture, because I don't plan on dating anyone. Watching you fools– *ugh!* Gross."

"C'mon." Willow yanks her baby sister from her seat, then shoves the plate into the girl's hand. "Walk and eat."

"This is not going to be pleasant," Essie whispers in my ear as she stands. "We just had this conversation with Willow a month ago."

"Hey, now!" Willow protests. "We already went over how you assumed what I was thinking. So shut your trap."

"So annoying." Violet rolls her eyes, setting her plate back on the table. Then she grabs the basket of muffins instead. "I'll listen, but I won't like it– broken record." The girls disappear to parts unknown, leaving me to deal with Ozzy.

"Sorry, Clover." I stand from the table, with Ren following my lead. "C'mon, boys, let's go out back." My eyes flick to Dad, who looks shell-shocked. "I've never been here before, so…" I trail off, looking for some help.

"Officer Devon's back in action." Seth gives me a toothy grin, looking relieved that I'm the same bossy asshole as ever.

"I'm sober and medicated." I ruffle the kid's hair. "I didn't have a lobotomy."

CHAPTER FIFTY-THREE

Kieren Mason

"Okay, what's up?" Devon says from next to me at the picnic table, with the three boys sitting opposite us, Ozzy in between our brother and stepbrother. Devon is vibrating a bit, drawing all eyes.

"What's up with you?" Of course, Seth has no tact– blunt little shit.

Old Devon would've lashed out. New Devon tugs his backpack off his shoulder, plunks it on the table, then starts digging around inside. We wait for close to three minutes while he does whatever he's doing, all sharing loaded looks. Watching Devon is like being intoxicated by an intriguing car accident– we can't look away.

After palming a foam stress ball, which suspiciously looks like a happy toaster, Devon flops his pack onto the grass. "We'll just get this out of the way right now– I have tics. Creepy crawlies is what I like to call it. I'm tripping a bit, sitting here. This is my family, but it's a new house with new problems, and it's going to take me some time to get used to it."

"Yeah, I could see that." Seth eyeballs the toaster covetously. He looks like a little kid, is curious like one too, but has the mind of a prickly old man. "You got any more of those things?"

"More than a dozen." Devon chuckles underneath his breath, refusing to give his toys away. No doubt, Seth will have his own batch soon. "Dr. Delaney passes them out for good behavior. The peach is my favorite, but I needed the toaster's bigger surface area because of the squeezing power."

"What's stressing you out right now?" I'm glad Weston voices my thoughts, because I didn't have the balls to ask.

Shrugging, Devon looks down at his fist while clutching and releasing the foam toy. "This new life was a progression for you guys. The melding of two families. The moving to this house. You were able to gradually let our old life go. I was torn from it without a goodbye, then dropped into a life that doesn't have room for me."

Turning to the side, I'm a hairsbreadth away from grabbing Devon. "Bro—"

"No, it's okay." Devon pats my hand so quickly, I'm left with the memory of his touch rather than the reality of it. "I have to pave my own way– make my own life. Anyway…" Sighing deeply, his hand starts manipulating the foam. "I'd rather help with what's going on here since my issues can't be fixed, only tolerated."

"Officer Devon," Seth's voice pitches high, like the little kid he appears to be, but there's ancient intelligence shining back.

One day, I asked the little shits what they wanted to be when they grew up, which truly does annoy the piss out of kids– too much pressure. Only the boys could answer me, both with equal passion.

Not that Violet isn't passionate or intelligent, she just hasn't found her thing yet. Why should she know a month before she starts freshman year in high school?

My baby sister was too embarrassed to voice what she wanted in a world that looks down upon women who want what Rae wants, because they don't think they're being empowered woman. Rae wants to be what she never had, what Clover is – a mother. The guidance counselor called at the end of last school year because Rae refused to sign-up for SAT Prep over the summer. The guy had a conniption when Rae said she wasn't going to college.

Clover and Dad fought, with Clover wanting Rae to take the course. Old-school Dad gave into his baby girl, perfectly happy if she becomes a stay-at-home wife and mother. Clover wasn't against Rae's future plans, but my sister is only sixteen and there is no guarantee there's a future husband and father. Clover wasn't real big on pinning a future on a guy who doesn't exist, when it should be Rae paving her own way through life. That's why Rae was put on birth control, and why Ozzy looks like he's about to be ill.

Weston's answer wasn't football, even though we know that's going to happen. He said he wanted to be Fairport High's gym teacher and coach, because kids shouldn't feel ashamed of their physical abilities, or lack thereof.

Seth's answer was far more gut-wrenching. A cancer research geneticist, and I don't doubt for a heartbeat that he'll do just that. Losing Sam to pancreatic cancer altered the lives of everyone in their family, and Seth has the brains and passion to want to put a stop to another family being decimated. It's no wonder Seth finds the interworkings of Devon's brain fascinating.

"Ginny said the medicine helps with how your brain misfires." Seth stares down at Devon's backpack, no longer coveting the toys– he wants to see the dozen or so bottles of pills rattling around in there. "The rest is just who you are. You don't need to be fixed or tolerated."

"Aunt Ginny was counseling you, I take it." Old Devon would have been pissed– this version seems to find our family talking behind his back as amusing. "Okay, youngest to oldest, tell me what's going on in your lives so I'm not out of the loop. Gimme something else to think about other than my narcissistic self."

"Not much, really," the youngest yet biggest mutters with a shrug, but his tan cheeks are flaming red. "Can't wait for school to start."

Seth chuckles, the amused tone nearly the same as Willow's voice. "West is *not* innocent." The soft ribbing is cut off by my baby brother's palm being smashed over the smaller guy's mouth. Ozzy elbows them both in the ribs to part them.

Laughing, eyes sparking with mischievousness, Seth has never looked more like Robin than he does now. No matter what, Seth and Weston have bonded as brothers, so that's all he's going to say. Instead he takes the limelight.

"We signed up for classes last week." Seth's enthusiasm is palpable. "Mom graduated when she was only sixteen, so I was allowed to pick classes with the upperclassmen."

"Seth's going to be in two of my classes this semester." Ozzy rolls with it, seeming unfazed to have a little shit hanging onto him, when anyone else would've been annoyed.

"I'm dipping into my *whatever fund* for a class at FCC. It has to be at the same time as one of Willow's classes– can't drive myself." Seth grins huge, reminding us how Willow never gave a shit about pesky laws. "We thought it would look good on my college applications, maybe help with scholarships."

"This dick keeps singing how he only has two more years living in the Pink Taco Hut, instead of four like Violet and me." West's words are taunting, but nothing but pride is shining from his eyes.

"I'm getting the hell outta Dodge before that baby is mobile." Seth flashes all of us a *'you feeling me?'* look. "It's not my kid– I'm not changing diapers or babysitting."

"You're going to miss out on some fun shit," I remind the kid to slow down. "Parties. Prom. Graduation. Skipping out to get away from our new baby brother or sister means you're jumping out of childhood into adulthood with no buffer."

"Do I look like a prom kinda guy?" Seth arches a brow at me, no trace of a smile on his chipmunk-cheek face. "My dad was a charming bastard, but he was dinky. I know my future is looking like Uncle Rob."

Head jerking up, mop of wild curls flying around his blade-sharp jaw. "What's wrong with how Rob looks?" Ozzy, poor deluded Ozzy.

"Everyone assumes he's gay!" Seth growls, the side of his fist landing on the tabletop. "Everyone assumes I'm gay because I'm small and smart. They think I'm a pushover. I don't need to stick around for parties and prom, because no girl believes me when I hit on her."

"Friend-zoned…" Weston drawls out, trying hard not to laugh. "I'm gay, and they don't believe it."

"By default, they assume I'm gay too." Seth narrows his eyes, trying hard to blame Weston but knowing it's not right. "Whatever… I'm so out of here."

"Just show the girls your real side." Devon tosses Seth his happy toaster squeeze toy. "For some bizarre reason, girls love a prick."

"Asshole!" Seth tosses the foam toy back to Devon, face lit up with laughter.

"Exactly– the worse you treat a girl, the more she'll fall all over herself to please you." They toss it back and forth while smirking at each other in understanding.

"Stop!" Hand snapping forward, I snatch the toy out of the air. "Don't you fucking dare do that," I growl in warning. "We have three impressionable boys here, and your advice is toxic."

"It's true though." Dev shrugs, completely unrepentant. "As I said, I'm sober and medicated. I didn't have a personality lobotomy." Mouth saying one thing, eyes another… "If you want more than to get into her pants, you should just be real with the girl. It will cause *way* too many problems down the road– let me be your lesson. But the truth doesn't change. I have no fucking idea why girls are pathologically drawn to assholes."

"You're in luck." Smirking, Weston points at Seth. "Because you're an asshole."

"Lucky me– I'm an asshole who's invisible, while the *sweet* guy is getting laid left and right."

"What?" Devon and I practically shriek in unison at our baby brother, who just blushes bright red and stares upward at the clouds.

Silence descends. Line drawn in the sand, clearly it's them versus us, even with the small age-gap. Ozzy straddles the line between, and he picks a side by distracting us.

"So I like working with Dave– he's a pretty cool dude. But he'll only let me work on small jobs on the weekends, because it's too much hassle to put me on the books. Something about red tape, never-ending paperwork, and worker's comp." After finger-combing his awesome hair, Ozzy tucks it behind his freakishly tiny ears. "Anyway, I need to bank some cash for my future, but Malcolm put his foot down. He lets me clean up around the Batcave, but won't let me get a fulltime job."

"Let me guess," Devon's voice holds twenty-one years of Malcolm Mason knowledge. "Dad said you need to concentrate on your studies, and don't worry about living in the Pink Taco Hut? I bet he said Mary and Clover love you as much as their own kids. Am I right?"

"Yep." Eyes downcast, I can practically scent Ozzy's pride flowing into the shitter.

"Dad's right." Devon stares the guy down. "It's not about you, so don't start wondering why Dad picked you and not someone else. As long as you appreciate it and do something with your life, don't sweat it. Go to school, get a future, and let them love you."

"I thought–"

"That'd I'd be an asshole about this?" Devon finishes for Ozzy. "I spent about six weeks wondering why me. Why Dad would pay for my treatment at the expense of his own future. I know he sold our house to pay for only eight weeks of treatment. I've asked why me, but it's not about me. Dad had to do it, so he did."

"But I…" Frustrated, Ozzy's chest starts moving up and down rapidly, so I toss him Devon's foam toaster. "I don't deserve it."

"Doesn't matter." Devon's stare is unflinching. "Do you like hanging around the Batcave?"

"Yeah, I love it there." Ozzy's blush is answer enough. "I feel like I'm a part of something when I'm there, even if I'm only scrubbing the toilet."

"Good." Devon plucks his toy out of Ozzy's hand. "Go to school. Graduate. Keep hanging around the Batcave until you're a permanent fixture. Working with Dave under the table may give you some extra spending money, but not as much value as scrubbing the drunk tank for free. Being employed isn't the same as having a profession– let them give you a future. Give you a home. Then pay it forward."

Until this second, I never understood Devon's obsession with the Batcave. I couldn't give two shits about being a police officer. Dad was always obsessed, spewing John-Mason-isms. Watching the odd connection between my brother and Ozzy has a thread of jealousy sparking to life. Then I realize I'm not meant to understand, because it's not my passion. They'll never understand when Weston and I go on a tangent about football, either.

"Now that that's off the table, care to explain what's going on with my baby sister?" Devon's tight voice is utterly frightening.

"Nothing!" comes from three sources across the table, all of them looking equally terrified of Devon.

"Nothing, like you and Sage?" Devon asks Weston.

"And Maddox," Seth coughs into his hand, then coughs for real as Ozzy elbows him in the ribs. After clearing his throat and swallowing a few times, Seth flashes us a patent-pending Robin Prynne smirk. "Sorry, the word slut was caught in my throat– thanks to Ozzy for dislodging it."

"You wish you were a slut," Weston breathes, trying hard not to grin back.

"Actually, I don't," and the kid means it. "I guess I'll explain. Ozzy's more like me– we have more important shit to deal with than boy-crazy girls… or boys." Seth mutters out the side of his mouth at Weston. "I want to graduate as soon as fucking possible, and our boy just wants to survive to see adulthood. West doesn't realize how good he has it."

"I never said that." Weston folds his arms over his broadening chest, glowering. "I know I'm lucky, so stop trying to get me into trouble. Leave me out of this shit."

Losing his patience, when it's in short supply to begin with, Devon makes sure he has Ozzy's complete and total attention. "Explain what's going on, because these fools are making it worse."

"I won't let anything fuck up my future." Determination bleeds from Ozzy's tone. "I never want to feel like I did after I lost my grandma. Foster home after foster home– some of them felt like homes, but most were only in it for the money. I like living with your family because they treat me like family. I'm not going to let Raven ruin it for me."

Heart beating extra hard, words spew out of my mouth before I can examine them. "Do you like Rae?"

"I don't know her." Ozzy's voice pitches high with frustration, nearly a whine. "I don't get it. Half the girls in school have crushes on me, and I don't get it. They don't know me. *At all*. So how can they like me?"

Eyes narrowed, I'm drawing a blank. "Umm…"

"OH!" Devon gets it, and the minions nod their heads, eyes glued to Ozzy.

"I'm lost," I mutter in defeat, confused. "That had to be the humblest, most bizarre way to express arrogance I've ever heard."

"I'm guessing those two are alike." Seth points between Ozzy and Devon. The grin on his face clues me in to the fact I'm going to hate what comes next. The little bastard is definitely his big sister's greatest creation. "You two slut-bags," he points between Weston and me, "Won't understand."

Eyes narrowed, I grumble to the little antagonist. "And that leaves you where?"

"Hopeless," Seth replies without missing a beat.

Smothering a laugh, Ozzy puts the train back on the tracks. "I want to like Rae as a sister, but I don't know her. I try to talk to her, but she hides after being caught staring at me. I don't date, and I sure as shit am not going to start by looking in the house for one." Whatever else he says trails off in an inaudible grumble.

"Do you like girls?" Devon puts out a hand to stop Ozzy from blowing up like I would have. "Not saying because you don't date that you're gay or whatnot. I didn't date in high school either. I get it, but my issues were way deep."

Blushing, Ozzy can't look any of us in the eye. "I like girls– I just don't understand this crush business, where they giggle when they look at me, then fight over who I talk to. It's insanity at school. I've lost real friends to the horde, like they own me because they have a crush on me, when they've never spoken two words to me. I don't get it, and I hate how they push my friends away, like what Rae's trying to do with V."

No way in hell am I going to voice how that was my favorite part of high school. I loved the way all those girls made me feel, only I took the time to get to know them before I had sex with them. I never used them– they got a boost in their popularity for banging me. We were friends before and after the deed, no hard feelings and no jealousy. If Seth wasn't a cute little bugger like a puppy, he'd be worse than me, only he'd be an ass about it. But I can see how a quiet guy like Ozzy would be uncomfortable by the primal dance.

"Last year, I tried to be Rae's friend at school, so I was happy that she was in the house with me– didn't feel so alone." Mumbling mutely again, it takes a bit to figure out what Ozzy says next. "I was terrified of Violet."

Devon's snort turns into infectious laughter.

"Rae's turned into a weirdo, and Violet actually wants to get to know me, hang out with me. Now I feel responsible for Rae and Violet being at each other's throats." Ozzy leans across the table, imploring Devon and me. "I have to see them as my sisters, no matter what. How I do or don't feel doesn't matter, so Rae acting like a stalker is making my life miserable. If V and I are in the same room, Rae loses her shit. Malcolm's going to get fed up and kick me out. Rae may be happy to get me away from Violet, but I'll be on my own, without a roof over my head and no job. I'm seventeen and still have a year of high school left."

Staring down at his hands, Ozzy draws in large breaths of air, then he stares me down, eyes flicking to beg Devon. "Make your sister back off. *Please.* I don't want to hurt her feelings. I don't want to be a dick about it. It hasn't even been a month, none of us can handle a year. This isn't about some girl having an unrequited crush on me– it's my life being fucked over."

Shuddering violently, Devon mutters from next to me, "Teenage girls."

To break the uncomfortable silence, I mutter, "Dibs," to be a snarky ass.

Laughing, Dev and I are holding onto each other, hamming it up. We're confusing the three idiots sitting across from us, but hopefully they'll never understand. Calming, I decide I better put the guys at ease.

"You're allowed to feel as you feel. You're allowed to like who you like, want who you want. It's not fair to be manipulated or emotionally extorted into dating someone, continuing to date someone, if you're not feeling it. This goes both ways. Hurting someone's feelings is not worth being with someone when you're not feeling it. They don't *own* you, and vice versa."

"If a guy or girl pushes your friends away out of jealousy, they're an asshole. Don't date that type of person." Devon's speaking, but obviously looking inward. "If you give in, it feeds the monster, turning them into a toxic person."

"Okay, but what do I do about Rae?" Ozzy's voice warbles, but it's Weston looking far too interested in this portion of our conversation. What kind of fucked up love-triangle bullshit does my baby brother have himself in now? Seth just looks amused by it all.

"Ignore it," I mutter with a shrug. "Don't feed the beast. Try to be Rae's friend, don't let her push Violet away from you. Wait–" leaning forward, I get into the kid's space. "You're not feeling Violet, are you?"

"*No!*" Eyes huge with terror, Ozzy's objection echoes around the backyard. "I want to be part of the family– I make sure to hang out with everyone, even Mary. It's fucked up that I have to look over my shoulder when Violet and I are playing Xbox."

"Rae's making the atmosphere in the house uncomfortable," Devon murmurs to himself. "If it doesn't get better after the girls talk to them, then I'll have a word with my sister." Scrubbing at his shaggy hair, Devon looks defeated. "Can't help how she feels, though. But that doesn't have a dang thing to do with you."

"Boys!" Thankfully Essie's voice reaches us before they do. "We have a lot to do today, so quit clucking like hens."

"We have jobs for everyone!" Willow's cackle has the boys' eyes widening, but has a smile spreading across my face. "Idle hands are the Devil's playground."

"We're atheists," I remind my girlfriend as she leans against my back.

"Hmm… last Sunday, more than half the people in this lawn shared a church pew with me." Resting her chin on my shoulder, Willow gets cozy. "Doesn't matter. When I say hop–"

"We say how high." Willow's mini zealot grins up at her. "I already told Violet what's going on."

"What now?" Looking over my shoulder at Willow, I notice Violet and Raven in a standoff with Essie standing between them. Over ten feet apart, both girls have their arms folded across their chests. Raven looks miserable, guilty, and ashamed, but Violet looks on the verge of violence.

"*Your* Spanky loves me best," Seth taunts, crawling off the picnic table bench. "Always will– called me first thing this morning."

"Suck up– when you gonna cut the cord?" Weston thumps Seth upside the head. "Essie called me, so there… then we told our counterparts."

"Then there is me." Dev grabs his backpack, shouldering it as he stands. "Always in the dark."

"I'll shed a little light." After a kiss to my neck, Willow pulls away to wrap her hand around Dev's wrist. "You're with me today, buddy."

"Well, who the hell is gonna clue my ass in?" I mutter in accusation, eyes flicking from person to person.

"That would be me." Essie puts me out of my misery. "Ozzy, you're with Willow and Devon– everyone else, come with me."

CHAPTER FIFTY-FOUR

Devon Mason

"You just couldn't help yourself, could you?" Willow and I are standing in the center of my new living room, staring down at the shit-brown stained carpeting. On the walk from the Pink Taco Hut to the Shithole– as everyone is calling my new home – Willow explained why we were evacuating the Spook House a week early, when I hadn't signed the paperwork on this house yet.

My aunt and uncles have lost their minds, and I don't want to be a part of whatever the hell they have going on. I even warned Willow I didn't want any details, because we have enough to deal with without their insanity added to the mix.

After touring the tiny two-story house, Willow brought me into the living room, all the while she kept blushing in shame.

"Let me guess," I gesture around the newly renovated house, with its fresh paint, refinished flooring, and bright and shiny surfaces. "You were going to leave me some stuff to do, but couldn't help yourself." I swallow a chuckle when I notice she even gave us fancy molding and a modern light fixture in here.

The carpeting is *way* out of place.

"What gives you that idea?" Refusing to look at me, Willow's cheeks are so red, I fear they'll catch fire.

In the background, Ozzy is hanging the resurfaced cupboard doors. Dave is running around with some kind of box to test the electrical current. One of Dave's fellas is testing the water pressure, while another is checking the pilot lights on the range, water tank, and furnace. Aunt Ginny is leaning over the counter with a bunch of paperwork spread out before her. She brought Opal for some reason, and a tiny old dude who is acting as the notary.

Ah! Opal leans forward to kiss the nape of Aunt Ginny's neck– and that explains that.

"Didn't know Aunt Ginny had a girlfriend," I mutter underneath my breath. "Sage's mom no less."

Taking a deep breath in relief, Willow seems happy I changed the subject. "They're attached at the hip." Shuddering in revulsion, I'm about to ask Willow if she has a bit of homophobia like Ren, which would be bizarre after I watched her mess around with Bethany. "I walked in on them making out– every time I see them, it replays in my head."

"Oh!" I drawl, then chuckle. The Playroom removed all my squeamishness when it comes to other people having sex. I've seen it all.

"On *the* sofa," Willow stresses, a shudder working its way along her spine. "So happy to be moving from the Spook House, if only so I don't have to see that dang thing."

"I have fond memories of that sofa." Now it's my turn to blush, while Willow pales. "So… the carpet?" I kick at the only thing out of place in our new home, changing the subject back because I know I have to have that conversation with Willow, like yesterday.

"I… um– I was going to leave you a bunch of stuff to do, and show you how to do it, but I… um–" Willow strides over to the corner of the living room, then crouches down. I follow, curious. "I couldn't help myself…" she trails off.

"Motherfucking déjà vu moment, we've got going on here," I mutter underneath my breath as I watch Willow pull up the carpeting. I'm transported back nearly a year ago, to a different time and place, where Willow and I were completely different people. We were becoming friends while she renovated the Spook House. Auggie was so terrified of Willow, he was shoving me at her as a lover.

"At least I'm not fuming over Auggie and wondering if you like me more than as a friend." Willow winks at me, then steps to the side. Gesturing at the edge of the carpeting, "I left this for you to do– an unveiling of sorts –but mostly I left it to protect my beautiful floor as we worked on the rest of the house."

In the past, it was me who sat on my heels, watching Willow pull carpet and attack carpet strips with a vengeance. Now is a different matter– Willow watches as I easily roll up the nasty carpet to reveal the refinished hardwood floor beneath.

"To make this a real déjà vu moment, you gotta shoulder the roll of carpet and toss it out the back door," I tease, half in the now, half in the past. "But I won't make you do that."

Laughing at me, or maybe herself, or maybe us from the past, Willow gazes down at me with fondness. "Do you ever wonder if Ren & Essie share moments like this together?"

Grinning up at Willow, purposefully hitting her where it hurts most, "Oh, most certainly." As I've said over and over again. I may be medicated and sober, but my personality didn't change. A part of me gets off on the pained look crossing Willow's face. Not because I want to hurt her, but because I love being the one to soothe her.

Kicking the roll of carpeting until it rolls across the floor near the front door, her sneaker getting scuffed by the backing, I recognize how Willow is going inward. "How is it that we ended up being the jealous ones?"

"It would've never worked out between us." I wait until I gain Willow's attention to finish what I started. Her head flips around quickly, with fury etched across her features. "Willow, we're too much alike."

"That's not helping, Dev," Willow grumbles, looking dejected and lost.

Shaking my head back and forth as I rise to my feet, I see too much of who I used to be echoing back from who Willow is today. "So are Ren and Essie– too much alike."

"You're telling me not to be jealous, so I'll help you not be jealous?" A grin of realization spreads across Willow's tiny face, enlivening her.

"True that, sister," I whisper in a teasing tone, looking around the room to ignore the intense emotions inundating me. I was taught to not run from my emotions, but I can't get into what needs to be rehashed with my aunt and her girlfriend in the next room, Willow's and my foster brother in listening range, and Willow's dad whistling as he works.

"Sister? In-laws… someday– as long as I don't experience fits of jealousy and possession, or hit my future kids."

"Ha-ha!" I bark sharply as the cavalry arrives, people pour into the tiny house carrying furniture. Stalking over to Willow, I whisper into her ear. "Sister no matter what, even if you and Ren don't work out," I remind her. "We're family– it's what you said to me as a goodbye. Words that gave me hope in the first few weeks when I was more animal than human. No, Essie and Ren don't share moments like this– never this intense, this important."

"Shit," Willow releases as a shaky breath. "Okay, work from the bottom up!" she shouts at her workforce. "Rugs, then furniture, then boxes." Tugging her general from behind Rory's mammoth frame, "Did you organize the flow of shit, so that they're not bringing stuff out of order?"

Essie levels Willow with a look that could incinerate the planet. "Same shit, different day, Willow. How many times have we done this in the past three months? It started with my parents' house, and it ends with this one."

"Okay," Willow backs off, looking sheepish, but Essie keeps looking between Willow and me with curiosity. I realize she may have seen me whispering in Willow's ear.

Innocent– I have no reason to feel guilty, shame, or worry. If anyone has a problem with whatever relationship Willow and I share, they can fuck off. I hurt her, and she was left dangling while I was being repaired. Now it's my turn to fix in her what I, and I alone, broke.

"Hey!" My voice is meek, and the little wave I give is lame. Too many people in such a small place. I feel invaded after already getting acquainted with my new home. It's mine, and there are too many people, too many clashing personalities, too many curious and eager eyes.

Shuddering, I slip my backpack off my shoulder, hugging it to my chest. Ren, almost taller than everyone in the living room, catches my eyes above everyone's head. "Get moving!" he orders, clearing out the space.

Some of our helpers linger, waiting to see how I'll react. Rory ignores me, but I can tell it's on purpose, giving me space. Bethany pats my shoulder and flashes me a knowing smile– after how we left things, where we beat each other up at the very playground where we met. My siblings try to hide how hurt they are that I've clammed up, but I know they understand.

Willow stalks off, leading the charge upstairs as bed frames, mattresses, and rolled up rugs flow by as I stand stunned in the middle of the living room, with Ren bringing up the rear. My brother flashes me a huge grin, winking on his way by, leaving me and Essie alone in our new home.

"Hey," I repeat, just as lamely as before. "One helluva turnout."

"I'm an expert now," Essie mutters sheepishly, blushing. "Let's see... how many houses have we moved recently? My parents. Dave and Mary's. Your house and Clover's. Now this one." Hand resting on her budding belly, my baby sleeping peacefully inside its momma, "I took over the organizational responsibilities since I can't lift anything. Willow still manages to micromanage me."

"Your job is probably harder," I admit, able to understand how Essie feels worthless and helpless right now, having to ask everyone to help. "I'm shocked so many people want to help us."

"I made sure the Pods were loaded with what gets unpacked first being loaded last– made it easier." Stepping forward, getting out of the way as the wave descends the staircase to flow back out the front door without lingering for my attention, Essie uses her body to push me toward the corner of the living room.

"You're more important than you believe," Essie whispers to me, not touching me but using her presence as a comfort.

Gazing out the front bay window, I notice the employees of Rush, half of Fairport's police force and their mates, my siblings, and a handful of Dave's men unloading five pickup trucks and a van. When I asked where my shit was earlier, Willow told me we had two pods stored in Prynne Renovation's parking lot across town.

Still staring, they troop back into the house, the empty trucks left lining the street in front of the house. "Too much. Too soon." Words barely a breath, my skin feels so tight, I fear it will burst from the emotions it can't contain.

"Here." Essie unzips the backpack I'm clutching to my chest, and I don't freak out by lashing out at her for touching something I hold sacred. "This may help."

Essie is squeezing my toys, hand hidden in my bag, then she comes out with the peach. "How did you know?" I murmur in awe as I slip my pack back on my shoulder, then palm my favorite of the stress balls.

Smiling serenely, "I could tell by feel which one you use the most." We both ignore the mass of bodies stomping across Willow's beautiful hardwood floor. "I've got to go with them," she warns, lightly pressing her shoulder to the side of my arm. "There's two more trips, and I have to make sure the right stuff is loaded in a specific order."

"Here," flows in an accented tone that draws a shudder down my spine, followed by a thump. "Something to sit on while we load the trucks." Colin and Rory both pat the sofa cushions after making sure it's not in the unloading path.

"Thanks," I murmur, embarrassed from everyone taking care of what I should be doing myself, but more thankful than anything. "It feels like forever."

Without a thought, I tug Colin into a hug. The guy isn't much bigger than me, so he's not intimidating at all. Plus, I've seen him nonstop since he came to Fairport more than a decade ago.

"I miss working with you," I murmur as I pull away from a stunned Colin, holding him at arm's length to get a good look at him. It's a relief to see the man hasn't changed, not even a single hair on his head.

"You don't have to miss that for long." Grinning, eyes wide with surprise at the affection I gave him, "You're due at the Batcave at oh-six-hundred-hours tomorrow."

"Really?" Now it's my turn to be shocked. "Thank God, I don't think being idle will be good for me."

"Your dad and I took care of your uniform, belt, and miscellaneous shit. But you won't be getting your gun back until after your probationary period."

"How long's that?" Yet again, I'm surprised, because I didn't think I'd ever get my service weapon back. Probation lasted three months before– the old Devon should've never been given a deadly weapon. Me, now, the fact that I'm worried about it, fearful on whether or not I'm ready, *if* I'll ever be ready, means I'm on the right path.

"One year." Colin winks, still looking surprised by my reaction. Old Devon would've thrown a tantrum, while I'm just thankful I'll carry eventually after the long list of felonies I committed. "See ya in about an hour," he says pointedly, like he's giving me a timeframe for something.

Turning, I notice Essie with her head pressed closely to Beth's and Rory's, discussing something. All three look up, guilty expressions written across their faces.

Colin walks out of the house, trailing ironic laughter, passing Willow as she heads back in. The idiots give each other high-fives– they became friendly at family game nights and barbeques after they discovered their undying love of competition.

Willow ignores us, walking through the living room to enter the kitchen. Beth gives me a wave, then disappears outside. Rory gives me a loaded look, one I can't decipher. I realize that just because I feel like a different person, that doesn't mean everyone doesn't see me as who I used to be. Even high out of my mind, I'd never hurt Beth on purpose. Rory no doubt wants to murder me after I put my hands on Beth– I was only defending myself as my ex-best-friend turned into a shrieking banshee, but he doesn't know that.

Essie's fingers curl around mine, squeezing in a comforting rhythm, then slip away. "Talk to Willow before we get back with the next load." It's not an order but a suggestion, one I understand.

Nodding in agreement, I walk away, headed toward the kitchen… it takes half an hour to sign all the paperwork and set up a payment schedule with Aunt Ginny. I promise to call all the utilities and switch them over by tomorrow evening. Being Sunday morning, this gives me a chance to spread all this stuff out over the next few days, instead of being bombarded with it.

Ren already gave Aunt Ginny authorization to use direct deposit for our payments. Which reminds me, now that I'm not losing my mind, I better get a bank account of my own and give the info to payroll at work.

Kieren may be babysitting me here at home, but I can handle my own financial obligations now. It was one of the things Delany stressed during our last session. I'd let Essie handle it, but we all know she's not the best at handling her own finances. I need to learn how to do this shit myself.

By the time Aunt Ginny and Opal leave, Dave and his crew are finished up with a few minor issues on the house. They leave Willow and Ozzy with me. Silent and contemplative, Ozzy looks uncomfortable being left without anything to do, so I don't protest when he starts opening boxes in the kitchen, putting dishes away.

"Who's the cook?" Ozzy asks, hand brushing his mop of curls away from his forehead. "I don't want to mess this up if it's… someone who's anal," he trails off, voice getting quieter and quieter, fearing it's me who will man the kitchen. But then I realize he lives with Clover, and the kitchen is most certainly her domain.

"Group effort," Willow mutters with a shrug and she and I share a look. We don't have a clue who will be cooking. Ren's food is passable if you want spaghetti every single night. Essie missed out on the cooking lessons because Violet would get violent when she showed up, so hopefully she's not cooking. Willow and I are okay, but we don't enjoy it.

"Just put it where it makes sense to you– we'll keep Weston on the next trip, and he and you can tackle it together." My baby brother is the organizer and cleaner in the family.

Fingers clenched, I have to stop myself from messing up Ozzy's hair even worse, in a gesture I reserve for my brothers. In a way, after less than twenty-four hours home, Ozzy does feel like he's one of us.

"Thanks for the help– really."

"No problem," Ozzy mutters in his soft-spoken way as he begins scouting out where best to put what in the kitchen. It takes me only a few seconds to get a feel for the kid– he wants to feel useful, make himself useful so we'll keep him, and he has too much pride to ask for help. No wonder Dad is nuts about the guy– Oliver Zephyr is a baby version of Malcolm Mason.

With less than twenty minutes until the horde returns, I decide I better rip the bandage off. "Willow, can I talk to you for a minute?" I realize Ozzy can probably hear us from the kitchen, but something tells me that kid's brain is a vault.

"What's up?" Willow bounces on the sofa, and the movements draw my attention to the pattern.

"Holy shit!" Scrubbing at my face with one hand, while the other squeezes my stress ball, I stare in wonder down at *the* sofa. "There's something about you and me and sofas."

"Oh," Willow mumbles, expression changing from open to locked tight. "Clover bought a new sectional for the Pink Taco Hut. Malcolm's and Clover's old couches are up in the attic for the kids to use– video games, studying, just vegging out. Essie took her parents' sofa for Primp, so I called dibs on Mom and Dad's for this place."

Willow's rambling, trying desperately to ignore what I said and why I said it. There's a reason Rory and Colin dropped this sofa in here, when it should have been delivered last. No doubt Beth and Essie thought it was time I had it out with Willow.

After drawing in a deep breath, I stow my foam peach in my backpack, then drop the bag on the floor next to my feet. While Willow tries to pretend she and I never dated, I take a seat next to her.

"We shared our first kiss on this sofa." I chuckle underneath my breath, realizing no matter where I moved, even if I didn't keep a single item from my old life, it would still haunt me because it's written on the canvas of who I am today.

"Yeah," Willow growls bitterly. "Because Essie told us to kiss."

"Christ!" Sighing, slumping forward to rest my elbows on my knees, I scrub my hands over my face. "About now is where I'd get up, run the fuck down the street, and I'd locate a dealer or user in under a minute flat. I'd jack them with threats of hauling their asses in. In less than five minutes, I'd be high, forgetting my pain. But the responsibilities wouldn't go away. The drug would make it worse... but it would feel *so damn good* while it lasted."

Voice slurred with a seductive cadence that rivals the intoxication of lust, breathing deeply, evenly, my mind reels as the cravings ripple over my flesh, causing a cold sweat to bead on my brow and in a long line down my spine.

Fight it, Devon.

You're better than this, Devon Callum Mason.

Fight it!

"I'm an asshole," flows from between my parted fingers.

"That's never been up for debate," Willow deadpans, causing me to bark a sharp laugh. The kid in the kitchen is trying hard not to eavesdrop, but the muted chuckling is undeniable.

"We spent four months nonstop with one another." Turning to the side to face Willow, I tuck my calf under my other thigh. "The only lie was my sobriety. I couldn't let you in, knowing I'd suck you down with me– it was my mental illness, and I wasn't willing to share that with anyone."

Staring at me with giant brown eyes glistening with tears, Willow manages to gut me with silence and the absence of violence. Someone other than me has been growing up.

"I know what someone like me can do to the people around them when they aren't properly medicated. Trust me, I do." Mind spinning memories of my mother like a kaleidoscope of misery and pain, it manifests into a physical ache deep inside my chest.

"I couldn't abuse you like that, so I lied– lying became as easy as breathing. But, no matter how off kilter I was, I never lied about how I felt about another human being. I'm an asshole– a dick. But I'm not evil."

"I know how you felt about me," Willow whispers, proving herself a liar too.

"You're hanging onto a twenty-minute conversation instead of seeing the truth of a four-month, nonstop friendship. What we shared wasn't a lie." I tug Willow into my arms, knowing she'll come freely. "I was being an asshole to push you away."

"You meant every word you said." Willow is seething in my arms, but she's not pulling away.

Holding this private conversation with Ozzy in listening range, I realize he can't hear Willow or me as we're hugging and furiously whispering in the other's ear.

"I did– I didn't lie, but I was an asshole about it." I admit without a shred of shame. "What I said about Essie, all of that was the truth. All. Of. It." Wounded, Willow struggles to get away, but I'd gained physical strength as I'd gained emotional strength in Arizona.

"But I did lie about how I felt about you," I admit to soothe the monster trying to erupt out of Willow. "I couldn't come to terms with being in love with two very different women, for two very different reasons. Loving and wanting Essie didn't erase what I felt about you."

"You bastard!" Willow yanks out of my arms, then throttles me in the chest with her balled up fists. Face etched with immense pain, it guts me to see the results of what I did. "You fed me the details!"

"And I gave Ren the details between you and me," I mutter without shame. Even after sixty days of intense therapy, nothing will get me to see it differently than I do. "Not knowing what happened between Essie and Ren had me trying to suffocate Ren in his sleep. I wasn't about to do that to you or Ren, so I gave you the truth. Why lie?"

"Motherfucker, you're still nuts," Willow growls into my face, but then she slumps back into my arms. "I still miss you– miss your hugs. I must be fucking crazy too."

"I give good hugs." Chuckling, I sound so dang arrogant that I can't believe my own ears. "I lied," I whisper into Willow's ear, not wanting Ozzy to hear this. "I lied to you, and it's hurting whatever you and Ren have going on."

"Lied about what?" Willow breathes back even more quietly.

"I don't know– it's just a feeling I get, like you and Ren are holding yourselves back. I talked to my therapist a lot about what happened between you and me. Ms. Amelia said I had to make it right with you."

"I just want you to admit you cheated on me," Willow mutters, tears of frustration thick in her voice. "I know we were going to break up, but the timing made it worse. If you'd just waited a day or two, I would've been hurt, but not homicidal."

There isn't a single cell in my body that sees what Essie and I did as cheating, but I can understand why Willow would see it that way.

"We wronged you," is the truth as I see it, because I won't admit something I don't feel I did. My regimen dictates that I remain strong in my ethics, and I refuse to say Essie and I cheated on Willow when I don't believe we did.

Willow and I were friends who kissed, and a few hours later we had sex. The next morning, after I heard Willow speak to Auggie, I knew it was over before it began. It wasn't going to work– never would –no matter if we loved each other or not, and Willow knew it too.

I don't hear Willow apologizing for how she used me to forget Auggie, to pretend she didn't want Ren anymore. I also don't hear her apologizing for what she said to Auggie while I laid in bed next to her, naked and smelling like sex, as she discussed my prowess. But I'm going to be the bigger person, because I don't need an apology. I know why Willow did what she did, said what she said, and I will never blame her for feeling as she does.

Someday I hope Willow will have the ability to see if from a view other than her own.

We weren't married, engaged, or exclusive, and I refuse to wear a mark of shame for life because Willow's feelings got bent out of shape because she didn't get to break up with me first. What I said when I broke up with her was wrong, so very wrong.

It was all a lie.

"When I said I never wanted you, I lied." I voice something that took me a long time to admit to my therapist. "Growing up a Mason, I believed in a husband and wife, and no one else. So it was hard for me to wrap my mind around loving you *and* Essie, so I was mean to you to push you away. Don't think for a second I wasn't saying worse to your cousin– not comparing, just admitting I was being a dick all the way around."

"I felt so…" Willow rasps against my throat, fingers twisting in the back of my t-shirt, as we hold each other tightly on the very sofa we shared our first kiss. "Broken," she breathes so softly I barely make out the word, but what she says next sounds louder than a gunshot, even if it's the quietest word of all. "Sexually."

"Willow," is a sharp bark as I tug her away, pressing my fingertips into her chin so she can't look away. "I said what I said to hurt you– it was all bullshit."

"No, it wasn't." Willow tries to break my hold by turning her head, but I refuse to relinquish my grip. "The things you said about Essie's tits… her pussy," she whispers like a filthy secret that makes her stomach curdle. "Ren thinks just like you do. You act like it's me and you versus Ren and Essie, but you know damn well you and your brother like the same shit… same as me and Essie."

Laughing, which obviously insults Willow more, I can't stop the bitter amusement from flowing out of my throat. "It'll take decades of therapy for me to work through what you just said, but here's the gist. We love you *and* Essie, in completely different ways– want you in completely different ways, and one doesn't cancel out the other, just like it doesn't for you or Essie when it comes to both me and Ren."

"Bullshit!" Willow spits into my face.

Anger boils in my blood, potent and intoxicating for the first time in months. I welcome it home, because it's a living, breathing part of what makes me who I am. I'm not medicated to the point where I'm numb, and I embrace the fire.

Grabbing Willow's hand, I press her palm to my crotch. The thin sweats hide nothing. "Anger always gets me hot," I whisper one of my deepest secrets. "Little girl, you have no idea what makes me tick," I warn. "But the truth is in my actions. I've never touched a woman other than you and Essie. I've never wanted another woman but you and Essie. So stop using me as a crutch when it comes to you and Ren. Stop this bullshit about hating Essie because the genetic lottery gave her big tits and you the perfect ass. Because the vapidness pisses me off– I lost the lottery where it counted."

Looking at me in horror, Willow snatches her hand from my bulge, realizing she was palpating my cock as I viscously spoke into her face. Important lessons come in many forms.

"I inherited a mental disorder, so deal with having a flat chest." Lashing out, I grab Willow's tit, only to be surprised that there's flesh giving beneath my fingertips. Laughing a choking sound, my hand lands in my lap, blazing hot as if burned.

"We have to let all this shit go, Willow– we do." Defiant, she glares at me. "It happened, and nothing can change it, whether it should've happened or not. We have to live together, and I can't survive bullshit stress. I'm sorry I hurt you by lying about what I felt for you, but I can't change it."

"You didn't want me." Flows so softly, I wouldn't have heard Willow speak had it not been for me reading her lips.

"Willow," I mutter pointedly, looking at her in complete and total exasperation. "From the age of fourteen until I was almost twenty-one, I was completely impotent unless I had wet nightmares. If anything, your ego should be gigantic for getting my dick hard, and keeping it hard enough to get me to come."

Blushing, Willow looks away from me, with Ozzy's snicker in the background not helping matters. No doubt the boy has heard my sordid history echoing between the walls of the Pink Taco Hut.

"Who are you going to believe? The four months of friendship? The twenty minutes with a drug addict tweeking, saying shit to push you away by having to hurt you on purpose? Or the sober and medicated person sitting here right in front of you?"

When Willow doesn't say anything, I realize she's going to believe whatever will feed into her insecurities. I know exactly how that goes, seeing as it took a team of trained professionals to get me to knock it the hell off.

"I'm not going to allow you to use me for whatever is keeping you and Ren apart," I warn. "I'm not going to allow you to use Essie, or what Essie and I did, or how Essie and I are today. Ren's not going to cheat on you, but he will be affectionate with Essie– I'm not jealous, and you shouldn't be either." Only a hypocrite would after she hugged me, loving every squeeze of it, then had no issue feeling me up when I pressed her hand on my bulge.

Glaring at me, Willow's mouth opens and closes, repeating for a good minute.

Smirking, I mutter, "Grow up," at the very second sound begins to erupt from her lips. "No one's cheating on anyone. We're all how we should've been from the beginning. There's no sin in loving someone, but there is if you're arrogant enough to think only *you* are the one allowed to love."

"Stop lecturing me," Willow growls as she lunges off the sofa. "You're no Mr. Kline."

"Thank fuck for that," with amused laughter releasing on its heels. "I'm your *friend*," I stress. "I love you– every part of you.

I want to you to be happy. But even after my mental timeout, I'm not altruistic enough to lie to your face to fix your butthurt feelings. If you know me so well, you'd believe me."

"I know you're an asshole." Willow reaches forward to grip my shaggy hair. Heartbeat accelerating, I have to push down the need to panic. "You're forgiven," is a whispered kiss across my forehead just as multiple doors shutting out on the street bang in unison.

"Thank God," Ozzy mutters as he slinks by us to slip out the front door. "I thought you guys got lost!" comes echoing back in the open door. Ever helpful, he begins unloading a truck.

"We don't have the excuse of rolling up carpet this time," I mutter wryly at Willow as she looks around lost, having no idea what to do or think. "Let's go help– get this stage over as quickly as possible."

"Okay," Willow whispers, still seeming stunned. Trying my damnedest to right our friendship, I tug her ponytail, then draw her underneath my arm. We walk out to the trucks together, with my arm slung over her shoulder and hers wrapped around my waist.

CHAPTER FIFTY-FIVE

Essie Prynne

"Is everyone else exhausted, or is it just me?" Back aching something fierce, I'm leaning on the countertop, eating a piece of pizza, instead of camping out at my parents' old dinette set in the corner of the kitchen. Legs flexing, I keep arching my back for some relief.

"You weren't supposed to lift anything." Ren's glare is piercing, but it bounces right off me.

Taking a huge bite of veggie pizza, I ignore the overprotective idiot and speak to Devon and Willow instead. "It was the repetitive movement of bending down to get shit out of a box, place it, only to have to bend back down again… in every room in this house. My thighs are burning something fierce from the decade's worth of squats I just did."

"Coulda had to lift shit like the rest of us." Willow's stuffing her face with Stromboli, voice gruff, but I know her moods better than anyone. She's happier than a pig in shit, but she's trying to hide it.

Ren kicks Willow underneath the table for being a bitch, and the glower is real on her face this time.

"Willow's right," I add to mitigate the oncoming disaster. There is no way in hell I'm going to let Ren and Willow use me as a reason to fight. "You guys must be paining too. Just commenting because I can only gauge how I'm feeling… wonder how much a hot tub costs."

"Pregnant women can't sit in hot tubs," Ren reminds me, face pinched like he thinks I'm an idiot.

"*I know*," I stress, not liking that asshole tone Ren keeps taking with me. For some reason, he honestly believes I'm going to hurt *my* unborn baby. "We're all exhausted, in pain, and starving. Let's just try to fill our bellies and relax, instead of fighting. We all have to get up early in the morning to go to work."

"Ms. Amelia would have a field day with you sick fucks." Devon's slowly working his way through a salad with grilled chicken. The rest of us ordered takeout, even bought Dev a veggie lovers, but Seth delivered a healthy, belly-friendly meal from Clover. The kid only came bearing one small salad– Clover hinting that the rest of us were on our own.

"If cohabitating is going to work, we have to have some ground rules." A notebook materializes from Devon's waistband. With a sharp rip, a piece of paper is slapped on the table, then the book returns to its hiding place.

"We'll post the rules on the fridge." Pushing his salad to the side, Devon leans over and begins writing. Willow, Ren, and I share glances for the next five minutes, all of us continuing to hog our food. Ren and Willow are sharing the Stromboli, with me having an entire veggie pizza to myself since Devon isn't eating any. By the way Ren's eyeing my pizza box, there won't be any leftovers for breakfast.

"There!" Devon announces, hand jutting backward to thrust the paper on the counter near my arm. Before I can even slide the paper over, his fork is spearing into the salad.

"If anyone wants me to add anything, we'll discuss it. What I wrote is nonnegotiable. The usual roommate shit goes without saying: Utilities are split four-ways and we'll make a grocery fund. There's no rent, because it's Essie's and my house. I'll pay it because I consider it a mortgage payment to Aunt Ginny– Ren, as soon as I get my new bank account, I want every penny you have of mine put in it, with the exception of what Willow used for home repairs. Make a mess, clean it up. If you're home earlier than everyone else, then you make dinner. If you cook, you don't clean it up, unless you're a hog. Stay out of other people's private spaces, don't snoop, and what happens in the Shithole, stays in the Shithole."

Holding my breath to stop the laughter from bubbling up, I have to bite my lip to keep from smirking. Ren had delusions when it came to Devon. Yes, Devon is a changed man, but his core personality is the same. I have no idea why Ren thought Dev would suddenly turn into a pushover who wouldn't mind being managed.

A drugged-out bossy bastard will be even bossier when he's in his right mind. A sober, bossier bastard.

Willow and Ren have started butting heads because they're posturing to see who's in charge. I noticed it last month when Ren and Willow blew up at each other in the Spook House, and Auggie had to intervene.

It's the same reason Willow and Auggie would've never worked. Willow was susceptible only because she was so young. As she's gotten older, she's gotten stronger. If anyone could recognize that Willow wasn't some malleable, weak creature, it was me.

With Devon and me, I've always known since we were five years old that Devon was in charge. If not Devon, Bethany was– they butted heads often because of this, with Beth bowing out because it wasn't worth the fight. With Willow, that fell apart, because as the eldest, it was me who had to take the lead, but I didn't have the temperament for it.

Devon and I are equals, in the way we balance each other, our strengths the other's weaknesses.

I'm staying out of the fight for succession between Devon, Kieren, and Willow, knowing that's a fight Devon will always win. Ren and Willow need to find their own sense of balance, and leave the rest of us out of it.

With a deep breath, I lift Devon's rules, instinctively knowing not a single one applies to me. I may not know what tonight and tomorrow will bring, but I do know how Devon operates.

#1: *No emotional baiting/extortion. If you don't know what this means, Willow's comment about Essie not having to carry boxes and furniture was baiting for a fight. Essie is allowed to feel pain, even if she didn't put in as much physical labor as someone else. It's not whining– it's expressing herself. She's growing a baby 24/7. None of us are doing that, so activity affects her differently. It's not lazy. I don't expect Willow to lift as much as Ren– that's not what carrying your own weight means. We're not having a competition, unless it's competing to see who the biggest asshole is.*

#2: *No lashing out at someone because you don't understand why you're feeling as you do. It's your problem, not ours. Don't make it my problem. Example: lashing out over lifting/not lifting. Willow & Kieren, I'm talking to you.*

#3: *If someone needs space, give it. Back off. Just because you have something to say, doesn't give you the right to force us* *to listen to it. If we want to hear it, we'll give you the floor. Your emotions matter, but not at the expense of our own.*

#4: *Today is the beginning, everything in the past stays there. No mentioning anything prior to this morning as ammunition in an argument. Some injustice from the past doesn't excuse you from being an asshole today.*

#5: *No controlling, manipulative, enabling, abusive behavior. Kieren, you don't get a vote on what Essie does or doesn't do with her body. It's insulting to her for you to keep telling her what not to do, as if she doesn't already know. It also rubs Willow the wrong way, which is part of the reason you're doing it. Caring for someone is not the same as controlling them. Insulting. Willow, this goes for you too.*

#6: *No alcoholic beverages. No addictive prescription drugs. No mouthwashes or liquid cold medicines. No street drugs. If you are prescribed a medication that is on the addictive substance list, you have to lock it in your vehicle, or buy a safe to store it in your bedroom. I'm not the morality police– I don't care what you do on your own time, just not in this house where I have access to it. Years from now, I may be strong enough, but that's not today. This isn't about the fear of falling off the wagon. Mood stabilizers mixed with drugs or alcohol is fatal. Not physically, mentally. Plummeting me into suicidal tendencies.*

#7: *We are housemates. Two couples. All relatives. There is no hierarchy. If it comes to a major change in the house, only Essie and I get a vote, and only we'll pay for it. All major purchases, unless in your personal areas, will be discussed prior to purchasing. In other words: don't buy a huge motherfucking television, then ask the rest of us for a cut, just because it's going into the living room, because I'll make you stow it in your bedroom, Ren!*

#8: *I don't need babysitting. That is on the no-no list from my team of doctors, which will be provided to you. The contact list for my team will be attached to the fridge, along with my medication schedule. I don't need monitoring, but if you notice I missed my schedule or an appointment, just remind me.*

#9: *When the baby is born, it will only have one mother and one father. Essie & me. You will be Uncle Kieren and Aunt Willow. If you try to parent our kid, see #10.*

#10: *if you don't like these rules, or if you break them, then you're behaving like a child. I'm not your dad– I'm your brother. Children live with their parents. Pack your shit, walk down the*

*street half a block, and then enter the Pink Taco Hut. Mommy &
Daddy will be happy to have you back.*

*I have to monitor every breath I take, I don't have the energy
to referee whatever insanity you keep engaging in. It's
exhausting to figure out if what I'm feeling is natural, or is it my
medication not working properly. Don't make life harder than it
should be as you nitpick, start fights, and act like assholes.*

Be happy!

As soon as I'm finished reading, I quickly hand it back to
Devon. It's almost as if he anticipated how long it would take me
to read it. We share a brief look, then I shove my pizza slice into
my mouth to cover my reaction.

It's an uncomfortable few minutes as Ren and Willow hover
over the list, their food forgotten. Devon tucks into his salad,
finishing it off, with my piece of pizza hitting my belly as if it
was made out of lead.

Queasy, I decide it's time I get acquainted with my own
kitchen, finding it beyond surreal as I shove the pizza box into
the empty refrigerator.

I have a house to call my own.

A house!

Ozzy and Weston were sweet, placing homey things in each
room, something representing each of us. The Mason dishes are
in our cupboards, the same ones John and Penelope used– maybe
even John's dad too. Welch's jelly jar glasses are lined up on the
shelves bordering the cupboards near the kitchen sink window–
Willow loves collecting eclectic things from Revamped, and
these glasses have cartoon characters on them.

I recognize my mom's cookie jar– Mom, Aunt Mary, and
Clover found a ceramic canister set shaped like ginormous
cupcakes at a flea market. They each wanted it, so instead of
fighting over it, they split the set up. Mom got the cookie jar, with
the flour and sugar going to Clover, and the tea and coffee going
to Aunt Mary. The entire set, except for the cookie jar, now sits
on Clover's counter at the Pink Taco Hut.

Tomorrow, on my lunch hour, I'll have to beg Clover to take
me to the grocery store, because I have no idea what you stock a
kitchen with– we have no food except for the takeout, a two-liter
of Coke, and a case of water.

I could live off grilled cheese, but we don't have the three
essential ingredients: cheese, bread, and butter. Add a jar of sweet

and spicy pickles, and I'll be a happy girl. I'm easy to please. By the looks of Devon, he'll be good with a bag of salad, a jar of dressing, and some type of protein. I can easily handle that, but it's the food addicts I'm worried about.

As payment for her help, I'm going to give Clover the cupcake-shaped cookie jar she's always coveted. It's the memory that matters, and Clover will make better use of it than I ever will.

We Prynnes believe in a bartering system, without money exchanging hands.

"Okay," Ren's voice flows low, with Willow looking sheepish next to him. I'd expected rage out of at least one of them, but they both look properly spanked. "I think, maybe Willow and I ought to be alone, give you and Essie some time alone. It's been a wild twenty-four hours."

"Yeah." Willow nods her head emphatically, ponytail bopping up and down. "Let's go for a walk– been a while since we were at the old bridge. Miss walking there with Seth."

Looking at the remains of the Stromboli with great longing, Ren swallows thickly. "Yeah, maybe stop for some ice cream first. A nice, big cone and a walk sounds great after a hard day like today."

Outrageously polite, Ren and Willow pick up after themselves, even rinsing out their Coke glasses. Willow locates the stash of magnets, then secures Devon's rules of conduct on the refrigerator as her nonverbal acceptance.

"So… yeah, we'll be back later." Ren's hand slips into Willow's, with neither one of them looking at us. "Night."

Chuckling to myself, I reach over Devon's shoulder to snag Clover's Pyrex dish. I'm still laughing as I wash it, silently reminding myself to give it back to her tomorrow.

Devon releases an audible gust of breath, body slumping in relief. "I can finally breathe– their moods were suffocating. I could literally feel it battering my psyche. They weren't like this before I left."

"They're trying to find their way, by simultaneously becoming the only obstacles in their own paths." At a complete and total loss of what to do next, I just stare around the kitchen.

Turning around in his chair to face me, Devon seems more relaxed now that it's just us. "Delaney warned me, now that I'm not drugged out of my mind, I'll be more sensitive to people's moods."

"I can see that– I may look like the bubbly type, happy to joke around and chat. But at family dinners, sometimes I could feel things riding the air. Willow has a lot of Sam's mom in her, and Peggy and Clover have never gotten along."

"When Willow and Ren started in on you, then ended up going for each other, it literally made my skin crawl." Dev raises from his seat, washing out his glass as an excuse to move around. "I can deal with it in small doses, but not if it's going to always be like that. Delaney said some people have a toxic personality– I used to be one, and could end up falling back into those same patterns. They just bring chaos into every room they walk in... I can't–"

"I get it." Shrugging, I think over the impact this is having on Devon, which is exactly why Malcolm sold their old house, and why Ren bought this one so Devon didn't have to be cloistered with almost a dozen people.

"I'm not the personality police." Devon returns to his seat, but his fingertips never stop moving against his thigh. "But I don't understand people who are so goddamn loud and obnoxious. Yelling is their form of chatting. I don't get it, and I can't be around it anymore."

Leaning with my back to the countertop, I fold my arms underneath my breasts. "Insecurity breeds clingy attention-seekers, that's why. In Willow's case, she's just frustrated because no one is listening to her– she's not being heard."

Devon's eyes snap up to meet mine. "I spoke with her, and I understand. I apologized and admitted to lying and hurting her on purpose. I do hear her, but she's past that point. I'm not going to sit around listening to it a billion times until she gets the reaction she's seeking. There is a difference."

"You don't give Willow enough credit." Devon appears shocked that I'm defending Willow. "But little digs are uncalled for– I think she stops herself most of the time, but some do slip out."

"If she's thinking of any, then the problem still exists." Devon stands, looks around lost, and then retakes his seat. "There was a reason the only interaction we had with other patients was during group therapy. They didn't want us shouldering someone else's burden, being infected with their bitterness– helping them at the detriment of our own sanity. I don't know if I can handle living with them. I can't do anything other than apologize– I meant it. It's in the past, and I can't change it. I'm trying to be healthy, and I still have some major hurdles in the way of my happiness. I can't bleed enough to satisfy Willow."

"It's not about you." I shrug it off.

"Maybe I don't want to sit around and watch it happen to *you*." Devon stands again, acts like he's going to reach out and touch me, then steps away.

"It's getting better, but Ren's keeping it alive by the stupid shit he does and says, then blames it on Willow. They've been together for months, living together for the past month. I've been around them nonstop since I moved into the Spook House. It is getting better, trust me."

"If it gets worse, I'll kick 'em out and not lose a second of sleep over it." Devon warns, and I don't doubt him for a second. "I appreciate that they're here to help me, but that type of bullshit will only make it worse. I won't walk on eggshells, and I don't want people walking around on them because of me."

"For me, actions speak louder than words." Now is my opening to speak my piece. Devon's right about the loud ones forcing us to listen, while I stand back in silence. "There's a lot of shit between us– all of us. But I'm not a grudge-holder. The slate is clean, and what happens from today forward matters. I understand Willow and Ren, and I don't blame you. I just want to move on with my life and live."

"No more talking about them," Devon decrees, expecting to be minded. "It's only eight. Even after this day from hell, I don't think I could go to sleep early. Are you tired?"

"Tired? Yes." The bedroom situation has been nagging me all damned day, and I don't have the balls to bring it up. So I change the subject. "Able to sleep? No. What's up with your hair?" My hand reaches out to grab a thick hank before I think the better of it. After watching Devon shrink back from touch all day, I feel guilty for doing it to him too. "Sorry."

"You can touch me." Devon's lips quirk up slightly at the corners, and I notice he didn't flinch or shudder beneath my touch. "I didn't want to cheat on my stylist, is what happened to my hair."

Sharing a laugh, I feel the weight of the world fall from my shoulders at the delicious, carefree laughter flowing from between Devon's lips– never have I heard him sound this way.

"Do you want me to cut your hair right now?"

"You're tired, and your back hurts," Devon reminds me.

"And I'll still be tired when I wake up, and my back will still hurt while I cut other people's hair tomorrow. Fact of life."

"Essie–"

"Colin brought your freshly-pressed uniform. Let's give you a haircut too. Tomorrow's your first day back to work. Be right back!"

It only takes me a few minutes to fetch my kit from the master bathroom. I'd unpacked the bedroom and bathroom while Devon unpacked his stuff. We don't have a lot, but it feels homey– a comfort to have familiar objects.

In the time I'm gone, Devon has relocated his chair near the kitchen sink and gotten a pitcher down from the cupboard. "Is this where you want me?"

"Yeah– perfect." Swallowing down the emotions threatening to spill out my eyes, I experience a déjà vu moment. I'm thrust back into the past, to the day Devon came to Salon for a haircut, with Isis and her gang watching.

Washing Devon's hair in the kitchen sink is a challenge, but a welcome and familiar one. Once he's seated with a cape covering his body, I get to work. The snick of the scissors lulls me into an uncomfortable conversation.

"What's the sleeping situation?" Devon's eyebrows hitch high with confusion. "We've never shared a bed before, and I understand if you need Ren, or if you want to sleep alone. I mean… it would be presumptuous of me to assume we would just fall into being a couple."

"And where would you sleep?" Dev's words are tight–controlled.

"I'm not sharing with Willow, if that's what you're suggesting. I didn't sleep last night after she invaded Isis's bedroom. I worked on the details, making lists of what needed to be done. Like calling all the utilities tomorrow, groceries, changing our addresses. Then I organized Beth and Rory's reception. That kind of thing."

"Where would you sleep?" Voice not as controlled, anger is seeping in.

"My health and sanity aren't in question, Devon. I'm fine– have been fine." Mind on autopilot, I cut Devon's hair by memory of the last time. "I've spent the last four months of my life worrying about being homeless, then being shipped back and forth between homes. I spent a good month sleeping on the sofa sitting in our living room right now."

Devon doesn't speak, but he isn't silent. The sound he releases is damn near feral, and I fear he'll snap. We've all been waiting on the emotional explosion.

"After Mom and Dad moved, it was a low point for me, and I'm not going to go into the why. It's no big deal if I have to sleep on the sofa. Aunt Mary tried to get me to stay in Willow's old room, but I couldn't. When Ozzy showed up a few days later, I forced him to sleep in there instead of taking my sofa. Uncle Dave was angry, but he understood. Then when I moved to the Spook House, I invaded Isis's bedroom– tainting it for her, so I never made myself at home. Now I'm here, and I'm okay with the sofa."

"I wish I had recorded what you just said," Devon mutters in a tight voice. "Delany used that trick on me. In my head, I thought I sounded rational, but when played back, I realized I was anything but."

"I don't... what are you getting at?" Squinting down at Devon, I try to wrap my mind around what he's saying. Beth and Devon are going to get along better than ever, with this psychobabble he keeps spewing.

"You always put up with anything I did to you, and I used to think it was because you loved me. Now I wonder if it's because you don't think you deserve anything better."

"Devon!" Snarling, I step away, fearful I'll clip him with the scissors. "That's not it at all. I'm being accommodating. I have no money, with every dime going into Primp. I'm living here because you're gracious enough to take care of me because of the baby. I've moved from living off my parents, my aunt and uncle, to Robin and Auggie– now you. The last thing I'm going to do is make waves, because there is nothing keeping me off the streets except for you putting up with me."

Sucking in a deep breath, Devon looks like I just sucker-punched him. Eyes slipping shut, his chest rises and falls in a rhythmic pattern. Fingertips clench and release on his thighs. I take a step back when the midnight blue of Devon's eyes laser a hole in my soul.

"For my sanity's sake, I'm going to pretend you didn't say any of that," Devon warns. "As for the sleeping arrangements, I stayed with Ren last night because I was in a house that held bad memories. With nothing of mine to anchor me, I used my brother.

Our bedroom holds both yours and my stuff, and you're going to sleep in it. Next to me. Not because you owe me anything, but because it's about fucking time. Okay?"

"Okay," I stammer, coming closer to finish cutting Devon's hair.

"This house is ours, no matter how we came to own it. My money is ours– use it to make the house ours. You're not living off me, taking from me– we're partners."

"Partners, okay."

"Don't let Ren or Willow bully you into anything, because I will step in, and no one wants to see that. Okay?"

"Okay," I repeat, more firmly this time.

"May I touch you?"

"Of course," flows without hesitation. "Why do you ask?"

"It's best to be sure," Devon mutters wryly. "Because you'd let me even if you wanted to say no."

Sputtering, I start to protest, but Devon flashes me a look that stops me in my tracks.

"I'm not going to force you to stand up for yourself, because it's who you are. But, maybe you better a bit, because I'm barely hanging on by a thread, and the next asshole who is mean to you may get the blast."

"I can fight my own battles," I promise.

"Good," is said with finality.

So engrossed in our conversation, I didn't realize Devon was griping my hips. Now that the scissors are resting on the counter, and I'm slowly combing his hair, Devon gets braver.

"Do you want a boy or a girl?" Devon asks, with a softness in his voice I've never heard before. "It doesn't matter to me. Do you want to name the baby after a relative, or give it its own name?"

"God, you know a way to a woman's heart," I tease, laughing. Tugged forward a bit, I look down in awe as Devon cradles my belly in his palms, as if he's holding our child. "I'm old-fashioned, so after a relative. But John and Penelope are off the table."

"Yeah?" Dev looks up at me, warm calm radiating back at me. "Dad and Isis, I suspect. So, I know you must have an idea."

Blushing, I can't look away from him. "With Beth spending a lot of time with Rory, which I think is awesome– not complaining –and with Willow not liking me until recently, I've had to hang out with different people than usual."

It's nearly impossible to hold a conversation with all of Devon's attention directed at me. Before, his mind was spinning like a hamster in wheel, but now he's able to focus on one thing at a time, with intensity.

"Uncle Dave is a hoot, and he talks nonstop about my dad," I mutter, words bittersweet. "With the big age-gap, Uncle Dave practically raised my dad. So he told me lots of stories, and of course it made me miss him all the more."

"Little Will, eh?" Devon whispers to my belly. "I'm down for that."

"Isis has been a surprise–"

"She's crazy over babies." Devon's expression shutters, letting me know Willow spilled the beans earlier today. I want to be there for Isis, but I know she'd never let me.

"Isis would come into the salon and watch Rob paint the murals on the walls. She gave me your entire family history, what little she knew about the Masons, but a ton about the Jamisons. I feel like I know them."

"Is Momma gonna name you after Aunt Ginny? A little Cammy? Nah," Devon purrs, face pressed close to my belly. Sneaky fingertips lift my shirt, then he rests his lips to my bare flesh, the touch scorching all the way to my heart. "Maeve. If it's a girl, you want to name her after Grammy Maeve."

"I thought it was fitting," I murmur, refusing to voice why. Maeve Jamison didn't struggle with bipolar disorder. She didn't allow it to stop her from living a full and happy life. She accepted it and went about living.

"Will or Maeve," Devon whispers to my belly, as if it's a secret. "Is your momma gonna make you come into this world a bastard, or is she going to let your daddy make an honest woman out of her."

"Devon, so much for changing your ways. Talk about manipulation and emotional extortion." I try to step back, but he doesn't let me budge. "It's not flattering that you only want to get married because you accidently got me knocked up."

"Accidentally?" Devon's laughter takes on a sinister edge. "A week before I turned fourteen, the sex was with intent. Coming down from a high, trying to outrun the darkness, I was still lucid enough to do you with intent. Just as I'm now asking you to marry me because I'm a selfish bastard who wants you, loves you, and will use anything at my disposal to keep you. I'm sober and balanced, but I'm still the same manipulative Devon– only more proficient and for the greater good."

Floored, the words tumble out of my mouth. "You really want to get married?"

"When I was fourteen, I would watch how you interacted with my siblings." Devon presses his face to my belly, but he holds my gaze. "It felt like home while you were with us. Then you'd leave, and Dad would be at work and Mom would be abusive, and I just wanted to run away and take the kids with me. So I came up with the plan to get you knocked up, not because I wanted the kid, but because I wanted to keep you– make you a Mason. Family."

"Jesus." Devon's words are raw and filled with a pain and longing so deep I'll never understand it. It's hard to ignore the truth when it's staring up at you with tears glistening in his eyes.

"You said you were shuffled from your folks' place, to Dave and Mary's, then the Spook House, and now here, never feeling at home. Maybe it wasn't that you needed a place to sleep, but you were missing home– missing *me*." Hugging me tightly, "I'm back– the same kid who loved you more than anything before all that bad shit happened."

"Okay," is a breathy form of acceptance, because I'm rendered speechless.

A noise draws Devon's and my attention, both of us looking up to see Willow and Ren standing in the entryway from the living room. "We're going to bed," Willow mutters, grabbing Ren's hand to pull him away.

Shocked, I watch their backs until they move out of sight.

"Why were they crying?" Devon asks in an innocent tone. "Do you think they're okay?"

"More than okay," I mutter, hoping they saw something in Devon and me that will help them get over whatever's blocking their growth. "Let's go to bed."

CHAPTER FIFTY-SIX

Willow Prynne

Devon's house rules hit me where it counted. I've been trying to be a better version today than the one I was yesterday. I always know the instant the words leave my lips that I took the snide remark too far. I know it's wrong, and I'd love to say I can't help myself, but that's a lie. Even when I'm thinking the things that will never be spoken, I feel like a nasty cunt for thinking them.

None of it has anything to do with my convenient target, and everything to do with me.

I'm not perfect, but I'm trying. What I thought was cute and badass– my sarcastic asshole vibe I leak out into the world –it's infecting Kieren. He's picking up bad habits from me. When he rolls his eyes as someone is speaking, even I want to hit him upside the head. If it's not cute on him, it's surely rude as fuck on me. The constant hovering, overprotective routine he's pulling with Essie, and now Devon, is utter bullshit.

It's a major wakeup call when you realize you're infecting your boyfriend with bitterness.

I want to be a strong woman, not a little girl hiding behind bitchy words and the promise of violence. Strength by using my intelligence, by being compassionate, by helping those who are less fortunate, and by not judging everyone who doesn't think exactly as I do.

My position is right for me, but that doesn't mean it's right for them. As a church-goer, I know I have no right to judge. If I get angry at someone for disagreeing with me, that makes me the asshole in the wrong, not them.

Dad taught me better than I've been acting. A tight ball of disappointment twists my guts, disappointment in myself. The very disappointment Clover felt in me when I beat Essie a few months ago– beat a pregnant woman because Devon had the gall to want her more than me, when I didn't even want him back.

I made a bunch of excuses, screaming how no one would listen to me, but there is no excuse on the planet for what I did. It didn't matter what Essie did or didn't do to me, it was *me* beating on a woman, someone I love, who was carrying a defenseless baby.

Two wrongs don't make a right.

Essie and Devon have both tried to make it right, Essie hundreds of times. Instead of accepting, I was getting off on wronging them to show them how much it hurts, doing things considerably worse than they've ever done to me.

That makes them good people who've learned a lesson, and me a bad person who is ignorant because I refuse to learn from *mistakes*. Worse, I'm evil for wanting to inflict pain on those I love.

We all do it– see a hot guy, who's probably a jerk, but that doesn't matter. Hottie's with a meh girl, someone we see as beneath us, and we think to ourselves... *Why is he with her? What does she have that I don't? How can that fugly, fat chick bag a man and happiness when I can't?*

The thing is, I fear girls are looking at me like that when Ren and I go out. He slept his way through Fairport High, and left them all satisfied. I know who every single one of them are, and I see their stares while we eat at the No-Name, grab snacks at the gas station, even when waiting in line at the post office.

They see me as beneath them. I see it– Ren doesn't.

The problem isn't how they see me. It's that I agree with them, when it's only Ren's opinion of me that should matter. Ren wants me, loves me, sees me as worthy, so why I am letting them win by believing in their jealousy instead of trusting my boyfriend? Trusting and believing in myself?

I'd be lying if I didn't admit to myself how Devon showing me he still wanted me wasn't a gigantic ego-boost. I felt like an asshole the second I realized it, like I somehow tied my worth to whether or not I could make a guy hard. I made myself sick.

Life isn't a competition, pitting woman against woman to see who can keep a man. It's not the men doing this to us– we're doing it to ourselves, perpetuating the misogyny as we make men the ultimate prize in the battles through life.

We don't even want the men. We just want them to want us, and no one else. Pine away, bleed for us. Because that means we're better. The best.

That's not the type of woman I want to be. I'm not in competition with Essie. I need to be happy for her, proud of her, help build her up because she's my cousin and fellow woman. Instead, I've been shredding the piss out of her to feel superior, all the while making myself sink lower and lower than I was the day before.

As Kieren and I walk in silence, both of us licking our triple-scoop cones, I decide to be a better person. The ice cream hits my stomach, roiling as if it's rancid, and I decide I'm no longer going to eat my feelings. I'm not going to scream them, or punch them into people, or be so narcissistic that I think everyone and their brother needs to know every emotion firing in my brain.

The only person who will know what I'm feeling is the one who made me feel that way.

I want things, things Kieren isn't giving me, and I have a feeling the reverse holds true for him too. We're so stuck in what we think we should be doing, we're missing out on what we are doing.

Everyone around us is getting married, buying houses, starting businesses, and having babies, so it feels bizarre that we're not. I could sense Kieren was trying to force it, and it's made him bitter.

I've finally realized I don't need those things to be an adult. It would just be playacting and a huge mistake because we're not ready. I *am* an adult, and I don't have to prove it to anyone.

I need to buy a vehicle before a house.

I need to graduate college before I run a business.

I need to learn to be a girlfriend before I'm a wife.

I need to get married before I have a baby.

I need to learn how to be a daughter before I can be a mother.

There's a reason it's called the natural order of things. *Don't shit on the gift I've given you!* The words Clover said to me the day I moved out of Mom and Dad's and into Auggie's world will forever ring in my ears. Only now they make sense.

I'm going to experience life in a natural progression, because Clover made the sacrifice so I could.

Our parents are in that stage, Kieren and I are not. Devon and Essie are a few years older, but the years between eighteen and twenty-one matter. If I'd shut up and pay attention, I'd learn a lot from them, so I won't make those same mistakes with Ren.

I have a feeling Ren's pondering the same things tonight. But, then again, maybe all Ren is thinking about is how tasty Black Raspberry ice cream is wedged between two scoops of Death by Chocolate.

"What?" Ren murmurs to me, a smudge of chocolate on his cheek making him look like a little boy. "Never mind, I know what." Arcing his arm backward, with a forceful snap, Ren flings his ice cream into the river.

Laughing, I do the same... only mine lands twenty feet from the water. "Wow! I suck."

"And I love how good you are at it." Ren waggles his eyebrows, innuendo thick in his voice.

Laughing, we race each other across the river rocks, scrambling as our feet slip. The one quality in Ren I admire the most is his playfulness– he brings it out of me.

"Hey!" I shout as Ren reaches my cone before I do. Smiling brightly, he gestures for me to stand next to him. Leery, I hesitate, then allow myself to be pulled to the water's edge. The cone is placed in my palm, with Ren arcing my arm back, lending me the force to lob the ice cream cone into the water.

"We make a good team." Ren's smile turns into an expression of contemplation.

"Yes, we do." My fingers slip into his, pulling him to walk with me along the river. In silence, my eyes continue to flick between the water and the rocks. In the waning light, it's easy to pick out the glittering rocks.

I miss my time with Seth, but I *need* this time with Kieren.

"Devon said he talked to you earlier," Ren seems hesitant. "In detail."

Blushing, I hiss, "Shit!" underneath my breath, knowing Ren will still hear me. "Yeah, Dev's always about the details... It was uncomfortable to say the least."

"I will admit two flaws," Ren says out of nowhere. "Fear is at the core of both. Homophobia, which sucks when you have a gay kid brother and an older brother who is fucked in the head."

Mind spinning, the terror in Ren's voice draws my feet to a stop. I just gape up at him, utterly speechless.

"I've seen things I can't unsee, things that ruined me. I've had things happen to me, things I can't escape. Things I've only shared with Devon– literally shared and in the aftermath. But I need you to know that someday I will share the details with you, when I'm ready. But not soon."

Knowing how he feels about possessiveness and jealousy, I realize patience is a virtue with Kieren Mason. "I've got a lifetime to wait– you'll get no pressure from me. But now I won't call you out when you act bizarre and homophobic."

Shame-faced, Ren refuses to look at me while he grumbles, "I know it's wrong the instant I say it."

"Been there, done that about an hour ago." I laugh without humor, and Ren joins in with me.

"Me too… Dad loved Mom, even though she acted horrific and treated him like shit. Mom tore Dad up, but a look or a kiss and he would be wrapped around her demented finger. That terrified me, and it's left a lasting impression. This fed into another issue caused by the nightmare."

"Your second flaw is fear of commitment while you not-so secretly crave it?" I offer up, not needing a degree in psychology for that one. "The other issue is how you *wouldn't* come with a girl, not that you couldn't."

"Nail. Head."

"I'm more perceptive than you realize," I mutter without a lick of arrogance. "I may look young and dumb, I may only be eighteen, but I am quite intelligent… just ask my professors and Mr. Kline."

"I've never doubted your intelligence, Spanky." Ren swats my ass, but the sentiment in his words is serious. "I'm just trying to explain why I'm having a difficult time letting you in. I want to connect with you so badly, but fear is holding me back."

"Then you're not ready." The words feel right. I'm surprised how that doesn't hurt when I thought it would. If anything, it takes the pressure away. I'm not ready to get married and have kids, but I do want to share all the moments between now and then with Ren. "Don't rush it. Let it grow organically. We're eighteen and nineteen. Let's just see where this goes."

"I don't want to lose you." The fear in Ren's voice rivals that of when he spoke of his homophobia.

"If you believe we should be together forever, then you don't need to worry about losing me. I'm going nowhere because I'm where I want to be. I left the Spook House, not because I wanted to rehab a new home, but because I wanted to make my home with you."

"This mature side of you scares me." Ren's voice warbles, and I don't know if it's with humor or terror. "I'm waiting for you to wish I was Devon, where you demand details of my time with other girls, where you force me to explain why I didn't want to get off with them… and I can't survive that."

Turning on my heel, I grin up at Ren as I point at my chest. "Intelligent, remember? I learned that lesson after you screamed in my face last month. Those moments belong solely to you, just as mine belong to me… which is why you didn't ask about me cupping Devon's bulge."

Panic overtakes my entire being as the verbal vomit flows from my mouth. In the stillness, I begin to wonder if Devon changed so much that he wouldn't have shared that detail with Ren. Then Ren returns to animation.

"I know you." Ren smirks at me, catching my hand again, then begins towing me back down the riverbank. "I know Devon. I know what each of you were thinking, so I didn't need to ask… doesn't matter."

"Good." Deep breath. "I've been a bad influence on you, and Devon's rules made me see that. So no more asshattery from either of us."

"Deal." Ren squeezes my hand. "I've been scared, so I've been acting like an asshole. I can feel it when I'm doing it. Bitter, I guess. Worried about Devon. There's been a lot of changes going on."

"Which is why I'm not pressuring you to tell me you love me." Smirking, I show Ren that he doesn't have to say it, because I can feel it and see it in his actions. "I like playing with you, hanging out with you, and that doesn't have to change just because you think being serious means something different. I'm not going anywhere."

"I like us too– just as we are."

"But less bitter," I tack on. "We're okay, and we're going to be okay. So we're going to make sure Dev and Essie are okay too. It's the right thing to do."

"Yeah, they have more shit going on than we do." Ren's fingers muss up his hair, tugging a bit. "I've been an asshole to Essie, resentful because she wouldn't let me help her. I'm done doing that."

"And I'm done being a cunt."

"We need to start working out." Ren pats his gut, then cups my tummy. "Healthy food. Devon's been detoxed to our nasty shit, so we should start eating like him."

"Agreed– it's the adult thing to do." Winking, I know damned well we'll have a food stash for our bedroom binge-watching sessions. "On our way home, let's hit the grocery store for healthy breakfast stuff."

"We'll get up and make them breakfast, show 'em we won't be shitty roomies."

"It helps that all we have to do is pull on ratty t-shirts in the morning, while they have to get dressed up. Devon and his anal uniform routine, and Essie having to do her hair and makeup so her clients trust her skills."

"Yeah, our lives are easier than theirs." Ren smirks at me, with an edge of mischievousness I'd miss if it was absent. "Let's keep it that way."

CHAPTER FIFTY-SEVEN

Essie Prynne

"I'm going to grab a shower first, if that's okay?" Devon turned jittery as soon as Willow and Ren came home. Maybe he can feel the energy they're giving off, or maybe it's just too many people in a confined space. His anxiety falls several notches as soon as we hear their bedroom door close.

"Sure." Curling my lips, I try to reassure Devon while showing him that I understand. "I'm just going to pick up the tools of my trade, then pop in to say goodnight to Willow and Ren."

Devon hesitates after shouldering his backpack. "This part isn't odd for you, is it?"

"First of all, your new haircut takes my breath away." Blushing, I can't help the fact that my heart is going all a flutter at the sight of Devon standing in the entryway to the kitchen. "Second of all, Willow, Ren, and I have been sharing a space for the past month. There's no transition for us, only for you."

"Good," Devon utters curtly, then does an about-face to head up the stairs. "I'll be out in less than ten minutes!"

Devon's moods would throw me for a loop, if I hadn't known him since I was in preschool.

After picking up the kitchen, I find myself knocking on Willow and Ren's bedroom door. I can hear their play-fighting– or as I've come to learn, foreplay –through the closed door.

"It's Essie!" Willow shouts at Ren. "The knock was too hesitant to be Dev."

"Up for a bet?" Ren's voice is deeper– as I said, foreplay.

"It's me!" I yell just to spoil their fun. "Just wanted to know if you guys needed anything before I called it a night."

"I love how she's treating us like guests." Ren's speaking over his shoulder as he opens the door. He flashes me a naughty smirk. "That will die out quickly."

"I'm not treating you like guests." All three of us share a knowing chuckle as I slip into their disaster of a bedroom. "I just knew you hadn't unpacked yet."

"Not all of us are as anal as Devon." Ren falls to the bare mattress, bouncing on his butt. "Nor did we have Wessie and Ozzy tackling room by room as a team."

"If you guys are hogs, I'm going to make you pay that kid to clean up after you," I issue a teasing warning. "Remember how Weston used to use Armor All on the tires of his Matchbox Cars?"

"The kid keeps the Pussy Magnet sparkling clean," Ren mutters with pride. "Ironic since he has no use for pussy."

"He's not old enough to drive yet, either," I remind Ren, since Willow never abided by those laws.

"What a car..." Willow's wistful comment has me wondering what exactly she's been doing in the Masons' vintage Camaro. Buried in the middle of a pile of boxes, Willow snaps out of it. "Yeah, this sucks."

Biting my lip, I try to stifle my laughter. "The Shithole is *thousands* of feet smaller than the Spook House... and you had such beautiful furniture."

"Someday I'm going to own a house like the Spook House, until then..." Willow wistfully looks around their tiny bedroom. "Storage unit."

"Anyone got a piece of paper?" I hold my hand out, waiting, as both Ren and Willow look at me like I've lost my mind. "I wasn't blessed to have a ginormous bedroom growing up. Also didn't have a bedroom inches smaller than the Spook House's master bedroom."

Willow's bedroom at the Spook House is the size of the entire second floor of this house– she must *really* want to live with us to give that up.

Ren passes me a dry-erase board. "I know how to situate furniture in a small room. Gimme five minutes, and you won't have to give up your major pieces. May have to pare down the decorations, though."

A few minutes later, I leave a very happy Willow and Ren, knowing they now feel welcome in this house after the damage Devon did with the list of rules. They'll be moving the furniture and unpacking for most of the night, but it will feel like home to them by morning.

Devon and I were lucky, because everyone concentrated on the communal spaces while Devon and I concentrated on our space. But we're all lucky to have so many people care about us, who are willing to help at a moment's notice. On a Sunday, no less.

"Hey!" squeaks out of me as I enter our bedroom to find Devon standing in the open doorway to the bathroom, with only a towel slung over his hips. He was always so modest, covering his body beneath hoodies as a teen, then his uniform as an adult. I've seen him naked twice in one day, and it's a nice sight.

"I promise I didn't use all the hot water." Devon teases with an odd glint in his eye. I'd almost say he looks how he did when we were kids. The thought simultaneously terrifies me as it enlivens me.

"I won't be long," I murmur as I slink past him, then close the bathroom door.

Staring into the foggy mirror, my visage warped, I can't believe this is happening. Over the months– hell, years –I tried to move on from Devon, but I just couldn't quit him.

It's surreal.

This is our bathroom. Our bedroom. Our house. Our baby. Our life.

It's going to take some getting used to.

Ordinarily I'd live in the bathroom, doing a beauty regimen that takes anywhere from a half hour to an hour. Tonight, I'm out in less than ten minutes.

Embarrassed, wrapped in two towels, I stick my head out the bathroom door and spot Devon tucked in bed. "I... um– didn't bring my nightgown in with me."

"Not a problem." Devon stirs in the sheets, and I assume he's going to get me my nightgown. "You can't wear it while I give you a massage, anyway."

Mouth gaping open, all I can do is stare.

"C'mon, don't be shy." He curls a finger in my direction, beckoning me. "We always fooled around in my room, fully clothed... then Willow's car and your backroom at the salon. I get how this is major. Only a massage– promise."

But what if I want more than a massage? I want to voice, but don't. It's been more than three months since I've been touched, touched him– since our baby was conceived.

"Can I massage you back?" I negotiate, starting to shiver as all the steam flees the bathroom.

"Yup." Dev says without hesitation.

"Deal." I escape the bathroom, no longer feeling awkward. "But we turn the lights down. You look better than ever, and I look worse."

Chuckling darkly, Devon takes on the cadence of a man who is thinking very dirty thoughts. "You've got that glow thing working to your advantage. Get in here." The blankets are thrust up, revealing that Dev is completely naked underneath them.

Mouth suddenly dry, "Nice tan lines," tumbles out as I crawl in beside him. He pulls off my towels and flings them in the direction of the bathroom.

"Incredible tits." I'm not the only one sounding like their mouth has gone dry, as is evident by how aroused he is. "Roll over on to your belly– we'll prop you up with our pillows."

Beyond exposed, I find myself with a pillow under my ribs and one beneath my hips, with my ass sticking too far up in the air, but I'm comfortable without my belly being smushed.

The first touch is a bit of a shock. Devon's hands are scorching hot, strong, and nimble. "I've missed this," he murmurs in a soft voice to match the dim lighting in the room. "Dad drove me nuts growing up with how clingy he was, but I didn't appreciate it until no one touched me in a kind way for months."

Eyelids droopy, mouth hanging open, the only reply I can give is a low moan as his fingers press in all the achy spots on my lower back. Neither one of us says anything for many minutes. I'm too blissed out, and Devon evidently enjoys his work. By the time he hits the soles of my feet, I'm bleating like a dying animal.

Skin on fire, I'm so sensitive, the brush of the sheets against my flesh ignites tiny sparks. "Jesus Christ, what would I have to do to get you to do my feet every night after work?"

Leaning over me, chest brushing against my back, lips fluttering against the shell of my ear, Devon whispers to me. "All you have to do is touch me back." The words elicit a shiver to work its way along my spine.

A pained whimper is torn from my throat as Devon stops me from reacting. I so badly want to flip around and touch him– touch all of him. He pulls away, hand pressed to the small of my back so I can't move, his arousal leaving a damp path across the back of my thigh.

"Let me touch you," is a raspy moan. "I know you want me to."

"Not yet," is gritted between clenched teeth, like he's struggling to maintain control. "Not tonight."

"You want it!" Devon ignores my pleas, continuing to manipulate the backs of my thighs, so very close to my ass cheeks and more needy places.

"I do." Now it's his turn to groan, even though I'm not touching him and I know he's not touching himself. Palms griping my ass cheeks, fingertips biting in, Devon parts me to his gaze.

"Oh, fuck!" is followed by a low moan of surprise.

Kneeling behind me, Devon presses his face against my upraised ass, parting me, he angles downward to lick at my slit. "You're fucking wet– I knew you'd be. You always were."

"Devon." Struggling to turn over, I want to see his face.

Voice taking on a chanting, coaxing tone, "I've missed this so much. Touching you… eating you out… having you touch me back… those memories are my happy place. Mixed with boring as all hell Monopoly with the kids, how you'd brush Rae's hair and help Ren with his homework… how you didn't think it was odd when Weston would offer to shine your shoes… how you'd hold me after Mom would scream in my face."

"Hey," is a gasp, because I'm moister than I ought to be– Devon's crying.

"I've missed you every fucking minute since that night, like a goddamn phantom limb." Nothing will distract Devon from his task, no matter what pleas I cry out. Giving in, I allow him to take comfort from touching me, from giving me pleasure.

What I thought would take a long time, because of emotional discomfort, turns explosive in seconds. Writhing on the sheets, pillows scattered to the floor, I find myself face-up with Devon crawling over me. He curls around my side, getting comfortable, as if he's ready to go to sleep.

"What about you?" Sensing something riding beneath the surface, I go with my gut-instinct and don't grab Devon's hard-on. It's pressed against my hip, leaking pre-cum and throbbing every few seconds.

"I'm good," is a drowsy slur of words, as if Devon got a high off eating me out.

"You're too hard, no way is it going down without getting off." I know I'm pushing it, but I don't want Devon closing me out so quickly.

"It's nothing new for me." Devon snuggles closer. "I was impotent from age fourteen until a few months ago. I could only get hard when I was angry, and I only got off during wet nightmares. So don't freak out if you wake up with cum all over you."

"I could take care of it for you," I offer, voice light so I don't sound like I'm pressuring him.

"Not now– need to take care of something first." Devon senses my next question, and answers it before I can voice it. "Tomorrow night, after massage time, there won't be an inch of me you haven't touched."

My meek, "Okay," is met with a snore. It's like Devon has an automatic off-switch.

I stare at the ceiling until time has no meaning, contemplating a whirling storm of emotions and fears. The concept of sleep feels foreign, as if I'm grabbing at it but it's slipping through my fingers like spider silk. Just as my consciousness dims around the edges, I'm startled fully awake by a soundless scream and claw-like fingertips clutching my back.

Terrified, feeling a pain so deep it's infinite, all I can do is hold Devon as he sobs in silent bursts of shuddering gasps. As quickly as it started, it's over.

"At least I didn't shoot cum this time." Devon jokes to make light of the fact that he was hard the entire time. After a few heartbeats of silence. "I'm glad you didn't ask if I was okay."

"Yeah, that would be pretty stupid." …because clearly he's not.

"There were a lot of things I didn't remember– blocked it out. So for me, this stuff just happened a little over two months ago."

"But your mind knew, which is why you had wet nightmares and were impotent?"

In the dark of our bedroom, after just experiencing the worst moment of my life, worse than being shoved into the grass face-first and raped, I've never felt closer to Devon. "How can I help?"

Huffing a laugh without humor, Devon snuggles back up to me. "You're the first person to ask me that." Before I can reply, he's pulling away from me, hand fishing beneath the side of the mattress. He comes back with his journal. "I trust you, more than Delaney and Ms. Amelia. They've only read parts I pointed out because I couldn't say it out loud."

"You want me to read this?" Floored, I can't fathom the amount of faith and trust Devon is placing in me. "I'll read it tonight."

"You don't have to do that," Devon mutters, sounding exhausted after his nightmare.

"This way you'll have it tomorrow, being your first day back to work and all."

"Thank you for understanding." The switch thrown, Devon's back to snoring again as if nothing happened.

I stay up until the sun breaches the horizon, long ago finishing Devon's journal. Silently weeping, I stare down at the man I nearly lost many times over, and I'm amazed he survived.

There is nothing I wouldn't do for Devon, now that I understand him inside and out, probably better than anyone ever will.

CHAPTER FIFTY-EIGHT

Devon Mason

"You did good today." Dad clasps my shoulder, squeezing in what he thinks to be a comforting rhythm. I'm sitting on the edge of his desk, looking out over the Batcave, with my nerves rubbed raw. My foam peach now has a hole in it from me working it all day.

"You seem surprised." I can't help voicing exactly what I'm thinking. "I don't blame you, and I'm kinda proud I survived the day."

Dad releases a dark chuckle, and I join in while thinking back over the day. It felt like the first day of school, the first day at the academy, and the first day of work all rolled into one. What should've been a comfort became a test of my abilities to deal with anxiety, all because I'm not the same person I used to be.

When I walked in the underground bunker known as the Batcave, I expected it to happen with little fanfare, but the guys and girls lined the tunnel with Chief Mason in the front. I was hugged, back-patted, grinned at, and kissed until I thought my skin was going to crawl off my body.

But I could recognize the emotion beneath the anxiety—pride.

A judgmental person would probably call me out for what everyone else considers normal. Why should I get a parade of Fairport's finest simply because I returned home from a sixty-day stint in rehab, after my county-wide crime spree?

I get it, and I feel ashamed of who I used to be, but I'm not him anymore. I'm not going to wallow in the past and bleed shame. I embraced my pride in order to get through a very emotionally and mentally taxing day.

Dad didn't take my job away, only my gun, but he wouldn't let me set foot back into the school. Instead, I took up residence at Kyle's desk, calling misguided parents about their absentee children. I filed paperwork while I waited for Kyle to come in, then we issued traffic citations and ran errands. There's no alone time like before, but I'm still doing as I had from the first day I began working in the Batcave.

Mayor Ross and Dad agreed with a year-probation before I'm allowed to carry a deadly weapon, with a note from my psychiatrist. I was given my Taser back– some idiot glued rhinestones on it. I was given a six-month-probation before I'm allowed back on school premises. I thought it was more than fair, when I expected to have my badge taken away.

There's added benefits with the job now. The vending machine is gone, with Clover providing a full meal and one snack at specific hours. Dad put it in our budget, with Clover only charging the cost of the ingredients. Lucky Clover's also provides meals to all the offices upstairs in the Courthouse, but they have to pay full price.

"You can go in a few." Dad's voice is more soothing than his words. No doubt he can feel my body vibrating beneath his touch. "Another round of hellos, and you'll be free."

Body slumping, Dad's hand falls from my shoulder. "Thank God, but tomorrow will be easier."

I wait for the changing of the guard– our shifts are staggered, with a few more guys coming in now. Colin comes in a few hours before Dad leaves, to get caught up on what happened all day. Colin mans the Batcave while Dad's at home. Once in a while they trust Kyle to babysit, so they can hang out together outside of work.

Eye's peeled for Ozzy's mass of hair, "Kyle's taking me car shopping tomorrow." Dad raises an eyebrow, but otherwise doesn't comment. "Just thought you ought to know why a cruiser will be at the dealership."

"Like it was at the post office and bank today?" Humor is lacing Dad's voice, but a bit of pride too. The entire county is keeping tabs on me, but I find it comforting instead of violating. "Accounting already got a call from the bank to change the destination of your direct deposit. I had Ren transfer all your money while you and Kyle sat at the S-curve on Paxton."

"Nabbed four speeders. Listened to a lot of music." Smile lingering on my lips, I look over at Dad. "Thanks– for everything."

The squeezing hand returns, only this time it doesn't make my skin do a quivering dance. But then I'm thrust into a fresh hell as three guys filter in, each giving me a backslapping hug and lingering to talk for too long.

Colin falls into the chair at his desk, but he's still close enough to have a conversation at normal volumes, so I don't wig out too bad. Kyle got used to the quieter me today, with Dad treating me as always, but the rest of the guys acted like I was a social butterfly. My battery is in the red, but I can handle Colin because he doesn't drain me.

Leaning back in his chair, feet propped up on his desk, Colin rubs his flat stomach. "I'm starving. Where's Foster."

"Foster?" I turn to Dad, confused.

"Oh, there he is." Colin's feet hit the ground with an audible thump. "My favorite time of day. Feed me, Seymour!"

Ozzy appears, carrying a tote of pre-packaged meals and snacks, with a smile so wide it's all we see through the hair. He passes food out to the guys as they move toward the tunnel that funnels into the parking lot. Then he visits the guys stationed at their desks.

"Ah, Foster– for Dad's foster kid."

Colin grunts, glaring at me. "Oliver Zypher is ours–" he gestures to the Batcave. "*We* adopted him."

"Probably why Clover feeds you twice as much as everyone else." Ozzy pulls out two meals and two snacks.

"Gotta stay awake all night. One of these is my breakfast." Colin pouts, but then his face transforms as he opens his supper. "Mmm… stir-fry."

"Malcolm brings you breakfast," Ozzy points out, causing everyone in earshot to chuckle.

"Where's mine?" Dad tilts the tote in Ozzy's hands, finding it empty.

"Clover said dinner is at seven." Ozzy turns to me. "Ready?"

I can't jump up fast enough. We're halfway down the hallway when Colin and Dad start bickering over a donut. "Hopefully I'll have a vehicle in a few days, so you won't have to cart me home."

"Don't mind." Ozzy's quieter than I am, voice soothing like rushing water. "Gives me an excuse to get out of the house."

"Plus you get to drive the Pussy Magnet." Laughing, I elbow the kid. "My sister is probably seething over that."

We wave to a bunch of folks on our way to the parking lot, and Ozzy and I both sigh in relief that we're not drawn into a conversation. He waits until we're headed home before he answers me.

"Rae's pissed I can't teach her to drive." Ozzy raises an eyebrow in my direction, sharing a private smirk.

That's a nightmare for a guy like Ozzy, being trapped inside a death machine capable of going over a hundred miles-per-hour, with a teenage girl who has an unrequited crush.

"Malcolm's already giving me academy textbooks, so the law's in my favor when Rae turns bratty."

"I'll talk to Ren or Essie," I offer.

"Not you or Willow?" he mutters knowingly.

"Nah… we're too impatient, and Rae is petrified of Willow. It'll be easier with Wessie and the twins. All three at once."

Ozzy shudders, then brightens. "I'll be at the academy by then."

We share an evil laugh as he pulls up to the Pink Taco Hut. "Willow can teach those fools to drive. She'll love it." I hop out of the car, wanting to get away before a houseful of people sets their sights on me.

"Go on." Ozzy's palms shove at my back. "I'll head 'em off at the pass. Your house should still be empty."

Walking off, I wave over my shoulder while saying, "Later."

Ozzy's, "Later," hits my ears just as indecision has my feet carrying me elsewhere. I'm across the street and up the front steps at the Spook House before I even realize it.

Last night disturbed me– the night before too. In a perverse way, I was happy to share the misery with Ren and Essie, so I wouldn't feel so alone. At the clinic, I'd wake screaming with no one to comfort me, and I couldn't fall back to sleep because of it. But I managed to lie for several weeks so I never once had to take an addictive sleeping pill.

Last night and the night before, the nightmares felt like a release with someone there to catch me when I woke, to the point I was able to fall asleep almost immediately.

They each gave me space, neither asking questions the old me would've lashed out about. But the current me needs to be pushed so I can't hide behind the fortress of my emotions. Delaney proved how letting it out sets me free, and bottling it up gives it power over me. That's why I suffered the humiliation of giving Essie my journal, because I needed her to push me for my own good.

There is something Essie can't help me with, a fear I wrote about in my journal. So I know she'll understand and won't think less of me or herself for what I'm about to do.

I was supposed to jerk off at the clinic– it's standard policy for victims of sexual assault. I needed to know whether or not I'd freak out, especially with my past. The Center prides itself on making their patients healthy in all ways. But I just couldn't– *wouldn't* –do it.

Control. I have to keep a firm grip on my emotions at all times. It's like a meter running in the background– I call it my battery. But it takes part of my physical energy to keep tabs on it. I can never be free. I can never let loose. With my disorders, mixed with recovery, my meds aren't a guarantee.

I need to be in control. I want to be in control. It guarantees the safety I lost, removing the powerless feeling I carry around like another skin. But during sex, absolutely no one is in total control.

I wouldn't get off at the clinic for the same reason I couldn't sleep there after a nightmare. What if I lose control? Essie will give me anything I ask for, put up with anything, this is a universal truth I've held true since we met as toddlers. She's not strong enough to keep me in check should I lose control. As Delaney said, there is a reason the French call the act of orgasming the little death.

I should've gotten off at the clinic, but I couldn't do it alone. I have no problem getting aroused, staying aroused, and shooting my load like I did before the assault. But there is no way I'm going to subject Essie to a freak-out of disastrous levels. The fear that I'll harm her overpowers all else.

There's a reason I knocked on the Spook House door, waiting for Robin to answer. I need to get off in a controlled environment this first time. Creepy, but nonetheless true.

Fingers shaking, I curl them into fists. A familiar sensation blankets me like a warm coat– it's the antsy feeling I had before a buy, the anticipation of taking my next hit. Breathing deeply, I put myself firmly in check.

Starling as the door opens, I know I look guilty as my eyes meet Rob's. "Hi."

"Back so soon?" Robin looks curious, but also suspicious. We haven't had the best of relationships. "Or did you guys forget something when you moved so abruptly without notice, without asking for our assistance?"

Clearly that left a lasting sting on the guy.

"That was up to the girls– Ren and I had nothing to do with it."

The truth in my words gains me admission. Rob steps to the side, methodically rubbing paint off his fingers with a cloth. "You're wearing the Mason '*I need a favor*' expression." Rob shuts the door, then locks it. "I hope you're visiting me, because Isis and Auggie will be at Rush for the unforeseeable future. I'm sure the girls told you why."

Wow. Auggie left his own fucking house?

"Yeah, but I wanted no details." Gazing around, the Spook House sounds so enticingly empty. I almost want to move back, just me and Essie. Serenity. But something tells me Robin Prynne would be harder to live with than Willow and Kieren combined. Breakfast was sweet this morning, but very loud and chaotic.

"Follow me." Robin ascends the staircase, expecting me to follow. "Just call me a mind-reader, but I have a good idea why you're here."

"I–"

"Wait," Rob cuts off my explanation. "Hold that thought until we're in the attic."

Winding our way up the staircase, then down the main hallway, we enter a doorway across from the master bedroom. Rob and I have no problem with the low-slop of the ceiling and the narrow treads as we ascend into the attic.

The Playroom.

I was a member of the Playroom when it was in the back storeroom of Rush. Dad forced Ren and me to go after Ren turned eighteen– if he didn't outright know the truth, then he must have at least suspected what happened to me. I hated my time in the Playroom, because part of me knew I belonged there.

I've never set foot up here. I was already too far gone to addiction and darkness, and it didn't open until after I was shipped off to Arizona. One step into the attic and I relax. "This is nice. You and Willow did a good job."

"Thank you." Robin preens, then settles his feathers– sits on a sofa. "Sit and relax."

"Motherfucking bizarre," I murmur beneath my breath, eyes flicking between the rich walls heavily shrouded in shadows, inviting play areas, and Robin Prynne wearing a paint-speckled t-shirt and an anticipatory grin. "This sofa is almost identical to the one in the living room."

"Willow upholstered them both." Rob shifts to face me. "But you didn't come up here to discuss fabric patterns, did you?"

"Christ," I snarl, going to attack my hair, only to find it shorter so the release isn't as potent. Giving up on that, I grab my riddled peach out of my gun holster and begin manipulating it in my fist. "I don't know how to begin."

"You start by taking off your utility belt, and placing it on Auggie's throne. Then you unbutton a few buttons on your shirt, so you can take a deep breath and relax."

Old Devon would have lashed out at being ordered around, then he would have used it as an excuse to run off and get high. Delaney broke that habit. Doing as I was told, I remove my belt, the telltale sound of my meds clacking around in one of the compartments. I gingerly set my belt and all of my things on the big, wooden chair. I even slip the foam peach back into the holster.

After slowly unbuttoning my shirt, I untuck my undershirt. Rob watches me as a hawk does prey as I remove my journal, placing it on the pile, then I cover it all with my uniform shirt. If I hadn't covered it, the sight of my things would've continually drawn my attention. Now it's safe and secure– out of sight, out of mind.

Taking my seat next to Rob, I turn utterly speechless. I stare at him, imploring him to help me, when I can't even voice what's wrong.

"You're here sooner than I anticipated, but I'm not surprised." Rob stares back at me, looking as if he can physically drill into my brain and steal its contents. "I'm a deviant. Back at Rush, I sat in the backroom and watched all of our members interact, including you. I'm not a voyeur, getting off on what I see. I'm an observer."

"I gave a guy a blowjob!" I blurt out rapidly, brain releasing it before my mouth can stop it.

A sinister eyebrow raises as Robin looks me over from the tips of my boots to the top of my head. "I'm not surprised. As I said, I'm an observer. Your reactions intrigued me. You were either numb, completely cut off and in your own mind, or furious, with no in between. Ren didn't need to be there, but he loved watching."

"I resented being in the Playroom."

"Because you didn't want to belong there." Rob's observation is correct. "Come sit with me while we talk."

"*I am*," I sputter, confused.

Rob shifts on the sofa, widening his legs, then he pats the space between his thighs. "This isn't sexual, but it's what you need. We'll talk– that's it. Sit. C'mon."

Some unseen force has me moving against my better judgement. My ass rests in the space Rob made, with the inside of his thighs bracketing the outside of mine, with my back resting against his front. We're nearly the same height, so his mouth comes to rest against my ear, with his chin on my shoulder.

"I know one thing that happened to you– I won't dick around and lie. Instinct had Malcolm figuring out you were forced to blow one, if not all, of your attackers. Watching your reactions in the Playroom, combined with you blurting out how you blew a guy, confirms that."

"I–" Shuddering, I can't stop shuddering. Lean arms wrap around my chest, pinning my arms to my sides, with the strength of steal bands. Legs slide over mine, knees hooking me into place. The shuddering is cut off immediately.

"Better?" Robin whispers into my ear, voice a comfort, not seductive. "Safe, like a swaddled baby…"

"I blew one of them to save Ren, but I… I did a guy just before I went to rehab. After I remembered." The flame of anger is instantaneous, nearly consuming me, and I welcome it home. "I'm so pissed at Ren, not because of what I had to do to save him, but because he looked at me every fucking day… all he saw was what I did, what happened to me, and he kept me in the dark."

"It was Ren's turn to protect you." Rob sounds rational, but I'm supposed to always protect my baby brother, not the other way around. "Tell me about the voluntary blowjob."

"Why do I like you holding me like this?"

Arms squeeze me tighter, just to the point where I can almost not breathe, then release slightly. "Because you trust me. Because you were a child, and no one protected you. Not against your mother. Not against the bad guys. You were a child having to protect the one person who was put on this earth to protect you. Not only didn't she protect you, she harmed you for fourteen years."

"I don't blame Mom." Even with my voice showing my emotional exhaustion, the anger simmering beneath is obvious.

"Doesn't change the truth, does it?" Rob squeezes me tighter. "You were still harmed. Mentally, emotionally, and physically abused by dear ol' mom. You were still raped." Rob ignores my gasp of protest and keeps speaking in a coaxing tone belying his words of rage. "It's why someone so brave, strong, and powerful needs someone to hold you together, to catch you should you fall."

Unable to handle what Rob's saying, my mouth spews things I'd rather never speak. "I blew Kurt. I'm not gay or bi. I didn't even get hard, but I loved doing it. I felt relaxed."

"That comes as no surprise, seeing as one of the two scenes that caught your undivided attention was always a guy getting blown. You would look so angry, and you'd leave with a giant wet spot on your jeans."

"I didn't want the girl… I didn't want to be the guy. It didn't matter who was doing it. I just liked how it made me feel." Panting roughly, I try to pull away but can't move. "Goddamnit! I'm not a submissive."

"No, you most certainly are not." Rob squeezes me harder, and it's like a switch was thrown. I relax immediately. "You need to feel safe. That scene reminded you of a time when you were least safe, forced to submit. Powerless and afraid. I'd suggest you have Essie stand at the end of the bed, with her foot on the mattress, while you feast between her thighs."

"No!" I bellow, warped voice echoing off the shadowy walls. "I'm not bringing Essie into this."

"Why not?" Rob sounds merely curious, with no judgment in his tone.

"She doesn't have the temperament for it. I'm supposed to keep her safe, not the other way around."

Rage whispers alongside Rob's words. "Essie's not fragile– we Prynnes may look small, but we're mighty."

"It's not that. Not the *make love to your wife, fuck your mistress* bullshit. I'll fuck her, make love to her, do anything I want to her, and she'll let me. But this is tainted, and I don't want to infect our life with it."

"I agree, it's compartmentalized. Some women wouldn't understand, but Essie will. It's not about sex." Rob's grip loosens, then a single fingertip taps my temple. "Humans are complex creatures, and the majority place us in tiny boxes with labels. When we don't fit in the box, they say we're not normal– they medicate us, ostracize us, shame us. But that's because we're using all three parts of the body that funnel into sexuality, where it's not so black and white."

Rob taps my temple again, tickling me. "While you were on your knees before Kurt, your brain was engaged. Ordinarily, your cock would come to the rescue to release what the brain summoned forth. The sex organs are merely a release valve for the brain and heart– soul and emotions. A physical release for a cerebral and emotional manifestation. Those who want to cage us, label us, they only think with their sex organs, not realizing it's way more complicated than that."

"I see married couples, and I know I can never be like that," I admit in defeat, fearing a lifetime of struggling.

"You aren't them, and that's not a bad thing." Rob stops playing with my scalp and returns to squeezing me in his death-grip. "I have someone perfect for you. Someone you can trust with your life and the contents of your brain. Someone who Auggie fucked up and I've been working for three months to help him cope. He's strong, strong enough to make you feel safe."

"I don't know…" I need to think, but Rob's somehow fogging my brain.

"It doesn't have to be sexual– like a sponsor. It can be sexual if you need it to be. It will be a different kind of intimacy, without romantic feelings. He needs to regain his power and you need to feel safe. Essie and his wife will understand. It's not unfaithful. It's survival. But he's not ready yet, and neither are you."

"I'll have to think about it, discuss it with Essie," I slur, feeling drugged on Robin's will.

"Good." He sounds pleased, squeezing me extra hard. "Unzip your pants, remove your dick, and jerk off."

"What?!" I squawk.

"It's why you're here, isn't it?" Maybe Robin Prynne is a mind-reader. "We'll finish our talk while you stroke yourself. I'm not doing it for you, so hurry up."

It's a struggle to mind Rob while he maintains his tight hold on me, but I'm relieved he doesn't let go. Groaning, I'm in physical pain after last night. My dick did eventually soften, but it's tender. Usually I shoot off in my sleep, just like Rob explained. My mind forcing a release through my dick. But that didn't happen, so today I've been hard off and on, when normally I'm not.

"Jesus Christ!" Rob hisses between his clenched teeth, breath tickling at my ear. "Did you see the episode where Jason Stackhouse drank an entire vial of vampire blood, and he jerked off until his blisters bled? Then Tara had to take him to the emergency room…"

"You're a goddamn sadist," I snarl, struggling to get away.

"I am, thanks for noticing," Rob purrs with pride. "Get to stroking your goddamn dick before it ends up looking like Jason Stackhouse's eggplant. Priapism is a real thing, dumbass."

"I was too scared to get off last night." Furious, I start jerking myself off, thankful Robin isn't at all aroused as he toys with me. I'd know. I can feel his dick pressing into the small of my back, but he's soft, which is a comfort.

Arms tighter, words low in my ear. "You're very brave, Officer Devon."

"No, I'm not," I mutter begrudgingly, trying my damnedest to get off as quickly as possible, which is nearly impossible with an achy dick.

"Brave but stupid." Words sinister, holding a sadistic delight. "All forms of anal sex made you enraged– fascinated." Leaning closer, holding me tighter, Robin's whisper snakes its way down my spine. "I remember."

"Shit!" Arching my back, I try to contain a deep, primal moan.

"I have a theory, because you're very brave and stupid, always having to be in control." Robin's words become a chant, flowing in time with the stroke of my hand. "After you blew the bad guy, you had to be a hero."

"Stop," I snarl, cock jerking in my hand.

"No– you called me a sadist, remember?" Squeezing so tight my breath catches in my throat. "You were a stupid boy who sacrificed himself for his abusive mother and a younger, yet larger brother who could take care of himself."

"I had to," I whine, hand picking up speed, slick with pre-cum. "I'd rather have nightmares than live with myself for not helping them."

"Your attackers stopped playing with Camille when you started blowing their buddy, I bet. But brave yet stupid Devon offered himself up if they'd leave Mom and Kieren alone. Too bad they were done with her already."

"Shut up!" I shout so loud my voice breaks.

"Did it hurt?" Robin whispers into my ear, breath dampening my skin. "Did they take turns, or was it just the one?" He shudders with me, bodies vibrating together. "Just the one, I bet. Even your mother's rapists didn't have the stomach for what yours was doing."

"Alejandro," I put a name to the face Rob is envisioning.

"Did it hurt?" He almost sounds as if he wished it did. "Did you bleed? It's an indescribable sensation to have someone force themselves into you, unprepared, unwanted. Unwelcome. The powerlessness. The rage. The fear. The way your life burns beneath your knees as you're assaulted. All trust flees with your broken innocence."

"It didn't hurt, not really," I yelp in reply, because Robin is going somewhere that has nothing to do with me, and it's making me fear he'll lose control. I admit aloud what I could never voice, what I only allowed my therapists to read. "Uncomfortable. I bled a bit the next day, but not much. I just knelt and rested my chest in the seat of my chair while Kieren screamed."

"You just thought about how badly you wished Ren would fucking shut up, didn't you?" Rob squeezes me so tightly, I fear I'll suffocate. "You couldn't escape into your mind because he was distracting you. Your instincts were to soothe your brother's fear, but it made it more difficult for you. It was worse because what should hurt didn't... there is no escaping it, awake or asleep."

"What happened to you, Rob?" I croak out, shocked, as if he's reading my words right back to me.

"You're free now– *safe*." Legs hooking over top of mine, Rob spreads me farther apart. "Come. Lose control. Fly, and I'll catch you before you meet the ground."

Too embarrassed to acknowledge the sounds I make, the way my body moves, or how much fluid my body releases, I come to lying on my side in the fetal position on the sofa, with Robin finger-combing my hair and crooning soothing words to me.

"Is Devon going to be okay?" Essie's voice filters into the fog. "Maybe I shouldn't have told you that stuff."

"Obviously you should have." Robin's arrogant words are a comfort as he touches me with sure strokes. "Dev showed up here all on his own, just like we anticipated. He needed this– he'll come down from the high in a few minutes. Just keep talking and touching him."

"High?" Essie's voice warbles as her fingertips skate across my brow. "That's not a good idea."

"Not the same, Ess." I can hear Robin rolling his fucking eyes. "It's a healthy high. An outlet for all the shit our boy has bottled up since he was fourteen. Dr. Delaney called me before Devon was released, asking me what I'd do if Devon came to me after he read it in the journal."

"I feel like I betrayed you," Essie whispers across my cheek as she kneels beside the sofa. "After last night... wanting to be touched but not allowing it, the nightmare, your journal... I had to ask someone what to do, I was so out of my element."

"S'okay." Tugging on Essie's hand, I pull her onto the sofa with me. "C'mere, join me... I feel so loopy."

"Enjoy it." The laugh Robin releases is pure sex. "It's the only high you'll get besides being high on life." Leaning down, he ruffles up my hair, then kisses Essie's forehead. "I'm going to be on the sunporch, finishing up a painting. You have to get off on your own before you leave this house."

"For real?" Then I realize it's Robin Prynne I'm talking to, and a strained laugh falls from my lips. "Thank God, Essie's with me this time."

"I was standing in the shadows," Essie admits, sounding guilty. Curling closer to me, she buries her face against the side of my neck.

"When you're done, just lock the door behind you." Rob stalks over to the door, then turns back to face us, as if he's debating to say more. "Be here Thursday night at eight. You can help me fix what Auggie broke in Rory."

My, "What?" follows Robin, then bounces back at me as he shuts the door.

"I didn't find out until this afternoon at the salon." Essie rolls over onto her side, because she was smushing her belly. "Willow and I kept seeing Beth and Rory coming up here, but I figured it wasn't any of my business unless she wanted to tell me on her own."

"What did Auggie do to Rory?" There's been no love lost between Rory and me, but I realize there wasn't much about me to respect. I was always annoyed how Rory straddled the line between my age group and Auggie's, but never wanted anything to do with me. It didn't help that my best friend was fucking nuts over him. But knowing Auggie hurt Rory, it causes possessive feelings to rise, an emotion I thought I'd smothered.

"I know you were in the Playroom with Beth." Not an accusation, merely fact. "So you know Auggie wouldn't let her go easily. Rory paid both the toll to the Playroom and let Auggie do him to cancel out what Beth owed. Now Rory's all messed in the head, but he's hiding it, and Beth's suffocating on guilt because he did it for her."

"Ass. Hole." Rage erupts, but I quickly dampen it down. Snuggling Essie closer, I breathe in her scent and bask in her warmth. "Auggie should fix it."

"Rory's too angry at him– Auggie's volunteered for anything Rory's willing to give, but Rob stepped in, saying it was toxic. So Rob's been walking Rory and Beth through it, but it's not working. He doesn't want Beth to be a part of it, only watching."

"No more talking– I'm burnt out." Knowing Essie's probably sore after being on her feet all day, after a night without sleep, I begin working on the knots in her shoulders. "Just hold me. In silence."

Understanding me better than anyone, Essie takes the initiative by massaging me back. Sneaky fingertips ruck up my t-shirt then slip inside as butterfly kisses are peppered along my jawline.

Eyes fluttering shut, I understand why Rory doesn't want Beth to be a part of what happens up here in the attic. What I just did is not the same as what Essie and I are doing now. The emotions are pure, comforting– healing.

Rob said our sex parts are the pressure release valve for our minds and hearts. Whatever needs Essie can't meet will be no different than releasing the strain my mind is under, the pain in my psyche, the pressure of unescapable emotions. None of which has anything to do with love, romance, fidelity, or loyalty, and everything to do with my very real nightmares.

We don't need help this time around. It's slow. Brushing caresses over needy flesh. Sucking, open-mouthed kisses. Biting fingertips. As always, when our bodies join as one, it's as easy as breathing. A comfort– a rebirth.

I have no fear of losing control. No worry over who will catch me when I fall. Essie and I fly together.

ONE YEAR LATER

CHAPTER FIFTY-NINE

Devon Mason

"You're such a dad." Taryn teases me about the three five-month-old rugrats I'm managing to hold at one time. "I don't know how you do it."

The sixteen-year-old girl is petrified of the babies, but she's hanging out with me for a reason. "They're less rowdy company than the yard full of partygoers."

"Oh, Gawd! Don't I know it?" Taryn's calmed some in the past year. I was so hyper-focused on helping the girl, I didn't realize she didn't need what I had to offer.

A few months ago, Taryn reluctantly came into Primp, wanting a professional dye-job. She left with a new confidence and a mentor. Taryn and I are still close, but she's Essie's purple-haired progeny now. Since Essie understands how to deal with me, and she's a girly girl, she had the patience to help Taryn be the best version of herself.

"This is the introvert section." Rae smirks up at me, tugging at the edge of the hammock to make me and the babies swing. Sitting on the grass, Rae and Taryn are leaning on one another, using the hammock to shade them from the judgmental gaze of our family and friends.

Rae needed a real girlfriend, not a sister, aunt, or stepmother. Taryn has brought out a girl in Rae who cares about what she looks like. Not in a vapid, vain way. Before Taryn, my sister wouldn't brush her hair, let alone wash it, wouldn't shower or wear clean clothing. We're not talking Violet and Essie primping, but at least the girls don't look like homeless people.

Rae's a beautiful girl who hides, and she's always surrounded by louder, more attention-seeking family. Taryn's a big girl, and doesn't care what people think of her. She changes her hair color more often than I change shoes. Together, they don't give a shit about anyone else, but at least they don't stink anymore.

There's dividing lines at school, and I see it every day when I walk the halls. Those lines keep kids who would 'get' one another apart. After a few times of Taryn being around, Rae warmed up to her, and they've been inseparable ever since.

"Jesus, the slobber monsters all look like you." Taryn tweaks John's toe, then quickly retreats before he can gnaw on her fingertip. "How do you tell them apart?"

Rae giggles at the growly sound I make from the back of my throat. "I have a son, remember? This child is obviously a girl." I pick up a lean and lanky Penelope by her armpits, and display her like she's Simba. "Notice the red hair and fuzzy eyebrows."

Busting a gut, Rae reaches up to steal her cousin from me. "Who's a pretty girl? You's a pretty girl," is murmured against a sweet-smelling tummy.

"This kid here—" I lift John up, and the kid just looks at me like I've offended him. It's past their bedtime, and they were ready to sleep. "Okay, he does look just like me, but I swear the mammoth beast is my brother." Will protests the loss of his best friend uncle, grabbing at John's feet to pull him back down.

"Yeah, that kid is most definitely *yours*," Taryn teases me, smiling. "You do realize that I work with your wife, right? All summer long I've been with Will at Primp."

"Fair enough. I'm being daft tonight." John and Will settle on my chest, tugging at a ring of key-shaped toys. Down below us, Penelope is being bounced on Rae's thighs.

"I don't get them." Rae is more talkative around me, less around everyone else. We share a sigh, looking out across Dad's lawn.

"They don't get us," I murmur with a sad smile, content to sit the party out with the babies and the less outgoing folks. We get visitors from time to time, but it's pretty dang comfy in this hammock, with a huge maple tree shading us… and a wife who brings me snacks.

This late-summer celebration is a joint endeavor, with Sage hijacking Ozzy's day because it's his birthday and he's leaving for California early in the morning.

Ozzy's leaving us to go to the police academy, but he's not going far. He'll be home every weekend. He saved up and bought himself a motorcycle, like the ones he's drooled over in magazines for the past year. Clover just about had a heart attack, but every family member with a Y chromosome, plus Willow and Violet, got a woody over it.

The party's winding down, with most of the food gone, the birthday cake already cut, and all the presents have been opened by both guys. The usual suspects are playing Ladder Ball, and I can hear Ren whining about his suckage from here.

A few of the guests broke out some beer and mixed drinks after the sun went down. They kept casting leery glances in my direction, but I'm good. The people who truly know me, they're drinking out in the open. My fellow officers, Dad, Auggie, and Robin, and a few of the women too.

A year ago, I couldn't have handled it, but now I have no desire for alcohol whatsoever. But I'd be lying if I didn't admit it's been a struggle, where I've come close to using but pulled myself back from the brink.

I've had three noticeable episodes this year, one manic and two of the darkness, which is okay for someone like me. Meds are not a cure. Being in recovery is not a cure. Being tempted is not a failure. We need weakness to reveal our strengths.

I'm stronger and healthier, because I've struggled, fought the battle, and won. I may lose a battle here or there, but that doesn't mean the war is over.

There are people out there who judge adversity, see us as less. But if I hadn't been shrouded in darkness, I wouldn't recognize and appreciate the light. If I hadn't struggled and pushed through it, I wouldn't know what real pride was.

There's no shame in living life on your own terms.

A trio of slightly lit mommas come toddling our way. If I ever hear my stepmother, aunt, and wife argue the validity of pump-and-dump again, it'll be too soon. It was the great debate of the party setup, where they tried to use me as an excuse to avoid wine to end their argument.

"Feeling good?" I tease. "You all look hella floaty."

"Miss that, dontcha?" Isis teases me, words slurring as she tries to fetch her baby from Rae.

"Nope," I pop the P on the word, completely relaxed and happy. "I've found other ways to get high." Essie giggles, but not because of the single glass of wine she had an hour ago.

"Auggie!" Taryn's big mouth shouts the word Rae wanted to say but was too timid to say it. It's like my sister is using her best friend as a puppet. I almost want to see if Rae's hand is lodged in Taryn's ass. They share one mind. "Your wife is too drunk– come git your kid!"

"I'm not too drunk." Clover had a few, but is still sober, so no one calls Dad to help. "How's my baby boy?" Kisses are given as hands scoop the heavy, sleeping weight off my chest. "Nighty night to my grandson too."

"Ready?" I move to sit up, passing Will off to Essie, but she presses me back down with a palm to my forehead.

"Hang out with your dad and brother– you haven't seen them all night." Essie leans down to peck a quick kiss to my lips, then snuggles our sleepy son to her chest.

"Singular– where the fuck are the others?"

Robin ambles up, interrupting. "Give me my baby." Penelope is in his arms, tucked in nice and tight, and fast asleep in a nanosecond, and I feel slightly jealous because I know how good and safe that feels. "Auggie will come home once a Ladder Ball champion has been crowned. Boring-ass game."

Holding Penelope in one arm, Rob presents Isis the other, and she scoots up to his side as they make their way across the street to the Spook House.

"You girls be good," Clover warns Rae and Taryn, passes kisses around to each and every one of us, then she sneaks inside to go to bed.

"Sleepover!" Rae jumps up, happy that since Clover left, that means she's allowed to scamper off too. "We'll be at Taryn's if anyone cares."

"I care," both Essie and I say in unison, which earns us a kiss from both girls. "Behave!"

"Not my dad!" Rae shouts back as the girls giggle and run like idiots across the lawn. Flipping around, they both shout, "Love you too!"

"Teenage girls, so glad we had a boy." Leaning up, I nibble at Will's tiny toes, and the fella kicks me in the forehead, peeved I'm trying to wake him up so he won't wake me later. "You're gonna be a naughty, naughty boy, I just know it."

"You have no idea how fucking adorable you are, do you?" Essie smiles down at me with an expression of utter devotion. My zealot of a wife.

"I know Will is," I tease. "We made him, so of course he's perfect."

"Ha-ha!"

"Why haven't you answered where all my siblings are? I can see Willow and Ren. Rae just scampered off, and John is cuddling with Clover. Where's Ozzy? It's his party for shit's sake. Where's Violet? Where's Seth?"

"Seth's at a friend's house. Weston disappeared with the birthday boy. When Ginny and Opal noticed, they hightailed it out of here like their asses were on fire."

"NO!" I'm horrified yet happy for my brother.

"Yes– motherfuck."

"Sage is eighteen as of today. West is still fifteen."

"Sums up why Ginny and Opal disappeared and Willow's been distracting Malcolm so he doesn't notice." Whispering like it's a secret, "I didn't want to say this in front of Rae, dummy. But Ozzy took Violet out for a ride on his new motorcycle. They've been gone for over an hour."

"Ooohhh… shit. There's something going on there, isn't there?"

"Hope not," Essie grumps. "Probably. I don't know. They both swear there isn't, but it looks like there could be… eventually. Sticky situation."

"I'm guessing there's a reason you're telling me to stick around to hang with Dad and Ren?"

"Yeah, eventually someone's going to notice Weston is missing, or he's going to come home, and shit will hit the fan. Ren's still skeevy about West being gay, you know that. Plus, I'd like you to imprint every detail of Ozzy and Violet when they get home. You know how much I love gossip."

"I love you so goddamn much." Eyes shining with pride, I'm so thankful every day when I wake that Essie's my wife, no matter how snoopy she can be.

"I love you more." I get a big, sloppy kiss for my sappiness. "We love him best." And then a real kiss from my wife. "I'll see you at home– every detail. Don't forget."

"Gossip!" I shout at Essie as she totes Will across the neighbor's backyard with ours as her destination.

Now that we don't have fifty people milling around, I flop out of the hammock and make my way over to the Ladder Ball tournament. Willow and Colin are playing against Dad and Auggie, with Ren as their disgruntled cheerleader. We have a Ladder Ball set in our backyard too, but only so Ren can practice… it's not helping.

"Dammit!" Auggie's shoulders slump when he misses. "Sorry, Malcolm." It probably doesn't help that it's now dark, and the light from the backdoor isn't illuminating much. They've been playing for hours, ignoring everything and everyone else.

"Woot!" Willow cheers, ponytail bouncing as she gives Colin a high-five. "Mr. Kline is getting rusty in his old age."

"Monster," Auggie growls as he tosses the bolo. "Eat that, little girl. Three points."

"I'll show you up." Willow sounds so haughty, we all laugh. No one calls her on it, because she does show her Mr. Kline up, making it nearly impossible for Auggie and Dad to win. She receives a slap to the ass from Ren and a high-five from Colin.

"I feel like our ref isn't being impartial." Dad glowers at his middle son. "Where is everyone?"

Chuckling, all I can do is shake my head to and fro. "Engrossed in the game, much? We're the only ones left."

"Did Isis and Rob go home?" In answer, I give a tilt of my chin to Auggie.

"Where's the party hosts?" Dad's eyes miss nothing now that he's alert.

"Shit," I hiss underneath my breath. "AWOL. Ozzy and Violet took off for a ride… and Wessie disappeared with the birthday boy," I mutter more and more faintly as I speak.

"Game over!" Dad announces. "You stuck around to wait 'em out?"

"Yup." … and to keep Dad from losing his shit.

"I want nothing to do with this." Auggie learned his lesson, and no longer sticks his nose where it doesn't belong. "I'll see you folks later– headed home."

"I'll follow." Colin pats Auggie on the back, then squeezes his shoulder. "You played good, but no one can beat Willow."

"Which is why she's always your partner," Auggie mutters back begrudgingly.

"We're the dream team of Ladder Ball." With a few back pats to the rest of us, and another high-five to his teammate, Colin and Auggie leave just us Masons alone.

"I'll take the hammock!" Willow bounds off, giving us some privacy. "This way they can't sneak in the backdoor."

Dopey-eyed Ren follows Willow like a dang tail, tackling her before she gets to the hammock. Which is Dad's and my cue to hightail it to the front. "Not gonna watch them make-out again today."

"Everyday occurrence?" Dad taunts me as we plunk our asses on the steps to the front porch. The kids can't get by us without stepping on us.

"Not really, thank heavens," I mutter dramatically. "They're easy to live with, most of the time."

"Do you think…" Dad pauses, turning his head away so I can't read his expression. "Do you think Weston is breaking the law right now? Ozzy?"

I tell one truth and a lie. "Weston? Yeah. Ozzy is too much like you." I chuckle as Dad flinches. "I don't mean trying to propagate the planet. Loyal and ethical." Not that having sex makes Ozzy disloyal and unethical, but we're not going there with Dad.

"Thank God." Dad slumps forward, resting his elbows on his knees. Ozzy breaking his trust is worse than Weston doing it, because we've been keeping Weston and Sage apart for almost two years. Ozzy and Violet would be a double-whammy.

We've gotten a lot of our shit aired out. My last dark period was directed at Dad, and I'm ashamed to say I freaked out at work on him. We're closer than I ever thought possible. I've forgiven him, even if I didn't truly blame him. But there are still things no man should ever share with his father.

"Spanky's staking out the backdoor." Kieren's blond head glows in the streetlamps, shiny white teeth flashing bright as he turns feral. "I'm going to murder Sage."

"No, you're not," West's voice flows from the darkness. If it wasn't so bizarre, it would be comical, how my brothers look just alike, but one looks spooked and the other despondent. "Sage already left."

"You okay?" I hop up from the stoop, pointing to the kid to plant his ass next to Dad. Weston does as he's told, knowing better than to fuck with me.

I'm shocked at how Dad's acting, angry but more disappointed. "Sage broke the law."

West flips around to glare at Dad. "I've been sneaking into Sage's bedroom for years, begging him. Always saying please and getting a no." Now my baby brother can't hide how dang cocky he feels. "I didn't get a no tonight."

"My comment was about you, not Sage." Disappointment bleeds from Dad, causing three of his sons to cower back. Ozzy should but won't be getting it when he comes home, Seth is too crafty to ever feel the shame, and John's a baby. But Ren, West, and me, we know this feeling well. Ren and I are feeling sympathetic to Weston's plight right now.

"You force my hand, knowing exactly what I'll have to do to your boyfriend, because you're selfish, Weston. I didn't raise you to be that way, only thinking of yourself, not Sage's future. It's not sneaky. It's not badass. It's disappointing that you'd beg Sage, feel entitled to something you shouldn't have, and force him to break the law. I blame *you*."

Ren and I wince in unison, because that was a rough comment, but it doesn't faze our little brother. "You're too late. Aunt Ginny and Opal walked in on us after we were done. They loaded the car while we said goodbye." The cockiness is replaced with tears. "They took off for an airport hotel, and Sage will be gone by early morning."

"Good." Dad's voice is filled with compassion. "I would've been forced to arrest him if this got out. But since he's gone, no one will be the wiser. Our family can't be above the law. I know you'll miss Sage– we *all* will. But what you did was wrong, and there will be consequences."

"Go ahead and ground me." Weston slumps forward, posture mimicking Dad's. "Maddox is gone. Sage is gone. The other gay kids are babies. I'm getting the fuck out of here as quickly as I can."

"You don't get it." Dad pulls Weston under his arm, comforting his son while punishing him. "You knew better, yet you preyed on Sage, and made him look like the predator. People do this every day, and I have to arrest otherwise innocent people while the snotty kid acts like a victim. I know you're mentally capable of consenting, especially physically, but the law says otherwise. Eighteen or not, maybe Sage wasn't mentally or emotionally ready to consent."

Ren's face is twisted with revulsion, no doubt thinking of things I wished he'd forget. "Kid, you better have been the one to top."

"Ren!" Dad and I shout in unison, both of us sick for West, but only me knowing why Ren says the homophobic shit he does.

"I'm a man now." West's lips curl up at the corners, trying his damnedest not to look too cocky with Dad's arm wrapped around his shoulders– Dad might act on wanting to strangle him. "It was fucking mind-blowing."

Creeped out, Dad drops his arm and moves a few inches away from Weston.

Losing it, Ren charges forward, seething. "I can't believe you let Sage fuck you! Did it hurt?" Towering over our seated brother. "Hmm… did it?"

"Whoa…" Lunging forward, I press my palm to Ren's chest, pushing him away from Weston's orbit. "Process before you speak, bro. Process."

Weston jumps up, enraged because he doesn't understand why Ren is attacking him. "I'm six-four to Sage's five-five, what do you think?"

Pushing at my palm, Ren tries to get at Weston, while Dad holds the boy back. "Sage has a tiny dick, and you've got a huge asshole."

"Shut the fuck up, Ren!" I try to snap him out of this fear-induced rage. "You okay?" I turn to Weston, only to find Dad losing his shit.

"You *are* staying here and finishing school, goddamnit! No running after Sage."

Several battles are waging at once, and I'm the idiot caught in the crossfire. Ren is fighting what Alejandro did to me, terrified for Weston to the point he's lashing out. Now Dad and Weston go for the other's throat.

"I tried to get Sage to stay with me!" Weston's voice warbles, tears steaking down his cheeks. "I tried to go with him, but he pushed me away. It took Aunt Ginny *and* Opal to tear me off him."

"Shit." Ren deflates in the face of Weston's pain, landing his big ass in the grass.

"What do you think?" Weston gestures wildly to his face. "Do I look okay to you?"

"I'd kill him. I'd arrest him. But right now, I want to find Sage just to give him to you." Dad pulls West back to the step, then smoothers the kid. "I never want to see that lost expression on your face again. You look just like I did when I lost your mother."

"It was goodbye, dammit!" Words strained because Weston isn't yelling, he falls exhausted against Dad's shoulder. "He's never coming back!"

"Did you tell Sage you were in love with him?" Keeping my voice level, I try to move this from negative emotions.

Weston's, "Yeah," causes Ren to hiss in pain.

"Did he say it back?" I coax, relieved to hear the sound of a Harley growling in the distance. Yet another shit-fest brewing on the horizon.

"No– he left. I was walking home, and he called me from the car. All he said was *I'll love you forever*. Then Sage hung up on me."

"You're the one who fucked him, right?" Broken record Ren mutters as Ozzy crawls to a stop out front. "How long were they gone?"

"Long enough," I murmur inaudibly. "More than two hours, maybe three."

"During his own party?" Ren looks confused, which is fucking hilarious under the circumstances.

Violet pulls a helmet off her head, then slips off the bike from behind Ozzy. After smoothing her dress down, she walks up to us with a vague expression on her face. Both look like innocent kids after a long drive.

Ozzy's a few feet behind Violet when they pass. My nose wrinkles with the stench. "Have a good time?" I try for light, because what was going down here is none of their business. It's only Weston's business. But we're Masons, so we made it ours. What Ozzy and Violet were doing is none of our business either.

"That bike is awesome." Violet's eyes twinkle, like she's making fun of us somehow. "See you guys in the morning." She leans down to kiss Dad's cheek, then scoots around Weston, who shudders as she passes.

"You have no idea how much I appreciated the party." As always, Ozzy is as smooth as glass, voice soothing and honest. "I never thought I'd feel like this, like I had a family, after my grandma died." The guy has a blush working its way up the back of his neck, and I can see the edges of a suck mark near his collar.

Dad falls for it, turning mushy, glowing his dad look, happily accepting a big hug from Ozzy. The kid slips inside after Violet. His words were genuine, the absolute truth, but used as a manipulative trick I perfected.

Mad props to Oliver Zypher.

"He's a good kid." Ren murmurs dreamily, like he has a bro-crush on the dude.

"You guys are so fucking deluded!" Weston blows up, but doesn't leave the step. I try my damnedest to have a silent conversation with my baby brother, but he ignores me. "They stunk like sex."

"How do you know what straight sex smells like?" Ren twists up his face in a grimace.

"No, they didn't." Dad *is* deluded.

"You have allergies." West pokes at Dad's chest, then points at Ren and me. "You bastards used to smell like yourselves, now you always stink like sex. Dev, back my ass up– I saw your nose wrinkle."

Ren and I share a masculine laugh that has Dad's eyes narrowing in suspicion and Weston getting enraged again. Can't wait until his testosterone levels out, but it's helping his game.

"Ozzy wouldn't do that." Dad looks inward, mind scrolling through past memories. "Violet is a good girl. She doesn't give a shit about boys yet. Ozzy is very dedicated to going to the academy."

"You were dedicated too, but Devon was in Mom's belly when you left for the academy... Or maybe Violet was telling everyone she didn't want to date yet, because she already had a boyfriend at home," Weston stresses, completely ignoring the conversation I'm trying to have with my eyes.

Violet is a girl– let her lose her virginity without it being a family affair, without her being interrogated by a stepfather and a gaggle of stepbrothers. Without Rae trying to kill her. Let Ozzy have something of his own for once.

"Nah." Ren decides Weston's losing it, and Dad slumps in relief. "They're good kids."

Denial.

"For fuck's sake!" Weston slams his curled fist on his thigh out of frustration. "Good kids have sex too! Who wears a dress on a motorcycle ride? Where did they drive to, Vermont? They were gone forever. Why was Violet's hair messed up if she wore a helmet?"

Do you want Violet to go through what you're going through? Shut your goddamn piehole before you destroy Dad's fantasy world. Nobody's hurt by this, so stop!

"You're just trying to get us to lay off you." Ren is inadvertently destroying all the work I'm doing with Weston. "I can't believe you had sex with Sage. You topped, right?"

That distracted our baby brother, and I almost think Ren is doing exactly as I am– protecting Dad from the truth.

"It's not any less gay if you top, asshole," West snarls, getting more and more angry, but at least he's not crying anymore. Better to hate Ren than mourn Sage.

A smirk curls my baby brother's lips, one I never thought I'd see him wear. He's going to terrorize Ren. "I did Sage first. Pinned him to the bed and had my way with him, then I let him make love to me, because I already knew this giant, goddamn body was a bottom."

"Jesus." Ren flinches back as if struck.

Dad and I just look at each other for help, wondering which of us has the tools to put a stop to this.

"Are you okay?" Ren's near tears, looking at Weston in a way I remember he used to employ on me, but now it makes a helluva lot more sense.

"Yeah, what the hell? Why are you so obsessed with this?" Weston and Dad don't miss how Ren's eyes flick toward me. "It's just how I have sex. It's normal."

Dad makes a move to stand, but I hold a hand out to stop him. Ren's on the verge of freaking out like I used to. "It doesn't hurt– it's not how you remember," I admit to get everyone to calm down. "I think Dad and Weston better go inside, figure out what Weston's punishment should be."

"I–" Weston goes to protest.

"You don't need our nightmares," I direct at my baby brother. "And there are some things grown men don't want their father to know," I direct at Dad. "I don't want to know what you've been doing…" I trail off as a hint, even though I do know.

We're only allowed in the Playroom on Thursday nights– the only night our other relatives aren't up there. Kyle babysits the Batcave on Saturday nights, meaning Colin and Dad are up in the attic with Clover. We ignore it, because we'd rather not know. I expect the same, because Dad can see us going into the Spook House on Thursdays, who's with us, how long we're gone, and how we look before and after we come out.

Wish Dad wouldn't sit on the porch and wave as we come out.

Dad remains silent, nodding in understanding as he hauls Weston inside. We can hear Clover at the door, asking what's going on, with John crying in the background. Weston's in for it now. In a way, it's not fair that Ozzy and Violet go free, but it's not the same with how predatory Weston was acting.

"I'm an asshole– I know it." Ren sniffles, looking up at me from the grass. "But I can't help it."

Eyes flicking up, I catch sight of Willow in the distance, looking out of her element. "C'mere, you need to hear this too." Flowing down, I take a seat on the edge of the sidewalk, only a foot between Ren and me. I try to keep my voice level and low, because this is no one else's business. I wait until Willow sits next to Ren, their hands immediately tangling.

Holding my brother's gaze, I pour it all out. "You have my permission to talk to anyone about anything between us, as long as it's to help you. It wasn't fair that you kept it bottled up, refusing to even speak with therapists."

"It belongs to you," is nearly a whine. "I couldn't betray you like that. I refused to even think about it."

"I think… it was probably harder for you to watch because you had no control over it. It was my bargain. That kept me sane during and after, because I made the choice."

"It wasn't a choice," Ren snarls, face warping with rage. "It was rape!"

"It was," I whisper softly, trying to calm Ren down. I ignore how Willow looks horrified. "But it was my choice to be raped–"

"To save me!" Ren pokes himself in the chest, tears streaming down his cheeks. "I feel so goddamn guilty every second of the day. It's why I was your perfect enabler. You could've killed me, and I'd understand. You could've shit on me, and I would've said thank you."

"Did you ask me to save you?" I try the rational route as Ren wigs out. "No, you didn't. I made the choice because I couldn't live with myself if I had to watch that happen to you after watching it with Mom. It was easier to be physically hurt than be powerless to help you."

"Don't I know it?" Ren jabs me in the chest. "You motherfucker. I can't let it go… how you looked."

"I hear your screams in my sleep, so let's not make this a competition," I mutter wryly, chuckling at the ridiculousness. "You need to be able to talk it out. I'll never be past it, because you can't get over something like this. But it's not ruining my life, it's not making me freak out on my gay baby brother."

"What are you doing? Is the therapy helping?" Ren looks so hopeful, it hurts my heart. Dad tried everything with us.

Therapists and therapists and the Playroom. But it's hard to heal when you keep the one thing that has broken you from your therapist. In my case, I didn't remember. It's why I got better after I did, after I let it out.

"My team changed my life," I say with all sincerity. "But being able to talk to Essie has helped the most." I tug Willow's ponytail. "Which is why Willow's sitting here with us now. But, what helped the most is rewriting that happened to me with good experiences."

"You mean with Kurt?" Ren's voice pitches high with fear. "I tried watching guys in the Playroom, but it didn't help me any."

"We're probably different– the situation we were in. Kurt, yes. But I've been going back to the Playroom in private. If you have any questions about what it's like, ask me. I'll be having the same conversation with Weston in the morning."

"You've…" Ren is rendered speechless, while Willow looks at me like I'm a rock star. "I don't want details. I just don't want to say hurtful shit to Weston, or sound like a gigantic ass of a homophobe."

"Tell Willow what happened to you," I blurt out, knowing that will help. "I'll sit here while you do. You'll feel better."

Shoving down the sidewalk a few feet, I give them some space, but I'm close enough to listen in. Ren has perfected looking perfect, to the point he holds it all in. He's got problems, but he won't voice them because they aren't as complex and nightmarish as mine. What happened to me shouldn't lessen the impact of what happened to Ren.

"I don't know…" Ren's words belie his actions as he yanks Willow into his arms, resting his chin on the top of her head. "You know how I used to have sex but not get off."

Snorting, Willow rasps, "No shit, Ren." Which is exactly what he needed to hear. Laughing with her, my brother relaxes.

"I get where West is coming from, how being horny was like a throbbing tooth. After *dates*, I'd jerk off in my truck before I got home. Sometimes I'd play around while we were at school. By the time practice came around, I couldn't take it."

Ren shores up his nerves, giving Willow and me time to stare at one another in perfect understanding. I'd given Essie permission to talk about me to Beth and Willow, because everyone needs to vent. I know Willow knows things Ren doesn't realize.

"I feel stupid that it bugged me so much, that I can't let it go. It's nothing like Devon went through, so I feel like a pussy for it bothering me."

"God, you misogynistic bastard," Willow growls. "Don't ruin this by being demeaning to women." Willow has been out-feminist-ing Beth this past year. "Competition is for sports and games, not horrible experiences."

"Spanky," Ren growls into Willow's ear, the sound too sexual and intimate for me to handle. "So I was jerking off, totally getting into it while in the shower in the locker room. Just as I was about to shoot, the dirty, nasty janitor grabbed my dick and kept pumping. I couldn't stop coming because I'd already started. I was screaming, batting at him. Coach ran in. It was even more humiliating when I had to tell Dad, the school, and a judge."

"I never heard– they kept it quiet," Willow murmurs. "I'm glad the bastard was punished. God, Ren... I'm glad you told me. Your fears make so much more sense now. We've got to work through this. Together."

"I don't want to talk about this anymore." Ren's words are drowsy, exhausted. Leaning down to whisper in Willow's ear, "I need to be deep inside you right now, show you how much I love you."

Blushing, feeling hella awkward, I jump to my feet. "On that note, it's time to go home." I take off like hellhounds are nipping at my heels. With Ren riding the high of sharing emotional torture with his partner, and an equally embarrassed Willow.

We may share a house, but we keep sex private. Randomly I'll catch them kissing, but that's okay. Our walls are thin, and we've all learned how to get off as quietly as possible. So it shows how *off* Ren feels right now that he'd say what he's saying.

A constant dialogue of sexual exploits is being whispered in Willow's ear behind me. I'm not going to lie, I'm hoping my son is down for the night, because I need to connect with my wife after this never-ending therapy session from hell.

Healing hurts, so we're all better off tonight than we were this morning...

CHAPTER SIXTY

Willow Prynne

"Oh, my God!" Ren tosses me on the bed, my ass bouncing on the mattress. "What has gotten into you?" In awe, I stare up at Ren and he stares down at me as if he's never seen me before now. Face flush, blue eyes bright, blond hair sticking out in every direction, Ren looks on the verge of losing it.

I tried to act surprised for both Devon and Kieren as they spoke about things that happened in the past, but Essie already beat them to it. Essie and I will never be how we used to be, but I think that's a good thing. We're closer in a more adult sort of friendship. Dealing with the Mason boys hasn't been easy, and we've needed each other as an ally.

All my life, I've said my cousin felt more like a sister, and now she truly is– my sister-in-law. I see Devon as my brother now, not only because he's my stepbrother, so I understand the toll he takes on Essie's emotions. I feel a bit bad that Ren didn't get to share his private moments with me, but Essie needed to vent to stay sane. A person can only hold so many secrets, and the pressure was getting to Essie.

"You look hungry," flows sluggishly from between my parted lips as I gaze up at Ren. I've never seen him look at me like this before, and it's making me squirm. In a good way. "Starved."

Emotions pour out of Ren in a rush like a wildfire eating everything in its path. He and I have always kept this wall up between us, emotionally speaking. Ren does all the right things, says what I want to hear, is supportive in the extreme, and always caters to my needs, but there's been something superficial about it. We both meet all the other's needs, but it's like we're just going through the motions.

Insecurities aside, I know Kieren loves and wants me, but it's been frustrating how he hasn't connected with me on a level

I see in others. I won't lie, the bond Essie and Devon share makes me jealous– I want it. I want it with Ren.

Petrified, I realize Kieren's finally giving me what I want.

"Are you tense?" More like *intense*. "Do you need a massage?"

Staring down at me unblinking, I shudder from the intensity of Ren's eyes boring into my flesh. From one breath to the next, he's on me, covering me with his body, mouth fused to mine. In shock, I realize he's whispering three little words over and over again as he kisses me, mouth trailing down the side of my neck while his nose nuzzles at my ear.

For the past year and a half, Kieren and I have shared the words. *I love how you make me feel. I love playing with you, talking with you, being with you. I love how you're a pain in the ass, douche-noodle. I love how you frustrate the piss outta me, Spanky.* In a mix of sarcasm and intensity, the words are either insulting or playful, but we never say I love you without something added to deaden the emotion behind the words.

Mind stunned, body reacting to how Ren is touching me, I can't believe my ears as he continuously murmurs *I love you* over and over again against my skin. The emotions aren't deadened as he explains why he loves me. If anything, they're intensified.

"You make me laugh when I'm sad." A kiss is peppered to my eyelid. "You always anticipate what I need before even I do." Sly hands creep up beneath my t-shirt. "*Gawd*, your little tits are perfect."

"Ungh!" is a grunt torn from me as Kieren's mouth latches onto my bare breast, tongue lapping at my nipple. Wiggling around on the mattress, I can literally feel my pussy dampening my panties. Never has Ren unhinged like this, losing all control.

"Telling you what I just did..." Ren's hot breath skates across my saliva-slickened flesh, dampening it in a cooling rush. "Dev and I fought for a long time because I told Essie about what happened to us. When it came time to tell you, he bowed out for me, knowing it would connect us. But I've always held back from everyone, because it wasn't my secret to tell."

"Oh, Ren." The compassion in my voice has my breath hitching in my throat. Ren's touch goes from lust-filled hotness to loving affection. "None of it was your fault– you need to talk about it. I'll understand if that person isn't me, but you have to let it out."

Head popping up, Ren looks down at me while straddling my thighs. "I want to share it with you, Spanky. Don't you see? I had a hard time not letting it all out. It was a struggle, and I know you felt it too."

"I did," I murmur, hands flowing up and down Kieren's forearms as he rises above me. "I know everyone thinks I'm a judgmental, little cunt, but I'm not. There's absolutely nothing you could say to me that would make me think less of you. Make me think more of you? Probably."

"I feel so close to you right now." Ren lifts himself up off of me, then attacks my jeans, fingers plucking the button then sliding down the zipper. The metal-on-metal grating sound causes a shiver to work its way down my spine. "I have this insane need to be inside you, like it will feel better than anything."

"Dev is always saying we've been doing it wrong," I murmur wryly. It usually pisses Ren off and makes Essie bay like a lunatic.

"Maybe our brother was right." Ren shocks the piss out of me as my jeans fly through the air to smack against the wall. "Maybe we better find out." Bending slightly, Ren wraps a hand around my ankle, lifting my leg, then he begins placing sucking kisses against my calf.

"Christ!" Neck arching, my eyes roll back into my head. Ren and I play in bed, but this feels different. Intense. Raw. Real. Like a forever whispered alongside the words *I love you* being placed on my flesh by Ren's damp mouth. "Oh, fuck!" Muscles locking up, my pussy clenches. I'm so wet, I can smell my own arousal.

Flowing back down to the mattress, Ren stares up at me with eyes gone feral. "I need to be inside you." But he makes no move to do just that. Sucking at my inner thigh, Ren's fingers flutter against my slit, parting my lips, then spearing me. "Yes... inside," is an intoxicated whisper.

Turning his fingers, tips brushing my g-spot, Ren finger-fucks me to the point of insanity. Writhing on the mattress, gushing words of affection, I turn into a creature I don't recognize. I left Willow the Wayward long behind. I'm no longer a good girl. I'm most definitely *not* Mr. Kline's monster. I don't turn into someone Kieren Mason owns, either.

Using the strength honed from years of fighting Violent Violet, I flip Ren over onto his back before he even gets a chance to protest. Straddling his hips, I impale myself on his rigid cock, shouting a harsh sound of elation to the ceiling.

In this moment, I realize I'm finally a woman. Not because I was waiting to grow tits, or have a job, or own major things, but because I finally know who I am inside and out. I don't belong to my father, my mother, to Clover, to Auggie, and I will never belong to Ren.

I finally understand what Kieren was trying to say to me for the past year and a half. It's not jealousy. It's not insecurity. To be someone's partner, there is no ownership– we're equals.

"This is what you needed." Eyelids shuttered, I gaze down at a shocked Kieren. "Someday you're going to realize I like those huge balls you have– I want you to just take what you want. You don't need permission. If I don't want it, I'll just knee you in the balls like forever ago in the hallway at Rush."

Even when we play, Ren is always so reserved, holding back the intensity of his need. Part of it is what happened at Rush between us, that ambiguous gray area that looked a helluva lot like attempted date-rape. But I know it stems from what happened to Devon, then what happened to Ren in the locker room by the janitor. I don't want a boyfriend who holds himself back from me. I need Kieren to unleash who he truly is.

"You wanted it then." Chuckling, Ren unfreezes, hands landing on my hips. Fingernails biting into my flesh, he thrusts upward into me, causing a violent shudder to roll through my body.

"Oh, I certainly did, Stud– *I certainly did.*" Leaning forward, Ren's dick almost sliding out of me, I whisper against his lips. "I want Date-Rape back, Stud. I liked that handsy fucker who was insane with lust over me." Thrusting slowly, lips never leaving his. "I won't say no– *ever.*"

Whimpering, Kieren looks on the verge of bawling, and I realize I've finally said exactly what he's always needed to hear. I've absolved whatever guilt he's been carrying, a guilt I didn't even realize he felt.

"I don't ever want to make anyone ever feel like that," he whispers, eyes turning glassy. "I was terrified for Dev, but I didn't realize until it happened to me how it truly felt. But what happened to me was nothing compared to what happened to my brother... then, when Auggie started that date-rape smear campaign, it killed me to think I made you feel that way too."

"No!" I cry, hand lashing out to grab a hank of blond hair. "*Never*. It was exciting. It was naughty and forbidden. I wanted you so fucking much, Ren, and I'm so goddamn sorry for everything negative that has ever happened between us. So sorry."

We've had a power struggle, Ren and I, trying to figure out how we fit in each other's lives. Everyone we know, one half of the partnership is the alpha and the other the beta. But we're not like that. As Ren stares up at me in awe, fingers flexing on my hips as he tries his damnedest not to thrust, I realize we need to stop modeling *our* relationship after everyone else's.

"You can top me when I'm good and ready," I warn I'm not giving my position away until I'm satisfied. This is one of the positions we don't use often because of the implications of who's in control. I understand how Ren's need to be in control stems from his past, but maybe it's time he dealt with it.

"*Top*," Kieren breathes, nearly silent. He shudders, and not in a good way, giving me a light bulb moment.

Sliding off his cock, I wiggle down the mattress near his feet. "You don't have to do that!" he protests, trying to push me off as my mouth descends. "You're on my dick."

"I don't care." Scrunching my eyebrows together, I gaze up at him, silently laughing. "You eat my pussy all the time, so why should it bother me to suck it off your dick?"

"Yeah, but…" Warring with himself, Ren just looks at me. "I won't kiss you after you suck me off."

"Maybe you should," I murmur underneath my breath, then I cover his dick with my lips, hardness slipping inside until the tip presses against the back of my throat. Working him into a frenzy, I don't mind the taste of me. I made it, so why is it gross? We're too hard on ourselves, and this is coming from an insecure freak.

Sucking Ren's cock, I slowly wedge his legs open farther, using my hips to make more room. Lost in the feel of my mouth sliding over his flesh, my tongue swirling around his head, and my teeth adding a slight edge of pain, I pray to God Ren doesn't kill me over what I do next.

High with the need to get off, Ren doesn't protest as I start sucking and lapping at his huge ball sack, going lower and lower with each pass. Setting my teeth into his taint, I bite down a little, causing Ren to arc off the mattress with a bellowed shout.

Chuckling, no doubt the movement vibrates against his flesh, I wonder what our housemates think of ever-silent Ren screaming in ecstasy. Getting braver, my insane version of therapy is to dart my tongue for a quick taste of Ren's pucker.

Moaning in pleasure, freaking the fuck out on me, large ball-catchers try to shove my head away. "What are you doing?" comes slurred from his parted lips.

"Relax." One hand stroking his harder-than-I've-ever-seen-it cock, while the other pets his thigh, I try to soothe him while arousing him to distraction. "You don't have to like it. We won't do it again, if you don't. We will, if you do. But I'm not going to allow you to freak out on Weston and every gay and bi guy for the rest of your life. Let me prove it isn't the end of the world– it doesn't hurt to have your ass played with."

"You don't have a cock," Ren says matter-of-factly between clenched teeth. His body is locked up tight, but his cock is jerking in my grip. "I don't see how this will help."

"Humor me." Rolling my eyes, I make sure he can see it. "This won't kill you. Just relax, and it will be over in a few minutes."

"So romantic," Ren mutters begrudgingly, but his body is telling a different story. "Whatever…" Legs falling apart, he closes his eyes nice and tight, like he's preparing for misery and terror.

I'm not a sadist. No way in hell am I going to shove my fingers into Ren's ass– we don't have any lube. I'd like to pretend this is my idea, but it was actually Essie's.

Bringing Ren back to the brink, I give him the blowjob of a lifetime, sucking his dick and balls and adding teeth to his taint. Saliva drips down my chin, speckling my tits, and I use it to pave the way of my stroking hand. The way Ren writhes against the mattress, his huge body knocking all the pillows and blankets to the floor, he forgets there is more coming.

I was a bit grossed out when Essie described how to rim an asshole. In theory, it sounds absolutely disgusting, but I'd do anything to make Ren better. In actuality, the way Ren reacts has me on the verge of coming. So aroused, I'm scissoring my thighs together, trying to rub at my own pussy.

Yeah, we both like it, and now I'm curious to see if I'd like it performed on me too.

Jerking him off as a distraction, I tongue his ass, surprised at the mewing sound he makes. After a few minutes of rimming him, realizing he's plateaued and won't ever come from it, I switch tactics.

Mouth engulfing Ren's dick to the point I'm nearly deep-throating him, I swirl two fingertips around his pucker, with no intention of breeching him. I don't want to traumatize him, because no doubt his virgin ass would burn if I tried for more. I just want to show Ren how it is supposed to feel good when not taken against someone's will.

Moaning and grunting, Ren's hips jerk up, shoving his dick down my throat farther than I wanted it to go. Choking, I pull off, gasping for breath. Lost in the act of struggling to breathe, I find myself pitched forward on the mattress, then flipped over onto my back.

Ren immediately covers my body with his, slipping inside. I'm so wet, there's no need to adjust to his size, when that was a fear I had when I was younger. Auggie made me feel like I was inadequate. Ren has a good sized cock, and we match up perfectly. I'm not inadequate– I'm perfect for Ren.

"Admit you liked that," I murmur wryly, chuckling. "Next time we sixty-nine, we need to do that to each other."

Kieren's reply is a feverish kiss, shocking me senseless. We've pitched our boundaries tonight. Ren has always refused to kiss me after I sucked him, even if I didn't get him off. As we slowly rock together, Ren kisses me with intensity, even though I not only sucked his dick, I rimmed his ass too.

Face pressed against the side of my throat, Ren's hands slip beneath my ass, holding me up for leverage. Head passing over my spot, pelvis grinding into my clit, the angle is sharper, forcing a cry to release from my throat. I don't even care that it's echoing through the house.

"I liked it," is whispered against my neck like a secret. "We'll do it again for round-two."

I respond in the only way I know how, saying it for the first time with no buts and no added sarcasm to lessen the emotion. "I love you."

Stilling, Ren gazes down in me in wonder. I fall back to the mattress as his hands leave my ass to cup my face. Affection, adoration, and love shine down at me with force enough to catch the breath in my lungs.

"I love you too, Willow." Staring at me unflinchingly, Ren allows his true emotions to warp his expression. "I love you so goddamn much, I'm thankful every single day I wake up that I have you in my arms."

Choking on a sob, I experience the real Kieren Mason for the first time ever. He unleashes the hold he had on himself, he tears down the barriers, and he shows me what he's made of.

The sex is no longer play. No longer a way to distance ourselves as we giggle during doggie-style, or tease each other over the gross sounds our bodies make. The play is no longer about getting off.

No doubt we will play in the future, but when you love someone, you should be able to open yourself up to trust them enough to make love to each other.

This doesn't feel like an act between teenagers anymore–we've matured.

We prove Devon right. We've been doing it wrong all along.

CHAPTER SIXTY-ONE

Devon Mason

Lying on my belly, resting my head in my palm, I find my wife and son the most fascinating beings on the planet. I could watch them for hours. It's a good thing it's a Sunday, because I have nowhere to go, nowhere else I'd rather be.

No work, or group sessions, or therapy sessions, or getting poked and prodded by my doctor. No family obligations or demands, outside of the tiny family Essie and I've created.

My belly rumbles, but I ignore it.

"Are you hungry too?" Essie giggles softly, barely a breath of a sound, but it hits me with the force of a hammer to the skull. "Hmm? This little fella is always starving in the morning." With two fingers near her areola, she adjusts her breast so her nipple is seated in Will's mouth better. "One of these days, he's gonna drain me dry."

Pretending to eat my son's leg, I make hungry, growly noises as I flow up to the head of the bed. "Little piggy ought to share Mommy with Daddy." Running my nose along Essie's cheek, I rest my chin on her shoulder, and stare down into my son's blue eyes.

"These milk bags belong to Will," Essie stresses, as she does every time I find her breastfeeding.

"I remember a time, long, long ago... when you hated your breasts." Nuzzling at the one not in use, it takes everything in me not to take a tasty bite. "They've always been one of my favorite things in the whole wide world, now you have to appreciate them too."

"Hardee-har-har," Essie mock laughs, still stinging over being bullied because of the size of her tits. The word *whore* never fails to elicit a visceral response in my wife. The sensation of being gutted alive overpowers me, then I realize those horrific acts were done by a different man. I'm not that Devon anymore.

"Hey, little guy," I whisper into Will's ear while he feeds. "I play with your toys at night while you're sleeping. Mm-hmm, I do." Nuzzling at *my* boob, "See this suck mark right here, Daddy gave that to Mommy last night. She liked it lots."

"You are so fucking disturbed," Essie drawls, but she's grinning down at me. "It's a miracle we got any sleep last night."

I'd love to take credit for keeping Essie awake, but between my meds and stress, I usually only have one pop in me. We do have sex every night, and sometimes it's just spooning with me inside her while we fall asleep, because we're that exhausted.

Because of Will, we spend more time cuddling and massaging each other, without the stress of performing weighing us down. Every two weeks, Clover watches Will while we go to *therapy* in the attic. But that's not the same thing. There aren't any all-night sex-fests on the horizon for us until Will's finally sleeping through the night.

Last night was an exception to the rule, but I still didn't have much lasting power to keep my wife awake all night. My brother, on the other hand, he seems to be a rock star in the sack. Ordinarily they're so quiet, I never know they were having fun until I see their idiotic, dopey expressions at breakfast. Last night...

"I've never heard them like that." Wide-eyed, Essie's biting back laughter. "I thought they were going to wake the baby."

"Me too," I mutter in awe. "That was definitely a first, and I tried my damnedest to sleep through it."

"You woke me up twice last night for sex." Essie's voice isn't nearly as smug as her expression.

"We had live-action porn playing on the other side of this wall." Hitching my head back, I stare at the wall separating us from Willow and Ren's bedroom, as if I can see them snoring in their beds through it. "No man could listen to that and not be horny... I even impressed myself."

"You lasted thirty seconds–"

"The first time," I banter. "It's more than we've been having, so I ought to make them a thank you breakfast."

"You ought to make *me* a thank you breakfast," Essie banters back.

Leaning forward, I cup my wife's cheek. "I do. Every. Single. Day." Our kiss gets interrupted by an impressive upper-cut to the chin. "Will's a scrapper. Rawh... rawh... rawh..." I pretend to gnaw on his fist. "I'll go make breakfast, I guess. Let this little fella eat in peace, since he gets territorial when Daddy tries to share."

Acting all put out, I crawl out of our nest, loving how Essie's eyes follow me– devour me as I get dressed. We have no issues with wanting one another, it's just finding the time and energy to put the effort into all the dirty things we want to do.

No one looking at Officer Devon Mason, his pretty wife, and their chubby baby, would think we're capable of the depraved acts we commit up in the Spook House's attic. Even the few Playroomers still in existence don't know what we do up there, not even Robin and Auggie.

Winking, I flash my wife the secret smile we share, and the one she gives back rocks my world to its core. "One thank you breakfast, coming right up, for my loving wife and our dipshit roommates."

"Let's see what Grandma's making special." With Will cuddled in my arms, I bounce him down the sidewalk toward the Pink Taco Hut. "You can fight your uncle over the stuffed Batman Willow bought you guys." Turning up the front walk, I mutter underneath my breath, "Who buys toys for babies to share? Only Aunt Willow."

Will blabbers at me, not making a lick of sense to my adult ears, but he's chattering like he's holding a conversation with his daddy. "I know, right? Why wouldn't she have gotten two of the same toy? Is that so hard to figure out?"

My son replies, slobbering on my shoulder as I let myself into the house. "I don't get it, either. Who buys a little girl a giant Chewbacca and names it Beast. Only Aunt Willow." Will yanks my hair. "I know. I know. Penelope loves it, thinks it's her daddy… I'm just jealous. I wanted one too."

A bunch of nonsense blabbing noises flows from the kitchen as we stride up the hallway. My son starts wiggling in my arms, expressing his demand to get to John. If I don't get him there quick enough, he'll start bawling like a siren.

"Hey." Clover turns to me with a smile, not surprised to see me in the least. She's bellied up to the kitchen stove, as always. "I'm glad you had Will. Now I can hear you approach."

Snickering evilly, I plunk Will's butt next to his uncle in the playpen. "Scaring people is fun." I educate my baby brother and my son. "They hop out of their skin, they do. If you walk really softly, hold your weight just right, you'll be as fluid as a dancer. Then you can scare your parents and siblings when you appear next to them as if by magic."

Clover's laughter is eclipsed by John and Will babbling at each other in their own language. I'd be jealous, but last week they each said their first words in human language. Da and Dev. I was told I spend too much time with the boys. Penelope's first word was no, said to the boys when they wouldn't share Batman with her.

The four-foot tall Chewbacca appeared in the girl's bedroom the next day. Willow's always going to have a devious streak, but combined with her newfound feminism… the boys better watch out.

"Hey!" Violet appears, carrying a stack of bakery boxes. She falls into a chair in the breakfast nook, then begins assembling the boxes. "I take it you're hungry."

Clover's snort sounds so much like Willow, I do a double-take. Even the boys are looking around for her, hoping for presents.

"Will and I made breakfast, then we cleaned the house. Essie's taking a nap, and the dipshits haven't left their bedroom since last night… so I came here."

"Are they starving to death in there?" Clover's cheeks are pinked as she pulls a tray of muffins from the oven. Violet pretends she doesn't understand what we're talking about, which is why I'm here in the first place.

"Nah." I chuckle in remembrance. "Essie nudged their door open and pushed a tray of food in there. A half our later, the tray was pushed back into the hallway."

"Empty." Violet giggles. "If they ever stop having sex, they're going to get really fucking fat."

"Essie and I were wondering how they're taking a piss." Reaching down, I tug a blankie free of John's foot as he tries to drag himself around the playpen. "We figure they're being stealthy and sneaking by us when we're not paying attention. I left, hoping it would draw them out so their room could be aired out."

"Eww." Violet twists up her pixy face, and I swallow what's on the tip of my tongue. I had to smell her stink last night. Talk about disgusting.

I watch Violet and Clover interact for a bit, as they work in tandem to fill bakery boxes with muffins for tomorrow. There's a huge stack of boxes already filled with pies that will be sold at the No-Name Diner. A sheet-cake rests on the kitchen island, ready to be decorated.

I'm in their way, but the kids are occupied and corralled.

"Where is everybody? It's quiet for once."

"Your dad's at work. Seth and Rae are still at their friends' houses, but they'll wander home when they're hungry. Weston's jogging off his rage, after being grounded until he's eighteen. Mom and Dad, Peggy, and the Dobsons are on a bus trip to a casino in Upstate New York. Ozzy's up in the attic, entertaining himself."

"And you want me out of your hair so you can get some work done while it's peaceful," I tease, rubbing the nape of my neck with my palm.

Clover laughs, not even bothering to argue.

"It's too bad I have nowhere to go, or anything to do," Violet grumbles, staring down at her work. "I need outside friends, but I'm not a joiner, and I can't use the excuse of studying because it's summer vacation."

"Your help is invaluable." Clover rubs Violet's back in a soothing gesture, when even last year she would've never reached out and touched her daughter with affection. Dad's rubbing off on her something fierce.

"I'll get out of your hair– I need to talk to Ozzy about the academy before he goes, and I'll catch Weston when he gets back. Then Will and I will go bother someone else."

"You're no bother," Clover finally argues. "You can stay indefinitely if you manage to change Weston's shitty attitude."

"Wish me luck," is my parting remark as I ghost down the hallway toward the staircase. Luck was on my side with everyone out of the house, making it easier for me to have a one-on-one conversation with Ozzy and Weston.

Smirking, I peer down at Ozzy as he plays some racing game on the Xbox. Ren and Willow are way into playing video games in our living room on a ginormous TV that just appeared one day, but I've never developed a taste. I watch Ozzy as he presses the buttons and flawlessly thumbs the sticks.

"Goddamnit!" Ozzy squeaks out, controller slipping out of his hands, and not because I just caused him to drive his car into a barricade. "You are like a fucking Ninja. It's freaky as shit."

Chuckling, I sling myself over the back of the couch to land next to him. "It's a special talent." Ozzy's feathers are never ruffled, even when he does ride-alongs at work, so his reaction is a gift. "Gonna miss you during the week, bud."

"Will they teach me how to be silent like you at the academy?" Ozzy's a quiet, introspective dude, but he becomes chatty if he's interested in a topic. He and I have gotten close over the past year or so, with him spending so much time with me. Essie's been mentoring Taryn, which made me jealous, so I put my focus into mentoring Ozzy instead.

"They beat it into you." My mind rewinds to the past, back to a time where I was lost, but found focus in the discipline. "Stepping lightly can save your life."

"I don't buy it." Ozzy saves his game, turns off the console, then pitches the controller into a nearby chair. "You were born walking that way."

"Not true." A sly grin pulls at my lips, knowing what I have to say will get Ozzy to feel sympathetic toward me. No amount of medication will ever remove my manipulative ways. "My mom was abusive, and she was always sitting on the couch– watching. I learned to walk on air as I snuck past the back of the couch."

"Oh, Dev– I'm so sorry." Ozzy reaches out to pat my shoulder, and I pretend I don't eat it up like candy.

"Eh, it's done and over with. My scars gave me some advantages, like my Ninja skills." My no bullshit stare slips into place, causing Ozzy's body to run taut with tension. "Did you have sex with Violet last night?"

"Shit!" The boy crumples, head landing on his knees, with his arms wrapped around his head like I'm going to beat him. Hating his reaction, I rest my palm between his shoulders, and he flinches before he realizes I'm comforting him. "Would you believe yes *and* no?"

"I'll believe anything as long as it's the truth." My fingers bite into his t-shirt as a silent threat not to lie to me. "I see you as my brother, no different than the rest of 'em. I'm not taking sides, and I'm not telling Dad or Clover. That's how family loyalty works. I'm sure after Willow tears herself out of bed with Ren, she'll be headed to have a talk with Violet."

"I like Violet, even though I shouldn't." Ozzy is gutted by his own admission.

"I know," I murmur in a soothing tone while I rub circles into Ozzy's back. Best way to get someone to open and up and tell you the truth is to be on their side. Good Cop– it's not an act for me. But I can play Bad Cop even better, if I must.

"We didn't have sex– third base." Ozzy shudders, either from fear, lust, or laughter, I can't tell. "Repeatedly." Ah, a mix of all three.

"How long's this been going on?"

"Twice, in the past few months– nothing before then. Violet and I are friends, and I was an idiot."

"Idiot?" That has got to be good. Since the kid still has his balls, I know it wasn't unwelcome attention.

"I'd get turned on when we were sparring– we have lots of common interests." Ozzy's blush burns my hand. "It's mortifying. Violet could tell because we were wrestling around. But she ignored it every time."

"That just happens to guys your age. Don't worry, it wears off, then you're gonna wish you had it back." Chuckling, I think of the difference between how I used to be when I was thirteen versus now, minus my impotency period. I know I'm a bit different than most, and Ren still seems to be operating like he's in puberty. Weston will cry the first time his cock won't get up because he's too exhausted.

"It gets worse, though." Ozzy groans, tugging at his mop of hair.

"Gonna miss your hair, bro. First thing they're going to do is buzz it off to your scalp." I can't help it, I have to muss it up more. "How much worse?"

"We were sparring in the backyard. I rolled Violet to pin her shoulders to the ground, and things lined up…" Ozzy gets quieter and quieter as he rattles the words off. "I popped off as soon as we made contact."

"OH!" Palm pressed to my face, I try to stifle my laughter. "How'd Violet react to that?" Poor bastard.

"She didn't tear my nuts off, so that was good." Ozzy shares a laugh with me at his own expense. "It was worse. I couldn't control it, trying to not make a noise or move, but she just instinctively knew what was happening. Some girl mojo horseshit. She flipped me around while I was distracted, straddled my hips, and didn't stop moving on me until I was done."

"Wow…" falls from my lips, completely floored. "Holy shit."

"Imagine being me in that moment– you have no idea what that was like."

"And last night?" I prompt, feeling like Dad. It's gross for the fact they're my stepsiblings, but no less intriguing. I'm a details kinda of guy. I love having the details, because people are interesting. How they act, react– the facets of their personalities.

I totally had Violet pegged right.

"Never put a girl you have the hots for on a bike, unless you plan on getting laid. I don't want to hurt our family, or my chances at being a cop, so Violet has to be completely off my radar. But I couldn't stop myself from asking her for a drive last night, knowing I was leaving this afternoon. It's why I'm hiding up here right now."

"I get it," and I do. But this is far too entertaining not to have the details. "What happened?"

"Third base. Repeatedly. Instead of sweats and yoga pants, it was a dress and panties with my jeans pushed down to my knees. That's why I said yes and no about having sex. I'd say it was sex, even though there was no in and out action. It was only by the grace of God I didn't slip in, because we were too distracted by how fucking awesome it felt."

"Let me guess, Violet is a baby domme." Suppressing a grin, I always knew she'd be a hellcat. "Violet attacked you this time. Rode you like your Harley?"

"It was like a goddamn bomb went off. Every time I got off, it's like V's claws were sinking into me deeper, but I couldn't stop. I wanted more. She's not even that type of girl. She's independent. She wants nothing from me. But every freakin' time, I wanted more."

"Ah… that's your brain fucking you up, bro. Welcome to my world– I'm the expert on chemicals the brain releases. There's a reason men have one-night-stands and women get clingy. When you get off with another person, endorphins flood your veins. The more you get off together, the worse it gets. Oxytocin is released, making you feel in love. When a boy your age gets around a girl like Violet, they go buy wedding rings. Trust me on that– Essie did the same thing to me, back when I was way too young to understand."

"So, you're saying it's not real?" Ozzy whimpers, looking devastated.

"Oh, it's real." I pat the kid on the back. "Best keep it in your pants until Violet turns eighteen, even longer than that. You going to the academy is the best dang thing that's ever going to happen to you, for more reasons than one."

"I know I have a lot to lose, and we agreed to never go there again."

"Never say never." Laughing, I just keep patting Ozzy on the back, finding the kid's drama entertaining. "You'll fuck up. A lot. Just be happy you're boarding at the academy. When you move back home, get your own apartment, and make sure Violet never visits. Just saying."

"You have *no idea* what it was like." Poor guy shudders.

"I've been there, and you can't blame your idiocy on mental illness like I could. I made a kid while being infected with oxytocin. Most of my decisions were based on tying Essie to me. So keep your dick in your pants. Don't hug. Don't spar. Don't kiss. Don't fool around. Hell, don't laugh together until you're ready. Dopamine. Norepinephrine. Testosterone. Oxytocin. Serotonin. Those chemicals are serious shit– they release when you're around someone you want and love, and they'll wreck your life. They're the best type of high you can find."

Looking up, I pin my kid brother in my stare. I'd heard him enter the attic a few minutes ago. Now he looks spooked and freaked out.

"Join us." I pat the sofa cushion. "How's your two and a half years of grounding treating ya?"

"Day one, and I'm already thinking up escape routes." Weston strides across the attic, balance still shitty with all the growth he's done in the past year. "They took my phone and laptop, then returned them."

"Returned them?" I try to wrap my mind around that as Ozzy jumps up from the sofa like his ass is being burned.

"I gotta– I gotta go take a cold shower." The guy jogs away, hiding his reaction to our conversation. "Especially before I say goodbye to everyone."

"I'd suggest no more than two minutes alone with Miss Violet, just saying."

"Agreed!" flows from the steps as Ozzy jogs down to the second floor.

Acting shady, and that's not how Weston has ever behaved, he refuses to look me in the eye. "My phone is programmed only to call specific phone numbers, all relatives. The data has been cut off. My laptop only has programs for school, with spyware on the internet browser. Everything I look up will go directly to Dad."

"Porn?" I feel bad for the kid, especially one who's wafting an excess of testosterone into the air. "I'm guessing you're being cut off from Sage and Maddox?"

"You came to lecture me too, didn't you?" Weston sighs deeply, falling back to land on the sofa. "I know I was wrong. I get it. I'm paying the ultimate price. So don't twist the knife in deeper. Tomorrow I'm changing my class schedule, so I can graduate sooner. I will not live under house-arrest."

"Hey!" Grabbing my brother, I tug the big guy into my lap, then squeeze the shit out of him. "I love you, kid– and you *are* a good kid." Smothering him like Dad would, I can tell it's making Weston feel better. "I came here to ask how you're doing, not rub it in. No lectures are coming from me."

"Dad and Clover are worried about me, so they're coming down extra hard on me. The guilt is killing me. In a creepy calm voice, Dad kept saying I took advantage of Sage. That if I cared about him, I wouldn't have pressured him. So now all I want to do is call Sage and ask him if he's okay, but I can't. I feel so powerless, like shit. Dad wasn't there last night, but now I question whether or not I assaulted Sage."

"Shit, kid." Sighing, I tug my cellphone out of my back pocket, then get to texting. Weston keeps angsting, oblivious that I'm waiting on a reply. After a few minutes, I wiggle my cellphone in my brother's line of sight, and it's snatched out of my hand in a heartbeat.

Gay Sage: *You're shitting me, right? Can you feel my eyes rolling? Tell Weston every boy who comes after him will have to live up to his expectations, and I doubt they ever will. Tell him to keep his eye on the ball, and don't worry about me. Someday I'll watch him play in a giant stadium with fans screaming his name, and I refuse to stand in his way. I'm hella proud to call Weston Mason my friend. My first everything. Tell him I meant what I said last night.*

With tears streaming down his cheeks, Weston holds onto my cellphone like he can physically feel Sage through the device.

Hugging him, rubbing his arms, I try so very hard not to laugh. I know how he feels, but it's truly not the end of the world. "C'mon, bub." A snicker slips out. "Your guy is off getting educated for your future. He's giving you an out. So what if you fuck other people in the meantime– it's all just experience. Tell me what he said last night?"

Sniffling, Weston wipes his nose on my shoulder. Yuck! "Sage said... he said I was his future, and he'd always love me."

"There. See, that sounds promising. So stop acting like you're on the verge of slitting your wrists." Squeezing him tighter. "And I get how wildly inappropriate that comment is coming from me, being said to a kid whose mom committed suicide. But you know my dark humor."

Chuckling, Weston pounds me in the chest as he pulls away. "Dick! Why are you even here? Looking for a free babysitter again, aren't you?"

"Nope." I shift on the couch until I can look Weston in the eye. "I came to talk to you about Ren." My brother flinches, so I know I made the right decision. "Ren loves you, and accepts you as you are, but he's terrified."

"Terrified? What the hell, Dev. He acts like I'm a predator." Tears drying up, with anger in their place, the kid's mood swings must drive him batshit.

"I won't go into detail, because you don't need to know." Sighing, I try to think up the best possible way to voice this without saying too much. "Homophobia is based on fear. Fear isn't always irrational. Ren had two horrific experiences that I hope you never go through. I was there for one of them– it happened to me, and he was forced to watch. We're wired differently, so it affected us differently. Gay men terrify him, especially tops."

"Tops?" Weston's eyes narrow as he tries to work out what I'm trying to explain. "I thought he was pissed, calling me out for not being manly because I like to bottom."

"No." I shake my head in denial. "In Ren's head, he was probably seeing tiny Sage being overpowered by you. Fear can't be helped. Obviously that wasn't the case, but it still ate at him. Ren loves you and accepts you. You need to love him and accept that traumatic experiences can't be erased, so his reactions aren't about you."

"It's kind of difficult to ignore when Ren's yelling into my face about me being gay." Weston hops up from the sofa, channeling all the hurt into anger. "I'm not stupid. I have a pretty good idea what happened to you. Everyone was talking around it when we went to Arizona."

"I'm not freezing you out. It's not me and Ren against you and Rae. I wish I didn't know, so why would I push that pain off onto you by sharing? So just ignore Ren when he says something stupid. Know he's probably thrust into the past and choking on fear."

"If it isn't about me, then Ren needs to work on not judging me. There's nothing perverse with what I like."

"I know." Closing my eyes, I hadn't realized how hard this would be to admit when I came here today. "Being gay must be very difficult in a town filled with religious nuts. I know you think us Masons are bigots, or whatnot. But you don't have to go to Auggie for advice– you can come to me."

"You're not gay," is almost accusatory as Weston narrows his eyes. He's waiting for me to judge him, I can feel it. "How can you help me? You're not bi, either."

"A week before I turned fourteen, I was assaulted. I'm sure it's all violence and bloodshed in your mind, but it was worse because it wasn't. That fucked me up."

Weston wants to say something, but it gets stuck in his throat, so he just stares at me in silent horror instead.

"No pity… Sexuality is fluid. Just because you're born one way, doesn't mean life experience won't alter you. Just ask Robin– he'll tell you he's straight. But no one listens, so he just says he's bi. He'll also tell you Auggie is more attracted to men than women. They'll both call you narrow-minded if you truly believe you'll never meet a woman and find her sexually attractive at some point in your life. Same goes with straight men with other men. So don't automatically assume just because a person identifies as one thing, that they haven't experienced the other. That's ignorant."

"I-I-I… I'm sorry," Weston stammers, dropping his ass into a chair, smashing Ozzy's controller beneath him. "You're pissed because I doubted you'd be able to help me."

"Damn straight." Snorting, I laugh at my own joke. "Happily married, straight man with a kid, sitting right here, but I've had more sex with men than you have, and I don't mean by assault. I've been with a guy for the past six months. A therapist, sponsor, and a lover all rolled into one. He's dealing with being bi, and I just so happen to need things that I wasn't born to want. So it's a win-win. So, yeah, don't fucking discount my goddamn advice, you little shit."

"You're what?!" Weston's outrage is the most hilarious thing I've seen all day. "Who?!"

Ignoring my brother's questions, I ask my own. "Are you okay after last night? Do you need to ask me anything? Do you need any advice?"

Relaxing, Weston starts lobbing questions at me left and right. I enter big-brother-mode, which isn't much different than Good Cop. By the time I'm finished with the kid, Clover hands me enough sweets to satisfy Willow and Ren for weeks, along with the promise to babysit Will whenever I need.

EPILOGUE

Kieren Mason

"Wow, I can't believe the turnout." I'm in awe as I stand on the steps, overlooking the backyard, with Willow leaning against my chest. "Essie knows how to throw a party– ugh!" is forced out as a sharp elbow digs into my ribs.

"I'll have you know, I organized this party."

After tucking away a strand of hair that escaped Willow's ponytail, I nuzzle my cheek against hers. "Spanky," I croon into her ear. "I know, that's why I was teasing you."

"Never gonna stop ribbing me, are ya?" My girl sounds defensive and annoyed, but I can feel her lips curling into a grin.

"Never," I vow. "Do we tell them?"

Willow and I both take a few silent moments to gaze out over the most important people in our world, contentment and pride flowing from the both of us.

Willow and I have been together almost five years now, taking it slow, more solid than we would've been if we'd jumped in head-first like fear was dictating we do.

Together, we've watched babies be born, graduations take place –including Willow's –weddings, college acceptances, football and academic scholarships, a renegade business partner on a world-wind band tour, and family members join the brothers in blue. But Willow and I have stayed the same, growing up while we grow into our relationship, and now that the attention-whores have worn-out their welcome in the spotlight, it's our turn.

Standing on the back steps of Essie and Devon's house, I'm proud to be a Mason. Proud of the painful journey and how it shaped me to appreciate the small things in life. The important things.

Dad and Clover are leaning over Essie, oohing and ahhing over their newborn granddaughter– Maeve. Devon's got his chest ballooned out like a proud peacock, and I can't help but chuckle because of it.

Isis, Auggie, and Robin are busy trying to wrangle the billion children running around screaming like chickens with their heads cut off. Maeve is too much of a draw, leaving misbehaving children unattended.

John and Will are exactly the same age. The uncle and nephew team couldn't be any more different. John's a strapping, big boy with a mellow yet firm personality, while Will is a tiny, cute shit with Devon's bossy attitude and Essie's charismatic charm. The boys are inseparable, much to Penelope's dismay.

The girl is the biggest of all of the kids, with red hair and giant blue eyes. She's also the kindest, most compassionate person I've ever met, which makes me wonder who Auggie was meant to be had life not kicked him in the nuts.

Since the boys want nothing to do with Penelope, she's latched onto her little brother, which is a good thing. David is a budding dictator. The three-year-old recently decided he hated the letter D, and has since demanded we all call him Avi.

Avi terrifies me, but it's no shock when his parents are Isis and Robin.

"Who's the little girl playing with Pen?" I whisper in Willow's ear.

"Sage's little sister." Willow's voice has an underlying edge of sadness.

Aunt Ginny and Opal came into sharp focus as soon as Willow said Sage's name. They're teasing each other with a cupcake, but the act seems intimate, like their revisiting the past.

"Is Sage here?" I can't help but sound surprised. The kid hightailed it out of here, landing his ass on a plane to California. I haven't seen him since, but I've played online video games with him for the past few years. Hard to believe, out of all the Masons, it was me who kept in touch with Sage. Even smaller world, we both play online with Toby Kline, Tina and Auggie's younger uncle.

"Yeah, over there." Willow points to where a professional yet dinky man is camped out under the maple tree with Rory and Beth. "Sage's dad is dying, so he had to move back to Boston to take care of the man. He's going to adopt his sister."

"Her name's Gemma," I murmur, remembering Sage saying something about having her all summer. He was going to take her on a cross-country road trip from California to West Virginia, then Dominion, New York to visit Toby, before ending back in Massachusetts.

"Is Franny here too?" I ask of Sage's roommate. I met him online too. He was one of the reasons West Virginia was on the itinerary. Sage wanted to meet all of Francis Parker's hometown friends.

"Yeah, Rory's big body is hiding him from view." Willow chuckles in remembrance. "Essie and Fran took one look at each other, and it was best friends at first sight. It was the funniest thing– sweet. He uprooted his life to help Sage take care of Byron and the little girl."

"They're not partners." I decide I ought to set Willow straight. "I'm not saying they don't share a bed sometimes. They're just living life together– partners in the truest sense, I guess. The guys I play video games with are always razzing Sage about Weston."

"I never would have imagined you'd get past your fear of everything gay while playing video games."

"They're good guys, even if one of them violated my baby brother."

"*Pfft…*" Willow scoffs. "Violated? Baby brother followed Maddox to Ohio State a year early."

"What can I say, we have many geniuses in this family and rampaging hormones." Willow's answering growl has my dick getting hard.

"Clover graduated early because she was determined. Seth was accepted into Harvard at sixteen because he's scary smart and going to change the world. Weston graduated at seventeen, not because he's hungry to play college ball, but because he's horny."

"Well, all he had to do is sneeze and the scouts and recruiters were pouring out of the bleachers."

"Yeah, but West picked Ohio because his dick led him there." Willow's voice is tight with rage while she stares at Sage with pity.

"Spanky… Spanky… Spanky…" Laughing, I trail kisses along her neck. "You need to watch football more often. There was no better offer than Ohio State. West's dick led him in the right direction, and Maddox is to make Sage jealous, the same way Francis is."

"He needs to grow up," Willow grumps, sounding like a petulant child. Then she wises up to her bad behavior. "I just don't like to see people I love throw their happiness away over petty, childish bullshit."

"West is young, living the life of a superstar, with his best friend beside him. He'll get to his future when he's meant to… like we did."

"True," Willow mutters begrudgingly, but whatever else she was about to say is interrupted by Violet skipping through the yard to greet Ozzy.

"You're home, safe and sound!" Violet comes to a standstill, then reaches up to rub Ozzy's shaved head. The guy is renting one of the lofts over top of Rush, and he must've come straight from the Batcave, because he's still in uniform.

"You don't greet us like that, young lady!" Dad shouts at Violet while pointing between himself and Devon. "Don't care if we make it home in one piece, I see."

"Dad…" Violet rolls her eyes, knowing she's being teased.

"Something's going on there," Willow mutters. "I know my sister."

"Nah, she's just excited."

Violent Violet, the girl who was crowned princess then queen in high school, with her good grades, pretty dresses, and no dating policy, has found a healthy outlet for her simmering rage and need for justice.

After the boys graduated early and moved away to college, we were all taking bets on what Violet and Rae would do with their lives.

I won.

On both accounts.

Back in June, Violet and Rae walked across the stage to grab their diplomas. Next week, Violet will be the first female member of our family to go to the police academy. Introvert Rae, she leaves the house less and less and has been helping with Lucky Clover's– the bakery and bag-lunch service Clover runs out of their kitchen.

Willow and I watch Ozzy and Violet interact, while Rae glowers from the shadows of the house. It's obvious they're friends, and they've bonded over their love of law enforcement. Dad and Devon are giddy, but they're veterans, so the youngsters bonded together.

"They're just friends."

"My sister is fiddling with the buttons on Ozzy's shirt." Willow glares as they chat animatedly, Ozzy telling Violet about all of his arrests today.

"And you're being overprotective." I chuckle at the ludicrousness. I've gained some of Willow's snark, and she's gained my enabling tendencies.

"Christ," she hisses. "You're right."

"I always am," I purr against Willow's ear, causing her to shudder. "Do we tell them?"

Good things come to those who wait. Every night after Willow closes up Revamped and I shut the bay doors on Wreck & Ruin, we walk hand-in-hand through town. We always pass this giant Victorian house that's on the Historical Society registry. Every night, Willow would gaze up at it with intense longing.

We're not attention-whores. Willow and I have gotten quieter over the years. We let nature take its course, instead of fear and the need to keep up with our family force us at a different pace.

Willow promised herself she'd do things in the natural order, so when a For-Sale sign was placed in front of that house, we got married without anyone knowing. The day the Sold sign was placed in the yard, we got even better news.

The natural order was waiting on us, then it moved us with super-sonic speed.

"Nah, we don't tell them yet." Willow's voice warbles with fear.

"Why? Aren't you excited?" Holding Willow tight, I gaze out at our family.

"It's Essie's day– let today be about Maeve."

"Ah, you've grown a heart," is said in a teasing tone as my hands slide around Willow's hips to cup her belly.

"Nah, I want our day to ourselves– no sharing." Laughing. Lying. "No, really. Our niece deserves her own day, as do Dev and Essie."

"You were always in such a hurry to shed the good girl– you're a good woman now, Willow Mason. A good woman."

Thank you for reading **WARPED**. Don't miss out on what's to come…

GOOD GIRL, Willow's coming-of-age tale.

WILDLY WEDDED WIFE, Rory & Bethany's novella.

WIDOW, Malcolm & Clover's journey.

WANTON, Opal & Ginny's tasty treat.

WARPED, Devon, Essie, Kieren, & Willow's future.

COMING SOON.

WOVEN, a novellas with surprising narrators.

WICKED, a novella showcasing Auggie & Tina's parents.

WAYWARD, Auggie, Isis, and Robin's angsty emotional roller coaster ride.

…and many more to come.

There was a thread in Warped that was left unexplored for a reason. While I gave enough information to give the readers a good idea on what happened between the scenes, I didn't go into detail. Devon and Rory. It isn't a romantic entanglement, and I didn't want their bond to cheapen what I'd been building between Essie and Devon. Originally, I was going to show this from Robin's point-of-view in Wayward, but then I realized these private moments would still go on behind closed doors. I felt the best people to express their thoughts and emotions on the situation were Devon and Rory. For those who would enjoy reading the dark and dirty, I will be writing a novella from both Devon and Rory's point-of-view, giving the details I thought were best left off the pages of Warped. **WOVEN**.

ACKNOWLEDGEMENTS

A lot of work goes into writing a novel, and it isn't just by the writer herself. **My parents:** for their unconditional support. **My readers**: thank you for reading my twisted words and spreading my books to the masses. For without you, no one would have ever heard of my stories. My readers are my lifeblood. A shout out to the members of the **M&M of Restraint Group on Facebook**: thanks for the endless entertainment and inspiration. **Wicked Reads**: (in all its incarnations) **Angela G.**, thank you for taking over and making Wicked Reads better than I could have done by myself. & thank you for helping promote my work and the work of other authors. Angela? Have I told you lately how much I appreciate you? A huge thank you to the **Wicked Writer's Betas** for keeping me grounded and encouraging me to keep trudging along when I get frustrated. Your thoughts and observations are invaluable. ((Hugs)) Beta readers: **Kris | Diane | Jacki | Linsey | Alexis | Judith | Jodi Lynn |** Someday, I'd love to meet you all in real life– it would be the experience of a lifetime.

ABOUT THE AUTHOR

Erica Chilson does not write in the 3rd person, wanting her readers to *be* her characters. Therefore, writing a bio about herself, is uncomfortable in the extreme.

Born, raised, and here to stay, the Wicked Writer is a stump-jumper, a ridge-runner. Hailing from North Central Pennsylvania, directly on the New York State border; she loves the changes in seasons, the humid air, all the mountainous forest, and the gloomy atmosphere.

Introverted, but not socially awkward, Erica prides herself on thinking first and filtering her speech. There are days she doesn't speak at all. If it wasn't for the fact that she lives with her parents, giving her a sense of reality, she would be a hermit, where the delivery man finds her months after expiration.

Reading was an escape, a way to leave a not-so pleasant reality behind. Reading lent Erica the courage she gathered from the characters between the pages to long for a different life. Writing was an instrument of change, evolving Erica into the woman she is today— a better, more mature, more at peace thinker.

Erica has a wicked mind, one she pours out into her creations. Her filter doesn't allow all of it to erupt, much to her relief. Sarcastic, with a very dark, perverse sense of humor, Erica puts a bit of herself into every character she writes.

I love hearing from readers. If you would like more information on release dates, works in progress, teaser chapters, and random bits of madness, please visit my Facebook Fan Page: https://www.facebook.com/thewickedwriter my website: ericachilson.com or please contact me via email: wickedwriter.ericachilson@gmail.com
DEVIANTS ONLY, if you'd like to join Erica Chilson's closed Facebook group, M&M of Restraint: https://www.facebook.com/groups/MistressandMaster/